THE DESTROYER OF MEN

By

Will Hathaway

MOST OF WHAT FOLLOWS
IS TRUE.

DEDICATION

To my family and friends,

who always encouraged me.

CONTENTS

ACKNOWLEDGMENTS

To everyone who helped me with the research, and to the artist, Stephen Whatcott, who provided the cover and countless beautiful illustrations to inspire me.

Chapter 1

From the back seat of the car, he could see other people dressed exactly as he was dressed. They hurried anonymously through the dusty sun-drenched streets, not making eye contact with anyone, not daring to talk to anyone, but he knew that they were women. No one noticed just another slight figure shrouded, for the sake of modesty, from head to foot in black, with an intricately carved mask across his eyes so that not even these were visible to strangers. He watched the world glide by outside the comfortable air-conditioned car, and he wondered if the women had their mouths sealed with tape as he did or whether their slavery was even more subtle than his own. What made them live not even a half-life in the shadows of their men?

Chapter 2

She collected waifs and strays. That was really all that she did. She lived alone. No one came to the house. Because she ate rice and cereals, she could just about survive without working, but her financial situation was always precarious, especially with the inevitable veterinarians' bills that her extensive menagerie required. The local vet was probably the only person she had actually invited inside her house since moving there. The postman came up the potholed driveway with rates bills and electricity bills, but often weeks went by, and he passed the gate without remembering that she existed. She had an old car that never went further than the nearest supermarket, which she preferred to the slightly nearer village shop, where people remembered her and spoke her name, and for some reason believed they were allowed to ask after her health. The supermarket was reassuringly anonymous. She liked it when nobody knew her name.

Chapter 3

Sunday, May 2006.

The forecast was rain, but the sun hung like a cold yellow disc in the sky at eight o'clock so she went out into the garden. It was late May. It had been the coldest May that she could remember after the driest winter ever. So the garden was a mess. The plum and cherry trees were full of blossom, but the apples and pears were almost bare, and there was not a bumble bee in sight. She did not know what that meant, but it had to mean something.

The ponds that she had dug out all by herself years before were still in turmoil. Early in spring there had been more frogs and newts than she had seen before, scuttling about in the bottom of the ponds. Spring had come so slowly, and the sun had hardly put in an appearance. It was mid-April before there was enough sunshine to draw out the buds and leaves. Then suddenly there was frogspawn. She had never seen so much, and the poor frogs had waited so long until they were almost dead from exhaustion and starvation that they just sat at the bottom like skeletal ghosts. There were hundreds of them. And it was all for nothing: the brief flash of sunshine disappeared again behind heavy grey cloud. The temperature plummeted. There were even frosts in the mornings. It was so cold that none of the frogspawn matured. It all turned a milky grey colour, and sank to the bottom of the ponds to form a lifeless smothering carpet which slowly poisoned the water. Then the water went green. There had already been four dead newts. She fretted that there would be more, and was convinced that all the emaciated frogs would die. They looked awful. She had never seen anything so thin, not even the children in Africa. They never moved. She nervously diced up cat food, and sprinkled it across the surface of the ponds. The snails ate it with relish. Their table manners might have been rather unattractive, but they were in the food chain. She had not known what else to do. The water became murkier, and began to smell so at last, reluctantly, she fished out all the remains of the frogspawn and refilled the ponds, being ever so careful not to harm any of the miserable frogs or increasingly aggressive newts. So far, spring had been a complete catastrophe.

Of course, there were hosepipe bans already in the south. That meant

3

London and Kent. It was apparently drier down there than in Ethiopia so she did not understand why the government was pushing ahead with plans to build another million homes in the area. The news was always depressing. It was always bad news. And the most depressing thing was that no one was doing anything about it. The government seemed to be full of idiots, who could not be trusted with a 'bring and buy' stall at a charity market.

She tried to read the newspapers on a Sunday, just to keep up with what was happening in the world, and to mark out the passing of another week. And it was Sunday, but she was already depressed so she had made the decision to work in the garden while the sun was shining, and not drive down into town to buy anything at all. As usual, she was a bit short of cash. That was the story of her life.

Her home was an old Victorian villa set way back off a country lane, and had once been a busy farmhouse. She still had the outbuildings though they were falling down around her, which she actively encouraged. Nature had reclaimed them. Every nook and cranny had cobwebs, birds' nests and the narrow little well-trodden pathways that promised rabbits, hares, foxes, and even deer. Beyond the buildings were several acres of woodland. She had altogether ten acres close around the house. She owned almost one hundred more, but had rented out everything else to neighbouring farmers when she first bought the place. They seemed to grow nothing but the yellow rape. There had been some lucrative offers for shooting rights in the woodland behind the house, but she refused to allow it, and promised to prosecute anyone who came near her land. Of course, it was a shrewd and intimidating solicitor who did all this. He was a Rottweiler that she could set on anyone who annoyed her, and after eight years there was no one left. She was allowed to withdraw into her private world, and nobody noticed that she had gone.

There had been no birds there originally. It was odd to live in the country and not hear birdsong. She realised afterwards that it was probably because of the shooting parties that had been held there through autumn and winter every year for decades. The guests would have been the young townies with too much money, and no feeling for the land. They would have shot anything that moved. No self-respecting blue-blood would have ignored the etiquette of a proper shoot. There were rules or there was anarchy.

So she had banned them. She had also sorted out the Lampers. That took a bit longer, and she had needed to be quite firm with the local police. It had taken them a while to understand that she was determined. Initially, she just called them out, 999 emergency, whenever there was the slightest suggestion of someone on her land with a vehicle. The police came late if they came at all. When they began to ignore her, she had to change her approach. So she cordially advised them that if they did not sort out the problem then she would do it herself, and be it on their heads. When they tried to take away her shotgun licence then she set Mr. Watchman, the Rottweiler, on them. The Lamper gangs, who seemed to be all of the same family, and had been active for generations were, of course, very well known to the police, but she made sure that they no longer turned a blind eye to their nefarious and dangerous activities. Uninsured and unroadworthy vehicles probably helped make a case against them. Whatever tactic the police used did, at last, warn them off even if they only ended up in prison for totally unrelated matters. It was hard not to point out that if the police had acted twenty years earlier then several people might have avoided being beaten up or stabbed or robbed.

Her life was full now. All of May had been a long hard slog to sort out the garden and the ponds. All that kept her going was the certainty that the sun would eventually shine. It was inevitable, hopefully. She had just finished reading a book about the island of Thera. It had been destroyed centuries ago by a volcano, and the book suggested that this natural disaster had caused the Bible's seven years of famine and plagues. She understood about global warming, and still did not understand why they simply did not ban all non-essential air travel. People did not need to fly to Thailand or to have stag parties in Malaga. It was surely easier than messing around with buses and trains that were always unreliable. And it did not matter at all how much we saved on our own personal carbon footprint when India and China were decimating the planet with their huge new power stations to build up their economies, which Europe could not compete with because they were scaling everything down. And the tsunami? Nobody was talking about that any more. Surely that rocked the Earth on its axis. Over and above and beyond the human lives destroyed and the misappropriation of aid money, there were the curiously darker evenings late last year. But nobody talked about it. She blamed the media. The recent scare stories about the Niger were also infuriating. If there were millions of people starving to death then why hadn't it been reported earlier? She had always assumed that foreign correspondents roamed about looking for the stories that needed to be told. They sought out injustice, and brought the light of publicity to the darkness of ignorance and corruption. It was a shock to realise they probably all lived in civilised Kensington, and were hand-fed stories by people with predetermined agendas. Starving black people were just not sexy, so they were not forgotten, they were simply being ignored.

Yes. She worried about lots of things. Why was there no respect anymore? Why was 'youth' celebrated and all things 'youthful' prized when they were actually stupid and shallow? Why were so many people so unhappy that they had to get blind drunk and fall down in the gutter just to have a good time? Multiculturalism was just apartheid without the need for legislation. How could misogynists still be ruling the world? And was that why the world was in such a mess? There were more wars and more natural disasters, and nobody cared. And then there was Barbaro. Would he survive? She worried a lot about Barbaro. And then there was the sublimely talented and mischievous George Washington. She had fallen in love at first sight with Gorgeous George, and the more he tossed his head and rolled his eyes and showed his temperament, the more she had loved him. He had brought Newmarket to a complete standstill at the 2000 Guineas, would not obey the rules, and looked utterly adorable. She was genuinely excited about seeing him again at Epsom. Could he cope with the track? Could he go the distance? Would he behave?

So she went out into the garden where she could think about the frogs and newts and birds, where she could actually do something and make a difference. Two cats followed her. There were a dozen about the place. She knew they were the greatest predators in the country, but her family were spoiled and old, and she compensated for them. All year round, she fed the birds which provided as well for the hedgehogs, squirrels and mice. There were rabbits, of course, and therefore foxes, and very early in the morning, she could sometimes see the deer on the lawn. Her one fear was rats, but between them, the cats and foxes seemed to have that situation under control.

She walked along the cobbled path from the back door to circle the walled garden. This area was older than the house. The walls looked probably seventeenth century. They were limestone. The sheltered spots had moss and lichen. There were numerous fruit trees, beds for wild strawberries and thickets of raspberries. Here herbs and roses grew with towering foxglove spires. Broken cold frames and discarded bundles of canes littered neglected corners. In the summer, she grew vegetables, but not today. It was too cold. There were green shoots coming, but the grey skies made everything so miserable and depressing. It was hard to believe that anything would grow. There was so much work to do. At the end of the path was a stout door. This was the only part of the garden kept safe from the rabbits. If she left the door open they did occasionally manage to get in, and always took some rounding up. She was more forgiving of the hedgehogs. Once upon a time, there had been so many hedgehogs. Where had they all gone?

She opened the door in the wall and passed through, emerging into a large open garden with a long lawn, and deep herbaceous borders that would hopefully soon burst into colour with foxgloves, hollyhocks, poppies and peonies and various hardy geraniums, but were now a wasteland spotted with fading tulips and hellebores. Everything looked forlorn. Ahead and to her left, the garden was bordered by her woodland. It was a wild wood. She had read too much about Ratty and Mole and Pooh Bear when a lonely little girl. She had always dreamed of owning her own wood, and it was broadleaf and ancient and truly wild. Immediately to her right, the garden swept down beside the long potholed driveway, becoming scrubbier as it reached the lane that divided her from the far horizon. Someone had cut down the hedgerows decades ago so she could see across the road, across several acres of yellowing fields to the sky. Being situated on the top of a flat-topped hill, she had no neighbours to look at. The nearest neighbours were in fact a mile beyond the wood as the crow flies, but much further by road. She knew them by sight. His name might have been Maurice or Morris or even Bruce. She found it easier to just avoid talking to them.

Further down to her right were various buildings. The nearest one made a passable garage. The doors just about closed, but the hinges were about to let go completely because the wooden frame was rotten. There was enough paint left to call them green, but it was a generous compliment they hardly deserved. There were stables big enough for three horses with a tiny garret room above where grooms had probably once been grateful to sleep. Beyond them, a large and refurbished barn loomed against the sky line. It had been rebuilt since 'the war', but she was never sure which war. It had two old brick walls, and one of metal sheeting which also made up the roof. It was certainly big enough to turn a tractor around in. It was empty now except for a hundred years of agricultural litter; bits of equipment she could not even name, heaps of old straw and leaves, long trails of ivy determined to turn the whole place into a romantic bower, and of course, owls. Later, there would be swallows, which were always very exciting, but the owls alone were a perfect treat. There were also various types of mouse and shrew and even voles as well as slow worms and the odd snake. About twenty yards beyond the barn were a sequence of long low buildings that her deeds told her were pig sheds. They were in a dangerous state of disrepair, and she hardly ventured down there more than a couple of times in a year. They were full of abandoned equipment that a museum might be interested in, but also covered in cobwebs and birds' nests so they were left in peace. Scattered about the buildings were several long abandoned frames for rearing game birds, which now reared themselves deep in the wood away from feline eyes. Behind the stables were the foundations of an extensive chicken house, which had been pulled down and cleaned up when she first moved in. Well, the smell was overpowering.

The first and one of the biggest of the ponds was on the north side of the lawn, indented into the flower bed so that three sides were overgrown with ferns and irises and yet bathed in sunshine, when there was a sun to shine. Initially, she had edged the pond with nice tidy paving, but the frogs had stuck to it, and were slowly cooked to death in even the mildest weather. So that was all dug up, and chucked away during the second summer that she was in the house. She still winced whenever she saw the liner edges, but the frogs and newts seemed to be able to scale it with ease so it stayed exposed.

The water looked dreadful. It was still murky with green frothy bits here and there. At the bottom, she could just about see the yellow and brown markings of the desperately thin frogs. The only signs of life were the flashes of movement and colour when the newts danced across the frogs in a courtship display, treating the frogs as if they were already just corpses in a mass grave.

Her heart ached. Her back ached. She had been toiling away to change the water for a week. Every day all day, she bailed water out as carefully as she could, not wanting to kill anything. The green blooms looked like algae, but she did not know. She had never had them in the garden before. There was nothing in her books about such a calamity. The frogs just lay there in heaps. They were all looking at her. Were they accusing her of disturbing them or asking her to try again? She was sure they were all going to die.

The next pond was smaller. It had originally been a backup for the first. There had never been any fish in this one so the newts and frogs had been more successful. Its smallness had originally been a problem so she had made it artificially deeper by raising the edges with rocks and bricks. Too much frogspawn was always a problem here. Once there had been so much, it suffocated all the newts underneath so now she always bucketed some out. It hatched out quicker in the scullery, obviously, and the tiny fry went easily back in warmer weather into the ponds and the food chain. Every year, she told herself that there were thousands of tadpoles because thousands had to die. This year, they had all died. This year, the one and only year when she had strenuously resisted interfering, and they all died. It was heart breaking. She knelt down and picked up a bucket to carefully scoop the green bloom of algae off the surface of the water. Even the lily plants looked sick.

She worked quietly for hours, so engrossed, so upset; she did not even feel the weather turn chilly. And then it rained.

She looked around, surprised. It was near midday. There were still swathes of blue sky, but the rain poured down. There were huge warm drops that just drenched her in a moment. It was not even like English rain that could last for hours and amount to nothing. It poured down like some Asian monsoon. Her clothes filled up with water. Her hair that usually just turned to frizz became rats' tails with rivers running through them. But there was nothing she could do. It was pointless thinking about seeking shelter. So she just stood there and drowned quietly.

And as suddenly as it started then it stopped. She looked up at the sky, wondering if there really was someone up there with a big switch. Then she tried to move. Even her shoes were full of water. When she stepped away from the pond, she saw that where she had stood and knelt, there were now little lakes. Then the birds started singing very loudly. She gazed down hopefully into the pond where she had been carefully bailing out water. It was still murky. The frogs had not moved at all.

She walked back towards the house. She was quickly cold and despondent and just plain tired. Around her, the lawn became suddenly alive with Blackbirds and Robins. In the trees, there were a variety of Tits and numerous Finches, full of song and suddenly ravenous again. There were nut and seed feeders in every tree and shrub strong enough to bear them. There were fat balls too inside the walled garden. Baby birds loved the fat balls so she bought them in bulk.

By the time she reached the back door, she was feeling a little better. In the scullery, she stripped off the heavy wet clothes and bundled them straight into the washer, then picked up a towel to rub her dripping hair. She was naked, but that was alright. No one had been inside her house in years. The last person was the Vet on a midnight call out. That cost a fortune and had been in vain. Even the infrequent meter readers did not manage to have more than a toe over the threshold. When she first bought the house, she had moved all the meters to the front door. Strangers were never allowed inside.

She pulled on dry underwear and jeans and a T-shirt then went through to the kitchen to make a cup of tea and sit down. She was still cold. Her hair was a mess. She hated it when her hair was a mess. She knew she was not an attractive woman, but her hair was a lovely colour and framed her face if she dried it properly. She chuntered on under her breath for a while then had another cup of tea, and reluctantly began worrying again about the frogs and the newts and the weather.

It did not matter how often she rationalised what was happening. Nature was cruel. Most living things existed in constant terror of being eaten by something else. Human beings were top of the food chain only because they were the monsters. All they had to fear was a natural death at the end of all things. No one knew about death. No one ever came back to talk about death. At least, no one that anyone believed. She had read a lot of books trying to find the answers. If only people would be nice to each other. Do as you would be done by. But then as Richard Bach pointed out: what about the vampires? If human beings became nothing more than fodder for another species how long would we even recognise the concept of humanity? It would be survival of the fittest. We would shed every single virtue that did not guarantee our survival. She worried about everything, and because she was completely alone, she had no perspective to balance her fears.

She knew she was too focused. Frogs died all the time. Dragonflies lived only a few weeks after spending nearly two years at the bottom of ponds where they devoured everything. Perhaps frogs only lived a couple of years? Perhaps only one year? But it did not make sense. She had been nurturing the garden for a long time. She had never known such a catastrophic failure before. Bill Oddie would know. She wondered how she could get in touch with him, knowing of course, that she never would.

The sun was shining weakly again when she went out, but the air was still chilly. The garden looked bathed and fresh whereas she still felt like a drowned rat. She set up the hose to replace the water she had bailed out of the pond. Fish liked quite a robust flow of water but the frogs did not, so she turned the tap on accordingly. It would take about an hour to fill the small pond again so she walked on across the lawn towards her woodland.

There were not really any words to describe how she felt about her woodland. It was almost religious. When she stepped across the threshold and entered the quietness, the peace and the beauty, it was as if she was entering a great medieval cathedral. The tall trees diminished her. They were already older than she would ever be. They cleaned the air and healed the planet, and she did nothing. She felt small and humble whenever she walked there. The trees were all as individual as people. They bore their years and their scars. In the spring, they seemed bursting with joy and life. In the winter, their mood was mournful and irritable as if their age had become a burden and their patience in short supply. It seemed a lonely place in the winter. Their boughs creaked like arthritic bones. Only the Blackbirds and Robins stayed to sing. But she loved it. She photographed it and drew it and wandered the quiet paths, always with a pocketful of nuts and seeds because there was always someone in need. She believed she was only alive to protect the sanctuary that she had found in the woodland. Some ancient power or purpose had brought her there. It seemed disrespectful to question what and why and how. The quality of sound was different too. In the woodland, she talked in a whisper. Even the birds seemed to sing more sweetly. If there was a sudden and startling noise, then she knew that it was a warning. Something was amiss. Someone or something had intruded. But no one intruded. No one came into her woodland. It was her place. It was a very special and private place.

A well-trodden path marked the route she took down through the trees going from clearing to clearing, taking her down into the dene at the bottom, where she had made a shrine. It was a small altar made of Cotswold stone that she had brought there slab by slab years before. There were dead flowers and obelisks and mementos that only she recognised now. No one else came there. No one else had ever been there. It was like her heart: closed and private and unknowable. She touched all of the obscure objects, and acknowledged all the memories that they invoked and quietly moved on.

It was not raining then, but she was cold, and the trees dripped endlessly. Little rivers still trickled across the hard ground, forming dams against the exposed tree roots then flooding over them and hurrying away. She ploughed through the puddles, trying not to splash childishly, but puddles were always fun, and her shoes were so wet already. For a while, she hopped and skipped and jumped then trotted away, embarrassed by her own behaviour yet laughing out loud.

Deep in the wood, there was a clearing, and in the clearing there was a pond. She would have liked it to be a lake. It was the biggest of all the ponds, and kept her employed several hours a week. When she first bought the farm, it had been nothing more than a mud hole that flooded whenever it rained, and she had spent ages digging it out, and building up the sides. The setting had a romantic quality. All it needed were gothic ruins for it to qualify as the resting place of the Lady of the Lake. It was beautiful, but she had never been able to sort out the balance. There were too many leaves. The water became acid. The oxygen levels dropped. She had to work hard to keep the water clear. She wanted a proper filter system and aeration and all sorts of modern conveniences, none of which she could afford or had the energy to contemplate. The child in her heart still enjoyed wading in barefoot, even in the late autumn when she needed to fetch out the leaves and dared to use chemicals because the suddenly fashionable barley straw was so expensive. On hot days, she paddled at the edge, and if she waited very quietly the foxes and deer sometimes came down to drink beside her, and this gave her joy.

There were numerous species of ferns planted along the banks. The Male ferns had done exceedingly well. In the winter when covered in early morning frost, they glittered majestically in the sunshine. In June, they were full and blousy, promising a safe habitat for so many creatures. There were always dozens of fat spiders with elaborate webs, ready to give birth. In her garden there was life in abundance. She had planted all of the ferns around the ponds and every plant in the garden, and every day admired her wisdom and their fortitude. This was her place. She had made it, and she felt it was a jewel. Even when it was freezing cold, and she was netting leaves, and it was too dark to see, she would not have asked to be anywhere else.

But it was only May, and it was cold, and so the ferns looked battered. The grass was not growing. The water was dark and foul even with the recent downpour. She knew the pond water was dead again. Her heart sank. Suddenly, it was overwhelmingly depressing. All she could look forward to was more hard work, long hours of it with no guarantee that she could stop another catastrophe.

And that was when she saw him.

*

In Great Britain, half a million people go missing every year. More than four hundred of the children are never found.

*

He was a beautiful child with big blue eyes, white teeth, and freckles across the bridge of his nose. His hair was a mass of unruly curls that gave him a delightful, mischievous look.

He was loved. Family, friends, teachers, even strangers were drawn to him. He had a grace, a shining goodness that was a beacon to others in a jaded world. When he was a baby, someone had tried to carry him off from the hospital. It left a deep, invisible wound with his mother. She was overly protective, suspicious of strangers, and unable to explain to anyone why she guarded him so zealously. His father was more pragmatic. He worked away from home a lot so had a certain detachment, and he viewed his wife's obsession with annoyance, but wrote it off as a 'mothers and sons thing'. There would be no other children. The father accepted unhappily his second place in his wife's affections, and later there would be rumours of affairs and prostitutes.

The child went missing before his seventh birthday. He simply disappeared.

Chapter 4

And then it rained again. It poured down. It was not just a shower, but a deluge. The noise was deafening. And it was cold.

A dozen feet away on the other side of the pond, a man lay on his back, half hidden by the ferns, almost invisible in his muted earth-toned clothes. He did not move. He did not seem to be alive.

Her immediate concern was that he was a rapist, pretending to be dead, waiting for her to approach so that he could attack her. Which, of course, was silly. But she could not move. She stood there riveted to the spot, just staring at him while the rain drenched her, and beat the ground like a thousand hammers. Was it the rain? It might have been her heart.

She was afraid of being afraid. Her imagination left her paralysed. She could not approach, not even to see if he was merely injured, or run away. Without touching her, he had managed to rape her courage and confidence. At that moment, she needed John Wayne. She had a long-standing relationship with John Wayne. It was a thing. She knew it was one-sided, but it was still a thing. The long years of reclusive isolation left her completely unable to function around real people.

"I can't do this," she thought, then said it aloud, hoping that she could merely blink, and the man would disappear like a bad dream. She peered away into the trees, as if looking for a brutal murderer. "I can't do this."

There were no alarms. She was alone. Surely, that meant he was dead?

She looked at him again, aware that she should be doing something, but too afraid to acknowledge her responsibilities as a decent human being. He was really just a body, something in the way and inconvenient and irritating. She was too far away to see his face, and the distance allowed her to remain detached. It was only the bulk and the clothes that declared that it was a man, but being a man he was the aggressor and threatening and dangerous.

Nothing happened. For an awfully long time, nothing happened. She did not know what she expected, but it felt ominous. She did not understand why he was there. It was bad enough that he had invaded her precious secret sanctuary, but that he remained there and did not explain was very irritating.

It took her a long time to overcome her nerves while the rain continued to pour down in torrents. It seemed to be harder and louder. Then she was shivering. It was so cold. It took that long for her to remember what she was supposed to do. Poorly cats and hedgehogs and injured birds were less complicated, and all that she knew. A human being in need was a totally alien species in her universe, but she had the cultural memory of Samaritans, and a maternal instinct that ran true even if a little rusty. She was supposed to help him. That he was trespassing and probably up to some mischief was irrelevant. It was a duty – an obligation, she had to do something, but she couldn't. She just couldn't do anything.

"I can't do this," she said loudly, trying to drown out the drumming rain, staring into the trees, wanting the game to end. It had to be a game. Someone was playing a cruel trick. She felt humiliated already and surprisingly angry.

He did not move as she approached. If anything, she was initially relieved to think he might be dead. He could not hurt her if he was already dead. As she drew closer, she saw that there were cobwebs over and around him like perfect nets. They were bowed under the weight of the rain drops, but the water glittered brilliantly like diamonds. She paused to gaze at them, imagining hurrying home for a camera. Beauty demanded a camera. On one of the cobwebs, a cloud of tiny spiders clung stubbornly. At the slightest disturbance, she knew that they would scatter across the web then slowly but surely return, guided by some instinct that she could not even imagine. How did they know the difference between torrential rain and a predator? The mysteries of nature never ceased to amaze her. That their home was undisturbed and perfect only reassured her that the man had not moved at all for a long time.

She, at last, stood over him, on her toes, excited with fear and ready to run. There was no blood. There should have been buckets of blood. His clothes were clean, not even a little creased. He was just laying there. The position of his head and limbs suggested he had carefully laid down. He did not look hurt or even ill. She breathed deeply, trying to find some logical justification for just leaving him there, but knowing that she did not want to do that. She wanted him to go away. She needed him to have never been there at all. She started to reach down. She wanted to touch him to be sure that he was real, but hesitated. He was so close. Her fingers trembled. Her hand shook. She could not do it. At any moment, she expected him to open his eyes, and make a grab at her. She withdrew, sweating and cold. Who was he and what was he doing in her garden? She walked up and down, staring at him, feeling absolutely lost. This was not in her repertoire.

She did not know what she was supposed to do.

The rain eased off, but she was soaked through and shivering. The trees dripped loudly again. The little rivers raced with renewed vigour.

The man lay motionless. If he was acting, it was a brilliant performance. It had to be drugs. Obviously, it was drugs. Her prejudice added conviction. She tried to recall what she knew about crack and cocaine and heroin, but all her information came from the newspapers and television so how could she know if it was true? Alcohol smelt. There was nothing worse than the smell of old beer, except perhaps cigarettes and urine. He did not smell, but the rain might have washed the aroma away. It had to be drugs.

Several minutes passed before she found the nerve to go back and stand over him again. He had not moved. He looked as if he was fast asleep, but he might have been dead. It dawned on her very slowly that if he was dead then there would be so much more trouble. She would have to tell someone. There would be police and doctors and a hundred intrusive questions. Strangers would trample across her land. It would be an absolute nightmare for her, and yet she could not abandon him in her precious woodland. That would ruin everything. She had to do something. Even in her confused terror she knew that she must do something.

Losing patience, she reached down and shook him roughly. He was alive. His head rolled. An arm fell limp to the ground. She was ridiculously pleased. He was alive. It was only then that she actually looked at him. He was not at all what she had expected. He should have been a homeless vagrant with smelly clothes, needle marks, ulcers and boils and most definitely a beard. Yet he was no more than mid-twenties. His face was smooth so she knew he had not been there more than a day, and his hair was clean and tidy, though of course, he was now thoroughly wet.

She tucked her own hair behind her ears, suddenly conscious of her appearance. Drenched twice on the same day: it was hardly fair. In comparison, the young man's clothes were very smart and well-made and looked new. He wore a pair of expensive shoes that were not even scuffed. The soles were unblemished. How had he walked miles into her woods without getting his shoes dirty? Leaning a little closer, she saw that his hands were soft with immaculately manicured nails. None of it made any sense. All he needed were a brace of pheasants and a spaniel to make him the perfect embodiment of a *Country Life* cover.

It simply did not make sense. Who was he and what was he doing in her garden? He was so young. Someone must be missing him? Such a good-looking young man must have a wife or lover somewhere. There would certainly be parents. He was too well-heeled to be wholly independent at his young age. Next to him, she felt like a motherly forty-something, wearing torn jeans and an old baggy T-shirt; and so wet and so bedraggled. He was much too handsome and too well-dressed to have any reason to be prowling around in her woods. It made no sense. There was no logic. She hated it when she did not understand.

She wanted desperately to go through his pockets, but that meant touching him. Stroking hair away from his eyes, and pressing her palm to his forehead was acceptable behaviour. It was not intrusive or intimate, but deliberately searching him when he was unconscious seemed a step too far. And she was sure that he would wake up the minute she started, and just thinking about that was embarrassing and quite unnerving.

There was something about him that made her think of a little boy sleeping in a leafy bower. Thick moss made a pillow for his head. The ferns drooped over him like exotic fans. The silver gossamer of spiders' webs covered him like ancient bejewelled lace. He looked utterly peaceful. As she stooped to stroke long wet curls of hair away from his face, she wistfully imagined that he might have been her own son. He was shockingly beautiful. For a while, she drifted in thoughts of what might have been. In the dark attic of her memory, ghosts stirred. Things that were best forgotten sought out the light of day. For a moment, she was weak and vulnerable, and her heart ached with loss, but only for a moment. This was not her son. They were not the same. She closed the shutters and nailed shut the door. The past was dead. No amount of longing could bring back what she had once loved too much and possessed all too briefly.

Standing up, she backed away from him, distracted by the memories, yet certain that they were false. She had been alone too long. She knew that it disadvantaged her, but she took in strays and wounded animals. She wanted to believe that she could help him. At the very least, she desperately needed to move him away from her land. If she left him there then she could never come back. It would never be the same.

It took her a long time to accept that she must leave. Even though he was unconscious, she found it impossible to trust him. She still suspected that someone might be hiding behind the trees and laughing at her. It was too easy to imagine that there was nothing wrong with him. Drink and drugs seemed a certainty. Nothing else made sense. She decided it was most likely cocaine. She had read something somewhere about cocaine chic. He could easily be one of those useless young men, who hung around parties frequented by equally useless supermodel types.

She did, at last, decide to go back through the woods to her house. It was such a long way when she was in a hurry. And she hurried. It had probably been years since she ran even a few steps, but she ran as fast as she could along the winding path. Her knees complained at once. Her ankles were decidedly wobbly. But she pressed on, suddenly overwhelmed by a sense of urgency that she did not really comprehend.

She went at once to the phone, but the line was dead. That happened frequently in the country. Farmers were constantly knocking down telegraph poles. Then she remembered that it had been dead the day before, and she worried that her inertia might now cost the young man's life. Her mobile phone was dead too. She could not find the recharger, and swore vehemently at her own carelessness and stupidity. There was a young man's life in the balance. But she prevaricated helplessly. Her nearest neighbours were a mile and more as the crow flies on the other side of the wood. If she went by road it was even further, and the nearest village was twice as far again.

It was hopeless. She stood in the hallway, dripping wet, her shoes leaving muddy footprints that a blind man could follow, and it was so hard to breathe. Her heart was pounding. Her head throbbed. Everything hurt. She felt sick and dizzy. She was ready to fall down, and she could not be sure anymore that she had not imagined that there was a young man unconscious in the garden. But there was nothing she could actually do. It did not matter about the phones. Damn the phones. It was not the distance to the neighbours or the village or the nearest town. She simply could not ask anyone for help. That would have literally killed her. Now, it would probably kill him. Whether it was chronic shyness or some genuine phobia, the end result was the same. She could not ask anyone for help. She had to believe that she could save him on her own. Her whole life, she had managed to survive on her own. It was not arrogance. She did not have the confidence to believe that she was better than everyone else; simply that she was equal to them. She had to believe that she was definitely equal.

She hardly knew what she wanted to do except that she would not allow him to die. She was not sure of her intentions. Obviously, it was important to save his life, but it was so much more complicated than that. He was perfectly lovely, sleeping like a nymph in the forest, but he might be anything when he was awake. If it was drugs... Imagining him as a sweaty, grey-faced schizophrenic drug addict stealing money and wielding a knife was very sobering. She was already making plans, worried about evicting him, and had not actually managed to rescue him yet.

In the end, she did the only thing that she could do. She took her old wheelbarrow back down the path, hoping at every step that she was dreaming. She was frightened of being mad. She argued with herself all the way about the pros and cons of being mad and not finding him, of being mad and failing to rescue him, and then about being sane and having to deal with another human being.

It was probably the hardest physical work she had ever undertaken. He was not that heavy, but he was too much for her. If he had not been unconscious to begin with, he would certainly have passed out during the hour or so she dragged and bumped his carcass into the wheelbarrow.

By the time she had him sprawled in the bucket like a lifeless doll, his immaculate clothes and luxuriant hair were dishevelled, and strewn with mud and leaf litter. He had never looked more dead. She checked his pulse frequently, pressing her fingers to his reassuringly warm neck, and gazing into his face with unbridled curiosity. There was no end to the questions that she wanted to ask him, but more important than any of them was her imperative need that he wake up and walk away. She was prepared to let him go without any explanation as long as he went quickly, but he did not stir.

The journey back up the path through the trees took until late afternoon. Several times, she almost lost control of the wheelbarrow, and only just managed to save him from being jettisoned across the ground. It hurt her back badly. His weight tore the muscles in her arms and shoulders.

As soon as they emerged from the cover of the trees, there was a dreadful hail storm. The ice felt like golf balls. She wanted to run away and take cover, but could not leave him. For more than five minutes, she stood stooped over him, shielding him with her own body, being stoned by the driving ice. It had certainly been a day for weather. Even after it stopped, she remained bent over him, her back raw and stiff with swollen muscles and frozen flesh.

Half way home, her knees and thighs succumbed to the pressure. Long before she reached the driveway, every movement was painful, and she could only manage a few steps at a time. She imagined that it must have been like this to be tortured on the rack in Elizabethan times. She certainly felt like a martyr.

Reaching the driveway and the front door, marked the end of her resolution. She left him in the wheelbarrow, and staggered into the house, collapsing on to the nearest chair, and then weeping almost hysterically. It was too much. The adrenalin that had carried her so far left her trembling violently, in physical shock and so much pain. She could not think rationally anymore. Her intense focus on rescuing him had triumphed, but at a terrible cost. For an hour, perhaps longer, she sat there in a wakeful coma, unable to function. She was exhausted and dehydrated, but too far gone to be able to walk from the chair to the sink and water.

Much later, she was able to think again. The old questions remained; the most pertinent now being what she should do with him. Stiff on the chair, with every muscle seized up and swollen, she did not know if she could do anything. She had never felt so completely disabled. When her cats came out to the kitchen expecting food because there was always food whenever she was in the kitchen, she tried to explain to them that there might be a delay because she was completely crippled by pain. The cats cried and purred and stared at her then went back to their beds, apparently feeling betrayed.

She never actually remembered how long she sat there. It was some time after her hands stopped shaking; a long time after her lips felt like sandpaper and her mouth dried to stone. By then the cats, almost all of them, had been to see what all the fuss was about. She knew she would have to overcome the pain to rise from the chair and to walk. Her thirst was driving her insane, but the pain was so intense she did not have the nerve to confront it. To even think about moving made her tremble. She kept telling herself that it was just pain, and pain was not a real thing, it was just a panic signal from her brain.

It took an awfully long time, and mostly sheer bloody-mindedness, to bring her gasping and grimacing back to her feet. It all hurt. Everything hurt. She stood there sweating and shivering again as more adrenalin coursed through her veins. Then she took one step and then another. Her hands were so sore, she could hardly close them around the tap or pick up a glass, but the water was delicious. It flooded down through her body like a cool balm. She could hardly believe that she had succeeded. Triumph made her dizzy. Then she felt sick.

*

There were mountains on the other side of a valley. They were bare rock without trees or snow. In the morning light, they glowed like heaps of burnished gold. The boy crept closer to the parapet, filling his lungs with the cold air, and curious to see everything after an eternity of darkness in the dreadful hood. He was on a rooftop. From his vantage point, he could look down on all the other rooftops in the town though there were screens and walls on many of them to cheat him of a clear view. Across the roofs and courtyards, and beyond the town's gates, there were date palms, fig trees and lemons because this side of the valley was fertile. There were wells amongst the trees, and beyond the orchards there were irrigated plots, but they were small, and did not reach more than a quarter of the way across the valley floor. The boy strained to see down to the street below him, but there was not enough slack on the chain to enable him to lean over the parapet or to show his face to the world.

From a white tower only a hundred yards away came the muezzin's call to prayer. It was eerie in the half light. He had heard it before, but always distantly. The boy did not understand the words, but if he stood up, he could glimpse people in distant streets winding their way towards the mosque. Below him, inside the house, were noises, the sounds of life, and occasionally there was the movement of a light in the stairwell. He turned about seeking a hiding place, not sure whether he wanted them to come. They had been so horrible. Everyone had been so horrible. For several minutes, he was genuinely afraid, then beneath him, the house slowly became quiet and still. They were not coming. He turned again to gaze across the roof tops towards the golden mountains. Then the scratching started. The smelly blankets were full of fleas.

Completely hidden beneath hooded black coats, women worked in the fields in the most intolerable heat. Some seemed to have proper hand tools, while others hacked at the ground with knives so that they could plant their crops one seed at a time. In all the months that he watched them, the boy never saw a tractor or oxen or even a plough. The few donkeys that he saw were as thin as sticks. He never saw a man there working with them. Yet the crops grew. The irrigated plots were soon green, and the sorghum grass shot away almost before his eyes. The women worked all day. There were often arguments. Two of the older women obviously bullied the others. There were often tears, sometimes laughter, but never fun. They only stopped working when the eerie voice wailed from the white tower summoning them all to prayers. He saw them looking after goats on the other side of the valley, and when they were so very far away they prayed by themselves, turning to the north west and kneeling down.

He watched them all day. He had nothing else to do. Most of them were indistinguishable from each other, but he knew that they were all women because they were veiled. Very occasionally he saw little girls helping with the goats, but never men and very seldom the younger boys. The men and boys never worked in the fields. On the roof, fastened like a dog, he only saw the women up close when they came up the stairs to lay out their washing. Even then they were veiled. Mostly, they ignored him. If he was lucky, they ignored him. When it was very hot, the men slept on the roof, but when it rained he was left there alone. There was no electricity in the town, though every house had a generator. Water was scarce. There were no toilets that would be recognisable to the boy. He was cleaned only when it was essential, and always with a bucket of already dirty water left over from someone else's ablutions. The women worked hard. He watched every day as they went to fetch water from wells and firewood from wherever they could find it, and he knew when the men went away because the women chattered loudly and gaily in the house beneath him. He came to know their voices. They did not speak to him. They never spoke to him. The food they gave him was almost inedible. The water was full of worms and bacteria and made him ill. And everything was full of sand.

Every gust of wind brought the sand. There were several small sand storms that he watched like a spectator in a grandstand as they bowled across the valley floor. The veiled women stood against them, turning into grey ghosts as their clothes were overwhelmed. One storm was so bad that he had seen it coming like a rolling fog, filling up the sky and obscuring the sun. From this one, the women and little girls had run, dragging their goats and sheep back within the walls of the town. He could hear it like a muffled scream long before it reached him. Then the air filled with stinging crystals. He could not see anything, but turned in panic, calling for help. No one came. The wind knocked him down. He shouted loudly, but could not hear anything but the wind. The sound was deafening now. He could not see his hand before his face nor lift himself off the floor. All he could do was pull a blanket over his head, and try to cover as much of himself as possible while the wind tried to snatch it from his grasp. The storm lasted hours. There was no rest. At some point, he fainted. Afterwards, he discovered that everything was covered with sand. He was buried under three or four inches, and from the rooftop he could see that the trees and crops were battered and grey. They stayed that way until the next rains. It was a terrifying experience, but no one had offered him shelter. They protected their livestock, but he was always on his own. When it rained enough to send flash floods down the nearby wadis, washing away everything in its path, he hid again beneath the blanket. Even in the most spectacular thunderstorms with lightning exploding down around him, he was left alone on the flat roof.

The only time he actually saw one of the women up close was when he screamed at the sight of a particularly monstrous spider. It was bigger than his hand, and stalked towards him with latent menace. The women had all rushed up through the house in a state of panic, but they froze in the stairwell. Not one of them wanted to come closer. The boy was as terrified of the faceless inhuman black creatures as he was of the spider, and screamed again hysterically. A stout wrinkled figure emerged from the pack, shouting in a high-pitched voice to quiet the boy, and to take some control of the heaving chattering mass behind her. The spider stopped, and seemed to reconsider its situation. The boy could see the hairs on its body quivering. His heart was exploding. He drew breath again. In one fluid movement, the elderly woman crossed the roof, and stamped on the spider with her flip flop then with the same weapon slapped the boy back to sensibility before whirling around to chase the other frightened women away.

The boy was left alone again so quickly, it was hard to believe what had happened yet his face stung, and the juicy mush of the spider remained. It was black and brown and surprisingly hairy. He sat in what shade there was for the rest of the day staring at it. That evening when a moustachioed man returned, he picked up the tarantula, and lunged at the boy with it then burst out laughing, and tossed the spider off the roof into the street below. The boy just wept tearlessly.

There were scorpions too. They always seemed to be more plentiful after dark, and he spent many fitful nights imagining that they were walking across his body only to discover that it was merely the wind off the desert with some chaff. He left off the blankets to escape the torment of the fleas, but without them he was cold and invariably attacked by a multitude of other creepy crawlies.

The wolves and hyenas were just unnerving. In the daylight, he knew that they could never enter the house, and find their way up all the stairs to eat him on the roof. At night, though, everything seemed possible. Their cries and howls carried so far on the desert air. He did not know that they were miles away, sniffing out where the goats had been that day, and no one ever explained.

He was miserable, and resigned to being nothing more than a chained dog. After months of dreadful heat and then rain, it did become cooler. The sunsets lost their violent orange hue, and the sky became a vast blue vault without a single cloud. At night, the temperature dropped down to nearly freezing. By then he had started talking to himself, and had welts on his arms from scratching himself with his long nails. He still spent every day staring down at the surrounding rooftops and the distant mountains, but he was in a daze of exhaustion and despair that completely overwhelmed him. He was only quiet when the men were there because they punished noise. No one was nice. No one liked him. In another life, he had only known love. Now, he was bereft of love. He was rudderless, abandoned and visibly damaged. It was during this period that he forgot his name.

Chapter 5

Pain was just a panic signal from the brain. But it hurt so much.

She tried to tip him out of the wheelbarrow with as much care and dignity as was humanly possible, but she hurt all over. Just lifting a hand to push her glasses back up her nose left her weak and dizzy. So the poor young man tumbled out in a heap, and sprawled across the gravel. She flinched for him, grimacing at every injury she was inflicting. He did not waken. His body was completely lifeless, but his skin though markedly paler was still warm, and he had a pulse. She pulled him by his coat up the steps and in at the front door. She was embarrassed to have to treat him so badly, but she had to do it. There was no other way. It took ages to drag him through the hall, then into the lounge. The thickly-piled carpet was like glue, and with every step he grew heavier. The effort almost killed her. She was almost instantly trembling violently and drenched with sweat that was so rank she could not inhale without gagging. The exertions sapped what little strength she had left. Her determination and her rage were totally spent. She had nothing left with which to lift him on to the sofa so she abandoned him.

She collapsed again into the nearest chair, and waited for the tremors to stop. Her head and heart were exploding so powerfully, she was afraid of passing out or worse - having a heart attack. She was almost blind with exhaustion. She could not move or think or be afraid. She had forgotten almost everything. She could not feel the triumph anymore. The acute paralysing pain resonated through every nerve and sinew.

She might have fainted. It was certainly much darker outside when she managed to open her eyes, and looked around the room. Her vision had recovered. Her heart was not thumping erratically in her chest anymore. But she could not move. Simply trying to lift her hand sent excruciating pain up her whole arm and shoulder. She gasped, froze then saw him lying on the floor where she had abandoned him. He was just a heap of soiled clothes and tangled limbs. There was no resemblance now to the young man she had found by the lake. And if he was dead now then hadn't she killed him?

She turned away, grimacing.

Her cats were congregating in the hall, staring at her, and emoting feelings of betrayal. They were convinced that they were hungry. Some of them were sure they were being starved to death. It was dinner time, and there was no food on offer at all. In their eyes, she felt sure they were expressing shock and disapproval. They had never had to wait before.

Feeling guilty, she struggled bravely to her feet, and limped in agony out to the kitchen. The cats milled around her, oblivious to her injuries, and not hurrying to move away even as she shouted at them. She could not believe that it hurt so much to do so little, and not moving made it worse because she was already feeling stiff and swollen. Her joints ached. Opening two tins was amazingly difficult. Placing the filled plates on the floor almost made her faint as lightning bolts of pain tore through her back, but she felt better. The guilt was assuaged as the cats hurried to eat. These were her children. She could not have denied them anything, no matter what it cost. If she loved anything then it was these soft and amiable creatures. For a moment, she lost herself in gazing at them, counting them and worrying about them. They were indeed her children. They meant everything to her.

She had to sit down. She was so tired; she feared she might be seriously and permanently injured. To be mad and disabled was more than she could bear.

Around her the cats moved from one plate to another, each aware of their status in the group, and every one of them convinced that the next plate had better food than the one they were eating from. She had studied them over the years. Whenever a new waif arrived there was consternation in the ranks, but because she remained ultimately dominant, the newcomer was shuffled in at a level acceptable to the group. The only aggression came from the two older males, who were rivals in her absence. The females all seemed to have territory issues. They needed to have their own space where they felt safe. She could relate to that. The upstairs rooms were allocated accordingly, although one of the males periodically liked to dispossess one or other of the females, but after a week or so he would move on.

It was becoming late. The May twilight still filled her rooms with light, but she felt the time in her empty stomach, and desire for a comfortable chair and a hot drink. Sitting in the kitchen, she tried not to think about the young man in the lounge. She knew that she should go in there and do something. She knew what she had to do even if she did not want to admit it. She did not need John Wayne anymore. The maternal instinct worked independently if a little erratically. The young man needed her. It was not complicated.

In great distress, she filled a jug with water, and took a towel with her as she crept back into the lounge. He lay where she had abandoned him. He looked uncomfortable. His clothes were awry. She was shocked to see how white he had become. In serious pain, she groaned and flinched as she dropped slowly down onto her knees beside him. She found his pulse then stroked loose strands of hair from his face, and gazed down at his lovely features, sure that he was the best looking young man that she had ever seen.

"What happened to you?" she asked quietly, not wanting to disturb his rest. "I don't know what you want me to do? You don't seem hurt. You haven't a temperature." She actually held her breath, expecting him to answer, but there was no response at all. She sighed and nodded. "I don't think I can move either. I'll have to have a long hot bath, but I don't think I can stand up. I've no idea how to climb the stairs. I'm getting old. It's not your fault." He had such a lovely face. "Do you think maybe you could possibly wake up now?"

She straightened his clothes and rearranged his arms and legs, then lifted his head so that she could place a cushion there. His body temperature was dropping. He looked quite ashen. She was worried about him now. He had become a human being. There was a connection even if she wanted to deny it. "I wish you'd wake up."

He did not even flinch as she soaked a corner of the towel in the water then stroked it across his lips. She repeated the process several times, carefully parting his lips to allow the moisture to seep inside. He needed to drink, but she knew that pouring water into his mouth would only flood his lungs, and he would end up with pneumonia. The patient's friend? She had heard a doctor call it that once. It was so easy to let someone die with pneumonia. Surely, that made it a bad nurse's friend. It was an all but legal means of euthanasia. But the man was young, and now, she did not want him to die. Her steely determination was returning. He would not be allowed to die.

She waited patiently for over an hour until her legs were rigid with stress then withdrew back to a chair. Later still, she made herself a coffee, and waited just a bit longer. When it was dark outside, she crept up the stairs and filled a bath. She was so tired. She could not remember ever having been so tired before.

It was then and only then that she remembered about the frogs and the water and the hosepipe. The pond would have flooded hours ago. There would be water across the lawn, in the flowers beds. Her heart sank as she thought about the poor sick frogs, the blood worms, the leeches and a dozen other creatures she could not even name. It was too easy to deny her responsibility, but she had worked so hard to save all the living things in the ponds. All the bugs and beetles were part of the food chain. If they had all been washed away then what would the frogs eat? If she was prepared to give up on them now then why had she worked so hard for the last few months to re-establish the natural balance? If only she had worked harder. If only the young man had not come into her woodland. If...

She struggled to her feet, and turned off the bath taps. There was no point in trying to forget about it. All night, she would toss and turn, imagining what was happening in the garden. Something might still be alive. She had to go out, and turn off the water, and try to save whatever was left.

Like a crippled old woman, she climbed back down the stairs. She cast barely a glance at the young man. He had not moved. He was very pale. At that moment, she almost hated him. Her world was the garden. Her children were the living things that she cared for like a benign goddess. She was in control of it, and responsible for it though it felt like a war against all the elements most of the time. Unable to bend down to pull on shoes, she went barefoot out the back door, taking a torch off the counter. The brilliant beam of light helped her pick her way across the cobbled path towards the door in the wall. Her shoulders and arms were so sore she could hardly pull it open, and she did not bother to try closing it behind her.

The tap was set against the wall about twenty feet to her right. The ground was rough and the tiny pebbles cut her swollen feet. With the water off, she cast the torch's beam southeast across the deserted farm buildings. Something white flashed across the dark silhouette of the immense barn. There were the telltale squeaks of numerous bats. In the undergrowth, hedgehogs rummaged noisily. She searched with the torch, but they were quicker. A cool breeze refreshed her face, and whistled in the tree tops as she crossed the lawn.

The ground became spongy long before she reached the small pond. It was cold beneath her feet and yet so soothing. She slowed down, desperate to know what had happened, and yet dreading it. The pond was full to the brim. Weeds trailed around it, snared by the flooded grass. There was a ring of spoil around the edge of the waterlogged ground, carried by the quickly rising water, but anchored by the grass which she had yet to mow. Her heart sank with every step. Everywhere she looked there were the tangled remains of dead frogs and toads. Their long limbs were bent and broken. They were dead. They were all dead. Her heart almost broke in two. The torch fell from her blistered hands. Distraught and exhausted, she just stood there sobbing, unable even to produce tears. It took a long moment for her to gather herself. She was too tired to be hysterical.

Slowly, she sank down on to her knees, no longer caring about being muddy or wet. She could have slept there. She could have died there with them, but she gravely picked up the torch again, and surveyed the carnage. What she could see were not frogs at all, but old leaves and pond litter. The relief was joyous. Her smile was childish and unashamed. Inching forward across the water-logged grass, she did find the odd snail which she tossed back into the water, but there were no corpses anywhere. Her excitement was palpable when she cast the torch's beam across the pond, and saw that there was still a carpet of frogs on the bottom, which were all alive, and everywhere there were newts displaying. The crystal clear water looked fabulous. She experienced such an overpowering sense of relief, she forgot completely about the hour and the stranger she had dragged into her home.

She had no sense of time in the garden, especially after dark. For nearly an hour and a half, she stayed there bent over the edge of the pond, entranced by the activity in the water and in the flowerbeds surrounding it. The sick frogs bestirred themselves to come to the surface. Some of them climbed out, and disappeared into the undergrowth. The newts came up for air only when they absolutely had to. They were driven by the sexual imperative. The males were assiduously courting the less flamboyant females, having stand offs with other males, and generally finding the females totally unreceptive. Their breeding cycle obviously started later than the frogs. The four dead newts that she had found the previous week had all been female. They appeared to have died while producing an egg. Some still had the egg. Where the frogs had failed because of the terrible spring weather, and almost killed themselves, the newts, at least, the female newts seemed to be having different problems. She had bought a book, but there was nothing in it to enlighten her.

As soon as the hedgehogs became used to her presence, and came to investigate the soggy grass, then the frogs hurried back into the safety of the pond. Nature abounded around her, and she sat still, completely perplexed but enthralled.

It was late when she returned to the house. The hall clock told her it was almost one in the morning. With her nerve recovered, she went to check the young man. He was still alive. He had not moved at all. She stood over him for a few minutes wondering what she was supposed to do next, but there was something quite harmless about him. She was so tired, she could not think rationally anymore. All the questions that had troubled her while she pushed and pulled the wheelbarrow back from the garden seemed insignificant now. She wanted a bath. She wanted to lie down. Like Scarlet, she knew that there was always tomorrow.

The stairs had never seemed so steep. The bath water was cold. She pulled the plug and started again. Every part of her body ached. Her thoughts were irrational and foolish. There was a stranger in her house. Had she locked the bathroom door? Did it matter? The frogs were alive. The water was clear. The newts were plentiful. Where were the cats? Had she injured her shoulder? Had she twisted her knee? What time was it? What day was it? Had she imagined it all? Was the beautiful young man just an impossible dream?

It was probably 3am when she dragged herself out of the scalding hot bath. There was no clock on the landing. She stood wrapped in a towel looking over the banister, straining to hear what she could not see. It was deathly quiet downstairs. There were not even any cats about. Sometimes, she wondered if they were also just a figment of her imagination. Was there really a man down there? Her nerve wobbled. Was it better for him to be real and dead or non-existent? That was too hard. She could not think about that.

She went wearily into the bedroom, and collapsed on the bed. Dying seemed quite good about then, but it did not answer any of the questions that filled her head. Was she mad? The locals probably thought so. She could imagine them gossiping about her in the local shop. The nearest village was very small with a close community. They all knew each other, but no one knew her. The family that she had bought the farm from had lived there for generations. She had intruded. One of the women in the village had once told her quite firmly that she and her husband had wanted the farm, and evidently felt that they had a right to it even if they could not afford the asking price.

But she could not sleep. She was too tired and too curious. Miserably and reluctantly, she pulled on clean clothes, and limped back down the stairs.

The lights being switched on disturbed the three cats in the lounge, but the young man did not move. She hobbled on swollen feet to stand over him then reached down with great effort and discomfort to feel for his pulse. It was worryingly weak. In the bright light, she could see how pale he had become. It was a significant change. In the woodland, in the dappled light he had appeared to have a healthy tan, but that seemed like yesterday. It felt like a week ago. She was worried about his condition, but strangely relieved to know that he was real. She gripped his shoulder, sinking her fingers into the expensive material, immediately recognising the very real quality of his clothes, and she shook him as if he were a sleepy old cat on her bed. He was out cold, he felt cold. His clothes were still wet.

It was decision time. She knew how to look after sick animals. She knew about shock. Somehow, she needed to get him out of the wet clothes so that she could try to warm him again. But it hardly mattered that she knew what to do because she was physically incapable of doing anything. She had not eaten all day. She needed sugar yet walking off to make a cup of tea seemed irresponsible when he needed her immediate attention. She sat down beside him again, and moistened his mouth then slowly wiped clean his lovely face. He could not have been more than mid-twenties. His skin was flawless. By morning, he would need a shave. Did she even possess a razor? Somewhere inside, she was aware of the strengthening resolve. She would save him. She would take care of him. He would be alright. She could do this, but not now, not at this moment. He was too big and too heavy. She could not move him. He would have to stay on the floor. If she could get him out of his coat, he might be dry underneath. She stared at him thoughtfully. That was just about do-able.

She unbuttoned the coat then climbed awkwardly back to her feet. In theory, it seemed straightforward, but the young man was effectively dead. Her joints and muscles protested as she tried to pull one sleeve of the coat off his arm. It felt like terminal arthritis. He did not help at all. She kept telling herself that it was just pain. Just pain. She could ignore it. She would. But she had to sit down again, because the slightest exertion made her dizzy.

*

The small plane banked steeply then descended between towering brown mountains. At the bottom there was a blue river with a small town clustering along its banks, and beyond it a terrifyingly small runway. The plane plummeted down at an alarming angle.

The child stood between the legs of strangers. He was frightened. Through the window there were green meadows, a playing field, a town laid out along orderly streets, but overwhelmed with brown buildings and tin roofs. They flew so low over the town that the child could glimpse people in the bazaars, the colourful hoardings and wares, red jeeps, and battered, garishly decorated buses. He grimaced, and sank his fingers into the arms of the men, who surrounded him. They laughed to conceal their own nerves, but they held him securely during the perilous approach.

Suddenly, the plane pulled up sharply then dropped as gracefully as a bird on to the runway.

The child was given a bundle of clothes.

"It will be cold," someone said in English.

The child turned anxiously to gaze out of the window. There were about thirty yards of scrubby grass, then a treeline, and beyond that the steep brown mountainsides that reared up to the sky. It did not look like anywhere he had been before, and all that he had flown over in the last few hours had been mountains that were covered in snow or cloud. Yes. It would be cold. He put the clothes on. They were to him no more than pyjamas. They were hardly more than cotton pants, a long loose shirt and a sleeveless quilted jacket. Being his only possessions, he stroked them as if they were the finest silk, and they would remain precious to him until they fell into rags.

One of the men reached out to take the child's hand. Overcome by the humanity of the gesture, the child gave it willingly. He was led to the exit, and they both went down the steps to meet a jeep that hurtled across the tarmac from the terminals.

The men in the jeep regarded the child with cold contempt, and talked to the Arab in a language the child did not understand. His hand was passed across, but the stranger seized his wrist as if the touch of his palm was poisonous. The child drew back, instinctively aware that there was danger.

Both strangers were small dark men, no more than five feet five tall, lean of limb and kindness, with deeply lined faces and darting black eyes. Their hair was long and wild looking, but they had neat trim beards, and only smelt of the previous night's curry, which was quite pleasant compared to some of the odours prevalent in that country. They wore the floppy beige-coloured hats common to the local people, and woollen pants, long coats and proper walking shoes, though these were very old. When they spoke, they always sounded agitated and angry. Their voices were raised, whining, and grew more shrill as their patience evidently became exhausted. The one that held the child seemed inconvenienced in the extreme at having to touch him.

The Arab turned from the Pakistanis, who he found irritating and loud, and leaned down to the child. He smiled with genuine sympathy. "Do not speak to the locals. They still believe in devils. And don't look at them. They'll send Jinns after you to bewitch you." As the child frowned, the man smiled again: "Devils," he explained. "They're a bloody superstitious lot." He laughed good-naturedly. "You must be careful when you get up there." And with that he ruffled the child's hair then waved to silence the two men before walking jauntily back to the plane.

As the child was led to the jeep, he longed to look back and see the Arab again, but he knew that it was useless. He had changed hands again like a library book. He would not cry. The others had made him cry. He could not count the men or tell them apart. He had cried until his face ached, and until long after he was too exhausted to produce a solitary tear. These new strangers lifted him into the jeep, lashed his ankles and wrists with sticky tape then covered him with a blanket. He was exhausted from travelling. It had felt like a thousand million miles. There had been so many different vehicles and planes; so many different men, and all of them had covered his face, and tied him up. Before the engine started, he was sure he heard one of them say: 'kafir'. He had heard it before. He wondered what it meant, and where he was being taken. The last bitter gasps of a guerrilla war in Afghanistan between the various tribes, some banded loosely together under the Lion of Panjshir, Prince Massoud and his Northern Alliance, and the evil Soviet Empire had kept the child stranded for months on a rooftop in Yemen with only scorpions for company. Now, he was being moved again. He just wanted to go home. He wanted his mummy and daddy. But he could not quite remember where – it was on the tip of his tongue, the very edge of his memory, but it was fragmentary, and it was all fading away.

Arguably the most dangerous road in the world followed a river that was wild and rough as it thundered down from the Shandur Pass. It was an ideal spot for seriously dangerous white-water rafting, but there was nobody there. The road was barely tarred, and only just wide enough for single-file traffic with white earth on either side that billowed up like smoke signals with every disturbance. As they moved further out of town, the mountains crowded in, forcing the road to carve its way like a deep scar through the landscape. The region's geology made rock falls and land slips a regular occurrence, cutting off the isolated towns for sometimes hours or weeks at a time. In the spring, rains and the melting snows and glaciers, brought flooding rivers and deep flows of mud that could wash away roads and bridges in a moment. Almost every day there were accidents.

They drove for six hours, turning off the Chitral road, and heading north into the Hindu Kush. There were isolated villages, made of the local stone. Children played on the roadside. As the miles slipped away beneath their tyres, the road deteriorated rapidly. Sometimes, it was no wider than the axles of the gaily-coloured and infrequent local buses that clattered between the various hamlets. The road was constantly being repaired. They crossed streams that swept all before them, and stopped to clear rock falls or just to examine the latest accidents. To their right were the Himalayas, and behind them the Karakoram Range and the Silk Road that led into China. And all around them were the bleak and magnificent Hindu Kush with the lost valleys of legend, and the burning sunlight and freezing moonlight that made an easy life impossible. As they climbed higher, they passed through a few tiny villages that clung to the steep mountains often on stilts or built back in to what must have been caves. Sometimes, there were people there, but usually they seemed deserted. As the road became suitable only for goats, the trees disappeared, and then the sparse yellow grass was gone too.

They drove on. There were no other vehicles. Above them the sky was a brilliant but pale blue. The sun was already disappearing behind the towering peaks to the west, and the temperature was falling. Ahead of them, the track picked its way around the enormous boulders and deep drifts of shattered granite that regularly came down the mountains in an avalanche of broken shards.

Long before it was dark, they came to the end of the road. The two men stopped and smoked a few cigarettes. They talked together in low voices as if they were scared of being overheard or just overawed by the impenetrable wall of mountains surrounding them.

Then, irritably, they lifted the child down from the jeep, and tore off the sticky tape that had disabled him for so many hours. He was ashen-faced and weak, anxiously taking in the bleak mountains and uninhabited valley. The men both looked at their watches then rummaged through rucksacks while the child turned to gaze back down the road. Where had they come from? Where were they going? These were the mountains he had flown over that morning. They had looked utterly empty. There was an argument. By the time the Pakistanis had stopped shouting at each other, it was too dark to begin a climb. They set a small fire, and ate their few provisions, allowing the child only enough water to keep him alive. It was a cold night. They sat in the back of the jeep, huddled together in thermal blankets, listening to the wind.

In the morning after prayers, the men shouldered their rucksacks. One of them took hold of the child's wrist again. Without a word to him, they set off up the almost vertical slope. He stumbled after them in horror. Beneath their feet, the loose dressing of shattered granite moved and slid like ice. They walked carefully and quietly, only raising their voices to the child if he was slow or clumsy. The climb was exhausting. The altitude meant they had little air, and the child was sick with fear. The sun was disappearing behind the mountain that they were trying to climb so the shadow was absolute, and it was still very cold. They pressed on relentlessly, taking a snaking path which caused less disturbance to the shifting debris beneath their feet.

They climbed one ridge then descended into a deep gully, only to be faced with another almost sheer climb. The child could hardly stand up. It was impossible to breathe. There was no air. He kept looking back down to see the valley floor receding, but they never seemed to get any nearer the top of the mountain. He could not breathe. His chest tightened, and a pulse in his head throbbed painfully, affecting his vision and his sanity. He began to whine and whinge. His feet were cut to ribbons yet he felt nothing because of the adrenalin and cold. He was just exhausted and completely dehydrated and only eight years old. The man holding his wrist dragged him onwards. They crossed a wide plateau, and forded a turbulent stream on a narrow bridge designed for nothing heavier than goats. The child could hardly put one foot in front of the other.

They walked on, reaching another steep wall of loose rock. They climbed again, weaving up the sheer face. It might have been half an hour. Then the child collapsed. The momentum pulled the man holding him back off his feet, and they both slid away down the mountainside on a wave of broken rocks. Both men shouted, one in shock, and the other in terror, but the tumbling man managed with difficulty to scramble above the moving rock, dragging the child with him like rag doll. There were cries of relief and then laughter.

The men fell to arguing amongst themselves about whether to find another route or to keep going. It was very cold. They decided to keep going. They each hooked an arm through the limp child's and carried him carefully back up to where they had been before the fall, then pressed on to the high pass.

They rested there, appreciating the late afternoon light, drinking from their water bottles, then descended a few hundred feet into a flat valley that was as usual a quagmire in spring, and grazed by several dozen sheep and ugly long-eared goats. The men walked across the valley. It was only a half mile at its widest point then started to climb another almost vertical slope. This time there were a few established trails, and they made easier progress.

At the top of the next slope, with the setting sun behind it, was an old colonial fortress with commanding views in all directions towards a dozen towering snow-capped peaks and the passes that they guarded. Its walls were weathered. Its round towers had never been attacked, but they seemed to squat on the mountain top ready to bare their teeth like snarling dogs. There was a gate and great high walls. It was impregnable.

As soon as the Pakistanis crossed the threshold, they were surrounded by numerous teachers and clerics excited to hear news of the outside world.

The mountains were full of rumours about the departure of the Soviets from neighbouring Afghanistan. Were they actually leaving? Could Gorbachev be trusted? They had shot down a Pakistani F16. They had launched raids across the border into Pakistan claiming that Pakistan was supporting the Mujahedeen. They had blown up an ammunition dump outside Karachi, which left hundreds dead. There were a lot of rumours that they had murdered Zia. There were as many more that it was the Americans who had blown up the plane. Were the Soviets actually going to leave? Had bin Laden really defeated them? What would happen to Najibullah if the Soviets were not there to protect him and his communist regime? Would there ever be an end to the fighting? Hundreds of thousands of Afghans had been killed. Millions more had been displaced as refugees into Pakistan and war-torn Iran. There were clans and tribes and Sunnis and Shias. While the Soviets were in Afghanistan, their enemies were united. If the Soviets were really leaving then the warlords and feudal clan chiefs would begin to fight each other again for power and territory and loot. It would be like the old days only worse. Everyone had bigger guns now. The end of the Cold War and the collapse of the Soviets was changing everything. In Afghanistan, the war against the Soviets had become a war to defend Islam. Religious fundamentalism funded by oil revenues was filling the vacuum. The battlefield was not just in Afghanistan, but Nagorno Karabakh, Bosnia, and out of sight in the backwoods of other less accessible Soviet republics. It had drawn in many radicalised young men recently released from prisons across the Middle East and Africa, and forced into exile. They had flocked to Afghanistan looking for a fight and found one. They had been bankrolled by a young Saudi with limitless wealth, which had made every dream achievable. Many believed that only the fundamentalists could save Afghanistan, bringing the people back to God, and writing a template for world domination.

To the teachers and clerics at the isolated madrassa, they were all righteous heroes. They wanted to hear about Mullah Omar, who was rumoured to be gathering a great army down in Kandahar. While the Soviets were still a threat, the seven main mujahedeen armies were all brothers. They were all products of the madrassas. For many of the young fighters, the madrassas had been the only homes that they had ever known, and the male teachers were their honourable fathers. There was a great deal of pride. No one wanted to acknowledge that after all the Soviets had gone, there would probably be another bloody civil war. Afghanistan had a restless soul. Her men knew nothing but fighting. The only hope was Islam and absolute submission to the Will of God.

The white child was quietly handed over without explanation. There were scores of boys dressed in the same white clothes, no older than the new student except that the others were nice local boys, and not a filthy ignorant kafir whose existence was an insult to God.

Chapter 6

The sun was rising. It must have been about 5 o'clock. She realised she had not drawn the curtains. She always drew the curtains. It was normal. Somewhere in her past, she remembered being told that she must always draw the curtains. It was something about neighbours and being overlooked. Well, the farm was not overlooked, but she felt that she should have drawn the curtains. It was normal. It was important to do normal things. It was hard to remember what had happened yesterday that had stopped her doing something so conventional. Then she looked down at the young man on the floor, and knew. It was his fault. She could not blame him really, but it was totally his fault.

She rose to her feet again, and picked up the sleeve. When she ignored the fact that she was in pain and that he was actually alive, then she managed to drag the coat off his back. It must have hurt him. She did not want to think about that, but it must have hurt. He flopped about like an old broken doll. His clothes were damp too. It was only when the sunlight brightened the whole sky that she realised he was actually very ill.

She found it hard to stand up, and could barely walk, but she went back out to the kitchen to turn up the central heating by a few degrees, and to fetch fresh water. Outside, the birds were singing loudly. She had no time to listen. He needed blankets, but she was too broken down to contemplate the stairs again. She collected towels off the radiators, and went back into the lounge. She tried to lay out his body so that he would be comfortable then covered him with the towels. Every movement was painful. She groaned and gasped and grimaced, but there was no relief. Sitting beside him again, she mopped his face with the clean water, and squeezed out the drops into his mouth. He made no sound, but he was breathing. She could see that his chest rose and fell, and there was the slightest throb of a pulse in his neck. She could not help imagining his name, creating a family and a life for him. His clothes were expensive, and his hair and face and hands were well-tended. There had to be money. Someone would be worried about him. There had probably been a party somewhere, and there was an accident with pills or needles or something like that. He must have been dumped in the woods as a joke. He certainly had not walked there, not in those shoes. It was all probably very funny, but she was too tired to be amused.

The hours were marked only by the cramp in her legs and back. She shifted and stretched, but was so tormented that she needed periodically to scramble to her feet, and pace up and down. She went to feed the cats. She filled the washing machine. Another time, she remembered to make a cup of tea then forgot to drink it. She kept returning to sit close beside him, holding his head in her arms. She wanted to make everything right. In her world, she could do that. It was not about lovely flower beds, but happiness and safety. The young man had invaded her sanctuary, but he needed help now. He needed help desperately. She could no more deny him than the other waifs and strays that she always took in, and strived to make safe and well. She knew it would be more complicated. She knew it was going to be hard work and worry, but she would make it right. Now, he was just a corpse, but he would become an independent, functioning, human being, a species she knew little about. It was quite terrifying. But she would not think about that. She studied his lovely face, and imagined a whole life for him while he slept safely in her arms.

Obviously, somewhere he would have family and friends. Someone somewhere must be worried about him. Good-looking people were never alone. They were like magnets. Families held on to them. Lovers clung to them. Strangers were attracted to the stardust that always seemed to surround them. Of course, when he was stronger, then he would be able to tell her his name, and who she needed to call. He would not be with her long. He would want to go home. Judging by his designer clothes, his home was somewhere rather nice and countrified. His mother probably wore lambs' wool and pearls, and was involved in the local pony club. His dad worked in the city, played squash, and probably had affairs. Her cynicism embarrassed her. The young man was so ill, and she was already ridiculing his parents. She was used to being free with her opinions. It was easy because she was alone, and being alone seemed only to encourage her to express them. She did not have to worry about offending anyone. She did not have to consider anyone else's feelings. The cats did not mind her high-handedness. They did not recognise the difference between confidence and arrogance. She sometimes suspected that they could recognise swear words, so she tried not to swear, and always apologised, which on reflection, she had to admit, was probably a little weird.

He did not stir. Cats came and went. She turned on the television, but being still was as painful as moving, and even his beauty could not stop her thoughts wandering out into the garden.

It was a very cold morning. She was vaguely aware of it being a Bank Holiday. That meant it would, of course, rain and be cloudy. Bank Holiday weather was traditionally bad, but it was late May so it should have been all sunshine and dandelions. She found herself eventually at the small pond. There were no newts. They often seemed to disappear in the daylight, but there were still frogs. Everywhere she went, she looked for dead bodies. It was a habit. She was checking all the time. Her nerves were now more ragged than ever. There was a young man in her house. He might be in a coma. He might be dead. The more she thought about it, the worse it seemed. If he died! Where could she bury him? Where could she hide a body so that it would never be found? Lime would dissolve a body, but how much lime?

Duty claimed her for a while. The cats demanded food and attention. She knew she should fill up the nut and seed feeders. The ponds needed checking. There might be a hedgehog drowning or a frog dying or another deceased newt. It was just too much. She could not cope. The pressure was immense. Her sense of duty was so strong, but she had no resources left. She gritted her teeth, and stooped to put two more plates of food down for the cats, then sank onto one of the kitchen chairs. She folded her arms on the table. She meant only to rest her head for a moment, but she slept for hours. Her whole body stiffened. Her hands ached so badly she could hardly open them. She was in a bad way. She knew that it would take a week, at least, for her to recover from the exertions of her stupid, foolish rescue of the young man by the lake.

Later, she dutifully fetched down blankets to cover him. Now, he was running a fever. Bravely ignoring her nerves and her own injuries, she sank back to her knees beside him, and began to bathe his face, and press drops of water into his mouth. Her resolution was set in stone now. She would take care of him, and make him well because in another life he might have been her own child. That he was lovely and helpless did not harm his prospects. She could have loved him if his hair had not been like silk or his features so soft and sensitive. Was he an addict? No. He looked like a choirboy. It was not even that he was a handsome young man because he was so much more than that. He was shockingly beautiful. If he woke up and was unharmed, she was already convinced that she could forgive him for having invaded her secret world, just as long as he went away quickly and without causing any trouble.

She placed a bowl of water next to his face, and used an absorbent cloth to continuously transfer moisture into his mouth. It was not perfect. It was hardly fool proof, but she knew he was dehydrating. If she kept the bowl full and the cloth under his tongue then he was getting something. It felt like an achievement. She checked it regularly, and was pleased to feel the difference it made to his mouth and lips.

*

A slender man of respectable appearance and considerable authority, stood in front of the child. Behind him were an assembly of teachers, and surrounding them were all the students of the school. They were in the courtyard. The air was crystal clear. The sky above was a cobalt blue. Every horizon was a wall of glistening icy peaks. It was a beautiful day, but it was cold.

The child swayed. Two older students held him upright. He had been brought from his tiny room to meet his peers. There were so many boys. They were all dressed in the same white pyjamas that he wore. Their ages ranged from about seven to seventeen. They were all alike, black-eyed and dark-skinned and unfriendly. He was the alien. He was their enemy.

Alternating between reasonable English and a translation for the rest of the assembly, the Head Teacher, Sheikh Achmed Qadri, said, "You have come here from far away to be taught the Will of God."

The child stirred at the sound of English words. He looked up with intense interest, desperate to believe he had found a friend and some protection at last.

"You will learn the Words of God, the only Truth. God, The Almighty, has decreed that you will be a servant to the Believers, Might and Strength be to God, the Prophet and the Believers. God, may He be Exalted, has decreed that the Believers will rule the world, and that on the Last Day, the disbelievers and the Jews and the Christians, who are base and perverted transgressors, they will be cursed, and those that conquer them will go to paradise. So that – while you live – you do not offend God, the most Compassionate, the most Merciful, you will learn the Teachings of His Holiness the Prophet, Peace and Blessings be upon Him. You will learn the wisdom of the Sunnah and the commands of Sharia. You will learn all the teachings of our great leaders. You will learn with these Blessed Believers. You will learn to respect God and the True Faith and all Muslims wherever in the world they live whether they be a venerable man or his new born son. We are of one family. We are the Ummah. You will show respect. As a disbeliever you are condemned. You are unclean. You are born of swine. You have been brought here to learn so that you may serve the Faithful, and not be offensive to our sight. You will learn. You will obey. You may not look into our faces or touch us or our food or our possessions. You will not speak unless we first speak to you. You may not walk in front of us. You may not sit in our presence."

There was a pause to allow the two boys holding the child upright to force him down to his knees. They pressed his forehead into the soggy cold ground, and forced his hands palm flat on the ground in front of his head. They held him there by force. The child started to cry, exhausted and frightened.

"God, may He be Exalted, will not allow vile infidels to have the upper hand over righteous Believers. This is how you will meet all Believers. You will bow down and hide your face so that we are not offended by the sight of it. You will not raise your head. You will not move until you are given permission to do so. You may not rise from the ground until we dismiss you. If you are beaten (and you will be beaten to encourage your resistance to the wickedness in your heart) you will submit, and you will be thankful. If you ever raise a hand higher than your shoulder it will be cut off. If you steal anything your hand will be cut off. You may never raise a hand against a Believer. You may not leave this place. You may not go out after dark. You may not wear shoes. You may not eat or drink anything unless we give it to you. You own nothing. You are nothing. You will obey or you will be beaten."

The child had heard almost every word, but he did not understand any of them. He was traumatised and quite terrified. It was too much to expect a child to comprehend total servitude.

Achmed Qadri, the Head Teacher, lapsed into a mixture of Arabic, Pashtun and Urdu. Then he dismissed the other boys, who disappeared into their dormitories to snigger and gossip about the nasty white infidel.

The Head Teacher understood the attention span of boys. Soon, he and the teachers were left in the courtyard. Only the two older boys remained, still holding the infidel down. The Head Teacher noticed they had its palms pinned under their feet. He did not approve, but then the infidel must learn to feel its inferiority at all times. Many fundamentalists preached that disbelievers had no rights, and were, in fact, only firewood destined for hell. The dogma of Islam proclaimed that it was the mission of the Islamic community to impose the Will of God on all Mankind. That meant subjugation, not incorporation.

The young kafir was pulled across the ground to the feet of the Head Teacher, and forced to bow down and press his forehead into the mud again. The rules of his narrow existence were repeated slowly for him. He was told to repeat each sentence, but it was still too much for him. He mumbled incoherently. It was hard to speak when bent low over his knees, and choking with sobs. There were words he had never heard before. But he tried to understand, to be helpful, to be nice, because he wanted to be loved. He needed desperately to be loved.

*

There was a westerly wind. She could see it running through the tree tops.

It almost called to her, but she was trapped by aches and pains and the strange young man. She sat across the room in a state of collapse, watching him and the television with heavy eyes and faltering attention. She wanted to go outside and escape, but her injuries foiled her, and it was so cold. She could not leave him. The programmes on the television were the usual holiday afternoon fare. She did not have digital because she could not afford it. She watched idly. There was a David Lean film. They were always good, but she was so tired, she could hardly keep her eyes open, too tired to be hungry, too tired anymore to be afraid of the young man.

The blankets and the hot radiators seemed to be warming him, but his face was now grey, and his skin felt like a dead chicken. She brought more blankets, and filled another hot water bottle, and though she was tempted to cuddle it herself and nurse her own wounds, she did press it against his chest, and gently tuck the blankets closer. Even the cats came to nestle against him, though not out of any compassion. Perhaps, because it was cold outside, but more likely because she was hardly able to move without whimpering, she stayed close and stared at him in dumb adoration. From the chair, she could see him laying on the floor beneath a mountain of blankets, pale and corpse-like, yet still beautiful and still breathing. Eventually, she fell asleep.

The television awoke her. There was tennis on somewhere. It hardly seemed warm enough. Was it really time for Roland Garros? Everything in the media was about the World Cup in Germany with Beckham and Rooney and the WAGS; the sex god and the potato head and the glamorous girlfriends. Tennis was not on the media radar. She struggled to find anything interesting in football though the trailer on the BBC was mildly engaging, and even a football atheist could appreciate Thierry Henri.

The first sign of life was when the young man's bland expression changed into a deep and unhappy frown. Then his head moved, but it was more of an involuntary jerk than an assertive nod. She hurried to kneel down beside him, hoping he was about to wake. She stroked his face to erase the frown, but he shifted again in distress, and made some inarticulate noise that reminded her of a dog whining. She realised he was dreaming. She stayed with him, holding his head in her lap, stroking his face, and assuring him over and over that he was safe, that he would be alright. Sometimes, he seemed to be speaking, but it was not a language that she knew. His increased anxiety and repeated attempts to raise his hands to fend off some imagined enemy only encouraged her maternal instincts. She bent over him, holding him still, and repeating her assurances.

Long after her knees hurt so badly she doubted she would ever be able to walk again, he fell limp in her arms. Her regard for him vanished. He was put aside and forgotten as she dragged her crippled carcass across the floor then struggled to her feet. Part of her almost envied him because he was unconscious while she was in pain. It had cost her dear to rescue him. In her socially crippled mind, he owed her big time, but as soon as her circulation improved, her temper softened. It was not his fault. She would make him well. She could easily play god in her universe.

When exactly the smell began, she did not remember. The heat generated by the hot water bottles and the blankets and her central heating system probably exacerbated it. She did not even think about it until the cats began to appear in the hall, all of them looking perturbed by something unpleasant in the air. She sniffed and grimaced. It was offensive. She recognised that it was not a feline smell. A quick sniff reassured her that she was not to blame. It had to be the young man. His face was now grey, and he looked bad, as bad as the smell.

She stared at him for several minutes, imagining the state of his bowels and his underwear. He was unconscious. She did not know if bowels moved when the vessel was unconscious. She knew that euthanized cats emptied their bladders. It seemed reasonable to consider the possibilities, but she knew she was only delaying the obvious. He needed the equivalent of a bed-bath, and she did not know where to start doing that.

So she went out. She needed fresh air, and to hear her birds sing. It still hurt to move. Her knees and shoulders and lower back were particularly sore, so it was hard to fill the nut feeders, and to carry even a half-filled bucket of seed all the way down the garden. But she did it. This was her thing. And once she had walked that far then she had to go down the path into the woods to visit the little shrine then on to the pond. She did not expect anyone to be there, but was still surprised by the relief that she felt. She was alone again. Her heart was restored. Forgetting all her cares, she sat down under the trees, and gazed away across the pond, lost in the reflections of light even on a cold grey afternoon.

Hours later, she limped back, soothed by the pleasures of her secret garden. She knew every leaf and bough. The fresh spring colours and textures that no one else had ever seen belonged only to her, and she did not need to share them to appreciate how wonderful they were. The ferns in the woods and the mosses along the waters' edge enchanted her. In every nook and cranny, she imagined a world of delight. It was so much more fascinating than the world of humans. She had stepped back. The world she glimpsed on the television hardly encouraged her to re-engage. People were not very nice. Children were usually monsters. The world she had created in the garden was a haven. She did not need anything else. She did not want anything else.

It was late. She had been gone hours though it seemed but a moment. He was still unconscious. She wondered if she had really expected him to disappear. Would she have actually been able to live with not knowing what had brought him into her garden? She told herself 'yes' but knew the answer was really 'no'.

The smell seemed infinitely worse after the fresh, cold air outside. She slumped to her knees beside him to check that he was alive. Her relief to find him still in the land of the living was, she felt, quite the correct response. As she peeled the blankets away, the smell grew worse. She inhaled through her mouth, filling her lungs with air then gazed at his still-clothed body. He looked suddenly crumpled and frail. His clothes were stained with soil and leaves and sweat and something else, something she could not quite recognise. She breathed again through her mouth. It was like peeling an octopus. The jacket came away first. Having removed it from his body, she was much less squeamish about going through the pockets, which all seemed to be empty.

Then she found a fifty thousand Euro casino chip. It was from Monte Carlo. There was nothing else. She stared at the chip in amazement. She had seen casino chips before, but never one of such a high value or from Monte Carlo. But then he looked like the Riviera. He had the fine clothes and the golden tan. She could not imagine that he had ever done a day's work in his life. Yes. He did look like someone, who would go to Monte Carlo, and play Baccarat with the rich and famous. The Monaco Grand Prix had been on at the weekend. Had he been there? He had a wristwatch that looked fabulously expensive, but she could not take it off his wrist. It was a Breitling. She was very impressed, and decided that expensive watches probably did not open like ordinary ones. She bit the casino chip just to make sure it was real, and wondered idly about the exchange rate. The chip seemed completely genuine. She slipped it into her own pocket. His appearance in her garden seemed even more baffling. For a moment, she stared at him, adding the new piece to the puzzle, but still knowing nothing at all. The waistcoat seemed to be glued to his back so she gave it a sharp pull. It came away, and hung stiffly in her hands. Then she saw his shirt. It was soaked with muddy red blood, and still horribly damp in places.

Blood. She had never seen so much real blood. She stared in shock, suddenly paralysed by disbelief, and afraid of touching him. His entire back seemed to be an open wound judging by the amount of blood oozing through his shirt, the fabric being completely undamaged. What could have happened to him? She drew away as much to find fresher air to breathe as to gather her nerves. His flesh was rotting. The smell was now unmistakable and quite sickening. All her good intentions disappeared. She was a coward. She had no idea what to do. Climbing to her feet, she backed away then fled the room.

In the kitchen, she had a drink of water, and leaned on the sink while she considered her options. Of course, she should have called the police when she first found him. After rescuing him, she should have driven him to the nearest hospital. Hindsight was a wonderful thing. She stared out of the window. She imagined how absolutely bloody awful it would have been to have big-booted coppers all over the garden, and their endless and annoying questions. Who would believe that he had appeared as if by magic in her garden, and that she had no idea who he was?

But he was injured. She could reel off a list of injured animals she had successfully nursed. Of course, some had died. And he was not a battle-scarred cat or a starving hedgehog. She remembered how lovely he had looked amongst the ferns when she first found him. Now, he looked really ill, and it was probably her fault.

It was decided. She had no choice. If he died, she would deal with it, but she couldn't ask for help, couldn't have strangers in the house, couldn't bear any questions. She filled a clean bowl with water, collected a pair of scissors and some towels then returned to kneel by the helpless young man. Without hesitation, she set about cutting the shirt off his back. She knew what to do. She had nursed a cat with horrific facial wounds, and it had survived, and all its fur had grown back. She could do this. She had to. She would not think about how her clumsy rescue must have made his injuries so much worse. She would feel guilty later. He would understand. If he lived, he would understand.

The shirt was glued to his back. She tried to peel it off then dampened it with water. Even when the material was wringing wet, she had to pull it away quite forcefully, taking skin and tissue with it. His back had been torn to shreds. Every inch was raw and still weeping with blood and pus as the wounds were inflamed, infected, and looked horrible. He had been whipped, but it was so much more than that. All her senses were revolted. The smell made the air unbreathable. Her eyes smarted and burned. She was at a loss to understand what could possibly have happened. Struggling to her feet, she hugged his clothes to her chest, and just felt sick and helpless. She had never seen anything like it, and could not imagine anything comparable. The clothes were full of blood. As she held them at arms' length, she saw the bloodstains had spread on to her own clothes. He must have been bleeding a long time. She shuddered, and dropped silently back to her knees as she remembered again how she had dumped him in the wheelbarrow and dragged him across the floor. She wept tearlessly. His blood was everywhere. It was on her hands and in her head and everywhere.

Chapter 7

Everyone said it started with the Gulf War, but for him it had become confusing long before that. In the Kingdom, it was always safe and quiet. The rest of the world seemed so far away. For many, the only foreigners that they had ever met were the few migrant workers allowed into the cities or amongst the wealthy, there were the servants, who came and went almost unnoticed. He knew that there were some people who had never met a foreigner. It seemed inconceivable on such a small planet, but the Kingdom had always been that way. There were certainly more pilgrims now. They came in their millions, and some were distinctly more foreign than others, but their strangeness was muted by the white uniform that all pilgrims had to wear, and they were never allowed to stray far from the Sacred Sites. He had annoyed his father by being different. He had wanted to go to school in America, and had defied his father. For a while, they had fallen out, but the seventies changed everything. So he went to live amongst the foreigners. He learned their ways, but he kept his soul. After university, he had gone to the West Coast in search of an adventure. There were still hippies and flared jeans, but the sex, drugs, and rock and roll lifestyle had become distinctly corporate. Everything was run by lawyers. Half the people that he met were, like him, from somewhere else, and had come west in search of a dream. For a while, he let his hair grow into a goofy mane, and dressed it with daisies. He could not play a guitar so he sat in the park quoting Omar Khayyam to the tourists. He had so many girlfriends, he hardly remembered all their names. For a while, life was good, but all too soon his father sent emissaries. His mother sent demands. He had to go home. Reluctantly, he surrendered. In the last precious moments of his freedom, he made the decision to go north to see the icebergs and polar bears. Under a transcendent midnight sky, he watched the Aurora Borealis, and fell in love with a golden girl with white hair and green eyes, who led him to Svalbard. Another year passed in the blink of an eye before he started south again. He crossed Europe in a rickety VW camper van that had the good manners to only breakdown conveniently outside of garages. He slept under the stars with an Andalusian gypsy while her people danced the flamenco and played their guitars during the Horse Fair in Seville. Spain delighted him, but he could not rest. He felt like a fleeing fugitive except that he knew in his heart that he was going home.

In Casablanca, he met some guys in a cafe. He had gravitated to them because they looked like students, and were much younger than the other patrons. When he offered to buy them a drink, they became surly and suspicious. He made a joke in English about all the gin joints in the world, but they ignored him. He quickly apologised in French, assuming they did not speak English, and explained that he was a tourist, and did not know anyone. They all looked at him as if he was some alien thing, but he laughed. He still had the blue jeans and the goofy hair, and cared not a jot about his appearance. He pulled up a chair and sat down, which unsettled them. He told them his name was Abdul Aziz, and that he had been travelling for months in an old van. It did not seem important then that he was a prince and wealthy beyond their dreams. They let him talk. They let him order a round of drinks. When they rose to leave, he rose too. A little desperately, he explained that he had not had a proper conversation with anyone for weeks, and that he thought they looked like students, and he was just a student.

"We are Saharawi," they had said. He always remembered that, but he did not understand. He sat down, and slowly, almost reluctantly, they had joined him.

"We are not Moroccan."

That still meant nothing. He told them that he was not Moroccan, but they already knew that.

They were not talkative. He felt sure they did not trust him, which was baffling. Later, he realised that they probably thought he was a spy. He talked for hours, filling their silence. He won them over a little with snapshots from his life in San Francisco. They relaxed slowly. While they kept quiet, they could not be betrayed. He was funny. Occasionally, he managed to make them smile. He alternated between French and English. Their French was better than his, but they did understand English. Talking made him feel better. His spirits lifted. For a while, he was able to forget that he was going home.

Later in the afternoon, he invited them to see his van. It was nearby. They were curious now, and followed him through the streets like a Greek chorus. It was very hot and dusty. The traffic was thick and loud with the cacophony of horns. He was surprised by the number of men in uniform. They were on every street corner, and they were all armed.

The van seemed to reassure them. He opened the side door to show them his home only to regret not having made any attempt to tidy up. It was squalid. There were piles of dirty clothes, empty tin cans and food wrappings. There was also a smell, which he had not noticed before. A few of them leaned in curiously then drew away smiling. They were all students. He closed the door again, and felt his face burning with embarrassment. He was surprised when, after a brief but unintelligible discussion, two of the young men climbed into the van. He hurried to sit behind the wheel. He was told to drive. The ones left on the pavement disappeared into the crowd.

For thirty odd minutes, he drove at a snail's pace through the crowded streets. He turned whenever directed to do so. There were no words. A finger pointed and he followed. He had no idea where they were taking him. At last, a finger pointed to a building. He squeezed the van into a tight parking space, and definitely bumped the old green Citroen parked behind. Nobody seemed to mind. He hurried to look. There were so many dents on both vehicles that it seemed better to ignore it. The young men were already walking away. Casablanca was not a particularly attractive town. They had not quite reached the suburbs so everything new was cheap and concrete. They led him upstairs to a first floor flat. The front door had been painted red, but everything else looked unfinished and rough. The flat was small and utilitarian. The walls were unpainted plaster. The only light came from naked light bulbs. There were cushions and rugs scattered across the floor. In one room, there was a small desk and chair; both were piled high with books. Everything about the place underlined the fact that they were students on a budget.

Suddenly, they were courteous. They bid him to sit down on one of the cushions. They insisted on making him a cup of tea. Their English vocabulary was formal and polite as if they had learned it from a guide book. When they were all seated comfortably on the floor, and beginning to feel at ease, the door opened and the rest of the group entered carrying bags of fresh produce. They were all smiling now. They were his hosts. Two of them immediately set to work preparing a meal. The transformation was remarkable. Again, he was embarrassed because they were obviously poor, and could ill afford a generous meal. There was nothing he could say that would not have offended them. For about twenty minutes, they sat in silence, all smiling, but no one knowing what to say. The smell of fried goat filled the room. From the spines of the books that he could see, it was obvious that they were studying to be engineers. Some of the books were very old. The others looked decidedly second hand. It was a world away from his affluent privileged life at Harvard.

A bowl of meat was placed on the floor between them. His hosts were deferential and smiling. One of them introduced himself then one by one his friends. They all insisted that he fill his plate first. He was hungry by then but he took a little and thanked them. They all ate with relish. Despite the humble surroundings, it was a meal fit for a king.

They began to talk. They were earnest and sincere. They were in Morocco legitimately studying at the university, but they were planning to join the Polisario Front, and fight to liberate their country from Moroccan tyranny. They were Saharawi. They belonged to the indigenous peoples of what had been called Spanish Sahara since 1884. He had vaguely heard of Spanish Sahara or now Western Sahara, but it was almost unknown compared to its neighbours Morocco and Mauritania. The call of independence had swept across all the colonies of the 'old world' powers encouraged by the United Nations. The indigenous tribes were the Saharawi, Berbers by extraction, and Western Sahara was at the top of no one's agenda. They were few. They had no voice. They had lived in isolated oases and in coastal villages. They were camel herders and fishermen. Their country was nothing more than a narrow strip of desert along the Atlantic Ocean, but they wanted independence.

He was shocked to learn that Morocco had managed to drive almost the entire population of Western Sahara across the border into Algeria. Modern jet planes and napalm had been used to attack unarmed civilian refugees. More perplexing was their assertion that the US and Saudi Arabia had supported Morocco's flagrant land grab. He hardly dared to ask if they were flag-waving communists. Nothing else explained why the Americans were supporting the aggressors. There was no oil. He would have known of the country's existence if it had oil. Aba explained that the King of Morocco believed his rightful dominions extended across all of the Sahara including Algeria and Mauritania. He was not going to stop at the borders of what he now called his 'southern provinces'. The Saharawi had formed the Polisario Front in 1973 when Spain was still the colonial power. They had established their claim to independence, and in the beginning the Franco government, under pressure from the UN, had provisionally agreed, but then there were claims that the land was Moroccan by right as the Spanish had stolen it in the nineteenth century. In the ensuing arguments, the people who actually lived there were ignored, and when Franco died, Spain handed over their colony for Morocco and Mauritania to divide between themselves. It was a done deal. Only the Polisario Front raised objections. What had been irritating occasional attacks became a full blown guerrilla war. The Saharawi had started their campaign with camels and muskets, but they captured vehicles and weapons from the Moroccans. Mauritania quickly retreated from the fray as their army had barely three thousand soldiers, and the country was effectively bankrupt. Algeria, never on friendly terms with her neighbour, quickly offered sanctuary and arms. The Saharawi were able to set up a government in exile that operated out of a refugee camp in southern Algeria. Col. Muammar al' Gaddafi was also happy to supply them with weapons. Libya was by then supplying most of the insurgents on the planet. Beyond these few allies, the Saharawi were completely on their own.

They talked into the night. Aba and his friends reeled off a list of villages that had been destroyed with the families left destitute when their livestock were driven off never to be seen again. They told him about the wall that the Moroccans were planning to build. It was to be fortified. There were already landmines. The Moroccans were already using napalm. They had flooded the western side of the country with Moroccan settlers. There were also more soldiers on the ground than civilians. The few Saharawi who remained along the coast or lived in the capital were worked harder and paid less than the Moroccan settlers who came down to bolster the King's claims. The Saharawi had been portrayed as impoverished nomads living in a wasteland who needed rescuing from their predicament. The Moroccans were investing. They were building roads and harbours. They were also reaping the financial benefits of a huge phosphate mine, and leasing out fishing rights to the Spanish. The Saharawi believed their country was being plundered. They were launching attacks on the foreign fishing fleets to drive them away, and they were doing everything they could to stop the resources of their homeland being looted. They called their country the Saharawi Arab Democratic Republic. Only the International Court of Justice had contradicted Moroccan and Mauritanian claims to sovereignty, and established the precedent that territory belonged to its inhabitants, which were and had always been the Saharawi. The Polisario Front was lobbying in European capitals while fighting to thwart Moroccan expansionism, but nobody was listening. They were so few. Morocco had powerful friends in the UN Security Council, but according to the young students, the Polisario Front was well organised, disciplined and determined. They would never give up.

Prince Abdul Aziz went home chastened. His father engulfed him in duty and protocol. His mother wanted him to visit the Scared Sites and get married. He had changed fundamentally, but it had less to do with the green-eyed beauty in Svalbard than the sheer hopelessness of the Saharawi people, who simply wanted to live their own lives even if that meant being poor nomadic camel herders. From boardrooms and offices around the world, he watched helplessly as Morocco engulfed almost the whole of the country, drove the Saharawi people into exile in Algeria, then built an immense sand wall to stop them returning to their homes.

While abroad, he had managed to take care of himself. He was awoken by a modest battery-operated alarm clock. That was now the job of a servant. He had successfully washed and dressed all on his own for years. Now, he had several households of servants, and their sole responsibility was taking care of him. He could not just boil a kettle and make a cup of tea. There were a dozen people involved in the process. He found it irritating in the beginning, but learned to share his space. He was a rich man. It was his duty to provide a home and employment and opportunities for 'his people'. On paper, he had nearly two thousand employees though the vast majority were bodyguards. Most were older than him. Some were foreigners. Some were not even that. As a child, he had been surrounded by servants. Some were his, but most belonged to his parents. His father upheld the old traditions, and while his father lived then he had to submit to his father's will. He had been given properties and shares in businesses around the world. His family were steadily extending their portfolios. It was no longer all about oil.

He lived a life of smothering comfort. In the Kingdom, his family focused on duty and pleasures. The strange stillness of life there was attractive on a planet consumed by violence and corruption. Religion restricted anything spontaneous or impetuous, but their extreme wealth made it almost painless. In the early days, whenever he tried to change something, he would be summoned before his father, and lectured as if he were still a child. It was humiliating. The only escape was to live on the move. He owned houses. His first few wives were chosen by his parents. He treated them honourably. He set them up in Riyadh or Jeddah or Medina, but he did not live with any of them. They were not unattractive. Some of them were intelligent and charming, but they were his political wives. He stayed with them long enough to get them pregnant. They did not complain. They had royal titles, luxurious homes and children. They knew their duty. He travelled with an entourage of servants and bodyguards. He bought planes, small jets then airliners. He had business interests from Chile to Indonesia. His circle of friends were all men he had met through his businesses though his father still insisted that he should limit his friends to members of his tribe.

International news focused on the Soviets in Afghanistan, American involvement in the revolutions in Central America, and the Iran-Iraq War. These were not the only conflicts, but they had the attention of the predominantly American Press. In the Kingdom, there was support for Iraq, but Saddam Hussein was considered reckless. When the old king passed away after a short illness, the situation changed. The new king was on friendlier terms with Saddam, and quickly agreed to lend him more money to finance the continuation of the war against the Persians. He also purchased AWACS from the US, with the long-term goal of having surrogate American bases inside the Kingdom. In Western Sahara, the sand wall was continually extended by the Moroccans to make an impenetrable barrier keeping the Saharawi away from the valuable resources discovered in the west. The Saharawi government in exile respectfully applied for membership of the OAU, which heightened tensions in the region. The Moroccans responded by resigning from the organisation in protest, then started firing ground-to-air missiles against Polisario bases on the other side of the wall. International criticism eventually forced the Moroccans to retreat behind their wall where they merely consolidated their defences. They had successfully populated the western side with enough Moroccan settlers to completely distort any referendum suggested by the OAU or UN as a peaceful resolution to the crisis. They were making friendly overtures to Algeria. Morocco was positioning itself as the major power player in the region while the rest of the world focused on the Death Squads in El Salvador or the courageous Afghan fighters, who were taking on 'modern arsenals with simple hand-held weapons'.

Prince Abdul Aziz had been to Tindouf, the isolated refugee camp in southern Algeria where most of the Saharawi population had taken refuge. The first time, he arrived with a few bodyguards and boxes of money. It was to be the beginning of a steep learning curve about the needs of displaced persons and the ineptitude of bureaucratic institutions. The UN had some people on the ground. They had set up a clinic. They were supplying food. When he offered them the money so that they could bring in more food and build more homes, the UN officials refused to take it. They had told him that he was complicating the situation. They actually asked him to leave and to take his money with him. They stalked him around the camp as he went to talk to the refugees. Many were hostile. His country was financially supporting the enemy. Even when he was handing out money, there was suspicion, then almost a riot.

Over the years, he made many trips to Tindouf, and during the ceasefires, he actually went to Tifariti. He improved the runway. He wrote a blank cheque for medicine, but the money was spent on latrines. A UN representative asked him to contribute to the aid being supplied to combat famine in war-torn Eritrea and Ethiopia. He bankrolled a vaccination campaign in the Upper Volta after an outbreak of River Blindness. During the eighties, he was constantly called upon to make financial contributions to the UN, but they did not like him going to refugee camps. They did not like him asking questions. They kept telling him that he did not understand the situation, and they politely asked him not to interfere. There was drought and famine across northern Africa. In areas where there was conflict, the supply of aid became another weapon. The UN provided no protection to the food convoys, which were often hijacked and looted. The vulnerable people in the camps were the young and the old. No one was protecting them. In the end, he was not just asking questions but constantly criticising their methods.

After one particularly long and bitter critique to yet another UN representative, he was invited to go to New York to see for himself what the UN were doing. He was in New York when Michael Buerk made his 'Biblical Famine' broadcast that changed the way many people felt about giving aid. Feeling that the tragedy in Ethiopia vindicated his argument, he attended a meeting at the UN believing he would be allowed to speak, but again they wanted him to be silent and not interfere. He could not even get a meeting with the Secretary General. The UN were struggling under the burden of more than a dozen wars, civil disobedience in numerous regions, drought and famine in Africa, kidnapping in the Lebanon, women's rights, modern slavery, poverty, corruption and the spreading epidemic of AIDS. It was easier to get a meeting with Donald Rumsfeld than with anyone with any authority at the UN. The Reagan Administration was busy with the Cold War, and the extremely violent civil wars in El Salvador, Nicaragua and Honduras. There were many who said that Central America had been completely destabilised by American interference, but the Americans believed they were protecting their rear. They were providing humanitarian aid to Africa, but their attention was definitely focused somewhere else. He had tried to bring up the subject of Western Sahara, but was told that the House of Representatives' Foreign Affairs Committee had prohibited US Military Advisors from working there so the UN and OAU were sorting it out.

When he went back to Riyadh, he was reprimanded first by his father, then by the King. It was a serious situation. He was going against the wisdom of the King. He could be stripped of his titles and his wealth, and sent abroad into exile. He could be sent to prison. His only defence was an eloquent description of the Saharawi as nomadic camel herders living in the vast inhospitable desert as Arabs had done since the dawn of time. It did not work with his father, but the King accepted his romantic explanation, and pardoned him with the admonishment that he must not interfere again in matters that did not concern him.

He focused on work. He remained abroad for long periods of time. There were many women in his life. His extensive network of friends and associates were always happy to introduce him to attractive women. They were always beautiful, always foreign, and always available. He had wives. He did not need long-term relationships. The sex was good. Having a physical relationship with an athletic woman who enjoyed the journey was marvellous. By the late eighties, he had become used to having a constant supply of women through his bed. He was gracious and charming. He bought them presents, but no one touched his heart. His various business enterprises were making so much money it was obscene. He bought even bigger houses and begat more children. His wives never complained, and they all dutifully professed their love for him. Only his mother constantly lectured him. She alone felt that she had the right to interfere in his life. There were more political marriages, and a spate of equally political divorces. Living in seclusion, his ex-wives behaved themselves or they lost their children. It was a harsh reality of life that everyone accepted. He never questioned how much money they spent.

Occasionally, he would give all his staff the day off then fly down with a few plainclothes bodyguards to attend a meeting of the OAU or because he wanted to talk to the UN representatives, who were visiting Tindouf. He had friends down there now who would tip him off when someone important was coming. He still felt impotent. The French were constantly shutting him out, and making snide remarks about his American friends. He did not have any American friends, at least, not in the way they were suggesting.

There was some shady deal going on with the Israelis. He had been invited into a meeting with some of the Reagan Administration, but he felt sure they thought he was someone else. The name Manucher Ghor Banifar was whispered several times in dark tones then they started saying that if they gave Noriega some money he claimed he could sort it all out. The Prince did not know what to say about that. When they said 'arms for hostages', he knew he was in the wrong meeting. Hezbollah were picking up hostages like cornflakes in the Lebanon. He was not sure if they believed he was a Shiite or an Iranian. Either way, they were misinformed. He rose to his feet feeling slightly insulted then introduced himself with all his titles, making it perfectly plain that Iran and Hezbollah were his mortal enemies. A few days later, McFarlane resigned.

The following year, the UN calculated that nearly six million people were dependent on food aid. The support available from the UN was directly linked to the contributions of the member states. As the largest contributor, this gave America a great deal of power, but its ambitions were continually frustrated by a pro-French bias. This bias also existed in the Lebanon where French hostages were rapidly released while American hostages languished for years. The top secret 'arms for hostages' scheme was obviously not working. But when France defaulted on a debt to Iran, five French journalists were quickly rounded up, which just proved who really pulled the strings in Hezbollah. The following month, within a matter of days, Brian Keenan and John McCarthy were taken alive while three university professors were killed. They had years of hell ahead of them, but the atrocities in the Middle East were totally eclipsed by a cataclysmic nuclear disaster at Chernobyl near the Belarus border. The Soviets tried to deny everything then just heavily disguised the truth.

In the autumn of '86, the Prince finally met Javier Perez de Cuellar, the Secretary General of the United Nations. They had a brief conversation about the situation in Western Sahara. It transpired that de Cuellar had met with the Moroccan king in Rabat some months earlier in an attempt to find a settlement that was acceptable to both parties, and he had failed. The King of Morocco believed he had every right to occupy Western Sahara. He was not prepared to discuss any concessions to the Saharawi. Even some semblance of autonomy inside Morocco was not on the table. A referendum, which was the UN resolution of choice was out of the question unless the imported Moroccan settlers were allowed an equal vote, which was totally unacceptable to the Saharawi.

*

At some moment in his silent life, the kafir had realised that he preferred to be with Prof. Shah, who simply hated him, and a prince, who had never actually acknowledged his existence. To everyone else, he was just an object. He was a thing. During the long years at the madrassa, he had been the sweeper, cleaner, fetcher and carrier, condemned to be despised and bullied and humiliated by everyone. Prof. Shah loathed him as an imperialist enemy, but the Professor spoke to him in English when no one else spoke to him at all. He taught him a dozen local dialects, and unconsciously allowed him an education that the other boys were denied. While the other teachers shunned the kafir because his presence defiled their classrooms, the Professor taught him enough Arabic to be able to read the Koran, and to understand why he was considered such a pariah. During long evenings and endless cups of tea, the Professor and Head Master sat together around a stove as old friends, and argued about life and death and their unfulfilled ambitions. The kafir was always there in the background, grateful to be overlooked whilst listening to every word. The Professor took great pleasure in berating him, but he had given him food and allowed him a blanket. There was a bond.

The Soviets eventually left Afghanistan, but continued supporting Najibullah, which enabled the communist government in Kabul to keep up attacks on Pakistan. Kashmir was still hot. There were pogroms in Baku. Iraq complained to the Arab League about Kuwait stealing oil and ignoring quotas, but when Iraq moved thirty thousand troops to the Kuwaiti border, the American imperialist infidels sent battleships to the Gulf. When Iraq invaded Kuwait seeking justice, the world forgot about the troubles in Pakistan and Kashmir.

At the madrassa, the kafir had always been the enemy. In the beginning, he was just the Soviet dog. During the Gulf War, he was the murderous crusader, who would be destroyed by the righteous Believers. He was a heretic, an apostate, a filthy infidel. He was always the outcast, always alone. He tried once to run away, but there was never a second chance, and eventually he came to believe that they had every right to treat him like vermin. He was a kafir. He was the disbeliever they were all taught to hate.

The madrassa's isolation meant that rumour was almost as rare as truth. The Gulf War was over quicker than the winter. The aftermath was shocking and confusing, and already consigned to history by the time the facts filtered into the mountains along the northern border. The clan allegiances of the shepherds, who carried the news, coloured everything. Pakistani politics were always a minefield. Zia's death was still an unexplained mystery. The daughter of the man he had brutally betrayed and publically hanged was now running the country. She was the first female to rule a Muslim country, and many loathed her as a foreigner, which was almost worse than being a woman, but she had that name. There was still endemic corruption and shocking violence. The feudal warlords were becoming more powerful again. The Generals only ruled effectively in the towns. India was still the dangerous enemy at the gates, and still armed by the Soviets. Everything had changed, but everything stayed the same. When the Soviet Union ceased to exist, Osama bin Laden claimed it as a personal victory. Najibullah's powerbase was disintegrating. The Pakistani Intelligence Services were openly supporting the Sunnis, funnelling money in from Saudi Arabia, though not all the money reached its legitimate goal. The Mujahedeen army was fragmenting into opposing factions based on ethnicity and religion and cold-blooded greed. The unifying common enemy had gone. Only God could save them now.

As the years passed, he had learned about the wars with India, and the constant threat of a nuclear conflagration. Benazir Bhutto's coalition government was eventually dismissed on charges of corruption, nepotism and despotism by President Ghulam Ishaq Khan. She was replaced by Nawaz Sharif and the Islamic Democratic Front. It was a surprise to many. There were rumours about vote rigging and backhanders. Overall, Bhutto's PPP party did not lose by many votes, but it translated into a major victory for Sharif. The festering corruption charges were damaging, but she was never charged. Her husband, a feudal aristocrat, ended up in prison for eight years. Her brother was accused of terrorism. The lawless Tribal Areas were unstable and basically racist because the clans and tribes naturally favoured their own people to the exclusion of anyone else. Many of the cities were riven with violent crime. The only real power was with the ISI.

When Bhutto tried to organise a protest march from Rawalpindi to Islamabad, she was threatened with arrest. They placed her under house arrest anyway. There were several attempts on her life. Despite the scandals, she was sworn in as Prime Minister for a second term in 1993. She chose a president who would tow the line. The consensus was that Bhutto and Nawaz had both done very badly in the past so it would be difficult for either of them to do any worse. If Bhutto failed there would definitely be a coup, and the Army would take over, helped by the shadowy ISI. There were uprisings in the Swat valley region where a religious cleric was calling for the overthrow of 'the un-Islamic rule of the Iron Lady'. In 1995, the Indian army fired off RPGs near the border. Pakistan started air sorties and patrols. Bhutto warned India to back off and behave, but India provocatively test fired more missiles. Pakistan retaliated, but did not escalate. For a long time, everyone was holding their breath.

Southern Afghanistan was, once again, a lawless hell hole run by Pashtun clan chiefs. There were rumours about a bunch of students, who had taken it upon themselves to bring back law and order. They became known as the Taliban, and the Pakistani Intelligence Service was sending them money and guns. It became very bloody very quickly, and Afghanistan returned to the Dark Ages.

Then there were the wars in Yugoslavia, Chechnya and Azerbaijan, and in all of them the Muslims were threatened with extinction. Apparently, President Mitterrand had been quite blunt about not wanting any more Muslims in Europe. Radovan Karadzic had boasted: "in just a couple of days, Sarajevo will be gone and there will be 500,000 dead, in one month Muslims will be annihilated in Bosnia and Herzegovina." Hardly anyone at the madrassa knew where these countries were, but the message was clear. Islam was under threat. It was every Muslim's duty to defend the True Faith even if that meant sacrificing their lives.

After his seventh winter at the madrassa, the kafir was collected without explanation then delivered like a piece of freight to another world, and a different climate. The isolated desert fortress had been modernised at great expense, but the kafir rarely saw the finery. He had become merely the plaything of some Pakistanis. He shared their beds. Quite often they shared him with their friends. Most evenings, he was required to dance for an aggressive all-male audience. The Pakistanis dressed him like a girl, and painted his pretty face. He learned very quickly that to perform and please brought rewards. He sought affection, but received none. Sometimes, there were apricots or honey. On very good days, there might be chocolates. There was very little food. Dressed as a brazen whore, he was pampered and desired. Men beat their breasts, and swore their undying love for him. Every night, after a lively auction, he no longer had to dance for the excited crowd in a smoke-filled room, but went away to entertain the highest bidder. Without the costume, he was nameless, and treated like a filthy scavenging dog. His days were spent on his knees cleaning floors or washing laundry. He had quickly learned the whims of his companions. They were not brutal psychos, but they loathed his blue eyes. He had to constantly subdue his eyes and bow his head. If he ever looked at them, even accidently, there was a howl of rage, and a barrage of abuse. He accepted it all without question. He knew no other life. The madrassa had ingrained the Truth into his soul. He was an infidel. He was hated by God, the All-Knowing, the most Compassionate, the most Merciful and the most Wise. It was written. The Blessed Prophet had been instructed by God to ensure that all those who did not believe in The One God or in The Last Day were to be killed or enslaved and humiliated. The Pakistanis were not being unkind. He was just a kafir with no honour. Every detail of his existence had been prescribed centuries ago by His Highness, the Blessed Prophet. He knew that he did legally belong to these Pakistanis. There was not a moment in his life when he had a choice about anything. He accepted it, without question, as the Will of God.

His companions never actually spoke to him. Whenever Mahmood, Waheed and Aziz talked about him, he was the 'evil blue-eyed jinn', and they discussed his body in the crudest terms like farmers at a livestock market, but everyone acknowledged that he was extraordinarily beautiful. Being beautiful was his only redeeming feature in a world of Believers. It added considerably to his value as far as the Pakistanis were concerned, which they exploited ruthlessly. Aziz was the disciplinarian. He was quick to punish cunning, laziness or haste. Waheed was always looking for ways to make some extra cash. Mahmood was put upon and did all the unpleasant jobs, but he was a kind man. The kafir learned everything he needed to know from listening to their endless chatter. He quickly learned about their families and their lovers and about their prince. From his first morning at the fortress, he had been educated to bathe his Pakistanis. Unlike many of the other servants in the household, they had a bathtub. The kafir had never seen a bathroom let alone a bathtub so he was a nervous pupil and a skittish subject. He was afraid of the water. He did not understand about soap and bubbles. Undressing and bathing his Pakistanis was a task loaded with danger, but one he was expected to master with the utmost skill and grace. When it was his turn to be bathed, there was brute force and a whipping for the slightest show of temper or fear. He quickly realised that one of his future responsibilities would be to bathe a dauntingly powerful prince whenever the great man came to the fortress.

From the crass jokes and sniggering, he took it for granted that the Prince might also want to use him as other men used him. Fortunately, the great prince was a very rare visitor, but the Pakistanis devoted every morning to honing the kafir's skills, and destroying his reticence.

Their first meeting had been a major anti-climax. The Prince's arrival sent tremors through the fortress that even the kafir noticed. The Pakistanis had barely a few hours to prepare their pupil. The kafir was a bag of nerves as he removed the Prince's magnificent robes then followed him into the bathroom, which was sumptuous beyond words. The Prince went to the bubbling hot tub, and sank into the water. The kafir followed meekly. Compared to his Pakistanis, the Prince was a monster; tall and powerfully built, and so intimidating that he quite overwhelmed the young and blushing kafir, who kept dropping the soap in the hot swirling waters.

If the Prince noticed the creature's awkwardness and nerves, he made no comment. He stood patiently as he was dried. He was almost docile as the trembling thing helped him into his plain white robes. When the Prince left for evening prayers, the creature cleaned the bathroom, collected the wet towels then presented itself at the servants' entrance. An aloof Arab took away the laundry. Concealed by a black burqa, the young creature was discreetly returned to the Pakistanis in the labyrinth below stairs. That it bore no wounds certified that it had not embarrassed them. They were delighted. They threw a party. The creature entertained their friends long into the night.

Chapter 8

By some miracle, he did not waken.

She recovered her composure slowly, quite daunted by the task she had undertaken. All the windows were opened. Suddenly, she did not feel the cold. She had clean water, antiseptic, a sponge and several towels. He smelt like sewage. The raw flesh on his back was already putrefying. It was no wonder that he had a fever. It was a miracle that he was still alive. Her hands trembled. It hardly mattered that he was unconscious. For several minutes, she just sat there staring at the immense open wound, not knowing where to start or what to do. Driving him to a hospital seemed suddenly ideal, but she did not know how to put him in the car or how to answer the questions when they arrived. The phone was still off. She had to accept that she was on her own. She had never felt more alone, but her resolve strengthen slowly. Nurses could do this. Doctors did it all the time. If they could clean horrific wounds then so could she. It was a trick that she used often, but her hands still trembled, and the smell made her heave.

It took a long time to sponge away the blood and rotten flesh. She knew she was working against the clock. She had to be finished before he regained consciousness, if he ever did. It was important for the wounds to be clean. Free flowing blood meant clean wounds so she was quite ruthless about scrubbing away the dead and dying flesh. She worked meticulously, leaning down close to his body, trying to deal with the wound in isolation, not thinking about him at all. Soon the water was scarlet, and the towels were stained with slimy gore. She went out to the kitchen for fresh supplies then came back to continue in silence.

Once he was clean, she poured rum across his back, swallowed some, then covered his wounds with a linen sheet. She had not finished, but she hardly dared continue. Removing his trousers might only offend his dignity, but she feared it would be much worse. While she considered her options, she made a coffee, and started the washing machine. He needed clean clothes. She needed to wash the blood away. His coat was hung up, and his jacket sponged down and aired. She searched for other chores, but knew that there was only one thing she had to do; that she must do. It was only prudent to check him all over. Someone had cruelly beaten him. It was personal and vindictive. There was no telling what else they might have done. Yet stripping him naked felt like a step too far for a middle aged woman living alone.

It must have been - well, far too many years since she had seen a naked man. Television did not count. There were all sorts of things on television that with hindsight she should have avoided. Seeing his back was something else it would be difficult to forget. Everywhere she looked, she saw the livid bloody wounds. Even with her eyes closed, she could not see anything else. It was as if the images were seared on the insides of her eyelids. Everything dripped with pus and blood, and smelt of putrefying death. The smell was everywhere. Even the antiseptic and the rum and the open windows had not overwhelmed it. It was him.

She dithered helplessly. Procrastination was a well-studied art. Surely, she could find something to do that would stop her seeing those awful wounds, but they were everywhere.

And he was ill.

She was responsible now. His life was at stake. She knew that she had to do something. He had been through a dreadful ordeal. She could not begin to imagine what had happened to him, but it must have been truly awful to have resulted in him being beaten so badly. A fist fight would have been understandable. If he had been a victim of mugging, she would have been shocked, but that was a modern crime. Flogging was not modern. It was so old. The word itself was invested with so many historical references. It made her think of mutinies at sea and convicts and the dreaded cat o' nine tails. He did not fit any of those scenarios. He looked as if he had just walked off a grouse moor or been playing polo before the Queen. He looked lovely. He looked harmless.

Reluctantly, she went back into the lounge to stare down at him. There were fresh bloodstains emerging through the linen. Her heart was heavy. She already knew that she was losing control. It was now or never. Once the wounds on his back stopped bleeding, it would be inadvisable to disturb them again. If she was going to strip him naked then she had to do it immediately. But her hands still shook. The thought of touching him again made her feel sick.

She knelt down again, annoyed that her body still hurt so much, convinced she was too old, and furious that it might be true. He was a dead weight. Her awareness of his injuries made her so much more respectful of him. Her fingers struggled with the belt and buttons. She raised a real sweat trying to peel away his trousers. The first thing she noticed was that he wore no underwear, which made her pause. Then she saw the tattoos along his lower spine. Then she noticed that his lower buttocks were discoloured. She leaned indecorously closer. Had he been conscious she would never have dared to study his bottom quite so intently. It was not just a stain. The tops and insides of his thighs were deeply cut and pitted with what she would have described as African Tribal Markings. Perhaps, with all his body art, he did not feel the need to wear underpants. It might have been uncomfortable. But he was not hurt there. The extraordinary decorations were all old. There were no fresh wounds though the Tribal Markings must have been excruciatingly painful when they were applied. She had always felt that only a masochist would want a tattoo. Having one's own skin carved up and whittled like a piece of wood needed a higher pain threshold than she could contemplate. Was it called scarifying? She could not remember. There had been a programme. Was it a Frenchman or a Belgian? And of course, they were doing it in LA. For a long moment, she sat staring at his decorated bottom, not quite able to believe what she was seeing. Taking a deep breath to steady her nerves, she reached out touch the markings. They were surprising soft. The detail was fascinating, but there was no infection. She was quite relieved. So far it had not been too traumatic for him, but she was still loathed to turn him over. The idea of his genitals terrified her. Every instinct told her that there would be something shocking.

She retreated to the kitchen, and washed her hands again then walked out into the garden. It was early evening and very cold. The weather made the twilight gloomy and ominous. She walked up and down, and took long, deep breaths. Rubbing her eyes, she knew she needed to forget him for a while. She felt overwhelmed. He was totally helpless and likely to die, but she was still terrified of him, and terrified of what she might do to him. He was obviously some deviant, narcissistic pervert, who was obsessed with sex. Experts on television said everything was about sex. Advertisements were always about sex. The only movies that sold millions of tickets had lots of sex. Wuthering Heights was about sex. Love had died somewhere in the early sixties. Sex was the only thing that anyone seemed to care about. Didn't his body confirm that? He might have the face of an angel, but his body was a pervert's dream. And his lack of underwear was surely emblematic. He was completely alien in her universe, not because he was so exotic, but because he was a man. There was no escape. But she did walk away. She needed to find her emotional centre again. She felt shell-shocked. Her quiet life had not prepared her for any of this. She was sympathetic, and she wanted to believe that she could care for another human being, but he was not just another human being. He was a pervert, probably an addict, and she needed to know why he had come on to her land. It still felt like a violation. Her hands were shaking. She was having trouble processing information. She was becoming obsessive. Her head was full of his face and his back and his arse. How could she keep him in her home? She needed him to leave, but more than that, she needed him to have never been there at all. She felt guilty about being so precious, but she knew that she was terribly vulnerable

"Oh, let me not be mad, not mad, sweet heaven. Keep me in temper. I would not be mad."

There was not enough time to have a rendezvous with Big Shoulders. She needed a quick fix. Walking down to the pond, she would find something or be inspired by something, and then know the answer or forget. Time stood still when she went into the woods where it was gloomy and cold. It was hard to believe that it was the end of May. She walked on stubbornly. Her footsteps were sure. She knew every path. It was not just another world, but a different dimension. She walked and walked, seeking solace, but even here the young man haunted her. Everything had been corrupted. He had ruined it for her, but it seemed so appalling to blame him. At the shrine, she wept silently, feeling nothing as she examined the treasures of a forgotten life, seeing their absolute decay and ruination for the first time. She had been violated. The frontiers of her quiet life lay in ruins. The world she had created and guarded so carefully for so many years had been invaded. She had no battalions. She had never had any kind of defence. In her heart, she knew that no one could mend what he had broken. The grief that she felt was real. Even if he survived, and she lived there another thousand years, there was no hope of restoring what had been lost. The spell had been broken. The magic had gone.

She walked back to face her worst fears. Emotionally, she was the one who was naked. It was not about clothes. It was not about being brave or smart or savvy. She was just totally alone. Human beings were meant to be paired. They were gregarious. They had advanced communication skills because sometimes there was an imperative need to communicate. She had been in denial. For most of her life, she had refused to accept that she needed anyone. Now, she had no one to share her fears and anxieties. Being alone sometimes became loneliness. Her loneliness had never been more acute. The futility of continuing crushed her. It was the black dog. Everything seemed pointless. She would become invisible. She felt it beginning. She would diminish mentally then physically then die. Eventually, the cats would eat her then leave to find another home. She actually envied them. She had always envied them. That they had stayed with her so long had given her a sense of worth, but it seemed so insubstantial now. Would they even remember her? No one remembered her. No one knew her name.

She returned to the house; the lights from the back door helped her find the way. Her whole body ached, every muscle had been punished to breaking point by her stubborn determination to save him. She would save him. Suddenly, nothing else mattered. It was as much about her pride, and her need to achieve something as it was about her not knowing how to give up. She would save him. He had no say. He would live and leave. Somehow, she would make it all alright, and fix what he had broken. Some cats appeared to greet her at the back door, and distantly she heard the foxes barking, and she knew that the world would go on.

He had not moved at all. The sheet covering him was stained again with pus and blood. She hesitated then went to fill another bowl with clean water and to collect the last of her towels. She cleaned his wounds then carefully rolled him over almost on to his back. Her breath caught in her throat. Her heart trembled. What she saw was shocking and puzzling. For a moment, she actually forgot how to breathe. Every part of her body blushed and trembled. She could not think. She could not even blink. She could not believe what she was looking at, and hardly had the vocabulary to describe it. Even late night television had not prepared her for this. She leaned a little closer, quite overwhelmed by revulsion, and yet embarrassingly fascinated. It was the most lurid kind of curiosity. A grimace lined her face. Her hands clasped and unclasped, but courage failed her. Her throat was suddenly dry. There were no words.

A metal sheath concealed all but the tip of his penis. It was smooth across the top, but heavily studded with fabulous jewels that glittered despite the grey slime of sweat and dirt and old urine. The sides and bottom were vented. It was held in place by an ornate bronze padlock. His flesh was red and sore from sweating. It was appallingly grotesque yet the jewels glittered beguilingly.

She was paralysed by embarrassment and shock. It was beyond her to touch the thing, but the smell was revolting. She had to clean him. She had to touch it. She could not just throw a bucket of water over him, and hope for the best. That it clothed his nakedness did nothing to ease her discomfort. Touching his penis would have been easier. A penis was ordinary. Half the population had one. She might have been exposed as a stupid old maid, but she could have pretended that she was a nurse or a doctor, and acted her role with, at least, some pretence of composure.

She drew back from him more than just physically, and took a long moment to study his face. He was no longer a young man. He was not even a drug addict. He was beautiful, but he was obviously someone's canvas. His skin had been heavily scarified and tattooed. His penis was held captive in a steel cage. And the skin had been flayed off his back. She could not begin to imagine why a young man would submit to such brutal treatment. The simplest explanation was that he had no choice. In the twenty-first century, that meant it was about sex. Everything was about sex. She could not imagine a woman demanding such a sacrifice so she accepted that he was gay, and that he was the submissive partner in a long-term relationship. If the jewels were real then the young man's lover was incredibly wealthy and cruel.

She sponged water across him, flooding his groin. The jewels sparkled brightly. If even one stone was real then it was probably worth a quarter of a million pounds. She was sure that the sheath was made of steel. Silver would tarnish. White gold was too soft. It might have been platinum, she was sure that it was steel. As she carefully cleaned him and his jewellery, she was reminded of a programme on body piercing she had found while cruising channels in the middle of the night. The fools on the television seemed to be just stupid drunks, who were prepared to do anything to be on TV. Nothing that they had endured came close to the mutilation visited on the young man's groin and thighs.

She had suddenly so many questions, and knew she could not ask him any of them. With the greatest care, she cleaned him again and wrapped his wounds. He was receiving moisture via the cloth in his mouth, but it hardly seemed enough. She understood the temptation to pour liquid down his throat. He was not strong enough to survive pneumonia. She stared at his face for what seemed to be an eternity, but there were no answers there. Slowly, she turned away, and switched on the television. Richard Hammond was on a horse, hunting for the Holy Grail. What on earth was going on?

But it was an engaging programme. The weather and scenery were easy on the eye, and the ongoing hype surrounding The Da Vinci Code made the teasing hypothesis seem less light weight. She recalled her conviction that the figure next to Jesus had always looked like a woman, but she had to admit that she had never actually counted the heads. Judas looked shifty. She had never really looked at the others beyond accepting that they looked more like Italians than Jews. She had looked at the cup only because of the legend and because of Indiana Jones. A group of unemployed Jewish males, mostly fishermen and artisans, would only have access to economy fare, and they were all of an age. If they had not all been married and had children then they would have been considered odd in that culture. So there would have been children somewhere, probably with the grandparents because the men had no income, and back then, women were invisible chattels so the wives were never heard about. So an apparently empowered Mary Magdalene had to be made subservient in a male-dominated culture so she was reinvented as a whore. It all made sense. It was the first big conspiracy if one ignored Gilgamesh and the

Greeks. Jesus was reinvented as a celibate bachelor so the Roman Catholics could enforce the same standard on their priests, but that was surely more to do with the Borgias, who were Popes and the most venal family in history: so little power, no sex and no dynasties in the Papal line. But Jesus must have fathered children unless he was infertile. In the context of the era and the culture, it made perfect sense that he would have a wife and children.

She shivered. It was really cold. The injured young man had not moved. She went around closing all the windows and the back door. The smell had dissipated. She hung the laundry on the radiators then put in another load. If she kept going through towels and sheets then she would need a tumble drier, but that was well beyond her means. Turning up the central heating again, she worried what the young man was going to cost. She focused on the financial implications, but knew her concerns ran deeper than that. Everything had changed.

Back in the lounge, she found a cat sniffing around him. She shooed the cat away, but it thrashed its tail about then leapt on to the sofa, and settled there glaring at her. She knelt down beside the young man, and pulled the blankets back over his body. He was infinitely more fragrant. After fondly stroking the cat's head, she picked up the cold hot water bottles, and retreated back to the kitchen. She boiled the kettle, made a cup of tea then refilled the bottles. She took them back into the front room to find the cat sitting, paws tucked in, on top of the young man. She lifted the top blanket, and pushed in the hot water bottles near his abdomen then deposited the cat back on the sofa. The cat was not impressed.

Turning to her comfortable chair, she found another cat stretched out to fill the seat. Any other day, she would have deferred to the cat, and moved to sit on the sofa, but she was extremely tired and sore. The cat was visibly surprised to be dispossessed. She sat with a sigh, and curled her feet in under her. The cup of tea warmed her hands. She watched the young man, almost certain that the grumpy cat would return to sit on him again, but neither moved. The face was still very pale. He had some stubble now, but it was uneven and unattractive. His hair was flat and heavy with sweat. She frowned, and felt the guilt that came with inertia. There was a long list of things she should have done, but almost nothing she could do now. He was clean. He was sleeping. He was absorbing water through the soft tissue in his mouth. For a long time, she simply watched him breathing. She still felt guilty. Her attention slowly drifted away to the television. It was Bill Oddie. She remembered her other troubles, and turned happily away from the ones she was unable to resolve.

She did dutifully glance across to him now and then between swallows and otters, and the strange osprey trying to haul his unfaithful mate off their nest by her tail feathers. That actually made her smile. The TV presenters commented on it being extremely cold. In Shetland, it looked more than cold. She was surprised to learn that in Shetland in late May, it never actually got dark. She switched the lights on then closed the curtains. She smiled again then returned to her chair. She had barely sat down when another cat leapt on to her knee. He was heavy, and liked to pluck with his long, sharp claws. Even through her jeans, it was painful. She winced, and put up with it for a moment then when the cat would not stop she gently pushed him away, and felt like a brute for rejecting him.

Apparently, the programme's audience was in the several millions. She liked it that so many people were interested in the things that she was interested in. It took the edge off her loneliness. It was like being part of a club. Her garden was much further north than Devon where the programme was being filmed. There were nest boxes with clutches of chicks that were much further advanced than her own. She had the Blue Tits and the Great Tits. She had numerous different Finches including the scarlet Bull Finches and the rarer Gold Finches. English birds were not known for their brilliant plumage. They sang like angels, but were often written off as merely brown. The Bull Finches were a complete knockout. Her extensive range of dilapidated buildings provided hundreds of nest sites. The garden and woodland provided all the materials needed to build excellent nests, and a constant supply of food. Some weeks ago, she had scattered hay and moss inside the barns so that it would stay dry and be available whenever the birds needed it. In the autumn, she also left out bedding material for the various hedgehogs. The rabbits were on their own. Well, they bred like rabbits, and never seemed to be in short supply. There were Swallows already nesting in Devon. She made a mental note to have a walk around the barns and sheds in the morning, to see if her own Swallows had come back from South Africa.

She was grateful to be able to forget the young man. That he was breathing steadily, but did not move, made it easier. She began to look at him in the same way that she looked at her cats. It was really nothing more than a cursory check that they were breathing, and not in any distress. She did not like interfering. She provided food and a safe home, and the cats and birds and everything else basically did their own thing. She had not even set up the bird feeders where she could sit and watch. All that she required was that they were happy and did not fight, and hopefully, did not eat each other. That had been a problem with a younger cat. He kept bringing baby rabbits into the house. She had had to drown them all because they had broken backs or legs. The cat had grown up, and fortunately realised he did not need to harvest the bunnies anymore. He still brought the occasional mouse and vole and shrew. The latter were savage little things. They tried to bite the cat, and invariably managed to bite her. She rescued what she could, and released them carefully back into her garden. Dead rodents were chucked away to feed other predators. There were less foxes about now because of the lighter evenings, but there were always hungry mouths to feed.

The programme ended. Suddenly, she felt alone again. With a frown, she turned back to the young man. Something was different. Had he moved? She rose stiffly, and went to stand over him. He looked the same. She stooped to feel his forehead. He was still very warm. She went to her knees, and reached under the blanket to feel the hot water bottles. They were still hot enough. She did not want to disturb him, but knew that she must. She rolled him on to his chest then carefully lifted away the blankets until only the sheet remained. There were blood stains. With a grimace and sigh, she lifted the sheet up to peer underneath. His back was raw. There were a few thin trails of white pus, but predominantly, he just looked like meat. It was better. It had to be better. Biting her lips, she lowered the sheet, and laid the blankets back over him. It would take time. There were no miracles in the real world.

After refilling the water being used to moisturise his mouth, she found her torch and went outside. It was really cold. She had paused to find shoes, but she needed a coat. She hurried away to the large pond, and peered down into the water with the torch. The clarity was still good although there was evidence of the frothy algae gathering on the surface. Across the bottom, there were still lots of skeletal frogs, and as she stood still and waited, the newts came out to display. She felt better, and attributed the improvement to an hour of wildlife on the telly. No one had mentioned newts, but perhaps that would happen later in the series. There were hedgehogs in the undergrowth. She could hear them and smell them. Further away, there were other night noises that suggested mice and predators. She stood for probably half an hour at each pond, and she was smiling when she turned back towards the house.

After another hot bath, she dressed, and went back down to the front room. She watched the young man all night. She watched him breathing. She counted his breaths. He did not move at all. She knew so much more about him, but did not know him at all. Her strangely distorted view of life coloured everything. Sometimes asleep and sometimes awake, she imagined the relationship between the young man and his lover.

Chapter 9

It was late in January 1996, a few days before eyes turned to the heavens in search of the auspicious crescent moon. The creature was about to be dressed for its evening performance. Its heavy makeup was still damp. Its hair hung in ridiculous ringlets, full of cheap diamante pins, and lashings of styling mousse. Mahmood and Waheed were just about to shoe-horn the creature into the tight scarlet dress that was two sizes too small, but very popular with the crowd, when the door was flung open. It was not Aziz. Two bodyguards entered. They were both armed and unfamiliar. Without hesitating, the creature dutifully hurried down on to its knees, and bowed to place its forehead and palms on the floor. The bodyguards tossed a black jilbab and a burqa at it. The creature flinched. It was the stunned Pakistanis who went absolutely ballistic. They swore and waved their arms about in righteous indignation. They made such a din that Aziz came running to see what was happening. The bodyguards explained curtly. The Pakistanis fizzed with rage. Aziz only added to the confusion.

For the first time in his life, the kafir ignored the supreme authority of his Pakistanis. The bodyguards had guns. He moved slowly back onto his heels, and picked up the clothes then silently pulled them on over his thin cotton shirt. The burqa was not unusual. He was smuggled through the corridors concealed by that. To be given the jilbab as well signified a journey. Around him, the screaming insults continued. Almost unnoticed, he rose to stand, his appearance completely obscured by the layers of voluminous clothes. It was a fait accompli. The bodyguards brushed the Pakistanis aside like annoying flies. There were no further explanations. The kafir quickly gathered up the acres of material from around his feet then was dragged away as quickly as the bodyguards could move him. They hardly broke stride until they reached the basement, and were confronted by a locked door. The kafir swayed on his feet, breathless and drenched with sweat.

The door opened into an underground car park. There were a dozen vehicles ranging from the most expensive sports cars in the world to utilitarian jeeps. They hurried the creature to a jeep, and shoved it so violently against the vehicle that it bounced back into their arms, and was then dumped unceremoniously on the floor. Unable to breathe, and handicapped by the enveloping clothes, the creature made no attempt to rise. The bodyguards waded into the yards of material to find limbs which were quickly bound with sticky tape. It was tossed into the back then pushed and shoved into the smallest space possible so that they could load over-stuffed rucksacks, bottles of water and provisions.

The kafir was not entirely uncomfortable, but he was frightened. He could rest his head against the back of the driver's seat, but whenever they hit a bump, his head whacked against the metal frame, which happened more frequently as he grew tired. The mask over his eyes meant that everything was a blur, but he recognised the road to the airport. He wanted to believe that it was just another sudden change of residence. There had already been several. The palace on the beach near the resort at Haqi, the cool summer palace in the mountains at Taif, another monstrously indulgent mansion in the sweltering desert city of Riyadh, and the old fortress near the Empty Quarter that was as lonely as the moon; he had been bundled up like an old carpet, and delivered to them all along with the usual retinue of servants. This felt different. Where were his Pakistanis? Where was the Prince? He grew increasingly anxious.

It took about an hour to reach the huge airport. The streets were almost deserted, but for a few men in their simple white thobes and red ghutras. Sometimes, if they were stuck in traffic or a car pulled up beside them, he saw the partial faces of women, and realised he had not actually seen a woman for many years. He vaguely remembered the rooftop in northern Yemen, but that was a lifetime ago. And these handsome women, if they noticed him at all, smiled kindly because they thought he was one of them. But he could not speak, and they could not see him. All that they saw was a woman from the country, whose husband insisted on the full veil.

The men had the right papers, and were waved through by the soldiers and police at the various security checks. None of them so much as looked at the obscured figure in the back of the jeep. Only the 'decency' police could touch a woman in a full veil, and get away with it.

On the airfield, they freed his ankles, and 'helped' him from the jeep, then steered him up the steps on to a small jet. There, he was bundled into a seat, and the belt held him trapped. It took a matter of minutes for the gear to be stowed, and then they were off. He was very tired, but even more frightened. In the tussle to get him aboard, the burqa had slipped, and now he could not see anything at all.

They flew east to the coast and stayed over the ocean, then gained altitude, then turned north. It was almost two thousand miles to Islamabad, with a complicated flight plan, and several nervous air traffic controllers wanting to know who they were. They had to divert to Chitral because of the weather. The clouds were impenetrable, towering over the glittering peaks, some of which were too high for snow. Chitral was already cut off by road so the airport was the only way in and out. It was not particularly busy because of Ramadan and the snow so the men were able to take a room in a cheap hotel near the airport, and had to wait it out. The men talked about the atrocities in Srebrenica and Chechnya during the summer which left several thousand Muslims dead, the bomb in Riyadh and bin Laden, and the insanity of Pakistan and India actually having nuclear bombs.

It was a tough week for the kafir. He was shackled beneath the sink in the tiny little bathroom, where he fretted and whined until the bodyguards made him stop. The wild borderlands of northern Pakistan only meant one thing. He did not understand what he had done to deserve banishment. He was not strong enough or brave enough to quietly meet his fate. He was not sane enough to hope that there was another destination. All he thought about was another seven years of constant brutal discipline. Life at the madrassa seemed like hell on earth after a year of hot baths and warm beds and flattering attention. He wanted to dance again. He wanted to be loved, and at that moment, the fucking felt like love. He would have danced naked and been grateful to be fucked by all of them if it meant escaping the madrassa. He could already hear Professor Shah's scathing comments about his murderous ancestors. The other teachers would encourage the younger boys to beat him with sticks and pelt him with stones because he was a despised infidel. He would be constantly dirty and hungry and loathed and cold. It would be so cold. He could not bear it. He wanted to go home. He needed Mahmood's gentle kindness. He needed reassurance. He became increasingly agitated as the stopover stretched into days. Most of all, he was tormented by fear of having upset his master. He had failed somehow. He had done something so terrible that he was being sent away.

Every day, it felt like every day, they concealed him in the burqa, and set off for the airport. There was deep snow on the ground. It seemed foolish to go out at all, but they packed up and set off. There were always arguments at the airport. Often, they went straight back to the hotel, sometimes, they actually managed to board the plane to have even more arguments with a pilot. Three times, they took off and headed east into buffeting storms. The kafir was terrified. They all were. Three times they had to return to Chitral.

It took four attempts over several days for them to find a window through to Gilgit. By then, they were all irritable and tired. They had all been prisoners at the hotel, but only the kafir did not want to escape.

Gilgit seemed exactly the same. They had barely enough visibility to land, and the snow had been cleared off the runway just minutes before they arrived. It was a terrible blow. It only confirmed that he was being taken back to the madrassa, but for what purpose and how long? His few fragile hopes were decimated. He had been confined there for seven years. How many more must he endure? The rules of his existence would be as harsh as before. It would be hell. It would kill him.

While one of the men sorted out the paperwork with a local official, the kafir stood motionless, staring up at the sheer walls of the towering mountains that were already choked with snow. He remembered his previous visit, and felt physically sick just imagining what lay ahead.

Once the permits were all stamped, a red jeep with a local driver came across the field to pick them up. The kafir in the burqa, obviously, had to sit hunched up in the back surrounded by the luggage, because a woman was not permitted to share a seat with a man who was not a husband or a close relative, not in the town anyway. One of the bodyguards sat next to the driver. The other perched on a jump seat, and hung on for dear life.

The three men talked about their trip and the weather as they drove through the busy little town. The shops were as colourful, but everything was ankle deep in muddy snow.

They took the same treacherous road following the river that was now a dull grey brown colour. The road had been recently tarred, but they had to follow in the tracks of the vans and buses that had forged through the snow before them. As they moved further out of town, the mountains crowded in. There was evidence everywhere of recent rock slides. There were potholes. There were abandoned vehicles that had been looted and burned. They drove for several hours, turning off the Chitral road at the same junction, and heading north into the white wilderness of the Hindu Kush. The scenery was as spectacular as he remembered. There were a few isolated villages that clung to the roadside. The buildings were small, made of local rocks, held together only by gravity. The slightest rock fall or tremor would have transformed them into piles of rubble. There was no one there. They appeared to have been abandoned. As the road climbed higher, the snow deepened and the trees thinned then disappeared. In the jeep, they drove on. There was no other traffic at all. Above them, the sky was a cold grey colour. Long before it was dark, they came to the end of the road, but they had gone further and were higher thanks to the slow expansion of tourism, and hence the marginally better roads.

The kafir was lifted down. He could not walk. He was thoroughly demoralised and physically broken. While one man stripped off the black veils to have a look at him, the others efficiently set up a blue tent, a cooking stove, and broke out the rations. They gave him a few mouthfuls of water, which he promptly threw up.

That night, they camped undisturbed by anything more than the distant eerie call of wolves. The local guide made a fire of dung and roots, and heated water and a lamb stew while they all chewed on old chapattis. They talked about predators. There had been talk in Chitral of snow leopard, but the guide dismissed it. No one ever saw them. If they did then it was too late. Crowded close together in the small tent, they managed to keep reasonably warm. It was the kafir who did not to have a fleece-lined jacket, thick gloves or even shoes. They all woke up with headaches, and only the local guide did not feel sick. During a breakfast of dried biscuits and apricots, they were being heckled by scavenging magpies. There was talk of a shooting competition, but even though they were surrounded by what looked like desolate empty country, they knew that there would be shepherds and nosey Western tourists with nasty foreign habits and cameras somewhere nearby.

After prayers, as the snow began to fall again, one of the bodyguards and the local guide set off up the mountainside with the reluctant kafir in tow. It seemed like insanity. The snow was thick upon the ground, and beneath it, the rock was loose and treacherous. It rose at an almost 80 degree angle with a snaking path creeping up its face. One wrong foot sent tonnes of rock and debris down upon anyone coming up behind. It was not just difficult to negotiate. There was no air. Gilgit was in the valley at 4,900 feet, and they had climbed much higher by road. The headaches that they awoke to at dawn became worse as the day went on. The kafir weakened quickly. He did not have the same level of fitness. After climbing barely a hundred feet, he had to stop and catch his breath. He was ridiculed by the local guide. The bodyguard, who was also struggling with the altitude, called him a typical example of Western imperialism: useless, stupid and soft. It did not strike the kafir as that insulting. It could have been worse. Bending over in distress and pain, he just concentrated on breathing. Staying conscious was hard. It would have been so easy to just topple backwards and fall to his death. He was allowed to rest, but the distances he could cover between stops diminished rapidly. He was too ill to realise that he was only allowed to rest because the muscular bodyguard was suffering too. The kafir collapsed several times, and was only brought around when they poured icy water over his face. He was given chocolate, lots of it, and commanded to eat.

It took all morning to reach the first ridge. By then it was snowing quite hard, but it was curiously warmer. They rested beneath an overhang that exposed the colours in the local rock. There were reds and blacks mixed in with the endless sepia tints, and bolts of orange that looked like gold. The mountains that surrounded them were turning blue with a curious heat haze rising from the valleys, and the distant snow-capped peaks brooded menacingly. They climbed down slowly and carefully into a narrow valley with a blue stream, and a meadow that had been trampled down to mud. They stopped for an hour. The local guide told the kafir to wash his feet in the stream. He did so. It was perishingly cold, but soothed his feet, and stopped the cuts from bleeding.

He was vaguely aware of the towering mountains becoming familiar, and had long since resigned himself to life back at the school. There was something like a path that weaved up and down through a succession narrow valleys and broken ridges. The passes were often choked with debris and snow. They made slow progress, and it was exhausting. The landscape was vast and inhospitable. They crossed an icy stream by way of a slippery wooden bridge that looked as if it had originally been a crude ladder. The bodyguard pulled him along by his wrist, and they both trailed behind the local guide. Beneath the snow, there was short grass which was springy and soft after the miles of broken rock, and the kafir tried to linger there, but they had another sheer wall to scale, and he was pulled relentlessly onwards.

He was so exhausted he could barely walk ten paces without becoming dizzy and distressed. He had to stop and lean on to his knees, and just suck air into his lungs, and hope he did not faint. The bodyguard was at his wits' end, and just wanted to shoot him and go home. Neither of them could speak anymore. It was all sign language, and the brandishing of a gun. The kafir kept raising his hands passively while he gasped for breath, and tried to blink away the clouds of fog filling his eyes.

When they crested the next ridge, they saw the valley below them where the ugly, long-eared goats and sheep came to graze in spring. The snow covered everything. Above it, squatting low across a mountain top like a stalking lion was the old colonial fortress.

It stopped snowing. The altitude made it cold, but the latitude made it warmer. Moving from sunshine to shadows could change the temperature by tens of degrees.

The kafir's heart sank. His legs nearly folded under him. He was still in shock when they reached the valley floor, and there he sat down, and would not move until he was given more water and more chocolate. His tantrum earned him a thrashing, but he had what he wanted, and the bodyguard stood over him, smoking marijuana while they all came to terms with still being alive.

The path from the valley up to the fortress weaved torturously. The guide boldly tried to scale the face, but was forced back on to the path because the loose rocks were so treacherous. The madrassa really was almost completely inaccessible. Devastated by the pain in his head and his chest and his feet, the kafir struggled to simply put one foot in front of the other.

When he crossed the threshold, he felt as if he had stepped back in time. The courtyard was exactly as he remembered it. There was snow and mud. It was an austere place. The faces at the windows might have been the same faces. It was certainly the same Head Teacher walking towards him, and most of the teachers and clerics looked familiar, although all of them now had the regulation beards and prayer caps. None of them looked welcoming. They had come away from their warm fires to receive the visitors, who promised news of the outside world. None of them were pleased to see the scandalous white infidel.

The bodyguard thrust the creature forward. The clerics stopped in their tracks then started shouting at him indignantly. Dead on its feet, the creature sprawled in the icy mud, hearing the word 'kafir' again and again, and fearing the worst. All it could do was creep on to its knees then bow down to indicate its complete submission. That did not seem to be enough, but there was nothing else it could do. The shouting slowly subsided amid accusations of carelessness and stupidity.

Achmed Qadri, the Head Teacher, gazed at the kafir in his thin shirt and bare feet. He could not help remembering the child that he had watched grow up. Had they been alone, he could have spoken freely. "Get up."

The kafir hardly had the strength, but he obeyed, and stood there on bleeding feet, swaying like a sapling, with his head bowed low.

"It's the middle of winter, has he no other clothes to wear?"

The bodyguard shook his head, and shrugged carelessly. "There is nothing."

The Head Teacher lifted his hand to quell the muttering rebellion from the other teachers and clerics. Jawad, his newly appointed assistant, was particularly aggressive. When there was silence, he said to pacify his audience: "Vile disbeliever, you will draw water and wash. Sort out your hair. You look like a Jewish harlot. I cannot have you seen by the students while you look like this."

The kafir nodded and bowed lower. He was too depressed to be embarrassed. His heart was breaking. "Please, yes my lord, sir, by the Grace of God, the most Compassionate, the most Merciful." He took a deep breath. He was too weary to raise his voice above a whisper. "Please my lord, I apologise." He tried to fill his lungs again. It actually hurt to breathe. "I beg your forgiveness, my lord. God is Great."

"Then you will wait upon Prof. Shah."

He stiffened, doubting his hearing. It couldn't be! But he bowed even lower, and nearly fell down because he felt so weak. "Please? Thank you, my lord." He gasped breathlessly. There was not enough air. "May the Blessings of the Beloved Prophet be upon you. God is Kindness and Mercy." He could not inhale. He could not breathe. His head was exploding. "Thank you, my lord. Thank you. God is Great."

They all answered: "God is Great." And then scowled because they realised what they were talking to.

He bowed again slowly then drew back, bringing him alongside the bodyguard, who firmly grasped his wrist. The kafir stooped, and kept his head down, following meekly as the Arab walked away to find the well and the water.

There was a round pool about ten feet across that was filled from the well. It was not very deep, and already had sheets of ice forming across the surface, which had only recently been broken. The kafir knew that the bottom of the pool had been lined with blue tiles. In summer, it was a thing of beauty. Now, it just looked grey and cold. This was where the whole school came to complete their ritual washing before going to pray. The kafir had never been allowed anywhere near it. Even when he was nursing the Professor, the water was forbidden to him. So he hung back, and when the Arab turned to take a swipe at him, he said: "Haram!" He pointed to the water, and shook his head. "Haram."

"Yes, it is forbidden."

The kafir wearily reached out to hold the bodyguard's sleeve then turned carefully to face Prof. Shah. His elation was unexpected. He was so surprised he almost fell down. He was certainly relieved to see him. No one else offered the remotest hope of sanctuary. But he bowed his head while grimly hanging on to the bodyguard's arm.

The Professor looked well, still pale and thin and elderly, but he was on his feet, and wrapped up in thick woollen clothes with a blanket around his shoulders.

"Fill a bucket. Give it to him."

The Arab did not know the Professor, but he respected his age. Negligently tossing the creature to the ground, he walked to the edge of the pool, and shoved a bucket into the icy water.

The Professor limped slowly across the courtyard to stand over the creature, which lay broken on the ground. He glanced across at the little group of teachers, who looked on with nervous disapproval. Then he gazed down witheringly at the creature's unkempt, but decidedly feminine hair. "You look like the filthiest whore from the town of Sodom. Are you the son of murderous crusaders or a vile Jewess?"

The kafir did not move. He had been brought from his Pakistanis, and climbed through snow in bare feet. He had a thousand excuses, but was not allowed to say a word.

The bucket was dumped beside him.

"Your great master sends you back to me. I knew he would."

The kafir gazed towards the Professor, but dared not look at him. He managed to nod to acknowledge the welcome then struggled awkwardly on to his knees. He was shaking as much from the freezing temperatures as from exhaustion, but hurried to dip his hands into the icy water then bathed his face. It was so cold it hurt his hands and face just as walking through the snow had made his feet lumps of raw agony. He rubbed his eyes, and tried to remove the black smudges that had once been immaculately applied makeup. He raked fingers through his hair, which felt like a mass of knotted string. His hands were shaking. He had no mirror or soap. He had no idea if he was just making it worse. Before he was brave enough to stop, the bucket was snatched away then emptied over his head. He shrieked in shock and horror, and started to rise, but the bodyguard caught his tangled frosty hair then hurled him skidding across the ground. The impact knocked the wind out of him. His skull felt encased in ice. He lay paralysed by pain in the muddy snow, too exhausted and frightened to move.

"Thank you," the Professor said irritably. "This thing has come here to be cleansed and purified. We must not waste its time with our idle chatter. There is much work to be done. Did you bring supplies? Did you bring food?"

The Arab gazed witheringly at the old holy man then shook his head.

"Then you can leave." The Professor turned away, dismissing him.

The Arab gazed up at the sky then at the local guide, who was already at the gate waiting for him. Almost reluctantly, he nodded to Achmed Qadri then walked idly away.

The kafir was still completely traumatised, but when he felt the

Professor's hand on his back, he had to stand up and bow then followed him submissively to his classroom. Every inch of his body hurt. He was shivering violently. His brain had shut down completely, and his skull felt as if it had been cracked open like a nut.

There were a dozen students, who all tried to avoid looking at the outrageous creature as it stumbled in through the doorway. It was as surprised to see them as they were shocked by its appearance. Suddenly turning on his heel, the Professor slapped it so brutally across the face that it fell down like a butchered animal. There were gasps from the students though none of them dared to rise from their studies. The Professor stood over the cowering thing. When it did not move, he grabbed a handful of the icy hair, and tried to dramatically drag it across the floor. It whined like a whipped dog, and he was too old so he swatted it irritably across the back of the head.

"Nazarene! Bow down before these righteous children. Show your respect." Prof. Shah slapped it again in front of the whole class, then walked back to close the door, and shut out the freezing air.

The kafir was barely conscious, but he bowed dutifully to his betters, and he stayed down while they sniggered and giggled. He was so cold. His head felt as if it had been split open. The pain was unbearable. He found it difficult to inhale. He did not know how he could be so cold and still be alive.

With the door closed, the Professor draped some of his own blankets around the creature's shoulders. "Get up now. Go to the fire. Get warm. There's some food left. You must eat."

The kafir slunk away to the back of the dark, badly lit room to rub life into his frozen flesh. The fire was hardly more than a few embers. The food was merely crumbs.

When they were alone, the Professor turned to him. "The dog returns to its master." He wheezed. It was meant to be a smile. His yellow teeth were long and pointed behind thin pale lips. "Is it another year?"

The kafir nodded. He could hardly move. He was almost sure that he was dying.

"I see that the jinn still possesses you. We will drive that out. You will read from the Holy Book every day from sunrise to sunset until your tongue stiffens. We will cleanse your soul. We will teach you to respect us again. Come closer so that I can look at you." He watched as the creature seemed to come back to the present. It lifted itself slowly from the floor and crept closer to kneel before him. It looked utterly broken.

78

Feeling worthless and condemned, the kafir pressed his forehead against the cold stone floor.

"Your feet are bleeding," the old man said as if commenting on the weather.

The kafir slowly drew back to sit on his heels. He could not speak. Even if he had been allowed such a privilege, it was beyond him. Nor did he have the courage to meet the Professor's gaze.

The Professor stared at him as if committing every detail to memory. Even a bitter old man could appreciate the extreme physical beauty. He noted all the cuts and bruises that marked his face. "This man who brought you here does not like you. You must not be troublesome. Childish tantrums and disobedience are never tolerated in adults, and you are an adult now, full grown and responsible for your own behaviour."

The kafir nodded, but did not raise his head. At that moment, he wanted to die. His sanity could not survive at the madrassa.

"I will allow you to rest until dawn, but you must apply yourself tomorrow. I am certain your schooling has been completely neglected so we must start again."

The kafir raised his hands to cover his eyes. He wanted to weep, but his will had been stripped away as easily as the burqa. He was so unhappy. He was choked by pain. His raw anguish completely overwhelmed him.

"Reading the Holy Book again will heal you," the Professor said compassionately. "You must bow down before us. You must not make trouble. Everything that happens to you is God's Will. You must bow down or they will beat you."

The kafir shivered then nodded then bowed down.

The kafir could not remember feeling warm during the next four weeks. During the daylight, they fasted. That was hard. The altitude and the winter weather kept him permanently exhausted. Not being allowed anything to eat or drink merely compounded his condition. He had the crumbs of breakfast and the evening meal, but it was never enough, and while the Professor and Qadri drank hot sweet tea in the darkness, he had only the water provided from a bucket, and usually covered in dirty ice. His days were spent in the Professor's classroom, studying the Holy Book, and demonstrating his understanding of it, and of the Sunnah and the Hadith. When there were no lessons, he had to translate tracts into English or German, which he had not spoken since leaving the year before. His palms were caned when he made a mistake, which happened frequently. Some other unfortunate little kafir was now doing the chores that had once been his so he was confined to the Professor's room during the day, and locked safely away at night. He often glimpsed the white-haired child across the courtyard, but was forbidden to seek him out. He understood that they were destined to be rivals.

The kafirs were not singled out for abuse. Even the Muslim boys were thrashed and kicked if they did not attend to their lessons. Discipline was swiftly enforced with violence. A few of the teachers were using techniques on the children that were brutal and inhumane. But no one dared to complain. The school was at full stretch. The number of students was dramatically increasing year on year. Achmed Qadri was under pressure to take on inexperienced teachers because of the volumes, but also because local warlords were exerting their influence, and were constantly threatening the supply chain that kept the school alive. Almost all of the young teachers were associating themselves with Al Qaeda, and it was not just the Americans who suffered from Post-Traumatic Stress.

It was a nightmare for the kafir, not because they were particularly unkind, but because he did not know what he had done to deserve being sent back to the madrassa. The rules of his existence had not changed at all. He was required to bow down to even the smallest child. The students were encouraged to exercise their authority over him in a thousand petty ways. Only the Head Teacher and the Professor actually shared their food with him, but even that was never enough. He was always hungry and so very cold, but it was being alone that destroyed him. He was so fragile, he could not believe in anything anymore.

Qadri was feeling marginalised. He had become a teacher because he believed it was a worthy profession to mould the minds of young men. The thousand or so madrassas that existed at that time offered free education to poor boys, who could not go to the State schools. Now, there were more than ten thousand, and though many were still offering a mainstream education, far too many were run by fundamentalists, who preached hatred and wanted recruits for jihad. But for the financial support of his patron and friend, Prince Abdul Aziz, he was sure he would have been forced to resign because he was completely out of step with the political situation brewing around him. He tried to temper the excesses of the newer teachers, but he could not be in every classroom, and none of the children were brave enough to complain. He spoke to the whole school at least once a day, and he always spoke about the family united in its duty to God, the All-knowing and Wise. It used to be Prof. Shah, who was the bitter radical. Now, it was the younger teachers, who preached about the necessity of jihad, and the supreme duty of all Muslims to kill disbelievers for God.

Mullah Omar and the Pakistanis were still fighting against the Northern

Alliance in Afghanistan. They had besieged Kabul for a year, but Prince Massoud had broken through. No matter what they did, the Lion of Panjshir always seemed to outsmart them. It had to be because of the Americans and all their spies. Bin Laden was still financing the war even though he had been living quietly in the Sudan for five years, ostensibly running a construction business. Benazir Bhutto was once again the Iron Lady in Pakistan. She was still surrounded by corruption scandals, but never charged. Her husband seemed to be the lightning rod. There were still terrible problems in Karachi, which was becoming the most violent city in the world, and serious unrest in the Swat Valley. Benazir was constantly under threat of assassination. But she was a Bhutto, and a scientist, and she was the leader of a Nuclear State. Even in the mountains, the Pakistanis were proud of being a nuclear power. It was the only effective deterrent to Indian expansionism. The population was heading towards one hundred and sixty million, but there was massive unemployment with many of them living in abject poverty. Aspirations were not being met. All the political parties were plagued by corruption scandals and relied on dynastic loyalties and clan allegiance to win power so there was never a cohesive society. The Mullahs and the Military were always at loggerheads. Pakistan was always teetering on the brink of civil war. Qadri wanted to believe that they were safe from it all on their mountain, but Professor Shah said that nowhere was safe anymore.

Just when the kafir was becoming resigned to his banishment, he was removed from it. One of the Prince's bodyguards and the same local guide arrived at the gates at lunchtime. It was a sunny day, but still very cold. Ramadan was over. Everyone else had celebrated Eid with a feast, but the kafir was still starving. He was always hungry. He was ravenously eating half a chapatti, which he had found on the ground, when he recognised the tall bodyguard striding across the courtyard. He choked guiltily and coughed. Within minutes, he was on his feet, and being marched out on to the mountainside. Not even Prof. Shah rose to say goodbye.

The descent was horrendous, but he would have endured anything because he believed they were taking him home.

Chapter 10

It was driving her mad just sitting there waiting for him. It was simply not in her repertoire. She just did not know how to wait for anyone. She did not actually know anyone that she liked at all or respected enough to make that kind of commitment, and being so close to another human being undermined her self-image. She did not know how to deal with him. It was a foregone conclusion that she would be exposed and humiliated. She knew she was gauche and not attractive, and despised anything that might be called 'cool' with the obvious exception of Steve McQueen, because she had no understanding of what 'cool' was, except that whatever it was, she was not it. Alone, she was not threatened. Alone, she was unique. Nobody challenged her view of the world. She was very comfortable being unchallenged. Even asleep, even deathly ill, the young man was a threat. It was inevitable that she would be measured against some unspecific, but accepted standard of normal behaviour. Comparison meant exposure. She did not want a confrontation. What right did anyone have to criticise her? But she felt it everywhere. It was in the way people looked at her. It was implied in the way the local shopkeeper asked after her health.

She needed to move, to walk, to go out into her garden, and try to remember who she was. In the house, close to him, she was not sure what she should be feeling. She did not like the confusion. Most of all, she needed him to go away. There was something about him that made her feel powerless. She knew he was ill, and she was concerned, but she could not bear just sitting there. It made her feel weak. She had to be in control or they were both in trouble.

So she wandered in and out, going down to the ponds, staring at the frogs then hurrying back to stare at him. He did not do anything. She spent another hour cleaning his back, leaving it dry where there was no infection, but ruthlessly removing pus and dead skin. She bathed his genitals, and tried to deny her increasing interest in the variety and value of the gemstones. If she had more confidence, she might have tried to pick the padlock and to remove the sheath altogether, but she was not averse to trying to jimmy the jewels out of their settings with a sharp knife. She failed, and on reflection was appalled that she had tried to rob him. The casino chip remained in her pocket. She had conveniently forgotten about that. After lunch, she crept away to her comfortable chair to switch on the television and search for Roland Garros.

A cold wind swirled around the red clay courts. The players' eyes smarted. The stands had rows and rows of empty seats. She watched the tennis with increasing interest. He was not moving. She had done everything she could to help him. She could not lift him on to the sofa. She could not make him wake up. As the hours passed, she almost forgot that he was there. After a particularly exciting point, she was perched on the edge of her chair with her fists clenched in triumph, when she saw that he was watching her.

She turned to look at him. He blinked slowly then lowered his gaze. He had the bluest eyes. She rose unsteadily to her feet. "Are you alright?" she asked, excited by the prospect of some answers.

He stared distractedly at the television then surveyed the room then lowered his gaze again. His face was a horrible colour. By the time she had crossed the room, his strength had failed, and he had lost consciousness again. She fetched clean water, bathed his face, and squeezed drops into his mouth. He looked awful, but the smell had gone.

Again, she was waiting for him. Her attention wandered back to the television. He did not waken. He kept breathing. Her lower back and knees began to protest. She returned selfishly to the comfortable chair, and forgot about him as a young Spaniard played a particularly brilliant point. The French Open followed by Queens and then Wimbledon, who had time for anything else?

There were moments when she was sure that he opened his eyes, but they were few and fleeting, and she might have imagined it.

When the match finished, she hurried to kneel beside him again, making a conscious effort to look at his face, to not see the bloodstains on the sheet spread over his back or his long slender legs. As she sought his pulse, the glittering blue eyes flickered open. He looked at her, dumb with pain.

She leaned closer. "Don't move. I've cleaned your back. You must just lay very still." Stroking his face, she was embarrassed by her inability to be of more help. "Could you drink something? There's water. Would you prefer milk? I'm sure there's some milk in the fridge. There's tea, but I don't think you could manage a hot cup of tea. You really need to be still."

His eyes rolled. She spoke so quickly, he could not understand. But he wanted a drink. He needed one. It was all he could think about.

She realised he probably was not able to reply. He was still very warm, but the fever was abating slowly. He was ever so slightly a little better. "I'll fetch some water. You have to drink as much as possible." She drew away from him. She really did not want to leave him alone, but it was vitally important that he drink.

He needed to move onto his side. The raging agony across his back threatened to overwhelm him, but he felt it was imperative. Pushing out his stiffened forearms, he managed to lift his chest off the floor. The effort was almost too much, but gritting his teeth and sucking in air, he clung on to consciousness. When his senses rallied, he twisted his legs, and folded them under him then rolled effortlessly, but painfully onto his side. It hurt. He groaned aloud and shivered.

"Are you more comfortable like that?" she asked, staring into his astonishing eyes. His awful wounds were concealed now, but something else was not. What she still preferred to discreetly call his private parts were covered only by the bejewelled sheath. She stared at it quite dazzled then turned away utterly confused and embarrassed. She could feel her face burning. "I've brought a glass of water."

He blinked slowly. He was barely conscious.

She moved awkwardly to kneel down beside him. "You must drink." It was almost as difficult to gaze into his eyes as it was to avoid looking at the glittering sheath. It was harder to lift his head and help him to drink, but she would not change her position. She was determined to delay as long as she could. Washing him while he was conscious would be a nightmare for her, but he still needed to be kept clean, so it was inevitable that she would have to confront her prudish innocence. She was no virgin, but at that moment, she actually felt like one, which was really annoying. And it was not a young virgin filled with curiosity about life and men, but a jaundiced old crone filled with revulsion.

He drank innocently. Nothing else mattered. He did not notice that he was naked. He was too ill to be aware of such trivialities. The shock and trauma that he had suffered had not lessened their grip at all.

She lingered, plying him with water until his strength failed again, and he started to choke. After placing a cushion beneath his head, she drew away to let him rest. Her heart was thumping like a piston engine. Now, she wanted him to be unconscious. The burning acid of bile soured in her throat. It was not within her capabilities to touch him there while he was awake. Imagining him watching her doing it, was too appalling to contemplate.

Once again, averting her gaze, she turned away, and quickly left the room. It was curiously easy to convince herself that she was not running away. She needed to go into the kitchen. She wanted to wash her hands. She needed to wash the glass. All the clean towels were in the kitchen. She could make a cup of tea, wipe down the sink, and stare out of the window at her garden. She liked being in the kitchen.

But she knew what she had to do. She knew she was only delaying the obvious, and embarrassed that she was just playing games that were so transparent. She filled up the bowl again, and collected the last of the clean towels. Her hands were shaking. Walking back into the lounge, she smiled bravely. Other people did this so she could do it. She could do it. She would not throw up or be embarrassed in front of him. He would not understand, and she did not know how to explain. Other people did this. They did do this. She could do it just as well.

He had passed out again.

Appreciating the reprieve, she bathed his body more carefully, as frightened of offending him as hurting him. His groin and thighs were sweating and reddened, but there were no wounds. She sponged down the bejewelled sheath, dazzled again by the beauty of the design, but disturbed by the cruelty of the padlock that kept his penis permanently inside a cage. She quickly pressed a towel over him to absorb the moisture, then settled him again, and pulled a blanket down to hide his flesh, and to keep him warm. She scurried out to the kitchen, her hands still trembling and her face flushed, then hurried outside in acute distress.

She was away hours. She walked through to the furthest side of her woodland to stare at her neighbour's house, which was still some distance across a ploughed field. Maurice, Morris or Bruce lived there with his wife and a dog. She imagined explaining to him that she had a sick, sexually deviant young man unconscious in her house. She tried to find a way of describing his deeply decorated flesh without sounding insane. What vocabulary could she use to coolly explain the bejewelled sheath that imprisoned his penis? Was it a chastity device for men? Was it a symbol of dominance or even ownership? She blushed, imagining the conversation. She would be the one who was humiliated. She would become the object of lurid gossip in the neighbourhood. It would be endless. It would be intolerable. So she turned around and walked home.

The blue eyes opened. He took in his surroundings. He had managed to move on to his side, which hurt marginally less. It was the same room. Cats kept trying to sit on him, and even after he screamed, they still walked across him as if he was part of the furniture. One or two had rubbed around his face, trying to encourage him to stroke and pet, but he just could not move. He could not even lift a hand to push them away. Pain paralysed him. Something had happened. He could not remember. Why couldn't he remember?

She drifted wearily into the room, and sank into her chair. She found the tennis again in Paris, and watched, wondering why she was so tired then realised that she had not eaten anything for days. She was too tired to think about food, too tired to think about why her nerves were shredding. It was more than the young man. No, she would not think about it. Everything would be alright. She fell asleep. She woke up. She watched the tennis. The tennis symbolised summer, and strawberries and cream. She just needed some sunshine, and to see her garden in bloom. Then everything would be alright.

He did not move at all.

She watched her tennis. She was too tired to even make a cup of tea. The sun was shining. The red clay was stunning. She preferred grass, but the clay was excellent for dramatic slides, and swooping to the net for a drop shot. There were always some really good matches. Because she liked grass she loved Federer, by far the most elegant player to watch, and recognised by his peers as probably the best player in the history of the game. Federer was Number One in the world. He was brilliant on all surfaces, but young Nadal was playing much too well. Barely twenty years old, he seemed invincible on the red clay in Paris. Federer was obviously the favourite, but Nadal was a very real threat. Just imagining their meeting in the final made her heart flutter with excitement. They were head and shoulders above the rest of the players. Their presence in the final was a foregone conclusion. It was bound to be a classic.

The dreaded World Cup in Germany was starting on the 9th June. It was everywhere. She hoped it would not affect the coverage the BBC gave to Queens and Wimbledon. The England team were scheduled to play Paraguay on the Saturday. If they were knocked out in the early stages of the competition then the coverage on national television would shrink significantly. She did not feel remotely unpatriotic for hoping they would not win. Every honest person knew that the top league clubs were only good because they had lots of foreign players.

She turned to gaze at the young man. She was sure there was a flash of blue, but when she looked again, his eyes were closed, and he seemed to be asleep. She went out to the kitchen to fetch a glass of water then returned to kneel beside him. She lifted his head. If he had been pretending then the deception was over. He groaned as she lifted his head a little higher then pressed the glass to his lips.

"You must drink. Please, try again."

He looked at her as if struggling to focus then lowered his gaze. He opened his mouth, and she patiently dribbled in a few drops. He swallowed with difficulty. She repeated the process until he remembered what he was supposed to do. With the glass half empty, he flinched, and tried to move away, but she pressed his lips again, and held on firmly to his head. He was not happy, but he finished the glass. She understood that she was bullying him, but reasoned that it was essential. She was so determined to make him better that his own feelings were irrelevant. Even if he had asked her to stop, she would have ignored him. Putting aside the glass, she lowered his head carefully back on to the cushion then re-arranged the blankets. The hot water bottles were cooling. She took them away, and filled them then returned to press them back near his body.

There was a roar of approval on the television. She quickly turned away from him to see a repeat of a match winning point: a deep serve followed by a blistering forehand down the line. She managed a smile of satisfaction then turned back to her patient.

"Are you feeling any better?" she asked, gazing into the young man's face.

His eyes were gorgeous. They twinkled. They were not just blue, but a mixture of a dozen different shades of blue and green, and full of reflections of light from the big windows. When she stooped to smile admiringly, he lowered his gaze.

"I don't know your name," she said, trying to encourage him. She smiled again for him, but it was a feeble effort. He was a man. She already felt threatened and humiliated.

He breathed deeply then closed his eyes.

That felt like rejection. She waited for him to respond, but he remained motionless. She stroked the loose strands of hair away from his eyes. Even ill, he was extraordinarily good-looking. He was, without doubt, the most beautiful man she had ever seen, not just in real life, but in movies or magazines. Her smile came easier because he had fainted again. For several minutes, she was happy to study his face while waiting for him to come back to her. The texture of his skin would have been the envy of most women. He had thick, long lashes. His hair was like strands of black silk. She could tell from the ends that it had been recently trimmed. He had fine bones, neat ears, clean well-defined lips and strong white teeth. He needed a shave. Not that she was an expert, but she thought his emerging beard was uneven, and definitely needed to go. Perhaps, it was hormones.

Not that she had ever noticed that gay men could not do beards. She was quite confident now that he would not die, and knew that it was, at least, partly due to her determination if not her skill. He was marginally stronger than he had been the day before. The nasty smell had gone. She just had to get him back on his feet, and quickly send him on his way. She wanted her house back. She knew she could not cope with him under foot or hovering around her. Just imagining it made her nerves jangle. Making him leave might prove harder than dragging him in from the garden. She drew away, irritated. Of course, he would leave her. She could not conceive of anything that might make him want to hang around. It was obvious that he loathed her. He would not even look at her. For one brief moment, she hated him. But she had only to look at his lovely face for her heart to melt. Yes. He was loved. She knew, with certainty, that whoever had hurt him also loved him. It would all turn out to be some tawdry homosexual parlour game. She was embarrassed again by her complete innocence. There were more things in heaven and earth, Horatio, than she had ever seen on late night television.

Another match started. She made herself a cup of tea, and sank down into her comfy chair. It might be cold in England, but in Paris it was a sunny if breezy day. For another hour, she ignored him, not even interfering as the black cat walked across his body, and settled on the very spot where she had put the hot water bottles. She had a little argument with herself about hygiene, but gritted her teeth, and left the cat alone.

It was another horrible grey day. It was the wettest, coldest May she could remember. Her body was still sore. She knew that she should have been physically working though all her aches and pains to make them go away. She did not have any broken bones, but she was distracted and unhappy, and the tennis was more inviting than a cold garden, and she did not really trust the young man. When another cat came to sit on her knee, she settled placidly. It hardly mattered that there were two Eastern European women on court. They looked great, but were both losing games and not winning them. It was still blustery, but the red clay and blue skies were more alluring than her grey, lifeless garden.

Now and then, the young man opened his eyes to stare at her, and to survey the room. The girls on the television held his attention longer than anything else, but he was still too weak to do more than sleep. He was in pain. He hardly remembered what had happened to him, and the woman and the strange room raised questions that he was unable to ask. So he drifted back to sleep, hoping that when he awoke again all the questions would be answered, but they never were.

That evening, she pulled the curtains, and switched on the lights then settled to watch the next instalment of her favourite programme. Dear Bill was still 'flipping freezing'. She smiled immediately. They were talking about otters and bats. She had bats, but they were too swift or too small to see. She had assumed they were the tiny Pipistrelles. They certainly made the same noises that she heard on the television. Up close, they were not as attractive as she had imagined, but perhaps even bats had bad hair days. And they were evidently very small as they weighed less than a 20p coin.

It was quite late when he started dreaming again. He flinched and trembled. Sometimes, he seemed to be trying to push away demons. There were times he actually spoke, but she did not understand any of the words except 'no'. He said 'no' a lot. He was increasingly distressed about something. She wanted to wake him, but did not have the nerve. At one point, he was shouting. She hurried to kneel down, and took him in her arms, but as soon as she touched him, he went rigid, and quickly passed out. Frightened of hurting him, she sat beside him all that night. Sometimes, his dreams lasted only a few minutes, but others lasted for hours as he shouted and struggled until exhaustion finally wore him out.

*

The old desert fortress was probably the safest place in the world for the kafir. There had been the huge bomb in Riyadh in November at a US-operated National Guard training centre. All the fatalities had been American. The men arrested all claimed to have been inspired by bin Laden, who was making a lot of noise about there still being infidels in the Kingdom four years after the Gulf War. Certainly, there were lots more foreigners about. The number of American troops was staggering, and amongst them were women in uniform, who drove vehicles and carried guns. Women in the Kingdom were asking why they were not permitted to drive a car if they remained veiled. Control of the media, and information generally, had also loosened up because of the presence of so many foreigners. Young people were listening to pop music. Many hardliners in the older generation were very upset.

The Irish were also leaving bombs all over London. In February, they had tried to blow up the prestigious Canary Wharf, and caused a billion pounds worth of damage, killing two people, and ending a seventeen-month ceasefire. Only ten days later they had detonated a briefcase bomb on a bus, meaning to cause the maximum amount of carnage. They were not the only terrorists busy that February. Libyan explosives were being exported all over the world. The US Embassy in Athens was attacked by mortars. In Sri Lanka, there was a bomb in Colombo that killed ninety, and seriously injured more than a thousand.

The Prince was still in Sarajevo with the UN Special Representative of the Secretary General, and a large team of UN personnel. The siege had ended after nearly four years. The considerable structural damage to the city was nothing compared to the psychological damage to the survivors. The Serbians had turned the city into a firing range, and could pick off their targets at will, and the UN had done little or nothing to protect the civilians. They had done nothing about the massacres either, as they had done nothing in Rwanda and Burundi and Western Sahara and Liberia. They had eventually sent Peacekeepers into Bosnia Herzegovina, but intentionally tied their hands with a mandate that did not allow them to intervene. Mladic and Milosevic ruthlessly took advantage of this. When UN soldiers did disobey orders, and actually challenged the Serbians, they had become hostages.

During the Srebrenica genocide, one French commander made a deal with Mladic, agreeing to stop NATO airstrikes against Serbian positions in return for the release of some French troops. Dutch troops were forced to stand down when the Serbians took over Srebrenica after having starved the town into submission after blockading it for years. Srebrenica was supposed to be a UN Safe Area, but one by one the UN outposts had been forced to retreat or surrender. There were reports of people actually starving to death in the town. The Peacekeepers were also suffering No supplies were getting through. But NATO refused to intervene. The Muslims trapped in the town had begged the Dutch soldiers to stay and protect them, but the UN Peacekeepers were not allowed to engage. They could only watch as men were murdered, and women were repeatedly raped in the streets. Their hands were tied by orders. It was an appalling situation. Tensions were running so high that two Dutch F16s using SAS co-ordinates launched an unauthorised attack on the Serbian artillery advancing on the town. NATO were compelled to offer assistance, but then it was a foggy day so no other planes could actually take off, and ultimately NATO did absolutely nothing because the Serbians threatened their hidden cache of Dutch and French hostages. Over the following week, the Serbians had murdered thousands of men, and buried them in mass graves. In the end, the United Nations and NATO had to accept that the Serbians were not going to stop their campaign to eradicate the Muslim population unless they were resoundingly defeated. An intensive bombing campaign had begun on the 30th August, and did not stop until the 20th September, when the Serbian forces did finally withdraw their heavy weapons.

The United Nations were all over Sarajevo now that the shooting had stopped. The journalists, who had been in the city throughout the siege, were happy to remind them of their failings. There were already some horrible statistics: about 200,000 dead, including those that were starved to death in the camps, and between 25,000 and 50,000 raped as part of the campaign of ethnic cleansing to guarantee a future population that was, at least, genetically half Serbian. And if asked every Serbian would say that the Croatians had started it.

Seventeen Greek tourists were killed in Cairo with a dozen more injured just because they looked Jewish. No one admitted responsibility, but the opinion of the servants at the palace was that it was the fault of the pro-Western government, and Mubarek in particular, who never dressed like a good Muslim so he was insulting God.

Egypt had been going off the rails for years. Sadat had been even worse than Mubarek. He had signed a peace treaty with Israel. Israel! He had betrayed the Palestinians. Sayyid Qutb had started the revolution. He had originally been a secularist, but working in America in the 1940s, he had seen how coloured people were treated in the great Western democracy. He had a very poor opinion of American morals, jazz music and haircuts. Returning to Egypt, he worked extensively with Nasser, believing that they had common goals, only to discover he was being exploited. He began to believe that anything non-Islamic was evil and corrupt. This simple truth inspired a generation. He condemned supposedly Muslim governments such as Nasser's regime in Egypt as being secular, and therefore illegitimate. He opposed Arab nationalism. He never married having never found a woman of sufficient moral purity and discretion. When he was arrested and charged with plotting to assassinate Nasser, the Egyptians put him in prison, and there he was tortured by the pro-Western government.. He wanted the world to submit to divine power. It was pure and perfect. True Islam would transform every aspect of society, eliminating everything non-Islamic, everything Western and modern and bad. According to Qutb, jihad was not about defending Islam from the Jews and Westerners. That was outdated and wrong. Qutb preached that jihad was the aggressive expansion of Islam to create a strong community throughout the Islamic homeland, which would then spread throughout the world. Islam had always been spread by the sword. The great leaders were all warriors. Those that did not convert died. It was absolute submission to the Word of God or death. There was no dilution. There was no middle ground. There was to be no tolerance. His philosophy inspired Ayman al Zawahiri, who became the esteemed mentor of Osama bin Laden.

The kafir was safe at home with his Pakistanis. He was surrounded by the people that he knew. The Pakistanis allowed him back into their beds as if he had never been away. There were never any questions. There were a lot of complaints about the state of his hands and feet, but no one blamed him. After the bleak conditions at the madrassa, he was happy to have lots of hot baths and massages, and be spoilt with treats when he entertained their friends. He was flattered by the attention. There was no humiliation. He did not feel abused. If he worked hard and submitted graciously they were merciful. Every day, he bowed down and submitted, and they were merciful. If he awoke in a cold sweat, frightened by bad dreams, there was always a reassuring embrace. His Pakistanis were always there to comfort him. He was never alone. For a long, long time, he never wanted to be alone again.

Early that same year, it was announced, to the dismay of many, that the young creature was required to accompany its master on a trip abroad. No one had anticipated that. Many whispered against it, but the Prince had made up his mind. For the Pakistanis, it complicated everything. They hardly had any warning. Their established and stable home lives were turned upside down. Mahmood's elderly mother was very upset. The complex dynamics of Waheed's life meant he was actually glad to escape the endless pressure and demands for money, but he would be constantly pursued by phone calls and messages. Aziz was simply irritated by the inconvenience of it all. Their unchallenged authority over the creature had allowed them a reliable source of income and some prestige. No one would have dreamed of suggesting that the Prince was not allowed to make use of his servants as he saw fit; they were all his to command, but it did cause problems for them.

They all travelled on the Prince's diplomatic papers. No one questioned them. No one searched their bags. That would have been impolite. The hotel was very grand. The Prince and his entourage often took over two or three floors, and within reason, the Prince picked up the bill for everything. There were armed guards everywhere. Security was always very tight. The servants were packed in like soldiers in a billet. The younger ones had to sleep on the floor. Food was flown in. Prayers were read. It was expected to be hectic and stressful, but the Pakistanis were determined to make the most of what might be a once in a lifetime opportunity.

With all their baggage safely stowed away, the Pakistanis were able to spend most of their first day sightseeing in Paris. They bought cameras and sent postcards, and went to strange new places to see exotic new things that even the colourful slums of Cairo and Karachi did not possess. They were like children again. Their joy and excitement was boundless. They had all made long lists of all the things they wanted to see and do, but there simply was not enough time. It did not matter how fast they ran from the Moulin Rouge to the Eiffel Tower to the Crazy Horse Bar. It was impossible to see everything, but they did try. After a long, weary day of adventures, they all met up back at the hotel to swap stories and show off their souvenirs.

At last, when they had all eaten their fill, and there were simply no more stories to tell, Aziz opened the closet, and carefully parted the drapes. From the depths of the shadows, blue eyes glittered as the creature lifted its head. Aziz loosened the gag then shoved the face away so that he could reach down to unfasten the clips that held its ankles and wrists to a belt. It had been immobilised for hours. Stiff and sore, it moved awkwardly. Its muscles were cramped. It was shivering and confused. It needed reassurance, but Aziz was brusque. He dragged it from the closet and dumped it irritably on the floor.

The kafir was used to being the centre of attention. At home, there was a routine. He knew what he had to do. In the bottom of the cupboard, all they required from him was silence. He had had nothing to drink for nearly eighteen hours. He was going insane. He was desperately thirsty, but dared not beg. He could hardly move, but knew he must never complain.

Before dawn and late at night, he rose from the stagnation of his existence to take care of his master. It did not matter that his master chose to ignore him. His master was a great prince. That his Pakistanis no longer took him into their beds left him desolate. He never considered for a moment that while they slept three or four to a bed there was no room left for him. It was his fault. It was always his fault. It was engraved into his brain that it was always his fault.

The gulf between the kafir and his Pakistanis widened with every day that they were abroad, but as soon as they came home, everything returned to normal. He was allowed to share their beds, and given treats when he pleased them. To him, it was forgiveness. He had done something. He had failed somehow. It reinforced his dependence. He needed their constant and unwavering approval. If he was left alone for even a moment, he became increasingly distressed and unstable, which was misconstrued as rebellion and temper. The security around him was continually strengthened. He was allowed less and less.

Amongst the servants, the ongoing Iraq disarmament crisis was viewed with a great deal of pride. Saddam Hussein was making fools of the Americans and the United Nations Security Council. They might have managed to destroy an abandoned factory at Al Hakam, but they had not found anything. Saddam was too smart for them. It was the number one topic of conversation. Saddam was their hero. He was cheered every time he appeared on television. They completely overlooked the little problems that had cost so many lives in Iran and then Kuwait. Only the Arabs worried about the bigger picture and the fracturing of Islam.

On his first trip to New York in October 1996, the kafir was surprised by the blatant animosity of the media towards Saddam. He was genuinely relieved when the American imperialists failed to bully the usually weak United Nations into supporting an invasion of Iraq. The Americans were rapidly falling out of love with the Secretary General, who was definitely pro-French, and they were using their financial clout to try and muscle through their own agenda. Everyone knew it was all about oil. The Americans were desperate to invade just to get their hands on the oilfields while accusing Saddam of having biological weapons, and heaven knows what else. Of course, it was all lies. Even if the Americans found something, everyone knew that it would have been planted there by the Jews. It was all another cunning American Zionist plot to destroy Islam.

The most shocking news of the year was the bomb attack in the Kingdom, which killed nineteen Americans, and caused catastrophic damage to the Khobar Towers in Dhahran. His master was upset that such a thing should happen. The opinion of the household was that bin Laden was right, the Americans had no place being there, and might now get the message and go home. The kafir hated the Americans because every man in his life hated them. There were many who considered it sacrilegious to have the infidels in the Kingdom. Some of the younger men, who felt their duty to God very keenly, were bold enough to even criticise the King. This was considered unacceptable behaviour, and many of them had, more or less, been forced to go abroad. Even the ordinary people believed that the foreigners only came for the money and the oil. Their women were all shameless whores, who flaunted their breasts and their legs, and the men were all drunks and liars, and had no honour. There were constantly rumours that the foreigners were smuggling liquor and drugs. The authorities were suggesting that there was some underworld war going on between gangs of bootleggers, who were all Americans. Any disruptive behaviour was blamed on the Americans. In fact, everything was blamed on the Americans. The kafir had never heard anything remotely complimentary about them, and would have believed wholeheartedly that they had two heads and horns and a tail if he had not actually seen them in the flesh. They were definitely friends with the Jews occupying Palestine, which condemned them utterly.

Chapter 11

She opened the curtains and windows soon after eight. It promised to be another cold grey day. She wandered alone to the kitchen, and gazed out of the window. There was so much to do. In her heart, she was already walking out to look at the ponds. The woodland called to her. But she could not go. It would have been unforgivable to abandon him. She resented it, and felt the guilt her humanity demanded. And she still did not trust him. He was conscious now. Leaving him in sole possession of her house and her secrets was too frightening to contemplate.

When she turned from the window, there were half a dozen cats waiting for her. "Yes, I know. I'm sorry," she said aloud. "It's my fault. I found him. What else was I supposed to do?"

Some smiled, some blinked, some glowered, but no one said anything. They wanted food. Her relationship problems were her own. They just wanted food.

She opened the cupboard. There were only a few tins left. That was a blow. She would have to go to the shops, and spend as little money as possible. Her only income was paid on the Quarter Days when other farmers paid their rent on her land. So until Midsummer on the 24th June, she was strapped for cash. It was still only the 31st May. She opened two tins, and put down the plates for the cats, then went back into the lounge.

She stooped to feel his forehead. It was still warm. He looked very pale, but his lips were not as white as they had been the day before. He was shockingly beautiful. She gazed at him, mesmerised by his sheer physical beauty. Her fingers strayed to sweep a few errant strands of black hair back off his forehead. She traced his cheekbones. She held her breath hoping to glimpse his exquisite eyes. When her back muscles protested again, she limped slowly to her comfortable chair, and sat down feeling quite bereft.

The morning news was on television. The headlines were obsessed with Rooney's metatarsal, but Real Madrid midfielder, a certain Mr. David Beckham, was assuring everyone that Rooney would be fit to play at the World Cup. She yawned. There was another story about Big Brother, a popular reality TV show that pandered to a certain section of the public that seemed to enjoy watching people be destroyed. The audience for the show was evidently made up of the same sort of people who had gone to the Roman arena to watch gladiators kill each other to escape a gruesome execution. All the contestants in 'the house' were chosen from the most vulnerable in society. According to the criticism on a rival channel, the current crop were either anorexic, suicidal, sexually confused, or had Tourette's. None of them were really fit to be put in a pressure-cooker environment, and shown 24/7 on live TV. The show had become something of a phenomenon, luring celebrities in by offering huge financial rewards for end of season specials. The clip of a politician pretending to be a cat, and licking milk from a saucer, was one of the more deplorable episodes that had become headline news.

So the world might have been coming to an end because of global warming or because of the ongoing problems in the Middle East, but the only news that anyone was apparently interested in was a metatarsal and a reality TV show.

The young man moved, but he was still asleep. She knew she had to make sure he stayed asleep while she went out to the shops. Now that he was able to drink, she could spike his water with pills. She could crush them under a spoon. He would not know. He might even be grateful. If he was asleep then he was not in pain. She nodded thoughtfully. She would keep him drugged. She would keep him, but then she realised where she was going, and radically changed course. As soon as he was well enough to give her a name, she would phone his lover or parents, and get rid of him. A wife had dropped off the radar. He did not have the body of a married man. He had a lover. What he needed were parents. He needed unconditional love and protection. Someone had hurt him badly. Someone had treated him appallingly. She had treated him appallingly, but she had not known that he was so vulnerable and so badly hurt.

She rose stiffly to her feet then walked back to stand over him. She bent to retrieve the cold hot water bottles, and limped back out to the kitchen. There were still a few cats eating. The ginger glutton was always hungry. She filled the kettle, and stood at the window while it boiled. There was still so much to do. She would have a bath, find some clean clothes, then go down to the supermarket. She needed food for her guest. She could exist on pasta and rice, but a man's appetite required protein and bulk even if he was gay. But if he was very ill, he probably needed fortifying drinks and medicine. She could not afford what he needed. The kettle boiled. She stared out of the window. She had no idea how much money she did or did not have in her account. Most trips to the supermarket were a battle of nerves when it came to the checkout. Would the card work? Would she be embarrassed? If it was the 31st May, then there should be something left in her account. She had been so careful. But if she needed petrol as well? She shook her head, and turned back to the kettle.

The young man stirred as she pressed the hot water bottles close to him. He was stronger. The fever was breaking, at last.

She made sure he was comfortable then went away up the stairs. She found her horde of pills. The ones she wanted were technically painkillers, but she used them to make sure she could sleep. She needed to sleep at least eight hours a night. She was already feeling the effects of not having slept properly for three days. The most obvious symptoms were irritability, and then increasingly irrational behaviour, and finally complete insanity. She had half a bottle of pills. She held the bottle like an addict. She needed them. She knew the tells. She was not prepared to share, but she had to. It was a tough choice. She needed to stay sane, but she needed to incapacitate the young man or her nerves would destroy them both. She counted the pills then counted them again.

Back in the kitchen, she sat at the table quietly crushing three pills to dust. She had a glass of milk ready. Three seemed to be the right amount. He weighed more than she did, but he was ill. He had an empty stomach. Eggs. She would buy some eggs. Whenever she was ill, she always liked scrambled eggs. A good maternal instinct made her feel warm all over. She would drop in at the doctor's surgery, and wheedle another prescription, then they would both have enough pills.

Making him drink required him being conscious. He took a moment to come around. As soon as his eyes opened, she started talking to him. He was not really awake, but she focused on his eyes, waiting for him to look at her, which he seemed curiously reluctant to do. "You must drink," she said, showing him the glass, which he did look at. "Come on, stay with me. This will make you feel better. You have to drink. Do you understand? You must drink."

He took a breath then tried to lift himself, but the slightest movement sent waves of pain flooding through his body.

"Just drink," she said. "Don't try to do anything else. You're not strong enough."

He glanced at her then focused on the glass. When she pressed it to his lips, he swallowed with a determination that had not been there before.

She was pleased that he drained the glass without being bullied. "That's much better. You look better." She smiled with genuine pleasure.

He looked at her again then quickly lowered his gaze. He had no idea who she was or why he was in that room. All that he knew was that he was in pain, and it engulfed him, keeping him a prisoner. He winced as she released him to lay on the floor, and tried not to flinch as she covered him with blankets. He felt her concern, but did not trust it. There were so many questions, but he could not ask any of them. He did not know how to ask, and while she was talking so quickly, he did not have an opportunity to try.

She sat staring at him, ignoring his discomfort, waiting for him to go to sleep. When he did not, she moved away irritably, and went out to the kitchen to crush a few more pills. When she returned with another glass of milk, he was happy to drink whatever her generosity allowed.

He still did not sleep. She sat staring at him from her chair. It took barely a moment for her to regret giving him the pills. She had given him too many. Not only would he sleep, but he would never wake. She had killed him, murdered him. She chewed her nails as her nerves frayed. She had killed him. It was only a matter of time. When he did go to sleep then she hurried to waken him, but he was ill, the drugs had no effect on that. So she woke him again, which frightened him. She assured him everything would be alright, but every time he drifted off to sleep, she woke him.

She held him in her arms all day. There were moments when she was crying. He hardly moved. Even when the pills had the desired effect she kept trying to waken him, but he was deeply asleep. She watched him breathing. For hours, she watched him, sometimes crying for him and sometimes for herself. But he kept breathing. He did not die. It was late in the afternoon when he moved restlessly in her arms and proved his consciousness. By then, she was a complete wreck.

She went out into the garden. She was too emotional to go out in public. She needed to go for a walk. She felt confined and her options were limited. With the young man in the house, she could not even chill out with Big Shoulders. No one would ever understand that. She needed *The Searchers* to combat the futility of her life, and loneliness and a crippling lack of esteem, and *She Wore a Yellow Ribbon* for – she hardly knew what, but she always felt better afterwards. There had been days when John Wayne was the only human voice in her life.

There was a dead frog in the small pond. It was like a knife through her heart. Without thinking she took off her shoes, and waded into the freezing water, placing her feet carefully on the pebbles. The frog was at the bottom, and she did not have a net. She reached down with her right hand. The water came up to her shoulder, soaking her breasts. It was so cold. The frog felt slippery, but it had not yet started to decompose. She stood examining it morosely. If she had come earlier? If she had paid more attention? Did everything have to die? There were no obvious injuries, but it was very thin. She decided it was a female. Life was always harder for the females.

She went back to the house. She left her shoes at the back door, but trailed through the hall, and up the stairs in her clothes. The young man might be unconscious, he might actually be dead, but she could not walk through the house naked anymore. It did not feel like her space now. His body had become a permanent fixture in her front room. If he died then he would become a permanent resident in her garden. She ran a hot bath then stripped off her clothes. She needed a hot bath. She felt that she had killed something or someone. Like Pilate, she desperately wanted to wash her hands.

The water was so hot her flesh turned red, but she still felt cold. She washed her hair, and scrubbed her skin. It made no difference. When she stood up, her head swam. She grabbed a towel, and hurried to her bedroom to lay down and cry. She had not eaten or taken her medication. She was ill. She was so very ill. It should not have been a surprise. Her set routine had been shattered. On the first day, when she found him, she forgot to eat, forgot to take the pills. She had a drawer full by her bed. There were pills for the morning, for the evening and for anytime in between when she did not feel in control. Here were the tells: she was crying. She felt as if she had been crying from the moment he arrived, but there were never any tears.

She took a cocktail of pills then went downstairs to find a glass of water. Her intelligence allowed her to function briefly once she recognised that she was ill. It did not stop her being a danger to herself, but it gave the young man some protection. Sometimes, she wondered how many people actually lived in her head. She had long conversations. On good days, everyone agreed.

The young man was sleeping soundly. She was relieved. Pulling on a coat and scarf to hide her hair, she went out to unlock the garage. The car started, which was always a pleasant surprise. She set off to the nearest town. It was not far. There was an all-night supermarket. She could buy what she needed to feed the cats and her young man. The prescription would have to wait for another day. Her doctor was very good. He did not put her under pressure to attend counselling or clinics. There was no cure for her condition. Only she could monitor it 'in the community'. She had proved to the doctor that she was capable of managing a routine. The young man had distracted her. She knew what she had to do. She had to take care of herself, take her pills, sleep and eat, and then worry about him. It was more important than ever that no one knew he was there. There would be alarm bells. There would be red flags. Social Services would come and take him away. There might be the police. She could not cope with that. No one would understand why she had kept him. And now she had drugged him. How could she explain that? How could she explain his body? Didn't she look guilty now?

Leaving him alone in her house was probably the hardest thing she had done. It did not matter that he was too ill to move. He was a man, and his reach was daunting too. Huddled up and sick, he seemed nothing at all, but one day, like a great eagle, he would stretch out his arms, and become immense. It was altogether too unnerving to contemplate how quick and agile he would be when back on his feet. How could she control him then? How could she maintain the balance of power, and stop it shifting to the stronger man?

She thought about him abstractly all the time. He had become an obsession. He was such a great secret that the power of it almost overwhelmed her. She did not know his name, but what he was physically had eclipsed all ordinary things. She almost suspected that she was still in shock. Nothing seemed real. He had taken over her life so completely that she almost resented it. Only the fascination saved him. His being so ill became quite secondary. She had to know. Late night television, that had once appalled her, now whetted her appetite. She needed to know exactly what he was, and what had driven him or tempted him to turn his body into a celebration of everything lurid and obscene. Clothed and clean, he had been so angelic, but naked he was absolute corruption. In darker moments, she thought of him as a whore, but suspected that he was so much more than that. Sex obviously obsessed him whereas she was filled with revulsion at the idea of something so private and intimate being so outrageously public. She found herself repeatedly condemning him. At times, she hated him, and wished she had left him there to die, but as soon as she looked at him and his lovely face, then all her prejudice evaporated and she was crushed by guilt.

The card worked. Her relief must have been apparent as the teller smiled knowingly then offered to help her pack the items into bags. All the local supermarkets were pushing the use of reusable shopping bags, but seemed to have overlooked putting them at the checkout. She considered herself a 'green' person, but never remembered to bring the reusable bags back when she came shopping. She had failed again. Thanking the woman on the checkout, she left the supermarket. The pills were not working yet. She was tense and agitated. She wanted to hurry home and lock all the doors.

The young man awoke on the floor. He felt curiously groggy. It was not unpleasant. He remembered his injuries, and was grateful to have escaped some of the pain. The television was on. It always seemed to be on. There were ugly miserable people arguing about ugly miserable things. He did not know if they were real people or just actors. He wondered where the woman had gone. Had she abandoned him? He had no strength, no reserves of anything. He was not even sure why he was still alive. He could not help wondering who she was, and what had brought him to this place. He studied the limited view that he had of the room, and learned very little. There were a lot of books and paperwork. The furniture was old. The curtains and carpets needed cleaning. She was not a tidy person. She seemed to like cats; there were lots of cats. He went back to sleep, woke again, then slept until the sound of her car on the gravel awoke him.

She hurried into the house, switching lights on and pulling curtains across. She did not need to examine the young man because he watched her every move. Seeing what was on the television, she grabbed the remote, and flicked through several channels until she found something interesting. It was a trailer for her favourite programme. She grinned at the young man as if he was part of the fan club then hurried away to sort out the shopping. Two of the cats that had been sleeping next to him, yawned and stretched. They knew where the food was. He watched as other cats appeared from other rooms, and all headed towards the kitchen. To him, they were all vermin. He had no idea who she was or why he was there so he stayed still and quiet and did not complain.

She switched the oven on then hurried into the front room to offer the young man a can of milkshake. He did not move. She hesitated, reading in his expression that he had no idea what was happening. She decided the rich really were different, and pulled the tab on the can then offered it again. "It's strawberry," she said, and smiled. "Drink it. You must drink." He still did not move or show any kind of recognition. She sipped from the can, and made a yummy sound then offered it again. He was looking at the can now, but he could not move. It hurt his back to move his arms. She suddenly realised her mistake, and leaned down to put the can in his hand, but he still did not drink. Without thinking, she knelt down, and lifted his head then pressed the can to his lips. He drank. He liked it. She knew then that he had never tasted a strawberry milkshake. She stared at him in shock. How could there be anybody on the planet who did not know about strawberry milkshake? McDonalds had reached everywhere. She wondered who he was, and where he had come from.

She retreated to the kitchen, shaking her head. She would not think about him. She cooked a nice meal, and sat alone at the kitchen table to eat it. All the pills she needed to take were in a line next to her knife. She took them all. She was a good girl. She was not going to be ill. She could be sane and sensible and normal. She could care for another human being.

Just because he had come crashing into her life did not mean he had to die. She was not a killer. She wanted to believe that she would not kill him, but who was he? How could he not know about a strawberry milkshake?

*

Long before dawn, before any other people were awake, the kafir was prepared like a princess. Scrubbed clean and in his best robe, he was returned to the anteroom where one of the elderly Arab retainers awaited him. In the early morning, it was now the kafir's duty to wake his master, bathe and dress him, then to withdraw so that the Prince and the other righteous Believers could answer the first call to prayer. Each palace had its own mosque. If they were abroad, an imam stood in the stairwell, and loudly summoned the Believers. Other guests in the hotel were too polite to complain. No one was ever comfortable about criticising any religion except their own.

The kafir had been taught to be a good Muslim, and he had been a diligent student. His education was considered more important than his looks or his talent as a valet because it was essential that he did not cause offense. The principal influence in his life were the ultraconservative Wahhabis, but he knew men who adhered to the Salafi doctrine and even a few Sufis. He could recite most of the Holy Book and Hadiths and spoke Arabic fluently, so he knew how important it was for his master to be clean and simply dressed. That was his responsibility. He took it very seriously. There were never any complaints about his work, but he was constantly faulted for being just too damn tall.

God was great. God was compassionate and merciful and kind. God hated disbelievers. The kafir tried to find private moments to pray for his soul, but they were few. He was kept constantly busy. He knew that there was no heaven or afterlife awaiting him. Only Achmed Qadri had ever offered him hope, but that had always seemed qualified. He was condemned to a cold grave while waiting for the Day of Judgement then an eternity in a flaming Hell. He was less than them, less than their horses or their dogs or their shoes. Their great god had dictated it to their beloved prophet a thousand years ago. They were the chosen ones. It was their duty to live as their prophet had shown them, to be kind and generous and obedient, and to be prepared to sacrifice their lives and the lives of their children for their god. All his life, every day, he was reminded that he should be grateful for simply being allowed to serve the Faithful in a world that would one day be wholly and completely Islamic. God had determined it. It was written. There would be peace and harmony and one god. For the Believers, it was to be a paradise on Earth, and something they must all strive to achieve. The kafir was not one of them. He could never be one of them. His white skin and blue eyes marked him out. His soul was impure. He had no honour. Their immense charity and compassion and mercy spared him, and every moment of his life was dedicated to proving that he was grateful.

After being forced out of Sudan in May by pressure from the Americans and Saudis, bin Laden declared war on them both when he wrote: "The Declaration of Jihad on the Americans Occupying the Country of the Two Sacred Sites." The kafir had heard the other servants talking about it long before he saw anything in the newspapers that were always on his master's desk. It frightened the servants, which surprised him. He had not been aware of an invasion. It took him a while to work out that it was a metaphorical occupation. He had thought bin Laden was a hero after single-handedly defeating the Soviets in Afghanistan, and subsequently destroying their evil empire that had tried for so many decades to deny the existence of God. Osama defied the disbelievers. He made them look weak and stupid. Rumour had it that he was starting training camps in Afghanistan to teach people how to kill the disbelievers. It was very exciting. Many of the servants proudly boasted of brothers and cousins going to join the cause. It was the righteous thing to do. There was no greater prize than giving one's life for God. To be a martyr was the highest of aspirations. No other human endeavour matched it.

Apparently, bin Laden had some arrangement with the Taliban. The kafir did not understand that. The Northern Alliance was fighting the Taliban. Surely, they were on the same side? The Pakistanis and the Americans had financed the Mujahedeen during the war with the Soviets. Now, the Americans were supporting the Northern Alliance against the Taliban. Half the Taliban were Pakistanis. Pakistan was an ally of the Americans. Nothing made sense. He had been so sure that bin Laden was a good guy.

When Saddam Hussein sent troops to Arbil in the northern No Fly Zone, there was much chuckling in the servants' quarters, and consternation everywhere else. Saddam had once instructed his men to drive their tanks over the Kurds because he was saving his bullets for the Persians. The genocide following the Gulf War had been widely reported. The poison gas attacks had caused outrage, but were quietly forgotten now. The No Fly Zone was actually inside Iraq, but the arrogant Americans had decided that it was completely off limits to Saddam. He had called their bluff again, and everyone hoped that the Americans would have to back down because the French would certainly stir up the UN into a hornets' nest of dissent. Saddam had long been an ally of the Kingdom. He had fought the heretical Shias in Iran, who called themselves True Believers, but were considered amongst the worst heretics on the planet by the righteous Sunnis. There was only one God, but there were so many churches, each one believing that all the others were wrong. Saddam had fought the Ayatollahs bravely for eight years until each country was on the brink of destruction, with children fighting when there were no men left strong enough to stand. Saddam had been financed and trained by the Kingdom's allies, the Americans. Now, those same allies, and the Kingdom, considered Saddam a dangerous enemy beyond their control. Allegiances were as shifting as the sands in the desert. The kafir remembered what he had heard about the Gulf War. He had been at the madrassa. At the madrassa, Saddam's young troops won handsomely, and so did the Kingdom's, but the kafir, simply because of the colour of his skin, had been forced to represent the Americans and the British, and been thoroughly vanquished. Much later, he was surprised to learn that the real war had ended very differently.

It took only a matter of days for the Americans to launch 'Operation Desert Strike' to punish Saddam's alleged impudence. That might have secretly pleased the Saudis and Kuwaitis. It only enraged the ordinary people, who grumbled that once again imperialist America was able to bully the United Nations into attacking another defenceless Islamic nation.

In late September, the Taliban captured Kabul, driving out the latest pro-western president, and executing the Soviet front man, Mohammad Najibullah. He had been given refuge for some years in the United Nations compound in Kabul, but the jubilant Taliban marched in and pulled him out. He was publically beaten, castrated in the street, dragged around town behind a truck, and then hanged like a dog from a street light. There was concern at the barbarity of his execution then jubilation. History was never likely to remember that he had once been considered a great administrator of a turbulent nation. Bin Laden was now thick with the Taliban.

Early in the winter, the United Nations Security Council announced that the weapons inspectors, that Saddam had been forced to allow back into the country, had at last actually found some missile parts. It was not the 'big gun' that had become the iconic image of Saddam's secret weapons horde. They claimed that munitions had been buried in the ground, but it was generally believed that it was all just another American Zionist plot. Iraq had oil. It was always about oil. The Americans had huge cars and refrigerators, and would simply die if they could not get their hands on the oil.

The recently re-elected President of the United States was still considered rather young, and as the servants pointed out, he did not have a beard so he would always be weak and dominated by women. Interest in the weakling president waned after only a few days when there was a mid-air collision between a Saudi Boeing 747 and a plane from Kazakhstan. Three hundred and forty-nine people were killed. There was a national outpouring of grief that the kafir had never experienced before, and a period of mourning for innocent lives lost. Not two weeks later, an Ethiopian plane was hijacked then crashed into the Indian Ocean just off the Comoros after apparently running out of fuel. One hundred and twenty-five people were killed. There were immediately rumours that the Saudi flight had been deliberately brought down. This caused consternation and outrage across the Kingdom. Prince Khalid, in New York, assured his father that the American-led aviation agencies were convinced that it had been an accident, but that there would be no absolute proof for months or even years. The Black Boxes were being investigated, but it might take some time to sort out all the evidence. The atmosphere was so tense. No one believed the Americans anymore.

Saddam's son, Uday, was seriously injured in an assassination attempt. He was shot eight times while out in his Porsche. It triggered terrible reprisals and much bloodshed. There were any number of suspects. Even Saddam had cause. Uday had killed his father's personal food taster in front of all the guests at a party given for Mubarak's wife. Rumour had it that the weapon of choice was an electric carving knife. It had been a horrific attack. At the time, Saddam had locked him up in a private prison then sent him off into exile in Switzerland, but the Swiss had deported him because he was always getting into fights, and allegedly spent his time prowling the streets looking for women he could abduct and rape. Stories were already circulating that Uday was a very dangerous psychopath. One particular story about his behaviour after the national football team lost a game was repeated so often it became truth. The team were known as the Lions of Mesopotamia. They had a proud history, and had been very successful. His idea of motivational speaking was threatening all the players with prison if not death if they did not win games. Any player that missed a goal could expect to be tortured. If the whole team failed to please, their heads might be shaved, and they were very publically humiliated. When Uday was put in charge of the Iraqi Olympic Committee, he was responsible for disciplining the athletes who did not perform to his expectations. The Olympic athletes and footballers both endured the painful but invisible torture of having the soles of their feet beaten if they did not run fast enough to please Uday. As the Kingdom also had a football team, and had often played the Iraqis, there were many who were well aware of what was going on.

In December, the Prince spent nearly two weeks lobbying various committees at the United Nations about the ongoing occupation of Western

Sahara. Kofi Annan was being confirmed by the General Assembly as the new Secretary General. The Americans had threatened to veto Boutros Boutros-Ghali if he tried to stand for a second term. The Prince was sure that Kofi Annan would be more useful than Boutros-Ghali. Perez de Cuellar had tried and failed. King Hassan II of Morocco had been allowed to dictate terms for more than a decade. He had promised to talk to the Saharawi then declared there was no need to talk to them. There were promises which led to ceasefires then renewed aggression. The Moroccans were controlling the agenda. They had used napalm and cluster bombs on civilian targets. They had built a huge fortified wall in the desert, and driven the Saharawi across the border into Algeria. They were looting the country's resources, and playing with the United Nations like a maestro on a violin. The Saharawi just wanted a referendum. They wanted to be able to vote for their independence. They wanted what the UN had been promising them since 1981. The Prince was determined to make the UN finally deliver on its promises. He had known Kofi Annan for years. It was Kofi Annan, who had involved him with the refugee crises. There was the earthquake in Armenia in the winter of 1988, when more than ten thousand people had perished, while all around them there was a bitter war that hampered the aid efforts almost as badly as the freezing winter weather. In 1990, it was Kofi Annan, who had to negotiate the rescue of nine hundred UN employees trapped in Kuwait. The Prince had managed to open a few doors, but Morocco had trumped him by sending troops to support the Allies in the Gulf War. When Kofi Annan was the UN Assistant Secretary General for Peacekeeping from March 1993, the Prince was frequently involved in dangerous situations. He had his own bodyguards, and enough money and power to solve most problems, but it was always a wakeup call when he arrived in Eritrea, Djibouti or Nagorno Karabakh, and could not just write a cheque. They were happy to take his money, but they still did not want him asking uncomfortable questions. He was told repeatedly that the biggest killer amongst refugees was Diarrhoea, Dehydration, Malnutrition, and Measles. He had a running joke with Annan that the UN only wanted his money to buy toilets.

For the Pakistanis, it was just another fabulous holiday. As long as they had their creature fit to work, morning and evening, seven days a week, there were no other demands on them. They were all staying in Manhattan. They were having a ball.

In Afghanistan, the increasingly resilient Taliban finally succeeded in retaking the Bagram Airbase from the Northern Alliance, which solidified their control of the area around Kabul. They began to issue even stricter edicts, banning everything modern except guns. Even the kites, which were so traditional and harmless, were banned. The Northern Alliance was complaining to the Americans that moral support was not enough. With the Soviets gone, it was hard to interest the average American in the fate of 'blanket heads' far away in a primitive country that did not possess any valuable resources. Liberals were moved by the stories of veiled widows starving to death because they were not allowed to work to earn money to feed themselves and their children. Feminists were outraged to hear that no girls were allowed to go to school. The Neo-Cons and the Money only had eyes for Iraq. Bin Laden had returned to Afghanistan after Clinton and the Saudis had put pressure on the Sudan. Hardly anyone in America even knew about bin Laden. Even after the bombing of the World Trade Centre in February 1993, he was barely on anyone's radar outside of the intelligence services, which were already stretched.

Only the Pakistanis were interested in the murder of Murtaza Bhutto. Benazir's brother had been in trouble for years. He disagreed with his sister on just about everything. Many accused him of being a terrorist, which he had always denied. The fate of his father had profoundly affected him. He had never really recovered, and had sought vengeance against anyone who had wronged his father. He had been shot dead with six friends near his home in Karachi by the police. There was conflicting evidence. Benazir's husband was implicated. They had never got along. The 'royal' family of Pakistan was in turmoil. There were a dozen conspiracy theories. The police had lied. Everybody lied. Evidence was contaminated. Like the plane crash that had killed Zia, it was another mystery never to be solved.

A few days later, some innocent Palestinians were shot down in cold blood by an Israeli soldier because he knew that they hated Jews. The fact that it was other Israeli soldiers, who overwhelmed him, and made sure that the injured were taken to hospital, did not stop the Muslims feeling even more aggrieved and victimised. There was talk of jihad and the glory of martyrdom. There was no mention of stopping the Palestinian kids lobbing rockets across the border in to Israel. Peace was not on anyone's agenda. If a Believer died killing Jews then he went straight to heaven, and could take ten companions to paradise. At such moments, there was always much talk of paradise, and the allures of the dark-eyed virgins waiting there for righteous men.

Chapter 12

The frogs in Devon were not doing any better.

Curled up in the comfortable chair, she watched the television. She knew he was staring at her. He would be comparing her with other women. How dare he criticise her when she had rescued him from certain death? She took a deep breath and tried to be calm, but she felt wounded and vulnerable. The show's presenters were still feeling the cold. Kate's hair was all over the place, but she still looked lovely. It really wasn't fair. She thought about explaining to the young man that she was probably old enough to be Kate's mother. She could not help trying to imagine what he was thinking. Her assumption was that he was being judgemental, but he was not. His eyes were open, but he was barely conscious. He really was too ill to be interested in anything.

There was snow in Scotland. It had to be a recording. It was the end of May. Surely, it could not all be about climate change. The wind howling behind the narrative made her shiver. Beautiful white hares floated across the top of the snow. Ptarmigan croaked. It seemed odd that such a beautiful bird could make such an ugly noise. Then they were talking about Jackdaws dying because of the wet weather and the lateness of Leatherjackets. She had a Jackdaw nest in a chimney in previous years. It was sobering to hear that they had probably starved to death. Nature was unbelievably cruel. There was never a backup plan. Too many babies or not enough food guaranteed deaths. It was mentioned that the human race could learn that lesson. She knew that there were far too many people on the planet, and that it was a situation that needed to be addressed, but it was unusual to hear anyone say it so succinctly on television. It was a topic avoided by all the politicians. Perhaps they were frightened of the solutions, which were bleak. No one wanted to be associated with Eugenics and Hitler and the Holocaust. Who had the courage to say that men and women everywhere should limit the number of children they had to those they could afford to raise and educate?

The results from a survey proved what she already knew, which was that spring had been a disaster. Apparently, cool in May used to be normal, but more recently May was expected to be warm. This year was a one off. The frogspawn suffered nationally. On the 14th February the frogspawn had 'peaked' across the country then cold weather and frost had killed it all. In Devon, there were still some tadpoles, but twelve months ago, there would have already been hundreds of tiny frogs. So the British Isles were having all the same problems that she was having in her own garden. She sat smiling. It was not her fault. She was not responsible. She waited in expectation of being told what to do to help, but the programme shifted off to the Shetland Isles again, and otters. She did love otters, but she was realistic enough to know she could not ever hope to have otters anywhere near her garden. Pied Flycatchers, yes, but never otters. There were badgers about judging from the young ones she saw dead on the local roads. The badgers seemed to have the same road-sense as fox cubs and squirrels. Baby birds were fledging in Devon. She shifted forward in her chair. Devon was weeks ahead of her garden. What delights she had to look forward to! Then the programme ended. She rose to her feet wanting to go outside, but it was dark and cold.

The young man was asleep. She stared at him, frowning, then went out to hide in the kitchen. She fed the cats and collected the dry washing off the radiators, then folded it up and piled it neatly on the kitchen table. She made a pot of tea, and carried the tray back into the lounge. The young man had not moved. His hair was dishevelled. He needed a shave. He needed clothes. She crushed another three pills into a can of milkshake then settled on her knees beside him, and lifted his head into her lap. It was easy to waken him. His initial shock quickly disappeared when he saw the can being offered, but again she had to hold it to his lips. He drank it all. Afterwards, she lifted back the covers to look at his back. The worst of the wounds still leaked, and made the sheet stick. She peeled it off as carefully as she could. New skin was growing. She knew it would heal faster if she did not cover him, but she could not carry him up the stairs to a bed, she could not lift him onto the sofa. He was on the floor. It was cold. Keeping him warm was as necessary as making him drink. She tenderly spread more Vitamin E cream across his back. The new skin was red and delicate. She did not dare apply any pressure. Allowing a few minutes for it to be absorbed, she took the soiled sheet out to the kitchen, and returned with a freshly laundered one. He was going through her linen at an alarming rate. When she returned, he had moved onto his other side, which put his back to the room and the light. His mutilated skin looked awful. Every movement must have been agony for him.

She knelt down again to spread the sheet across him. "Who did this to you?" It hardly seemed enough. She was so angry, she needed to demand an answer, but she could not shout at him. "It must hurt. It must actually be very painful! It's so horrific." She tried to smile, but it was utterly pathetic.

"You must know who did this. You must know. We should call the police." She stopped. That would never happen. "I'm sorry. You're being so brave."

He flinched when she touched his shoulder.

She straightened the sheet then laid the blankets over him. His rejection hurt. She picked up the two cold hot water bottles, and retreated to the kitchen. At the window, she steadied her nerves. She needed to take some pills, but her self-destructive temper argued the necessity. Like a wilful child, she went to the back door, shoved her feet into some shoes, found the torch, and ran away into the garden.

It was as cold and dark as she knew it would be. She walked down the cobbled path to the door in the wall then passed out into the garden. Away from the shelter of the walls and the back of the house, it was even colder thanks to a piercing wind. She stopped to listen, and surveyed the sky. There were some stars visible through gaps in the shifting cloud. It felt like there was rain in the air. In the distance there was the urgent call of a fox, but the owls were quiet. Nothing else stirred. She crossed the lawn slowly, feeling the tug of the long, wet grass. She found the first pond, and peered anxiously into the water, looking for death. There was still a carpet of skeletal frogs. They did not stir as she bathed them in torchlight. Even the aggressive newts barely missed a step. She marvelled at them again, not even considering that to them the beam of a searchlight was utterly normal because she had subjected them to it every day of their lives. Minutes passed. She was not intentionally counting, but she peered at every creature that came into focus to make sure it was still alive. She repeated the process at the second pond. It was more than an hour later when she moved on across the lawn to find the pathway down through the trees.

She was so cold her bones ached, but she did not want to be in the house. She went down through the trees to the place where she had found him. Not even aware that she was looking for something, she went to stand by the ferns that had almost hidden him from her sight. She did not want to remember that finding him had been just a lucky accident. He might have lain there for days undiscovered. He would have died. Shivering, she experienced the horror of death again. He was not a slimy frog or a bloated hedgehog. Imagining his corpse, she shivered, and the torch slid from her grasp. She cursed her clumsiness and stupidity. The impact put out the light, but it came on again quickly enough. The torch did not travel far in the dense undergrowth. Still muttering curses, she reached into the shadows. Her muscles were still sore, but she forgot all her aches and pains as her fingers closed around something that was not a torch. Holding it up to her eyes, she was so startled, she very nearly threw it away.

It was a gun. It was not a big gun, but it was a gun. She was surprised by its weight. It was not until she had the torch in her other hand, and was examining the gun that the relevance of finding a gun where she had found the young man dawned on her. It had to be his gun or, at least, have some connection to him. The odds of the two things being at the same spot had to be in the millions to one. She did not really know anything about guns. She could hit a barn door with a shotgun, but that was her limit. She did manage to roll out the cylinder, and discovered that there was only one bullet. Almost instantly, she had made the assumption that it was a suicide attempt or Russian Roulette. That just gave her more questions. She was more confused than ever about his motives. Pushing the bullet deep into a pocket, she shoved the gun into her belt with the feigned confidence of John Dillinger's moll. Walking back to the house, she tried to understand what had or might have happened, but she became more upset and distressed, and then just despaired because she was not smart enough to decipher any of the clues.

It was past midnight when she reached the kitchen. All the lights were on. There were cats loitering everywhere. It had to be curiosity because it was absolutely impossible for any of them to be hungry. She waited only to take off her shoes then hurried through to the lounge to confront the young man with her groundless accusations and wild conjecture. She had the gun in her hand. All the courage she possessed was red hot in her veins.

"You have to tell me! I've waited long enough. You owe me an explanation." But he was asleep, barely conscious because of the pills, and when he tried to turn to look at her, he was so obviously unwell that she hid the gun behind her back, and smiled sheepishly. "Would you like a drink?" she asked.

If he shook his head it was imperceptible. He lay back on the floor, and quietly drifted off to sleep.

She stood over him for a moment then turned away. She circled the house, making sure all the windows and doors were secure, then went upstairs. While she ran a bath, she sat and counted out her pills. She did not want to be ill. It would be too dangerous for him. From her pocket, she retrieved the bullet. It was curiously fascinating yet did not really look extraordinary. She pushed it under her pillow then hid the gun on the top of her wardrobe.

That night, she slept soundly in her own bed. She was so tired, but she had taken enough painkillers and antidepressants to guarantee an undisturbed sleep. It was bliss.

*

The kafir was taken by surprise. They had only been back in Jeddah a few weeks. It was warm and sunny. He had succeeded in persuading himself that he was absolutely safe. He had worked hard to make sure his master was happy. His Pakistanis were established and in funds, and beyond the usual family complications, they were also very satisfied with their lives. There had been no indication that he was in any kind of trouble, but the same bodyguards came with the burqa, and he knew.

It was the same as before, the jeep, the road to the airport, the flight and then Gilgit. They actually had to sit and wait at Chitral for more than twenty-four hours for the weather to lift so that their plane could make it through the mountains. It was the same local guide, the same muddy roads. The mountains seemed taller than ever, and the snow deeper everywhere. The three men talked about their trip and the weather as they drove through the busy little town. The stalls in the market were as colourful. There were more signs in English, and more hotels, many of whom had signs saying: 'Backpackers Welcome.' The kafir had no idea what that meant.

They reached the end of the broken track and parked. After he was taken down from the jeep, the burqa was pulled away, and his hands untied. They gave him water and a chunk of gritty bread. He had to accept that he was going back to the madrassa again. It had been decided. During Ramadan, the Prince did not want him around. It was because of his blue eyes and infidel's soul. During the month of Ramadan, the Prince and the household contemplated God, and measured their lives against that of the Holy Prophet. All men had to model their lives on the Prophet's. He was the image of perfection. The kafir understood what was required. During Ramadan, a man might kiss his wife, but only chastely. There was to be no casual fucking, not even a harmless bit of sport thrashing around with an infidel. The kafir was abandoned again, and climbed into the mountains with a heavy heart.

The altitude sapped him immediately. It was freezing cold and muddy. The view was frequently obscured by sleet and snow. It was a barren wasteland of ridges, crevices and defiles with the mountains rising almost vertically, and crowding claustrophobically around them. He climbed, stopping regularly to catch his breath, and to wait for his thumping heart to slow down. The local guide seemed impervious. The bodyguard sweated like a grumpy pig.

The gates were open when they reached the madrassa. They went inside, the kafir dragging his feet as he thought about what he would have to endure. He was more hopeful than certain that it would be only for the month of Ramadan. Four weeks plus or minus a few days depending on the weather, he told himself he could survive that, but it would still be tough.

The courtyard was deserted, but a shout went up, and suddenly there were teachers in their traditional white robes and prayer caps, emerging from half a dozen doors. Then the faces of students pressed against windows.

The kafir grimaced, and leaned down on to his knees, feeling suddenly overwhelmed by exhaustion and the altitude and despair. As soon as the lights had stopped flashing in his head, he tried to straighten up, but the bodyguard took hold of the back of his neck, and compelled him to kneel. He dutifully went down and bent low, placing his palms on the ground in full view to signify his absolute submission.

The last to arrive, Achmed Qadri, asserted his authority over the younger, bearded teachers and clerics by walking calmly to the front, and placing himself between them and the new arrivals. Polite greetings were exchanged with the Prince's bodyguard. They were not friends, but they were not strangers.

"May the Blessings of the Prophet be upon you. You will eat with us before you leave," Qadri said to the two men, who had brought not only their patron's white servant, but also all the precious news of the outside world, which was of great interest to everyone. Gazing at the creature, he could not help frowning. The white ones were the most difficult. "You will go to Prof. Shah," he said quietly. "He has been ill."

The kafir lifted his head enough to speak, though his voice was still strained from exhaustion and disappointment: "Please? God is Great." He shuffled forward slowly like a cowering dog then formally bowed down, and kissed the man's dirty boots. "Yes my lord, by the Grace of God, the most Compassionate, the most Merciful." He kissed the boots again for good measure then surreptitiously drew his sleeve across his lips to remove the dirty, slushy snow. "God is Great."

Qadri turned away with distaste, and walked back to his office, but other teachers and clerics drifted menacingly closer, glowering at the creature that remained bent over its knees on the muddy ground. Jawad, the new Deputy Head, began talking loudly about Crusaders and Jihad.

"We must put an end to the sovereignty and supremacy of these disbelievers. The authority to rule must only be with those who follow the True Faith. We will not be humiliated. They have stolen our lands, and raped our women. One day, there will be an Islamic State for all those who follow the True Faith. This day will come. Didn't we destroy the evil empire of the Soviets? Isn't it written, that we must fight to the death those who do not believe in God or the Last Day, nor hold that forbidden which has been forbidden by God and His Messenger, nor acknowledge the religion of Truth."

The kafir felt the crowd circling around him. He stayed motionless. If he had even glanced in their direction, he was sure they would have beaten him to death.

Also sensing the danger, the bodyguard moved resolutely to stand beside the creature. He had a gun, but he did not really want to shoot Believers. He reached down, almost negligently, to tap the creature's back then held out his hand. The creature rose slowly, head bowed, shoulders rounded, turning towards him. It placed its wrist into the outstretched hand. It was brought to its feet, and stood submissively, staring at the ground. All the teachers and clerics took a step back, surprised by how much taller the creature had grown since they last saw it. For a moment, there was absolute silence. The creature waited dumbly for a command, trembling under the burden of its obedience. The bodyguard tightened his grip. He surveyed the hostile faces, recognising that Jawad was the ringleader. He stared at Jawad with menace until the man backed down, then he led the creature through the crowd to the pool of water in the centre of the courtyard. He broke the ice with a bucket, filled it, then put it at the creature's feet. He did not let go of its wrist. He still felt danger. The mere presence of the creature had upset everyone. While it stooped to dip a hand into the water, he turned to watch Jawad approaching.

"Its blood is immoral." Jawad was still enraged. "God's Curse be on it. It may not touch our water. It may not touch our food. It must be barred from the company of our students. And if it touches any book or page that contains verses of the Holy Book or the sayings of His Holiness the Prophet Mohammed, then both its hands should be taken by a sword. We must instil terror into the hearts of these infidels." He gazed at his audience, scowling at those who did not nod vigorously. "Once we have established one Islamic Caliphate for all the world then there will be no sanctuary for them or their wealth. The infidels will be slain, and their women taken into slavery. God has decreed it. This great day will come. Allahu Akbar. Allahu Akbar."

Then they were all saying it.

The kafir tried to be even smaller, crouching down on his heels like a monkey. He retreated slowly behind the bodyguard's boots, but there was nowhere for him to hide. The grip on his wrist was so tight that it restricted the blood flow to his hand.

Like millions of moderate Believers, the bodyguard was caught in a dilemma. If he protected the outcast creature then he was condemned as a traitor to Islam. Yet he had a duty to his master.

"Allahu Akbar. Allahu Akbar."

It was getting louder. The kafir could hear them approaching. The heat of their rage filled his nostrils. His heart was pounding. He was afraid. From behind the bodyguard, he risked one quick look around then lowered his gaze again, and braced for the attack that he was sure was coming.

Jawad was inching closer, weighing up the Arab's mood. "We must slaughter the Jews, infidels and crusaders. We will not be humiliated. We must kill all the kafirs. We must strike their heads off. God has decreed it."

"Allahu Akbar. Allahu Akbar."

The kafir closed his eyes, and braced himself. He was trying to rationally calculate whether they would actually kill him or if they were mad enough to just cripple him then throw him off the battlements. It was a familiar threat, but no less scary. Somewhere back in the past, it had apparently been a popular custom. And there were the wolves, and always the rumours about a leopard.

Then the chanting stopped.

The kafir breathed again slowly, not daring to hope. It became so quiet. He could not hear anything at all. His wrist was released. He retreated away from the old bucket and the forbidden water. He was reasonably confident that the bodyguard would not allow him to be killed, but a thrashing was definitely a possibility. Then something touched his back. He started in alarm then froze. He tried not to grimace as someone fumbled the back of his neck, seized the irksome collar that he was obliged to wear then pulled. Scrambling on to his feet, he quickly tried to ease the pressure on his neck, but stooped to stare at the ground so that no one would be offended by his height or his blue eyes. The collar tightened. He could not breathe. Then he was jerked backwards, and lost his balance. He fell awkwardly, the collar biting into his neck. Around him, he could hear voices muttering threats again. The bodyguard loomed. Feeling cornered, the kafir quickly gathered himself back on to his knees, and bowed down, his forehead and palms pressed into the freezing ground. The tension around him did not ease.

"Get up."

It was Prof. Shah.

But the kafir hesitated. His nerves were in shreds. He knew he was surrounded. Somehow, the irascible old man had risen from his sick bed, and the magnitude of his achievement overwhelmed them all. Gazing around at the feet of his enemies, the kafir tried to gauge their mood without having the privilege of being allowed to look them in the eye.

Slowly and carefully, he regained his feet then felt the Professor's sure hand on his arm. To appease everyone, he stooped then showed them his empty hands.

The Professor tightened his grip on the creature's arm to demonstrate ownership, and to conceal his frailty. He walked it slowly backwards away from the grumbling mob.

The kafir focused on placing his feet carefully, and keeping pace with the sick old man. He could hear the Professor's ragged breathing. The old man sounded as if he was at death's door. The kafir was genuinely concerned. The Professor was the nearest thing to a family that he had, but he dared not look at him.

Prof. Shah led the creature into his room then closed the door. There were no windows. The only source of light came from a lantern on the floor beside a badly made up bed. A young child sat in the small pool of light, reading the Holy Book. He looked up as the Professor returned then went docilely back to his studies.

"There's water." The Professor pointed weakly towards a bucket on the floor beyond the bed.

The kafir nodded and bowed then limped across the familiar classroom to squat down beside the bucket. He drank deeply then washed his face. There was a sliver of soap, which he used sparingly. Such luxuries were hard to come by. The Professor would not approve of him wasting it. When he turned around, he saw that the small child was helping the Professor to lay down in his bed. In the feeble light of the old lantern, he was amazed to see how the Professor had been ravaged by his illness. He moved to assist, daring to touch the old man, immediately slipping back into his role as carer.

Prof. Shah looked at him. "I knew you'd come back, Nazarene. I knew it."

The kafir smiled, but kept his head down. He was pleased to see the old man, and knew he should have been grateful to be allowed to return to the madrassa, but he would have been happier to stay at the house on the Red Sea or even in Riyadh. They had electricity and running water, and it was always warm. At the madrassa, it was always cold, and he was always desperately hungry.

"There's trouble brewing." The Professor surveyed him thoughtfully. "I hear things. The mountains are full of fanatics. They're even here." He was as irritable as ever. He did not like being fussed. "We have to be careful. They are determined to destroy us all. Are you listening to me? It's dangerous."

The kafir bowed. "Yes, good uncle, may peace be upon you. God is Great."

Prof. Shah grumbled and swore. He felt he was being ignored. "When you go back you must tell him. It's not safe here anymore."

"Yes, uncle. God is Great."

The Professor scowled. He would have cuffed the creature about the head if it had been near enough. "The boy will fetch fresh water and food. He'll make a fire. You don't go outside. I can't believe I saved your life, Nazarene. I must be a crazy old man now." He lay down, suddenly, laughing. It was good to hear him laugh. He looked sicker than anyone alive.

The kafir moved closer, and firmly placed a hand across the old man's forehead, then leaned down to stare into his eyes. "Please, master. You need a doctor. You need to go down the mountain. There are good hospitals. If you stay here you will die. We could make a litter…"

The Professor gazed into the blue eyes then smiled. "Who gave you permission to speak, vile blasphemer? And lower your gaze. You are a kafir; you know you may never look upon us. If only I wasn't sick. I'd take a whip to you myself. Three hundred lashes." He was still laughing, but very tired.

The kafir did not even blink. He stroked the old man's forehead, and frowned unhappily. "Please, good uncle. God is Great. You're running a temperature. You need a doctor."

"Don't think you are allowed to be impertinent just because I'm sick."

"Please, good uncle," the kafir insisted.

"Murderous crusader," the Professor said darkly. "Do not touch me."

The kafir drew away, and bowed reverently then sank to the floor exhausted. He knew how vindictive the old man could be. His feet were swelling up. His whole body ached, and it still felt like someone was repeatedly banging his head with a hammer, but worse than everything else was the despair. He had been sent back to the madrassa. He did not really know why, and had no right to ask. It was Ramadan. He had to believe that it was simply because it was Ramadan. They did not want him in the Kingdom during Ramadan. He shivered unhappily. He had been banished again.

At that moment, the door to the school room opened, and the sour-faced bodyguard walked in.

The kafir had completely forgotten about him, but dragged himself on to his knees, and bowed. Every movement hurt, and he was so very tired, but these were the rules he had to live by.

"You stupid bastard," the Professor shouted irritably when he saw the Arab. "The damn thing's your responsibility. How would you have explained such a loss to your master?"

Somewhat taken aback, the humourless bodyguard stared down at the sick old man, and wondered what all the fuss was about. He was just an old man. He did not look like a great holy man.

The kafir sensed what was running through the bodyguard's mind. He rose with difficulty, and limped on his swollen feet to stand in front of him, then sank slowly down on to his knees, then bowed until his forehead rested on the cold floor. For good measure, he reached out tentatively to touch the great big boots, and begged solemnly for forgiveness.

It worked. The Arab reached down to seize the collar then dragged him outside. He was hauled across the courtyard, bent double, unable to breathe, terrified of passing out. It seemed the place was deserted, but the kafir was blinded by tears, and had no idea what peril he faced. When he lost his footing and fell down, the Arab lifted him by the collar, and dropped him back on his feet as if he weighed nothing at all. He struggled on, choking and coughing, almost hysterical with exhaustion. They mounted some steps and crossed a threshold. He was flung to the ground.

"You are here because His Highness, Prince Abdul Aziz, has insisted."

The kafir blinked and tried to focus. There were bells ringing in his head now as well as the hammering. Barely conscious, he quickly bowed to perform his regulation act of submission. Before he had even pressed his forehead to the floor, Qadri was speaking again.

"I have two choices. I can lock you up, and feed you, and keep you safe or you can be out there, and take their abuse."

The kafir focused on the floor. He was in the Head Teacher's room with the man glowering down at him. The bodyguard stood to his right. A little overwhelmed, the kafir made a conscious effort to be smaller, convinced he was about to be punished just for being alive.

"You have no honour so there is no oath you can give me that I could trust."

The kafir crumpled lower then stretched out his arms to touch Qadri's boots with his fingertips. "Please? Arjuu-ka. My lord, Sheikh, by the Grace of God, the All Knowing. Please?"

"Be quiet!"

The kafir trembled.

"You must not be killed, do you understand?"

"Please, yes my lord, sir. God is Great. Allahu Akbar." But he did not understand.

"Allahu Akbar." Qadri sighed bitterly. He did not feel it was appropriate to offer further salutations to a blue-eyed infidel. "The students have been told to shun you. You will avoid them. No matter what happens, no matter what the circumstances, if there is any trouble at all then you will be blamed. Radical young men are spreading their own puritanical version of the True Faith, and they intend to convert or kill everyone in their path, even their own brothers. They are even here in this school. Hatred is a sickness. It is contagious. These men here will seek your destruction. They believe they are fighting a holy war. Jihad! Do you understand? You will be humiliated and degraded. You will take their abuse. Whatever it takes. You will submit. It is written. Do you understand? You must prove to them that there would be no glory in killing such a wretched and miserable thing. There is no shame for you. Your master did not send you here to be murdered so you will make sure that you give them no cause to kill you. Stay close to Prof. Shah. He is a holy man. You'll be safe if you stay with him. If you make any attempt to leave his room, you will be shackled there like the outcast dog that you are. You will not give them cause to kill you, do you understand?"

"Please, yes my lord. God is Great."

"Fortunately, this is now Ramadan. Even these fanatics must respect that. Jawad is a bully, but he isn't stupid. If you stay out of his way, you should come to no harm. Take care of Prof. Shah. He is very frail. He has the boy, but he is young and dyslexic. That means he cannot read very well. You may help him. There might be some redemption for you. It can do no harm. Some of the other students believe he is possessed, but they are country people and superstitious. If we send him away, he will starve. Above all, you must obey Prof. Shah, as you would your own gracious master, His Royal Highness, the Prince."

"Yes, my lord." The kafir moved slowly to kiss Qadri's boots then settled bent over his knees with his arms outstretched so that Qadri could step on his hands if he chose to. "Please, yes. By the Grace of God, the most Compassionate, the most Merciful, I am honoured to be his servant. May peace be upon him. May the Blessings of the Holy Prophet protect him. God willing, he will live forever. God is Great, my lord. God is Great."

Qadri studied him for a moment then murmured softly: "I have told him that you are the bravest boy here. It takes more courage to forgive than to fight. We can all kill our enemies. How much harder is it to live with them? You think he hates you, but he hates himself. His family were murdered. He took a terrible revenge. When he was a younger man, he found it easier to blame the British. The British divided India and Pakistan, but he knew, as everyone of his generation knows, that it was India that demanded independence, and Pakistan that demanded partition. History has been rewritten. His family were massacred by Hindus. His revenge – I cannot tell you what he did – but it was Indians and Pakistanis murdering each other, not the British, not your people."

"My people?" the kafir asked in absolute bewilderment.

"It was not your people, your tribe. You are truly a vile blasphemer, but you are not responsible for the past. Prof. Shah looks at you and feels shame, and he's too proud to know it. He's an old man. You must be patient with him."

"Please? My lord, before God I swear, I am his servant," the kafir declared, but continued staring at the floor, and did not lift his head.

Qadri gazed down at the creature, penitent on its knees then sighed again. "I know you are a cunning devil. You must trust me. And remember what I have said."

"Please? My lord, by the Grace of God, how may I defend myself?" he asked quietly, not daring to move a muscle.

Qadri stood over him. "If you retaliate you will be killed, this is written. You cannot raise a hand against them. Do what you must to stay alive. Do you understand?"

The kafir shivered. He was really too exhausted to comprehend the immensity of the danger.

Qadri leaned down and whispered: "You will hide like a Jew, and if you are discovered, you will grovel and weep and beg for mercy. You have no honour so there can be no shame for you. You will bow down before them, and beg for mercy, and they will pardon you because God is Merciful."

"God is Merciful," the kafir whispered, then his collar was seized, and he was yanked violently back on to his feet though not permitted to stand upright.

"You!" Qadri wearily turned his attention to the bodyguard. "That guide you brought here. He is a smuggler, a womaniser and a lover of boys. He must be gone in the morning."

Over the following weeks, the dyslexic child brought them food and water at dusk. A month of fasting was particularly arduous in the winter. Prof. Shah would not hear of any special consideration due to his health. He tried to teach for four hours a day when he was strong enough, but that was increasingly rare. Most of the time, he lay on his bed. Sometimes, when he was frustrated with being ill, he would demand the kafir give up his blanket or he would throw things at him to drive him from his room, but the kafir always managed to sneak back in, and shiver in the shadows until the mood passed. The Professor never knew that when he was delirious and trembling violently, it was the kafir, who held him in his arms, and tried to warm him. And it was the kafir, who sent messages to Qadri asking for better food, more fuel to burn, and lots of hot tea and medicine.

Chapter 13

The television had been on all night, but it was not loud. The young man was sort of asleep, facing the television, but with his eyes closed. She went to switch it off only to hear that someone had tried to kidnap David Beckham. That arrested her attention immediately. England's favourite player kidnapped! But it was a joke. She frowned. Who would think that was funny? The newsreader explained with a smile that Rio Ferdinand had arranged an attempted kidnapping, and it had been so realistic that Beckham had escaped by leaping out of the moving car. She shook her head. He could have been killed. He was lucky not to have been injured.

She turned away to open the curtains and stare out at the sky. Low cloud made the yellow rape fields look dull. Normally, they were dazzlingly bright. Once upon a time, it had been a rare crop, but now the yellow fields were everywhere. She guessed that farmers probably had some European subsidy for growing the stuff.

The young man did not move until she disturbed him by reaching down to feel for a pulse in his neck. He awoke with a start, quickly took in his surroundings, and again declined to look at her. She felt it was a rejection, but it seemed cruel to criticise him after all that he had endured, not least, the trip in the wheelbarrow, and being dragged across the gravel.

"How are you feeling?" she asked, and paused to let him answer.

He tried to move, but it was beyond him. His face lost what colour it had. Beads of sweat prickled his forehead. Slowly, he lowered his head to the floor, and firmly closed his eyes. She could hear him breathing. He was still in a lot of pain.

She felt a heartless bitch for expecting so much from him. "I'll bring you a drink, and something to eat. You should be able to digest something now. A banana, maybe? You must try."

The eyes flashed, but he did not attempt to look at her.

Dithering, she suffered the guilt of the damned then her maternal instinct stirred again. She stooped to lift the blankets away, and collect the hot water bottles. The exposed linen sheet had fewer bloodstains. She almost lifted it up, then lost her nerve, and hurried out to the kitchen to find

122

herself immediately surrounded by cats. They were starving. She was cruel. It was the usual story. She fed them because that was her job, then put the kettle on, and moved to look out of the window. There were Robins and Finches in the fruit trees, and two Blackbirds on the path. Perhaps, it would be a nice day. She could just about see the sun above the trees, but it still looked like a winter sun. She realised it was June. That meant the Derby on Saturday and Gorgeous George, if he was still running. Her heart fluttered a little. She would enjoy that. The Guineas had been so exciting. She was still smiling when she sat at the kitchen table with a cup of tea, and counted through her pills. Three more were crushed. She collected the dust, and mixed it with a little milk then let it stand while she swallowed the cocktail of drugs that she needed to take to stay in control. She was still sore all over, but it was not crippling. She could walk back into the lounge, and kneel down, and hold the milk to his lips with barely a grimace. He drank politely. She suspected he was disappointed that it was not the strawberry milkshake, but that cost money, and money was scarce.

"I'm sorry," she said, imagining that he had spoken. "I really have to go shopping. Is there anything else that you'd like? I'll try and find you something to wear."

His head rolled in her lap. He looked awful, but the fever had passed. There was an odour. She lifted the sheet a little, and glanced underneath. He had wet himself. She pulled a face. At least, it proved he was taking enough liquids. It took only a few minutes to soak him with clean water then pat him dry. She had to be a little more considerate when she rolled him this way and that to remove the layer of soiled towels under him, then to replace them with warm clean ones off the radiator. He remained conscious, but did not lift a hand or make a sound. She could almost feel his pain, and hurried away, wiping her eyes, to fill the washing machine. Recovering her nerve, she returned, and with a great deal of care, she managed to peel the sheet off his back then bent over the immense wound, and gently spread a coating of Vitamin E cream across his back. He still shuddered and groaned. There would always be scars. If he was lucky, it would be one immense blurred disfigurement rather than a hundred deep welts that would forever advertise what had happened to him, and declare him a victim.

She diligently made a shopping list. He needed so much, and she could not afford it, but she had taken on the responsibility. He was a guest. Etiquette demanded that she provided clothes and medicine. But for every two things she wrote down then one had to be deleted. She planned her route; first the doctor, then the pharmacist, then the supermarket. The latter had basic clothes, not that she had ever explored the range. They would stock shirts and underpants. She needed him in underpants. As soon as he was strong enough, he would be on his feet, and able to prowl around her house. It was alarming to contemplate. He certainly had to have some clothes.

She went to say goodbye, but he was asleep again, which was a relief. As she went out to the garage, she was surprised by the sunshine. It was also significantly warmer than it had been first thing, but she did not dare to hope that it was a sign of things to come.

She did not go straight to the doctors' but instead went to the nearest cash-point. Her heart was in her mouth as she waited to find out the balance on her account. It was such a surprise, she put in two requests then worried that not only had they made a mistake, but would swallow her card so she drew out cash, and hurried away.

The doctors' receptionist was the usual obstructive wall. She wondered if they went on training courses to learn how to be so unhelpful. No, she could not see the doctor. No, they could not tell her which day her doctor did emergency appointments. No, there were no appointments available with any of the doctors for two weeks. No, she could not book an appointment two weeks in advance. Could she phone and make an appointment in a week? She offered her most menacing smile, and asked them to ask her doctor if he could see her or write a prescription. No, that was impossible. She smiled again, and suggested that as it was very nearly ten o'clock that someone would be taking various cups of coffee into the various doctors so it was perfect timing to put a note in front of him or pass on a message. Still nothing. She leaned over the counter. "I'm mentally ill. My doctor has told me that I can see him whenever I need to see him, but I hate coming here. He would be very upset to know that I had come all the way here because I needed to see him, and you had turned me away, and not told him." A darling little old lady appeared behind the receptionist with a tray of cups and saucers. "Perfect timing," she said, and smiled again. The receptionist rose huffily to her feet, collected a cup of coffee, and walked quickly away. She went to the doctor's door, and knocked then took in the cup. Barely minutes later, the doctor himself came to the door, and smiled genially, mouthing the question, "Everything okay?"

Five minutes later, she had the repeat prescription, and was on her way.

It was nearly lunchtime when she returned home. The hedgerows were full of cow parsley. The potholes in the driveway were as deep as ever. The sheer neglect visible in the garden lessened as she neared the house. She did not like working down near the road. She did not like being watched. Not that anyone came along the road. That was one of the most attractive features of the house.

In the hall, she stood gazing suspiciously down at him. The change of scenery had fuelled her paranoia. It had allowed her to distance herself from him again, to be dismissive about his wounds, and to remember that he was potentially dangerous. The sound of the front door and the trillion plastic bags had awoken him.

"Are you alright?" she asked, trying to pitch her voice somewhere between a whisper and a polite inquiry.

He sighed heavily. That was the drugs. His heart was thumping sluggishly, and it hurt him. He knew she was standing there, but he could not turn his head to look at her. What did she look like? What was her name? Who was she? He wanted to look at her, and try to remember her face, but the pain and stiffness across his back kept him still.

She edged cautiously into the room. Her fears and prejudices were hard to overturn. It was not in her character to take any unnecessary risks, and he was a young man, possibly a very weird and deviant young man. Someone had beaten the crap out of him. Perhaps, they had cause. It was much easier to believe he was trying to deceive her. As she moved in front of him, he groaned again and stared anxiously, but always avoiding her face. He had the most dazzlingly blue eyes, and he was frightened. She drew back. He was so very frightened. She did not know what to say. They were both frightened. She covered her eyes and turned away, wondering again at her motives.

He just lay there, not understanding anything. Then she turned again and smiled at him. It was such a smile as he had never seen before, and he began to hope that she might explain.

But she hurried out to the kitchen to boil the kettle, and stared out of the window. Without thinking, she reached for the bottle of painkillers, and began to crush another three pills to dust. He needed no encouragement to swallow another strawberry milkshake, but she had to lift his head and hold the can to his lips, and he soon tired. He looked like an old man, wrinkled and sallow-skinned with rheumy eyes. She hardly recognised the beautiful youth that had slept amongst the ferns and mosses like a nymph in faerie land. He had lost weight and deteriorated so quickly. Her only hope was that while he stayed conscious, she could ply him with drinks and drugs, and then he would slowly mend.

"You'll be alright," she lied, stroking his white face. "Can you drink some more? You've been ill. You need to drink. Please, will you try again?"

He drank. It did not require a conscious effort. He knew he was ill. He wanted to believe her, but he no longer cared about truth or lies. At that moment, he simply wanted to live.

"That's better," she said, looking at him, but really talking to herself. "You'll feel better now. In a few days, you'll be back to normal. We'll get some food down you, build up your strength. And I've bought you some clothes. I know you're not well enough to think about that yet. You should just rest. I'll look after you. Can you drink some more? You must drink."

He could hear her voice and the soft lilting tone, but he had no idea what she was saying. Like an automaton, he drank everything that she offered him.

She wiped his ashen face again, hoping that she could expose the beautiful young man beneath the ravaged visage. He was not there. It would take more than a cloth and a bowl of water to find him again. "You should go back to sleep." She stroked his face as if he were one of her cats. "There there. You'll feel better soon." The eyes closed. He was drifting away. "It's alright," she said, letting him settle back on his side. "Could you – do you think you could get on to the sofa? I can't lift you. I'm sorry, but I have tried. I didn't mean you to stay on the floor."

He could not think, could not comprehend what she was saying, and was so mentally pulverised that he did not know why he was so ill, and in such terrible pain. He simply endured. There was nothing else he could do. It was almost more than he could do.

She was very pleased that he was able to drink so much. He must have had nearly a pint. That had to be good, but her optimism was erased by his dreadful pallor. She could see that he was completely out of it, which might have been the drugs. He did not even know that she was there. She stroked his face, and felt so sorry for him. In that moment, he reminded her of her failures, of the futile visits at all hours of the night to veterinarians, and the lonely drive home with a dead animal on the seat beside her. She had seen too much death. It had become a sixth sense. She could tell when something was going to die.

*

In the middle of the night, when he was too cold and hungry to sleep, the kafir remembered his happiness with the royal prince, and the comfort and companionship of his Pakistanis. He had always felt safe. He had always tried to please everyone. He had absolutely no idea what he had done to deserve being sent back to the madrassa. It had to be Ramadan.

Late in the second week, the Head Teacher came to visit Professor

Shah. A note carried by the dyslexic child, written in a beautiful Arabic script by the kafir, had brought him through a snow storm to the side of the old holy man. It was bitterly cold outside, and not much warmer in the Professor's bleak room. The kafir had built a fire, and had the Professor wrapped up in all the blankets, but he looked terrible. With barely a condescending acknowledgment to the kafir and the child, Qadri focused immediately on the Professor, recognising he was very seriously ill. He spoke to him as he would to an old friend, making gentle jokes about his shameless malingering and hearty health. Later, while the Professor slept, Qadri stooped over him, but talked to the kafir in English.

"You must be careful. Jawad is watching your every move. He has some of the older students spying on you. They tell him that you leave this room late at night, after your curfew and alone, which you know is forbidden. He plans to capture you. It will be the excuse he needs. You will have your throat cut, and be thrown off the battlements for the wolves to feed on."

The kafir bowed down as the law demanded. "Please? Please, my lord by the Grace of God, the most Compassionate, the most Merciful. I must go out to collect firewood for my good uncle."

"Must?" Qadri demanded harshly. "Must we shackle you like a dog?"

The kafir wearily rested his forehead on the ground. The cold earth smelt foul. "Please no, sir, my lord by the Grace of God. Thank you. Glory be to God and His Messenger and all Believers."

"You will not go out!" Qadri warned irritably.

The kafir rose slightly so that he could be seen to bow again. "Yes sir, my lord." He bowed again. "I am your servant. God is All Knowing. God is Great."

"But you will still ignore the curfew?"

The kafir sighed. He could not tell if Qadri was really angry or just making idle threats. He rose from his reverential bow just enough to be able to study the man's worn old boots. "Please, my lord. Please forgive me, my lord. I must keep a fire to warm my good uncle. I may not command the child. I may ask for nothing. It is forbidden."

"Yet you write to command me."

The kafir sighed again. He was trapped. "Please? For my good uncle? God is Great."

Qadri clasped the Professor's cold hands, and rubbed them gently.

"Please? My lord, please, you must allow me to leave this room. Please,

I beg you. Please? For my good uncle?"

"No." Qadri was adamant. "There is no excuse good enough to permit you to ignore the words of the Beloved Prophet, Peace be upon Him. They are the Commands of God. What you ask is absolutely forbidden. It is written. It is the Will of God. Prof. Shah would never allow you to use his health as an excuse to flout the law." He gazed witheringly at the creature. "You forget what you are."

The kafir bowed, and placed his hands flat on the cold floor near Qadri's feet. "Please? I beg you to help us. There isn't enough food. My good uncle is not strong. Please, my lord by the Grace of God, the most Merciful."

"It is forbidden. You will stay in this room or I will hand you to Jawad myself." He paused to study the Professor's ashen face. "But I will send food at sunset, and make sure that there is enough fuel to keep a fire."

The kafir slunk forward like a stalking leopard, staying low to the ground, conscious of the need to be below Qadri's eye-line, and he kissed his boots, then he took hold of the hem of his coat and kissed that too. "My lord, I thank you. May God the Almighty and the Holy Apostle bless you and your family. Prof. Shah will thank you. God is Great."

Qadri relented: "You're a good boy, but you must obey. This isn't about punishing you. It is about God's Will. You must obey. We all must obey. The Holy Prophet was not given these commands for us to pick and choose what we will obey. It is written. If you obey and serve the Believers with a good heart then when the Last Day comes, God will know all that you have done, and judge you accordingly. There is honour, even for such as you, in being a good servant."

The kafir moved to kiss the hem of his coat again. "Thank you, my lord by the Grace of God, the most Compassionate, the most Merciful. I am here to serve. I am the humble servant of all Believers. God is Great."

Qadri rose to his feet, and walked to the door. He took hold of the door handle then turned to look back at the creature, which quickly lowered its gaze. "It's snowing. In the morning, in the daylight while the students are at their lessons, and Jawad will be otherwise engaged, you may go outside, and spend a few hours clearing away the snow. Then the Professor can walk about without leaving footprints." He waited for an acknowledgement.

The kafir looked quickly at his expression then lowered his eyes again, and bowed. "Please? I thank you. God is Great."

"But you will have no reason to break your curfew. I will make sure that there is plenty of food. You will not go out, do you hear me?" He smiled as the creature nodded and bowed. It did not matter what it did or the oaths that it swore, it was a kafir so it was incapable of being honest, and had no understanding of a man's honour. "Nothing will excuse you breaking the law, but if you are caught, you had better be coming to my door with grave news."

The kafir bowed again then settled back to sit on his heels. He did not look at Qadri. He had been lucky to do it once, but twice would have been considered too offensive to pardon. "Please, I will clear the snow. I will take care of him. He will thank you. God is Great, my lord. God is All Knowing and Merciful."

Qadri left. A gust of wind filled the room with snowflakes. It was so very cold.

The next morning, Qadri watched from a window as the creature hurried to clear a wide tract of ground. It ran directly from his own door to the Professor's. He wondered if the creature was being sarcastic. Disbelievers were known for their strange and perverse sense of humour. He watched it working. It was barefoot which was correct, but it was inappropriately dressed for the weather. When it had almost finished, Jawad appeared from his classroom so Qadri went out to intercept him, allowing the creature to retreat back safely into Prof. Shah's room.

Jawad never caught the creature prowling around at night, but Qadri was almost certain that it did venture out. Often, he found notes pushed under his door. It was too cleverly done to be the child. He provided the supplies as promised, and made sure he found the time to visit his old friend. He could not condone the creature's behaviour. Nothing excused disobedience, but he never felt the need to speak to it again.

A few days after the school had celebrated Eid, which marked the end of fasting, on an unexpectedly sunny day, a group of men in western-dress arrived in the courtyard. They stuck out like sore thumbs, wearing jeans and quilted jackets, baseball caps, dark glasses and first-class hiking boots. The kafir glimpsed them from the shadows of the Professor's doorway, but had the door closed in his face so he was left alone in the darkness to contemplate his fate. He knew it was the right time to leave, however, his self-esteem did not allow him to believe that so many men had come simply to collect him. A thousand fears made him shiver in ignorance.

Qadri brought the strangers over to the Professor's room nearly an hour later, after they had the usual cups of tea and swapping of news. The Professor was too ill to move. The child was sent away. The creature was ordered to its knees. It complied obediently. They held it down anyway while one of them prepared an injection. It cowered before the needle, convinced it was about to be murdered, but there was nothing it could do. A cold chill spread throughout its body, and then it lost consciousness.

When the kafir awoke, he was laying on the floor. The room was known to him. The people sleeping with him were known to him. The arm draped across his chest was known to him. The shock became surprise and then relief. He was at home. A strange sense of well-being smothered him. The confining belt held him again, but he strained against it, enjoying the burning sensation it produced in his cramped muscles. Then the arm tightened across his chest, and a voice whispered: "Sleep. Sleep now."

All that day, they bathed him in waters scented with jasmine oil. His hair was encased in expensive creams, and his skin was scrubbed and exfoliated, then they removed every trace of body hair. Restoring his hands and feet took hours, but concluded with one of them carefully painting his nails in a gorgeous shade of shimmering pink. As far as the Pakistanis were concerned, it was simply unthinkable that he should ever look masculine.

And they talked gaily amongst themselves while they worked. One of Waheed's sons had followed tradition and married a cousin. She was very beautiful, but Waheed's wife thought she was too interested in continuing her education and having a career. So many young women were going to college, but it was a waste of time because no one would employ them. There were too many unemployed young men for anyone to bother employing a stupid, selfish girl. Waheed's wife said it was alright for her to read and write, but anything after that was willful extravagance. For Mahmood, life was simpler. He had no wife. His mother looked after his home in Hail. He had no cousins to marry, and when he was younger had few friends with sisters, so there had been no opportunity for him to see a girl let alone marry one. Mahmood listened to Waheed's tangled web of relations, and often felt sorry for him, but he longed for the companionship of a family. His mother was almost completely blind with cataracts, and since his father's death was totally reliant on a child that Mahmood had found orphaned in the streets of a northern Iraqi town. He was paying to have the little boy educated, and intended to raise him as his son. Compared to Waheed's complicated family life, Mahmood had few headaches, and he did still have hopes.

Chapter 14

To build up his strength, she woke him every hour with either a glass of water or a milky drink fortified with all the minerals and vitamins he could possibly need. He drank without the slightest protest. It was to become a routine. She plied him with yoghurts and baby food. He could not sit up. He could not feed himself. She had to believe that anything that did not need chewing would be easily digested, but would still give his stomach some protection against the strong painkillers she was forcing him to take.

He was still so weak he could barely lift his head. He could not even brush away the cats, and they all took this lack of rejection as positive encouragement. There were always at least two of them near him, one usually behind his knees, and another on the sofa above him.

Less frequently, she had carefully lifted back the linen sheet to examine his back. She cleaned his wounds, and covered them with cream, and tried not to be obsessive. She was only nursing him. She was doing the right thing. Eradicating the infection had brought down his fever marvellously. Making him drink replenished his fluid levels, and washed the toxins out of his system. Letting him sleep, encouraging it with painkillers, allowed his back to heal undisturbed. She worked diligently. She was out there in Oscar territory. It was a performance worthy of Meryl Streep. He was too ill to notice that her hands were shaking every time she touched him. He did not see the hunger in her eyes. His raw back demanded her respect, but the rest of him was a banquet of curiosities. It was not the sheath and the jewels that captivated her, though that did give her pause. It was the rich tapestry etched into his flesh that she returned to again and again. It was extraordinary and so intricate. Imagining the pain of its application left her breathless. Yet, it was so soft and so lovely. She simply had to touch it and admire it. She resisted in vain. Her curiosity was insatiable, and her guilt made her cunning so it was easy to justify giving him more and more pills.

They watched the television together. She watched the tennis from Paris whenever she could find it. The news headlines were still dominated by a metatarsal, and some comedian was going to swim the Channel for Sports Relief. She turned to smile at the young man: "I always wanted to do that. It takes about fourteen hours. It's only twenty-one miles, but it's the temperature and the jellyfish that put me off." He stared at the floor while she spoke then gazed back at the television. The presenter on the television continued the story, explaining that less than 10% of the people attempting it actually reached France. Later, there was another World Cup story showing Peter Crouch, who was 6ft 7ins tall, doing a peculiar dance for Prince William. It was funny. She had to accept that she did not need to like football to laugh at that. She turned again to look at the young man, wanting to engage his attention, wanting to make a connection, but he stared at the floor. The only story that elicited a response from him was the American President George W. Bush making a statement to the effect that US Troops would have 'ethics training' as a result of what had happened in Haditha in November. The President had vowed that everyone involved in the shameful rampage through Haditha would be punished. She could not have sworn to it, but she was sure that the young man had sneered.

She completely lost interest in him when the scenery shifted again to Devon and the Shetland Isles. The promiscuous male Pied Flycatcher had abandoned the female. There had been six eggs, but a Wood Mouse had predated two, and one had simply not hatched so the three surviving chicks had only the female to provide food. It was a potential disaster, another single mother and absentee dad. The cameramen down in Devon had located the male in another nest so there was much talk about his disreputable behaviour. They were sure it was the same bird. He had quite distinguishable juvenile feathers. So another camera was hurriedly set up in the new nest box, and it became very obvious that this new brood were actually older than the three in the other nest. So it was quickly decided that the male Pied Flycatcher had a wife and a family, but had gone off and got his new mistress pregnant, then abandoned her and the kids to return to his wife. He was seen to be providing food for his original family, but had left nothing for his mistress's kids.

She grinned for an hour, enjoying the pictures of Jackdaws in a sunny field of celandines; otters in the Shetland Isles catching swimming crabs in driving rain, Red Kites in Rockingham, and the amazing endurance of the Brent geese. The latter were on their annual migration from Ireland across the North Sea to Iceland, then across the vast ice field on Greenland to the east coast of Canada where they would spend the summer. Some of the geese had been caught then had trackers fitted to them. One, Floyd, had already disappeared. Most of the others were somewhere between Iceland and Greenland. The Oyster Catchers were having entirely different problems. The spring lambs were gambolling through the long grass right next to the nest. Whenever they came too close, the Oyster Catchers tried to stab them between the eyes with their long red beaks. It looked not only painful but dangerous, but it did not seem to bother the lambs at all. Bill went to London Zoo in search of Cockney Sparrows, which had once been prolific in the city, but were now quite rare. In the zoo, the remaining few had found the habitat they required, and lots of free food. There was dung and straw and the equivalent of hedgerows. They were doing very well in the zoo. But even in Devon, they were scare. Kate went swimming with the second biggest fish on the planet, a Basking Shark, in the waters off Mull. She was either very small or the shark was unbelievably big. Fortunately, it only ate plankton as it liked shallow water, and could have scooped up and swallowed a dozen children with ease.

After an hour of sunshine in Devon, she felt restored, and took a torch outside to have a wander around her outbuildings. It was quite noisy in the twilight until she approached, but that might have been more to do with the cats that trailed behind her. A few bats soared through the beam of the torch, but all the other nesting birds were evidently shy or sensibly on their nests. She could see what looked like the nest sites from the previous year, but she knew the Swallows often came back to exactly the same nest. They had not arrived yet, but she was happier to know that they were still coming.

It had certainly been a better day. She walked across the lawn to the ponds, and stood for more than an hour watching the frogs and newts. There were blooms of algae, but she was too tired to take it on. In the morning, she would come back. In the morning, the sun would shine, and it would be a lovely day. Her confidence was wafer thin. Even if it was pouring with rain, she would come back, and bail out the green stuff, and she would keep doing it until the water was crystal clear again. Her worst fear was that her constant meddling was causing the problem. But she could not stop herself. She was obsessive and compulsive and utterly driven. She knew what she was capable of, and knew that she should never have taken the beautiful young man into her home. Many years ago, she had received counselling. In an early group session, she had been asked to suggest a fictional character that she felt best described herself. It was supposed to be all friendly and elementary, so the suggested characters came from children's stories. She immediately thought about the giant spider in Lord of the Rings, but smiled sweetly and said, Rabbit, because everyone knew that Rabbit was OCD.

*

During 1997, they travelled together, the Prince, his servant and his servant's servants with an entourage of at least thirty. The Prince had diplomatic credentials so no one checked if the tall figure beneath the black burqa was really a woman. Nor did they search the men in suits and dark glasses, who were invariably armed. There were earthquakes, floods, and wars. They spent weeks in New York because of endless talks at the UN about Iraq. The British gave Hong Kong back to the Chinese. Che Guevara's body was given back to the Cubans. The Prince took over houses in Germany, villas in France and palaces in Italy. Money was no object. Prince Abdul Aziz was one of the richest men in the world, but he still expected to receive some form of tribute from his hosts. It was something in the culture of the desert. It was about the generous hospitality of a host to his guests. To the Europeans it was a bribe, but to the Arabs it was just good manners and patronage.

Yasser Arafat had returned to Hebron on the West Bank for the first time in thirty years so the talk amongst the servants was about the imminent creation of a Palestinian State, the end of Israel, the death of Jews, and the return, at last, of the Palestinian families to their homes. When two helicopters collided carrying Jews to the Lebanon, there was rejoicing.

The kafir had stood in the cool darkness on the flat roof of the desert palace with his master searching the sky for a comet. The wonder of it was lost on him. He had no concept of time or understanding of the cosmos. He simply could not grasp that he was experiencing a moment of history because no one had told him what it was that blazed slowly across the star-filled sky. News of a fire in Mecca was received with tears and heartbreak as three hundred and forty-three pilgrims were killed and countless more hurt on the plain of Mena as a fire swept through their camp. The massacres in Algeria had become so commonplace that they hardly made the news anymore, even when the majority of the victims were children.

That year, the Prince's diary kept them abroad more than they were at home. The kafir withered under the strain. He never saw anything of the outside world except through the black gauze-covered letterbox in the burqa. He wore so many layers of clothes that Waheed said he looked fatter than his father's best cow, but it was all to confuse the curious. His mouth was covered in sticky tape. His hands were anchored at his sides. At airports or security checks, no one came near him because they were afraid of doing something politically incorrect to an obviously devout and respectable Muslim woman. So it was perfectly easy to take him anywhere in the world with no questions asked. Even when he collapsed on a pavement in Paris, no one stepped forward. He was carried into their hotel by one of the bodyguards, and disappeared again.

In May, there was another immense earthquake in north eastern Iran with thousands dead or missing. The Prince and his creature were in New York, attending meetings at the Security Council where Saddam Hussein's disarmament was still the main focus of world attention simply because it was on America's agenda.

The continuing massacres in Algeria, though horrifying in their intensity, received significantly less attention. The kafir learned from reading upside down, and blatantly eavesdropping, that the fundamentalists in Algeria had been in bin Laden's army in Afghanistan, and that they wanted to restore Algeria to the True Faith, which banned everything modern and Western, and restored the Sharia. To them, being involved with politics was a denial of the Holy Book, and that meant that all the politicians and every single voter had to be killed. Anything and anyone that criticised or undermined the teachings of the Blessed Prophet, which were the actual Words of God, was condemned. Anyone who disagreed with their strict interpretation of Islam could be killed on sight. It was righteous. Unfortunately, every sect and every faction believed they alone were righteous. In Algeria, almost on a daily basis, there were horrific massacres. The pictures were appalling. There was no censorship. It was as if the pictures were also weapons to terrorise all who saw them into submission to the various distilled versions of Islam being espoused by the various warring factions.

Then some beautiful, young, white woman died in a car wreck in Paris, which wiped all the other news off the front pages of the European and American papers. The kafir enjoyed looking at pictures of her. She had the same blue eyes. She had sons. She was a princess. And she was lovely. He did not understand what made her so famous. She was only a woman. According to one article, she had been killed by photographers. Some of the older Pakistani servants believed that if they were photographed their soul was stolen from them. It was all very confusing for the kafir. He had never seen a camera. Nowhere in the Holy Book had he read anything about cameras or the dangers of being photographed. In the Holy Book, good women were recognised by their modesty and submission, and they lived out of sight. Bad women were punished harshly because they brought shame on their fathers by not subduing their eyes or hiding their flesh. He had heard old men say that daughters had to be killed at birth. Some boasted that a daughter was not worth the price of a bullet. The same men were disturbed at the very idea of their daughters having sexual relations with a husband. They counted their sons as a blessing from God, but honour was everything. Having a daughter was perceived as a guarantee that their honour would be slighted. The kafir had not seen a woman since leaving the rooftop in Yemen, except as glimpsed black shapes from a moving vehicle. He had never spoken to a woman, rarely thought about them, and had no sense of a connection with anything resembling a mother. In the male-dominated culture in which he lived, it was hardly surprising that he, and many of the men around him, held women as a species in absolute contempt.

Then another eighty-seven people were murdered in Algeria for belonging to the wrong clan, and the beautiful blonde princess disappeared. He never saw her again. The troubles in Egypt came to a head with nine Germans being murdered, but Mubarak would not come to terms with what he called extremists, who seemed to hold sway in the south. Thousands of lives had been lost in the troubles, but only the death of foreigners made headline news.

Saddam kept up his delaying tactics with the weapons' inspectors. A heroic Iraqi escort tried to take over the controls of an airplane, and almost crashed it in an effort to stop them reaching one of the sites. In another incident, the inspectors were kept outside while Iraqis destroyed the paperwork and evidence. At the end of October, Saddam boldly threatened to shoot down any foreign planes, even in the No Fly Zones.

In November, Ramzi Yousef was found guilty of masterminding the World Trade Centre bombing in New York in 1993. The servants grieved that he would languish in a prison instead of being executed, which would have enabled him to go straight to paradise as a great martyr. Yousef was later sentenced to two hundred and forty years in a special prison in Colorado that would keep him "quarantined like a person which if loosed would spread plague and pestilence." The Judge said that Yousef "was not fit to uphold Islam. Your god is death. What you do you do not do for God, you do it only to satisfy your own twisted sense of ego." To the Americans, he was arrogant, but to the Brothers of Islam, he was a proud man, who had sacrificed his life and liberty to promote his faith. Nothing was more important. It made him righteous, and it did not matter that he had failed to kill thousands of Americans because he had told the world that they would all be killed if they did not submit and become Believers.

A week later, sixty-two foreign tourists were killed by six freedom fighters outside the Temple of Hatshepsut, in Luxor, Egypt, to protest at the widespread corruption of the Egyptian government, and the decadence of the increasingly secular population. As in Algeria, the young fundamentalists were trying to awaken the Islamic conscience of their countrymen, to lead them on to the right path, and save them from perpetual torment and hellfire. They demanded the release of righteous brothers, who were being tried for murder, and had certainly been tortured. The young men had killed only to show the Truth. The English 'papers called it a massacre, and were outraged, which meant little to the servants, who only saw the six men as their brothers, who had killed the disbelievers for God.

*

The sun was shining. She had fed the young man enough painkillers to knock down an elephant then had spent a lovely morning out in the garden, which was beginning to flourish with the improved weather. Later in the afternoon, she had almost missed seeing the Sadler's Wells' filly, Alexandrova, win the Oaks at Epsom for Aiden O'Brien. Her routine had been completely turned upside down. She might have been angry about it, but really she was just tired. The lovely weather reminded her of all the jobs that still needed doing in the garden. When it was cold and raining, she did not feel guilty watching the tennis or the horse racing. The usual daytime telly was so appalling, she rarely had it on, but now she was losing track of the programmes she watched almost religiously. She had nearly missed the Oaks. It was one of a dozen races that she never missed. But she had only to look at the young man to feel guilty and selfish. He had lost so much weight. He was as white as a sheet. His Riviera tan was a mere memory.

"You can talk to me, you know," she said, for possibly the thousandth time, wanting him to take the initiative. He had to explain. She felt that he needed to justify to her why he was there, and why he had a gun with one bullet. And all that artwork? Though she would have denied it, she was actually intimidated by his body. Familiarity had not bred contempt. The extensive artwork and unusual jewellery were something he really needed to explain. "I'm just trying to help you. Isn't there anything you want to say?"

He stared at the floor.

She was kneeling beside him, and leaned down to tenderly stroke his face. It did not matter if he was a sex fiend. He had a lovely face, made more masculine by his need for a shave though the stubble was still patchy. "I know you can speak. I've heard you. And I know you can speak English. Why won't you talk to me?"

He blinked, and stared away at the window then shrank from her touch, and closed his eyes.

She did not understand. "My name is Jane Howard. This is my house. You speak English, don't you? I've heard you."

He totally ignored her.

She fumed silently. Not only was he a sex fiend, but his manners did not match his Barbour clothes either. "You owe me an explanation. Who are you? What were you doing on my land?"

He glanced in her direction, obviously hurt by her tone, but when she looked into his eyes he bowed his head and looked away. When she reached out to comb her fingers through his hair, he drew away, trying to avoid her touch.

She eased back, surprised by his reaction, and trying not to feel offended. She hoped it meant he was about to say something. Biting her lip, she waited full of expectation and nerves.

All on his own, he managed to sit up though he was slewed over and ashen, and it nearly killed him. He could not look at her. He was so completely lost, he did not know what he was supposed to do let alone understand her expectations.

She hardly dared to breathe as she watched, desperate to help, but sure of being rejected. "You poor thing," she whispered, not really wanting him to hear. "Who did this to you? It must hurt so much."

He was shaking like a leaf. He took a long moment to recover, sucking in air through gritted teeth, waiting for the cold sweats to stop. Then he lifted his head, but dared not look at her. His face was a white mask. His eyes were almost raw.

"I'm so sorry. I should take you to a hospital." There were so many things she wanted to tell him to justify why she had not been able to do the right thing.

He breathed deeply, anxious about niggling pains in his chest, and overwhelmed by the raw agony that still raged across his back. The word 'hospital' accelerated his heart, and made the strange pains more acute. He shook his head then noticed for the first time that he was naked. He looked at her accusingly then lowered his gaze. He gently tugged the blankets closer, and groaned as even the slightest movement hurt him.

She nodded. This was the nearest they had come to a conversation. "Okay. You don't want to go to hospital." She tried to smile, but it was a pathetic, twitchy leer. "You'd have had to tell them your name," she said rather harshly. "They would have insisted."

He still did not look at her.

She tried another smile. He was going to be alright. She had pulled him through. He would heal, and grow stronger, and leave. Her relief was tangible. "You'll be alright," she told him happily. "I know, you still feel pretty terrible, but you will get better now. The fever's broken. Your back is healing over nicely. I wish I could tell you that there won't be any scars." She gazed at him thoughtfully then sighed. "Whoever did this to you did get a bit carried away." She tried another smile. It was horrible.

She was talking quickly again. He winced and slowly drew away, then his back touched the side of the sofa. The pain was shocking. He jerked violently and gasped, almost fainting.

She stared at him, biting her lips as he slowly settled again, still breathing hard and sweating. "I'm sorry. I'm an idiot. I don't know anything about – well, you know. I live here rather quietly. Tattoos and S&M games: it's just not my thing. I guess, it's all about Miss Whiplash and Madame Dominatrix." She tried a smile. "When you're better, you can tell me all about it. You could tell me anything, and I'd believe it." She smiled a little easier. "I have 'gullible' written across my forehead."

He blinked and frowned then slowly lifted his eyes to stare at her forehead, and had no idea what she was talking about.

Her smile faded. She had run out of things to say. Babbling was so embarrassing, and she knew that she was over her quota on being embarrassed. She felt uncomfortable. It was odd, but he was so different sitting up. He had become, suddenly, three dimensional, and he was mobile. He was no longer just another wounded stray, but an adult human being. He had thoughts. He had needs. Wondering what sort of person he really was, she looked wistfully at his lovely face, and tried very hard not to be prejudiced by the extraordinary body.

Then, unexpectedly, he smiled, and it was so soft and gentle and sweet.

Her heart throbbed powerfully. No one had looked at her like that in decades. Her reaction to it was shocking. A surge of heat went through her body, every inch of her skin tingled, her heart fluttered, her pulse raced, her cheeks burned red, and all her defences crumbled. For one brief moment, she was absolutely lost. Blushing and stammering, she was a little girl again with a thousand hopes and dreams blossoming in her heart. Before she could recover, he had reached out to clasp one of her hands, which he then drew carefully to his lips and kissed. Utterly enthralled, she was trembling and vulnerable and incredibly flattered. She smiled back as coyly as a Victorian maiden, then suddenly realised that it was utterly false, and that he was just predatory. She withdrew her hand, and glowered. "Please, don't do that."

She might as well have struck him. What little strength he had conjured up seemed to evaporate. He withdrew into himself, and stared at the floor. Before her eyes, he shrank away, and became very pale. Knowing she was responsible made her pause. This was her fault. She had been alone too much. It simply never occurred to her that other people might be sensitive and fragile too. That body declared him to be wanton and promiscuous. It was impossible to even consider that he might have a sensitive soul. She was prepared for the obvious: he would turn out to be a callous and manipulative sexual predator, but while he was ill, he was definitely at her mercy. That really made her pause.

"It's alright," she said, almost apologetically. "Do you think you could get onto the sofa? You'll be more comfortable, and I'll help you." He did not seem to hear. "Come on. I'll help you." She rose to her feet then seized him under the arm. He made the most awful noise, but she had gone too far to back down. He was so heavy and unwilling. "Get up!" She shouted into his ear: "Come on! Get up!"

He shuddered, but his will rallied, and life, however diminished, surged through his veins. He rose unsteadily into her arms. She held him tightly. She could not move him. He was far too heavy. It was nothing but gravity and luck that made him sway backwards so she could half lower and half drop him down onto the sofa. He cried out pitifully as his joints were jarred, and the massive scar on his back tore open.

She helped him to lay down then lifted his feet up, wanting him to be comfortable. He was shivering. "It's alright. You're safe now. Let me cover you. You'll be better up here. I'll fetch you some milk. Do you think you could eat something? You've been here nearly a week, and you haven't eaten anything at all."

He looked awful. His face was white. He was shivering badly, but he ground his teeth, and managed to firmly shake his head.

His back was bleeding again. It was too late to feel guilty. She laid the linen sheet over him, and then a blanket, and tucked them in around him as if he were a child. There was a sudden flood of memories. Here were the ghosts again. She trembled then shook her head. "Not mad," she whispered, "not now, not mad."

He was barely conscious. He was in agony again.

"I'm sorry." She carefully knelt down next to the sofa, and gazed beseechingly into his eyes. "There must be someone I should call? If I knew your name? I wouldn't tell them anything that you didn't want me to. Someone somewhere must be worried sick about you. What about your mum?" She swallowed a lump of embarrassment. "Or your girlfriend? Or your wife? Are you married? You're very good-looking, I'm sure you must be very popular." His face was carved from stone. He was as white as snow. He was hardly breathing. "Is it a boyfriend? That's alright. It's not a problem. I don't mind. Really, it's absolutely alright. There must be somebody that I can call?"

He ignored her completely. He was totally focused on containing the agony that had gone through his body like a bolt of lightning.

"It's alright." She pulled the covers higher over him. "I don't mind."

He just closed his eyes. The pain engulfed him. He could not cope with anything else.

After he had seemed so well, she found his sudden relapse disconcerting. But, of course, it was her fault. She was a bully. She was a heartless bitch. She went out to the kitchen to fetch another glass of milk, and to crush some more pills. The phone was working. She had no excuse not to call an ambulance. Did she want to hand over the young man? He would end up with Social Services in a hospital, and eventually the police. They would probably 'section' him. With that body and the enigmatic silence, they would surely lock him away, and when he was well enough to speak, he would be lost in the system with no way back.

He drank the milk because he was compelled.

She must have picked up the phone a dozen times that day

Later, when he was asleep, she went back out into the garden. She filled the bird feeders then went to stare at the frothy green algae in the ponds. The weather had improved. It was a lovely warm evening. There were increasing numbers of Starlings about. They always arrived early in June, usually in great numbers which increased daily as their young fledged. They mobbed the bird feeders for two or three weeks then vanished. It was another of those mysteries that she just had to accept. She had been out there nearly two hours before she found the dead hedgehog. That grounded her. Any pride she felt for having saved the young man turned to ashes in her mouth. Bereft, she carried the prickly little creature back to put it into the incinerator behind the garage. What should have been a good day became just another lost battle in what felt like a war.

Chapter 15

She woke early, and hurried downstairs. It was Derby Day. Seeing the young man stretched out on the sofa distracted her for a moment, but she hurried to pick up the remote, and flicked through the channels on the television. "George isn't running," she said to anyone that was listening. "It'll be Sir Percy or Horatio Nelson. Frankie never wins. We all want him to. Everyone puts money on him, but he never wins. But what's really annoying is when a French horse turns up that you've never heard of, and just flies home."

She turned to survey the room. No one was listening. She pulled a face then moved to stand by the sofa. The young man was playing dead. He had moved in the night, but she could not tell if he had managed to stand. Lifting back the covers, she could check his wounds easily. It was much kinder to her back to have him up on the sofa. However, getting him there had torn a gash through the delicate new skin. It had bled during the night, but there was no sign of infection yet. She fetched the Vitamin E cream, and applied a liberal coating before replacing the sheet. He did not make a sound as she tended his wounds. Even when she carried on her usual one-sided conversation, he made no attempt to join in or to acknowledge her presence. Working on his back always silenced her criticism of him. She could not begin to imagine how painful it was, but simply looking at it made her grimace. If he did not want to move again, she would not make him.

She stood behind the sofa watching the tension ease out of his shoulders as he slowly relaxed after what probably felt like a mauling. She was ill at ease. His physical body confused her. She recognised her imperative need to touch him. It was obviously inappropriate. It was more childish curiosity than carnal. He had a long lean body. He came from a warm climate, and had the classical features of some Renaissance Christ. The jewels glinted and glittered in the pools of sunshine that filled the room at noon. The channels and ridges of the Tribal Markings looked as if they should have been rough and uneven, but were deliciously soft, and the pattern was anything but arbitrary. Once during a visit to Cordoba, she had seen many saddles that had been tooled and routed with the same ornate geometrical designs. It was Moorish. The Moors had ruled Spain for hundreds of years, and left their signature on not only saddles, but beautiful architecture and glorious gardens. The young man's lovely flesh bore almost identical markings. They demanded admiration. She could not resist tracing the patterns with her fingertips. The skin was so soft. It was quite beautiful, and endlessly fascinating. From amongst the pattern, she had discovered the roots of a great tree that must have been tattooed across his back. That was now almost completely obliterated by the deep welts of the whip. Lost in the detail, it was too easy to forget that the amazing canvas was the living body of a human being. She shyly restricted her explorations to moments when he was unconscious or drugged, but these moments were becoming rarer, and she was struggling to justify giving him more and more of her pills. Religiously, she rubbed moisturiser into his skin, all the time imagining the canvas before it had been destroyed by some brute with a whip. It had to be about sex. She could not imagine why anyone would want to hurt him. He was extraordinarily beautiful. Why would anyone want to destroy a thing of beauty? It had to be sex. It had to be because he was gay.

She did not understand the contradictions. He was so young and lovely with expensive clothes, yet he had been mutilated and whipped. That was recent, but so much else was not. The tattoos and scarification were so much older, and must have taken hundreds of hours to complete. He must have consented. His hair and his face and all the manicures spoke of a comfortable affluent lifestyle. His hands were too fine to have ever done a day's work. He spoke English. His clothes were English, but the suntan was too good. He lived abroad or he had daily visits to a salon to top up his tan. No. He lived abroad. He spoke other languages too. He had been to Monte Carlo. Perhaps, he lived there. She could not help wondering how he had managed to come through an airport without all that jewellery setting off the metal detectors. It was not difficult to imagine the security officers politely drawing him to one side then making him strip off his clothes. It made her smile to imagine their faces when they discovered his adornments. It was probably not illegal, but it was hardly normal. And still she did not understand why anyone would go through all that. It had to be sex. It was always about sex. She felt like a middle aged virgin again, and resented it. Almost every day, she found something new and extraordinary. He had to be unique. It was impossible to sustain the suspicion that other men were being carved and branded quite so liberally without her having been aware of it. Channel 4 would certainly have made a programme about it. There had to be consent.

She took a long walk down through the trees just before lunch. Watching the Derby was one of her highlights. She wanted to be able to savour every minute of it without thinking about homosexual sadomasochism or the difficulty of etching intricate patterns on to human flesh. It was all just too distracting. Plants that had seemed dormant if not dead only days earlier were now covered in buds. The leaves in the trees were lusher and greener. Everywhere, there were birds singing loudly, collecting food for their young. All the feeders were busy. Even the bumble bees were busy. It was to be a lovely day, but for all the delights of the garden, she could not quite forget him. Her fingers remembered the texture of his skin. Her heart hungered to experience the rush of pleasure that his kiss had produced. There had to be consent. His body was a priceless work of art. It must have taken years to produce such a treasure. There had to be consent. It was hard not to think about him, but she was ashamed because she was not thinking about who he was but always what…

*

It was just another day. Every day was the same. On holy days there was often no food at all and more tension, but otherwise the kafir's days all ran seamlessly together. It hardly mattered what country they were in. He was never left alone.

After Paris, Omar had made the decision to change the routine imposed on the creature. Perhaps because of its age or its nerves or the constant confinement, it was perceived to be suffering real psychological damage. The Pakistanis were not deemed to be at fault. It was obviously a flaw in the creature. Omar assumed control. He was an ex-soldier, as loyal as a son, and well educated. He knew that the Prince had no interest at all in the creature as long as it served its purpose, which meant keeping it fit and well and sane, and not having it fall down in the street. Omar shared responsibility for the creature between the Pakistanis and the Prince's personal bodyguards, who were all men from the Kingdom. A rota was set up. Immediately after First Prayers, the creature was delivered to the bodyguards. Before sunset, it was sent back. They always had a gymnasium set up. The equipment had been a gift to them for their service, and it travelled with them everywhere. Many of the bodyguards were semi-professional wrestlers. At home, they took part in competitions. They all knew about the creature. Many had fucked it, but no one laid a hand on it in the gym. In the gym, they were professional athletes. They were certainly capable of setting up a well-balanced but formidable timetable that would keep the creature physically fit and mentally occupied.

The rooms changed. The landscapes changed. Sometimes, the Prince had to leave them behind in a foreign country, all of them far from home, as he attended quickly arranged meetings to solve some international crisis often at the eleventh hour. At such times, the bodyguards depleted in number, but there were always enough to keep the creature focused on the timetable.

The kafir only marked the changing days by the changes to the plumbing and facilities that he had to work with. What happened, happened. The new regime of constant physical activity improved his health which strengthened his nerves, but the rules remained the same. He might be spending several hours of every day with men in a gym, but none of them actually spoke to him. Wrestling on the mats, adrenalin coursing through his veins, he might in a fleeting moment of triumph forget that he was not allowed to look them in the eye, but no one else forgot. There were definite boundaries. Sometimes, he forgot to mind his manners because he was invariably tired, and he would be punished, but it was never unfair. It was never malicious. Having never known another life, he accepted his circumstances without ever imagining that he was unhappy. Because he accompanied the Prince, he had better clothes. He was even allowed to wear shoes, which was a great privilege. He felt Omar's absolute authority, but did not fear it.

He had worn collars for a number of years. As he grew bigger and stronger so the collars had evolved. When he was little, the Pakistanis and their friends were brave enough to bully him. Now that he stood as tall if not taller than all of them, they used the collars to command and enforce. At that time in his life, he had two. One was a steel choke-chain placed around his neck when he was a child, and now too small to be removed without proper tools. It was slight, but strong enough to break his neck. It did not bother him as long as no one touched it. It was for a dog. He had never seen a dog. In the eyes of his Pakistanis, he was their dog. If he displeased them, they had several cruel names for him. The second collar was the latest in a long line supplied by the Master of the Royal Horses. It was thick and heavy, a combination of reinforced leather, hinged metal plates and rings. The Pakistanis kept it round his neck all the time. In the gym, it was ignored. It would have been unsporting to take advantage of it. When he was dancing for their friends, it was carefully concealed by a scarf. All the men knew it was there. It excited them, and it was something they could hold on to when he was wet and slippery.

Then everything changed. It had started like a thousand other days. The Pakistanis had him up very early to complete his chores. Then he was taken down to the gym where he spent the day. He looked very fit, but he was never strong. It was the considered opinion of his late-night audience that the hours in the gym had improved his performance. He certainly thrived on the attention. Once again, apricots and dates were available. He felt good. Even Aziz was being nice to him. With the Prince away, he was already focused on the dance he would perform. One of the bodyguards had whispered a request. There was the promise of mango. That was a rare treat. His hair was already piled up on his head. His face was rouged and powdered. Immense false lashes framed his eyes. His lips and nails were as scarlet at the tight burlesque costume that pinched his masculine frame. It was new, but much too small, which made it difficult for him to breathe. All the men loved it. They roared every time he stepped on to the stage. And their hunger burned him to the bone. He liked it. It nourished him. Even with the collar, he looked ravishing, but no one was fooled. He was not a girl.

They were preparing to leave for the gym, the only room large enough for the servants to gather en-masse. The Pakistanis were babbling with excitement. The kafir stood quietly, a little breathless, his pulse racing, the centre of attention, but excluded from it. They were all taken by surprise when the door was flung open, and Aziz stood there.

The Prince had arrived. The creature must attend. It was not optional.

They had barely a minute to rip off the tight dress, and pull a plain white shift over the creature's head. The Pakistanis were screaming that they must wash its face and brush its hair, but Aziz merely threw the old black burqa at the creature then led it away.

The Prince was in his private suite. He was at his desk, studying his computer, and did not even look up as the kafir was shoved into the room.

The kafir was completely unaware of his outrageous appearance, and went straight through to the bathroom to prepare the hot tub for his lord and master. They were in Jeddah so the bathroom was opulent. It was brilliantly lit and extravagantly furnished. Every wall was a mirror. The kafir was instantly brought to a standstill by his own reflections. There were so many. Everywhere he looked, he saw painted dolls. He hardly recognised the things that stared back at him. He was still standing there utterly shocked when the Prince entered.

The Prince had come expecting to find a bath prepared, but he found a slightly dishevelled but glamorous showgirl, except that it was not a girl. He stared at the creature, seeing it for perhaps the first time. Such servants were commonplace. It was not the white skin or its sexuality that arrested the Prince's attention. It was the face. He could not quite believe his eyes. It was extraordinarily beautiful.

The kafir was rooted to the spot. He quite forgot everything else, and just stood there dumbly staring at his own multiple reflections. There were so many. The image was bounced around the mirrored walls. He was at once captivated and appalled. He could not turn away. He could not even blink. It was only when the Prince moved to stand in front of him, blocking his view, that the kafir realised he was no longer alone. In absolute panic, he fell to his knees then stooped to kiss his master's feet in the desperate hope of finding forgiveness.

The Prince grinned. Only good manners prevented him from laughing out loud. He knew exactly what had happened. Even in his exalted society, he had heard about the Pakistani passion for dancing boys. He was just a little surprised that the inconspicuous creature that had sorted out his bathroom and toilet for so many years had cleaned up quite so well. Having never in his life spoken to one of them before, he was surprised to hear himself saying: "It's alright. Go back to work."

The kafir kissed his master's feet again. He was genuinely terrified. He was ashamed and embarrassed, and convinced that his master would be grossly offended by his shocking appearance. "Please, Your Highness, my master by the Grace of God, the most Compassionate, the most Merciful. Forgive me. Please, forgive me. I'm so sorry. God is Kindness. God is Forgiveness."

Appalled, the Prince merely lifted a foot to gently push the grovelling creature away. "Get on with your work."

Grateful for the reprieve, and almost in tears, the kafir withdrew then rose to his feet. He bowed again and again then hurriedly backed away until he felt able to rise to his full height without it being considered disrespectful or threatening.

The Prince stood watching it. He was smiling again. He was actually struggling to contain his laughter. The cares that had burdened him for days and weeks simply faded away. The creature looked about twenty years old, but the heavy makeup made that impossible to guess with any certainty. The carefully arranged hair was beginning to fall, giving the impression of wildness. The makeup was smudged and smeared, suggesting disreputable behaviour. The plain white shift had obviously been hurriedly pulled on, and was hitched up, showing rather a lot of leg. Despite its dishevelled appearance, the creature was very good-looking. The Prince could not help speculating on what it would look like on a stage in some exotic costume. He tried to remember when he had looked at it before, but could not. He had never actually looked at it. That would have been impolite. One was not supposed to notice servants. The most perfect servants were the ones that remained invisible. Did that make the creature a perfect servant? That was unthinkable. Imagining the protests from the Pakistanis and his Arab retainers, the Prince could only shake his head and smile. The pretty thing was absolutely adorable.

The kafir was a bundle of nerves. He made a huge effort to ignore the mirrors. He kept his eyes down. He meticulously went through all the procedures. He turned on the water jets. He checked the temperature. He fetched soap and oil and towels. When he was ready to bathe his master, he waited, slightly stooped, trying not to fidget, and still hoping he would be forgiven.

The Prince approached it, sensing it was as nervous as a wild bird. He was curious. There were a dozen questions. Hardly any of them were appropriate. He was intrigued. He wanted to see its face. He wanted to know if it really was as beautiful as it had seemed. In the plain white shift, it was impossible to admire its figure. He needed to look into its eyes. "Are you a good dancer?" he asked pleasantly.

The kafir trembled and shook his head, not daring to look at the Prince.

Amused, the Prince regarded it for a moment then grimaced, imagining a rather grotesque bump and grind routine that would delight the Pakistanis. He moved closer. He noticed the collars, and wondered what else he had been too blind and pre-occupied to see. The leather collar was ugly, and incongruous beside the false eyelashes and red lipstick. He reached out imperiously to touch it, and recognised it immediately. It was heavy and stiff, nothing more than a completely utilitarian noseband for a horse. The metalwork glinted coldly under the bright lights. It was tarnished steel. It should have been brass. Brass would have suited the creature so much better. He understood that his people had probably recycled some old bridle, but the pretty thing definitely required something more decorative if it was dancing every night before an audience of sex-starved men. His close attention spooked the creature, which started in alarm and trembled every time it was touched, but was too well trained to run away. The Prince caught the flash of incredibly blue eyes. He offered a smile of reassurance, but the creature still shivered. Disturbed by its obvious fear, the Prince was reluctant to imagine the cause. When he stepped back to allow the creature some space, it collapsed to its knees, and pressed its face to the floor.

The Prince realised he had caused a situation. The traditions that dictated the rules of their relationship were as old as Time. Not even the Prince had the right to sweep aside customs, which protected both servant and master.

"Come and undress me," the Prince said kindly, and turned away to leave the room.

Forgetting everything but his duty, the kafir hurried to follow. His hands were shaking. His heart was beating way too fast. For the first time in a long time, he had been absolutely terrified. He had been shocked by his appearance in the mirrors. The Pakistanis always kept him away from mirrors. They felt he already had too many vices without encouraging vanity. His master's reaction had completely unnerved him. He could not count how many times he had been alone with his master in an intimate situation. He had never been afraid before. The man had never looked at him before. Now, he desperately needed to be allowed to disappear. Being quiet and obedient had always been his only shield.

The Prince was standing where he always stood to be dressed or undressed by his servant. Beneath his tribal clothes, he wore a western suit. He had flown in from Schiphol, and would fly out again within a few hours. The creature was so skilled and dexterous; it could strip off the Prince's clothes without him feeling anything at all. It had the light fingers of a thief, and the slow lithe movements of a cat. The Prince watched it closely. Every day of his life, some servant had undressed him. In his various houses there were many such servants. Some were coloured. Some were white. He never asked where they came from or inquired when they disappeared. His father and all his forefathers had white servants. They were more numerous then, but they were always nameless and disposable.

For a while, the Prince closed his eyes, but curiosity overcame good manners. He watched the creature gently pull away the belt then unbutton his fly. He experienced a sudden swirl of energy as the creature brushed against him while drawing his trousers down. The Prince sank on to the bed, and lifted one leg then the other so the creature could gather the garments into its arms. He watched it rise to its feet, and turn away to fold the trousers carefully over a press. It opened the jacket around the frame, and brushed down the fabric with languid strokes. The creature had no idea it was being observed. It knelt down again beside the bed, and stooped over the feet, drawing off the socks carefully then placing the feet back on the carpet. When the Prince rose to stand his penis was inches from the creature's face, but the creature coolly drew down his shorts, and waited for the Prince to step away.

The Prince stepped to one side, but did not leave. Lost in its task, the creature straightened up too, and suddenly found itself face to face with its master. Though taller, the Prince was able to stare into the luminous blue eyes. They were exquisite. He saw every fleck of azure blue. His breath caught in his throat. His heart actually stopped beating.

For the briefest moment, the two men were transfixed.

It was the kafir who blinked first. Terror overwhelmed him. He ducked away and bowed down, his heart racing, his limbs trembling.

The Prince stood perfectly still. He was still dazzled by those eyes. The shades of blue and green were as gorgeous as a tropical sea on a sunny day. A wave of affection swept through him. He actually smiled then blinked, and realised that the creature was on its knees, cowering in fear. The reality of their relationship was a cold slap across the face. He stared down at it, feeling a dozen conflicting emotions. Amongst them was a prejudice that shamed him, and a compassion that tradition and culture and an ancient code of honour despised. He hardly knew what to do next so he just stood there, willing the creature to look up, knowing it would not. The eyes were like diamonds. Even behind the monstrous, theatrical, false lashes, the eyes were dazzling. He remembered vaguely some protest from the older Arab servants about the creature being too tall, and suggesting that it was time to bring in a younger replacement. It seemed so ridiculous. The creature's height was immaterial. It was utterly beautiful. The blue eyes were exquisite. The Prince waited breathlessly, but the creature remained huddled over its knees, obviously too frightened to move.

Confused by his emotions, the Prince walked back into the bathroom. He was naked. He had a powerful physique, helped by the best food, and a lifetime of muscle building exercise. Without waiting for the creature, he stepped down into the bubbling waters, and settled on one of the seats. He stretched his legs out before him, and enjoyed the effects of the powerful jets around his back and groin. But he was waiting for the creature to join him. It must come. It must share his bath. He would see those eyes again. The creature must come and fulfill its duties. It was not allowed to refuse.

The kafir came submissively, afraid of the reflections and of the Prince, who was watching him intently. He knew what he had to do. It did not help that he had built up an imaginary relationship between them. It was unconsummated, but it had always thrilled his heart. His only hope was that the Prince would not be angry with him. But surely, the Prince had guessed. Nothing else explained the sudden interest, and his quickening pulse. As he sank into the hot oily water, his white shift clung to him. He kept his eyes down. He sought the soap. He knew his task. He focused on being the most perfect servant in the world. Nothing else mattered. He needed to be invisible again. He needed to hide.

The Prince found its diligence amusing, and studied its face with rapt attention. He knew that the creature was desperately trying to avoid a confrontation. It would not look up. It hardly dared to touch the Prince, which made washing him clinically from head to foot more than challenging. The Prince reached out to catch its wrist playfully only to let it struggle free. He touched its face. He reached for its thighs. The creature squirmed and panicked like a little girl. The Prince's hands were quicker, and he had the authority of a dictator. More forcefully, he caught the edge of the shift, and slowly tore it from hem to neckline. The movement brought the creature close against him, but he merely laughed, and let it squirm free only to trap it again and reel it in. For several minutes, the little game continued. The creature strove admirably to do its job despite all the distractions. The Prince merely played with it, trying to make it drop the soap, laughing at its confusion, watching it get more and more upset and agitated. But it would not look up at him.

At last, his nerves ragged, the kafir drew back, and sank on to his knees in the water to await a command. The swirling waters lapped his jaw, and buffeted his naked body. He knew the Prince was happy and laughing, but he could not reciprocate. His training had not prepared him for games. The Prince had to behave with absolute decorum or the kafir was lost.

The Prince took a moment to study the downturned face, the sadness, the running mascara and the smudged lipstick. He slowly reached out to grip the creature's shoulder then rather irritably took hold of the collar instead. It seemed to frown, but it was almost impossible to read anything into the mask it turned to the world. He imperiously drew the creature in by force, having failed to beguile it. It would not look at him. It would not lift its gaze. When he used the collar to force up its head, it merely closed its eyes. The Prince took another long moment to study its face. The wrecked makeup was hardly flattering. The false eyelashes looked like dead spiders. The lipstick was smeared across its face like a rash. Beneath the mask there was a perfect storm of anguish and fear. He leaned closer. The creature was trembling. He clasped the face in his hands, dragged a thumb across the lips and glimpsed the perfect white teeth. Trapping it between his thighs, he carefully caught the edges of the eyelashes, and slowly peeled them off. The creature was overwhelmed. Its lips trembled. Its breath came in ragged gasps. The Prince stared at it, mesmerised. He explored the lovely face, the bone structure, the flawless skin, but the creature kept its eyes shut tight. He knew it was frightened. He almost felt guilty for causing it so much distress.

The kafir was compelled to surrender the soap. There was no escape. There was to be no evasion.

The Prince carefully lathered the solemn face. His thighs held it still. He had big strong hands, but was gentle and considerate as he washed away all evidence of the garish makeup. The creature did not raise its eyes. It did not resist at all. It knelt like a martyr at its master's feet as its tangled hair was carefully pulled down and finger-combed. Its disguise was slowly, but completely washed away. The Prince smiled with genuine pleasure. The creature was really more beautiful without the makeup, but seemed overwhelmingly sad. It was as responsive as a corpse. Such behaviour seemed at odds with its role as a promiscuous dancing boy, kept to satisfy the needs of the allegedly sex-mad Pakistanis. The Prince took control of the collar again, and compelled the creature to lift its head. The eyes stayed closed. The planes of the face were clean and perfectly symmetrical. It was almost too good-looking to be real. The Prince moved its head about, trying to trick it into looking at him, but the creature was too well trained to respond. For a while, the Prince let it be. He was content to just stare at its face in frank admiration. It was shockingly beautiful.

Unable to escape, the kafir toiled over his predicament. At last, perplexed, he lifted his head, and coolly surveyed the Prince. He knew what his Pakistanis would expect. To do nothing seemed unthinkable. He was never allowed the luxury of doing nothing. He could not withdraw from his master nor leave the tub. The Pakistanis had trained him very well.

The Prince smiled. The eyes were extraordinary. He was the lonely mariner coming upon a lighthouse in the darkness, long after giving up all hope. The luminous eyes shone like diamonds. He could not stop smiling. He felt elated. He actually laughed with unashamed pleasure.

The poor dumb creature lowered its gaze submissively. With trembling hands, it reached out to do what it had been taught to do to appease other men. Its hands moved delicately to locate its master's knees then travelled along his thighs to caress the penis.

Utterly shocked, the Prince drew back. He was appalled and indignant then just bloody livid. His first instinct was to knock the creature away, but he saw the eyes again. Without the trashy makeup, the creature was astonishingly beautiful. His heart accelerated. His flesh burned. Curiosity overcame reserve. He took an immense deep breath, and spread his arms wide along the rim of the sunken bath then waited to see what the exquisite creature would do next.

With barely a few strokes, the kafir had produced an erection made of iron. He worked it efficiently, never lifting his head, never changing his bland expression. He looked the picture of innocence, but his hands were working the blackest magic beneath the surface of the swirling waters.

The Prince resolutely kept still as his body revelled in a tumult. He could feel all the strength he possessed being drained from his limbs. A roaring combustion of power focused in his groin. His eyes rolled. His stomach somersaulted. But the joy became agony as the creature tortured him relentlessly by keeping his climax at bay. The frustration sent explosions of pain through his heart and daggers through his brain. He was ready. He wanted it. He did not care anymore that it was just the Pakistanis' rather vulgar toy.

And still the kafir's expression remained disarmingly bland.

Unable to endure being humiliated a moment longer, the Prince lunged forward, and struck the creature across the face. When it collapsed backwards into the swirling waters, the Prince was almost mad enough to drown it. He loomed over it, searching the water for the collar, found it and wrenched the creature up from the depths. For a brief moment, he struggled to get his hands around the creature's throat, but the thick collar thwarted him. Enraged, he hurled the lifeless thing across the side of the bath. The white rump loomed like a girl's breasts. Without even thinking, the Prince seized the soft flesh and tore the creature open, then forced his erection inside. Unable to keep its head above water, the creature flayed about wildly then sank like a stone. The Prince scooped it up again, and beached it securely across the side of the bath, forced its legs wider, then drove into it again. He eased back slowly then punched his way in again and again and again. His temper, and the ferocity of his penetrations, provided his release. He began ejaculating, at first in a frenzy, then with immense energy sapping bursts. Almost immediately, he experienced a deep sense of relief that soothed him, and made his flesh burn all over. Every fibre of his being registered the most profound pleasure. He experienced a joy that was beyond human comprehension. It was the most perfect rapture. It was a hot, dark and dangerous ecstasy that seared through his heart and soul like a flaming thunderbolt. Under his hand, the creature stirred only to brace itself. Soon the only sounds were their laboured breathing, and the heavy, wet thud of the Prince colliding against the creature's backside, venturing deeper and deeper within.

An eternity later, when his sanity had been reduced to ashes, the Prince leaned forward. Like a cruel tyrant, he greedily seized the collar to keep his victim trapped. He was shattered. His brain no longer functioned. He could not think, could not breathe, could not let go, but he was immensely satisfied. His legs were like jelly, but his whole body throbbed and burned red hot. He had been firing off like a rocket launcher. He had been in tears. Lodged deep inside the creature, he was loathed to disengage. There was something unusual, he hardly knew what, but he was strangely comforted. If he tried to pull away, he knew it would be painful. He was shaking uncontrollably. They both were.

A sudden pain in the pit of his stomach focused him. With a terrible groan, he pulled away, seized its hips then drove into it again. Their bodies collided. The impact was devastating. The creature cried out in agony. It was so sweet, so musical. The Prince slid deeper. He pounded it again and again. The same sweet sound chimed in his ears. He launched into it so powerfully, he felt sure that it would be cleaved in two. It wept. It cried and gasped. The music was delightful. He forced his way inside. He drove harder, went deeper, reached further. Was there no end? The creature's channel housed him perfectly. The walls were firm. But where was the bottom? He slapped the creature's flank, and thrilled as the startled muscles contorted around him. He struck it harder. It was thrilling.

Every assault left him quaking. The kafir was powerless, but this had been his dream.

When the Prince failed to climax quite as spectacularly as he had done the first time, he took it out on the creature, beating it across the back, and almost rupturing it. The creature just stiffened under the blows. The lack of any response was annoying, but he drew away, and staggered out of the bath. He could hardly walk. Once in the bedroom, he threw himself down across the vast bed trying to understand what had just happened. Never in his life had he plundered another body so completely. There was no respect, and very little tenderness. It was just sex. He had violated the creature. He had thoroughly vanquished it. It was only sex. It was not even desire. His huge penis was burning and sore. The exaltation that he was experiencing was extraordinary. He remained motionless, breathless, hopeful that the surreal contentment would last forever, but it ebbed away much too quickly. When the nervous creature appeared hesitantly in the doorway, the Prince turned wrathfully to study it.

Completely naked and utterly spent, the kafir stared at the floor. He could not leave until his master dismissed him. He felt very vulnerable. For years, he had dreamed of being the lover of the great man. His imagination had not prepared him for the reality. The Prince was certainly passionate, and as strong as the kafir had hoped, but the raw lust had destroyed all his illusions. He knew that he meant as little to the mighty prince as he did to the excitable Pakistanis, who used him as casually as a cheap toy. With the shattering of his illusions came the loss of his sanctuary. Now, there was nowhere for him to hide.

"Go fetch a towel," the Prince said. "Cover yourself."

The kafir doubted his hearing, but bowed gravely and backed away.

Chapter 16

It was a lovely day at Epsom. The sun was shining on the Queen, and the sky was blue. Perhaps summer was coming at last. The ladies were all out in their posh frocks. Many had suntans. Many must have been fake. To her surprise, the young man actually turned to watch. She almost asked him if it was the horses or the girls, but knew that he would not say a word, and very obviously did not want to be noticed. All the men wore morning suits. He would have fitted in very easily with the beautiful people in the paddock. Monte Carlo, the Riviera, he was obviously very comfortable in that milieu. The Epsom Derby was all part of the same Society Season, and would soon be followed by Royal Ascot. She enjoyed the spectacle on television. In the crowds, she would have become increasingly distressed. It was the same with Wimbledon, she could dream of affording tickets, but the crowds would have destroyed her.

To guarantee that she had a quiet afternoon, she went out to the kitchen, and crushed some more painkillers. He was stronger so she gave him four. It was suddenly annoying that he would not take the can of milkshake. He was perfectly capable even if he was still in some pain. But she submitted again, and held it to his lips. How could she argue with someone, who had apparently taken a vow of silence, and refused to look her in the eye? She made a cup of tea for herself then returned to curl up in her comfy chair. Within a few hours, she had a cat on her knee, and one on the back of the chair. Two sat on the sofa around the young man. The ginger glutton sat in the doorway, waiting for her to go back to the kitchen and provide food.

At four o'clock, the horses were circling at the starting gates. Horatio Nelson was being checked by the Vets. Sir Percy had the biggest fan club. The French horse that she had never heard of was getting rave reviews, and was a firm favourite. The little horse, Horatio Nelson, was continually being trotted up and down in front of the Vets. Kieren Fallon, the jockey, did not look happy. The odds on the horse were drifting out. They were all good-looking thoroughbreds with excellent pedigrees. From experience, she had learned that the really good-looking ones seldom won races. It was all very exciting. A dozen pundits all had a dozen different opinions. Along the rail, the ordinary race-goers were shouting for Sir Percy. His nervous owners were thrilled and anxious. He was so special. Owning him had been a dream come true. As long as he was alright! Aiden O'Brien quietly insisted that Horatio was fine and would run. She was worried now. If she was betting, she would have chosen Horatio, Dylan Thomas, Sir Percy and Papal Bull. Sixties Icon was in the field, the son of her all-time favourite, Galileo, but he did not seem to be favoured over the trip. Clair was saying that all the horses were looking warm, but it was 'a very very warm day'. It had to be global warming. Only two days ago, it had been too cold to go outside.

They set off. Epsom was a difficult course. It was full of hills and corners, and really tested a horse's ability to keep its balance and gallop. A furlong and a half out, and Horatio Nelson broke down. The crowd gasped. The commentator barely missed a beat. Sir Percy won, third was Dylan Thomas, but Horatio was back up the track with a broken leg. It ruined everything. She leaned forward in anguish as the screens went up around Horatio. She was reminded of Barbaro. She would have to search around for an update about him. He was not in the news anymore. The media were so fickle. She hoped he was still alive. His owners were spending a fortune trying to save his life, but it was worth it because his stallion fees would be huge if he survived. She wasn't sure that Ballydoyle would be so philanthropic. In England, racehorses were swiftly destroyed if they were injured. They fared better than greyhounds, which were shot if they were not fast enough.

She leaned forward to switch off the television, but there was an interview with the winning jockey. He was thrilled to have won the most famous horse race in the world, and was waxing lyrical about his horse, and declaring that Sir Percy had only been beaten in the 2000 Guineas because the horse that won was exceptional. She smiled happily. "That was George, Gorgeous George, George Washington!" But no one was listening. Her joy vaporised, and she left the room.

There was a friendly football match between England and Jamaica, which the young man would probably want to watch, but he was still not talking so she changed channels to avoid a confrontation.

When he was asleep, she went outside to incinerate the hedgehog. She was upset that she couldn't cry, but she knew that was her medication. She went to sit on the bench near the wall, and stared into the darkness. One of her cats came to sit beside her. The night was full of noises, but none of them were frightening. What frightened her was inside the house. She had lost control. There was a beautiful, naked, vulnerable, young man in her house. She wanted to touch him. She wanted to kiss him as she had never kissed another living soul. All that stood between him and her ravenous desire to consume him, were his pitiful injuries. She was the great black spider again. She would spin a web of shadows around him, and he would simply disappear…

An hour later, she returned to the house. Her hands were shaking. She had managed to vanquish her desire for him. She had punished every weakness. In her own universe, she was the goddess of everything, but he was beyond her power. He was too beautiful. He was too young. He was too vulnerable. Even in her imagination, she could not hurt him. It might have been nothing more than her maternal instinct or her guilt, but she had to protect him even from herself.

At the backdoor, she heard him shouting. She ran into the front room expecting burglars or worse, but he was alone, struggling in the grip of some terrible dream. She rushed to his side, and grabbed hold of him. Her own fears were forgotten. "Are you alright?"

At her touch, he flinched. His back was still raw with pain. He went rigid. She released him slowly, and pressed him carefully back into the bedding. He came around slowly, struggling to focus, and was alarmed to find her so near.

"You were dreaming," she explained, offering her best smile.

He sort of nodded, but could not immediately recognise her or his surroundings. "Please? Please, where am I?"

She froze. She hardly knew what to say. From his expression, it was obvious he was still half asleep and confused. "You've been ill," she said, and kept smiling. "You were having a bad dream."

He grimaced as the pain awakened across his back.

"What's your name?" she asked with practised innocence.

He managed to look at her then he remembered. It was like a curtain being drawn across his face. The shutters came down. His whole body seemed to shut her out. She did not need to understand 'body language'. He did not answer. He lowered his gaze.

"My name is Jane Howard."

He blinked, understood and looked away.

Realising the moment had passed, she went out into the kitchen to fetch him another drink. It was the middle of the night. She was dead tired. Her sugar levels were low. She needed to go to sleep. Being tired always made her bad tempered. If she was seriously over tired then she was prone to lapses into increasingly irrational behaviour. She knew the signs. The feelings that she had for him were totally unacceptable. He was just too naked and too good-looking. She needed her pills. He needed clothes. He needed to leave. She made a cheese sandwich and poured a glass of milk.

She took out a milkshake for him, and sat quietly eating the sandwiches while she crushed some more pills. He had spoken. She should have been pleased. It was progress. It was a beginning, but it had taken a week to get four words. She could not wait much longer. He might be helpless, but he was not innocent. He might not have moved a muscle or said a word, but he had taken over her house. Drugging him had become a habit. She knew it was excessive and unacceptable, but her nerves were beginning to shred. These were the signs. It was beginning.

After eating, she went into the lounge then knelt down beside the sofa. "Here, drink this."

He lifted himself and grimaced. She held the can to his lips. He drank without making any attempt to take the can from her. He did not look at her. It was bizarre.

"Will you be alright?"

He had remembered. He was still very drowsy, but he knew who she was, and that she had been taking care of him. His fears were too easily seduced by the drugs and the delicious cold milkshake. He desperately wanted to say something.

"You just rest," she reassured him. "You'll be better soon. The fever's gone. You're going to be fine. You're safe now."

"Please?" His throat was so sore. "Please, are you a doctor?"

She was so surprised that she hardly knew how to answer. It was almost too easy: "Yes." It was a lie, but she could not take it back. "Yes, I am a doctor. Do you remember now? You've been very ill."

He nodded. He still could not look at her.

"Do you want to tell me who did this to you?" she asked quietly.

He shook his head.

She wanted to tell him that he should go to the police, and report what had happened. She had only to look at him to know that he would refuse. He was consenting. Nothing else made sense. It was some deviant sexual practice that she could not begin to understand, but still found intriguing. She had never credited herself with such a lurid curiosity, but it must be true. She wanted him to explain everything. She had to know every sordid detail. If she promised not to tell anyone then she might be able to persuade him to speak, but she still felt like a ghoul. Because he was obviously gay, she was not physically afraid of him, but it made him a curiosity in her quiet life, if not a complete freak. "You should go back to sleep. Think of nice things. Try not to have nightmares. You need to be quiet and still."

She reached out hesitantly to stroke a few strands of hair back off his face. She so wanted to kiss him. Her need was mystifying. Surely, if he was gay? "There must be something nice you can think about. What about your family? We'll get in touch with them when you're a bit stronger. I should think you can't wait to get away from me and all the cats." She made a huge effort to smile. It was truly terrifying.

He just closed his eyes, and wished her away.

"Okay, yes," she said, understanding completely. "You go back to sleep. It's alright. Everything will be alright."

She would go up to her own room, and lay down alone on her immense and comfortable bed – after she had locked all the doors, and taken all the keys to make sure he could not leave. "I'll be upstairs. If you need anything then you'll have to shout. But don't worry. You go back to sleep. You're safe now. No one is going to hurt you anymore."

It was an expression she used so often with the waifs and strays. It had a cadence that was soothing, and required a tone that was soft and smooth. There were no harsh consonants. Understanding was not required. It was the sound and the rhythm. She said it to the cats and the birds. Now, she was saying it to him. He was not something small and pliable. She could not overwhelm him with physical power or lock him inside a cage to keep him safe. Keeping him safe would be far more challenging. He was so ill. He needed her. Tomorrow or the day after, or even the day after that, he might be well enough to trouble her, but she was not yet ready to consider it. She was the doctor and the nurse. She had enough pills to sedate an elephant. While he kept swallowing them, she could control him. If she looked after herself then she could look after him.

Walking away from him, she realised that her hands were shaking. She felt sick. It was madness to have a stranger in the house. It was a thousand times madder to keep someone like him. She took all the precautions she could, and went upstairs. She did sleep for a few hours. She needed it. When she came down again it was about eight thirty, and he was still fast asleep.

She fed the cats then went out into the garden. The sky was blue. It looked like it would be a lovely day. She would mow the lawn before it became a meadow. There were a million things to do, and it wasn't raining so she had no excuses. The ponds were turning green again. She stared down into them, lost in thought. There were still frogs at the bottom. Her heart was burdened again. She was too involved. She took it too personally. She turned away, and hardened her heart.

The lawnmower was about ten years older than Moses, but it still worked very well even if it was rather noisy. She had excelled herself by cleaning all the moving parts during a period of frenetic activity at Easter so all she needed to do was top up the petrol, and then it was all systems go. She raised the blades to the highest setting then set off. As usual, she went neatly up and down until she was too tired to care, then it was just a chore, which she wanted to finish as quickly as possible. The grass was too long, and still rather wet so it was hard work. She soon had backache. But she persevered. It was nearly lunchtime when she returned to the house.

"Are you going to speak to me today?" she asked, smiling as she went into the front room. He was sitting stooped over the arm, supported by a cushion with the sheet draped over him like a Roman toga. The blankets were dishevelled, and she knew that he had been on his feet. "Are you okay?"

He did not look at her. He had the remote in his hand. The television was on. He stared at the floor, his face completely expressionless.

"I've been taking care of you. Don't you remember? I want to help you."

He lifted his gaze just enough to see whether she had brought him anything to drink. There was the familiar can of milkshake. His face melted for a moment. He licked his dry lips.

She raised the can, wanting to look into the blue eyes, but he lowered his gaze, and shrank back on the sofa. Someone had hurt him badly. Even her cold heart understood that he was a broken wreck. She took a moment to consider how much power she actually had over him. It was daunting. She was suddenly ashamed. "I've been alone too long," she said aloud. "I'm probably the least competent person you could have found. I'm so sorry."

He shifted uncomfortably, keeping his back untouched, trying to keep his nakedness covered.

Her granite heart pulsed again. He could have been her son. He was almost the right age. She frowned, and shook her head to banish the ghosts. "I'm sorry. I wish I could help you, but you won't tell me anything. You're afraid. Please, don't be afraid of me. I won't hurt you. I promise."

He remained motionless. His eyes were locked on the floor somewhere between them. He seemed to be barely breathing.

"I'm sorry." She gave him another moment, but he might have been carved from stone. She understood that something compelled him to silence. He could speak. He understood when she spoke. She lifted the can of milkshake. "Do you want this?"

The eyes darted, but did not move from the floor. A morbid frown darkened his features. She could see the muscles across his torso tightening. His fine hands turned to fists then opened, and his fingers stretched like talons to seize his thighs. He shuddered and bowed his head, then slowly looked up at her. He possessed the most luminous blue eyes that she had ever seen. The perfect bone structure, the flawless skin, and the quality of his eyes made him, without doubt, the most beautiful creature on the planet.

Her heart pulsed again. She wanted to kiss him. The ugly black shadow of the spider made her shiver with dread. She would have done it, but his face registered his awareness of her desire, and he lowered his gaze, and shrank back within himself. She shivered. "I'm sorry." The beauty had gone out of him. She hesitated then took a step forward, and offered the drink. "Do you want this? Take it. You're strong enough to drink it yourself."

He stiffened again. He cast a glance towards the can in her hands then turned slowly to face her.

She almost took a step back because he seemed ready to rise to his feet, which was something she was totally unprepared for.

The young man moved slowly and awkwardly forward to let one knee rest on the floor then he bowed to her. With two hands clasped together, he reached up to receive her gift.

Aghast, she took a step back. He was begging. It was a posture she had not resorted to since Holy Communion when a child. She had knelt down and bowed her head, then held out her hands cupped together in supplication for the Blood and Body of Christ. She was appalled. Swaying on her feet, she stood over the beautiful young man. He was silent and motionless. He was naked. The sheet had fallen away. Completely embarrassed, she just shook her head. There were no words. She pushed the can into his hands then stumbled backwards. She was trembling. She just did not know what to say. It was so much worse than handling the bejewelled sheath. Hot and bothered, she turned away, and retreated to her chair, then stared out of the window until she was sure that he was back on the sofa, the blankets carefully arranged over him, and his attention somewhere else.

It was too much information. It was compounded by his awkwardness opening the can. He managed. He did work it out, but the process proved his inexperience. That he drank it with relish just proved again that he had not been exposed to such an ordinary everyday thing in his ordinary everyday life. She rose to her feet, and hurried from the room. She went out to the kitchen, but it just was not far enough. She went out the back door and walked and walked, through the door in the wall, across the lawn then away into the woods.

*

"Go fetch a towel," the Prince had said. "Cover yourself."

No one had ever given him anything before. And it was such a gift. It was a moment of consideration. It was a precious acknowledgment that he was entitled to a little dignity. He went to the mirror to study the thing that he lived inside like a parasite. It was such a pretty thing. He stroked the hair then peered into the eyes. The Prince had made a good job of cleaning away the mascara and eyeliner. The kafir's hands were shaking as he picked up one his master's towels then wrapped it around his master's creature's body.

The Prince lay back amongst his pillows. The utter contentment that warmed his body deceived his mind. He had a wide circle of women in his life, amongst them wives and girlfriends and whores. Though many of them were very beautiful and accomplished, he could not recall ever feeling as he had when embedded deep inside the creature. The creature? It was surely male. Even in a dress, it was definitely male. That was disturbing. The self-deception ended. He had entered a male body. That was sodomy. That was haram. It was the most forbidden of all things. There was no excuse at all for what he had done, but he tried to find a defence. He did not feel like a homosexual. He was sure that he was definitely not a homosexual. Never before had he gazed at a man with desire. Curiosity had gotten the better of him. It was just a moment of weakness. It had seemed so harmless. It had all started as a game, a bit of fun, but now he had committed the most dreadful of sins. He could hardly remember what had possessed him. When had curiosity become desire? Was it even his fault? It was the creature. It had done something. It was the hands and the collar and those luminous eyes. It had tricked him into doing something filthy and depraved. His intelligence was appalled, but his body burned with pleasure at the very thought of it. He hardly knew how to rationalise his feelings. He was experiencing the most perfect rapture. Every nerve and sinew quivered with joy. His groin was a fireball of molten magma. His disgust could not quench the desire that still raged through his flesh like an inferno. By the Law of God, he was condemned to perpetual hell because of one brief moment's madness with a worthless kafir. The Holy Prophet had declared that the act of sodomy was an unforgivable crime against God. And before the sinner went to the eternal fires of hell, he was either literally set on fire or thrown off a cliff, and the honour of his family was irreparably scarred. He was already trying to write it all off as a moment of complete insanity that only a great deal of prayer and charity and a pilgrimage would absolve, when the creature returned.

The kafir stood just inside the doorway. His head was bowed. His hands hung languidly at his sides. A white towel had been wrapped loosely around his hips. His torso was hard with muscles. He had clean lines, and those perfect, classically symmetrical features. He could not have looked more attractive or more vulnerable.

Disconcerted, the Prince turned away, and pulled the bedspread across his body. His usual composure and self-assurance had abandoned him. His groin was already on fire. His flesh craved to be plunged back inside the creature, deeper and deeper. He ached with longing. It felt like insanity. It was a necessity. He had to look, and was appalled to discover that he had the willpower of a child. It did not matter how often he reminded himself that the creature was utterly forbidden. Just looking at it was a sin. But the creature stood there, staring at the floor like an innocent as if totally unaware of its beauty, and the effect that it had on everyone around it. The Prince stared helplessly. He was captivated. Echoes of the rapture scorched through him again. His fascination slowly devoured his guilt. In agony, he explored the limits of his self-control. He took a long torturous moment to study the strange alien thing that held his sanity in the palm of its hand. The Pakistanis had certainly earned their pay keeping it fit and well. There was not a mark on it. The skin was flawless. The muscle tone was exceptional. Its beauty and gentle silence were absolutely enthralling. It had been in his service for years. It had shared his bath, washed his body, been as tender and caring as a mother with a child, yet he had never looked at it until that day. He was almost sad. He had possessed a thrilling jewel, and until that moment not been aware of its power. Echoes of his conquest became an inferno. He was compelled. It overwhelmed every vestige of guilt that his rational brain had demanded. He knew that such liaisons were not culturally uncommon. Recognising the realities of life did not absolve him or quell the passion in his belly. Boys had always been the scandal of Islam. They were still beautiful and available when girls reached puberty and disappeared behind veils. And they were not yet men, so even the great and the good had managed to argue that pretty boys were okay. Sexually, the pretty boys had the same currency as pretty girls, and inherently less complications. He could not help believing that it was his guilt that had made their encounter so potent. The whole adventure had been electrically charged.

The lovely catamite stood motionless, gazing at the floor, perfect in its beauty and silence and shining innocence. The Prince's aroused sex was as angry as a bear. It had never been so proud or so hungry. He impatiently rose on to an elbow, and drew breath to speak then hesitated. There was a protocol amongst servants. The foul infidel did not qualify as the lowest of the low, which was why the Pakistanis kept it like a pet. It was unlikely they ever spoke to it. So he snapped his fingers, and watched as the creature's head lifted though its eyes never left the floor. Somewhere in his DNA, he knew that a kafir was forbidden to look at him, forbidden to speak, forbidden to raise a hand even in defence. The Prince pointed to the floor beside the bed, and was rewarded when the creature crossed the room, went to its knees, bowed low then submissively kissed the ring offered for it to worship. Every movement was fluid and graceful. Watching it do the simplest things gave him unexpected pleasure.

Again the electricity. The Prince drew back awkwardly across the bed, patting the mattress, commanding the creature to join him. He was so aroused he could barely command his own limbs.

Without a murmur, the kafir climbed on to the bed and lay down, turning his face away so as not to offend his master. He was young, but his figure was manly rather than boyish. His body was long and lithe, all muscle and bone. It was apparent that his Pakistani handlers were experts. He had the look of a great athlete or perhaps a dancer. All his body hair had been removed. His skin looked waxed and polished. His hands were particularly fine, and his hair shimmered like strands of ebony silk. He looked pampered. He was sublime.

The Prince moved to sit so that he could admire the extraordinary creature that stretched out beside him like a cat in sunshine. It was so much more than beautiful. It was deliciously perfect. When he reached out to stroke its back, it arched beneath his hand with evident pleasure. He slowly pulled away the towel then explored the exquisite flesh like a connoisseur examining a rare and priceless work of art. Even up close, it was flawless. Perceiving the intention, the creature moved to lay face down, and clasped its hands above its head. The Prince ran his fingers down its spine, and smiled as the creature stretched contentedly. There was certainly something feline about it. His guts twisted. He was struggling to maintain his self-control. It had to be witchcraft. There was no other explanation.

He succumbed. He straddled the creature. His phenomenal erection breached the barrier with alarming ease. The descent was so swift and sudden. He almost lost his balance, but reached out to seize the creature's flesh, and saved himself from a fall. His sex was painfully engorged. He adjusted his position, following helplessly as his fearsome weapon ventured deeper into the vault. He crashed against the creature several times like a sledgehammer. There was a dull smack every time their flesh collided. The creature did nothing. It just lay there while the Prince slugged away like a punch-drunk fighter. More than irritated, the Prince sank his fingers into its flesh, determined to cause it pain. He felt it shudder. That was thrilling. He hurt it again. There was that addictive little cry. Suddenly, he wanted to experience something forbidden. This white thing was utterly forbidden. It was positively foul. It had been fucked more often than he cared to imagine, and always by righteous Believers. They had set the precedent. They used it without a second thought because its entire existence was nothing more than a matter of interpretation. It was a creature. It was a thing. It was neither male nor female. Did they ever have second thoughts? Did its beauty not persuade them that it was not just a worthless kafir captive that could be used and abused and thrown away? The Prince withdrew. He felt raw. He wanted to fuck it again so badly, but he wanted more than that. He wanted some cathartic mind-expanding experience. It was not just about the sex, but about changing the creature so fundamentally that he would never be attracted to it again. He wanted to ruin it, deface it, spoil it. He failed. He fucked it brutally, but conventionally until they were both drenched with sweat, panting like dogs, and too physically wasted to break away, but there was no climax, just violent agonising graft. A lifetime later, he collapsed across the creature, wrapping his arms tightly around it. He was embedded so deep inside it he did not know how to find his way back. And he had missed his flight, forgotten everything, everything but the joy of ravaging that beautiful body.

The kafir was stuffed full to bursting, and squeezed into submission. The weight of his master's body crushed him into the mattress. The powerful arms held him pinioned. He made no attempt to move. He could breathe. He needed nothing else. The moment he had dreamed about had come to pass. The mighty prince had thoroughly fucked him. It was everything he had hoped it would be. The raw power of the assault had erased every petty and inconsequential fuck he had ever had to endure before. Never had he felt so completely consumed by another man's passion. Was it love? He did not know the meaning of the word. All he knew was that his master's physical strength had burned him to the bone, and left him wanting more. He would have lain there locked in his arms until the world ended, and been content to burn in hell for the pleasure of that moment of perfect happiness.

Chapter 17

The kafir knew he had done nothing wrong, and fretted, overwhelmed by the invisible, but inescapable constraints that held him powerless. He could not run away even if he had wanted to. He had no thought to struggle though he feared the whip, and hated the pain he knew it would bring. It was inevitable. He understood that he would be whipped brutally and savagely, and it was his fate, his destiny, almost his necessity, as much as it was to give them pleasure. His body belonged to them. They used it entirely for their recreation. They had every right as they paid for the food that he ate, the clothes that he wore, and the roof that sheltered him. It was not in his power to consider, for the briefest moment, that he might deny them anything. But he thought about the pain, how bad it would be, and how bravely he must endure it.

It had become a custom. He was whipped slowly over perhaps an hour late every afternoon. It was always after sunset but before dinner. It might have been New York or Kathmandu. Wherever in the world they were, every afternoon, it was the same. He moved furniture to make space. He spread a plastic sheet on the floor. Then he took off his clothes. He stood bent forward, gripping the side of a table. One of his Pakistanis delivered the blows. Usually it was Aziz, but Waheed was always keen. Mahmood did not enjoy the chore, and happily deferred to his friends. They were directed to his buttocks and thighs. It was not a flogging. He was not being punished. It was done slowly and carefully like a sacred ritual. There were even candles, and the air was always thick with incense. There might be five minutes between each powerful blow, during which the kafir was allowed to gather his nerves, and wait in anticipation of the next, never knowing when it would come.

The whole procedure was supervised of Omar, the Prince's trusted right-hand man, who directed the Pakistanis, telling them when and where and how hard. And it was never private. There were always, at least, half a dozen men who drifted into the room to watch. They stood around smoking cigarettes, flinching as the whip cut into the soft flesh, gasping as the creature gasped, then slowly, reluctantly, the men disappeared back to their duties. Every day there was an audience. Afterwards, the kafir had to roll up the plastic sheet, then clean the whip, then go back with his Pakistanis.

166

The kafir understood why he was there. Prince Abdul Aziz had taken the time to politely explain the necessity for the marks. It was not about punishing him, but it was essential that he was marked. The livid red welts across his backside were a warning sign for those who saw them that they were offending God. Homosexuality was a sin. It was forbidden by God. The men were allowed to continue fucking him because he was an infidel, that was their right, but the Prince did not like it. Unfortunately, the bloody welts did not deter the legions of admirers. But the injuries made the Prince pause. He could not touch it. He might hunger for it like an addict, but it was forbidden to him now. The need that twisted in his gut like a festering wound was his penance.

Each blow was agony. The long pauses were a bitter torture as the kafir waited, barely able to breathe, expecting at every moment that he would be hurt again. Just when his sanity began to crack under the strain, the whip would cut into him like a knife. He was allowed to cry out. They liked him to moan. He could weep as much as he liked. Screaming was forbidden. There was a device that they used to make him quiet, which was worse than any whip so he never screamed. He never ever screamed.

After the show, the creature was quickly cleaned up and dressed to attend the Prince at dinner. Later, it would be made available to bathe the Prince, and either dress him for final prayers or for bed. They were like a divorced couple forced to live in the same house. The Prince loathed having the creature anywhere near him, but could not bear to be parted from it. In the privacy of the bathroom, he crudely examined its backside to make sure it had fresh wounds. Once, he sent for Omar to complain that the creature had not been beaten harshly enough. He never had to complain again. It felt like righteous anger, but was only jealousy.

Omar recorded the procedure on a digital camera so that the Prince always had proof that his orders were being carried out exactly as he would wish. The camera was small and discreet. Initially, the creature had no idea it was being filmed, but its every grimace and shudder and tear were recorded in close-up so that the Prince could gauge whether its suffering was absolutely genuine. Omar felt some compassion. He could see that the creature was confused and often distraught. He could not explain, but now and then, he took the time to reassure it with a pat on the shoulder. It would look up at him with eyes awash with tears. For Omar, the whole ordeal was distasteful, but the infidel could not be spared. There was to be no mercy. That was haram.

*

Later that afternoon, she returned to the house. She had no answers, only more questions than she could ever ask. He was laid out on the sofa, on his side, and probably as comfortable as he could possibly be with his extensive wounds. She gave him a glass of milk, which she had already drugged. To avoid the discomfort of watching him kneel down, she had pressed the glass into his hands before he was fully awake. While he gathered his senses, and rearranged his blankets, she turned away to switch on the television. It was Songs of Praise. It used to be on at prime time after six o'clock, but had crept earlier, almost as if the BBC was embarrassed to have to broadcast a Christian programme. Since 9/11 there had been lots of well-made and well-intentioned programmes about Islam, but Christianity seemed to have become a dirty word. She had always believed that the BBC were anti-Semitic and anti-American so it should not have been a surprise that they might also be anti-Christian.

"Please, talk to me. I know you can speak. You have bad dreams. You talk in your sleep. Why won't you talk to me?" She felt helpless. "Do you actually know what strawberries are?"

She was talking too fast again, and it just made his head spin. He glanced at her, wondering if she would pause to inhale. It did not seem likely. He shut her out, and turned his attention back to the glass of milk. It was not pink.

"You do prefer the strawberry milkshake," she said with relief. "You see! I'm not a complete idiot. Some things I do know." She watched him finish the drugged milk then rose to collect the glass.

He released it, and bowed his head respectfully, then turned to watch her walk away. She returned moments later with a can of the delicious milkshake. He was gathering his limbs to kneel and bow, but she quickly forced the can into his hands then walked back to her chair. He watched her for a moment in absolute confusion, then opened the can and drank.

"Okay," she said. She watched him with a mixture of emotions. "So you need to explain to me who you are. Your name would be a good place to start."

He stopped drinking, and stared at the floor. Every muscle stiffened. If it were possible, he might have grown paler. For a moment, he waited breathlessly for her to continue, but understood that she had made herself perfectly plain. He shivered visibly, and shook his head then lay down on his side, and folded an arm across to obscure his face.

She moved closer, and went down onto her knees beside him. It was easy to lift his arm away. He was weak and pliable. He did not resist. "It's alright. You're safe now. You don't need to be afraid. You're safe here. I won't let anyone hurt you." She gazed at his face, moved by his obvious distress. "You can tell me anything. Who would I tell? I just want to help you." She stroked his hand then rubbed and patted his shoulder comfortingly. "You can tell me."

He closed his eyes, and tried to turn his face into the cushions.

"There's something very wrong here." She ran her fingers through his hair then brushed his cheek gently. He was rigid with tension. "What happened to you? Someone has hurt you so badly. You can tell me. I want to help you. I will protect you." Her voice was now as soft and cooing as a dove's. Her heart was literally swelling in her chest. "I will protect you. I promise. Please, tell me your name?"

His face crumpled, and he sighed raggedly, but he could not do it.

"What is your name? Why won't you tell me?" She realised even this was too much to ask, and that she must respect his limitations. "It's alright. I won't ask you any more questions." She rubbed his shoulder again then pulled the covers higher. He looked as if he was almost in tears. His face had crumpled up into an ugly bawling grimace. His whole body trembled. She felt ashamed. "I'm sorry." She patted him sympathetically then bent down to kiss his forehead. "I'm sorry. I won't ask. I just don't understand." She wanted to kiss him again. If he had been a cat, she could have wrapped him up in her arms, and stroked him and kissed him to her heart's content, but not a naked young man.

She backed away and sat down. She already regretted saying that she would not ask him anything. Part of her hoped he would quickly forget, however that did not seem likely.

It took him a while to recover his composure. It took longer for him to sit slumped over the armrest. He arranged the sheet and blankets with particular care. She was a woman. He was very uncomfortable in her presence. Being naked, made it worse. That she was a doctor did not lessen his embarrassment. He stared at her as she stared fixedly out of the window, convinced he was about to faint, and terrified of being helpless. He tried to calculate the risk involved with telling her anything. He was not sure whether he was more afraid for her or for himself.

"It's alright," she said reassuringly, turning slowly to meet his gaze.

He drew a hand across his mouth. Even after the milkshake, his mouth felt dry. His heart was emitting bolts of pain across his chest, which worried him, but it seemed inconsequential compared to everything else.

She leaned forward, sensing that he was about to say something, almost trembling with anticipation.

"Please? I may not. I cannot…" He stopped, gasping like an asthmatic. He breathed deeply, watching her, keenly aware of her curiosity. His nerves were not good, but he had a plan. There had always been a plan. Yet he accepted that he needed help. He did not really know anything about the woman, but he did not know anyone else at all. "I have no name."

She bit her lip, not actually able to believe that he had spoken, and unconvinced by his words. Easy ridicule filled her thoughts. She was so close to belittling him. Only his wretched despair made her silent. The pain that she saw in his face was so real she had to believe him. She wanted to say that everyone had a name. Even the most ignorant beggar had a name. Most babies had names before they were born. Everyone had a name. Yet his face assured her beyond all reasonable doubt that he was being sincere. "I'm sorry. I don't know what to say. I don't understand," she said quietly and respectfully.

He moved with great difficulty to set his feet on the floor. He remained slumped over the armrest. The exertion left him breathless again and sweating, but he gazed at her with great determination. "Please, I have no name."

"But," she could not help herself, "everyone has a name."

He shook his head, devastated. "Please, no."

"You're joking, right?" She could not imagine what he meant. "Everyone has a name."

Feeling diminished, he stared at the floor. He did not know how to explain what he was.

"Is it amnesia?" she asked hopefully. If he was mentally ill then she knew she would have to call the police. Even someone mildly delusional exceeded all her capabilities. "Maybe you just don't remember?"

He shook his head.

She began to understand his silence. "I guess there are a lot of things you need to explain."

He sat before her, swathed in sheets and blankets, yet all she saw were the tattoos and tribal markings and the dazzling jewels. She was embarrassed. It was about sex. It was some weird cult thing involving sex.

He nodded slowly.

She was at a loss to know what to say. They could sit for hours with her adamant that he must have a name, and him staunchly denying it. She was reluctant to push him. He might stop talking again, and then she would never learn anything. She looked at him and frowned. "I wish I knew what to say." It seemed so pathetic. "But you are safe here. You know that. I'll take care of you. It'll be alright. All that is important now is that you get well."

He slowly sank down on to the sofa, and pulled the covers around him. Her words were nice. The reassurance was incredibly comforting, but he felt completely alone.

She collected the shirt that she had bought for him from the kitchen. As he struggled with the drink cans, she did not even bother giving him the packet. She pulled it apart then opened out the shirt, removing the pins and the clips and all the tissue paper and card. It was only when she actually offered it to him that she wondered if it was the right size. His neck was probably the only part of his body she was not familiar with. He gazed at the garment. His confusion and anxiety were clearly reflected on his face. Her heart fluttered again. To kiss him – she would have given her soul to be able to kiss him then have him forget. Frowning, she turned away to hide her embarrassment, then focused on unbuttoning the shirt. It was a good shirt. It was a delicate shade of pink. She opened it out, and held it up for him. "Up you get. Let's get you dressed." She stood behind the shirt. Her face still burned. She really did not want to see him standing up, completely naked, but for the jewellery and the tattoos.

He rose slowly to his full height, which allowed him to see her blushes. Now, it was her turn to stare at the floor. He was as weak as a kitten, and every movement hurt the tender new skin growing across his back. With gritted teeth, he carefully inserted one arm into the shirt. The other was almost too painful to contemplate, but he persevered, breathless and sweating. It took him more than a minute to regain his composure. He stood mute as she moved to quickly and prudishly button the shirt, and make him presentable again. She held his arm as he sank carefully back on to the sofa then slumped across the armrest. He was as white as snow. His eyes were raw. It took him some minutes to recover, but his heart steadied, and his hands eventually stopped shaking.

She left him watching a programme about antiques. There were things she needed to do. Being alone with him when he was conscious made her feel gauche and embarrassed. It was easy to find something to keep her busy, but impossible to forget his eyes or the texture of his skin or his soft voice.

She remained outside. It seemed safer. There were shoots on plants that had recently seemed dead. The frogs were slowly disappearing from the ponds. The newts were still courting. She watched several females laying eggs then wrapping them securely amongst the weeds. It was always a great temptation to bring the weed into the scullery, and to the safety of tanks where the baby newts could hatch out without being in danger. She had always been very successful with the baby newts. After the failure of her plan of not interfering, and consequently not having a single tadpole, she was seriously tempted to interfere with the newts. There were no dead bodies. She could hear hedgehogs in the undergrowth. Earlier in the evening, she had heard a lot of birds, but by ten o'clock there was not a sound beyond the odd hoot of an owl.

He was asleep. The excitement of the antiques had worn him out. She placed her hand on his forehead as much to test that he was genuinely asleep as to feel his temperature. He was recovering. She was almost shocked. Just remembering the state of his back when he had first arrived made her hands tremble again. She had been lucky. She did not believe that she deserved such luck. He should have died. She had no skill. All that she had was her bloody minded determination not to ever give up. She was too insecure to believe she had done anything but harm. The dead hedgehog had been her fault; the newts the week before and every bad thing ever. It was guilt that kept her a prisoner on her own land. Her inability to communicate made her captivity solitary confinement. All that she knew of the world came via television and newspapers, and she was too cynical to believe any of it.

*

He stood there like a statue as he had been taught to do. Almost every evening, when his master was in residence, the kafir served him at table. Only when there were visitors was he excused. It was another of his increasing number of duties. The Prince was demanding more and more of his time. With his hands clasped behind him, and his gaze fixed on the Prince's glittering ring, he was the perfect servant. His clothes were made by the tailors of the future king of England, but that meant absolutely nothing to him. Every evening, he was dressed in a black morning coat with tails over a black satin waistcoat and trousers, a hand stitched white linen shirt, with a black cummerbund, a fashionable black tie with tiny polka dots, handmade leather shoes, and mother of pearl cufflinks, and white gloves that buttoned at the wrist. Every day, he had new gloves. Beneath the carefully tailored shirt, he wore the thick leather collar. It was now a much heavier collar with cold brass fittings. It was a thing of beauty, and it never came off. Across his backside were a dozen fresh welts from the whip. The pain had become as constant as his companions, and took its toll on his nerves. But with his master, he affected the manners and poise of an officer with a stiff back, jutting chin and emotionless visage. In the sombre costume, he looked considerably older, but no less handsome. His long hair that usually flowed across his shoulders was slicked back with cream, and neatly bound with black ribbon in the style of a bull-fighter. It did not matter how hot it was in that room or how tired he might be, it was his duty to stand there in absolute silence.

Seated in a throne-like chair before a table that was twenty metres long, the Prince dined alone. He wore the long formal robes of his ancestors, the beard of his prophet and simply exuded the wealth and courage and intelligence that ran in his veins. He ate from gold plates. The food was varied and international. More than a dozen dishes were prepared at every meal to tempt just one man's palette. Yet he was always more interested in his books. He loved poetry. He loved reading. These quiet evenings were precious to him.

From his place beside the chair, the kafir watched. His eyes never strayed from the Prince's hands. They never made eye contact. They never spoke to each other. The Prince never acknowledged that the kafir existed, but there was a recognised code. If the Prince wanted to see a dish of food then a finger pointed subtly, and the kafir stepped up promptly to fetch it. If the Prince's napkin slipped from his lap then it was the kafir, who came and knelt down to pick it up then graciously offered it back. Even when they were close enough to feel the other's breath, and hear their hearts beating, not a word passed between them. The Prince took back his napkin or his book, and the kafir withdrew to stand silently in his place. The atmosphere was always electric. They did not need words.

If the Prince was hungry then he ate voraciously, and the meal ended quickly, but more often than not, a dinner could last up to three hours. No one else ever entered the room. For the kafir, it was arduous. He had to keep his wits about him. If he missed a cue then he would be in trouble, but he had never missed a cue. He never made a mistake. It would have broken his heart to do anything that might offend his master even though he knew that it was his master, who insisted that he was marked every day with a camel whip.

The meal was finished only when the Prince laid his napkin across his plate. The kafir would move immediately to stand behind the chair, and when he perceived that his master was ready to rise, he drew it back. It was a great, big, awkward chair, but he always managed to lift it away so that his master was not inconvenienced for even a moment. From the Pakistanis, the kafir had the hope of scraps of food that were his reward for good behaviour. From the Prince, there was not a crumb. The laden table, still groaning with food, was left for other vultures to clear. The starving kafir had to follow his prince.

Chapter 18

The week started with a nice warm day. She threw back the curtains, and gazed out at the view like a queen surveying her realm. From the front room windows, she could see to the distant horizon, and knew that there was not another living human being in her sight. The yellow rape fields gleamed in the sunshine. The sky was an immense vault of blue without a single cloud. She knew it was just a trick of the topography, but she puffed out her chest, and rested her hands akimbo, and smiled. Yes, at that moment, she was a queen.

She turned to survey the room. There were numerous cats. There was also the young man. He was sitting on the sofa, leaning across the armrest for support. One of her sheets was drawn across him. The pale pink shirt set off his eyes beautifully. It was surprisingly less awkward for her to have his flesh covered up. She was not caught staring at him with her mouth open, almost too stunned by his beauty and adornments to remember to breathe. His face was a better colour, and less drawn now that his fluid levels had improved, but he needed a shave, and to have his hair washed. She felt diminished. He also needed strength and fortitude, which she simply did not possess.

"How are you feeling today?" she asked, and tried to smile.

He glanced towards her nervously then lowered his gaze back to the floor. He managed to shake his head.

She noticed he was trembling. She quickly took in the condition of the blankets and the cushions, and knew that he had been on his feet. "You're very weak, you know. You shouldn't expect to be up and about quite so quickly." She tried another smile. "It's been a week. You had a fever. It'll take time."

He nodded only because he felt she required a response. He did not lift his gaze. He was barely breathing.

She wondered if he was afraid of her. It was so much easier to stare at him, and not feel like an inappropriate adult with a child, now that he wore a shirt and kept the sheet drawn across his legs. Not that he had the body of a child, but it was in his manner and his innocence. "It'll take time. You've been very ill." She tried yet another smile. "Would you like something to eat? You must be hungry."

He shook his head, and still did not look at her.

Rather annoyed, she walked away. She fed the cats then sat down to eat a proper breakfast and take her pills. It was important. It did not matter whether she felt ill. It was the routine. It was paying attention to the details.

And amongst the details that morning was giving him a bed-bath. She gave him a can of milkshake then regretted her generosity because she had not crushed any pills. It was also the last can so she would have to go to the shops. Quite suddenly, she resented the time she was investing in him.

"Can you stand up?" she asked.

He had just opened the can, and was about to take a sip. He froze. His eyes swept across her then focused on the floor. He slowly lowered the can, and waited for her to explain.

She repeated the question. "Can you stand up? I'll help you. It just seems silly that there's a bathroom across the hall. As you get stronger then it'll get easier, but we could start right now. I'll help you. I don't want you to fall down, and I know, for sure, that you'd rather go to the bathroom yourself than have me fussing around you."

He had not moved. There was not the least change in his expression. He stared at the floor. But he was listening.

She was more annoyed with herself then with him. This silence was obviously his usual manner. She had no right to be cross with him, but she felt that he was not grateful enough. Carefully, she reached down, and took the can out of his grasp. He let it go. He might have blinked. "You can drink this later." She made sure she was smiling even though he was not looking at her. A smiley voice was more attractive than a bossy one. "Let's get you cleaned up." Bigger smile. "You know that you'll feel 100% better when you've been to the bathroom and had a wash."

Despite all his confusion and anxiety, he could not find fault with her logic. He took a long deep breath then started forward. The taut new skin across his back made every movement difficult, but he leaned forward over his knees, and used his legs to lift him off the sofa. Before he was upright, he was sweating and shivering.

"It'll get easier, I promise," she said soothingly. She clasped his left arm and, more or less, forced him to accept her assistance.

He was only marginally taller than her, and they were so close. He could see that she was nervous and distracted. He recognised that she was afraid. It took him a little longer to comprehend that she was afraid of him. Never in his life had he imagined that he might inspire fear. Why was she afraid? He had not done anything. He did not know her. He did not remember. Was he supposed to remember? Was that why she was so afraid? He wanted to tell her that he did not remember, but he could not. He was not ready. He still had no idea why he was inside this house or with this woman.

She felt he was staring at her, but when she lifted her head, he had withdrawn again. She tried another smile. "Are you ready?" she asked.

He nodded hesitantly. The eyes flashed.

He was surprisingly heavy, but after the first few steps he found his balance, and would have tried to walk unaided, but she held on to him. They walked together slowly. He was grateful. She was relieved, and then afraid because she was making him independent. Her control was slipping away. Being mobile would improve his confidence. That was all part of being independent. He needed be independent if he was ever going to be able to talk about what had happened to him. He had to be able to explain or it would destroy him. He said that he had no name. Everyone had a name. Someone had beaten the crap out of him, but he had more than just physical wounds. He was so damaged and yet so lovely. It was in the silence. The silence: it was a door she could not open. He was a puzzle she could not solve.

"Let's go," she said quietly. "That's it, just one step at a time. You can climb every mountain if you take one step at a time."

They reached the bathroom. She pushed the door open, and let him take hold of the doorframe then she backed away, and let him go on alone.

She lingered a moment, rationalised that he would probably be ages, then went back out to the kitchen. At the table, she sat counting out her pills. She crushed three painkillers. Obviously, he was in pain. The wounds on his back were healing, but still qualified as a major injury. She was being kind. She was doing the right thing. It just felt like expediency. She poured the powder into his opened can then stirred it around carefully with the handle of a teaspoon. He would be grateful. Of course, he would be grateful.

At the sound of the bathroom door opening, she hurried into the hall. His shirt was wet. The sheet was wet. He looked pale and exhausted. She took hold of his arm, grinning triumphantly. It did not matter that he had made a mess. It was proof positive that he had made an effort.

"That's great," she said. "You've done very well. It will get easier, honestly. I know it doesn't feel like it, but you're getting better."

He sort of nodded. He did not dare look at her. Walking took all his concentration.

At the sofa, she let him take the lead. She supported him. He found his balance. He made the decisions. His back still screamed with pain as he lowered himself down. His face went white. The pain was excruciating. For a long time, he sat upright, unable to think about moving. Only when the pain began to ebb did he carefully lean down across the armrest which enabled him to relax.

His obvious suffering was daunting, but it eased her guilt about the pills. She pressed the can into his hand then dithered then retreated across the room. He drank slowly and carefully. From her chair, she watched his every move, hoping he would look at her, hoping he would speak. He did neither. He was visibly exhausted. She felt guilty again, and turned away to stare at the television. Had it been on all night again? She was sure that she had switched it off. Rooney's metatarsal still dominated the news. Bored, she went out to the kitchen, stood at the sink, and stared out of the window. There was so much to do.

The car started. The card worked. She still did not quite believe how much money she had in the bank, but she had no intention of questioning it. Anyone monitoring her spending, which, according to the media, was the whole point of loyalty cards, would have been struck by her sudden need for men's clothes and baby food. Usually, it took five minutes to unload the car, and it was 99% cat food. Now, it was a major chore, and it was still all for her guests.

He was asleep. She gently felt his forehead then pressed two fingers against his neck to monitor his pulse. Asleep, he looked like a child. He was lovely and harmless and manageable. Someone somewhere must have loved him. Someone must be looking for him. It was inconceivable that he had been abandoned in her garden by strangers. He had been brought there. She remembered his immaculate shoes. He had not walked across the fields for miles to come and find her garden, and then laid down beside the pond, not with those shoes and those injuries. Someone had brought him there. Had they meant her to find him and take him in? Had he been abandoned there to die? There were so many questions. She did not know how to ask them, and was loath to explain about the wheelbarrow and everything else. How could she explain that she had dragged him across a gravel path after dumping him like compost from her wheelbarrow? How could she justify abandoning him on the floor when he was already so badly injured? That she did not know excused nothing. She should have known. She should have checked. He might have died because of her negligence.

He slept on, safe from her curiosity.

She spent most of the morning mowing the lawn then working from the back of the garden towards the house. There were wild 'forget me nots' flourishing in the borders. The foxgloves were shooting skyward. Peonies were just about to burst into flower. Groundsel had appeared almost overnight to fill every nook and cranny. The dramatic changes brought about by only a few days of good weather filled her heart with joy. Even the cats had moved outside. She disturbed several sleepy characters in the undergrowth. Like the hedgehogs, they had trodden down little nests to curl up in, which explained why they had been coming into the house with old burrs and last year's seed heads stuck in their fur.

By two o'clock, she had managed to stop thinking about him, but it was more an act of will than inclination. She was tired. She needed to eat something.

He and three of her cats were watching television. He had changed channels. She wondered again about men and remotes. But was he really interested in antiques?

She made a pot of tea, and a plate of cheese sandwiches. There were enough for two. She filled the coffee table with cups and saucers and tea plates. He stared at the floor. He declined to acknowledge her. Becalmed by the sunshine and the joy of gardening, she did not press the point. She went out to the kitchen to fetch him a bottle of baby food, a can of milkshake and a teaspoon. She gave them to him. He gave her the remote. She retreated to her own chair, flicked through half a dozen channels, found the tennis, smiled, then poured a cup of tea.

Nothing troubled her except for two female cats, who seemed to be able to smell cheese from a mile away. She had never had a male cat that liked cheese. One of the females even liked very rich blue cheese. She was not sure whether it was actually good for them, but all her cats were fit and well. Some of them were nearly twenty years old. Her Vet always commented on how well she looked after them. That was always very flattering. She felt that she was a failure on so many levels so to be praised on one that was so important meant a lot.

The tennis was great. The weather in Paris was glorious. There were some of the best players in the world out on court. It was the beginning of the second week. Everyone had found their stride. Even the girls were making loud grunts and growls as they hit the ball. Had Navratilova done that? She could not remember. There were still empty seats. Perhaps, there were not enough French players to lure in the crowds?

The young man watched. He did not fidget or raise clenched fists in triumph or despair, but he remained mute and motionless, and did not distract her from her obvious enjoyment of the matches. Once, later in the afternoon, he rose slowly to his feet then walked stiffly out to the bathroom. She had hurried to steady him as he stood up, and rose again to help him sit back down. It was very obviously painful, but he did not complain, and she could not give him any more of the pills than he was already taking.

By then, the spare sandwiches were beginning to curl. She took them out to the kitchen. The ginger glutton wanted food, but turned his nose up at the cheese. Cats were certainly intelligent. They knew what they liked. They knew where they were comfortable. If human beings were wiped out, it would be the cats that ruled the world.

She went back into the front room. The sunshine poured in through the big windows. It was hard to remember that a week ago it had been too cold and miserable to go outside. Now, she did not need the central heating on during the day.

"Okay, so we have established that you can talk. Aren't you going to speak to me ever again?" She leaned over the back of the sofa, smiling kindly, holding a glass of milk, but not offering it to him. It was a carrot.

He looked at the bribe. In his nice new shirt, he almost looked normal if anyone with that face and those eyes could be considered normal.

"You speak in a foreign language when you're dreaming." She reached out to feel his forehead again. He was too polite to pull away, but he stared resolutely at the floor. "It sounded like something from the Middle East. Do you speak other languages?" She still smiled. "You obviously have a natural aptitude for languages so you must talk, and actually talk quite a lot."

He wanted the drink, but could not move to take it.

"Why won't you talk to me?" It was a very direct question, almost an accusation, but her tone remained warm and friendly. "You really don't have a name?"

He blinked then shook his head slightly. He could not look at her.

Her imagination had already supplied several suggestive scenarios, but none of them were repeatable. She felt like an inappropriate adult again. She was certainly disapproving. The evidence was that he was sexually active, which at his age was quite normal, but it was not normal sex. She kept returning to the weird homosexual sadomasochistic cult. "What is it you're so afraid of? It can't be me. I want to help you. You're in some kind of trouble, aren't you? There must be someone I can call for you? What about your parents?" His head went down. She sighed. "I just want to help you."

"Thank you," he said, but it was hardly more than a whisper.

She suspected that he was being insincere, but his frailty protected him. She was at a loss to know how to proceed against the wall he had erected. "Please, tell me what happened to you?"

He flinched then shook his head slowly once.

She felt rebuffed. He had taken control of the situation. Feeling provoked, she changed her tactics, leaning forward to hold the glass almost within reach.

He relented, surrendering the high ground to accept the bribe. He dared not turn to look at her. He had to believe that she intended to give him the drink, but irritation made her move it away. The fleeting look he gave her was surprisingly reproachful. His eyes glowed like hot coals. She wilted instantly. Her hand trembled. She watched helplessly as he leaned closer to make up the extra few inches, and she could not cheat him again. Once had been bad enough. She pressed the glass into his hand then drew away to watch him recover. He was as white as a sheet.

"You've been in the Middle East?" she asked casually. "It didn't sound like Hebrew, but then I don't know Hebrew. Was it Iraq?" She stared at him, trying to read something into his blank face. "Were you a hostage?" Her sympathy increased a thousand fold. "It's a bloody nightmare over there. Did someone do that to you in Iraq?"

He had raised the glass to his lips, but lowered it. He wanted her to stop talking, but he was powerless. Taking a long deep breath, he turned to stare at her, searching in her face for the answers or at least for some compassion. He had come so far to tell the truth, but realised that he did not know what was true or false or just his hopeful imagination. And he still did not know who she was or why he was there, wherever there was. Despite all the drugs that he knew she was feeding him, he was afraid. He had never been so far from feeling safe. He did not know what he was expected to do. He understood only that for the first time in his life he was completely on his own. Everything that he had ever been taught seemed suddenly, utterly pointless.

"You don't have to say anything, but it would be so much easier if I knew what happened. I want to help you. Haven't I proved that?" She could not conceal the hurt in her voice.

He merely lowered his gaze, though it felt like a confession.

"Is it amnesia?" she asked again, reluctant to give him such an easy way out, but desperate to make him say something - anything.

He just stared at the floor. He was not ready.

She tried to imagine what he was thinking, but he was just too alien, too extreme in her quiet, reclusive world. Sid Vicious would have been easier, and she was younger then. She could predict his behaviour, and understand his motives even if she disapproved of all of them. Her guest was an enigma. She kept thinking that he was at best just extremely promiscuous or at worst a cold-blooded sexual predator, but she knew that was too easy, and she really did not want it to be true. The maternal instinct kept sparking into life, and it melted all her prejudice. Having him in a shirt made her so much more comfortable. And he had such a lovely face, and the bluest blue eyes. Why would someone have whipped him so badly that he had almost died? In Iraq, they just chopped people's heads off. It seemed to be almost a daily occurrence. There was no mention of flogging. He became a victim again at such moments, then she remembered the ornate sheath and the jewellery, and he was as quickly tainted and condemned. If only he had been a cat or a hedgehog. She could have stroked and petted, and spoken in soothing tones, and expressed everything that she felt in her heart without needing real language or any explanations. Why was it so important that he explain? She was not ready yet to acknowledge her fears.

He glanced across to see if she was looking at him, and being discovered he stared back at the floor.

She sighed unhappily. His reticence was infuriating. "I've seen you naked. I have washed and nursed you. I've seen it all. You can tell me anything."

He did not respond.

"You are very handsome." She hesitated and smiled, hoping to flatter him into looking at her, but his head bowed lower. "You obviously have money. Your clothes are very expensive. I'm sure I couldn't begin to guess how much that wristwatch cost, and everything else?" She ran out of words, and blushed as the images glittered and gleamed in her mind's eye. Speaking casually about his private parts was still too difficult to contemplate. "All that jewellery and those decorations: that sort of thing must be really expensive. I've never seen anything like it before." She tried to smile, but it was weak and wobbly. "So you obviously have money. Someone somewhere must be worried about you. Do you have a girlfriend? Are you married? Or a boyfriend? That's okay. Honestly, I don't have a problem with that. There must be someone that I can call, who will look after you? You need someone to look after you. Surely, you want to go home? I know you don't want to be here. I understand. It's a normal reaction. You are getting better, but it'll be weeks before you can safely look after yourself."

He glanced across the room again rather slyly, but dropped his gaze as soon as she looked at him.

"You're sick," she insisted, carried away by her own authority. "If you're in trouble then I'll help you, but you have to explain all this. You're being totally unfair to me. I'm not asking for all your darkest secrets, I just want to know what is going on. I've spent money. I nearly killed myself getting you back here. I've nursed you all this time. Why won't you talk to me? What have I done to you? Are you in trouble? Wouldn't it be better to call the police? If someone's hurt you?" She sighed, and shook her head unhappily. "You are in trouble. You must be in trouble. Is that why I can't take you to hospital? I think I should make you go." She smiled when he looked up, suddenly alarmed. "You're not strong enough to stop me. I could drag you out, and put you in my car."

He shook his head slowly, lips compressed, brow deeply furrowed, but still said nothing.

"Is all this about drugs? Are you wanted by the police? Is that it?"

He shuddered, but merely shook his head, and stared back at the floor. The idea of being examined by strangers appalled him. That a woman had touched him was bad enough, but he knew, he understood instinctively that she hated doing it as much as he loathed it being done.

She moved to kneel down in front of him, which forced him to shrink back against the cushions. She stared up into his face. She was so close. She could see his luminous eyes and long eyelashes. She could have kissed him easily. She could have done worse. "It's alright. Don't worry. I'm not going to hurt you." Pulling the blankets up around him, she was disappointed to see nothing but apprehension in his face. "You could lie to me. I wouldn't know. If it made things easier for you, then that's okay. I want to help you. That's all I want. What is it that you are so afraid of? It can't be me." She laughed at the very idea of it, but he did not laugh. "I'm sorry. I wish I knew how to help you, but really I don't. You have to help me so that I can help you." She reached out tentatively to stroke the wayward strands of hair away from his eyes. "You're very attractive, but it's like you're a child. Yet how can you be a child with that body. You must be easily in your mid-twenties. And you understand everything that I'm saying, so what is it that's frightened you? Who hurt you? You know who it was! Can't you tell me? Can't you tell anyone? You nearly died.

You must know how bad it was. It must still hurt terribly. Why would you protect the man who did that to you?" She gazed at him, marvelling at his lovely face, and she longed for him to look at her so that she could swim in those big blue eyes, but he ignored her, staring down at nothing. She sighed again. "It's alright. I won't make you leave or call the police. You can stay here until you are strong enough to move on."

He sucked air into his lungs, and shifted uncomfortably then his blazing eyes locked on her like car headlights. "Please? Please, I cannot tell you," he said, his voice breaking. He searched her face for answers, but found none. "Please? I do not remember."

Her heart fluttered. Not remembering his name was bad enough, but if he did not remember anything then it had to be amnesia. While she sat there quietly panicking, she covered her eyes to avoid his gaze, and regulated her breathing, and accepted that she was totally out of her depth. Slowly and methodically, she reviewed what she actually knew. That was scary. "Okay, so you have amnesia. You don't remember your name or where you live. It has to be drugs. Someone's beaten the crap out of you. Is it what they call a 'bad trick'? But that wouldn't make you lose your memory unless it was some temporary reaction to shock. I don't know." She sighed in despair. "Are you seeing a doctor? Is it, maybe, a side effect of some medication? Has this happened before?" She lowered her hands then gazed into the lovely blue eyes with bitter disappointment. "It's drugs, isn't it! You're an addict!" She tried to smile bravely. "Do you need methadone? What is it? Crack? Cocaine? Heroin?"

Her words hurt him, but the look that she gave him pierced his heart. It seemed so unfair. To be condemned so completely on no evidence at all, destroyed his naïve hopes. How could he overcome all his disadvantages and so much prejudice? He did not know how to answer her. He was simply not equipped to eloquently defend himself.

She confidently assumed that his discomfort was because she had so perceptively unravelled his mystery. "So it is cocaine? Crack's lethal. You'd have needle marks from heroin. You're covered in artwork, but none of that is new. I didn't find any signs of recent needle marks. So it is cocaine." She watched unhappily as he lowered his gaze and frowned. He was upset, which genuinely surprised her. "I don't really know how these things work, but you know, it's all on the TV these days. There are all sorts of weird and not very wonderful things on the TV."

She was talking quickly again. He glanced at the television then chewed his lip, and waited for her to draw a breath. He felt it was imperative to correct her before she became obsessed. Drugs were always denied him.

He needed to explain. It surprised him how much he actually wanted to tell her that she was completely wrong. "Please?" He looked at her again, waiting for her to listen. "Please? Drugs are forbidden."

She stared at him, open-mouthed, surprised that he had actually said something. After so much silence, it was shocking. "Okay." She was almost lost for words.

"Please? It is not drugs," he repeated slowly, speaking carefully, remembering to inhale. "Please? He will not tolerate addicts. You must believe me. It is important that you believe me."

She felt the pressure. She almost said that, of course, she believed him, but it made her angry because she did not. She did not trust him.

He stared at her while she struggled against her prejudices. While she felt guilty, she was unable to look at him, but as soon as her morality reasserted itself, then he was the one who lowered his gaze, and silently deferred.

She wanted to explain that she simply did not understand, but said instead: "I do want to help you. I really do. You're just so different. It's been a bit of a shock for me. I live very quietly here. Well, you've seen what it is like. You're rather exotic by local standards. We're very provincial. Country people, you know. The jewellery and all that sort of thing: we just don't do that around here. I'm sure it's not all that unusual at all, especially in London or somewhere like that. It's just that I've never seen it before, not in real life anyway. There was something on TV once, a long time ago, but nothing like yours, like what you have had done, which is, I'm sure, absolutely beautiful artistically speaking, but it is just not my thing." She smiled bravely, knew she was blushing, but smiled anyway until her face ached.

He blinked slowly. There were too many words again. "Please? Where is your husband?" he asked quietly.

She froze in alarm. The question was so unexpected. For a minute she forgot to breathe. Why would he ask her about that? Every instinct warned her to beware. Suddenly, he was the enemy. It was all she could do to stand there. She was more than afraid, more than suspicious. Who was he and what did he know?

Realising, almost at once, that he had miscalculated, he lowered his gaze. He should not have dared to ask a question. What right did he have to ever ask a question?

His anxiety and frailty eased her fears. What could he possibly know? Breathing again, she rubbed her chest, and listened to her heart beating.

Then she sighed. "My husband does not live here." She waited nervously for him to look up, but he was shivering. "He's not here," she said firmly. "Did you come here to meet my husband? I don't understand." Again he cowered. "Did you know my husband? He never lived here. He's never been here. Did you know him?" She waited for a response then shook her head, and shrugged stiffly, then stared at him. "You can't possibly have known him. I don't understand. Did someone send you here to ask me about him? Please, you must tell me!"

He looked up fleetingly then drew away. "Please? Please no. I cannot." He shook his head. "I cannot."

"My husband's dead. I know he's dead. Why did you ask me about him? He was a complete bastard, but he's definitely dead. I know he is dead." She was actually trembling. "Is that why you are here? Is this about my husband?"

He cowered, broken by fear, but compelled by her absolute authority. "Please? You are a woman," he whispered. "Women must not live alone."

She filled her lungs then exhaled to settle her nerves. He did not know anything. She almost wilted with relief. His explanation was still puzzling. She tried to think of a reason that might make this true. "No. I live alone. As you see, there is no one else here. That's actually insulting, you know! It's quite normal for women to live alone. Men also live alone. It's very popular these days. That's probably why there's always a housing shortage."

He frowned, and shook his head, but dared not look at her.

"Okay. Yes, that really is annoying. You can't remember who you are or where you live, but you've got the nerve to make some crack about women being inferior."

He winced. "Please? I do not understand."

"No, you don't. You really don't!" She was livid.

"Please? Please, do not be angry with me."

She drew away, and walked across the room to stare out of the big windows. There was the immense sky and the acres of yellow rape. It was a lovely day. But now, she was too angry to notice any of it.

He moved awkwardly on the sofa, checked his shirt buttons, and arranged the covers over his legs, then breathed deeply. He felt her anger from across the room. He felt compelled. "Please? I am sorry. Please? I cannot. I do not understand."

She turned slowly to stare at him for a moment, which made him shift uncomfortably. She was really very upset. It took a long time for her temper to subside. In her chest, she could feel her heart racing. She felt sick and dizzy and angry and ridiculously afraid. At the mere mention of her husband, she was overwhelmed with anxiety. Rubbing her chest, she watched him shiver with apprehension.

He had made a mistake. He literally cowered.

"But you must remember something! You can't possibly have forgotten everything."

He shook his head. "Please? I do not understand. I cannot…"

"You can," she insisted, then tried to smile. "I want to help you. You have to trust me."

He flinched.

"You've been very ill. Let me help you. There must be something that you can tell me? You can't possibly have forgotten everything." She started towards him. "Just talk to me! You have to tell me what's going on."

"Please? I have not forgotten," he protested. He was frightened. He was not strong enough to fight with her. "Please? I do not have a name. I do not know why I am here. I do not understand." He was desperate. He was really and truly desperate, but there was nothing he could do. "Please? I was in Paris. I can remember being in Paris. But I do not know why I'm here or how I came here. Please? Should I know you?" His voice was thick with emotion. "Should I remember you?"

She moved to sit down. He did not know anything, but what he said was heart breaking. "I'm sorry."

He breathed in and out. His chest was tight. He took a sip of the milk then moved to ease the stiffness in his back. Had he been alone, he would have laid down, and stretched out along the sofa. Rather anxiously, he risked looking into her face then focused again on the carpet. He could still feel her anger. He could almost see it radiating from her. "Please? I do not remember you. I was in Paris. I do not understand. Please? Why am I here? How did I come here? Please, I do not remember you. Should I remember you?"

She slowly shook her head.

For a long time, neither spoke. He turned away to drink the milk. She turned away to watch the television. Later still, she helped him to walk to the toilet. Their silence became a wall. The day passed slowly. Even taking a long walk down through the woodland, she could not forget him. She spoke only to offer him something to eat, and he declined as she knew he must.

Later, she remembered that it was Monday, and found her programme. It was a lovely, warm, sunny evening in Devon. The Shetland Islands were not quite so sunny, but were much further north. There was another episode in the saga of the Pied Flycatcher. A couple of nest boxes were being used as props. It was like watching a card trick except they weren't cards. Dear Bill was having fun. The promiscuous young male was having a great time. Not only did he have a wife and family, but also a mistress and family that he had abandoned. The wife's chicks were close to fledging. The discussion was about whether he would go back to the mistress, and help her with her chicks. He had been named Casanova. He had been to visit the mistress's family when she was away from the nest, and had not even left a caterpillar. Bill was being positive. Maybe Casanova would do the right thing when his wife's chicks fledged. There had been no indication that he had a conscience. Domestic bliss was evident with the Moss Tit family in their beautifully appointed nest box. All the chicks were thriving with obviously successful parents. The chicks looked very beautiful, but were decidedly more yellow than blue. In a rather shabbier nest, the Humble Tit family were distinctly less photogenic than the other Tits, but they would be fine in the end. The parents were just younger and less-experienced. One of them had brought in an unsuitably large caterpillar, which just stuck in the throat of one of the chicks. It looked very dangerous. If they had been human children, someone would have called in Social Services already. The chicks were a few days behind the Moss Tits, and their feathers were still in pin. Then it was the Swallows. Bill rhapsodised over the five chicks in the Swallow nest. He had to admit that they weren't at their most attractive yet, but their feathers would appear soon. It had been a hot day so they had been panting to keep cool, but were thriving and well fed. The extraordinary Red-Throated Divers were making spooky noises. Why nature would have given them blood-red throats seemed an odd piece of evolution, and because they lived on the oceans they could hardly walk so were extremely vulnerable while on their nests.

The young man rose unsteadily to his feet, carefully straightening his back, and disturbing the new skin growing across his wounds. He paused to find his balance, and to secure the sheet around his waist. She turned from the television, staring at him anxiously. He checked her with a look then raised his hand. He took one step then another. She started forward, but he raised his hand again. It was his determined frown that made her pause. She watched in silence as he walked hesitantly across the room. She heard him cross the hall. He went into the bathroom. Her heart wanted to follow him, and make sure he was alright, but he could not have made it plainer that he wanted to go alone.

Henry was having trouble with his fish. She sat down again. Henry the Osprey was in trouble again. His wife was definitely unfaithful. Two of the three chicks were not his. There was speculation about whether or not he knew. Henry had brought in a huge fish, and nearly knocked all the chicks out of the nest. Mrs. Osprey was playing the exasperated wife, but Henry did not care. Then there were pictures of the unfaithful Mrs. Osprey having some sort of chat with another male. Was this the father of the other two chicks? It was a soap opera with feathers. She liked Henry a lot.

She had a moment of perfect clarity. She watched Springwatch religiously because it always made her feel better. It was therapeutic. She knew all too well that nature was cruel. Life for most creatures was too short, and fraught with danger. They were risking their lives every minute of every day, not just facing predators, but freakish weather and speeding cars. It did not matter that her contribution was not even a drop in the ocean. It was something. She had fed generations of birds and mice and hedgehogs. She provided water. She raised frogs and newts in her scullery. She had done something positive for the greater good, and it made her feel that she belonged to the army of enthusiasts even if she never paid the fees or attended the meetings.

The bathroom door opened. She blinked and drew back. She wanted to be smiling when he returned. He needed encouragement. She rose slowly to her feet then sat down again. She did not want him to think she had been waiting. She settled into the comfortable chair as if she had been there for hours. Her face set into a smile just as he walked stiffly into the room.

She kept smiling and raised her eyebrows, but the young man returned slowly to the sofa, and carefully sat down. There was some talk about hating winter, and always looking forward to the first snowdrops in February, and she could relate to that. She hated winter. She hated the dark evenings.

"Okay?" she asked, leaning towards the young man, speaking softly.

He raised his head and nodded, but did not look at her. He was breathless and grimacing, leaning over the armrest as if in pain.

Suddenly concerned, she rose to her feet, and walked across the room. Without considering his dignity, she gripped his shoulder, and forced him to bend so that she could take a look at the back of his shirt. There were creases, but there were also smudges of blood. "You're bleeding again," she said ominously. "It's not bad, but you have to be more careful. It's important that there is no infection. If you take off your shirt, I'll put some more cream on, which will help you."

What could he do? He was loath to speak, and unable to physically resist her. He started to fumble with the buttons.

"Take off your shirt. Here, let me help you." She walked around behind the sofa, and reached down to literally peel the shirt off his back. She knew it would hurt. His back was scarlet. A few new tears in the fragile skin were bleeding. With the lights on, and a tub of ointment, she was able to examine his back, and apply a thick coating of cream while he was flinching and grimacing and trapped. "It's a lot better." There were so many questions she wanted to ask. "Another week and you'll be as good as new." That was a lie. She closed the jar, and carried the shirt away to lay it over a radiator. "You keep still for a while, and let the cream be absorbed. That's it. Don't move."

There were Emperor Dragonflies on the television. She was torn between him, and the beautiful insect. She knew it was a monster. It lived barely a few weeks, and was a killing machine after spending two years as an inappropriately named nymph that lived at the bottom of ponds where it devoured everything, even tadpoles. It was certainly one of those miracles of nature that never failed to impress, but apart from its beauty and its amazing aerial acrobatics, it was undoubtedly a monster.

The young man remained motionless. Even the gentlest touch made him quake. She had administered the cream as carefully as she could, but it still felt like a mauling. His heart was thumping. A cold sweat made him shiver. He cast a suspicious glance at her, she was watching the television again, then closed his eyes, and screwed up his face in an attempt to master the pain.

There were Pipistrelles pupping, except there was no sign at all of the pups. The producers were hoping to show actual births. What they did film was the completely unknown behaviour of mutual grooming, which had never been witnessed before let alone filmed. The bats were tiny. They were in the dark. It was impossible to tell if they were even pregnant, but they were definitely rubbing noses. She glanced across at the young man. He was as white as a sheet. She wanted to interrogate him again, but knew it was the wrong time. It would probably always be the wrong time. The cameras in Devon did a sweep of the various nests. There was a lot of activity. In the morning, she would take a tour around the garden and outbuildings to look for Swallows. Surely, they had to arrive soon if they were going to have any chicks this year.

The young man had not moved. She rose to her feet, and walked around behind the sofa to examine him. He trembled before she even touched him. She drew back then walked out of the room. She put the kettle on then quickly crushed some painkillers. She put them in a glass of milk. She still found it awkward to give him anything because she knew he would try to go down on to his knees. She rushed to his side, and pushed the glass into his hand before he could do anything embarrassing.

"Just drink it. You'll feel better."

She fetched a clean sheet off the radiator in the hall then laid it over him. She lifted his feet onto the sofa then arranged blankets over him. He did not make a sound. She went around, drawing the curtains and locking the doors. She had a cup of tea, then satisfied that he was asleep, she went upstairs to her bed.

She had so much to think about. She was no further forward in understanding what had happened to the young man. He remained a complete enigma.

Chapter 19

At some time in the night, he must have woken up, and gone to find his shirt because when she came down the next morning, she found him wearing it. She had to insist that he take it off again. She needed to look at his back, and carefully spread more cream across the enormous wounds. While the cream was being absorbed, she kept his attention with milkshakes and baby food. After that she helped him back into the shirt. They were both more comfortable with his flesh covered up. While the painkillers took effect, she sat in the kitchen, and ate a proper balanced breakfast then took her own pills, and was ready to take on the day. He was left alone with the remote.

She went out to run a perforator over the lawn. It would improve the drainage. The lawn did look horrible. There were patches of yellow grass, and many bald patches that were just mud. In the garden, she could focus on other things. In the house, all she had was him. Even the cats were relegated. They did not seem to mind. They were definitely co-ordinating a campaign to overwhelm the new visitor. The more he resisted their attentions, the more they were intrigued and curious.

She spent most of Tuesday morning working around the ponds. Most of the frogs had gone. The green algae bloom had also stopped appearing. She still had no idea what had caused it. The cold weather seemed the most likely suspect, but that made no sense at all. She made an effort to go back and check on the young man, making sure he always had something to drink, and that he had not fallen over, or worse, that he had run away.

A few days of sunshine had transformed the appearance of the garden. The lily leaves in the ponds were unfurling. Californian poppies had appeared almost overnight to fill the edges of the paths with colour. Wild Aquilegias in a thousand pastel shades filled the garden with confetti. The Hawthorns were a mass of white and pink flowers that filled the air with fragrance. A dozen Lilacs were drooping under the weight of plumes of buds. Rhododendrons and Irises filled the beds bordering the walled garden. Yellow Broom sprouted from the drier beds surrounding the garage and outbuildings. The acid-green of Euphorbia mixed with the spotted leaves of Hostas. A spectacular Acanthus stood where days before there seemed to be hardly a trace of growth. From amongst the fallen Daffodil leaves came the jutting spires of Day Lilies. The bed of Hellebores still flowered profusely. There were a dozen varieties in a spectrum of colours varying from cream to burgundy. Giant Oriental Lilies shouldered aside ferns. Early Peonies held aloft their firm scarlet buds. And in the woodland, suddenly the foliage was dense and vivid. It was as if she had come to a theatre, and had sat in the gloom, waiting for the curtains to open and the spotlights to come on. Suddenly, everything was beautiful again. The sun was shining. It was warm, and she was very happy.

*

That the kafir anticipated it hardly made it any easier to bear. It was the end of December 1997. They had just arrived back in Riyadh after extended trips to Paris then New York then conferences in Ottawa and Kyoto. Everyone was tired. Everyone was making complicated plans for Ramadan, the holiest month of the year, and already looking forward to the celebrations of Eid. For many of the servants, it was their best opportunity to go home and be with their families. Prince Abdul Aziz also had a lot of family commitments. Prince Khalid, his eldest, was flying in from New York with the latest grandchild. There were going to be huge celebrations. The Prince had also discovered that a secret party had been planned on the 6th, which he was not supposed to know about. The kafir observed their growing excitement with trepidation. He was excluded from it. The Pakistanis all buzzed around him like busy little bees, but they were making plans that did not include him. He grew more and more anxious. He knew he should be grateful. A four week retreat to study the Holy Book was an expensive privilege he was expected to appreciate, but he did not want to go. And when the bodyguards appeared with the burqa, he collapsed and very nearly threw up. The Pakistanis thrashed him with their camel whips to quell any rebellion then he was covered up and dragged away. He knew the danger that awaited him. The journey was as perilous as before. He longed to hear that the weather was bad, and they could not fly through to Gilgit. He hoped they would be stuck in a hotel. When the gaily-coloured jeep arrived to drive them into the mountains, he prayed for a rock slide or a broken bridge or a flat tyre. Nothing impeded them, and he became more and more afraid. The two bodyguards knew him very well. One of them had been a lover. The local guide also remembered him. They read his anxiety as easily as a ten foot high signpost. They had never seen him so afraid. When they camped that night, they were expecting him to make a run for it, and he did. When he begged and pleaded with them not to take him to the madrassa because the clerics would kill him, the bodyguards just put him in handcuffs, and gagged him with his own tie. To slow him down, his fine handmade

Italian shoes were thrown into an icy river. The freezing temperatures and altitude did the rest.

He was delivered in handcuffs, and thrown to his knees. Jawad was running things. When the kafir bowed down, and made his usual pledge of submission, Jawad kicked him in the head. He explained to the Arab that Qadri was away in Islamabad then declared pompously that no one was expecting the kafir, and that it was totally unacceptable to have such a perverted creature anywhere near the pure and righteous students. The Arab explained politely that he did not care: every year he brought the creature back to school for a month of fasting and contemplation. It was the express wish of His Royal Highness, Prince Abdul Aziz, son of Faoud, nephew of the King, Defender of the Faithful, who paid Jawad's salary and sponsored the madrassa, which enabled hundreds if not thousands of poor boys to acquire a good education.

Jawad reluctantly took custody of the creature. He was quietly incandescent with rage.

The kafir was taken down into the cellars, and shut in a tiny room. He was almost grateful to be alone. No one could get at him through the locked door. Jawad was a fanatic. If he actually needed an excuse to kill a kafir there were enough in the Holy Book to justify killing one a dozen times over. It was literally sanctioned by God. The Blessed Prophet had decreed that every infidel should be destroyed. It was the most sacred duty of Believers. It hardly mattered that God's servant and messenger had only condemned the true followers of Abraham when he was actually trying to rally his troops before a battle. Jawad and his fellow fanatics took the words literally. To contradict them invoked a death sentence. No one was allowed to criticise the Prophet. Trapped in the dark room, the kafir shivered all night. There was to be no rescue. Achmed Qadri had gone. The Professor was probably dead. Nothing but the locked door stood between him and certain death. He was distraught. Terrified. He had no self-confidence or self-esteem. He did not have the luxury of being able to trust anyone. At his worst moments, he suspected that his master had actually sent him there to be executed. There was not the smallest crumb of hope that he would be spared. It was written. He almost hoped that Jawad would quickly cut his throat, and throw him off the battlements because being buried alive was his greatest fear. He had heard too many stories about sinful men being buried beneath walls, and surviving two or three days, and only then to have their skulls crushed if their accusers were merciful. That filled him with horror. There was nothing he could say. He was a kafir. His blood condemned him. His very existence was an insult to God. Being a good servant was the only protection he had, and here at the madrassa that had no currency at all. He was bereft of everything, having never known a friend or received a kindness or felt that he belonged anywhere. He could beg for compassion and mercy as he did every day of his life, but he knew it meant nothing to Jawad. He was not a Believer. That was the capital crime which Jawad could not forgive. Like a dumb animal, he had to wait in misery and confusion for someone else to decide how he must die.

Jawad came with a torch. He was not impressed by the foul blasphemer's desperate attempt to kneel and bow at his feet. He beat it about the head with a stick whilst explaining that it must behave and show respect or it would be killed. Hardly believing that it was to be spared, the creature promised faithfully. It was forced to confess all its failings, and had to admit that it was the vilest and most treacherous of imperialist crusaders, and that it was a living insult to God, the All Knowing and most Wise. Jawad thrashed it again because it was obviously a boastful, decadent infidel that only knew how to lie and deceive. He warned it that it would be watched every minute of every day because it had no honour, and had surely raped many dark-eyed daughters of Believers.

Huddled on the floor, bleeding from his wounds, the kafir would have sworn anything just to see the sky again.

Prof. Shah was even frailer. He stared at the man that Jawad dragged into his room, seeing only an unknown enemy that he instinctively despised. The European in western clothes was kept on his knees by Jawad. There was no recognition in the Professor's face, and no curiosity at all. He started to turn away and close his eyes. He was sick. Why were they bothering him? He was so sick.

"Uncle?" the kafir murmured, desperate to find sanctuary.

Jawad struck it across the back of the head. Speaking was forbidden. He jerked the collar, crushing the creature's neck, and shouted threats as it cowered at his feet.

But the Professor had glimpsed the flash of blue eyes, and he knew the voice. With a great sigh, he turned back to stare at the creature then laughed drily. "Nazarene, you came back." He saw that the hands appealing for mercy were locked together. "You have committed a crime?"

Jawad beat the creature about the head again, and pulled the collar even tighter. Unable to breathe, the creature tried to ease the stiff leather and metal plates away from its throat, but dared not provoke Jawad, who was seething with indignation and rage. "If the kafir leaves this room it will be killed. There will be no sneaking out after dark. It is a kafir. There is a curfew. There are laws. What is forbidden must stay forbidden. It is written. It is a Commandment from God. You need someone to look after you. It did it before. If you wish it, it will do it again."

Prof. Shah was almost too weak to lift his gaze up to Jawad's face. "Thank you. May peace be upon you. May the Blessings of the Prophet protect you. Thank you, my son."

As the collar was released, the kafir huddled down at Jawad's feet to avoid further blows, but dared to hope that the Professor would insist on the handcuffs being removed, but he did not, and the moment passed.

Jawad reached down to grasp the shackled wrists again, and loomed threateningly, but the creature cowered and stared at the floor. Jawad vented his spleen with a torrent of abuse then slapped the creature about the head before turning irritably away.

Battered and bruised, the kafir slowly found his knees, and moved closer to the Professor's narrow cot. He was disturbed to see how much thinner and sicklier he had become. "Please good uncle, are you well?" he asked anxiously.

"Why are you here?" the Professor asked, but before the creature could answer, he had drifted away into a troubled sleep.

The kafir searched the room for something to unlock or break the handcuffs, but there was nothing. He found a jug of water and some dry bread. He was starving. He built up the fire, and tried to make the Professor more comfortable. Then he ate all his food and drank all the water. Later, when he tried to replenish the supplies, he found the door blocked by a group of aggressive students.

"Kill all kafirs," they shouted. "The world belongs to God. We will kill all the disbelievers for God."

He bowed down to them, and asked for mercy, but begged to be allowed out. When he tried to explain that the Professor needed to drink, he was accused of being a murderous crusader, and thrashed for stealing the Professor's food, and daring to insult God with complaints. He was trapped. There was no way out. He stayed with Prof. Shah, watching him sleep, dreading that every breath would be his last.

At night, when it was almost too dark to see, Jawad came and shackled the kafir to the cot on which the Professor lay. Enough food and water were left for the Professor, but he was too ill to feed himself, and in the handcuffs the kafir was powerless to help him. In the morning after prayers, Jawad returned to see if the Professor still lived. He then freed the kafir from the cot, but kept both his wrists in handcuffs, and made him confess that he was a blaspheming son of swine then made him swear again that he would not run away. Then he set spies to guarantee it. The untouched food and water were taken away. There was nothing left for the Professor.

The dyslexic child came sometimes during the day, and read verses from the Holy Book. He was bullied by the other boys, and picked on by the teachers. It took time to overcome his fear and prejudice. He had been taught that all kafirs ate babies and drank blood. In a rare moment of clarity, the Professor explained that this kafir, despite the suit, was nothing more than a worthless outcast banished from its exalted master during Ramadan. After a few days, the child was happily sitting with the kafir, who patiently read with him, never mocking him when he struggled with the bigger words. This filled the kafir's days, and the child was the only human being who did not treat him with contempt. After dark, when they were allowed to eat, the child went out to gather the meagre rations. Invariably, it was the kafir who went hungry. Every night, Jawad came to shackle his wrists to the cot so the fire went unattended, and by dawn the room was freezing cold. The Professor grew sicker by the hour.

It was the longest month of the kafir's life. He lost weight. His clothes were slowly destroyed. All that kept him sane was his fragile hope that he would be rescued after the Holy Month had passed. He just had to stay alive. That meant surviving Jawad's fanatical interpretation of the rules governing the treatment of disbelievers. They were all legitimate. They were all ordained by God. The kafir knew them by heart, and never thought to question them. His Pakistanis allowed him their companionship, but all the customs and traditions and laws were observed. The slightest transgression had always been punished, but it was never malicious. They were never cruel. However, Jawad wanted obedience to the letter of the law, and abused his authority over the kafir by making an example of him on the slightest pretext. He made the kafir kneel down for hours in the icy snow. He denied him food for days on end. When the kafir begged like a starving dog, he abused him before the whole school. The smallest child was encouraged to pelt him with stones. He was vilified. When Achmed Qadri finally returned, he brought medicine for the Professor, and some desperately needed respite for the kafir. The handcuffs were removed. He was given a change of clothes. He was given food. The Professor's health improved marginally. Qadri insisted that Prof. Shah did not fast at all, and made sure that the kafir had the resources to take proper care of the old man, but everyone knew he would not survive another year.

There was a lot of news about the troubles in Afghanistan. The most beloved of God, Osama bin Laden, was now involved in a protracted civil war with the Afghan Northern Alliance led by Ahmed Shah Massoud. According to bin Laden, Massoud was a traitor to God, and a lackey of the Americans. Late at night, in the Professor's room, he and Qadri discussed the situation. They were both old men. Prof. Shah was a Hindustani Fanatic. He had been in exile almost his entire life. He spoke of Patna as a homesick Frenchman would describe Paris to wide-eyed children. Qadri had only ever wanted to be a good teacher. His Islam bore little resemblance to the creed being espoused by bin Laden and al Zawahiri. The kafir understood from the comments that passed between Qadri and the Professor that they rather liked Massoud, and that Jawad and his radical friends were firmly behind bin Laden. The kafir was disappointed. He had always believed bin Laden to be a hero.

To avoid the encroaching bandits that were roaming deeper into the mountains, and made travel increasingly dangerous, the kafir was collected by helicopter. He was too weak to be a threat to anyone, but they still stabbed a needle in his arm then carried him away. Concealed by a specially lengthened black burqa, he had passed through security checks in Islamabad in a wheelchair. Drifting in and out of consciousness, he had little opportunity to raise any alarm. The midnight trip across Riyadh from the airport to one of his master's many huge and secluded palaces was by limousine. Slumped on the floor like a sack of dirty laundry, the kafir kept quiet. The subdued lighting and the mask across his eyes restricted his vision almost to nothing. There were men around him. There were voices that he was sure that he recognised. The idle chatter was comforting. He was going home. He wanted desperately to go home.

The Pakistanis were summoned down to the basement to reclaim their property. When they arrived, it was lifted out of the limousine then settled on to its knees. The drugs were wearing off. It wanted to be free of the burqa and the tape that held its arms pinned at its sides, but it dared not make a sound. The Pakistanis fussed around it, concerned there might be real damage hidden beneath the burqa, but the burqa was mandatory. It could not be removed in public. They were told to just hurry up and take the creature away.

The kafir was almost too weak to stand, but as soon as he felt hands under his arms, he struggled gamely to his feet where he stood swaying and breathless. He felt sick and had a headache, and needed to go back to their room where he would be released from the unnecessary restraints, and allowed to rest. "Please?" he whispered.

Mahmood patted its shoulder. "Shush. Quietly," he whispered, then coaxed the creature to walk. "Come."

The kafir shuddered, but he followed obediently. His legs were like water. His circulation was badly impeded by the hours he had spent crumpled up in planes and cars as he was brought home. "Please?" he said again then slumped into the arms of his companions.

They held it securely, suddenly concerned. Its loss of weight was apparent. They could feel its emaciated limbs through the black cotton. One of the Arab bodyguards moved quickly to scoop the creature up in his arms, and carry it away towards the elevators. It might have been an act of compassion, but felt like someone sweeping the garbage out of sight. The Pakistanis followed, imagining shattered limbs and horrible disfigurements that would surely affect its marketable value.

The Prince was out of the country so the Pakistanis had, at least, a few days to sort out their charge. The creature was in a terrible state. It had lost so much weight. It looked haggard, and its hair was thick with grease and dirt. The shaggy beard was removed immediately because facial hair was a symbol of manhood. Nothing was ever allowed to suggest that the creature was male. They would have castrated it a decade ago had the Prince allowed it. They scrubbed and exfoliated the skin then covered it in a cream to remove every trace of body hair. Then it was lowered into a hot oily bath while they tried to restore its hands and feet. Aziz was concerned that it would no longer fit into the dresses. Waheed was concerned only that it was too frail to entertain their friends. There were already rumours. Confirmation of its return had aroused expectations amongst the regular clientele. There was a bidding war to be the first. Money had already changed hands, but some of the officers were trying to pull rank.

The Pakistanis worked through the night, but the creature grew sicker and paler. By dawn, they began to realise that it was actually seriously ill. They stood around shouting at each other before grudgingly accepting that it was no one's fault. There was no hope of a doctor so Aziz sent out for some medicines, while Mahmood lay down beside it, holding it in his arms. The creature was still ashen, still shivering, and locked in a fever, when Omar appeared at the door to demand an explanation. It was late in the afternoon, and he had orders to resume laying the stripes across the creature's backside. He was concerned to learn that the creature was sick, and really annoyed that no one had bothered to tell him. He did not have the discretion to ignore his master's commands nor did he dare to presume that his master would not have compassion. He left the squabbling Pakistanis to make a call to the Prince, who was angry when informed that his creature was ill. He almost did not believe that it was possible, but he knew that Omar would never lie.

The Pakistanis were informed that their creature's backside must be clearly marked with livid red welts from a whip before it was allowed to entertain their friends. That was never going to be negotiable.

Chapter 20

In the garden, the baby Starlings were much more prolific. She could hardly keep up with the demand for fat balls. The more she hung out, the more Starlings appeared, and they were always very noisy. The walled garden was beginning to sound like the Tower of Babel. All the small songbirds that usually filled the trees and shrubs had retreated as the annual invasion took place. For a few weeks only, the Starlings took over everything. Between them, they could eat four large fat balls in a day. It was not cheap, but according to her favourite programme, the Starling population was in serious decline. The great gatherings that were one of the most amazing natural phenomena on the planet were apparently usually made up of foreign birds coming to the UK from colder climates.

The ponds were going green again, but for entirely different reasons. She ran the hosepipe across the lawn, and pumped fresh water in while scooping out the blanket weed. She tried to search out the newts' eggs, and carefully put them back into the pond. There were no fish anymore. There was no evidence at all of tadpoles. There were leeches and snails and the dragonfly nymphs as well as dozens of tiny shrimp-like creatures. They were so delicate they almost disintegrated in her fingers so she had learned how to manoeuvre them from place to place. There were still a few frogs. The others must have disappeared into the flowerbeds. They could not have all been eaten. She had not found any dead ones, so she was happy to delude herself into believing that they had all survived.

The lawn still looked terrible, but that was all her fault. The borders were full of flowers. Every day, there were more. If it did not rain then she would soon have to start watering the garden. She walked down through the woodland, dazzled by the wealth of leaves, the different textures and colours. In the canopy above her, she could hear numerous different birds singing. The sunshine had produced a bumper harvest of insects so the birds were busy collecting food for their young. Now that the trees were full of leaves, she could not see the nests that had been so visible in the winter. There were nest boxes nearer the house, but not in the woodland. She could only gauge the number of birds by the cacophony of their calls. Now and then, a Robin would flit from branch to branch above her head. Sometimes, she might glimpse a male or female Blackbird searching through the leaf litter. The Robins were all identical, which must have made courtship rather complicated. Male Robins had been known to fight to the death over territory. In the spring, the females had to somehow prove that they were not marauding males so that they could have sex and get pregnant. She had seen them doing the wing shivering that was usually associated with juveniles wanting food. Perhaps, it was actually more about being vulnerable and asking for mercy.

She went back into the house as often as she remembered. Sometimes, it was almost hourly, but she was often so distracted and busy outside that she simply forgot about him. Her life almost returned to normal, but then she remembered. Then she was resentful, then angry, then stricken with guilt. So she hurried back to fuss around him, and make sure he had a drink. The television was always on. He had mastered the remote quicker than the can of milkshake. He managed to walk to the toilet, but he never took anything from the fridge, and she was sure that he never filled a glass at the tap. If she took off his shirt to rub cream into his back then went away, he was always wearing the shirt again when she returned. He kept his groin covered by a sheet. If he had to stand up, he was adept at pulling the material around him like a sarong. She had his trousers somewhere, but he never asked for them. He never asked for anything. His silence was infuriating. Her natural scepticism made her doubt everything that he had said. He must have a name. He must know what had happened. He said that he had been in Paris. She knew he had been in Monte Carlo. Every instinct told her that there was a story. It might be just some tawdry homosexual affair that had gone horribly wrong, but she needed to know every sordid detail. Yes. There was a lot of guilt. She had never considered herself an inquisitive person, but with him, her curiosity knew no bounds.

Later in the afternoon, she sat with him in the lounge. She had made a pot of tea and brought two cups. Watching him move made her wince. Laid out on the sofa, he was able to sleep or watch television. Whenever she came into the room, he always curled his legs under him, and struggled to sit up though he inevitably slumped across the armrest. It seemed to be too uncomfortable for him to sit upright though he never complained. When she offered him a cup of tea, he was completely nonplussed. She had loaded the cup with sugar, but that was not what stopped him dead. Not prepared to go through the whole milkshake can scenario again, she reached down to lift his right hand, and forced the saucer into his grasp. He blinked and stared at the cup, but did nothing else. She went back to her chair, and picked up her own drink then showed him what to do. He blinked again. His eyes were amazing. She could have stared at them for hours. But he lowered his gaze back to the cup. Moving made him flinch, but he straightened up slowly then passed the saucer into his left hand, and nipped the handle of the cup between his fingers.

"It's hot," she said quietly. He actually sniffed it, which made her smile, but he did sip it with due care. It had so much sugar in it that it must have been ghastly, but he drank it. Sip after sip, he hurried it down, not even waiting for it to cool. "Slowly," she said.

He stopped immediately, and held the cup awkwardly, not knowing what to do with it.

"So what happened in Paris? Do you live there?"

He leaned across the armrest again, grimacing, and not looking at her.

And his body language told her that he had no intention of saying anything so she finished her tea then went back outside. Later, when she came in to make a dinner, he declined the offer of food. So she ate alone in the kitchen surrounded by cats, who were all convinced that her three minutes in a microwave was better than what she had put down for them. She took her medication. She told herself that she was feeling better, but it was a lie. The garden had lifted her out of the gloom of her confusion and despair, but the effects wore off as soon as she came back into the house. She knew the pills would take a while to have an effect. She needed to keep to a routine and protect herself, and be very, very careful about the young man. She had reduced his painkillers by half, which brought them in line with safe prescription levels, but that left him more or less active. Now, he was sleeping because he was ill, and not because she was drugging him. Her control was slowly crumbling away.

The television programmes were beginning to focus more and more on the football. It was annoying now. Of course, he would want to watch the football. That was obvious. She absolutely resented it. If he had not been there, she could have sailed blithely through the whole World Cup experience, and never had to watch a single minute of it.

She had to ask him for the remote when her programme was due on. He gave it to her immediately, and bowed his head. She could not fault him. He was quiet and respectful, but she did not trust him. He was a man.

It was lovely in Devon. Casanova was still sticking with his wife, and ignoring his mistress and her family. As Bill delicately described it, Pied Flycatchers liked putting it about a bit. Damien, the Jackdaw chick was growing rapidly and very handsome, but spoiled by his very attentive parents. There had been three eggs. Jackdaws often had as many as six. Bill was still convinced that the other two had not hatched because nature somehow knew that there was not enough food about to safely feed three chicks. Good news for Damien. He was a magnificent-looking bird.

Out on the Isle of Mull, there was an update about Itchy and Scratchy, the stars of a previous series. Scratchy had island-hopped from Mull to Skye. Itchy had apparently disappeared about six months ago, but it was quite normal for young males to explore their territory. They were juvenile male Sea Eagles. Their territory was huge. It could take years to tour majestically around it. They were simply awesome birds. Their parents were still on Mull. The mature male kept trying to build a new nest, but his DIY skills left something to be desired. Two of his latest projects had been destroyed by bad weather. The female stayed stubbornly with the sturdy and functional old nest where they had raised chicks successfully for many years. She did not help with her partner's constant attempts to establish a new home. Once again, he had come back to the old nest where she had been patiently waiting for him. It was a secure relationship. They worked well together. They sat close together and groomed each other. They were obviously devoted.

An equally gorgeous bird was the Buzzard. Originally, she had two chicks, but one had eaten the other. There was a comment from Bill to children in the audience about not doing this at home. The adult female did not seem at all perturbed to have lost one chick entirely or by the unexpected weight gain in the remaining one. Like with the caterpillar, the surviving chick had swallowed its sibling with no ill effects despite its size. Both parents were feeding the chick. Frogs seemed to be the flavour of the moment. When a toad was brought in by mistake the chick positively turned up its nose at the offering. The toad crept slowly, but resolutely across the nest, and launched itself off the side. There was a sixty foot drop to the forest floor. Apparently, the toad survived. Unlike the frogs, the toads had glands in their skin which released poison when something tried to bite them. It seemed very likely that toads often found themselves abandoned in nests up in the treetops. They must have evolved some way of surviving the falls. There was no evidence of them being found dead in any great numbers to suggest it was a common cause of death.

The most charming moment was supplied by a viewer's home movie of a Grey Squirrel family being launched into the world. They had been living under the roof. The four youngsters were probably very happy to continue living under the roof. It was warm and safe and dry, and as long as Mum kept bringing in the food, they could have stayed there forever. The people living in the house might have found them an inconvenience, but as far as the squirrels were concerned it was the des-res. The female was repeatedly showing the youngsters how to jump from the guttering to the nearby conifers and laurel. They watched, but were not at all encouraged. She climbed up the drain pipe then jumped into the trees then came back up the drainpipe to jump again. No one followed her. The youngsters were very nervous. When Mum grabbed one of them, and forced it to the edge, the poor thing wrapped itself around her, and held on for dear life. She pushed and shoved, but it clung on to her. She released it then jumped again, called again, then hurried back up the drainpipe to prove that it was easy and safe. They just did not believe her. Two of them hurried back under the roof. In frustration, she grabbed another, and pushed it over the edge. It plummeted into the laurel. She leapt after it. It was safe. It might not have wanted to jump, but it knew how to grab hold. Mum hurried back up the drainpipe. The second youngster was petrified. She grabbed hold of it. It wrapped itself around her shoulders, and held on to her as if its life depended on it. Without hesitation, she leapt from the guttering, holding the child in her arms. The third was even more reluctant. It clung on to the roof tiles as she tried to dislodge it. She pulled and wrestled with it until it had to let go then leapt into the trees with it wrapped around her face like a muff. The last one emerged from its hiding place beneath the roof. It stared forlornly from the guttering, all alone, and too terrified to leave the safety of its nest. Probably exhausted, the mother did not climb the drainpipe again. She had three youngsters to hide safely somewhere. It was reported that the last one stayed in the guttering all night. At some point, it disappeared.

She thought about the young man's wounds. That had to be something weird. It could not be just because he was gay. Under her severe scrutiny, he stared at the floor, and literally quivered like a leaf. It almost made sense that he would be a member of some secret satanic cult. Perhaps she should have called the police. It was too late now.

She went straight out to the kitchen and crushed four pills, then mixed the dust into a milkshake. She gave it to him then sat and watched, waiting for the drugs to take effect.

*

The kafir understood when he was taken to the Prince's study. He had been granted a reprieve for eight days. He did not feel strong enough to endure it, but had no choice. He was still coughing, still breathless, still dead on his feet. He was not restrained. The Pakistanis played around with the whip while he walked across the room, hoisted up his shirt then bent forward to grip the edge of the desk. Omar had already set up the camera. Waheed had won the toss of a coin so he stepped forward with the whip. The kafir trembled. He could still hear his master explaining why it was necessary for him to be beaten every day. Apparently, it was his fault that so many men wanted to fuck him. He was allowed to deny them nothing because they were Believers, but it was imperative that they were forewarned about the perils of entering his foul body. He was filthy. He was a morally corrupt thing. That the Prince had decided that he enjoyed his degradation guaranteed that the punishment was relentless and severe. The whip screamed. It sliced through his soft flesh. The pain scorched through his entire body like a fireball. His heart stopped. He could not breathe. Sweat instantly drenched him. He almost fell down, but he grimly held on to the desk. It was worse than he remembered. The pain, the torture of having to wait between each blow for a few seconds or minutes or what felt sometimes like an hour, destroyed him. Long before Omar was satisfied that he had fulfilled his duty, the kafir was slumped across the desk, sobbing silently. There were tears on his cheeks. The new scarlet stripes on his backside were livid and raw.

His coughing annoyed them. His loss of weight made the dresses much more comfortable, but it was a small point against everything else. Mahmood worked in silence to paint his pale face, and pin up his tired hair. Aziz and Waheed were constantly shouting and screaming at each other about the damage done at the madrassa. He might have given the worst performance of his life, but no one ever asked for their money back. The wave of emotion came across the footlights like the blast from a furnace. It scorched his heart. He heard the declarations of love that drowned out the loudest music. Grown men stood there beating their chests, grinning wolfishly, adoring him with their eyes. No one here would hurt him so he danced and danced and danced, spinning faster and faster, whirling around until he was so dizzy and light-headed that he was happy to fall into any man's arms.

For the next few weeks, he simply existed, but his health did slowly improve. He was freely given supplements and treats that he normally had to work hard to earn. There were lots of pills and foul-tasting cough mixture. More importantly, the Pakistanis gladly took him back into their beds, and seduced him with attention which healed most of his invisible wounds. Being alone was still the one hell he could not endure.

The President of the United States of America had been on television denying that he had sexual relations with an intern at the White House. The very next day, his wife had been on the Today Show defending her husband, and saying that the accusations were all part of some 'right wing' conspiracy. It was front page news. There were soon charges that Clinton had murdered someone, that he smuggled drugs, and that he was being investigated for fraud and deception. He was being described as a psychopath. It was utterly unbelievable, but it was also hysterically funny, and the servants made jokes about it for months.

The Republican Party was actually waging a war against the leader of their own country. It became the only story. The American media feasted on it like wild dogs on a carcass, but Clinton was not dead, which made it all more appalling to watch. There were earthquakes in Afghanistan. The insurgency continued in Algeria with an ever-increasing death toll. Women and children were hacked to death with axes and knives. There were claims and counterclaims. The Russian President was a drunk. The world was full of uncertainty and violence, but the only story anywhere was Bill Clinton having oral sex with a giddy girl.

Early in February, the Prince was in Damascus when news came in about yet another massive earthquake, this time in north eastern Afghanistan. It was 6.1 on the Richter Scale, and had devastated a large area. The estimates of casualties ranged around ten thousand, but as the aid poured in, it was believed that five thousand had died with tens of thousands displaced. The kafir worried about the madrassa. At every opportunity, he eavesdropped on conversations. No one was interested in Afghanistan. Several of the Pakistani servants knew families near the border, but they were not affected. Most of them came from the south. The kafir did not know if Gilgit was near the border. He had never seen a map. There were no maps at the madrassa, and only one text book: the Holy Book. And he could not ask. He was not allowed to ask for anything.

The kafir and his Pakistanis remained in Riyadh. It was late in February before the Prince came back, but he was still preoccupied with more important matters. He was constantly taking conference calls from the United Nations. The Secretary General, Kofi Annan, was negotiating with Saddam Hussein to allow the UNSCOM Inspectors back into Iraq. The big stick was that America was threatening to invade. Countries were taking sides. Saddam was increasingly isolated. His sabre rattling and bravado made him very popular with ordinary victimised Muslims. He was standing very publically against Western oppression. It was blatant grandstanding, which alienated many in the Kingdom, who were the most moderate and respectful of people. The Prince had been appointed as a UN Ambassador, which was a tremendous honour, but it was a role that took all of his time, and kept him away from his home far more than he would have wished.

Even as the creature was brought to him late at night after his family had retired, he was still on the phone asking for patience and tolerance and not war. Omar salaamed his master respectfully. The pretty creature bowed and knelt then bowed again to press its forehead and palms to the floor. It remained there. It would have remained there forever. From the conversation, Omar and the creature learned that the war-mongering Americans were primed to lay waste to the Middle East. The Jews occupying Palestine were on high alert. All that Saddam possessed was an overinflated ego. The Prince put down his phone. He turned to acknowledge Omar with a smile, then surveyed his most troublesome servant.

"What happened?" he asked.

"Your Highness," Omar said, and bowed again. "My Lord, by the Grace of God, the most Compassionate, the most Merciful, may peace be upon you, my lord. May the Blessings of the Prophet protect you and your family." He paused to shrug inoffensively. "He was sick. It was probably a virus. I took the liberty of organising some blood tests. He's clean."

"And may peace be upon you," the Prince responded and smiled. "Thank you." He turned away to lift a box from his desk. It was about four inches square, and made of the most exquisite inlayed wood. The marquetry was highlighted with gold filigree and geometrical patterns. He gazed at the beautiful box then looked at the creature, which was barely breathing. To Omar, he said: "You understand the function of a tracker?"

"Yes, Your Highness. Yes, I understand." Omar looked at the box as the Prince slowly opened it to reveal a fabulous wristwatch.

The Prince smiled, and shook his head. It was a most ostentatious piece. "Always," the Prince said. "It would be a mistake to lose it."

Omar nodded, and bowed as he was given the wristwatch. His eyes were dazzled as he examined it. He glanced towards the Prince, who had already walked away to the other side of his desk. He summoned the creature with a click of the tongue. It crept to him, and slid close enough to suggest a kiss at his feet then rose gracefully to stand, its hands clasped together in prayer, its head bowed. Omar demanded that it surrender its left wrist, which it did without hesitation. There was the slightest gasp as the cold metal bracelet was threaded over its hand. Omar took a moment to fasten it securely. There was the usual clasp, but also a pin that once pressed could not be released. It was slack on the slender wrist, but Omar checked to make sure it would not slide over the hand. A curt word sent the creature back to its knees with its forehead pressed to the floor.

"Thank you," the Prince said. His phone started ringing again. He nodded. "I will bathe. Tell them we are leaving tomorrow."

Omar nodded, and salaamed again. He muttered a command, and watched as the creature rose slowly then stole away to the bathroom to prepare the bath. He turned back to the Prince, but his master was already on the phone. As he went out the door, he heard the news that Saddam had agreed to let the Weapons Inspectors back into Iraq.

The Prince took several calls over the next hour. He spoke a dozen languages fluently. Most of the time, he kept his eyes closed. He did not want to be distracted. He hoped that he had the self-control to resist the creature, but this seemed to be the wrong time to test his powers of concentration. The creature delicately stripped off his clothes then led him into the bathroom, and guided him down into the sunken tub. The water was just the right temperature. The creature's hands were impersonal and gentle. The Prince was able to conduct complicated diplomatic negotiations, and completely ignore the presence of the creature that obsessed his soul. When, at last, he was in bed, and had put aside the phone, he turned to survey the gorgeous thing that knelt beside the bed waiting to be commanded.

The Prince offered the ring. His heart twisted as the creature crept forward to kiss the jewel. He felt the electricity again. It singed every nerve. He knew he would know peace if the creature looked at him. He had but to look into those luminous eyes to know perfect contentment. It had to look at him. It must. It must, but the creature had been forsaken for too long to hope for a grain of kindness. It could not even trust the fabulous wristwatch that was still cold as ice around its wrist. Offended, the Prince snatched back his hand. He would have brutally struck the creature, but for the glittering teardrop that trickled down its cheek. He wanted it so badly. His flesh hungered for it. It was slowly driving him mad. It took all the jealousy twisting up his brain to empower him to lean closer and growl: "Go away."

The kafir shuddered then sobbed wretchedly once. His heart was bursting. He was so unhappy he thought he would die. "Please?" He stared into the Prince's eyes. The emotion he saw there almost made him retreat. "Please?" His whole body trembled. He frowned then took a deep breath. "Please?" He wanted to swear his undying love, but he could not say it aloud. It was forbidden, and there were no other words in his head. His nerve failed for a moment. His emotions overwhelmed him, but he gazed back miserably into his master's eyes. There was a change. The black eyes had softened. The dark wrath that always terrified him had mellowed into something warmer. "Please?"

The Prince did not hear a word. He was drowning in the luminous blue eyes. He was powerless, becalmed, drugged. He could not move. He could hardly breathe.

The kafir's heart swelled. On his master's face was every expression of kindness and love that he could have hoped to find. He could not believe it. He smiled shyly, then reached out to grasp his master's hands. He kissed each palm then pressed it to his face. He did not dare blink. He knew the moment would pass. He knew his master would always turn away and abandon him.

Prince Abdul Aziz smiled. He stroked the beautiful face but saw only the extraordinary eyes. They were swimming with tears.

"Please?" the kafir asked quietly. He still could not say the words, but he hoped that his master would simply know that he loved him.

The Prince smiled. He lifted his hands only to gently brush away the tears.

"Help me?" the kafir asked. He felt the moment was passing. "Please, help me. I don't know what to do." He clutched the Prince's hands again, and held them against his face. "I don't know what to do. Help me."

The Prince awoke from his dream. He eased his hands from the creature's grasp then drew away more than just physically.

The kafir's heart broke. He was suddenly desperate and lost. "Please? You could stop them. You let them use me then you punish me. I don't know what to do. Please, help me."

The Prince blinked again. The blue eyes were still mesmerising. He was vaguely aware of the creature saying something, but that was impossible because it was never allowed to speak. The eyes were shining. They were so deep and so blue. He reached out to take hold of its head then drew it closer to him. It came willingly on to the bed. It lay down beside him. It was still talking. It was still making a noise. He covered its mouth. The eyes shone even more brightly. The Prince was already imagining plundering the creature's flesh. He was breathing hard. He was distracted and impatient. He mauled it hungrily.

Suddenly, the phone rang loudly and intrusively.

The kafir shook his head to dislodge the hand that was smothering him. "Please?"

The Prince drew back, allowing the creature to roll down off the bed onto its knees. He watched it with some aggravation as it moved to pick up the phone then with perfect manners offered it to him. He took the phone then turned away to take the call.

Utterly overwrought, the kafir waited on his knees. The minutes felt like hours. There were so many things he wanted to explain, but the words just turned to ashes in his mouth. When his master came back to look at him then reached out to surrender the phone, the kafir seized his hand. He stared into his eyes, willing him to listen. "Please, help me. I'm begging you to help me."

The Prince frowned then took a deep breath. He was surprised then embarrassed. It spoke. He was momentarily ashamed of his manners, then remembered that the creature was condemned. His honour required that it be condemned. It had a sordid past and no semblance of a future.

"Please?" it asked again.

He should have struck it for being impudent, but the eyes ravished his soul.

The phone rang again.

"Help me," it said. Its broken voice added a depth of misery that no words could have conveyed.

The Prince could not answer. His culture forbade him to acknowledge that any wrong had been done.

The phone continued ringing.

The kafir read his master's dilemma in his proud face. "Please? You let them use me. You allow it." He stifled a sob. "It isn't fair. Please, help me. I don't know what to do."

The Prince eased his hand from the creature's grasp, and turned away again to take the call. It was longer. He paced the room then stared out of the window. He discussed the most delicate matters with frankness and clarity. He was perfectly polite, considerate, and never lost his temper. When he returned to his bed, the creature was asleep. He drew breath to wake it up and send it on its way, but he remembered it saying 'help me', and he simply could not let it go.

There would be many nights when the kafir was allowed to sleep on the floor beside the Prince's bed. No one could challenge the Prince's authority though they were all curious about what was going on behind the closed doors.

The next day, the Prince returned to New York, taking the creature with him. Omar showed the Pakistanis around the penthouse apartment that the Prince had rented. It had views over Central Park. The Prince's entourage was set up in smaller apartments on lower floors. They were crammed in as usual. They were all in New York when Ali Abu Kamal started shooting 'the enemies of Palestine' on the observation deck of the Empire State Building. It was only the next day when they heard that bin Laden had issued another fatwa ordering the killing of all Jews and crusaders. Fortunately, New York was a melting pot of immigrants so the Arabs and Pakistanis went completely undetected. The fatwa was generally ignored.

Chapter 21

She was eating properly and taking her pills. She was constantly reassuring herself that she was okay. If she was outside, she almost believed it. But sitting in the lounge, she knew that she was in trouble. She could still watch her favourite programme, and almost forget that he was there, but he was always there. Whenever he rose to his feet, she stiffened. She could not relax until he returned to sit on the sofa. He never spoke. He never asked for anything. He always wore the shirt, and made sure that a sheet was securely fastened around his waist. There was nothing to see, but she had already seen everything. It was too upsetting to question whether she actually wanted to explore his extraordinarily decorated flesh once more. She knew every mark. Her fingers still remembered the texture of his skin where it had been burned and pierced. Every facet of the jewels glittered in her eyes. She had forgotten nothing. Just remembering made her shift about on the chair, ill at ease, guilty and obsessed. Her thoughts were inappropriate. All that she was exposed to now were the exceedingly pink wounds on his back. At least three times every day, she helped him take off the shirt then carefully applied a coating of the Vitamin E cream.

She should have taken pride in the fact that the grotesque wounds had healed so well. It was nothing short of a miracle. But she had lost confidence in herself. She had lost control. In her determination to not hurt him, he had gained some independence. Because she wanted to treat him with respect, she had completely deferred to him. So they would watch the football. He would command the remote. Like a servant, she ran around providing him with nutritional drinks and jars of baby food. The small victory of making him feed himself seemed inconsequential. When in the pit of despair, she forgot that he was a victim. Whenever she looked at him, she imagined him naked and brazen. She wanted him more than she had ever wanted anything in her life. That he never met her gaze now signified his contempt and rejection of her. She was definitely spiralling down into a serious psychotic break.

She could not even reclaim the remote to watch Federer or Nadal in Paris. She had missed the matches against Massu and Berdych. There was a pain where her heart should have been. She was genuinely upset. She was becoming increasingly irrational. That she knew what was happening did not help her control her emotions. He had become an intruder, and not a guest. She started increasing the number of pills that she crushed every time she gave him a drink. He needed to sleep. He was still in pain. She needed him immobilised, not even sitting up, perhaps, not even alive. Yes. She knew she was in serious trouble.

The Humble Tits were looking good. Damien was still being spoilt by his overly attentive parents. The saga of the Pied Flycatcher continued. It was better than a soap opera. His wife's seven chicks were close to fledging. The mistress's three were a few days behind. They were all unbelievably cute. There was a curious segment supplied by a viewer about cuckoos. It was well made and poetic, but surely the cuckoo was not to be admired. It was a cold-blooded murderer, and an appalling parent. Ebb, the otter, was teaching her daughter how to catch fish. The Merlins in the Shetlands were a devoted couple with a nest full of eggs. They were apparently the smallest raptors in the UK, with the male no bigger than a Blackbird. It certainly was not big enough to nestle all the eggs under its breast. And it was curious how the programme's editors always seemed to find the predators more interesting than the vulnerable smaller creatures that they ate. It was the same with the mammals. Lions were trailed across the savannah from birth to death as if they were all cute and cuddly. No one looked at the wildebeest or zebra unless they were being killed. The Skylarks, which sang like angels, barely had a mention though their effective Merlin deterrent was to sing very loudly and boastfully while being chased about the skies by the agile little predators.

She wanted to be alone. She needed to watch Natalie Wood being swept up into John Wayne's arms. She gazed at the young man. He was lying down. He might have been asleep. If she made up a bed for him upstairs then he could sleep all day. And he would not be in the way. Then she could blissfully watch the tennis, and have a thing with Big Shoulders, and avoid a confrontation that she knew was brewing.

By far the most beautiful creatures on the programme were the Kingfishers. It was another older piece of film. She was sure she had seen it before, at least once, but it was still lovely. Charlie Hamilton James disguised Bill as a haystack then left him beside a stream. Charlie went off to hide in his hide with a camera that was to die for. Between him and Bill there was a perching place for the Kingfisher. It did look as if Charlie might have placed half a branch strategically in the middle of the stream. Bill sat still for a while then for a while longer, trying not to move, and prohibited from talking. Both of which were impossible. The Kingfisher arrived. It was so beautiful. The colours were amazing. The proportions were perfect. The males and females were exactly the same, but for the latter having an orange lower bill. In the sunlight, they gleamed like jewels. Bill was enchanted. There was a male and female. They caught fish and flirted. They could not have been any more attractive. For once in his life, Bill was speechless. The whole programme was an absolute joy.

The iridescent blue reminded her of his eyes. He was too beautiful. It had to be surgery. Like the Kingfishers, he was simply beyond compare. Having him in the room was so distracting. Even in the shirt, he seemed to be naked. She did not actually blush every time that she looked at him now, but when she thought about him he was naked. He was always naked. She wondered if she would ever be able to forget his extraordinary body. Just thinking about it made her gut twist and her mouth go dry, and she wriggled uncomfortably on the chair. He had to go. If she started fantasising about having sexual relations with him, then she would definitely be in real trouble. She had already worked out that bolt-cutters would set him free.

*

"My cousin has one."

They had been at the hotel in Brussels for three days, each one of them packed with meetings and functions. The Prince knew everyone of consequence. He moved with effortless grace from high finance to climate control to sustainable agriculture. He was well informed, courteous and charming, even to those who were not intellectual or remotely tolerant. He received many of these people in his suite where he could talk to them quietly and privately. It amused him that some of them initially treated him like an upstart Bedouin when his ancestors had ruled kingdoms with doctors and scientists while their people went barefoot and probably lived in caves. In his own rooms, they were served refreshments by his servants, and could speak freely and candidly because the Prince had no agenda but progress and peace.

"He insists that I have one. He speaks of the honour of my family." The last guest was a small man in his late fifties. He had a rather hawkish face and dark wiry hair, slicked back with some fragrant oil. His beard was thin and neatly trimmed, but streaked with grey. He wore a nice charcoal grey suit and lilac tie, but his appearance did not fool anyone. He was a Turk with no ancestors worth claiming.

The Prince merely nodded and smiled, and gazed away out of the windows across the rooftops of the city.

The guest picked up his half empty coffee cup and stirred it delicately, then put it down. There was a long pause as if he was expecting something to happen, but there was no response. "I first saw one at Nad al Sheba, and I did not understand. I had no idea. My cousin explained what they are. I felt foolish." The guest smiled to conceal his embarrassment. "I follow the camels: Saudi, Bahrain, Kuwait, and even the Sudan. It is my passion. I feel the memories of all my people alive in my blood when I see the camels come out of the dust and sand of the desert. The excitement. The shouting. The kinship of men." He blushed at his secret vice. "It is my passion." He sighed then stared again at the Prince. "But my cousin insists. He says it is permitted by His Holiness the Prophet, Peace and Blessings be upon Him. He says it is written and is therefore the Will of God."

The Prince frowned, but did not look at his guest.

"So I have come to you, Your Highness, to ask your advice."

Prince Abdul Aziz nodded. He still did not look at his guest for fear of revealing his disappointment. "It was written thirteen hundred years ago. It is also written that what you are suggesting is a great sin." He took a moment to sweep his hand down his robes as if brushing away crumbs. "The world has changed. The True Faith brought to us by His Holiness the Blessed Prophet was written for nomadic tribes in violent times when there was conflict and endless blood feuds. His Words might be interpreted differently if He came amongst us today."

"Forgive me, Your Highness, but the Words of His Holiness the Prophet are the Truth. We cannot doubt them. We must not deny them."

The Prince nodded. "Yes, of course, we must not deny them."

The Turk smiled, and toyed with his cup again. There was still no response. A little disappointed, he leaned forward to engage the Prince's attention. "My cousin was able to purchase one from a dealer in Djibouti. He's raving about it. He's insisting that I must have one for my house."

"Really? Then your cousin is a very fortunate man. I have heard of them being passed from father to son, but very rarely sold." The Prince smiled graciously. "I had no idea that any were available at the moment."

"I hope you do not mind my asking, Your Highness?"

The Prince took a moment then said: "Old families such as mine cling to their traditions, but when my father passes..."

The Turk still smiled. His eyes were bright as stars.

The Prince frowned again. He did not want to insult his guest, but felt it was imperative to prevent him making a terrible mistake. "It is a custom older than Alexander, but seldom practiced now, and so rarely understood. It is something of an acquired taste: much too rare and too expensive for many to contemplate. In my grandfather's time, they were certainly considered a more common convenience. Everyone understood what they were, and there was no scandal attached to them. These days, I fear that is no longer the case. It is a tradition that has become tainted." He gazed at his guest. "Our culture is so rich, but even our own children are losing their respect for these old traditions, and forgetting so much that is relevant to understanding who we are and where we came from." He brushed away more imaginary crumbs. "And foreigners have never understood. And forgive me, but I seriously doubt that your cousin found one for sale in Djibouti. The trade there has always been for blood and muscle. What you speak of is caviar to the general."

"Yes, Your Highness, I understand." The Turk tried to smile. He was acutely uncomfortable. "I am not like my cousin. That is why I have come to you."

"We live in such difficult times." The Prince nodded sagely. "Islam is under threat. It would be a mistake to celebrate such an old custom, which many will find distasteful now." He paused to study the Turk then shook his head solemnly. "Too many of our younger brothers are more interested in dying than in living. This love of death is troubling. It is very sad. In their hearts, are they already dead? It is a sickness. It is a pestilence of hatred and intolerance. There is something seriously wrong with our culture if our young people are so obsessed with death." He gazed away across the rooftops. "There is something wrong with our lives. We have abused our wealth and our power. The world has changed, and we haven't changed with it. Why do our children not want to live? All they speak of is jihad. How can we speak to them of joy and honour when they do not want to grow old and be wise?"

"But to the young there is no greater duty than jihad. It is an obligation. Jihad will make Islam supreme. There is no greater goal." The Turk smiled resolutely. "Martyrs are truly the beloved of God."

"But they are children." The Prince frowned then gazed across the coffee table at his guest. "They are taught that if they go on jihad, there will be virgins and paradise. If they do not go there is only hell. They are told that virgins will come down to wait for them to guide them to paradise. They are told that God will ignite the bomb. They are told that they have to do nothing. They are not murderers. They are not committing suicide. It is all God's Will. This is preposterous. They are innocent fools who have been lied to by older men who preach hated from their comfortable homes, and risk nothing of their own. Surely, it is better to be wise, and strive with all our strength to make a better world than be dead even if we go to paradise. And God, the All Knowing, has forbidden suicide and taking the lives of innocents. He will not be happy with the death of so many innocents. A thousand years ago... We no longer live in deserts. We no longer have to wage war on our neighbours simply to survive. All this killing must stop. It is genocide. It is hatred. It is not God's Will."

"But to kill disbelievers?" the Turk insisted. "Killing a Jew brings you closer to God. It is clearly written. And all martyrs are loved by God. We are only here to worship God. We have no other purpose. You are not a Muslim if you do not believe in jihad. These martyrs are our hope. They are our path to victory over the disbelievers. God willing, all the imperialists will be destroyed, and the Jews will be wiped off the face of the earth, and then peace will come, Your Highness. Then we will have paradise." He smiled wistfully. "Everyone wants to go to paradise."

Prince Abdul Aziz nodded, but turned away in dismay. He had dedicated his life to peace. "God willing," he said half-heartedly.

The Turk stared out of the window, seeking what had distracted the Prince. "My cousin recommended that I come to you. For generations, all your family have..."

"The world has changed. It is not like taking a wife or buying a falcon," the Prince explained carefully. "Forgive me, but you must not even contemplate such an acquisition if you cannot provide adequate care. Only last year, I had to arrange for a friend's zoo to be destroyed. He had spent years collecting some of the rarest animals on the planet then suddenly became bored with it all. We saved what we could, but most of the animals were half starved, diseased and demented from bad treatment. They had to be destroyed. It was a terrible waste."

"So I have come here to ask your advice, Your Highness. I wish to do the right thing," the Turk insisted earnestly. "I am an honourable man."

The Prince nodded and sighed. "I was not aware that there was any product on the market now. As you know, my father and my father's fathers observed the custom. There were agents. It was done quietly and professionally. Old families like their traditions. Old men can be stubborn. But when my father passes... The world has changed."

"But if God wills it? It is written."

The Prince frowned again. He understood the temptation. "Have some compassion, Rifat. They are removed from their natural environment when very young, and deprived of normal social contact. We have forced them to become entirely dependent on us. We have imposed our will on them, not allowing them to think, denying them independence, and keeping them as nothing more than domesticated pets. We have taken away their ability to fend for themselves. Because of this they never really mature. We must accept responsibility for the negative effects this has had on their development." He sighed and shook his head. "Many will call them stupid and lazy, but they are only as intelligent as we have allowed them to be. It's not their fault. There must be some compassion."

"Yes, I understand. My cousin has likened it to keeping falcons."

"There are some parallels. When they are young they will form an attachment. If the relationship is nothing more than a battle of wills then they will never respect you, and you will never be able to trust them. And if you indulge in teasing and tormenting them then they will become unstable and dangerous. We have made them this way. Making them so dependent is a double-edged sword. You have a young family, Rifat."

The kafir stood a little to the left and behind his master's chair. In front of him was the low coffee table with the silver pots and fine china. He had served the Prince and his guest, and now stood motionless watching the glint of the ring on the Prince's hand. The huge windows, overlooking heavy clouds and the historic rooftops of Brussels, were not for his eyes.

"So you will not sell it?" the Turk asked with regret.

The Prince glanced across to acknowledge the question, but shook his head. "It has been in my household for several years. I could not part with it for something as ordinary as money."

"It is very beautiful." The Turk clasped his hands, and shifted on his chair to stare in admiration at the handsome creature in its expensive suit. "Does it never think to run away?"

For the briefest moment, the kafir turned to survey him, their eyes met. The Turk licked his dry lips. The kafir lowered his gaze instantly while his heart quickened with anxiety.

The Prince caught the look, and frowned. He irritably rearranged a cup in a saucer. A teaspoon chimed in the quiet room. The creature focused. It was his again. "You'll need good people to look after it. They'll need to understand the psychology. Some people seem to have an instinct for it. We use Pakistanis. Observation is everything. Daily grooming and handling will reinforce the bond. It is essential that there is a bond. If there is no rapport then you'll need to make changes, bring in new people. And you have to be able to trust them. I've heard cases of exploitation and cruelty. You'll soon know if it's going wrong. All of this costs a great deal of money. You'll need somewhere secure to keep it that won't damage it psychologically because you want it well-adjusted and calm, but you don't want it playing with your children." He paused to gaze witheringly at the Turk, but the Turk only had eyes for the gorgeous creature. "They are not machines so no two are alike, but in many ways it will be exactly what you make it. Too much kindness will spoil it as quickly as neglect. Don't bribe it with titbits because it will quickly learn to manipulate you." He smiled, knowing that the creature was listening. "They are all as cunning as monkeys, but you must be the master. You must be firm. They will understand that. Because we make them totally dependent on us so they look to us for constant reassurance. It must be reinforced every day. You must be consistent. They must be able to trust you. If you neglect them then they will revert." The Prince paused to consider his words: "Then they must be destroyed."

"Destroyed?" the Turk asked doubtfully.

"You must destroy it, Rifat. You could not have a dangerous dog loose in your home or allow it to go into another man's house."

The Turk started to speak: "My cousin said the Chinese would..."

Prince Abdul Aziz concealed his disappointment by gracefully stroking imagined creases from his robes.

The Turk realised his mistake. "It is certainly very beautiful. If not money then perhaps..."

The Prince merely smiled and shook his head. He could as easily have considered severing his own arm.

"It travels with you then?" the Turk asked conversationally.

The Prince gazed across at his guest. "You should not do this, Rifat. You say it is written. It is also written that there is one devil with every woman, but there are seventeen devils with every boy. It is unlawful to even look at it to appreciate its beauty. Homosexuality is a crime against God, and is absolutely forbidden. It is a vile perversion: the most hideous of sins."

"Oh yes. Yes, I agree. But I'm not a homosexual," the Turk declared confidently, and he was grinning proudly. "I have a wife and children, Your Highness. I have sons. My cousin says this is not the same. It is allowed because it is not the same. I could never love a man. That's utterly disgusting."

"God has made Heaven difficult to reach, but He has surrounded Hell with delights and temptations."

The Turk still smiled, his eyes ravishing the exquisite creature that stood as if fashioned from marble. "And in Heaven they shall be attended by boys graced with eternal youth, and as beautiful as virgin pearls."

The Prince considered terminating the conversation. It was more than delicate. It was extremely dangerous.

"He is very beautiful," the Turk repeated, gazing at the creature, no longer disguising his true intent. It was on the tip of his tongue to ask if he might borrow it. Only good manners prevented him, and the unhappy certainty that the Prince would refuse.

"Three men that I trust look after it for me. They are all Pakistanis. They have a feel for this which cannot be taught. My family have employed them for generations. They are loyal and devoted. They manage it perfectly. They keep it quiet and calm." The Prince gazed at his guest, and saw his puzzlement. "It can be as highly strung as any colt. It has to be trained. You have to teach it when it's young otherwise it can be very difficult later on. Drugs are never the answer, and I will not tolerate addicts. You have to get its head right before you can do anything else. This one found it difficult to cope with the arrangements required for travelling, all the hotels and airports, and the sensibilities of my devout servants... I could not allow them to be offended. What has been forbidden must remain forbidden."

The kafir suffered in silence. He was deeply humiliated.

"How old is it now?" the Turk asked. "It seems so serene."

"Unfortunately, I am always travelling," the Prince confessed, ignoring the question completely. It was absurd to think he might know or care about such an inconsequential detail. "My schedule is extremely demanding. Tonight, we fly to Johannesburg then Nairobi then Addis Abba. In three days, we have to be back in New York. Next week, I must be in Hong Kong then on to Shanghai. I know how difficult it is for my staff. They all work extremely hard for me. I am full of admiration for them. But this one has struggled. We had to find a solution. It must travel. It must be able to deal with the airports and flights and hotels. That's all part of the job now. It had to learn, and quickly." He paused to move the ring on his finger, to make the point, and turned slowly to look up into his creature's gleaming blue eyes. A flood of emotion burned through his flesh, tingling his skin, teasing every follicle. "Fortunately, we were successful, but it did take quite a long time." The Prince smiled as he remembered some of the more bizarre remedies suggested. "I sometimes think that it requires more maintenance than my wives." He gazed back out through the windows. "Of course, I don't get involved anymore. I have good people. They keep it busy. It can't be left alone for a minute because it will always get into some mischief." The Prince paused to smile as he looked at his guest. "This is no beardless boy, Rifat. It has a specific job. It works hard. It has to work hard to justify the cost of keeping it. The Pakistanis know how to deal with it. It has a routine. It has a diet. No one is allowed to spoil it. There are no treats or titbits. If it fails to perform its duties then it is punished. When it excels it is praised. There can be no other reward. It has a job, which is all very humdrum and boring. It does what it is unseemly for a brother to do. There is no scandal. What has been forbidden by God must remain forbidden. Please, do not be misled by its smooth face. We are not Pashtuns. We don't go around buggering little boys."

"Yes, of course, I understand, Your Highness. I'm sorry, I never meant to suggest…"

Prince Abdul Aziz gazed at him steadily. "You cannot be a homosexual yet you have offered me money?"

The Turk hesitated then shook his head. "My cousin." He turned awkwardly to look at the beautiful creature. "He speaks so highly of them."

"If you want only a doe-eyed dancing boy then go to Pakistan or Afghanistan, they are as plentiful as the sands of the desert, but they are rife with gonorrhoea."

The Turk visibly shuddered. Reluctantly, he turned away from the creature, and stared down at his manicured hands. "I wanted something clean and beautiful and uncomplicated that would never criticise me. My wife is bad tempered and jealous. My cousin said that I can have this with a boy."

"It is far from uncomplicated." The Prince smiled almost fondly. "Truly, it belongs to me. It knows that it must obey. In many ways, the relationship is similar to that of the snake charmer and his cobra. They are not like us. You will never understand them. You are the master. They will understand that. If you care for it and protect it and are consistent then it will trust you and serve you. But it will constantly surprise you, and not always in ways that you will find attractive. It is a wild thing harnessed by your will. There must be no evasion or hesitation. It must obey without question like a soldier. It must attend with devotion like a wife. You see a smooth-faced, white-skinned boy, but this flesh is just a product, something that you can buy. But in its head it is always the cobra." The Prince leaned towards his guest, and whispered: "I think when you have paid out millions of dollars to acquire one of these then you will understand exactly what they are."

"Millions of dollars?" the Turk asked, crestfallen.

"You want a decent white skin, clean and untraceable, that is the price. This is not back-street human trafficking. For $20 you can have a Thai boy, and fuck him to death." The Prince paused to let his guest absorb the information. "Do you think your cousin has perhaps exaggerated the quality of his purchase?"

The Turk said nothing.

The kafir trembled, but he could not leave.

"You belong to me, don't you? I take care of you." The Prince did not even turn his head. The huge gemstone on his finger glinted. He smiled.

The kafir moved in an arc around the Prince until he stood before him then he bowed at the waist, then went to his knees, and pressed his forehead into the carpet, and placed his hands flat in front of him. There was a pause. It felt like an age. Then he lifted his head, and slid forward to kiss the Prince's shoes. "Yes, my lord, Your Highness, my master by the Grace of God, the most Compassionate, the most Merciful. Please, all that I am. I am here to serve. God is Great."

"It belongs to me," the Prince said with emphasis.

The kafir kissed the shoes again then reared slowly back on to his heels. Bowing his head, lifting his eyes only to find the ring, he moved gracefully to kiss it. He took the hand in both of his, and kissed the ring again.

The Prince felt the raw passion unleashed by the kiss like an electric shock. Arrows of desire burned through his entire body. It took all his will to keep his face expressionless.

"Please, all that I am," the kafir repeated. His blue eyes blazed like white-hot coals as he looked up into the Prince's face. "Please, Your Highness, my master by the Grace of God, the most Compassionate, the most Merciful. Please, all that I am. God is Great."

The Prince smiled. He could drown in those eyes. A wave of pleasure surged through his body, but he shook his head. There was an obvious understanding between them. The creature sighed and nodded, then bowed respectfully, and lowered its gaze. It was not allowed to look a Believer in the eye. It was considered grossly offensive. Anyone else would have knocked it down, and kicked it senseless for daring to look in their eyes.

"It is truly beautiful," the Turk said in breathless admiration.

"Yes, it is certainly very decorative." Prince Abdul Aziz sighed, gazing down at his creature, intimately familiar with its body, knowing its every thought. Their eyes met again. There was a wonderful, secretive smile then the creature lowered its gaze in submission, and pressed its forehead back to the floor.

The Turk wanted to touch it, but good manners made that impossible so he devoured it with his eyes. "It's not been castrated then?" he asked, his voice husky and low.

The Prince was surprised by the question, but shook his head slowly. "No. My grandfather forbade it in our family. It is useful when they are small, but causes so many problems when they grow up." The Prince gazed thoughtfully down at his creature. "I am blessed. It is devoted to me. I wouldn't want to spoil it."

The Turk stared covetously at the European boy in his expensive suit, who bowed down at the Prince's feet.

"If you want passion," the Prince explained, "then race with your camels. These things cannot be loved. That would offend God and all honourable men." He glanced towards his guest then stared back at his creature. "They will do everything in their power to bewitch you. You must constantly be on your guard. If you begin to desire them or your heart is moved by some remembrance of them then you belong to them. They will own you, and command you to some hideous perversion. What is forbidden is forbidden. They cannot be loved. That would be like loving a dog."

Smarting at the insult, the kafir buried his face deeper into the carpet. It was painful. It hurt so much. His pride and joy were destroyed again.

The Turk was also appalled, and drew back, his fascination extinguished as easily as a candle. "An unclean beast," he said, his eyes now glinting with hatred.

"Yes, that is exactly what they are," the Prince said, turning to smile at his guest. "We dress them up, and teach them our ways so they do not offend us, but they are no better than beasts. That is why it is essential to take them at an early age. They become so easily corrupted. This one is invaluable to me." He felt the electric shock of raw emotion as the trembling creature rose unsolicited, and kissed his hand again. "But I must take care of it. I must protect it." The Prince smiled, and turned away to study his guest. "It is like a greedy child. It constantly wants attention. It wants reassurance. If you give it a reward then it wants ten more."

"But a cobra?" the Turk asked, bitterly disappointed.

"Indeed, a very expensive but deadly cobra." The Prince continued to ignore the creature. He knew it was listening. He knew it would be sighing and fretting and squirming with embarrassment. "Could you afford to keep such a dangerous animal in your house?"

The Turk shook his head. He avoided looking at the creature, and could not bring himself to meet the Prince's gaze. "I am sorry for troubling you, Your Highness. I should not have come. I should not have asked you. Please, forgive my indiscretion."

The Prince nudged the creature at his feet, and with a subtle movement of his hand, dismissed it. No one watched as it withdrew, and bowed then rose to its feet then hurried from the room. The Prince smiled as the tension lessened markedly. "What you speak of is a fable; something from the Arabian Knights. I have in my houses forbidden things, which I am obliged to keep while my father lives. I protect them. I make use of them as respectable servants. I must keep them safe. In another generation, they will all be gone. When my father passes there will be no further need for them. You will understand about honour."

The Turk nodded. "I understand, Your Highness. I will not mention it again." He rose slowly to his feet. He tried to smile. "I do love my wife. She has borne me sons, but before we were married I had barely glimpsed her face. She came from the country. She was veiled, but she is my cousin so I could not refuse." He shrugged a little, and managed to smile wistfully. "Beauty? Why are our hearts so captivated by beauty! Even the beauty of a boy!" He turned away to hide his blushes, and quietly left the room.

Chapter 22

It was another lovely day. She had spent the morning in the garden. Mostly, she was just tidying up, but using her discretion. A tidy garden was not a happy wildlife garden. Most of the cats were outside with her. All the garden chairs were occupied. The suntraps were booked up too. The musical soundtrack came courtesy of the Blackbirds. Everywhere there were flowers, and, amazingly, bumble bees and even butterflies. She had half an idea that Federer was playing that afternoon or evening, so she had a plan about what she needed to accomplish before she could justify sitting down and watching television for possibly four or five hours. Her various wheelie bins were already full, and were not due to be emptied for another week. And again she was irritated because the local politicians had all promised that the bins would always be emptied once a week, and had again failed to keep their word. She started collecting refuse to burn behind the garage. She liked a good bonfire. She knew to collect and burn quickly to stop the hedgehogs moving in. It very quickly grew into quite a large heap.

By then she was thinking about the young man and the remote. Of course, it was totally inconsequential that he was dictating what was on the television. She had only to take it away from him. What could he possibly do? But she felt mean doing it, and then angry.

Lunch was late, as usual. She made a pot of tea. He politely received the bottle of baby food and a can of milkshake. She made a sandwich for him, but he declined to eat it.

Federer was not due on court.

Having settled in her chair, she was loathed to get up. She was physically tired, and being in the garden seemed to upset the birds, which were all desperately searching for food to feed their young. That was the only excuse she really needed. Her attention immediately shifted back to the young man.

He did seem better. His skin had lost the dead chicken look. His movements were more fluid. He could stand up almost without grimacing, but he was still in pain, and the skin across his back remained fragile.

"I found you about ten days ago in my garden." She started speaking.

She wanted to build a bridge. It seemed to be an appropriate time for a chat. She was prepared to believe that her nerves might have made her seem aggressive and openly hostile, which he might have found difficult to overcome. When he looked towards her, she managed a very nice smile. "Well, actually, in the woods on the other side of the garden. You were just laying on the ground, half hidden by ferns, and in the shadows. I might as easily have not noticed that you were there. Your clothes blended in very well, all muted colours, you know." She smiled again. He visibly settled, listening to her, but staring at the floor between them. "It was really just an accident that I found you. Even now, it makes me shiver thinking that you might have lain there undiscovered for days. It was just luck." She hugged herself, rubbing her arms vigorously. He looked at her, staring with accusing eyes. She lowered her gaze. She did not want to know just then what he was thinking or feeling. "But you were still alive. I honestly thought you had just fainted, and I was ready to give you a good telling off, but you didn't wake up. It was very strange. You had no obvious injuries. I couldn't see your back, not then, and obviously, you had clothes on." She smiled, and risked a glance. He was studying his hands. A deep frown darkened his face. "And they were really nice clothes; very expensive. And your shoes weren't even dirty. I couldn't work out how you had walked across the field, and into the woods without even getting your shoes dirty. It didn't make any sense. And I couldn't imagine why you would have gone into the woods. You were just laying there." She looked at him, but he was still staring at his hands. "I don't know how long you had been there, but you barely needed a shave. Which by the way, you do need a shave now. You look like Robinson Crusoe." She glanced across, wondering if he knew the name, but there was not a flicker of recognition on his face. If anything, he looked angry. He was grinding a thumb into the palm of his hand as if to erase a cramping muscle.

"There was a spider's web in the ferns above you, and a nest full of baby spiders. It wasn't disturbed. So I believe that you had been there somewhere between six and ten hours. I brought you back here. You were unconscious for days. I tried to get you to drink. I didn't really know what to do. My phone wasn't working then, and then when the smell got really bad, and I had to take your clothes off to wash you, - by then I really didn't know who to call." She stared at him, hoping he would acknowledge what she felt was an apology. He was totally focused on massaging his hand. His frown was still dark and full of foreboding. She took a deep breath. "I cleaned you up. It was a horrible mess. Someone hurt you very badly. They flayed off most of your skin. Most of the tattoos have gone. There are - some bits - left. You can't really tell what it is anymore." She glanced across the room again then focused on the floor or the ceiling, anything except his face. "Most of the welts are healing over. It must still hurt. It'll probably be sore for a very long time. You'll need to keep rubbing cream in to keep the skin supple otherwise it will restrict your movements. And there'll always be scars. I think you know who did that to you. You were in Paris?" He did not even flinch. She licked her lips. Perhaps, just a sip of tea? She focused on drinking tea for several minutes.

He said nothing. He just sat there and suffered.

"I'm trying not to be judgemental, but it seems obvious to me that you're part of some sadism masochism sex game thing that went horribly wrong. You nearly died. Was it worth it?" She looked directly at him. He had stopped fidgeting. His eyes were closed. The frown had become anguish. "The rest? Well, I was shocked and appalled, but that isn't your fault. That's all about me. I don't know anything about what people your age do now. It is probably all perfectly normal, but it upset me. It was such a surprise. I can't even imagine what it feels like. I thought it was painful having my ears pierced. That's a work of art, isn't it? It's so immense and – what's the word that kids use today for everything – awesome. It's awesome. I suppose it is beautiful, but I can't pretend to understand or approve. I never knew it was possible. Not like that, anyway. It's so detailed. Of course, I've seen African Tribal Markings. The Kikuyu were very much into that sort of thing, but I thought it had died out now. I believe the Maori are pretty good at it too. It must have taken ages to do. And it must have cost so much money. It must have cost a fortune. And it must hurt every time, well, I suppose all the time. And I guess you have to be a homosexual. That's fine. I don't have a problem with that."

He glowered at her. It was a fleeting glance, but loaded with emotion.

She was so shaken by the look that she found it difficult to inhale. For a moment, she completely revised her opinion of him, but he settled again, and stared back at the floor. "Well, you are, aren't you! That thing that you wear! It's physically impossible for you to have any kind of," she exhaled loudly and frowned, "well, you can't penetrate can you! You cannot have sex with a woman." She gazed at him, desperately wanting him to say something, anything, but he did not appear to be listening anymore. "If I was ever rude then I do apologise. I was shocked and tired, and I was frightened. You might have died. And I suppose, I was afraid because I'd brought a stranger into my home, and I didn't know his name. And you tell me now that you don't have a name. Everyone has a name. Well, it's all very confusing, but I did my best." She paused to look at him, expecting him to, at least, acknowledge that she had tried. He stared fixedly at the carpet. He did not seem to be listening. She took a moment to breathe. She was fairly sure that he was not being completely honest, but felt unable to accuse him so she smiled bravely. "So between us, we don't really know anything at all."

He lifted his head slowly, and stared at her, feeling that he had been condemned with every word. "Please? I am sorry, but I cannot," he said. His soft baritone voice was unthreatening. His accent was untraceable. The blue eyes were full of light, reflecting the sunshine from the huge bay windows.

She nodded and frowned. So it was all true. She was disappointed. He was a deviant sexual predator, and probably delusional, but at least he was gay. That made her feel a little safer. "I can't pretend that I approve, but if you want to go back to Paris, then I can contact your friends. If you tell me their names or his name and the address, the International Directories will be able to find them. Or if there's someone in this country that I can call for you or a place you want me to take you, then I'm happy to do whatever is necessary to help you get safely home."

"Thank you. You have been very kind."

His cool response surprised her. She thought they had moved passed reticence. "So who is in Paris? He must be rich. I don't know how he brought you all the way over here or why he dumped you in my garden. I guess the rich really are different. Was it just some completely silly game? I think if you say 'yes', then I'll be annoyed. It was dangerous. You were so badly hurt you could have died. And what on earth made him choose to dump you here in my garden? It has cost me a lot of money, and a great deal of time to nurse you. Was I supposed to just hand you over to the police? Was that it? Was it some cruel joke against you? Your lover is insane if he thought it was funny. And I'm quite sure that he's not your friend. He flogged you. We don't treat dumb animals that badly. I suppose, it was to have some heightened sexual experience? I've heard about that asphyxiation thing. People have died doing that. It's so dangerous. Well, it really isn't just a game when someone is whipped the way that you were whipped. You could have died. When you see him again, you can tell him that I said that it just wasn't funny, and if that's how you people have sex then it's disgusting. But I'm sorry. It's history. You'll be alright now. We should let him know that you are okay. If he really is your friend then he must be concerned. He should have come back to find you, to make sure you were okay. But never mind. You were probably all drunk. Yes. That's probably it. I suppose, it might have been some great party game that went terribly wrong. I'm sure, he'll be pleased to know that you are okay. Is he like you with the jewellery?"

He slowly shook his head, flinching under her critical gaze.

227

"Personally, I'd dump him, and find someone better. You're very good-looking. There must be a lot of gay guys out there, who wouldn't dream of hurting you the way that he has. You should try to find someone nice and ordinary, who doesn't like all this sadomasochism stuff, who would probably be rather boring in comparison, but who would love you. And it would be safer. You'd live longer." She tried to smile. Her maternal instincts were working well. She was very good at giving advice, but knew that she was wasting her time. Was he even listening? She smiled again, but he was staring at the floor. "I'm older than you are. I suppose, I don't understand the attraction of such high adrenalin activities. He nearly killed you. You must know that. Why did you consent? You couldn't have been that drunk. Is it really all about sex? Really? Does everybody do it like that? It makes me go cold just thinking about it." She looked at him, her thoughts running on to questions she could never actually ask him. Perhaps he understood because he bowed his head, and lifted a hand to cover his eyes. "I don't care if I am old fashioned. I don't care if you are a homosexual. It just isn't right. It can't be good for you. It must have been absolutely excruciating."

With a dark frown and compressed lips, he lifted his head to look at her. "Yes." His face paled as the echoes traumatised him again. "Please, do not be angry. You have been kind, and I am very grateful." He paused to rub his eyes, trying to erase so many other memories too. "I do not understand what is happening, but this is my fault." His hand shook so badly that she could see it from across the room. "Please, do not be angry." He took a deep breath, filling his lungs then shivered as his memories assailed him again. For a long moment, he could not find the right words then sighed: "I want to go home."

The words softened her heart as nothing else had done. She yearned to cross the room, and wrap her arms around him, but she just could not be so forward. "I'm not angry. Please, don't think that I'm angry with you. Someone has hurt you terribly, and I just wish that you were as angry about it as I am. Okay, so I am angry, but it's not at you. We should be reporting this bastard to the police, but you won't do that."

"Please, I cannot!" He did not know how to explain. "Please? I am sorry."

"But why not?" she demanded.

"Please? I am sorry."

She felt helpless. "I'll get you a drink. Later on, I'll help you upstairs. I'm going to make up a bed. You'll be more comfortable. Pretty soon you'll be well enough to have a proper bath. You'd like that, wouldn't you? It'll be much easier for you."

"Thank you. You have been very kind." His tone had become flat and cold.

"Thank you?" She sighed, feeling exasperated. "It's alright. We don't have to talk anymore now. We'll watch the tennis. Honestly, I wasn't angry. I just get upset. I promise, I won't bully you anymore."

He slowly leaned down across the armrest.

She went out to the kitchen, and stood staring out through the window at the garden. She felt physically sick. Without thinking, she put food down for the cats then tidied up a bit, but it was hopeless. She needed to get away. She needed to stop thinking about him. It was too much. He was taking over. He would not do what she wanted. Her nerves were beginning to fray. She kept telling herself that it was not his fault, but somewhere deep in her subconscious was the niggling doubt that it actually was his fault. There had to be consent. Was he dangerously delusional? There was no telling what he was actually capable of. A catalogue of monsters and their nefarious crimes filled her head. They all suddenly looked like him. Suddenly, he was Norman Bates. He was Bundy. He was bad.

Without a backward glance, she threw open the door, and went outside. She walked and walked until she was physically exhausted. Through the garden and through the woodland then on and on over the neighbouring fields, she walked blindly and angrily. Depression had long been a part of her life. She knew its calling cards. She had to put him away somewhere safe for a while. She needed some time with Big Shoulders. She needed to sit and count the bumble bees. But knowing what she needed did not make anything happen. He had to go. He had to disappear.

It was almost dark when she returned. He was on the doorstep, leaning against the frame, hugging his knees. She saw him as soon as she entered the walled garden. She could not tell whether he was asleep or not. Beside him there were two cats, the ones that had obviously taken a liking to him because they were always in the lounge. As she drew nearer, she could not help smiling. He was fast asleep. It was surprisingly sweet. She leaned down to study his face. How could a man be so beautiful? She gently combed her fingers through his hair. He came around slowly. He was adorable.

"It's alright," she said softly, and stroked his face as if he were a beloved pet.

He could not look at her, but he stretched out his legs then clasped his hands in his lap.

"Can you get up?" she asked. She knew he could not. "Please, let me help you. I want to help you."

With a grimace he nodded then offered an arm.

It made her very happy to take hold of his arm, and brace herself so that she could literally and figuratively help him back on to his feet. All her maternal instincts were gratified. When he stretched an arm across her shoulders, she was immensely proud.

They turned together into the house. He was a little taller, but she was stronger. She knew that he was no threat to her. That he was gay was just a bonus. A gust of wind could have knocked him down. His injuries kept him impotent. Without her, he would not have been able to survive. These things she knew. She knew as well that she was teetering on the brink of a complete breakdown. She could not, would not, must not lose control. His very stillness had saved them both. As she held him steadily, and did not hurry him, she was able to experience a rare moment of fulfilment. She almost wanted to thank him, but what could she say that would not expose her emptiness? Compared to her barren existence, he was the luckiest man alive. He was loved. She had no comprehension of what it was like to be loved as he was loved.

He settled carefully on the sofa, leaning across the armrest. She made him comfortable, fetched him a drink, then turned away to find the remote.

It had been a very hot day in Devon. Dear Bill did not really have the knees for shorts, but he was giving out the equivalent of Health Warnings so that was alright. Casanova had become Super Dad. The intrepid cameramen had found another Pied Flycatcher nest with another seven chicks. There was absolutely no doubt that it was the same male. His plumage was certainly distinctive. That took Casanova's tally up to seventeen chicks in one season. In nature that was a tremendous success story. Had he been a human being, he would have been politely despised. Bill had joined a shrew survey, and was bitten by a Water Shrew. They were ferocious little creatures. Only afterwards was he told that the bite of a Water Shrew was actually poisonous, but only slightly. Bill wanted to quantify 'slightly'. It was funny. Everyone laughed. The two presenters were like an old married couple. They talked in half sentences and at the same time. In the dappled woodland, life was grand.

Long before the programme ended, the young man had fallen asleep.

She went out into the garden. The twilight was lovely. There were still a few birds singing. It was a balmy summer's evening. She walked across to the first pond, and stared down into the water. The blanket weed was growing too fast. There were still some frogs. She hoped the others had not died. The second pond had less blanket weed, and there were half a dozen newts. She would have cut her arm off to have Great Crested Newts, but the Common Newts were still thrilling. While she stood there, one of the cats came to rub around her legs. That was unexpected and nice. Since the young man had arrived, she had basically abandoned all of them. She picked up the cat then carried it back across the lawn to the bench. They sat together, listening to the birds singing, and watching the light disappear from the sky.

It was nearly midnight when she started the bonfire. It took all her supplies of newspapers and a whole box of matches. The rubbish was too green and moist, but by the time she had stuffed the heap full of paper and cardboard, she could have set fire to water. The smoke hung in the air. There was no wind and the clouds were low. Wherever she sat or stood, the smoke always found her. By the time she had reduced the rubbish to a small heap of ashes, she smelled like a kipper, and her face and hands were smeared with soot.

When she returned to the house, the young man was waiting for her again. She helped him back to the sofa. She made him a drink, and gave him some pills then hurried away to have a bath.

*

They had been in Iran for nearly a fortnight. The damage from the earthquake might have been catastrophic had the area not already been devastated by previous quakes. The towns and villages had not been rebuilt so the death toll was minimal this time. In Afghanistan, they were still finding bodies after the February quake. The death toll there was expected to exceed nine thousand. There were seven days of aftershocks. Aid efforts were hampered by sub-zero temperatures, the remoteness of the epicentre, bad weather, and the Taliban. There were at least fifteen thousand homeless people in Afghanistan, but the aid workers were only allowed to deal with the men. In Iran, the situation was much more straightforward. For Afghanistan, that was to be a year of natural disasters.

Shortly after arriving at the airport in Paris, the Prince had turned unexpectedly to Omar, and pressed a wad of Euros into Omar's hands then directed him to take the creature somewhere safe. They were all tired. Half of them had been living in tents. All of them were looking forward to hot baths and warm beds. Omar turned on his heel, caught the veiled figure by the arm, and started walking away. In the Arrivals Lounge, they passed the sizable entourage of Princess Noor. She was one of Prince Abdul Aziz's many nieces. She spent most of her time in New York. She was glamorous and intelligent, had made a career of being a celebrity, and she was never going home.

Omar walked the creature out through the doors and hailed a taxi. The respectable Arab and his equally respectable wife climbed into the taxi, and were driven away. Omar had been in Paris before. He gave the taxi driver an address in the suburbs. They changed taxis, walked down tree-lined boulevards then took another taxi. They travelled away from the fashionable areas frequented by tourists. After more than an hour they were in an area with a large immigrant population. It was poor and overcrowded, and a perfect place for Omar to conceal his veiled companion.

It was raining. Paris in March was all grey stone beneath a grey sky. The people that they passed were all wearing black or grey clothes. There was very little colour. The population was a rich mixture of Blacks and Eurasians and Arabs. Everything began to look grubby and dissolute. The architecture became less classical and more concrete block. The open spaces became lifeless and littered instead of manicured and green. There were elevated trains. Blank walls were decorated with graffiti. Some of it was very good, but none of it was beautiful. The general theme was rage and protest. France was still in love with anarchists and the idea of revolution. There were numerous white police cars prowling the streets. Almost every face belonged to an immigrant. There were men, women and children. The slums where they lived, trying to eke out a modest living, were crowded and not even French anymore. There were millions of them, all of them bound together by poverty and one common language.

Omar and the creature walked down grubby streets. Omar's phone rang. As he lifted the cell to his ear, he reached out to catch the creature's elbow, and drew it closer. The Prince issued a few curt orders and rang off. Omar turned to survey the street then studied the creature that was completely concealed beneath the long black robes. It was tired and nervous. It shifted about as if its feet hurt, and visibly jumped at every sudden noise. Omar was uneasy about exposing the creature to the world and vice versa, but he knew it needed water and to rest. It must be exhausted. They had all had a tough few weeks.

They walked on. Omar needed to find a quiet secluded place. He knew from experience that the Parisian ghettos were not only crowded with immigrants, but also with undercover cops and state of the art surveillance. They found some shops. There was a group of itinerant youths hanging around. Omar led the creature inside. He was a big guy. The youths were hostile, but they let the strangers pass by. The man running the shop was suspicious and moody. He probably had a gun under the counter. There were cameras. There were iron bars on the windows. The door was made of reinforced steel. For all the security, the shop only sold basic foodstuffs, cheap work clothes, cigarettes and alcohol.

Omar bought jeans, a T-shirt, bread, and water. Purely to continue the illusion that the person beneath the veil was a female, he also bought sanitary towels and soap. The shopkeeper was surly and unhelpful, but happier when Omar paid in cash.

They left the shop under the eagle eyes of the youths, but walked away unmolested. Omar headed east. They needed to find a safer neighbourhood. The Prince wanted the creature kept out of sight for twenty-four hours, which was much longer than Omar had anticipated. They needed a cheap hotel, something respectable but off the radar. They passed a row of garages that had been vandalised and adorned with political slogans. Many were heavily secured. Some had been broken into. One stood empty. Omar hurried the creature inside. While it sank to its knees, Omar watched the street and surveyed the surrounding tenements and blocks of flats. It was impossible to tell if anyone had been watching. Reluctantly, Omar turned from his vantage point to rip away the burqa. The creature was ashen. He thrust the jeans and T-shirt at it, and ordered it to put them on.

The kafir was frightened. He had no idea what was happening, but he understood that they were hiding. He looked to Omar to provide everything so he was quick to pull on the new clothes, and cast off the thobe and burqa. He watched like a starving dog as Omar opened the bottle of water, and took several deep swallows. While he waited on his knees, his absolute faith in Omar was briefly shaken, but Omar offered the bottle to his lips. He was allowed as much as Omar had allowed himself, but whereas Omar had only been thirsty for a few hours, the kafir had not been allowed anything to drink for nearly eighteen.

"It's alright," Omar said reassuringly.

The kafir nodded and sighed. He was too tired to walk another step.

Chapter 23

All Friday morning, she worked in the garden. The sunshine was glorious after so many months of gloomy rain. She mowed the lawn again. It still looked awful. The weeds were growing everywhere faster than anything else. The flowerbeds were filling up with groundsel, nettles and brambles. There were enough bees to keep her happy, and numerous butterflies, but simply not enough hours in the day to keep on top of the work. It was certainly lush. Having once been plagued by rabbits, she knew what she could safely plant, but even these were susceptible to the snails and slugs that appeared as if by magic in the evenings. She worked quietly and patiently, talking aloud to herself and her constant companion, the black cat with the yellow eyes, about her backache and her tired old hands.

In her head, she was in the garden, but he dominated even here. She loved her cat and the flowers and the bumble bees, but if she did not concentrate on her work then he was increasingly luminous in her thoughts. He was magnetic and she was powerless to resist. Her eye searched for him amongst the leaves and the shadows. He was everywhere, but it was never really him, not the vulnerable young man who lay on her sofa like a corpse. If only he had been older. If only he had been ordinary. If only he did not have those eyes and that face and that decorated flesh. He was so lovely. She knew every curve and dimple and facet. The exotic markings were fascinating. The jewellery was dazzling. He was a work of art, honed and sculpted and yet flesh. He was so far out of her league that it was difficult to even fantasise about having sex with him. She had tried. She had tried so hard but his youth and beauty and fragility had awakened her guilt. Knowing he would be repulsed by her advances had not helped her confidence. He never looked at her. No one had ever looked at her in the way that she was looking at him. She kept reminding herself that every lascivious thought was inappropriate, but her mood fluctuated between giddy girlish excitement and predatory desire. She wanted him to take her in ways that she had never dreamed of before. Her imagination left her sweating and breathless, her heart pounding against her ribs like canon fire. But she had only to look at him while he lay broken on her sofa to know that she was a monster, and he was really no more than a child.

The garden. The garden. Thank God for the garden.

He would never look at her. She could not stop looking at him. He did not even need to be with her for her to see the freckles across his shoulders or the fine bone structure or the sheath. All the damage was on his back. Everywhere else, he was perfect. The wounds were spiteful and cruel and personal. That someone could have hurt him so badly was shocking. But for that one defect, everything about him proclaimed that he was loved. He was adorned and decorated. The athletic physique, the expensive clothes, the perfect manicure, the freshly cut hair, all declared that he was affluent, comfortable, pampered. He was a thing of beauty, but more than that, he was obviously – she hesitated to find exactly the right word – precious. He was precious. Someone somewhere would be heartbroken at the loss of him. She recognised that there was one significant influence in his life. All the artwork spoke of a singular preference. That was very specific. He had been redesigned and enhanced for one person to appreciate and admire. His body was a work of art. He had been sculpted over a considerable period of time so that proved a long-term relationship. His flawless features had to be the classiest cosmetic surgery that she had ever seen. No one could be so beautiful. It simply wasn't fair.

She needed him to look at her with those eyes. They had to be real. Everything else might be fake, but those eyes had to be real. She wanted him to take her in his arms and ravish her. It would be splendid. It would be so hot. Just imagining it left her weak at the knees, breathless, and on fire from the tips of her toenails to the very ends of her hair. Alone in the garden, she was embarrassed by her desperate desire. But it was so much more than that. In the garden, she was capable of devouring him. She was struggling to keep a material instinct alive. Her undeniable lust just overwhelmed everything else. She was losing control, but he was slipping further away. In her imagination, he was awesome and whole and resilient. She could not initiate anything. She could dream about it until she went completely insane, but she could not actually do anything. And when she went back into the house, he was just a frail shadow of the creature that lived in her head. He was beautiful. But he was so fragile and so vulnerable that she cringed with guilt, and smothered him with drinks and pills because she had no understanding of ordinary human kindness.

The fistful of pills that she took every evening at eight o'clock were the only things that saved her from the torment of twisting and turning in her bed, awash with sweat, distracted by her need to consume and be consumed. She hardly knew how else to describe it. She wanted to devour him. She wanted to absorb him into her own flesh. It was not about kissing. It was not even love. For years, she had never thought about having sex with anyone. Now, she had that constant niggling but totally addictive pain in the pit of her stomach. She wanted him so badly. It was so powerful. It was actually frightening. She knew it was inappropriate, but it was also deeply humiliating because he was so obviously gay. He had to be gay. Nothing else made sense.

His silence and secrets were also alluring. The latter she had to have. They were her fee. When she was coldly rational, she was determined to make sure that he was safe and well. She wanted to take him home. She wanted to take him to Paris, but that was impossible. Going to the supermarket was an ordeal. Asking for help was quite beyond her capabilities. She could make detailed plans about going abroad. She had lived abroad, but that was a long time ago. While it was an abstract idea in her head, she could dot all the 'I's and cross all the 'T's, but she knew somewhere in the recesses of her consciousness that she would not go anywhere. She could promise him anything, and want to deliver with all of her heart, but it was simply beyond her. She could book the tickets, make all the plans, but not leave the house. She might manage to keep it all together as far as the gate, but no further. She was in denial. She was pretending. It did not matter that she wanted it to be real. He had completely destabilised her. If he explained everything then she was sure that she would be alright. She just needed to understand.

She knew she needed some space. Her nerves were all over the place. Her resolve changed with the weather. She wanted Big Shoulders. She wanted her life back under her control. She needed her routine and her fixes. She understood that with her delicate mental condition it was actually dangerous having him there. Only his injuries kept him safe. Had he been whole, she did not want to imagine what she might have done to him. But had he been whole, he would never have come. She would never have found him. When she was tired, she was frightened. If she hurt him then she was doomed. He was the precious, and she was so near to being the monstrous evil spider that devoured everything...

In the lounge, she watched him walk carefully out into the hall then on to the bathroom. If he could do that then he could manage the stairs. There were spare rooms. She could make up a bed. He would be comfortable. She could hear him saying that he would be happier upstairs in his own bed, and out of her way. The more she thought about it, the more reasonable it seemed. Of course, he would approve. She was sure she could hear him agreeing with her.

He must have forgotten his name. No mother could have borne him and not loved him and named him. That was inconceivable. It was not even possible that he had been given up for adoption or lost in a handbag at Victoria Station on the Brighton Line. It had to be amnesia. It was probably induced by shock. The flogging that had almost killed him must have been excruciating. The brain had so many defence mechanisms. If she could just keep her distance, and allow him to recover in his own time then there was every chance that he would remember everything. Her doubts returned. His appearance in her garden, his strange behaviour, the gun – she had almost forgotten about the gun, that he really needed to explain. Her delicate sanity depended on it. But first, he had to disappear. She needed to repossess her house and her life. She would take her pills and eat properly and sleep eight hours out of twenty-four. She would be a good girl. She just needed to have control. Control was everything. Only then would he be safe.

When he walked back into the room, she made a tremendous effort to smile then turned away to stare at the television. He sat down very carefully. He was obviously still in a lot of pain. She made up her mind. He would be alright upstairs. He could be as silent and enigmatic as his heart desired. She was not being selfish. She was not being unkind. She gazed at him thoughtfully. He immediately stared at the floor. How could she help him if she was stark raving mad?

"Would you like something to drink?"

He looked towards her, but not at her. His head moved slightly. "Please? No, thank you. You have been very kind."

She marvelled again at his beauty. He was interestingly pale. His cheeks were slightly flushed. His inability to hold her gaze suggested anxiety and vulnerability. She felt he was lying. "You should drink, you know. It's important to flush out all the toxins in your system. Are you sure?"

He stared at something on the floor somewhere between them. His eyebrows had raised a little. Through his parted lips, she could glimpse the strong white teeth that proved he had a fantastic dentist.

She waited expectantly, but he could not volunteer a single word. "Are you feeling any better?"

Only good manners compelled him: "You have been very kind."

She took a deep breath. "Do you want to tell me what happened?" She knew he would ignore that one. "Or if you can tell me where to find your parents? You must want to go home. I can phone Directory Enquiries. I'm sure, you'd be much happier at home."

He glanced briefly up at her face then resumed his study of the floor. "You have been very kind."

She took a moment to consider the wonder of his eyes. Perhaps, it was simply the reflections of light from the big bay windows. His eyes seemed luminous. They had to be real. She followed his gaze down to the carpet. It was grey with dust. She was immediately embarrassed. "Yes, I'm so sorry. I need to vacuum. It's a mess in here, but I didn't want to disturb you. You've been so ill."

He was leaning across the armrest. The only indication that he had heard and might actually be listening was a weary frown. He did not lift his gaze. There was no shrug. A graceful gesture arranged the blankets closer around him, but he was utterly subdued and silent.

"I'll make up a bed for you." She produced a lovely smile. This was appropriate and motherly. She was ticking boxes again. "Then I can get stuck in down here and have a good tidy up." She managed to sound encouraging.

He merely stared at the floor.

She had been alone in that house for so long that she was used to her own company. Of course, there were the cats. Sometimes, there were hedgehogs in the scullery or tanks with tadpoles or baby newts. But she had never had another human being there. Now, she had him. He was there on the sofa, utterly beautiful, too beautiful to be real, and she could not touch him. She dared not consider the hours that she had spent just admiring him as if he really was a piece of art in a museum. He was much better looking than the Mona Lisa, but then it was said that one had to see the Mona Lisa to really appreciate her beauty. Perhaps, she had been spoiled. Her eyebrows had certainly disappeared in one too many cleaning processes. He was simply breathtaking. It was too easy to believe that he was not real. There were moments when she was almost certain that he was another of those Prozac-induced hallucinations. Her imagination had never been this good before. There he was on the sofa barely twenty feet away, but he did not actually seem to be there at all. He was so remote and distant and almost disinterested. She could stare at him for hours, and he never flinched.

She felt her gut tightening painfully. Another thousand inappropriate signals were transmitted from her brain. Her body was flashing. Her husband had never touched her as the mere image of this man touched her. She was on fire. The first time that she had seen Russell Crowe in the Gladiator, she had experienced a similar reaction, but he was older. He was a movie star. He was in Australia. That had been a rollercoaster. She was instantly on heat. She was sure she was ovulating. She was obsessed and distracted, deliriously happy and yet miserable. What she felt now was even more powerful, more primitive, and her faltering maternal instinct was just blown away. He could not hide anything from her except the truth. The silence was agonising. She did not have the tools to explore his mind as thoroughly as she had delved into every sumptuous piece of his amazing body.

She rose unsteadily to her feet. If she stayed there with him, she knew that something awful would happen. Her legs were like jelly, but she walked away. She walked and walked, out of the house, across the garden, through the woods then away over the fields. Her body was saturated. She was trembling and exhausted and half mad. He could not possibly be gay. Surely, her hormones were capable of detecting his gayness. There would be no attraction if he was gay. Parts of her body that had been dormant for decades were pulsating with life. She finally understood the remark that horrible men used so indiscriminately to criticise unhappy women: *she just needs a good fuck!* She desperately needed a good fuck. It was not just a sexist slur, but apparently a legitimate medical condition. She ached with loneliness and longing. She was ravenous for him. She needed to consume him and be consumed. Her muscles cramped. Her knickers were wet. She could hardly stand upright. It took almost five miles of walking for her to find her composure. He had to go. If he was not well enough to leave then she had to put him away somewhere safe for a while. She might yearn for him to the point of madness, but what she needed desperately was control. It might have been the meds or the splintered voices of her demons, but she would have control. While he was so near her and beyond her, she was lost. She was middle-aged, unattractive and lonely. He was a delicious boy. No matter what it cost, she would not become the spider that ate her mate.

He was asleep when she returned. She was briefly thrilled to see what looked like relief on his face when he opened his eyes and saw her there. Had he actually missed her? In her misery, she reasoned that it was only the chilled can of milkshake and the painkillers that he wanted. She turned away from him, and went upstairs to excavate a room.

The house had two double bedrooms and two singles. An estate agent would advertise it as four doubles. One of the single rooms was only just big enough for a double bed but no other furniture would have fitted into the room. The second single was wide enough for a double bed and long enough for other furniture, but the bed could only be accessed from one side. She had a big argument with the seller's agents when she bought the place about being honest and having integrity, but then they were estate agents so honesty and integrity were both probably alien concepts. Her own room was on the right front corner. The other double room was on the left front. They were both south facing and had huge windows which allowed amazing views. In his room-to-be, there were very nice oak wardrobes and a dressing table in the Arts and Craft style, a broken television, a vacuum cleaner, and several boxes of books and video tapes. She had always meant to redecorate, but it had never been a priority, and it had always been a convenient place to dump stuff from other rooms. So she would dump him in there too.

She sorted out the floor space by stacking the boxes then turned the mattress over and went to find sheets. There were no cats about, which was unusual. She worried that some of them might have trailed along behind her when she went for her long walkabout. It had happened before. She tried not to worry. She had lived there for so long that all of them must know the neighbourhood better than she did. They would come home, but only when and if they wanted to. More anxiety. More guilt. It was just something else for her to obsess about. She quickly made up the bed. He would be very comfortable. He was nearer the bathroom. He could actually have a proper bath or a shower. It was such a good idea. He would be fine.

"I've made up a bed for you," she announced when she returned to the lounge. "You'll be more comfortable." It was a command. She was grinning with confidence. She was genuinely proud.

He stared at her, his face white, his eyes widening with horror. He was so tense he could hardly shake his head. "Please?" He did not want to understand.

"Honestly," she said, still grinning, and she reached down to take hold of his forearm.

"Please?" he said again. He hung back. He shook his head firmly. He could not look at her, but he resisted. "Please? No, I cannot."

She tightened her grip. She was surprised, and not a little annoyed. "Up you get. Come on, you can do it."

But he could not. "Please, let me stay here?" He made no attempt to rise, but he could not find the courage to pull his arm free.

The desperation in his voice was surprising. She stepped back, frowning. This was not going according to plan. She had not anticipated him refusing to move. Was he refusing? "I'll help you up the stairs. You won't fall down or anything."

He shook his head urgently. "Please? No, I beg you. I will be quiet. I will not disturb you."

She stared at him, baffled and hurt. "You don't understand. It's not about the noise. You're so quiet! I just – well – I made up a bed for you. You'll have your own room. You'll be more comfortable. Then I can get out the vacuum." He was trembling. "It's not about the noise."

"Please?" He looked earnestly into her eyes. His expression appealed. His voice asked for mercy. He was suddenly very vulnerable. "Please, let me stay here?"

She drew back another step. She did not understand. All that she knew with certainty was that she needed him out of sight. More than anything else, she actually wanted him to have never been there, but how could she explain that when he had switched on those blue eyes like car headlights? She filled her lungs to forcefully explain, but her courage vaporised. "I'm sorry," she said. She did not know where to begin. He had to go away to stay safe. Perhaps, the truth? "I've been ill." She drew a hand across her face, utterly self-conscious now that he was looking at her, and grateful that she had taken the time to wash and change before coming downstairs. "For a very long time, I've been ill." She tried to smile bravely, but he had already resumed his study of the floor. She tried even harder not to feel the rejection. Obviously, he was bored already. "How could you possibly understand? You're so young and so good-looking." He did not even blink. She filled her lungs then sighed miserably. "I'm completely alone here. I have no one. No friends. No family. How could you possibly understand what that is like? Look at you. I don't have anyone. I'll never have anyone. You wouldn't understand. I'm sorry."

What could he say? How could he explain? He stared at the floor.

She started forward, meaning to catch his wrist again and draw him to his feet, but he evaded her. Feeling rebuffed, she retreated unhappily to her chair. "I made up a bed for you."

He glanced towards her, and clearly saw her dismay then it was his turn to inhale deeply. "Please? Please, do not be angry with me."

"But I'm not," she insisted.

He all but looked at her. His nerve failed again. "Please, let me stay here." He swallowed a lump of anguish that was almost choking him. "Please, do not leave me alone. I cannot..." words failed him. "I cannot," he repeated doggedly. "Please, let me stay here with you. Please, I do not want to be alone."

She thought about Garbo, but that seemed flippant. His admission surprised her. He was absolutely serious. She sank back into her chair, marvelling again at his suddenly tragic beauty. Was it Olivier and Leigh? She half remembered a comment about beauty and tragedy. Was he doomed? It was her turn to shiver.

With a perceptive glance, he read her expression. "You have been very kind." He tried to meet her gaze, but he was afraid of her. "You have saved my life." He shook his head then offered an awkward self-effacing shrug. "Please, let me stay here? Please?"

She leaned towards him, ridiculously encouraged by the number of words he had managed to string together. "I'm sorry, but I don't understand. I'm trying to help you. Why won't you tell me what happened?"

He drew back physically. Mentally, he had retreated behind a wall. It was fortified. There were gun towers and searchlights. There were landmines. Nobody was going to breach his defences.

She took a moment to study his face. It was as if someone had pulled the shutters down and switched off the lights. There was no one home. "Why were you in Paris?"

He stared at the carpet. He was cold and remote. The shining beauty was just a mask.

She was amazed by the transformation. "You'll be more comfortable in a proper bed," she said encouragingly. "A sofa is okay for the odd night in an emergency, but you can't be comfortable? I'll help you up the stairs. You'll be alright. I'm just trying to help you."

A sixth sense rang an alarm in his head. He did not look at her. Mechanically, he responded: "You have been very kind."

"But I don't understand," she said sharply.

The tone almost drew blood. He shivered. He slowly wrapped his arms across his chest as if he was suddenly cold. He could not describe his fears. There was nothing that he could say. He offered the slight shrug, and hoped she would leave him alone.

"I really don't understand," she said rather irritably.

"You have been very kind." It was his only defence. He glanced desperately towards her then lowered his gaze again, and squirmed uncomfortably. "Please, let me stay here? I will not make a sound. I will be quiet. Please?"

She rose to her feet, feeling cheated and indignant. "I'm going shopping. We'll talk about this later. You need to think about what you want." She tried to restrain her temper. "I'm trying to help you. I made up a bed for you."

"You have been very kind," he repeated mechanically as she drew closer. He was rigid with fear. He could barely breathe.

If he had not been so frail, she would have cuffed him across the head, not to hurt him but to underline the message. She had never hit anyone or anything in a temper, unlike her own father who had been known to vent his rage with blows. Her husband had only communicated through violence. For a while, she had felt that she only attracted violent men. Her memories sobered her. She sank down on to her knees beside the sofa then reached up slowly to clasp his face in her hands. It was such a lovely face. The eyes glittered like diamonds.

He tried to avoid meeting her gaze, but was anxious not to offend.

She was hurt. "I don't understand." She tried to smile. She could have wept. "I'm trying to help you."

There was nothing he could do. It was not a lie: she had saved his life. But he did not recognise her. He did not know why he was in her house.

"I'm not very good at this," she admitted unhappily. "I'm actually totally useless, but I do want to help you." She pulled his face closer. She needed to see those luminous eyes. She would have forgiven him anything, but it was useless. So she reached up to carefully plant a kiss on his forehead. "You must believe me."

He could not even breathe.

His bone structure, his flawless skin, his thick eyelashes and what she could glimpse of those startlingly blue eyes: mere evolution could not have created such a face. It had to be surgery. Now, he needed a shave. His beard was something of nothing. She did not want to imagine just how good-looking he would be when clean shaven and in good health. "You have to understand that I'm not really strong enough to do this. I've been ill for a long time. I want to help you. Really, I'll do everything that I can do to help you, but I'm terrified that it won't be enough." His eyes flashed. She lost her breath, but recovered. "Yes, I'm terrified. You'll have to help me." She combed her fingers through his hair, which was wild and unkempt. She smiled. She felt like a mother with a child. It was so nice to comb his hair. "Do you understand?" she asked. "You must understand."

She was too close. He could not look at her. He managed to breathe deeply, but his heart was racing, and he felt horribly sick.

She took a moment to study his expression. She could read every degree of his anxiety. The muscles in his jaw moved tensely. His nostrils were flared. She could almost smell the adrenalin coursing through his veins. She could have kissed him then, not chastely on the forehead but full and hard on the lips. She could have rolled him down onto the floor and wrapped her body around him then devoured him. But it did not happen. He was shivering again. She was embarrassed then quietly appalled. She did not need mirrors to know that she was too old and just completely unattractive. It would have been utterly ridiculous and wholly inappropriate, and in her heart, she feared that it was just obscene. Her hunger for him vanished like smoke in the wind. At that moment, her self-loathing filled her stomach with acid, and she turned away from him wanting to be sick. She drew away more than just physically. She was again the monstrous evil spider, and he was a delicate shining jewel.

"Please?" he said.

There was desperation in his voice, which made her pause, but it was her turn to stare at the floor.

"Please?" he repeated. "I am sorry." His eyes were pools of light. "I cannot tell you anything."

"You have to trust me. I saved your life. You can tell me anything."

He lowered his gaze anxiously. "Please, I cannot tell you. I am sorry. I do not know why I am here. I do not understand what is happening. I do not understand anything. I do not remember you." He could not look at her.

She felt cheap and dirty. Her usually brittle self-confidence had been decimated. She really did not want to stare at him, but those eyes were addictive. His face was extraordinary. In that lovely face, she found beauty and empathy and compassion. She reached out to brush a fingertip across his forehead then caressed his cheek. It just wasn't fair. Even unshaven and unwashed, he was so beautiful. As if perceiving her desire, he bowed his head, and drew away enough to make her feel that he had read her darkest thoughts.

"I'll buy some ice cream. Summer's here." She tried to smile. "Everyone likes ice cream."

He stared at the floor. He had overstepped the mark. He could not do it twice.

*

They had been running. Omar suddenly caught the creature's sleeve. "Okay, let's go - this way - now!" He dragged the creature in through a darkened doorway then forced it behind him while he peered back along the street. The drab buildings were defaced with graffiti and crude posters carrying political slogans. The street was deserted but for a few parked cars, and some distance away, a group of immigrant children loitered beneath a half dead tree. It seemed all clear. Behind him, the creature shifted anxiously. Instinctively, he tightened his grip then turned irritably to command obedience.

Almost dead on his feet, the pale kafir gazed about wildly. He could not breathe fast enough. His head was exploding. Pain tore across his chest. He started to lean forward onto his knees.

"Are you alright?" Omar caught it by the throat, and pressed it flat against the wall. "Stay there," he ordered. "Calm down. If you get upset there'll be nothing but trouble." The creature nodded, but it was very obviously distressed. "Okay? Listen to me. Don't get upset. Calm down. I don't want to hurt you." Omar's hand squeezed the soft throat again. "Calm down. Don't make me hurt you."

The kafir risked one searching glance into Omar's eyes then sighed again. He nodded. But his nerves and the adrenalin that flooded his body kept him agitated, and made meek obedience completely unattainable.

"Calm down!" Omar shoved the creature violently against the wall. He heard its head smack the brickwork. He felt it go limp, but he kept it upright and on its feet. "Don't make me hurt you. I don't want to hurt you," Omar said soothingly. "Okay?"

The impact had eclipsed everything else. His head was still ringing. The kafir nodded slowly. He felt sick and dizzy, and so terribly frightened, but he had absolute faith in Omar.

"Now, calm down." Omar squeezed its shoulder encouragingly. He did not need a degree in psychology to understand that it was confused and frightened. They were both in danger, but the last thing he needed, at that moment, was the creature dissolving into a bundle of nerves and forgetting its manners. "No one's going to hurt you. Don't do anything stupid."

The kafir hesitated then gazed earnestly at him. He visibly shivered. "Please?" he asked. He was begging. "Please, I can't. I can't do this."

Omar's tone changed. "I don't want to hurt you." He bounced the creature against the wall again, and stared menacingly into its eyes. "Calm down!"

Lifting his hands to pacify Omar, the kafir looked into his face again then lowered his gaze. "Please?" He nodded. He did not want to complain. He was not allowed to refuse. He was just so tired. "Please? I can't run anymore." And he slid down the wall to sit on the filthy broken tiles that covered the floor. He glanced anxiously up at Omar, who was visibly annoyed. "Please? Please."

Omar turned away to peer around the doorframe. The street was still quiet. He took in their surroundings. They were far away from the Paris that he and the millions of other tourists knew and loved. Half the buildings in the street looked deserted. Most of the windows were boarded up. The doorway that had given them sanctuary was the only open door in the street. He glanced down at the creature that remained huddled on the floor then turned again to explore the building that they had entered. There was a long corridor. It was drab and dark. The few visible doors were metal and all of them were shut. The only visible decoration on the limed concrete-block walls were the left-wing slogans and posters advertising political rallies and raves. The floor tiles were all smashed and disfigured. Drifts of cigarette butts, and the detritus of various unattractive addictions, and hurried sexual encounters covered the floor, discoloured by decades of neglect.

*

If it was possible, he became even quieter, and hardly moved at all. When forced to go to the bathroom, he rose stealthily like a patron stealing out of a theatre during a show. She made an effort not to stare at him. When she did, he always shivered like a beaten dog. While the tennis was on, she managed to completely ignore him, but she was still struggling with the basic concept of having a man in her house. But he asked for nothing. He said nothing. He just huddled against the side of the sofa like a wild bird with a broken wing. She gave him a drink whenever she made one for herself. He was never given the opportunity to decline. When she had offered him a sandwich he had recoiled. He shook his head. He trembled. When she pressurized him, he just turned on those blue eyes and she capitulated. He did not eat. He never ate. She plied him with bottles of baby food, yoghurt, milkshake, which he accepted politely, but never real food. While he was still ill, she was too anxious to upset him, and loathed to be a bully. His dreams were less frequent but still terrifying and foreign. The only English words that she recognised were 'please' and 'no'. He said 'no' loudly and desperately and often. Everything else was in a foreign language that she did not understand. Something terrible had happened to him, and he was constantly reliving it.

Chapter 24

They watched the television, and now and then each other. He always deferred. It was unmanly, but he was gay. She could not help suspecting that he had a guilty conscience. And of course, he was hiding something. His extraordinary body and terrible wounds guaranteed deep, dark secrets. She kept making excuses for him because to acknowledge that he was telling lies would have completely undermined her good intentions. There could not possibly be an adult male on the planet, who did not have secrets. That went hand in glove with having a highly tuned autonomous antenna stuck down their pants. It was not just the heterosexual men who were ruled by their dicks.

He had to be gay. She kept coming back to her original premise. He absolutely had to be gay. He was too good-looking to not be gay. It was her hormones that were completely up the creek. It was probably a side effect from all the pills she was taking. Perhaps, she was 'going through' menopause. But she had only to look at him to know that it was nothing more complicated than lust. It was about her, and not about him. Her certainty allowed her to watch him without flinching. She was allowed to be curious. She felt she had earned the right to be judgemental. So he was gay. He was gorgeous. It was a given. She could laugh off her burning desire as some ludicrous side effect of menopause. She was not a raging inferno of passion, but having a hot flush. If she concentrated very hard, she almost believed it. She wanted to believe it, but it was a lie. He might be gay, but she still wanted to have sex with him. She was not foolish enough to think that the love of a good woman would change him. She felt less threatened acknowledging that he was a homosexual. It did not make him any less attractive.

When the exquisite pain in the pit of her belly was unbearable, she went out into the garden. There was always so much to do in the garden.

She missed Federer's game, which was rather annoying, but he was through to the final and the long anticipated confrontation with Nadal. The World Cup was seriously beginning to clog up the channels, and absolutely dominated the news. She had actually managed to avoid watching any of the previews and 'friendlies', but had often heard the television on when she was not in the room. He had mastered the remote. She wanted to be easy-going about it all, but that was annoying.

"What were you doing in Paris?" she asked after watching the tennis highlights. She was smiling. Federer was being hailed as the greatest tennis player of all time. Every shot was a masterpiece. The superlatives were like honey to her ears. "Did you live there?" She was determined to be convivial, but there was no response. "Do you ever go to watch the tennis or the horse racing? The course at Longchamp looks lovely. That's in Paris, isn't it? Do you ever have the opportunity to go?" She felt she could carry a reasonable conversation on these topics. Small talk was not in her repertoire. The World Cup was banned.

He stared at the floor. For a while, he did not move at all, but he understood that she required him to say something. After a long, strained silence, he moved stiffly to place his feet on the floor then tried to sit upright. His face whitened. Pain tore across his back, forcing him to lean down across the armrest.

"You said you were in Paris," she reminded him gently. "And you've been to Monte Carlo recently. You were at the casino. Did you go down for the Grand Prix? It must have been packed out with tourists and spectators. I watched some of it on the television. When I was a little girl, I was a big Graham Hill fan, and then Damon, of course."

They were not questions. He understood that she was prompting him. He could not remember ever mentioning Monte Carlo. "Yes," he said quietly. He did not feel able to elaborate.

"What were you doing in Paris?" she asked, trying to keep the same warmth in her voice.

He was breathing hard. He was staying conscious. Looking at her was too hard, but she was just sitting there smiling. Why couldn't he remember her? Why was he in that house? Anxiously, he pulled the blankets around him. He just wanted to sleep. He wanted more pills. He needed the pills. "Please?" He shook his head then offered his self-effacing little shrug. "Please? I am so sorry. I do not understand what is happening."

She understood that he was frightened. She could not think of anything to say that would not have ridiculed him. And he was being totally sincere.

"Please, I want to go home," he said quietly. He was still staring at the floor. He could not look at her. He hardly dared to breathe.

She gave him the respect that he deserved. She was not sure why it was so significant, but his body language made it profound. She let him have the moment to gather his nerves and fill his lungs. When he managed to lift his head, she smiled kindly. "I will take you wherever you want to go."

Emotion flushed his face. His glittering eyes flashed. Were there tears? He simply nodded, unable to speak and utterly overwhelmed.

"I want to help you," she said resolutely. "I just want you to be happy."

A single tear rolled down his cheek to nestle amongst the stubble. She was promising him everything that he could hope for, but there was nothing that he could say. The muscles in his throat had contracted. His heart was breaking.

His silence surprised her. She wondered if he had not heard. "I want you to be happy." She leaned towards him. "But I can't help you if you don't tell me what happened. You need to tell me who to call. Someone somewhere must be worried sick about you. If you just give me a name then I'll be able to find the number. There must be someone that I can call for you." She tried a warm motherly smile. "You have to trust me. You have to tell me what happened."

He shook his head. "Please? I-" A fine hand dashed the tears from his eyes. "I cannot tell you anything." His breathing came in ragged gasps. "Please...?" He took a moment to try and find his nerve. "Please, I cannot. I am sorry." He nodded slowly. He did not know what to say. "It is forbidden." He shivered and sighed. "I took an oath. It is forbidden."

She frowned. That sounded ominous. "This is your lover?" she asked, trying to keep her voice soft and seductive. "He made you swear an oath not to tell anyone what he did to you? Well, he's not here, and if he was you should just tell him to fuck off. He nearly killed you."

He flinched then shook his head unhappily. His chest was bruised and sore. His lovely face was broken. "No. Please no, he did not hurt me." He cowered under her piercing gaze. "He never hurt me."

It was a declaration.

With all her assumptions blown out of the water, she had to sit in silence, staring at him, waiting for him to elaborate. She tried to read the story of everything in his grotesque and broken face. His eyes were red now. All the grace and beauty had vanished. He was hardly a shadow. "Then who has hurt you?" she asked gently. "Who could have done that to you? You must know. It's very personal. It's not as if you were just mugged. You must know. If I hadn't found you, and brought you back here into my home, you would have died. You must know who did that to you? You must have been conscious."

It took him a minute to find his voice. He was totally overcome. "He never hurt me."

For a moment, she almost believed that he was lying. There was desperation in his tone. He wanted to be believed. After all that he had been through, she felt obliged to give him the benefit of the doubt. It was not for her to start psychoanalysing his relationship with his lover. She had no experience to draw on, but she had seen all the American procedural cop shows. Victims aligned themselves with their abusers. Everyone knew that. It almost made sense. She tried to smile encouragingly. "It's alright."

He was staring at her now. His eyes were sharp with intent. He was agitated and upset, but determined. "He never hurt me."

She felt his need for her to believe him.

"He would never hurt me." He tried to control his emotions. He was terribly upset. The soft baritone voice had changed to that of a child. In his distress, he had become a child.

She could not bear to look at him. He was in a terrible mess. He was crying. For her sake, he had to stop crying. "It's alright. You're safe now." She did not know what else to say. "Really, it's alright." She looked up again to try and read him. "Please, don't cry. Please, don't be upset. I want to help you. You're safe here. No one will hurt you. Please, don't cry."

"Please? You don't understand," he said. He had his face in his hands. He was trembling, struggling to breathe, and in agony.

She said nothing. Clasping her hands in her lap, she waited for him, but she was too embarrassed by his distress to survive that. She went out to the kitchen to make a pot of tea. She gazed out of the window into the garden, but all she could see was his rotten putrefying flesh. Someone had beaten the crap out of him. That was sobering. The jewellery and the scarified skin were something else. He had been whipped. That was personal. It was vindictive. Everything else was just some adult sex game. She wanted to believe that his lover had not hurt him, but it all seemed connected.

She splashed a generous shot of rum into his cup and loads of sugar. It would probably make him sick, but it would settle his nerves. She carried the tray back into the lounge.

He was sitting on the edge of the sofa bent forward over his knees. When she entered, he retreated to lean across the armrest, but the sudden movement sent bolts of pain across his back. It was excruciating. A cold sweat drenched him. The shock was as startling as a slap across the face. For a moment, he had to stop breathing, and just focus on not passing out.

She fussed around the tea tray. She could see that he was in distress. When he had regained a little colour and managed to inhale, she turned carefully to press the cup of tea into his hands. "Here, drink this." He looked absolutely lost. Her heart melted instantly, and she gently ruffled his hair. "It's alright. You're safe now."

He managed to smile, but he could not look at her. His hands were shaking. The cup and saucer rattled in his grasp. It was all he could do to hold them.

She retreated across the room to her own chair, pushing a cat out of the way. She curled her feet under her. She tried not to stare at him. There was some mindless violent movie on the television. Without hesitation, she switched it off. The silence was profound.

"So who did hurt you?" she asked gently. "Someone took all the skin off your back. That must have taken hours. You know who did that. You must have been conscious, at least, at the beginning. Someone wanted to hurt you, damage you very badly. It was personal. You know who did that." It was not a question.

There was a long and uncomfortable silence. At last, regretfully, he nodded. He could not look at her. He felt her eyes penetrating his skull. Trying to deflect her attention, he turned the cup around in the saucer. The china grated delicately. The teaspoon tinkled like a tiny bell. Across his back, the agony was slowly ebbing away. He could just about function. He knew almost nothing, and could say even less. The strange pains in his chest twanged like guitar strings. He took a deep breath. "I was in Paris to see a doctor." He looked at her, daring her to contradict him, then nodded affirmatively. He knew that she knew he was being evasive if not actually dishonest. "I was ill."

She was still dazzled by his blue eyes. She managed to nod then was vaguely aware of being surprised. "You were ill?" She tried to smile sympathetically, but still felt like a rabbit dazzled by headlights. "I'm so sorry. What was the matter?" She hardly dared to hope that he would suddenly tell her everything.

He took a deep breath then turned to stare at the blank television screen then almost shook his head. He did not know how to explain. It took him a long time to admit: "Please? I don't know." There was a long pause. He understood she was waiting. "They sent me away."

"They sent you away?" She wanted to repeat everything that he said, but it hardly aided her comprehension. "Were your parents there?"

He found that baffling. Frowning, he slowly shook his head. He did not understand the question, but he was sure that it was important.

She could see that he was trembling. Perhaps, that was different in France? "I thought," she said, by way of explanation. She did not want to frighten him. "I thought that the doctor might have wanted to talk to them – if you were so ill. Was your lover there? Your partner? Is that what boyfriends are these days? I know you're gay." She tried to smile. She wanted to be terribly modern and broadminded. "In this country, doctors will only discuss your case with your next of kin, which is traditionally parents or spouses."

He had no idea what she was talking about, but he was breathing steadily. Some of the anguish had drained from his face. He was quiet, almost composed, but not relaxed. He was just very still. And he had aged a thousand years. "Please, I don't know. I was always sent from the room. The doctor asked me many questions, but he never told me anything."

She studied him for a moment. It was too easy to believe that he was telling lies. It might have been kinder to say that he was confused about the facts. He did not seem confused. So he was a liar or he was delusional. "So who did the doctor tell?"

He stared at her. He felt like a gutted fish. "Please? I don't know." He made his awkward shrug then frowned then shook his head then frowned again. "He told my master," he said, in a flat confessional monotone. Her reaction made him flinch. His nerve failed completely. His gaze fell back to the floor. "He only talked to my master. No one said anything to me."

"Your master?" she whispered. It was a cult. It was some weird foreign homosexual cult. She was pleased with her cleverness then appalled by the implications. "Your master?" Her breath caught in her throat. Her heart seemed to stop beating. She looked at him and saw a victim. The grace and beauty were just the wrapping. It did not matter that he was loved because she knew that he was loved beyond measure. He was a victim.

He stared at the floor. He was physically in the room, but really he was somewhere else.

"So tell me about your master then?" she said, trying to sound as if it was a normal topic of conversation. "Is he tall, dark and handsome?"

He shook his head. "Please, I cannot." He was in a mess. "I do not know what is happening to me. I do not understand."

She gave him the moment. "It's alright. You're safe now. No one can hurt you anymore."

He nodded, but he did not believe her. There was so much he needed to know before he could let go of his fear. He gazed at the teacup. He stooped to put it on the floor then stared at his hands, which were shaking, then trapped them between his thighs. He was so afraid. "There is a clinic in Paris. There were always tests, lots of machines, and I was sick the first time." He paused to carefully drag air into his lungs. There were pains in his chest again. His heartbeat was erratic. He glanced towards her, but not at her, in an appeal. "When my master came to meet the doctor, I was always sent away to wait with Omar. The last time, we could hear my master shouting. He was so very angry. I had never heard him shouting before. Later, Omar took me back to the house to wait with the Pakistanis, but my master never came."

"Your master?" she said again, staring at him, not wanting to hurt him, but knowing he would be hurt.

The young man moved forward on the sofa to convince her that he was in earnest. "My master? Yes, he is my master. He is a great prince. I take care of him."

"Your master or your lover?"

He was completely lost. He searched the pattern on the carpet for an answer. He did not understand what she was asking him. For a moment, he was a child again, and his heart was broken. "Please, I cannot… You are wrong. Please, I am sorry, but you are wrong. Please? You do not understand." He filled his lungs, and shook his head in despair. "He does not love me. He could not. He could never love me. That would be a great sin."

She was nonplussed. "A sin?" So it really was some weird foreign homosexual religious cult. "This is the man who beat you?"

He shook his head. He was terribly agitated. "Please? No. No. It was not like that. You do not understand. He would never hurt me. He is a great man. He would never hurt me."

"This is your lover?"

He started to shake his head. He did not know how to make her stop asking questions. He tried to hide behind his hands, but he was too weak to make such a dramatic gesture. She had to stop. "Please? I was in Paris," he said very quietly, trying to remember. "We were in Paris." He frowned and shook his head, but felt compelled to explain. "I carry his briefcase. It is very heavy. We were leaving a restaurant. There was a very loud noise. It sounded like an explosion or a gunshot. It was very frightening and confusing. Someone pulled me into a van. I did not see them. It was dark, and they wore ski masks, and it happened very quickly. They pressed something over my face. It smelt of something unpleasant. I must have passed out. I woke up later at the clinic. Omar had found me buried in a garbage skip. They had cut my master's briefcase from my wrist. My master was very angry."

"Did he blame you? That hardly seems fair."

He shrugged awkwardly, but lowered his hands. "I never saw their faces. Omar asked me so many questions, but I could not remember. He said they had used a drug. He said it was – chloroform?"

"That's the smell that you noticed. A cloth would have been soaked in it." She tried to smile encouragingly. "Was there something valuable in the case? They must have been an organised gang if they came with the chloroform and the equipment to cut it from your wrist."

He shifted uncomfortably. "Please? I don't know. When I came around I was very sick. Omar took me to the clinic."

"Probably a lucky escape... But somebody punished you?"

"Please? You don't understand. It wasn't like that. Omar took me home while my master stayed with the doctor." He paused. His head hurt. His brain was engulfed by fog. "I was pleased to be home." He brushed an errant tear from his cheek. "But then I felt ill. I was sick again." He looked at her anxiously. "Then I am here with you. Please, I do not remember you. Should I remember you?"

There was accusation in his tone, but she was not afraid of him. He was too frail to be a threat to anyone, and apparently, he had every right to be upset. "So what is wrong with you? You said you were ill."

He was struggling to calm down. He was confronted again by his need to know why he was in that house.

"What is wrong with you?" she asked again. His body language informed her that he was too upset to speak. She let her thoughts wander. "You went to a clinic in Paris? A clinic? In Paris? That's where Rock Hudson went. He had AIDS. He was one of the first great celebrities to die of AIDS. You're too young to remember. It was awful. The public reaction was appalling. For a while, they were dropping dead like flies. No one would touch anyone who was gay because it was a foregone conclusion that they were contaminated." She turned on him like a surgeon with a knife. "You're gay. You're sexually active, well, you are, aren't you! What was wrong with you?" He wilted under her gaze, which just proved his guilt. "Bloody hell, this is serious. Do you have HIV? Is it AIDS? You're sexually active so you could have God knows what wrong with you." She was angry now. She wasn't worried about him at all, but entirely focused on the risk to herself. "This is serious. You have to explain."

He shook his head. He rubbed his chest. "Please? I do not understand. It was not..." He hardly knew what to say. "Please? My heart. It is my heart."

It was not AIDS. She was alright. She would not die horribly. For a moment, she was embarrassed by her prejudice, then just relieved. "I'm sorry." She tried to smile. He was not looking at her, but she wanted him to hear that she was smiling. "I'm sorry about that. There are just so many horror stories about AIDS. They're saying now that it was a genetically engineered disease." She shook her head in dismay. "Are you alright now? Are you supposed to be taking some medication? You didn't have anything with you when I found you."

He shook his head. He was totally lost. "Please, I do not understand."

She needed a minute to find her equilibrium. Her palms were still sweaty. She had been genuinely afraid.

While she was lost in her own head, he reached down to collect the cup of tea. He was so thirsty. He drank it down without registering that it tasted of sugar and rum. As predicated, it hit all the right spots. The sugar went through his bloodstream like hot treacle. The alcohol took the edge off his nerves. Another cup would have made him quite happy. He could not ask. He dared not look at her.

"So you were in Pakistan?" she asked gently. It was an almost neutral question.

He was calming down. It still took him a minute to admit: "Yes."

"So your 'master' is a Pakistani?" She was surprised. Perhaps, it wasn't a cult? The Tribal Areas in Pakistan were as inaccessible as the Dark Ages.

He was adamant and anxious. "Please, no! No. He is a great prince. His uncle is a great king, the defender of the faithful."

She regarded him doubtfully. He was a liar or he was delusional. She really did not want to have to choose. "You're kidding right? A prince? Like a proper prince?"

He waited indignantly for her to stop laughing. It was loyalty that drove him to explain: "He is a great prince. He has many houses and many servants. He is one of the richest men in the world, and beloved by his people. He is a great man."

She tried to wipe the smile off her face. She could not tell if he was telling the truth, but he obviously believed it. That did not, however, make it the truth. "And you were his…?"

It was a leading question. It hung in the air between them. He did not want to own it. She could not take it back.

He clasped and unclasped his hands. He turned hopefully to find more refreshing tea, but the cup was empty. He wanted to search her face and look into her eyes. He needed to know her, but he could not lift his gaze from the carpet. Feeling cornered, he said: "Please? I take care of him."

She leaned forward. "So you are his servant?" She was watching him like a hawk. He was definitely shifty. He was not quite squirming with a guilty conscience, but he was in trouble. "All that jewellery and those decorations, and you are his servant?"

Completely confused, he stared at the floor. His brain was fog-bound. He just couldn't think fast enough. Every word he had said felt like a betrayal.

"You have a Breitling watch."

He did not even look at his wristwatch.

"So your lover is not some psycho Russian oligarch?"

"Please?" He felt every syllable like a nail through his heart. "I do not understand."

It was her turn to stare at the floor. He was trembling. His pale, tragic, beautiful face had disappeared into a tortured grimace. He needed the gentlest care and consideration, but she needed answers. She had to know what had happened. She had to know if he was telling lies or merely delusional. Merely delusional? It was her turn to shiver. Someone had hurt him. That was a fact. She had the evidence. She would probably never recover from the shock of seeing his flayed back. But all this stuff about a prince had to be nonsense.

"So who is Omar?" she asked. "Is he also a prince?" She felt like the Gestapo.

"Please, I'm sorry. No." he said. He glanced towards her, hoping to find clemency. He was exhausted. He felt pulverised. He could not escape her curiosity just as he could not escape that house. "Omar takes care of me," he explained defensively.

"I see," she said. "So is he your lover?"

He shuddered as a spasm of pain went across his back. He moved carefully to lean down across the armrest. Asking for mercy was beyond him. He could not even ask for a cup of tea.

"Well?"

He simply did not have the vocabulary to describe his relationship with Omar. "Please? He takes care of me."

She did not understand. Obviously, he was being evasive, but she did not have the skills of an inquisitor, and could not pin him down. And he was a victim.

"Please? I just want to go home."

She was quite taken aback. "Of course." She tried to smile. She could hardly believe that he was about to give her an address. All she could see was the top of his head. He was staring at the floor like a miserable penitent. "And where is that?" she asked gently.

He visibly withered. He could barely move enough to shrug. Looking at her was totally beyond him. To acknowledge the truth would destroy him. He felt she had betrayed him, but then he had betrayed everyone. When he shook his head, it was a confession.

He did not know.

She left him alone to recover his composure. She filled the kettle, stared out of the window, put food down for the cats. Only the ginger glutton was there. She was not really thinking. It was pitch dark outside, and she was simply too tired. Some horrible little voice was telling her that she could not run away. He needed her. She was too frightened to contemplate just how much he needed her.

He was grey-faced when she returned to the lounge. He was exhausted. She pressed him to take a can of milkshake and some painkillers. His nerves were at breaking point. She did not dare put him under any more pressure. She would have liked him to eat something, but his total lack of appetite seemed vindicated by his illness so she could not bully him anymore. Everything he had said just prompted more questions. He looked awful. She gently ruffled his lank heavy hair, then said goodnight.

*

The room smelt of stale cigarettes and mould. The kafir sat beneath the window, his knees drawn up, and his head resting on his folded arms. He did not need to worry about anything. Omar was there to protect him. But he could not sleep. When Omar moved about the room, the floorboards creaked. Whenever Omar peered cautiously out through the shutters to observe the street below, the kafir stiffened with apprehension, knowing he would be expected to run for his life at Omar's command. They had been in that room for a few hours. It was the fourth or fifth room. They were moving from one hiding place to another. It seemed to have been going on for days. He was so tired, and thirsty enough to drink poison. As the night lengthened, he began to shiver as all his resources drained away.

After his long vigil, Omar settled on the filthy floor next to the creature, opened his arm around it like a great wing, and drew it in. Not for the first time, he was reminded that the creature was barely twenty years old. He drew it closer, pressed its head down onto his chest then stroked it comfortingly. The creature grew heavier. Like a child, it sought reassurance. Omar pulled it in closer, lifting his chin to allow it to stretch across his chest. His own children clung to him with the same innocence. It was easy to forget that the creature was not a child. He squeezed it again, and stroked it gently.

The kafir could sleep now. Omar's steady heartbeat soothed him. He was not alone. Omar would never abandon him.

Outside, rain began to fall. It drilled chillingly against the shutters. A cold wind rattled through the gaps. The temperature dropped. Omar gazed at the shutters. His instinct was to take another look around, but the street had been empty for hours. Only a fool would stray out in such horrible weather. The creature slept in his arms, disturbed by bad dreams. He felt its every tremor. It was cold. It probably had good cause to be frightened. Omar held it tightly to reassure and arrest. It had been quiet and calm because he had insisted on its absolute obedience. He could not credit it with any sense of loyalty. It could easily disappear in Paris. It must have considered its options. That it had remained with him like a shadow proved only that it felt safer with him while they were both in danger. He did not trust it at all even while it slept in his arms like a child. It was as deceitful and cunning as a rat. It had no understanding of honour. It many ways the creature was still just an immature and opportunistic child.

Long before dawn, the streets filled with noise. The rain had stopped. Vehicles appeared to pick up immigrants, who emerged from the apparently empty buildings like an army of ghosts, to be carried off for the day to toil long hours for a handful of coins. Omar watched from the window. The immigrants and their dubious employers were better than watchdogs. They assured Omar that no one stalked the shadows. There were no police or strangers lurking behind corners. Omar sent a text message. He stood at the shutters, lifting his eyes from the phone only to take in his view of the street below him. There was no reply. He checked his watch. He stared down at the creature, who sat placidly at his feet. They had not had anything to drink since the previous afternoon. Omar could not remember when he had last eaten.

The phone did not ring. Omar had switched off the ring tone, but he kept looking at the screen even though the handset was lifeless. The sun rose over the harsh concrete skyline. There were no churches there, no architectural marvels. The ugly grey buildings were uglier in the light of day. The sun shone poorly. The temperature did not rise. Brown-skinned children came out to play in thick warm clothes. Malian women in quasi-traditional costumes emerged to watch their children, and gossip with their friends. There were some men still loitering. They smoked cigarettes. They watched everything in the way that all criminals did. During the morning a steady stream of cars used the road. A few drew up near the men, windows rolled down, packets were exchanged, then the cars drove on. A van appeared and parked. The street emptied. The van waited and waited then moved on. Omar watched. The children came back out to play. The men returned to watch the world go by.

"Please?" the kafir asked. He sat on the floor, his knees drawn up. He did not dare look up at Omar. "Please? I'm thirsty. Please, may I have water?"

Omar did not even look at him. "So am I. Don't make such a fuss."

The kafir ran his fingers through his hair. His hands were shaking. He felt very frail. "Please?" He was cold and tired, and did not like being adrift in an alien world. "I want to go home," he whispered. "Why can't I go home?"

Omar stepped back from the window then stooped to give the creature a backhander across the face. "Be quiet." It was not a savage blow. "Don't make a fuss. Don't make me hurt you."

Utterly forlorn, the kafir nursed his face. He curled up like a child, hugging his knees and rocking silently.

Omar checked his cell phone again then glanced down at the creature. He recognised the signs. He reached down to grip its shoulder, and brought it to its feet. It staggered wearily, certain it would be hit again. Omar forced it backwards into a wall, and pinned it there menacingly. "I don't want to hurt you. Okay? You have to calm down. We have to stay here for a while. You'll be alright."

The kafir stared down. He was shivering. He nodded dumbly.

The cell phone trembled in Omar's hand. He stepped away from the creature though he kept hold of its arm. There was a message from the Prince.

The kafir watched the expressions on Omar's handsome face. He read the concern and anxiety, which disappeared as the Arab lifted his gaze. The kafir's head bowed. He stared at the floor, round shouldered and submissive. He was not allowed to look, not allowed to ask.

Omar tightened his grip, and drew the creature across to the shuttered window. He gazed down into the street. They could not go out the front door. It did not seem likely that it would be any safer leaving at the rear. He surveyed the creature, speculating on whether he could risk leaving it alone while he reconnoitred the exits. There was nothing in its demeanour to inspire confidence. He glanced down into the street, and tightened his grip again. He saw the eyes flash as the creature looked towards him, but not at him.

"We're moving again. You stay with me, okay? You stay with me. You don't wander off." He gripped its arm tighter until the pain made it nod and gasp. "Come on. God willing, we will be back with His Highness by nightfall."

The cell phone trembled again. Omar gazed irritably at the screen. His face melted. His eyes lit up with joy. As he read the text, a great smile broke across his handsome face. For that brief moment, no one else existed. "Aysha?" he whispered. His whole body thrilled with pleasure.

The kafir watched him in silence. The man he knew had been transformed. Only the grip on his arm was familiar. He stared at the cell phone, trying to imagine what could have made a grown man so very happy. Curiosity almost overcame his reserve. He was almost rising on to his tiptoes to try and see what Omar could see that had made him so happy.

Omar turned abruptly. "Get down." The look he gave the creature was anything but kind. "Get down now. On the floor."

The kafir felt the impatience in his tone. He went down placidly. He stared at the floor.

Omar stood over him, but he was quickly typing out a message. His joy had become anxiety. He sent the text. Moments later, he had a reply. He read it unhappily. He ran his fingers through his hair then strode back to gaze out through the shutters. He typed another message. There were several over the next ten minutes. At last, he came back to grasp the creature's shoulder. "We're leaving."

The kafir rose slowly to his feet. Something was wrong. He stared at Omar, compelled to silence, but desperate to know what had happened.

Omar took hold of the creature's elbow, and led it away. In his left hand, he held it securely. In his right, he had his gun. They went out the front door. Everyone on the street stepped back when they saw the gun. Omar was a mountain of courage and fortitude. Nothing in his demeanour invited the strangers to risk a confrontation. They stepped back again, and by the time that Omar and the creature were turning the corner, they were completely alone.

Weak with hunger and completely disorientated, the kafir hurried along to keep up with the Arab, who strode purposefully down the ugly streets that were awash with squalor and vice. Omar was in unfamiliar territory, but kept moving forward, using the bleak sun to find his way. He made no attempt to hide his gun until they had been travelling for half an hour, and had reached a neighbourhood where French citizens lived, where there was traffic, and the hope of a taxi. There were the remnants of gardens. The windows and doorways were not boarded up. The locals were not rich, but these houses were homes, and they were all occupied.

Omar holstered his gun. Ahead of them was a weather-beaten bench under a poplar tree. Omar stopped, and pressed the creature to sit down. He took out his cell phone, and tapped out a number.

The kafir was exhausted and anxious. He watched as Omar's face lit up with joy. He liked Omar's smile. He had no comprehension of what could have made him so happy. It was so lovely, he found himself smiling too, and had no idea why.

"Aysha," Omar said, grinning foolishly. He saw the expression on the creature's face, but was too happy to be annoyed by its impertinence. "I'm looking for a taxi. I'll be there, I promise. It'll be an hour. There must be a taxi around here somewhere."

"My darling, I'll wait for you. We are safe now, but please hurry."

"Aysha, my love, are you comfortable?"

"The children are tired, but they are so excited about seeing you."

Omar turned to survey the neighbourhood. "We'll find a shop. They'll have a number for a taxi. I'll be there." He grinned again and felt foolish. "I love you so much, Aysha."

The kafir observed it all in a fog of exhaustion. He could hear the faint musical whisper of a female voice. He had no real experience of females. The few he had seen were concealed by veils. Recently, while travelling abroad, he had glimpsed foreign women, but they were always at a distance; and from the conversations of the men around him, he understood that they were all diseased whores, who were immoral and not fit to be the wives of righteous men. For years, he had listened voraciously to the stories that Waheed and Mahmood told about their families. Aziz was more reticent. He talked about his sons with pride. He kept his women under control as befitted his honour. Waheed's daughter-in-law wanted a career. The kafir had no conception of what that meant. He wondered idly whether Aysha was Omar's wife or a lover. If the former, she would be veiled and respectable. If the latter, she might be anything.

They found a taxi. It took more than an hour to reach the small, but respectable hotel in the western suburbs.

Aysha was a Believer. She wore a jilbab. Her face was astonishingly beautiful. She had three young children, who were wide-eyed with glee at seeing their father. Omar lingered in the doorway. He had the creature behind him. He had dictated terms to it while they were climbing the stairs. All of the terms were underlined with the threat that Omar would be forced to hurt it if it did not behave. Omar held his family back by raising a hand then he drew the creature from the shadows. He felt the shock in his wife's eyes. The children were confused, but still bubbling with excitement at having their father back with them. They all stared at the creature, a pale youth in a T-shirt and jeans. The creature stared at the floor. Occasionally, it looked towards Omar. It saw everything, but looked at nothing. Under their scrutiny, it seemed to shrink with apprehension. Omar moved it across the room. They had a suite. There was a small sitting room, a kitchenette and two bedrooms. He commanded it to sit on the floor in the corner furthest from the door where it could not blink without being observed. Then Omar turned to open his arms to his wife. She flew into his embrace. They kissed. The children scuffled around them trying to be included, their wild excitement suddenly unleashed.

The kafir had never been kissed. Even from across the room, he felt the flood of emotion. He was excluded again. His insignificance was underlined. He was too tired to be upset. At such moments, he yearned for the attention that he received when he danced for the Pakistani men. Their passion for him then was genuine. In their rough love-making, he felt their hunger for him. It was brutal, wounding and real. Those were the only times that he felt valued. Sometimes, he was allowed to fall asleep in their arms. He hated sleeping alone. He hated being alone. He hated being cold. Huddled up on the floor, he observed Omar and his beautiful wife and noisy children. They shared a joy that he could not comprehend. It was delightful and spontaneous. The man that he had known for years as the strictest disciplinarian was now blushing with happiness, almost speechless, overwhelmed by excited kids, and being kissed repeatedly by a very beautiful woman. It was a picture of domestic bliss and contentment. The kafir filled his lungs. He was so very tired. He could hardly keep his eyes open, but he watched them being happy, and they were so obviously very much in love. And he yearned to be loved like that. Somewhere in his heart, he felt the absolute loss of something he could not even remember. There was something missing. He watched Omar and his family, and he felt the warmth of their love like a roaring fire. Was it jealousy? He did not care. He wanted to be loved as they were loved, but knew it could never happen. He was not like them. They were Believers, which meant that they were the Beloved of God. They were righteous. They would all go to Paradise. In comparison, he was nothing at all. He was not considered the same species. They kept him and fed him as long as he was useful to them. He strove to be useful. He tried not to be too tall.

Later, when Omar was seated on the sofa with his children around him, his wife asked if he would like a cup of tea. She hesitated then glanced at the creature now curled up on the floor. Omar rose at once. He took his wife out to the kitchen. He filled a glass with water then went back to rouse the creature. It was pale, but not asleep. He held the glass while it drank. A curt command made it lay down again. It said nothing. It dared not look at Omar. It dared not betray the fact that it had been watching him and his family for hours. There was no malice. It was simply bewitched by the affection and tenderness that this man had for his family. Like a devoted dog, it lay on the floor, silent and motionless, watching everything, waiting to be needed and included, but it was quickly abandoned again, and forgotten as Omar turned away to rejoin his family.

Omar easily distracted his children with promises of all the wonderful and exciting things that they would be able to do and see in Paris. Everyone was happy. They were all excited. They were together and on holiday. It was perfect.

There were several calls over the next few hours. Omar's family went sightseeing. Omar kept the Prince's property safe. He could not leave it alone nor could he take it with him and his family up the Eiffel Tower. It was late in the evening when a bodyguard arrived with a new burqa. The creature was quickly covered up again, and taken back to the Ritz. Omar took a long anticipated week's holiday with his family, all expenses paid by the Prince.

It was only much later that the kafir learned that there were enemies searching for him in Paris. Princess Noor had been spreading lies about life for women in the Kingdom. She had apparently accused the men of hideous crimes against their wives, and insisted that the scandal of underage boys continued unchecked. She had published two books, and exposed her family to shame and scandal. If she went home, she would be arrested, publically flogged and possibly beheaded. There was no punishment harsh enough to restore family pride. According to the Pakistanis, she had spies scouring Paris for a beautiful infidel that had bewitched a prince.

Chapter 25

She was in the bath when she remembered that she had bought him a razor. That would surely cheer him up. A nice shave. He would be rid of all that itchy-scratchy stubble. He would be restored. He would be even more beautiful. He would be happy. That made her smile. And there were the clothes. Why hadn't she given them to him before? Because he was ill? But he was better now. There was absolutely no reason for him to be wandering around in a sheet like some bronzed waiter at Club Med. He would be happy about that too. Of course, he would. He was probably feeling quite awkward being semi-naked in a strange woman's house. She wanted to rephrase that.

She felt like some crazy old dame in a scary Grimm's fairy tale. The Grimm's stories were often quite gruesome. There was always a lot of vengeance and retribution. They were really not fairy tales at all, and seemed totally unsuitable for young children. But then most cartoons were incredibly violent. And there were far too many sadistic children about, and all probably brain damaged because their mothers took drugs or got drunk or chain smoked while they were pregnant. Children were not all universally sweet and kind. They could be unspeakably cruel for no other reason than to enjoy inflicting pain. She had once seen a young boy repeatedly smash a frog with a tennis racquet. He had only stopped when his racquet broke, then ran to his mummy in a temper and tears.

She put on some clean clothes then went back downstairs. He was asleep. He had not bothered to switch the television on. Obviously, he did not know that late night television on Fridays was invariably filled up with quasi-documentaries about giant penises and drug-fuelled orgies on some island in the Mediterranean. She had a feeling the giant penis was in New York. She shook her head. It was full of too much information. With a bowl of water, towels and some soap, she went to stand over him. She was grinning. She had had a good idea. He was really still asleep, but he rallied quickly.

"It's alright." She pressed his head back down on to the cushions. "Just stay there." She was smiling like a cat. "Lay still. I should have done this days ago."

He succumbed to the pressure, but his eyes swept over the equipment that she had brought. He was hardly reassured.

She showed him the razor then wet the soap, and rubbed it into his beard. His eyes were open. Now and then, he flinched. She could feel his breath on her hands. She could smell him. "I've never done this before." She paused to reflect. "Yes. That's true. I've never done this before. So lay still." She was enjoying herself. "Aren't you pleased it isn't a cut-throat razor?" She laughed. His pupils dilated in alarm. "It's not going to be great, but as long as I don't cut you, it will be an improvement. It's alright. Don't move!" She felt his anxiety as she pressed down on his left cheek bone to keep him still. Her heart was fluttering like a bird inside her rib cage. The razor slid down into the bristles. She could hear the hair snapping like wheat stalks beneath a scythe. Her initial plan had been to quickly and efficiently clean up his face, but the very first stroke of the razor revealed that it would not be so straightforward. The razor quickly clogged up. She had not used enough water to gain a good lather. She was loath to get her sofa wet.

He was rigid. If he had been half asleep, he was not now. Had she seemed remotely competent, he might have been able to close his eyes, but she was a bag of nerves, and kept squeaking with excitement. So he kept his eyes open while strenuously avoiding meeting her gaze.

His face was too dry. After every stroke, she had to clean the razor and lather his face again. And the razor was so sharp. She was terrified of cutting him. He remained as meek as a lamb. He hardly seemed to be breathing. As she worked, she was again reminded that his skin was flawless. His eyelashes were thick and long. It was almost as if he was wearing makeup. She was immediately reminded of Elizabeth Taylor. There was the legend that she had double eyelashes. As a child, she had auditioned for a part in the film '*Jane Eyre*', the Darryl F. Zanuck version with Joan Fontaine and Orson Welles. Like many Hollywood movies, it had cherry-picked the most dramatic elements of the story and ignored most of the sub-plots. Elizabeth Taylor was up for the part of Helen, who dies as only a Victorian heroine could die, but Elizabeth was sent packing because they believed that she was wearing makeup. It was not true. She won the part. Later, she acquired the height necessary to be '*National Velvet*'. After that, she grew up to become the biggest movie star of all time. Did the young man share the same genes? It would explain so much. He certainly had the remarkable eyes.

Her good idea took over an hour to accomplish. She did not cut him, but it was probably the worst shave since Stone Age Man tried it with a dull flint. She wiped his face carefully with a towel. Her heart was thumping. Her hands shook. He was so attractive. Her whole body was on fire. She drew back, biting her lips, offering an apologetic smile.

He immediately sat up, but he lifted one hand to stroke his face. The hand trembled. The tension in his body was making the wounds across his back throb with pain. "Thank you."

She shrugged, and shook her head, utterly embarrassed. "It's not great. I…" She ran out of words. She was babbling. Clean shaven, he looked so much younger, and he was far better looking than any man had a right to be. She felt diminished. She wore no makeup. Her hair was wet and flattened across her head. She reached out in awe to trace her fingers slowly across his cheek. The eyes closed. She felt him shudder. "How old are you?"

The shoulders moved. He shook his head.

He did not know. She was shaken to the core. It had to be amnesia. But she managed to smile, then climbed awkwardly to her feet. Her knees were shot. She walked unsteadily out to the kitchen with the razor and towel. She hardly knew what she wanted to do. It was very dark outside. She could not run away and hide. Killing time, noisily opening cupboard doors, she found by chance an old bottle of shampoo. It was half empty. It was years past its sell-by-date. She could not even remember when she had bought it or why it was stuck away behind a tin of chestnuts.

He was still sitting there when she came back. He looked lost and anxious. He kept touching his face. He did not know what to do.

"I thought we could wash your hair?"

He blinked, glanced searchingly into her eyes then stared back at the floor.

She could see the muscles in his jaw flexing. The perfect symmetry was there again. Her heart actually skipped a beat when she had looked into his eyes, and her whole body burned with pleasure. His eyes were so bright and blue and dazzling. He might have smiled. She might have imagined it. She almost suspected that he had only allowed her see his eyes because she had earned the privilege. It seemed arrogant, but it was less humiliating than believing he did not look at her because she was so unattractive. She had to make a conscious effort to breathe again. "Yes, we'll wash your hair." She was on a roll. She was ticking boxes, but her hands were shaking badly.

He barely flinched as she carefully wrapped a dry towel around his shoulders. She did not want to make his back wet. The new skin was so very delicate. The slightest abrasion would erase it as easily as a spider's web. She poured a good handful of shampoo on to his dry hair. It was thick and inert. It would not work up into a lather. She added more, then more again. She emptied the bottle on to his head. She worked the liquid into a dense foam which covered his whole scalp. Standing behind the sofa, she had to reach forward. She was very tired. She massaged with restrained aggression. He flinched and grimaced, but never made a sound. She did not want to see his face. She so wanted to do it really well, but knew she would fail miserably. To rinse out the shampoo, she had to ask him to bend forward over his knees, which was painful for him. Then she poured water from a jug over the back of his head, and caught it in a washing up bowl on the floor. It was awkward rather than difficult. She did not care about splashing water into his ears or over the carpet, but it was absolutely critical to keep his back dry. When she had finished, she gave him another towel then hurried away.

He rubbed his hair tentatively. When she came back, she gave him another milkshake and more pills. She took the towel without asking, and quickly finished drying his hair. He looked and felt like a drowned rat. He did not protest when she quickly finger-combed his hair. She was not smiling now.

"Thank you." He looked up at her, and tried to smile as he had seen a man smile on the television. "You have been very kind."

She could not look at him. It was nearly 3am. She was beyond tired, and frightened of doing something awful. Washing his hair and giving him a shave still seemed to have been the right thing to do, but not in the middle of the night. It ticked all the boxes. It was just the wrong time. She was so tired. She was almost sure that she was dreaming. Her maternal instinct was working quite well, but she knew that she was being totally OCD. She should have done it in the morning or the following evening, but not now. She just couldn't stop herself. As long as he kept covered up, and she did not have to gaze at that perfect face then there was still the smallest chance that she would not go completely insane.

Without acknowledging him, she quickly tidied up around him then hurried to the light switch. "I will see you in the morning." She switched off the lights, and ran away up the stairs.

He sat for a while in the darkness. He heard her going up the stairs. There was some movement on the landing. He could hear water running. The toilet flushed. Doors opened. There were footsteps. Then all the lights went out. He waited a moment more to be sure then slowly rose to his full height, and stretched very carefully. The pain across his back was intense, but it was less than it had been only days ago. He ran his fingers through his hair. It was a real pleasure to have clean wet hair. He felt revived as if he had just plunged into a swimming pool after a long hot day. And the shave saved him from the constant irritation of an unfulfilled beard. In the doorway, he stood listening a while longer. There were no sounds from upstairs. He walked across the hall to the bathroom, put the light on in there, then stood staring at his reflection in the mirror. He inspected her work critically then tiptoed across to the kitchen. Again he stopped to listen, then switched the light on and waited again. She was not coming back. He only disturbed a cat sleeping on a chair tucked away under the table. The razor and soap were on the draining board.

He had never shaved himself before. He had never needed to comb his hair. Was this independence? Tidying his appearance seemed acceptable. He could not contemplate opening the fridge to find a drink or attempting to remove the sheath that kept part of his body off limits. He did not feel independent. Until he knew who she was, it was not safe to do anything. But he shaved his face very carefully. He raked his fingers through his hair, and he smiled at his reflection because he knew that he was beautiful. It was the only currency he possessed.

In the lounge, he sat in the darkness. He swallowed the pills and the delicious cold milkshake. He did not know why he was in that house, but every day he was growing stronger.

*

They spent most of the summer in New York and Washington, with only the briefest trips back to Riyadh or the desert palace.

There were many scares that year. Pakistan and India played games with their nuclear toys while in neighbouring Afghanistan there were earthquakes that left thousands more dead. There were estimated to be forty-five thousand homeless refugees. The aid agencies were struggling with the usual cultural issues. Everything they brought in to give to the refugees was stolen and sold by profiteers. They were still not allowed to talk to the women. The decades of war had destroyed the basic infrastructure. All the while, India and Pakistan were test firing nuclear missiles at each other near the border. Oil production was to be reduced for the second time in a year to raise prices in order to reduce the Kingdom's national debt. On the eighth anniversary of American troops arriving in the Gulf, the US Embassies in Nairobi and Dar es Salaam were attacked. The mastermind behind it all was bin Laden. He had apparently been planning it for years. Prince Turki was trying to start a conversation with the Taliban about bin Laden. Two hundred and twenty-four people had died in East Africa, and thousands were injured, but in America, the nation and the media were still obsessed only with the moral character of President Bill

Clinton. A tsunami in Papua New Guinea hardly made the front page because Secret Service agents would be compelled to testify before the Grand Jury about the conduct of their President, and Monica Lewinsky was given immunity if she would testify against him.

The kafir actually watched on television as the President of the United States of America, the last remaining superpower on the planet, was forced by media pressure to confess on television that he had had 'an improper relationship' with Monica Lewinsky, and that he had 'misled' the nation regarding that relationship. Even to the kafir, it seemed ludicrous. He hated all things American because they loved Jews and murdered Believers, but surely having sex with a girl was too small a thing to pillory a man for in such a dangerous world. And it was endless. If anything the confession made it all worse. The kafir found it utterly distasteful and self-indulgent because while America turned in on itself and obsessed, the rest of the world was in trouble. There was a huge bomb in Omagh. The Russian rouble was devalued so savagely that tens of millions of ordinary people lost all their savings as several of the largest banks collapsed. The American President approved attacks on al Qaeda bases in Afghanistan and a pharmaceutical factory near Khartoum in retaliation for the attacks in Nairobi and Dar, but he was accused, at home, of only trying to deflect attention away from his own personal problems. Even UNSCOM's Scott Ritter had a go at Clinton and the United Nations Security Council for not forcing Saddam Hussein and Iraq to comply with the rules set down at the end of the Gulf War. Ritter was adamant that Saddam was not disarming, and still had the capability to launch a chemical strike, but the media were only interested in finding out how many other women had been seduced by Clinton, the psychopath, and what did Mrs. Clinton think about her philandering husband?

In September, the Prince and his entourage went down to the University of Stellenbosch for the International Peace Conference. It was ostensibly to commemorate fifty years of UN Peacekeeping, but the Prince had gone to have the official update on what was happening in Western Sahara. He had flown down in his own 747. They had parked up on a runway in Cape Town then driven every day across to Stellenbosch in UN designated vehicles. There were a lot of important people there. Security was tight. The Prince met his old friend Kofi Annan, and he was honoured to be introduced to Nelson Mandela. The situation in Western Sahara had not improved. The UN Special Envoy, James Baker, was struggling to reconcile the two sides. The UN team on the ground had successfully registered 147,350 voters, which was nearly 60,000 more than their previous best. The situation was complicated by sub-tribal factions, and the number of armed combatants in the region. The Saharawi felt too many Moroccans had been registered to vote, while the Moroccans felt they did not have adequate representation.

The dampener on the whole conference was that the UN Security Council's demand for a ceasefire in Kosovo between the Serbians and the ethnic Albanians was totally ignored. The following month, NATO airstrikes were authorised against the Serbians, but Milosevic quickly came to the table, and agreed to give autonomy to Kosovo so the airstrikes were called off. True to form, Milosevic reneged on the deal. A few months later, the Serbians sealed the borders, and went in to wipe out the Albanians.

For about six months, the UN focused a great deal of attention on Western Sahara. While the world watched the fracas of the Weapons Inspections being on again and off again, and the humiliation of President Clinton, Kofi Annan tried to speed up the registration of voters, the appeals process and ultimately the referendum. Polisario signed off on James Baker's revised package, and agreed a date for the referendum, but again, at the last minute, Morocco wanted some changes. In November, Annan went on a ten day North African tour. He spent the second day in Western Sahara. The Prince was sitting on his hands. Much as he wanted to be there, he could not sweep into the refugee camps at Tindouf or the capital, Tifariti, and overshadow the Saharawi people, who were struggling to keep their dignity in desperate circumstances. He was on the phone to his various friends down there, receiving a blow by blow account of what was happening, but he knew he had to keep a low profile, at the very least to pacify King Hassan, who was not above complaining to King Fahd.

The situation in the Kingdom grew increasingly tense. Whenever they went to the airport there were more policemen on the streets. They would not shoot at Believers. That was unheard of because the clerics would never allow it. The servants talked about troublemakers and bin Laden. In the palace he was feared, but there were many in the Kingdom who did not fear him. Change was needed. Everybody agreed. Nobody quite knew what that meant. They were an extremely conservative and hospitable people. It shocked them to talk about what was happening across the Middle East. There was so much violence. It could not all be because of the Jews and Americans. Bin Laden and the young men he led seemed determined to turn everything upside down. It was upsetting. To even talk about change as an abstract concept felt like disloyalty to the King, but the world had changed already. Those that wanted to keep it the same faced calls for modernisation, and also calls for strict adherence to the laws of Islam as dictated to the Beloved Prophet by the angel Gabriel. No one had the right to defy the Words of God. No one was permitted to question them. The goals of the two factions were poles apart, and there would be no negotiation only slaughter and martyrdom.

In Kabul, the Taliban had declared that bin Laden was 'a man without a sin', so there was not any hope of extraditing him to face charges for the bombings in East Africa.

The kafir hoped the airstrikes would prevent him having to spend Ramadan at the madrassa. The tension had been increasing for weeks. The Americans and British were determined to bring Saddam Hussein back in line, but he was still making outrageous statements, and having boisterous photo opportunities with crowds of loyal supporters. It was common knowledge now that he had a team of lookalikes, some men had even undergone plastic surgery so that it was impossible to tell which of the boastful characters popping up all over the country was actually the real Saddam. The French were undermining the Americans. The Russians and Chinese had their own agendas. No one wanted war, which had allowed Saddam a great deal of latitude. But the Americans and British were determined. The airstrikes had started on the 16th. Those first planes were probably still airborne when the same bodyguards came again to collect the kafir for his annual sabbatical. He tried to resist, but even his own Pakistanis turned on him. His master's wishes were sacrosanct. Not only did he leave covered in a burqa, but beneath that he had a blindfold and handcuffs. They had not forgotten his mutinous behaviour twelve months previously. Any professional courtesy that he might have received as the personal property of the Prince was forgotten. Now, he was just a prisoner.

He was given homespun clothes bought cheaply at the market in Gilgit. He was given boots. The snow was deep. The handcuffs remained. If he kept quiet he was allowed to eat apricots, and to share their water. The moment he started to speak, to complain, to beg for a reprieve, he was gagged. The blindfold remained. It had been a week. It felt like longer. He was in hell. His nerves had begun to destroy him. He simply did not have the emotional resources to survive his continuous analysis of his predicament. It did not matter how he changed the parameters or the facts or the statistics. Prof. Shah could not possibly have survived. Without the irascible old man, he had no hope of finding a sanctuary. It was too easy to imagine what would happen if Jawad was in control of the madrassa. Jawad had no loyalty to Prince Abdul Aziz. And the blindfold reinforced his feelings of isolation and despair. All of the structures that Omar had carefully built into the kafir's life to stabilise him and protect him had been left behind in Riyadh. He was disintegrating rapidly. He had an escalated heart rate. He wanted to throw up. He was so distressed he was close to passing out. They had not even left the hotel in Gilgit, and he was already breaking down.

They did not remove the blindfold until they were ready to start up into the mountains. The climb was even more difficult. The whiteness hurt his eyes. There had been a lot of snow over the last few weeks. It was a long, exhausting haul through sometimes a few feet of snow that had been turned to ice by the sunlight and the altitude. His new tribal clothes were better suited than the thobe that he usually wore. It was bitterly cold. The boots saved his feet from frost bite. His hands suffered, but not enough to trouble his bodyguards. Mentally, he was dead already. If the treacherous climb did not kill him then Jawad certainly would. It seemed pointless to even continue but they bullied him along. Whenever he complained, the gag returned, which made it harder to breathe, and denied him the ability to drink. He accrued cuts and bruises from falling down, but they never slowed down.

It was dark when they reached the valley at the foot of the mountain on which the old fortress rested like a slumbering beast. There were no lights. There were no stars. It was as silent as the moon, and so very cold. Not even the wind blew. The three men crossed the flat meadow that in springtime was lush with grass. The kafir was too weary to focus on anything more complicated than putting one foot in front of the other. He was propelled along by the bodyguard, who walked behind him. They were all tired, but only the kafir did not want to reach the safety of the high walls, and the warm fires that the madrassa promised. The final torturous climb sapped all of them. It seemed to take hours to weave their way up the almost sheer face. No lights came on. There were no sounds from inside.

At the gates, the kafir's strength failed completely. He was trembling and incoherent.

The bodyguard let him fall to his knees while he went forward to push on the immense doors. In the darkness, he was on top of them before seeing that one door hung aslant from its hinges. The other was badly shattered at the top. He turned to raise a finger to his lips, commanding his companions to silence, then pulled a heavy automatic pistol from his belt. The local guide also drew his gun. While the bodyguard peered through the splintered wood into the darkness beyond, the guide quickly forced a gag back into the creature's mouth then dragged it to the base of the wall. He left it there, with its shackled wrists knotted down into its bootlaces. The bodyguard had a torch, but he trusted his eyes to search the deserted courtyard. There was a deep carpet of snow. Something had happened at the madrassa, but whatever it was had been days if not weeks ago. He went from room to room, using his torch only when he was inside, and sure that he was alone. There were bodies. Someone had survived to lay out the bodies, perhaps attempt to nurse the wounded, but only the dead remained. There were bullet wounds, and the mutilated flesh resulting from explosives. The majority of the bodies belonged to children, but there were several men. None wore a uniform that the bodyguard could recognise, but then the insurgents dressed like civilians so they could infiltrate anywhere. In the darkness, it was difficult to make a judgement call, but the result was obvious. Everyone left at the madrassa was dead. Knowing that the insurgents invariably left booby traps, the bodyguard carefully retraced his steps to the gate, and climbed out through the shattered hole.

"They're all dead," he said quietly, then checked the creature's position before staring away into the darkness. "We need to find somewhere safe to spend the night then go back down in the morning."

"All of them?" the local guide asked in shock. "You're sure? All of them?"

The bodyguard nodded. His first responsibility now was to protect his master's property. An hour ago, his mission had been to transport its sorry arse to the madrassa for a month of religious contemplation and reflection. Now, his only concern was returning it safely home.

"My wife's cousin has a boy..." The local guide leaned anxiously through the broken gates.

The bodyguard caught his arm. "Don't go in there."

The guide turned to survey the darkness. "We can't stay out here."

It was the condition of the kafir which decided it. He was barely conscious and weakening fast. The freezing temperatures only compounded his condition. The bodyguard lifted him in his arms, and carried him through the gates. Using the torch, he carefully retraced his steps across the courtyard, and entered the nearest building. The guide followed, scared and hysterical, covering his eyes whenever they came upon a corpse. There could be no fire. There was nothing to burn.

They spent the night huddled together. The bodyguard held the creature in his arms. He never slept. He kept his gun close and the creature closer. At first light, they crept back down the mountain, and returned to Gilgit.

While the local guide took responsibility for reporting the massacre to the police, one of the bodyguards phoned Omar for instructions. They did not have the authority to make a decision about anything, but even they knew that the creature could not be in the Kingdom during Ramadan. The police ordered them not to leave town, and when the Arabs tried to insist, the police threatened to arrest them.

They sat it out in the hotel for nearly a week. The police wanted to interview everyone, but it was unthinkable that they would interview a woman. They made a big drama of demanding information from the local guide, but he had nothing to tell them. The Prince's bodyguards resented being shouted at, but it was a national trait. The police wanted to be seen to be doing an in-depth investigation, but they were not prepared to go into the mountains because everyone knew there would be booby traps and IEDs. The local police did not have the resources to deal with that, and the army were always busy somewhere else. Then it snowed, and the airport closed, and the atmosphere in the town became quite threatening. Stirred up by the mullahs, the locals believed they were above any secular law, and they despised the government, and particularly Nawaz Sharif. Everyone was becoming super-religious. It was not just because it was the holiest month of the year. It was a political statement. It was a declaration of their independence. They might be illiterate, unemployed and dirt poor, but they all had guns, and could all be fearless warriors for God. When there was no real information, there was always gossip about the foreigners, and then speculation about the reason for a woman going to a madrassa. There was a lot of talk about the mysterious figure in the burqa. Initially, everyone assumed it was a married woman, but then it became a cause for concern because the two men sharing the room were not related so, at least, one of them was not related to the woman. Someone at the hotel boasted that it was, in fact, a white-skinned foreigner, and possibly not a woman at all. Suddenly, there were always, at least, a dozen suspicious men loitering on the stairs. They never did anything. They just hung around menacingly, curious about everything but too sullen and proud to speak. The Arab bodyguards and the kafir became virtual prisoners. The situation became increasingly perilous as the silent multitude remained ominously blockading the stairs. There were a lot of anxious phone calls. They were running out of food. The manager wanted them to hurry up and leave because more men were arriving every day to blockade his hotel. As soon as the weather lifted, Omar arrived with a squad of towering bodyguards in white thobes and lavishly decorated jubbahs. The locals backed down before the impressive strangers. The rescue was successful. The kafir, concealed by the burqa, was escorted out of the hotel with all deference due to a respectable woman. As far as the resentful locals knew, he might have been a princess. An army helicopter took them all back to Islamabad. Omar and the kafir flew on to Paris in the Prince's private jet.

The kafir did have his regulation four weeks of fasting while reading the Holy Book from dawn until dusk, but it was in a Parisian garret, and it was Omar who set the curriculum. He did not allow the kafir even a moment to dwell on the past. He was a stricter disciplinarian than anyone at the madrassa. No one came to disturb them. No one ever found out what happened to the men and boys at the madrassa. It was never mentioned again, and the kafir had no right to ask.

A week later, gunmen opened fire on Shiites worshipping at a mosque in Islamabad. Sixteen were killed with another twenty-one injured. A Sunni group claimed responsibility.

Chapter 26

It was not quite so warm, but the sun was shining. From her bedroom window, she could see tractors in the distant fields. It would be an early crop of hay or a late crop of winter wheat. In the hedgerows, the cow parsley was falling over with the weight of the flower heads. Everything looked lush and green and stuffed full of life. She went to the bathroom, and it was not until she was inside with the door shut that she thought about the consequences of having him sleeping in the next room. When she had been downstairs, it seemed to be a very good idea. Perhaps, leaving him on the sofa was safer? He might be totally gay. He might be the most ardently homosexual man on the planet, but he could still be an axe murderer.

With some war paint on, she went downstairs. The cats were spilling out of the kitchen. There were several loud meows, a few choking cries, and a few more that sounded like bleating sheep. The black cat was sitting on the kitchen table. He was comfortably superior. He knew he did not have to make a sound. She picked him up and carried him through the throng then deposited him gently on the draining board. From the cabinet beneath the sink, she found three tins. She shared two and a half around two plates, which she put on the floor. The remainder went in a saucer for her yellow-eyed best friend. He purred loudly. She left him to eat in peace on top of the counter.

The television was on. She missed a step. She was sure she had switched it off the night before. The young man was asleep. She found the remote on the floor beside the sofa. She flicked through a few channels. The Morning Line was on, which more or less decided what she would do on a Saturday afternoon. Of course, that Saturday there was the Ladies' Final in Paris, England's first game of Group B in the World Cup, and the practice session to sort out Pole Position at the Grand Prix at Silverstone. It was a tough call for the horse racing to compete with all that.

He woke up with a start then moved diligently to place his feet on the floor. He was too sore to sit upright for more than a minute. It was easier to lean across the armrest. As she opened the curtains, he watched her every move, but as soon as she turned to face him, he bowed his head and stared at the floor.

"How are you feeling this morning?" she asked pleasantly. She did not look at him though the temptation was almost unbearable.

Clean shaven, and with full-bodied hair worthy of an advert, he was transformed. He was still encompassed by his wounds, but he was significantly better. He glanced towards her. "Thank you. You have been very kind." He tried to smile, but she was ignoring him. He fidgeted with the collar of his shirt then rearranged the blankets that covered his bottom half.

She almost blushed. "You're looking better." But she stared at the television. It was already an advert break. "I didn't mean to bully you last night. I was just, well, you know, I was very tired."

He watched her for a while. He did not understand.

In an attempt to reassert her authority, she walked around behind the sofa so that she could take a look at the back of his shirt. "It's not bleeding," she said. She was undeniably relieved. If all the rigmarole of washing his hair had opened his wounds, she did not believe he was strong enough to survive a new infection. His immune system had already taken a hammering. "If you take your shirt off then I can apply some more cream. It has healed amazingly well. It must be feeling a little better?" she suggested hopefully.

He glanced across his shoulder to acknowledge her then began to unbutton his shirt.

Having bullied him into a conversation yesterday, she had hoped for a verbal response. Perhaps, he was not a morning person? She pursed her lips, watching him start to take off his clothes. He was always so ready to take off his clothes. She walked away. For several minutes, she wandered in and out, watching the television, clearing up and washing up whilst strenuously ignoring him.

When he had taken off his shirt, she returned with the fat tub of Vitamin E cream. He was still an eyeful without his shirt. From the front, he was all abs and tight skin. Not for the first time, she focused on his injuries, and strove to ignore everything else. His back was very pink and uneven. Some of the welts had healed as lumpy ridges. Others were merely stripes on the paper thin skin. She lavished the cream on him. The slightest touch made him flinch, but he never made a sound or lost his temper. She was so gentle and so careful. She had seen what he never would. The putrefying flesh falling off his bones was something she would never be able to forget. It was not just a visual scar. The smell had been revolting. Even now, when his back was covered in the delicate new skin, all she could see was the original wound. Every time he started to unbutton his shirt, she was subconsciously anticipating having to deal with that wound. That it had healed at all always surprised her. For the rest of his life, he would carry the horrible scars on his back, but he had survived. She had been so lucky. Every day, she was thankful for being so lucky.

"That's much better," she said blithely. She was smiling with triumph and not a little relief. "You'll be as good as new soon." Now, it was her turn to tell lies.

He trembled. He needed painkillers.

"Keep still for a while." She was still smiling. She was way out there in Meryl Streep territory. "Let it all be absorbed. Give it about ten minutes." She stayed behind the sofa while she replaced the lid on the jar. At that moment, she did not believe that she could look into his face and stay sane. "And then you could get dressed? I bought you some new clothes. You could, maybe, go outside. It's a lovely day. You must be getting a bit stir-crazy in here." She was doing the smiley voice thing, but knew he was not listening. "I'll fetch you a drink. You'd like that, wouldn't you? Then you can rest. You don't really need to do anything except get well. I'll look after you. It'll be alright. I won't let anyone hurt you. You're safe now. You do know that you are safe now?"

He leaned across the armrest. He was so tired. He wanted a drink badly.

"I'm so sorry," she said. She did feel guilty, but she had to walk away. His naked torso was like a huge electric light bulb. She was dazzled. She just could not see anything else.

She made a sandwich, and ate it silently while she counted her pills. Somewhere in her head, a strident little voice argued about the necessity of taking all the damn pills. She felt controlled by the pills. There were so many. If she threw them all away then nobody would know. She counted them. She counted them over and over again. Her fresh cup of tea cooled. It was only when one of her cats tried to jump onto her knee that she realised that she had been sitting there for more than an hour. It was the black cat. He was as black as night. In his huge yellow eyes, she was sure that she could see love. This cat loved her. That was undeniable. And more than anything else, she loved the cat. Was it smiling? She was sure it did. She was a child again being gently scolded. Without further prompting, she swallowed her pills even though her throat muscles contracted and her tea was stone-cold. She knew. Of course, she knew. She had to take her pills. It was not just her life that was threatened if she did not take the prescribed medication. Her life was meaningless without the responsibility that she had assumed for the cats and the wildlife and now, the young man,

She crushed some more painkillers into a glass of milk. He drank it down without hesitation, but watched her with some concern. He thought he had been promoted to pills. She was obviously distracted. There was nothing he could do. When she picked up the shirt and opened it for him, he carefully bent his arms into the sleeves.

"I've bought some underwear for you." She tried to smile, but she could not look at him until he had buttoned up the shirt. "And I have your other clothes here somewhere. They're nice and clean. We could get you all dressed up then you could come out into the garden with me. Would you like that? The roses are coming into bloom. The birds are singing. It's lovely."

"You have been very kind." He was sweating profusely from the effort of putting on a shirt. Like a decrepit old man, he leaned back across the armrest.

It felt like a brush off. She took a minute to really look at him. He was ill. After everything that he had been through, it was a miracle that he had survived. She was not a doctor. She was still appalled by her inability to call the police or an ambulance. If he had died, she was not sure how she would have justified her failures. "I'll leave you to rest," she said. "Look! Here's the remote." She fetched it, and pressed it into his hands.

He stared at the floor. Putting on a shirt had left him drenched with sweat. He was absolutely exhausted.

She went out to the kitchen then opened another tin of cat food. The ginger glutton was always there. A few others appeared, but only because they were curious. They had all had breakfast.

When she heard the young man going to the bathroom, she lingered. It was not that she was curious about what he was doing in there. She just needed to know that he was coping. She had basically bullied him into going to the bathroom so that she could avoid having to wash him and keep him clean. She felt that she had been bullying him since he arrived.

When the bathroom door opened, she turned to watch him walk carefully back into the lounge. With the sheet knotted securely around his waist, he did look very oriental. Without the beard, he looked so much younger and thinner. His hair was luxuriant. It was styled to be quite long on top which allowed wayward strands to fall attractively across his eyes, but cut short around the nap of his neck. Even more than twenty yards away, she could not refrain from raising a hand to brush the loose strands back into place to restore perfection. It was an irresistible impulse. It felt like witchcraft. She clasped her hands in her lap. The cold thing in her chest was racing. She did not regret having washed his hair, but wished she had done it at a more conventional time. She shook her head. She was definitely in trouble. Why were her palms clammy when her mouth was so dry? She was in so much trouble. He was gay. Deep in her belly, the exquisite pain sent out a dozen assurances of penetration. Her muscles contracted. It was not real, but it was so real. She could not breathe. She could not move. Her whole body convulsed. Her fleshed burned red hot. He was gay. He was definitely gay. She could not possibly be getting all hot and bothered about some gay guy. It did not matter that he was so damn gorgeous. He was gay. She was obviously sickening with something. Her hormones were firing off like rockets on the 4th of July. The delicious pain went through her again. She writhed involuntarily. She was hot. She was so hot that she suddenly believed in spontaneous human combustion. At that moment, she would have let him do anything. Front, back, top, bottom, she would have done absolutely anything if he had only embraced her and kissed her.

In misery, she reminded herself that he could have been her own son. It did not matter that his eyes were the wrong colour. She had to believe it. It was possible. It was absolutely possible. He was her son. The delicious agony became crushing regret. Every nerve took a hammering. She beat herself up. She was a monster.

She could hardly stand up, but she went outside. It was still early. The sun had not warmed the air. The Starlings were monopolising the bird feeders. Robins and Blackbirds were searching through the undergrowth to find bugs and worms to eat. The other songbirds were keeping a low profile still on their nests. Carrying buckets of seeds, nuts and dried mealworms, she trudged around the walled garden topping up the feeders. Out in the main garden, she repeated the process. It was amazing how much the tiny birds could eat, but they were all spoilt for choice. There were always little piles of discarded seed beneath the various feeders, which the hedgehogs and mice tidied up at night. There were often foxes about on the lawn. They were particularly partial to the peanuts.

Her brain was not really engaged. That was part of the joy of being in the garden. It was always a complete distraction. She could be thinking about a dozen different topics and hold opposing opinions on them all. In many ways, she was like a butterfly going from flower to flower or a child in the biggest sweetshop on the planet. There was so much to do. There was so much choice. She could have a caramel here then a pear drop there, a few fruit gums then find a whole box of chocolates. Hours passed unnoticed. Then she would attack a patch of nettles, and reality dawned again, and she cursed her lack of gloves. She had gloves. She had lots of pairs of gloves, but she did not like wearing them. She liked to feel the good earth between her fingers, and be able to find the tiny firm eggs in the blanket weed.

She disturbed a hedgehog in the flowerbed behind the small pond. That was a bad sign. They were not supposed to be about during the day. It was quite small. It had to be a juvenile. She had several rabbit hutches which she had used over the years to keep unfit hedgehogs in over winter while she fed them up to the required weight to guarantee their survival. Curiously, her Vet had told her not to feed her elderly cats processed cat food because it was full of cereals and additives which the elderly cats found difficult to digest. It was hardly surprising that she was always teetering on the brink of bankruptcy.

She did not go down through the woods. He had changed it irrevocably. Perhaps, after he had gone? Perhaps, when enough time had passed? There were so many questions. She already knew more than she really wanted to. She was not sure whether she would ever be able to recover from the damage that he had done. Her absolute control over everything was an illusion. She thought about her land and her trees and her wildlife, but nothing was really under her control. Life was brutal. Nature was cruel. She was actually fighting a war, but she still persisted in believing that she owned everything and could command it all to her whim. She was still trying to justify why she had gone down in the middle of the night to give him a shave. It was so OCD. But he had needed a shave. He looked so much better for having been shaved. But in the middle of the night? She needed Big Shoulders. Her hands were shaking. They burned with nettle stings. Why hadn't she worn gloves?

When she went back into the house, the cats were gathering en masse. There was yet another football show on the television. Grinding her teeth, she gave the young man some more pills and a milkshake then returned to the kitchen. She fed the cats again then microwaved a quickie pasta meal, and ate alone. An hour later, she was still there. She had made a cup of tea. She had taken enough painkillers to settle her nerves. But she was still angry. This was her house. It was her television. Bloody football! Damn bloody boring World Cup! And damn the bloody nettles! Her hands were still burning from the nettle stings. She used some of his Vitamin E cream, which took away much of the heat.

The pills started to quell her black mood and helped with the nettle rash. She calmed down. She knew the young man was damaged more than just physically. He might be gorgeous and desirable, but he had been hurt in ways she could not begin to imagine. So he was watching the television? She had no right to dictate what he watched when she was not in the room, beyond the fact that she owned the television, and he was technically just a guest. But it was really not important. She had a little fight in her head. It was bruising. Out loud, she said: "It's just a bloody television!" So she had to acquiesce. His future weighed heavily on her now. He was in trouble. She could not be sure anymore whether it was some secret satanic cult with terrifying indoctrination rituals. She had crossed off the Buddhists. Opus Dei was still on the list. She remembered something about self-flagellation and hair shirts. They really liked to hurt themselves. And the Catholics were having a lot of trouble with celibacy and little boys. Someone had hurt him badly, and the worst pain had probably been years earlier when his skin was routed and tooled like a piece of leather. He must have consented to some degree or he would not have survived. Again, she felt the singular influence. It was all to a pattern. When he had said 'master', she had immediately made the leap to paedophile. So he was in real danger, and so was she. Victims became abusers. It was not guaranteed, but it was certainly possible. She hardly knew what she could do for him beyond offering sanctuary. The thought of sharing her home with another human being scared her silly, but sending him away was unthinkable. She could not abandon him any more than she had been able to ignore the sick animals and murky ponds. Compared to most people, her life was totally empty, but she was always busy, and always deeply involved in everything around her, but none of the things around her were human. Now, she had him.

*

Prince Abdul Aziz collected the disconsolate kafir from Paris. Mahmood had already gone on ahead to New York in anticipation of his arrival. While the Prince spent most of his days at his office in the UN building, Mahmood was tasked with teaching the kafir to read aloud in English. It was a skill he had only ever required when at the madrassa with Prof. Shah. The lessons were harder. His vocabulary was so limited. Mahmood spent hours translating verses into Arabic or Urdu so that the kafir could understand the meaning of the words before he learned to read them eloquently in English. Eventually, he could read and comprehend directly from the English text, but it took a long time.

The only subject was love. Every text was a love poem. For two months, the kafir lived in paradise. He was loved and cared for. Even his master, the Prince, was considerate and kind. No one hurt him. No one was unkind. All day, he read poems about beauty and love. He took care of his master, and all that the Prince required of him was that he recited the poems as he fell asleep. Now and then, when the Prince had to travel to a meeting, he was allowed to share Mahmood's bed. If they remained aboard the 747 then he no longer had to wear the burqa. If there were guests, he was kept out of sight. There was only one occasion when he was required to present himself to strangers. And this was hardly a stranger. It was the Turk, who had come bearing gifts. The kafir was flattered to be told that he was even more beautiful, and full of gratitude when the Prince turned down an offer of one million dollars in diamonds. The Turk went away disappointed, but with the promise that if the kafir was ever to be sold then the Turk would be first in line.

There had been calls for an Islamic Legion, similar to the French Foreign Legion. It would be an army of foreign volunteers. They would liberate Chechnya and Dagestan. They would travel the world protecting Believers from the bloodthirsty infidels, who wanted to destroy Islam. So they would destroy the Serbians, but no one knew how they would deal with the Shias or the Sunnis or the Sufis or the seventy-odd other factions that made up the church of Islam. In Algeria, the Believers were still killing each other. Almost every Muslim country was dominated by one sect or another whilst the minorities suffered exclusion and hardship. In March, the Kingdom had allowed eighteen thousand destitute Iraqis to cross the border and travel to Mecca. There was discontent everywhere. It was easy to blame specific key players in the region, but it was as much to do with several distinct plots coming to a head at the same time.

The newspapers and television programmes were full of lurid stories about the beardless president. The consensus was that it was inevitable. The man was obviously weak. He was obviously hammering the Muslims in the Middle East just to deflect attention away from his own personal problems. The media were full of stories about his imminent impeachment. Senators and Congressmen where grandstanding about his philandering ways only to be exposed themselves as being less than honourable when it came to marital fidelity. It became increasingly sordid and unpleasant, and cringingly embarrassing. In the corridors, everyone knew that women should not be allowed out of their homes to bring dishonour on men. The President's predicament proved it. Monica Lewinski had wilfully dishonoured her father and the President of the United States by not behaving modestly. Under the Sharia, her fate was sealed.

When the US House of Representatives' Judiciary Committee began impeachment hearings against the President, Iraq ended its cooperation with the Weapons Inspectors. The President ordered American and British airstrikes. All the inspectors were pulled out of Iraq. The President was impeached by the House of Representatives. The Vice President of Iraq announced that the UNSCOM mission was over. The impeachment case moved to the Senate. France, Germany and Russia called for sanctions to be lifted from Iraq, and for the UNSCOM mission to be disbanded and recast as it was obviously pro-American. The President announced that the

US would veto the lifting of sanctions. Some claimed that the hardships suffered by the Iraqi people because of sanctions constituted a war crime. Iraq declared it would shoot down any American or British planes, even in the No Fly Zones.

Chapter 27

When she went into the lounge, he gathered himself together, put his feet on the floor, tried to sit upright then offered her the remote.

She resisted taking it, and ignored what was on the television. "I'll put some more cream on your back."

He said nothing, but immediately started to unbutton his shirt.

She was embarrassed. She had not meant it as an order that had to be instantly obeyed. His response made her feel like a bully again, and his willingness to obey what might be considered an inappropriate command gave her pause. He was definitely the submissive. He had consented. Without hesitation, he was taking his clothes off in front of a stranger. She stared at him, chewing her nails, not sure if she really wanted him to stop. She could not say anything. But she closed her eyes and turned from him then found her way around to the back of the sofa. His mutilated back grounded her. It was the chalk to the cheese of his perfect abs. She could not count the times that she had spread the Vitamin E cream over his back. She was already on the third tub, each one bought from a different shop. She still did not know whether it was the expensive cream that had had such a miraculous effect, his youthful resilience, or her dumb blind luck. In two weeks, the infection had gone and a delicate film of skin grew across what had been raw muscle and bone. After ten minutes, she was Florence Nightingale, and he was safe again.

She moved to kneel in front of him. He was ashen and sweating, too overwhelmed to have any semblance of a defence. She had the most fleeting glimpse of his lovely blue eyes before he locked them to the floor. She grieved. She wanted to forgive him. He was in pain, he was lost and damaged, and he had done nothing wrong. "I'm sorry," she said. She tried to move closer to be able to see his eyes. They closed. He flinched. "I'm so sorry," she repeated. "I've been ill too. I'm a complete wreck. I do want to help you, but it is so hard for me."

He tried to draw away. Even a few inches would have made him feel safer, but when she seized his head, he turned to stone.

She was smiling, desperately smiling because she was hanging on by her finger nails. "Aren't we a pair? We've both been ill." She knew she was too close. She wanted to see his face, just his face and those glittering eyes. Almost in a dream, she stroked his face, his lips, and she could not breathe, but she ran her fingers through his silky hair.

He steadfastly ignored her.

She looked at his mouth, his eyelids; his lovely mouth again then slowly rose up to kiss his forehead. It was soft and delicate and chaste.

In that moment, he was her son.

He looked at her, confused by the tenderness.

She could see every shade of blue and green in his dazzling eyes. She smiled valiantly. Her body flooded with warmth. This was what motherly love felt like. It was intense and all-consuming and safe. "Please, don't be afraid of me. I'm a complete klutz. I always say the wrong thing and do the wrong thing. I really am the least competent person that you could have come to for help, but please, let me help you. You have no idea what it means to me to be able to help you."

There was something in her voice that touched him. He was almost prepared to let her kiss him again. No one had ever kissed him like that before. He studied her face. She was close to tears. "Yes."

But for the medication, she would have been weeping. "Thank you. Forgive me. If I've said anything or done anything that offended you, please, forgive me. I don't know how to talk to people. I'm just useless. I never know what to say. You need someone stronger and wiser than I will ever be, but I will do everything I can to help you. I promise. Please, let me help you?"

"Yes," he said again with surprising gravitas. He stared into her eyes as if she were some gypsy's crystal ball. His being there in that house only made sense if she was capable of taking him home. It was the only thing that he had ever asked for.

She was embarrassed, and blushed hotly. Her nerves were all over the place again, but she was happy.

Behind her, somewhere in Germany, a goal was scored. The rapturous cheering broke the moment. The young man's gaze drifted away to the television screen. "Damn bloody football," might have passed through her mind, but she just rose to her feet and walked away.

"Please?" he said urgently.

When she turned to look at him, he was leaning towards her, offering her the remote. She took it from him then turned back to the television then flicked through a few channels. Justine Henin Hardenne had just retained her French Crown. No one had done that since Steffi Graf back in 1996. That seemed like yesterday. Henin had beaten Kuznetsova 6-4 6-4, and it had apparently been a great game. "Damn," she said. "Damn. Damn. Damn." But she took a deep breath and smiled, then passed the remote back to him. "I don't care what is on tomorrow. I am – we are – watching Roger Federer. Absolutely no excuses."

He smiled. He actually smiled. "Yes."

Her heart melted completely. She was a human being. She was a woman. Once upon a time, she had been a mother. At that moment, she was ready to believe that he really was her son. It did not matter that he was the wrong age. His hair was the wrong colour. His eyes were not brown. "Yes," she said. She felt whole. She was smiling with joy. "Yes."

He warmed to her immediately. "Please? You saved my life."

She was blushing with embarrassment and sheer pleasure. It seemed wrong to agree with him, but only she knew what it had actually cost. She was his mother now. She could adore him from head to toe without craving his flesh. "So you like the football?" she asked, desperate to deflect the attention.

He shut down again. He stared at the floor.

She still could not read him. She did not know what she had done, but she was still feeling warm and fuzzy. She was his mum. "Well, you watch whatever you want, my dear." She pressed the remote back into his grasp. "And I've bought you some clothes. I hope they will fit you."

The generator clicked on again. He came to life. He looked up at her as if squinting at the sun. "Thank you. You have been very kind."

No. She could not read him at all. She started to leave then turned around and came back to stand over him.

His nerve crumbled. His gaze crashed back to the floor.

She reached out to delicately stroke a few wayward strands of hair back off his face. He was frowning. His lips were compressed. His brow was deeply furrowed. He did not like being touched.

"That thing – the sheath? It must be uncomfortable." She waited for him to respond, but he was carved from basalt. She took a big deep breath. "You were all red and sore when you arrived. It must be worse now." She paused again in vain. She was horribly embarrassed. "And it's locked. I couldn't find – you didn't have a key." He might have inhaled. There was no other response. She fidgeted anxiously. "It can't possibly be meant to be worn permanently." She stared at him. "Can you take it off? No.

287

Obviously, you'd have done that already. It must be uncomfortable?"

He was breathing slowly. His eyes were open, but he had resumed his perpetual study of her carpet. A slight grimace might have been an acknowledgment of her question.

"Are you any good at picking locks?" she asked cheerfully. It was meant as a joke. She was trying to be funny. Her face was scarlet.

His back was beginning to hurt. Had he been alone, he could have leaned down across the armrest, but not with her standing over him. He did carefully tug the blankets closer around him. He found the edge of the sheet which he slowly pulled up to cloak his chest. He was very conscious of the effect that his beauty had on the people around him. It was a burden he had to bear every day of his life.

Not understanding, she stepped closer and reached out to catch the edge of the sheet, but he leaned away, and tore it from her grasp. Her nerve failed. She had not meant to steal anything. She did not need to examine the bejewelled sheath. She knew every facet. And she could not work on it like Raffles, the Cracksman, while he was conscious. Even with him unconscious, she was not sure that she had the nerve to attempt something like that. She could not have done it even if he was a girl. But he was not a girl. He was not even an ordinary man. She needed tools. She had tools. Not the right tools, but she had pliers and wire cutters. The young man could do all the fiddly work. He could liberate himself. He had the time, and surely, the inclination.

She went out to the scullery. She had a mahogany tall boy where she kept a collection of screwdrivers and spanners and a host of other useful things. She had quite a good eye so easily picked out the right set of pliers, some strong wire cutters and a long slender screwdriver. When she gave them to him, he was surprised.

"Look," she explained with embarrassment. "I can't do this." Her hand waved vaguely towards his groin. Her face was scarlet. Her pulse had quickened alarmingly. "Please, try on your own. You must want to get it off?"

He looked candidly into her eyes.

She did not want to look at him then. He was her son. He was definitely her son. This was not a conversation she could have with her own son. Even a few acting lessons from Meryl Streep could not carry her through this conversation.

"I'll leave you alone." She started to leave, but came back to stand over him again. "Don't do anything stupid." She waved her hand vaguely again.

288

"You know! Be careful! Just cut the metal. I'd focus on the padlock. But be careful! I don't want any more of your blood on my carpet." She looked deeply into his eyes, and her legs turned to water. He seemed to be enjoying her confusion. For a moment, she could not function at all. "I – you should – please." She had to breathe. "It'll be fine." He was smiling. Why was he smiling? He was so damn attractive. "No hurry. Just break the padlock." She was as weak as a kitten. Her face was so hot it felt like serious sunburn. "I'll be in the kitchen. I'll put the kettle on. Tea? Call me when you have finished." That would never happen. He only raised his voice when he was dreaming. "Call me anyway."

She backed out of the room, leaving him alone. She did not know why she was suddenly so frightened.

For a long time, he stared at the tools. It was beyond him to do what she asked, and it was entirely outside his area of expertise to do any DIY. The tools were heavy and substantial. They looked new. Of course, he wanted to be free. She was quite right. He was red and sore around the metal, and he craved the dark solace that the sheath's presence forbade. That secret pleasure had always been forbidden.

He went into the bathroom. The light was better. He could lock the door, and guarantee that he would not be disturbed. His hands were shaking. Before he even started, he was absolutely exhausted.

It took more than an hour. He emerged sweating and breathless. She had waited in the kitchen, and invited him to come in and sit down. "Are you alright?"

He could not look at her, but laid the tools down on the table. Then he placed the sheath between them. There was no blood on it, which was a relief. The jewels glittered brilliantly, refracting and amplifying the light. She picked it up as if it were the finest crystal glass then carried it to the sink. She poured lots of soap over it then held it under the hot tap. In a matter of seconds, it was simply dazzling. It took all of her willpower to leave it in the sink. He was sitting forlorn at the kitchen table. She took him a glass of water, and put a comforting hand on his shoulder.

"Is everything alright?" she asked again.

He still could not look at her, but he might have nodded.

She pressed him to drink. There was no blood on his hands or the sheet. "You're alright," she told him. "I have your clothes. Do you want to put them on? You'll be much happier in your own clothes."

He watched as she fetched a pile of garments that had been by the kettle. Some of them he recognised. He was too tired, but dared not refuse in case they were never offered again.

"They're nice," she said soothingly. "I've looked at the labels: very expensive. Most of it is original. I've had to add items that were too damaged to clean."

He nodded. They were not his clothes. He wore them, but they were never his. "Thank you. You have been very kind."

She smiled. "Off you go then. Get dressed. Then we'll go for a walk outside."

He rose slowly to his full height. He was tall and slender. He had the physique of a dancer, but he was completely uncoordinated, which was hardly surprising after being so ill.

She waited to hear the bathroom door close then hurried back to the sink. In scalding hot water, the metal sheath had cleaned up beautifully. The stones were phenomenal. They radiated the sunlight that was pouring in through the kitchen window. With no effort at all, she could scratch the glass window pane with each of the stones. That made them priceless. She would never have to worry about money again. She would be safe. At long last, she would be safe.

*

One evening in April 1999, at his son's request, Prince Abdul Aziz allowed his white creature to serve at table. Officially, it was a respectable page or valet. Historically, it was a ghilman, usually foreign, always attractive, famously loyal. Now, it was just a scandal waiting to happen. His son and brother and brother-in-law were curious about his previously unseen, but notorious trophy servant. The tension in the room was palpable. They all watched him. They were the predators waiting to strike. The Prince's attempts to divert the conversation away to more neutral topics were generally ignored.

The kafir, to his credit, rose bravely to the occasion. Wearing a stiff white shirt, black tailcoat and dove-grey gloves, he served in silence, a perfect study of English reserve and professional polish. Though he was aware of the hostility that bristled amongst his master's guests, he never betrayed his concern. He stood at his master's left hand, and stared downwards, awaiting a command. That every eye was focused on him did not affect his manners, but it made his heart race, his palms clammy, and his face slowly whitened under the strain.

"Please, my father, give up this ignoble creature," the son said beseechingly. "He cannot remain here. Our brothers are insulted by him. He is an embarrassment to us. What he does for you is an embarrassment.

Our people do not cling to these old ways as you do. Keeping him with you is now considered scandalous. You must know this."

"My son, we should not talk of these things. It is not suitable for this table. Did you bring the drawings of the new hospital wing?"

Prince Khalid found it difficult to focus on his father when the creature lurked beside him as pale as a ghost and as still as stone. "You must understand, my father. You must understand. He is white. The colour of his skin makes us all targets. The world is changing, my father. In your heart you know this. His own people will hate us, and the fanatics will accuse us of dreadful crimes abhorrent to God. The family will be shamed." He struggled to find polite words. "Please, my father, see reason. He does not belong here. If the British and Americans find out that you keep him for your pleasure, how will we defend our honour? They will be outraged."

Prince Abdul Aziz gazed at his son then leaned back in his chair. "It simply isn't true, and no one will be outraged. No one will say a word."

"But he was stolen from his family. They will not have forgotten him. You cannot pay them off with a few rupees as if he were some peasant's child from Bangladesh to be glued on to the back of a camel. There will be a scandal if he is ever discovered."

"There will be no scandal."

Prince Khalid shook his head in bewilderment. "There will be a scandal. No one will do business with us. We will be ostracised by our own brothers. The Americans will be furious. You will not be welcome there ever again. They will take away your diplomatic status."

"They will do nothing."

His brother leaned forward, mystified. "You cannot seriously believe that there will be no repercussions."

"There will be none. They will deny it if they are asked. They have ignored everything so far, and some of your cousins have been quite brazen. They might complain about parking tickets and speeding fines, but we all know it's drugs and prostitution. There's child pornography now. They are even kidnapping white girls just to provide playthings for their friends. It all goes on. We all know about it."

Prince Khalid looked in torment at the vile creature. "But this is us. This is our family. Please, give him up. We are in the midst of negotiations with an American corporation for a hotel and residential complex that is worth billions. We must be able to do business with them. We need to prove that we are honourable, peaceful men. We want to be equals. You know how hard it has been for us because of Al-Zawahiri and bin Laden. Please turn away from this thing. I have men waiting in the courtyard. He will be gone tonight. It is arranged. Please, let me call them. The time for such traditions has passed."

The Prince gazed at his son then surveyed his other guests. "This is your mother talking. She was always a spiteful woman." He idly pushed his napkin off his knee then watched their faces as the creature gracefully bowed then knelt down and retrieved it. "Yes. You have been listening to the gossip of women." He reached out to gently rest his hand on the creature's back, effortlessly pinning it down on its knees. "Why are you all so worried about a kafir? He is nothing. Why are you not telling me about the Half Year Profit or the Futures Market? Are the results so bad that you have all come here to distract me with this nonsense?"

"The results are good," his brother assured him earnestly. "Our liquidity is excellent. We have come because we are concerned, Abdul Aziz. You know that it is becoming dangerous. You keep him with you. You even take him to New York. What if someone had seen him?"

"It would have made no difference. No one would have said anything."

Prince Khalid was upset. He loved his father, and it broke his heart to criticise him, but then if not him there was no one else to plead for the honour of the family. "You are a great man. We all love you, and we have sworn our loyalty with blood. We ask you this – I ask you as your son – to surrender him to us. He need not die. He must be sent away." He looked at his father's smile and completely misunderstood. "Give him up, my father. You do not need this vile thing."

"I suppose you have been to see your mother recently. Is that why you have all come here?"

"My mother loves you," Prince Khalid said emotionally, then paused to shrug. "All your wives love and honour you. They would never complain, my father. They know their duty and would never be indiscreet. I ask you, my father," he said earnestly. "Please consider the consequences. Imagine how the British will react after discovering you have kept him a prisoner here all these years?"

The Prince laughed heartily as if hearing a great joke. "They will do nothing. Appeasement runs in their veins. They would not have stood against Hitler but for Churchill. Morally, they are cowards. Their men have too many vices. They drink and whore like beasts. The ugly ones buy eastern women for a pittance. Their queers rush off to Bangkok to fornicate with children. They are a despicable people. So much ignorance. So much

arrogance. Do not fear them. They will do nothing. They will say nothing."
He patted the motionless creature's shoulder as if it were a devoted hound.
"It doesn't matter what we do. They must show us respect. When we shut
off the oil in 1973, and grounded all the American helicopters in Vietnam,
we proved our power. When the French came grovelling to us, and offered
carte blanche to guarantee the continuing supply of oil to Europe, we knew
we could force them to accept anything. And we have. We have. They
know this."

Prince Khalid shook his head and sighed. "Yes, the Euro-Arab
Dialogue. Submission without war."

"Overnight we were taken seriously. The money flowed into our
pockets. We bought property, businesses, and increased our influence. No
one dares to criticise us, and if they do then they are rebuked publically as
racists or fascists. We can go anywhere and do anything. We have
infiltrated every corner of their society. We have made sure that Europe is
anti-American and anti-Semitic and loudly pro-Palestinian. At our
insistence, Europe is firmly committed to the creation of a Palestinian state.
They have recognised Arafat as a great statesman, and the sole
representative of the Palestinian people. The Jews are hated once again,
and but for the memory of the Holocaust there would be no Israel, but
every day Israel is vilified, and Islam is declared perfect." The Prince
smiled. "And we all know that Arafat is no better than a terrorist. We
would not have him at our table, but the Europeans must treat him as a
king. They will not say anything that might upset us. Their democracies
will slowly disappear, and before they even notice they will be firmly
under our jurisdiction."

"What? That's nonsense." Prince Khalid dragged his eyes away from
the incredibly beautiful creature to stare again at his father. "I have men
waiting in the courtyard. Please, let me call them."

The kafir remained motionless, accepting that he must stay there
because his master's hand rested lightly on his shoulder. The words were
making him dizzy, but he did not feel threatened. He knew that his master
would not give him up. They were bound together. It was a complicated
relationship, but the kafir was devoted to his master. His only wish was
that these guests would depart so that he and his master could be alone.

Prince Abdul Aziz shook his head slowly. He was also wishing that
they were alone. "You fear shadows." He almost shrugged. "No one cares.
No one notices. He is a servant. My valet. He does not suffer. I'm sure he's
quite content." He gazed around the table at his son and brother and
brother-in-law. "You all listen to the idle tongues of spiteful women."

"It is no secret what he does for you. Your family knows. Your servants know. How many other people must know?"

"And what do they know?" the Prince asked, beginning to feel deeply humiliated. "He is no more than a servant. Yes, he belongs to me, but that is not illegal." He turned to regard his son sternly. "It is written in the Holy Book that I may keep slaves. The Blessed Prophet, Peace be upon Him, kept slaves. He sold slaves. That was His trade. No one may criticise the Holy Apostle of God."

The son shook his head slowly. "No. This is different. And the Kingdom outlawed slavery forty years ago."

"That is not God's Law. This thing is no more than a servant. I don't have sexual relations with it, if that is what you are implying." He was angry. "Why are we even talking about this? It's just a servant. It's just a bloody servant."

There was a hush.

"But no one will believe that." His brother-in-law spoke for the first time.

"Why?" Prince Abdul Aziz demanded. In his agitation, he brought his fists down on the table. "Because it is so beautiful? Because every servant fucks it?"

The kafir immediately rose gracefully from his knees, and returned to his post at his master's left hand. He stared down. He did not acknowledge anyone in the room. The guests were all watching him. He felt their disapproval like an icy fog.

"Because it is so beautiful?" the Prince demanded with a knowing smile. "You think I'm fucking it because it's so beautiful. If it was ugly, we wouldn't be having this conversation."

They were staring at the creature, but acknowledged the challenge by immediately lowering their gaze. Just looking at it made them all feel uncomfortable. It was probably the most despicable creature any of them had actually met, but it was astonishingly beautiful. In their culture, it was worse than a mass-murderer or a brutal rapist or an apostate. Being in the same room with it made them feel violated. It was corrupt and without honour, and yet looked perfectly innocent, and it was without doubt the most beautiful thing any of them had ever seen. Its submissive stance only added to its allure. But to its enemies these contradictions only proved that it was a manipulative predator completely in control of its environment.

Prince Khalid leaned towards his father. "Because that is the history.

No one speaks the word, but -"

"There are no women so we take teenage boys as our lovers? They wear makeup. They hold hands. They dance for us. I do not believe that was ever true. We are not Pashtuns. And I have not done this thing. I have no need of the delights you speak of."

"My mother believes," Prince Khalid said unhappily.

"And she is wrong."

There was a long silence as Prince Abdul Aziz recovered his temper, and his guests politely toyed with their food or sipped from the crystal goblets that contained nothing stronger than water.

Prince Khalid waited for his father to meet his gaze. "A thousand years ago, we were the leaders of the world, but somewhere we lost our way. Now, the Americans lead the world. Their country is only a few hundred years old. It is a child and we are the old men. Now, we run after them. We cannot insult them." Prince Khalid held up his hands, knowing that his father was about to ridicule his argument. "We should not want to insult them. They are our friends. They are our brothers on this planet. Bin Laden and the criminals and fools that follow him want to destroy everything, and they will end up destroying each other. We cannot allow them to drive a wedge between us. Yes, we have the oil, but when there is no more oil or they finally invest in the technology to find a new fuel source, where will we be? Surely, we should wish to be good neighbours to everyone on this small and fragile planet." He glanced at the beautiful creature, who stood like a statue, remote and unattainable. "This creature of yours will insult them. I live in New York. I can assure you that they will not understand."

The brother leaned forward too, his face a mask of woe. "We love you, my brother. All of my life, I have admired you. You will always be cleverer and wiser than I am, but God willing, I am an honourable and devout man. I do not want more than I have. I am not jealous. The same blood runs in our veins, Abdul Aziz. I know you. You take pleasure in this vile thing. I know you may quote from the Holy Book to justify all that you do to him, but you take pleasure in it. Your son has come here because he loves you. You should be proud of him. He works tirelessly. He is a great ambassador for you and all our brothers. He is a good man. Let him take this thing away. You have become bewitched by it. Take back your wives. Love them again."

"I have done nothing to be ashamed of. He is a kafir. He is just a servant. He does for me what it is unseemly for an honourable man to do. He exists only to spare my servants, who are true followers of the Blessed

Prophet, Peace be upon Him, from dishonour. He bathes me. He dresses me. There are such servants in every country of the world. You know this. You all have such servants. Even Her Gracious Majesty, the Queen of England, has such servants. Do you insult Elizabeth with this slander?"

"He is different. He is white. The stories about him and the others are shameful. When a man loves a man-"

"Do you think that I love this thing?" the Prince demanded in absolute astonishment.

"He is an infamous whore," his son whispered miserably. "We have all heard about him. They say he is insatiable, and that he was fucked by a bull when he had exhausted all the men. He is utterly disgusting. He is the worst kind of whore. He has no shame, and cares nothing for the good men that he corrupts with his wickedness. When a man mounts another man, then the Throne of God shakes."

"You are deceived," Prince Abdul Aziz explained unhappily. It was laughable, but he could see that his son believed every word.

"And you are misquoting the Words of God," his brother said quietly. "You are a great man. It is, surely, beneath you to use the tricks employed by the fanatics to incite a mob."

"Please, my father, you must send him away before it is too late."

Prince Abdul Aziz was utterly humiliated. "God willing, I am a good Muslim. I love my wives. I love God above all. I have never had any unnatural relations with a man."

Prince Khalid shook his head, his voice was full of pain and distress. It was hard for him to say the words aloud. "He's a catamite. I have been told that he is available to all who want him. The law that condones slavery condemns him to death. That is demanded by God."

"You cannot believe that I would do such a thing." The Prince's heart ached for him. "You are my first born. We must be of one mind. How can you believe this outrageous slander?"

"It is disgusting," his brother insisted quietly. "One of my own servants was told that this creature is so willing he will open his mouth and his anus at the same time. I too have heard about this bull. The story is everywhere. His very existence is offensive to God. He offends all of us."

"But it is not true. How can you believe such nonsense? This thing about a bull is simply ridiculous. It's just a sales pitch."

"I have heard it. In New York, I heard this." Prince Khalid looked at the creature with increasing distaste. "Why must he stand there? He is unclean.

He should not have served our food."

"He is clean. You have nothing to fear from his touch, and you asked for him. You insisted. What am I to assume from that? Do you want to fuck him? Is that why you have all come here?"

His brother continued in a low monotone: "A man cannot love a man. It is unnatural. It is disgusting. It is the most evil act. You deny it, but please, see how this looks. He has bewitched you. You are not yourself. He has caused some aberration. We, who do love you, merely wish to drive out the madness and return you to God. You cannot love this foul kafir. It is impossible."

Prince Khalid gazed at his father, hardly knowing what to say. "Please, give him up. Please, I beg you. If you are sentimental then he need not die, but give him up. He can be taken away tonight. If you love him," to speak the words pained him, "then I will make sure he is kept safe and well. No harm need come to him, but he must go far away from here and from all temptation. You must promise me that you will never see him again."

"But I don't love him."

"This is the twentieth century, brother," murmured his brother-in-law darkly. "Our friends in America and western Europe will call this thing that you do with him evil. They call it paedophilia."

The Prince shot to his feet, enraged. "How dare you say that word! I am no paedophile. You offend my honour to suggest it. If you were not the brother of my wife I would kill you for such a slander. You call me a queer, and now say that I am a paedophile. This is too much. You all go too far. I have not forsaken women. I am still a man in every sense, and a good Muslim. I know my Hadith, and have observed the laws of our Blessed Prophet, may Peace be upon Him. You shame me to suggest that I love this thing. I have had many such servants. I know what they are. My father presented me with my first when I was four years old. They have all been devoted to me, and I have never mistreated any one of them in the way you suggest. I am appalled. Do you know nothing? Khalid, my son, you have had such servants. My brother, Feisal, our father gifted you many servants. Yes, they are sometimes white and sometimes black. You still have Yusuf. I have seen him. Is he not devoted to you? We know what they are. They are not our equals. We could never love one of them. That would be like making love to a horse or saluki. It sickens my stomach to think of it. It is appalling and degrading. But my father still has such servants. They care for him as tenderly as his wives. Do you intend to call your grandfather a paedophile and a queer? He will strike you down for saying such a thing. Though he loves you, he will have you killed. Read your

Holy Book. Read all the sayings of the Blessed Prophet. Speak to the holy men. I cannot love him as I do love my God and my family. I know the words of the Blessed Prophet and the Wisdom of God. I have always insisted that all our kafirs understand the law, and their status in our culture. I have spent a great deal of money on their education. Every year, during Ramadan, even this one returns to a madrassa to study and learn, and to receive the Blessing of the Word of God. They are under no illusion. They are all taught to behave as good Believers so that True Believers are not offended. They must be quiet and modest and respectful, and are treated with compassion. It is not his fault that he is condemned. I cannot punish him for his white skin and false heart, but pity is not love. I am honour bound to protect him. We all have a duty to our subjects and our servants and even to the kafirs. You shame me." He gazed witheringly around the room. "It is not love. I am truly ashamed that none of you seem to understand our traditions."

"The world has changed, my father," Prince Khalid said quietly. "His skin condemns us all. There can be no honour in this. Please, let me send for my men."

"You do not listen. This is an old tradition – older than Islam. There is no harm in it. I am your father. You must listen to me."

"Yes, my father, and that is why I ask this of you. Please, give him to me. I ask this as your son."

"You want him then?" There was an unpleasant suggestion in his tone.

"I have men in the courtyard."

Prince Abdul Aziz breathed deeply, controlling his temper. "You don't understand. This one was given to me by an old family friend. It was an honourable gift. A very expensive gift!" The Prince looked at his guests, wondering if he had ever really known them. "Who amongst us has not been gifted or inherited a servant or slave? I also have land and jewels and even wives that were all given to me as honourable gifts. To decline them would insult the giver. What of our honour and good manners then? Your mother was given to me to end a blood feud." He gazed at his brother-in-law. "I married your sister to seal a treaty between my father and yours. I have been given many respectable girls as pledges of loyalty. They do not love me, but I give them my protection and honour them. You have all done this. There are many boys that I have raised as my own, but which a cynical man might acknowledge were mere hostages. I pay for their education, and they prosper working for me in offices or colleges or in the army. They are all my sons, and owe me their allegiance. Am I accused of abusing all of them as well?"

"It is not the same." Prince Khalid was miserable. "I love you, my father. You are a great man, beloved of your people, but it is not the same. You know, it is not the same. Please, let me summon my men. He can be gone in the hour."

"It is the same. It is your perspective that makes it different. It is the white skin that you fear. If I dyed his skin, and made him wear coloured lenses then no one would care at all. You are afraid of the Americans. You have become weak living amongst them."

Prince Khalid was furious. "You cannot use the threat of oil shortages to conceal this crime. You have a reputation. He should not be here. We have filled our pockets, and indulged ourselves like spoiled children since the King demonstrated our power in the seventies. What do we not own? What can we not possess or experience? Who would dare say 'no' when we can stop oil production at any moment?"

"What you suggest is appalling, but there is some truth in it. However, His Holiness the Blessed Prophet has said, and I can quote you the passage, that as the creature is my property - it may be used as required."

"Please, my father. We must be of one mind. Take back your wives, and give up this vile thing that has corrupted you. You do not need him. You do not want him."

The Prince turned his head slightly, and was acknowledged by the creature with a poised bow. "You will leave us."

The kafir straightened slowly then backed away, retreating to the door before bowing again, and letting himself out.

The Prince sat down slowly and inhaled deeply, filling his lungs with air, and his heart with courage, then he looked at his son, then his brother and brother-in-law.

"Please, my father. He is no better than a whore."

"He is no better than a whore because the Pakistanis, who care for him, rent him out amongst their friends. It is no secret that they have a thing for pretty boys. It's part of their culture. It's a tradition commonly practiced on every street corner. They are not ashamed. And men sleep with men all the time. They want to have sex. They fuck other men because there are no women. The women trafficked in to fill the brothels are too expensive. So the men fuck each other. They don't consider themselves homosexuals. They would be very insulted if you told them they were homosexuals." He almost laughed, but it just was not funny. "I have heard that men bring their sons to visit him – to teach them how to fuck. I have tried to put a stop to it, but they insist they have the right to observe their customs, and we must respect that. I believe they also dress him up as a jezebel, and he dances for them. The Afghans are the same. Wars have started over the possession of some pretty dancing boy. Are you satisfied now or is my complete humiliation not enough?"

The brother-in-law sighed unhappily. "This is not the same. He is white. They will call you a paedophile."

Prince Abdul Aziz shook his head, exasperated. "I have never touched a child. A paedophile is a foul thing. You insult me to suggest it."

"It doesn't matter anymore what you have or have not done. He is white. You must surrender him," his brother said flatly, "for the honour of the family. We don't want to be associated with those princes, who live abroad and drink and whore like dogs. They are an embarrassment to us all, but if you are caught with this kafir then it will destroy us. You have a reputation. Do you really want to jeopardise that?"

"Please, father," Prince Khalid said with regret. "We must be of one mind. I am sorry for you, but my uncle is correct. His white skin will condemn you. Let me call my men. He need not be killed."

"This is nonsense, but you are my son."

Chapter 28

She was still cleaning the pretty stones when he returned. By then she had been grinning like a lottery winner for so long that her face had set into that expression. Hearing him behind her, she shoved the sheath under a tea towel then spun around to confront him. Her nerves were ragged. She immediately suspected he had been creeping up on her with evil intentions then realised he had come only to show off his clothes. She relented.

He was so tired, he could hardly stand upright, but he had made an effort to brush his hair, knot his tie, fasten all the buttons.

She suspected he had even checked to make sure that just the right amount of cuff was showing beneath his jacket's sleeves. He looked fabulously elegant but ill. He tried to turn gracefully, and almost fell down. She started towards him, but he had taken hold of the doorframe. She backed away. Her face ached from smiling. She felt as guilty as a thief running off with the Parish Poor Box. She was going to rob him. She could not actually believe that she was going to rob him, but it was already written in stone. Her manic expression fractured then softened. "You look great," she said.

He stood still, holding on to the wall. The clothes were elegant. They were excellently made, and tailored to perfection. It was a very, very expensive suit, and much too classy for the off-the-peg shirt that she had bought at the local supermarket. The cut of the suit made him appear taller and broad-shouldered. He looked older, and he was still an absolute feast for the eyes. But he was ill now, and he did not know what she wanted him to do next.

"Go into the lounge," she said. "You look exhausted." She tried to smile warmly. "You've done really well today."

He managed to lift his gaze, but not high enough to look at her face. He might have nodded.

"Here, let me help you." She took a step closer, but he shivered. "It's alright." She lifted a hand to pacify him. "You can lay down on the sofa, and go to sleep. You don't have to do anything else. You've had a big day."

His strength was draining away. He allowed her to take hold of his arm. He walked slowly back into the lounge, and sank heavily onto the sofa ready to pass out.

She lifted his bare feet on to the cushions. She went to switch the television on then gave him the remote. He could hardly lift it so she quickly found the football. She fetched him a glass of milk. He did not need painkillers to sedate him anymore. His forehead was cold and damp. She pulled a blanket over him. She fussed around for a few minutes until she realised he was watching the football, and not actually taking any notice of her at all.

In the kitchen, the jewel-encrusted sheath shone like the crown jewels. Her broad grin returned, but she felt sick acknowledging that she intended to rob him. She had the casino chip. Now, she would take the jewels. Of course, she would help him. She would make sure that he was safe and well, but she was keeping the treasure.

With the loot safely hidden away, she went out into the garden while he watched the review of the game in Frankfurt. She simply could not bear to sit through it. The highlights were repeated on every news programme for the rest of the day. England won. Paraguay had scored an own goal in the third minute. But it was from a Beckham free kick so there was some national pride. The metatarsal had not healed sufficiently to allow Rooney to play. Lampard had been noteworthy. Sven would probably be happy just to have the points. The fans were going mental. Of course, there were other important events in the world, but the media were pandering to the masses as usual, and not brave enough to attempt to broaden the horizons of their audience with anything contentious or challenging.

Later that evening, they were in the lounge. He had recovered. He looked infinitely more comfortable. She had the black cat on her knee. She was at peace with the world.

"So you like the football?" she asked, after probably the thousandth replay of the winning goal.

He was still hunched over at one end of the sofa. The sheet and blankets were gone, but he was still a frail invalid.

"You watched the game?" she reminded him.

He did not look at her. He did not look at the television. There was that peculiar awkward movement, which was not even a shrug.

She tried to smile. "You can talk to me. Come on, we know you can talk. It's perfectly safe. There's no one else here."

He made an effort to sit upright, but the pain made him shudder. "You have been very kind."

She studied him for a while. It was so much easier on her nerves having him clothed. It also signified that he was on the mend, which meant that he would be leaving. She was suddenly quite ambivalent about that. She was not sure that she actually wanted him to totally disappear. Having him about the place had not been that unpleasant. His manners had allowed her to flaunt her authority over him as if he was just one of the cats. Of course, the only real authority that she had over them was that she was bigger and stronger. They still believed that they were in charge. They made demands, and she always obeyed. It was exactly the opposite with the young man. She told him to take his clothes off, and he did. Of course, he was sick, and she was pretending to be a doctor, but the outcome was the same.

"Have you ever been to a match?"

There was the same awkward, restrained gesture.

"You seem to be interested in it." She was puzzled now. "If you don't like it then why are you watching? There are other programmes."

His eyes flashed. He sighed heavily. "Please? He might be there." It was a confession.

She gazed back at the television. It was just talking heads now so she gently pushed aside the cat then rose to cross the room and actually turn the sound down. She turned to look at him. He was uncomfortable under her scrutiny. "Him?" she asked. When he did not respond, she took a step towards him which elicited a nod. She felt as if she was torturing him for state secrets. "Your lover?"

He went white, but shook his head urgently.

"Your prince?" she asked. When she returned to her chair, he managed to nod more comfortably. "You were looking for him?" She was more than surprised.

His nerves were shredding. "Please? No, that is impossible. There are so many people." He took a deep breath then found the courage to look up at her. "I could not." He shrugged uncomfortably. "It was such a long time ago."

"You were happier then?" she asked. "You went with him?"

He stared back at the carpet.

"Aren't you allowed to tell me?" she asked quietly. She did not want to start feeding him with suggestions. He had to find his own words, his own voice. She wanted to say that football was just a game, but knew that for many men it was a full time religion that demanded devotion and sacrifice.

He did not know what to say. He could not vocalise his thoughts. In his head, he could recite Shakespeare and Hafiz, but speaking to a stranger made him quake with fear. He was not gifted with the knack for conversation. He had no opinion about anything. He did not own anything. The clothes that he wore allowed him respectability, but they were not his.

"You went with him to a game? That must have been exciting," she said.

His brow furrowed.

"So you went with friends? That must have been nice. Was it a big game?"

He managed to shake his head. He took another long deep breath, but he still could not find his voice.

She waited. At last, she said: "It's only a game."

That normally drew an excited response, but he shrank before her eyes then slowly shook his head.

She felt he wanted to say something. There was a long silence. He settled again slowly, but could not lift his gaze until she turned away to look at the television. Then he could look at her. But the silent talking heads were redundant, and as soon as she lost interest, he had to stare back at the floor.

"We were in Japan," he said, after a long pause.

She nodded, trying to conceal her surprise. "Well, that was exciting." Somewhere at the back of her mind, a little voice in her archive reported that there had been other World Cups. "Was that four years ago or eight?" she asked.

He grimaced. He did not know.

"Well, come on, tell me about it. Football in Japan? That must have been very exciting?"

"Please, I cannot."

"Come on," she said. "You can talk to me." She was smiling broadly. If he started talking about offside rules or penalty shootouts then she was in trouble. "You were in Japan?"

Very reluctantly, he explained: "My master was an honoured guest. He was in the stadium." He hesitated then added slowly: "We remained at the hotel, but there were many empty seats. So my Pakistanis were invited to go." He clammed up, but the sudden and prolonged silence warned him that she expected him to elaborate. "I may not sit with them." He tried to shrug, but his back hurt too much. "I may not sit with them or be left alone so Mahmood stayed with me at the hotel. Omar insisted." He might have smiled. "We watched a television. Mahmood said they played very badly. 3-0. They did not score any goals." He managed the faintest most wistful smile as he remembered his friend. "He told me that cricket is the best game. He said it is worthy of a gentleman."

She smiled. The happy memory had transformed him. "Yes, cricket is a game for gentlemen. There is a saying that football is a game for gentlemen but it is played by hooligans. Is that what your friend meant?" She gave him a moment to respond, but he was silent again. "Japan was 2002. So Mahmood was your friend?"

The invisible shutters came down again. He stared resolutely at the floor.

She kept smiling. "What harm can it do to tell me about Mahmood? He was kind to you? He was your friend?"

He shook his head.

"Why is it a secret? Why can't you tell me?"

"Please? I can't! It was a long time ago," he said evasively.

"It was four years ago," she corrected him.

He flinched. He was exercising all his will power to keep her out of his head.

"You liked Mahmood. I can tell by the way that you say his name that you liked him. I'm sure he didn't do you any harm. Why can't you tell me about Mahmood?"

There was the slightest inclination of his head. He could not repair his defences fast enough to keep her out. He leaned forward to wrap his arms around his chest. His heart was beating rapidly. He wanted her to stop.

"So he was one of your Pakistanis?"

Flinching again, he managed another stifled nod.

"So he looked after you?" she asked, but she had no idea what that really meant.

He looked at her desperately. "Please, I cannot. I do not remember. Please, do not ask me any more questions."

"But why does it matter? You haven't really told me anything. Did you have all that artwork done in Japan? They can be quite kinky. I believe Japanese porn is in a league of its own." She watched him closely. "How long have you been working for the prince? Do your family even know what you've been doing? That you're lovers? That you like to play dangerous games? That you're gay?"

That hurt him. He lifted a hand to hide his face.

"So it's been a few years? If you want to go home, you must know that you'll have to be able to explain why your body is a billboard advertising sex. They're your parents. They love you. Haven't you told them anything yet? Didn't you keep in touch?" She was surprised. "I should think they'll be very upset. You've been hurt. You'll have scars for the rest of your life. They'll probably insist that you report all of this to the police."

"Please, do not... I cannot...." he whispered. He did not lower his hand.

"You've been badly beaten. I know you have money, but I don't think there's a surgeon anywhere in the world, who can fix all that. It just can't be done. You won't be able to just whitewash it by saying you walked into a door or fell down stairs. This isn't domestic violence, but it was your lover. It must have been. You'll need a very good excuse for not calling the police because I'm sure that the beating you took constitutes grievous bodily harm, assault, and possibly even attempted murder."

He was hunched up, hugging his chest, shaking his head.

"And you don't eat enough to keep a child alive."

"Please? I cannot. I cannot eat," he said quietly.

She paused to study him while she tried to calculate how that could be true. "Because you're ill?" she asked. "Is it an allergy?"

He shook head. He was trembling. "Please? Please, I'm very tired now."

She understood he was asking her to leave him alone. She wanted to pet him, and offer comforting words, but he just wanted her to go away. "You're probably very confused by all this, and just need some time. You do the enigmatic silence very well, but it'll help you to talk about it."

"Please? Please, I do not understand."

"Why won't you tell me what happened?" She tried smiling.

He shivered. "Please? I cannot. You have been very kind. I cannot tell you. I cannot remember. Please?"

"But you do remember because you're having nightmares. It's probably just shock. They probably gave you a bang on the head when they stole the briefcase. In time, you'll remember everything. Don't worry about that. It'll all come back."

He stared at the floor, shaking his head and shivering.

She felt guilty, but leaned towards him, desperate to reassure. "It'll be alright. You're safe now. You'll get better and grow stronger, and honestly, everything will be alright."

He shook his head more emphatically, but could not lift his gaze. "Please? You don't understand."

"Yes, well obviously, but you're safe now. You want to go home, and I want to help you, but you have to give me a clue. There must be something that you can tell me? There must be something that you remember? You remembered being in Paris with your prince and your Pakistanis. You remembered the football. It'll just take time. There must be lots of nice things you can tell me about that won't upset you too much. I just want to help you. You can tell me. There's no one else here. You can tell me anything."

"Please? You have been very kind."

She shook her head, exasperated. She wanted to shake him roughly, but he looked so fragile she did not dare breathe on him in case he completely fell apart. "So tell me about your prince? You've been in the Middle East. Was it Egypt or Syria or Saudi or Jordan?" She spoke slowly, waiting for him to react, but he had battened down the hatches again. "Qatar or Yemen? Iraq? It couldn't be Iran. Nobody goes to Iran." She shook her head again. "This isn't difficult. You were in Paris. You said he had a house. Did you live in Paris all the time?"

"Please? I'm tired. I cannot tell you anything." He took a deep breath then shook his head. "I don't know what I must do."

"You've been in the Middle East?" she asked sharply.

"Please, I cannot tell you. I don't understand what is happening. I don't know why I am here with you." His eyes never lifted from the floor.

His whole manner confused her. He seemed so guilty. Every word was a confession. But he was not actually saying anything. "What is his name?" she demanded rather sharply. "I'm sorry, but I'm taking it as read that the prince is your lover and therefore your master. That's alright. If that floats your boat then that's great, but why does it have to be such a big secret? Is it because you're homosexuals? I guess the Middle East is Islam, isn't it, and in Islam then - being gay is a real problem. Isn't it actually totally outlawed? Don't you get your head chopped off or something equally barbaric? Islam's not the most tolerant of religions. That's what you meant about being forbidden, isn't it?" She stopped talking. She felt it was inappropriate to hijack the conversation, and start lecturing about her problems with Islam. She wanted to. It was almost too tempting, but she knew that it would have been unfair.

He watched her taking a moment. He had no idea what was running through her mind. She was distracted, but not for long. As soon as she turned back to him then he lowered his gaze. "You have been very kind," he said for the thousandth time in an effort to placate her. "You have saved my life. I am very grateful."

She studied him for a while, trying to not be annoyed. "So you're not going to tell me anything?" she demanded.

He felt her unhappiness. "Please? You have been very kind."

She swallowed her temper.

"Please, I'm sorry. I can't tell you. You must believe me."

She was too angry to say anything.

"Please, I'm sorry. I'm very tired."

It was late. She rose irritably to her feet, and walked to the door then hesitated. Without saying a word, she walked to the sofa, ruffled his perfect hair then leaned down to kiss his forehead. "Goodnight."

"Goodnight," he repeated mechanically, but could not draw breath until she had left the room.

*

The kafir stood quietly. He could not turn around. He could not see what was happening, but he knew that voice. When the fingers sank into his arms, holding him tighter, his worst fears were confirmed. He was walked backwards, unbalanced and frightened, easily controlled. His heart was imploding. He could not breathe. Briefly, desperately, he imagined throwing off the Pakistanis and running, running so far and so fast that no one would ever find him, but he knew there was nowhere to hide. When Aziz turned him around, he was face to face with Prince Khalid.

Thick strong fingers circled his throat then squeezed. He hardly noticed as Aziz tactfully disappeared. Suddenly, he was pushed backwards. He slammed into the wall. The impact knocked the wind out of him, and killed whatever courage he had left. He could not look at his master's son. The rage in Prince Khalid's face burned white hot. He was saying something. He was so angry, but he whispered. He did not want to be overheard. The kafir did not understand. He wanted to drag the fingers from his throat, but knew that to seize a Believer meant the loss of that hand if not death. He could not move. He could not cry out. He could not stop his clothes being torn away, sending buttons raining to the carpet. His waistcoat, his shirt were all ripped open then the belt was crudely wrenched away, and his trousers were dragged down.

"Look at you! You're a whore," Prince Khalid whispered emotionally. Up close, he could see the classical beauty, every fleck of colour in the extraordinary eyes, and the stillness. It was frightened, but remained absolutely docile. He savagely took hold of the collars then crushed them against the wall. "You've driven my father insane."

Unable to breathe, the kafir could not answer, but he had nothing to say. He had been violated. He stood there exposed for what he was. As his trousers were forced down to his ankles, he felt sickened with shame. What he did for his master was intimate and private. This was brutal and cruel. When a hard, unforgiving hand gripped him, he wanted to die. The pain was extraordinary and savage. He closed his eyes. As his master's son pried and pawed, he trembled like a frightened little girl, but he never raised a hand to defend himself. He was choking, but he had been trained too well.

"I think it is you who wants to fuck it. You have lived in New York too long. They say half the whores in New York are transvestites. Perhaps, you have a taste for it," the Prince said, emerging into the corridor. "This is your obsession not mine. Take this thing, if you must. It will not resist even if you mistreat it, but please, not in the corridor."

Tears filled the kafir's eyes. The betrayal was complete.

"He is obscene," Prince Khalid said venomously. He wanted it to fight back. He needed to be able to attack it, but it was so still and so quiet. It hardly seemed real.

"Your thoughts are obscene."

"Look at him!"

"At what you are doing to it?"

"But look at him!"

"It is a servant. You dishonour me by touching it. It only obeys. Is that its crime?"

"He obeys because he must. He's a servant," Prince Khalid explained irritably. He did not know what he was searching for. Perhaps, it was the mark of sin though how would he know it? Perhaps, he merely wanted the depraved creature to fall apart and confess.

"So you must show mercy. That is your duty. God demands mercy."

Prince Khalid let go of the heavy collar, and drew back as the creature slumped against the wall, gasping for air. It had the temerity to actually look at him. No one had ever looked at him quite like that before. The exquisite eyes were full of reproach and understanding. He was overwhelmed with indignation. "Oh my father, he has driven you mad. Please, let me take him away, now, this minute."

The Prince was actually livid, but found it appalling to be at odds with his son. He was still shocked by the allegations. How could anyone believe such a thing? Yes, there was a tradition of teenage boys. It was a notorious habit, entrenched in the Islamic culture by the invisibility of women, but it was not considered a common practice anymore. Amongst men, it was forbidden. Between a man and his servant, it was discouraged. But between a man and a possession, especially a gift or something taken as loot then it was actually condoned by the Blessed Prophet though that had been so long ago. Islam was conceived in a male dominated world of nomadic bandits and constant warfare. Almost every family had a slave, clan chiefs had dozens; and women, gold and slaves were still the most highly prized spoils of conflict.

The Prince could not quite bring himself to give up the creature yet, even though his son's request meant he was honour bound to surrender it. Seeing the beautiful creature standing there, pale and dishevelled, with half its clothes torn away, being crudely manhandled by his son, aroused a flood of irrational emotions.

Prince Khalid grimaced then hurled the creature to the ground, and stared at his hands, not knowing what to do with them.

The Prince was furious. If it had been anyone else, he would have knocked them down and cursed them, but not his son. He was almost blind with rage. "I will give it to you then, this whore, but first I want to see you fuck it. I want to watch. I want all of us to watch."

"Father?" Prince Khalid was shaken to the core. At first, he thought his father was joking, but looking into his face, he realised he was in deadly earnest. "Please, my father. I cannot do that. Please, do not ask me to do that. Let me take him away. You need not fear. He will be cared for and kept safe. No harm will come to him. He is a slave. He will be pitied not punished. Please, do not ask me to do that. It revolts me. I am sorry if I have offended you. You are my father. I love you. Please, do not ask for this heinous thing."

"You have asked me to give you a whore. You will fuck the whore.

That is my request. You have accused me of this same heinous crime so you will fuck it or you will apologise to me, and never speak of it again. You will apologise?"

"Please, do not do this to your own son," his brother pleaded.

They both turned to look at him, but the Prince was unmoved. He nudged the motionless creature with his foot. "Get up. Ask Aziz to dress you as a whore then go back inside, and wait for us."

"Father," the son begged, but watched helplessly as the white creature crept away from his feet like a beaten dog. "I cannot do this. This is horrible. This is a sin."

They all watched as the humiliated kafir wriggled to pull up the trousers that had wrapped around his ankles. He moved awkwardly to his feet then carefully tried to restore his appearance in the torn and buttonless clothes. Faced with an audience, he kept his head down, and stared at his feet then bowed respectfully to each of them, and attempted to edge his way between them, desperate to escape.

"Pick up the buttons."

The kafir froze and stood a moment, shivering, wanting to disbelieve the words.

"Pick them up."

He trembled as his legs wobbled beneath him. Shame made his stomach somersault and knot. Sucking air into his lungs, he turned to acknowledge his master, and bowed again with the utmost respect. Then he gracefully dropped down on to his knees to grovel around their feet searching for the buttons. No one moved. No one could look at anything else. In silence, they watched him weave around them, brushing against them as he struggled to account for all the small, barely visible buttons.

"Please, my father," Prince Khalid said, staring at the creature. "I cannot do this. Before God, I cannot do this."

The kafir carefully collected all the buttons. It felt like hours, and all the time the four men watched him. He felt their hatred. He was afraid. They had him corralled between them. He knew he was only alive because his master wished it. He had no other protection. His life hung by the slenderest thread. At any moment, he might be cast off. There were men in the courtyard. He might die there in the corridor or later be abandoned in the desert. Shivering and almost incoherent, he struggled to stand up, and tried very hard not to be too tall. He dared not move again. Sweat prickled across his flesh. He felt a drop trickling down his forehead. In his chest, his heart was pounding like a hammer. He was in agony. It might have been only a minute, but it felt so much longer. He was shivering. He had never felt so violated. He stood motionless, awaiting a command, dreading what it would be, but no one spoke. They were all staring at him. His master watched him suffering, but did nothing. At last, emotionally ravaged, his face white, his eyes swimming with tears, the kafir went down to his knees, and settled his forehead on the floor.

"So?" the Prince asked, lifting his gaze to Prince Khalid's ashen face. "Well, there is no sin in fucking a kafir, male or female, if you are not in love with them. It is the Will of God that we humiliate all the disbelievers. Jihad. It is written. We must kill them all or take them into slavery and humiliate them. It is written. God wills it. His last words to the Blessed Prophet commanded it. Do you hate this pretty white thing enough to do God's Will, my son?"

"My father, you shame me," Prince Khalid raged hotly.

"As you have shamed me!"

"This is unseemly," warned the Prince's brother anxiously. "We must adjourn to somewhere more private."

"Do you also intend to sample its infamous delights?" the Prince demanded. "I wonder how many affairs you have had with women in New York, and how many times you have lied about them? Were they Apostates? Were they Believers? Were they all girls? I believe with Americans it can be hard to tell. And were they white?"

"Father," Prince Khalid said sharply. "Please, enough. Enough!"

The Prince glowered at them all, hurt beyond words, but he took a step back and then another then snapped his fingers at the creature, and with a subtle wave sent it away. "Using such a creature in time of need is not a sin. This is written. He is a kafir. This is written. According to you, he is kept for this purpose. You have decided that I love him. I deny it before God. I could not. He is a disbeliever. He is male. He is white. The Pakistanis are not offended by his sex or his skin. I have no knowledge of what they do with him, but I can guess. He is very beautiful." He gazed at his son. "We all know how they prize their libido. It is the stuff of legend."

"This is shameful, father."

The Prince glowered. "You have grievously insulted me."

Prince Khalid stared at his dirty hands, and grimaced again. "I am cursed."

"Yes, I curse you." The Prince stared at his son, feeling betrayed and disappointed.

There was a long and painful silence. They were all hurt and insulted and enraged.

They turned only when a mortified Aziz and the creature reappeared at the end of the corridor. It wore its gaudiest, tightest dress, and had the most lurid and hastily applied make up. It looked every inch like the most venal harlot imaginable.

Prince Khalid turned away, and covered his face with his hands. "This will be so embarrassing."

Aziz shoved the creature forward, and watched as it walked through the dazed crowd of onlookers, and into the dining room. It did not acknowledge any of them or lift its head. Aziz had heard enough to comprehend that he should leave the princes to their sport.

Prince Abdul Aziz followed the creature, surprised by the excitement and expectation that warmed him. He settled in own his chair, and directed the subdued and trembling beauty to remove any plates and dishes that might interfere with his son's enterprise. "Now, kneel down. You must help him." He watched his son come nervously closer. "He is a virgin, and you are a whore. You must be fucked. I insist. Do you understand?"

The kafir's nerves were running wild. He could hardly hear the words for the beating of his heart, but he bowed to his master then slumped to his knees, and stooped to kiss his feet. "Please? Please?" He was almost in tears. He lifted the hem of his master's long robe, and crushed it to his lips. "Please? Please, I'm begging you. My lord, Your Highness, my master by the Grace of God, the most Compassionate, the most Merciful. Please? Please? I really don't understand."

"You don't need to understand," the Prince growled. "You're a whore. Apparently, you're known everywhere as a whore. His Excellency, Prince Khalid, my son, asks for you. D' you understand?"

The kafir buried his face in the material, smudging it with his makeup, and wept like a child. When the Prince tore it from his grasp, he cried pitifully: "Please, no. It is a lie, my lord. Please, I beg you to be merciful. God is Merciful."

"You will be fucked by all of them. I insist. They all say you are a whore."

"Please? Please? I don't understand."

"Silence!" He kicked the creature away. That was the only time he had ever been intentionally vicious. "How dare you speak! You'll give yourself to my son. You'll encourage him. You will seduce him. And you will excel. Do you understand?"

The cold tone hurt more than the kick in his ribs. The kafir's nerves were shredded, but he turned obediently to kneel down before Prince Khalid, who was without doubt a very handsome young man.

"Father?" the son asked a little desperately, but he could not take his eyes off the painted harlot in the glittering dress, whose face was shining with tears.

"Brothers, please take your seats. I was offered a million dollars in diamonds for this whore only a few months ago, but I will give it to my son if he will do this. You've all supported him this evening with these false and despicable charges. Now, I think, he'll need your support a little longer."

"Father," the son asked again, unable to take his eyes off the creature. "Please, I cannot do this. I cannot. It is not in my power. It truly is a sin."

The Prince shook his head. "You must know the shame that you accuse me of. Either you want him or you retract your accusations and apologise."

The son swayed, and when the kneeling creature inched closer, he could not stop himself from stepping back. "Not like this."

"Hold your ground, you bloody coward."

Prince Khalid stared brokenly at his father then more distractedly at the creature. He knew he was trapped. He had used honour to force his father to surrender the creature. His father had neatly turned the tables to have his revenge. Prince Khalid was already humiliated. It did not seem likely that it could get any worse. Although his limbs were leaden, and the only emotion he felt was dread, he stepped closer to the creature until he stood over it. How bad could it be? There was no desire in him. He might be violently ill, but he could never actually be sexually aroused by any dirty white kafir.

The kafir was experiencing similar emotions. His only shield in a hostile world was to make men desire him so he strived to please them all. His every instinct told him that he was in danger. He could not understand what he had done that had brought him to such a perilous confrontation. His master was livid. He was commanded to perform, but knew that to obey put his life in danger, and to fail was unpardonable. He had to obey. His master had given him a specific instruction. He was not allowed to misunderstand or delay. Taking a deep breath, he looked at the men surrounding him. They were revolted and appalled by his rudeness. His master glowered. The kafir's hands were shaking. With regret, he gently ran his hands up Prince Khalid's legs then caressed his mighty sex. He felt him flinch and shudder, and had to acknowledge that neither of them wanted to be there. He looked up anxiously into the stranger's face. He wanted to apologise. He wanted to explain that he had no choice. The poor man was traumatised. Warming his hands against the soft material, the kafir tried to smile reassuringly then gently opened the trousers, and delicately reached inside.

Prince Khalid shuddered violently then struck it across the face. He had never hit anyone like that before. He wanted to scream and shout then turned away to cover his face as bile filled his mouth.

"Hold your ground, you bloody coward," the Prince roared at his son, then he reached down to seize the creature by the heavy collar, and forced it back on to its knees. "Stand here," he yelled at his son. When his son turned, he thrust the creature's face into his groin to continue its scandalous performance. "Now, fuck it! Fuck it so hard that you draw blood. It's a whore so treat it like one. Come on, fuck it! Make it bleed! Hit it again! That's what whores are for. Fuck it! Come on, fuck it! Harder! Fuck it!"

Chapter 29

She slept well thanks to her medication, but she found him very tense and sullen in the morning. He had slept on the sofa as usual. She knew he had slept in his clothes. He was probably too tired to undress. She felt that she had given him a bit of a mauling. That just hardened her renewed resolve to move him upstairs.

Sunday was full of the sad tales of fallen heroes, and lost opportunities in Frankfurt. It was reported as if the fate of the Free World rested on the performance of a dozen men. They had not won well enough. They had escaped an ignominious defeat only because a Paraguayan had made a mistake. She went out to the village shop, and bought a Sunday 'paper, hoping to find some good news. There wasn't much.

The young man sat quietly in the lounge while she read the 'papers. He read whatever came within range, but he did not venture to touch any of the pages that she tossed across the floor in exasperation and contempt. She was frightening when she was upset. For probably an hour and a half, she scanned every page. She ranted now and then as articles annoyed her. There were, of course, some opinions that matched her own. The media had so much power. There was always an agenda. They seemed to be happy just slagging off everyone else, criticising people who were trying to do something as well as those who did nothing at all. But it all came down to words. They could destroy people's lives with their words, but they never actually did anything. And waving banners demanding free speech, they could get away with saying anything. She only became angrier when she saw what a mess she had made. He curled up in the corner of the sofa as she hurried to gather up the loose sheets, wrapped them up into a roll then went out into the kitchen to shove them all into a bin.

After a series of loud bangs and swear words, she reappeared in the doorway with the vacuum cleaner. It was old and dusty and unloved. He had no idea what was about to happen. Suddenly, there was a loud roaring noise. Cats, that had been asleep in secret places, fled the room as if their lives depended on it, which was not far from the truth.

She did not actually dislike doing housework. That was just one of her tells. When she was well and happy then even the windows were sparklingly clean. When she was ill, and spiralling down into a serious

316

depressive state, then the washing up could gather for weeks, and the vacuum cleaner stayed under the stairs. It did not take long to go round with the vacuum, but it was so noisy, and the cats hated it with a passion so it was easy to justify not bothering.

"Just go and sit in the kitchen." She was angry.

He rose slowly to his feet. She was filling the doorway. In her hands was a growling cumbersome beast with a long hose. He anxiously wrapped his arms across his chest. He could not approach. There was nowhere to hide. He backed away from her, putting the sofa between them, ready to drop to his knees and take cover if she went berserk.

Absolutely livid, she surged into the room. The vacuum cleaner bashed against the doorframe then scuttled after her. She drove the brush across the carpet. She did not even notice as the young man fled almost as quickly as the cats. She bashed about furiously, but did slowly calm down. She vacuumed the carpet then moved all the furniture, and did it all again. She changed to the soft brush then went over the furniture before stripping it down, and thumping all the cushions. She cleaned the furniture again then put everything back together then went round again. By then she was hot and sweaty, and her heart was thumping in her chest. She could not breathe very well. She felt dizzy. Actually, doing the housework always felt like a victory. But she had to sit down. The room cleaned up well. As soon as her heart settled, she picked up all the rubbish off the coffee table, and carried it through to the kitchen. The young man was sitting at the table. She put the rubbish in the bin, and everything else went into the sink. She went back to fetch the vacuum cleaner. She quickly went around the hallway, but by then she was exhausted, and the vacuum went back under the stairs.

He sat quietly waiting. He had his hands clasped together in his lap. His head was bowed. He might have been asleep.

She turned on the cold tap, and lifted a handful of water to her lips then splashed another over her face. She was hot and bothered, but not angry anymore. She was full of good intentions about doing the housework properly and regularly, but it would never happen while she lived alone.

Turning around, she saw the young man at the table. He was perfectly still. He had his head bowed as if in prayer. She wondered what he was thinking. Her peculiar, twisted thought processes guaranteed that he had to be thinking about her. At best, he might be being kind, but she lacked the confidence to believe it. She was too old and too ugly, and just not attractive in any way that would appeal to such a good looking young man. He was calm, but she had never seen him relaxed. He was so beautiful. As her pulse steadied, and the sweat stopped trickling down her torso, she felt increasingly awkward and uncomfortable. It simply was not fair that he was so perfect. Even if he had been her own son, she would have believed that he was ashamed of her. She was always such a complete bloody mess. She was always conscious of being unattractive. She had never overcome the emotional damage done in her youth, which was then compounded by a bad marriage and almost fatal heartbreak. No one had ever been kind to her so the young man would be no exception. She could not take down the barricades. She did not know how to let anyone in. That was beyond her. His perfect manners had probably saved his life. She had not hurt him. She would not. He was not her son, but he could be a surrogate. For a few more weeks he could be a son. Someone had loved him. Everything about him proclaimed that he was loved, but it was not a love that she had ever known or would recognise. He was precious to someone. They would be desolate at the loss. No one had ever loved her like that. She had never experienced it. The cats? Yes, some of them loved her. Even her cold granite heart believed implicitly that they loved her, but not all of them, and not a single human being anywhere.

She sniffed loudly then drew a hand across her face. She did not want to imagine what she looked like. She tried to smile then changed her mind. He was not interested in her. She might have been standing there naked, and he would not have looked. She needed to go away, have a bath then paint on a new face, and try desperately to be someone else. Anyone else would be an improvement.

"Go and watch the television," she said, but moved to put a light hand on his shoulder. When he flinched, she tried to ignore it. "I'm going to get changed then we'll watch the tennis."

He nodded, but did not lift his head. He was afraid of her. There was something wrong with her, and he did not know what to do.

She felt his anxiety, but misread it. She paused, wanting to reassure him, but hurried away. She went up the stairs like a coward under fire. In her bedroom, she found the pills. She counted out what she needed then added a few more. While the bath filled, she swallowed them. In the mirror, she saw her face. It was a white mask, splashed with red blotches with oily smudges of mascara around her bloodshot eyes. Her hair looked like a bird's nest after a gale force wind. She looked demented. She almost smashed her fists against the glass. But it was pointless. The meds stopped her crying. She could get just so upset, but never enough to cry. She could almost get really angry, but never enough to do herself any harm.

She had a long hot bath while she kept a cold flannel on her face, and dreamed the dream of looking like Michelle Pfeiffer. But no amount of surgery could work such a miracle. She sank under the water then held her breath. It was supposed to be a relaxation technique, but she did not have the patience to persevere. She counted for as long as she could. It was supposed to clear her mind of extraneous problems. But she could not erase the young man. She just lost track of the numbers, and drifted off to appreciate his perfect symmetrical features and those amazing eyes.

An hour later, she was back downstairs, had the coffee table laden with cups and saucers and tea plates. She had made sandwiches. She had bought packets of crisps. Her biggest pot of tea was covered in a hand-knitted 'cosy'. Of course, she had provided tins of milkshake for him. The first had pills crushed in it. Everything was ready. She was ready. There was the tennis in Paris. At Silverstone, there was the British Grand Prix. Perhaps, she would be able to lure him into a conversation about Alonso and Button. He had been in Monte Carlo. He must have an opinion. He must have a team. He must have a favourite driver.

But first, there was Federer, and she was genuinely thrilled.

Federer's silky smooth forehand was acknowledged to be the biggest weapon in tennis. He had prepared for his match against Nadal by practicing against some strong left-handers. The French crowd were divided. They adored Nadal but they admired Federer. Their respective styles were evident from the start. Nadal bounced up and down on his toes like a boxer while Federer stood motionless and composed on the other side of the net. One was fearless and audacious. The other was a king. There was the awkward photo moment at the net. It was impossible to tell then that they were friends. They were both focused. In their minds they were already playing the game. Around them, the packed stadium was a frenzy of shouting and raw emotion. Only the two men were impervious to the clamour and noise.

For Federer, this was the Day of Days. Could he become only the third man in history to hold all four Grand Slam titles at one time? The only obstacle on his journey was Nadal. Most of their meetings had been on clay, but Nadal was irritatingly 5-1 ahead. No one else had beaten Federer that year. Without doubt, Federer was the class act. He was the thoroughbred, but everyone knew that Nadal relished adversity. The court felt like an arena. The atmosphere was electric. The heat sizzled off the baking red clay.

Federer played like a god. He showed his complete repertoire, taking the first four games with sublime ease. From pillar to post, he was driving Nadal about the court. Nadal did manage to land the odd forehand, but Federer was hitting clean winners all over the place. The variety of shots was impressive. He was giving a masterclass. But no one could discount Nadal. He was just twenty years old, and rippling with muscles. He might have been dripping with sweat, but he never seemed to lose his belief. In the fifth game, Nadal actually had break points on Federer's serve, but Federer held on. The French loved style. When the match started, the crowd had been split down the middle, but by the beginning of the sixth game, they were in love with Federer. Nobody did style like the great Roger Federer.

Nadal won the sixth game, but Federer won a perfect first set. Praise was heaped on him, but no one could quite believe that Nadal would not come back. It was a five setter. Perhaps Nadal was just toying with him?

Barely two hours later, Nadal came out to serve for his second French title. After another fabulous rally in which Federer ran down every single ball, he broke Nadal's serve then went on to hold his own. There was to be a Tie Break in the Fourth. The spectators went mad. Federer had come back again. Perhaps, there would be a Fifth set. It started well, but Nadal would not be denied. He did believe in destiny. The French was his.

She was almost in tears. Every nerve had been shredded. She had so wanted Roger Federer to win. It was not that she disliked Nadal. It was about History and Tradition. There was only one positive. No one believed that Nadal could be that good on grass. Wimbledon was a couple of weeks away. Federer could go to Halle, and effectively have a whole tournament to polish his grass court game. No one would dare to defeat him in Halle. It was his tournament. He probably owned the grass. Apparently, Nadal was going to Queens to do much the same. In only a few days, the world would see if Nadal could play on grass. And every game would be on television.

*

Prince Khalid sat on a table in his suite. He had tried waiting on the sofa, but he was too tense to sit still. He swung his legs, thinking about what had happened as dispassionately as possible; trying to rationalise his feelings. The whole evening seemed more like a dream. It was almost as if he had been watching it happen to a third person. His behaviour was so out of character. He was sure that he had been tricked. He was almost able to believe that he was the victim, but that the guilt that he felt was vividly real. He had done that shameful thing in front of his father and uncles. What had happened afterwards was too awful to recall. It was inconceivable that the others had simply followed his example. His feelings of guilt and embarrassment and shame were equally matched by self-pity, regret and betrayal. The confusion was a strange new experience for him. Usually, he was so sure. His instincts were so good. He needed desperately to understand what had made all of them behave so badly. He knew that they were men of honour. It troubled him greatly that they had all done something so despicable. He could not quite recall at what point he had lost control. In the space of a few minutes, they had all become violent predators. They had all lost every vestige of their self-control. It had to be witchcraft. They had been tricked, there was no other explanation. The dreadful creature had done something. He could still hear his father shouting: "Fuck it! Fuck it! Make it bleed!" He could not remember how the creature had ended up naked. But in the end, it was naked, and covered in blood. He remembered hitting it so hard, and his hand still burned. His knuckles were grazed. And the rest? His penis was red and sore, and he knew that he had probably fared better than his uncles. They had all gone stark raving mad. And through it all, the creature had obeyed every order and performed every deed. It had bewitched them, and no matter the punishment meted out, it never held back. It was as insatiable and greedy as its reputation, but that hardly absolved them. He knew it would take a great deal of penance to remove the stain from his honour, but as he would never be able to forget what he had done, then how could he ever hope for absolution and paradise?

The doors opened. Aziz, in his smart white thobe and taqiyah, entered the room. Behind him was the tall willowy figure in the black burqa. Aziz held its wrist. At a sign from Prince Khalid, he turned to make the creature kneel down and bend over its knees. Then Aziz bowed to the Prince, and greeted him with all due reverence.

Prince Khalid stared at the creature, unable to recognise it beneath the all-enveloping burqa. "Thank you," he said to Aziz. "I will speak to him."

Aziz bowed again. "It cannot speak, Your Excellency. It is forbidden."

"He will speak to me," Prince Khalid said curtly.

Aziz hesitated. It was not his place to question the whims of a great prince. He had brought the creature to be fucked. It had no other purpose. He had brought it back with some pride because he had assumed the young prince wanted another poke. "Then with respect, Your Excellency." Aziz turned to the creature then heaved it back on to its heels, and carefully lifted away the burqa.

Prince Khalid shifted his position to see what the servant was doing. He was just in time to glimpse a broad piece of sticky tape being ripped away from the creature's battered lips.

Aziz quickly crumpled the tape in his hands then adjusted the burqa to make sure his source of income was respectable and presentable. He turned back to the Prince with a smile. "Then it will speak, Your Excellency, but it is a lying infidel, and you should not listen a word that comes from its foul mouth."

Prince Khalid nodded and smiled. "Yes. Thank you." He did not approve of keeping the creature veiled like a decent, modest woman. It seemed wrong. It felt deceitful. Nor did he like Aziz's callous treatment of the creature, but he hardly felt able to criticise. "God is Great."

"May God the All Knowing, and the Holy Prophet bless you, Your Excellency." Aziz bowed again, and withdrew. He had no qualms about leaving the creature there. It was completely broken. He could have left it safely with a child. The young prince would be disappointed if he was anticipating another violent conquest.

The kafir had not moved from his knees. He dared not look at the Prince even from behind the mask that obscured his eyes. He did not feel he knew him well enough to risk such an indiscretion. His body was still stiff with injuries. Every movement hurt him. He believed he had been brought back to be raped again. There was no other possible explanation.

"Do you know why you are here?" Prince Khalid asked politely.

The kafir doubted his hearing, but bowed down to press his forehead to the floor, and flattened his palms. "Please? Your Excellency, by the Grace of God, the most Compassionate, the most Merciful, please forgive me. God is Great. God is Merciful,"

"You have been here a long time."

The kafir hardly knew what he was talking about, but he glanced slyly across to try and read the Prince's face. That did not help him.

Prince Khalid gazed at the black wraith on the floor. It looked like a heap of laundry. "Do you remember anything from your past life?"

The kafir shook his head slowly. He had no idea where this was going. He had been brought there to serve the Prince. His body had been repaired and prepared. Though he was hurt and tired, he was determined to satisfy him. The dreadful threats of the previous evening began to ring in his ears. This was not right. He lifted his head, and looked up anxiously at Prince Khalid. "Please? I must go with you?"

Prince Khalid frowned. No servant had ever audaciously asked him a question before. That it was the ignominious whore made him pause. That the repellent creature had dared to look at his face was unforgivably insulting. He cleared his throat. The creature clearly did not deserve his compassion. "You have shamed my family. There is no punishment harsh enough to satisfy my honour."

The kafir trembled. He was shocked to be accused of such a terrible crime. What had he done? His sense of duty was so strong. He remembered the threat of the men in the courtyard, and gasped: "You will kill me? Did I not please you? I have obeyed. I must obey. I must always obey. Please? Your Excellency, my lord by the Grace of God, I tried to please you. Please? God is Merciful. God is Compassionate. Please? God is Great. God is Merciful. Please…"

Prince Khalid found it difficult to look at the crumpled black shape that writhed and trembled on the floor. It did not even look like a human being so his temper was not soothed by any misplaced compassion. He could not erase the appalling images or emotions from the night before. This hideous wriggling thing had corrupted them all. "No."

The kafir was in turmoil. There were men in the courtyard. He looked up at the Prince then lowered his head then in absolute despair slid forward to try and kiss his feet.

Prince Khalid shrank away then lashed out angrily. "Don't touch me!"

Caught by a blow, the kafir drew back to cower over his knees. "Please, Your Excellency. God is Merciful. Please, I beg you. Don't do this. Please, Your Excellency. Please, be merciful. God is Merciful. Please, God is Merciful. I beg you. Please?"

Prince Khalid glowered at the heavily veiled figure on its knees before him. It revolted him. He felt dirty being near it. He wanted it to shut up and stop whining. He wanted to beat it with his bare hands until it ceased to exist. Only then would he escape the shame. He shuddered violently. The shame! How could he live with the shame?

"Your Excellency?" the kafir implored. He started to inch closer on his knees, his bruised and cut hands clasped together. The burqa snagged and tore. He was immobilised by the yards of material that wrapped around him like a shroud. "You mean to kill me? I beg you to be merciful. God is Merciful. God is Compassionate. I will do anything. Anything. Please, don't send me away. Please?"

Prince Khalid shivered and drew back. The words were sour to his ear. The pictures they painted in his mind were so loathsome, he had to turn away.

The kafir lunged forward to grasp a slipper, and pressed it to his lips.

Prince Khalid whipped around and punched him, knocking him down, and sending him tumbling across the floor. At that moment, he hated him.

The hate became absolute detestation, and then he was once more ashamed. He groaned aloud, raising his fists to flail at the air, knowing he had committed another monstrous crime. Turning away from the cowering thing, he leaned down on the table, and hung his head. He did not understand what was happening. It was as if he had become another person, one with no honour and no compassion. He had become a base, violent and godless man.

The devastated kafir did not move until he was sure that Prince Khalid had lost interest in him. Then he slowly crept back towards the door, and rose unsteadily on to his feet. He diligently straightened the burqa, but did not lift it. He was shivering. Everything hurt. He hardly had the strength to stand, but he had to stand there, and wait patiently to be commanded.

Prince Khalid turned regretfully to look at the veiled figure. He was surprised that it could just stand there so calmly when it was effectively sentenced to death. He shook his head. His own servants were altogether different. It was like stepping back centuries.

"Come here," he said, and pointed to a spot only a few feet away.

The kafir bowed, and moved placidly to obey. He observed every elegant gesture that took him to his knees, with his head on the floor, and his hands outstretched. He did not move to kiss the Prince's feet, and no ring was offered for him to worship.

"You cannot stay here. You have corrupted this place. You have brought dishonour to my family. By rights, you should be taken out and executed. What you do is a sin and unpardonable, but I cannot now allow your execution. You are really no better than a slave. There must be some leniency. You have been obedient. But you have revelled in your debasement. I cannot reward such vile behaviour, nor can I allow it to continue. You will not stay here. I will not have you in my household. I am only telling you this because I should not have used you. I should not have struck you. I was unwell. I behaved badly." He paused to stare at the creature's hands. No other part of it was visible. "I am sorry for what I did. I must now make amends and pay penance. Because of that, and because you had no choice, I am sending you away."

The kafir stared at the floor. He could not believe it. "Please? Please, I am sorry, but my master-"

Prince Khalid swallowed with difficulty. He could hardly say the words: "You belong to me now." Acknowledging the legal niceties turned his heart to stone. His chest tightened. "My father has given you to me. Now, you must obey me. You belong to me as you belonged to my father.

Do you understand?"

The kafir shivered, but he moved slowly across the floor to insinuate a kiss close to Prince Khalid's feet. His heart was breaking. The words rolled around in his head like marbles in a tin cup. He did not want to understand what was happening, but he said: "Yes, Your Excellency." Then he leaned forward, and carefully offered another soft kiss. "My lord, Your Excellency Sheikh Khalid bin Abdul Aziz, my master by the Grace of God, the most Compassionate, the most Merciful. All that I am." It marked his capitulation. His allegiance was transferred. His heart shattered painfully into a million pieces. Tear drops rained down behind the veil, but nobody noticed. Nobody cared. "God is Great, Your Excellency. May God bless you and your family with peace and prosperity, my lord."

"You won't be hurt," Prince Khalid explained uncomfortably. It took all his nerve to stand still while the creature had grovelled and humbled itself so completely to pay its respects, and obviously, in a calculated attempt to gain his goodwill. When it had said his name with the required deference, he still felt insulted then was ashamed of his blatant prejudice. "I give you my word that no one will hurt you. You'll be taken away to a safe place. They'll look after you. You won't be used like that ever again, I swear. They'll find you something better to do. Do you understand?"

The kafir had given up. He did not understand what he had done to be so harshly punished. In the dark loneliness of the burqa, he could find no consolation at all.

"You should never have been brought here. I wish I could make amends, and return you to your home, but I'm afraid that is impossible. I could not allow it. For the honour of my family, I must send you away. D' you understand?"

The kafir bowed and salaamed then crept tentatively closer to kiss the Prince's feet again. He was weeping. "Please, yes my lord, Your Excellency. All that I am. God is Great. Don't send me away. Please, have mercy. Don't send me away."

Prince Khalid was surprised that the creature was so upset. Servants could be so callous. Their loyalty was invariably fickle. "I can't promise that you'll be happy, but you'll be kept safe and well."

"Please? I beg you. Please, don't send me away. Please, let me stay here. I'll be good. I'll do anything to please you. Please, my lord, Your Excellency, my master by the Grace of God, the Compassionate, the Merciful. Please, I'm yours. I'm your obedient servant. I'll do anything you desire. Please, let me stay. Please, let me stay here. Don't send me away. I beg you, please don't send me away. This is my home. Please? Please, my lord. This is my home."

"Do you love him?" Prince Khalid asked in shock. He could hardly say the words. "You love him?" He was absolutely appalled.

Chapter 30

That evening, she found a little hedgehog on the lawn. It could hardly walk. She quickly carried it back to the house. In the kitchen, she examined it carefully. It had curled up tightly into a ball, and there was no way of opening it out without doing it harm. She could see that it was dripping with bloated ticks. She fetched an old washing up bowl, and placed the hedgehog in one corner then poured olive oil over it until it was thoroughly soaked. The hedgehog grunted and moved irritably, but it did not unwind from its prickly ball. She used almost a whole bottle of oil, and held the washing up bowl at an angle so that the creature was bathing in the deep oil, but not drowning in it.

She carried the bowl into the lounge, and sat with it resting in her lap. The black cat came to sniff and sneer. No one else was interested. She watched the hedgehog. She did not care anymore about the football or the metatarsal or even the young man. He might have been curious, but he never moved to look. He was quite startled when she forced him to hold the bowl when she left to go to the toilet. It smelt. He had no idea what it was. He was visibly relieved to hand it back when she returned minutes later.

She had the rabbit hutches ready for just such an emergency. It was easy to stuff one of them full of hay then burrow the creature inside. A bowl of water and cat food were placed in the run. She retreated to the doorway then switched off the lights. Within a few minutes the ravenous hoglet was tucking into a free meal.

The young man was asleep. It was very late. She hurried around tidying up then locking all the doors. There were already four cats on her bed. Two of them took the huff when she moved them aside to make room. So she lay down with her black gentleman and a deaf old lady. She drifted off to sleep listening to them purring. She could take care of them. She knew how to look after the hedgehog. For the first time in weeks, she did not go to sleep consumed by thoughts of the young man's lovely body. She slept well. She was still sane.

*

It was so overwhelming; he almost believed that he had died and gone to heaven. The room shone with so much light and colour. Rough red gemstones studded the walls. There were veins of gold. Everywhere, there were thick seams of lapis lazuli. Decorative tiles gleamed on the floor. After all the blackness, he struggled to find any definition or detail. It was too much, too dazzling, but he dared not close his eyes for even a moment in case it all disappeared. It was one of those moments which are etched so deeply into the memory that they were always fresh and vivid. He would never forget her or that room or the sweet fresh water that seemed so plentiful.

"You no understand they language," the woman said, leaning down towards him, her tone betraying contempt. "This is you problem. I am no speak." She was a strikingly handsome woman, no longer young or beautiful, but with a commanding appearance. She wore a rich blue robe and a great deal of jewellery. Her name was Leila. She was a princess in her own right and a queen by marriage. She had lost a husband to cancer and two sons to the Soviets. "You must have words. You must have respect my people. You must have know you no leave here." Her realm had once been a vast metropolis high in the lost valleys of the Hindu Kush, but that had been thousands of years ago. It was rumoured that the descendants of Alexander the Great had settled there. Certainly, the locals had fairer hair and paler eyes than the other tribes in the area. They had a distinct monotheistic religion that was at odds with the puritanical Islam sweeping through the mountains. They had withdrawn into their mountain, which had provided their wealth, and now gave them security. Inside the mountain, they guarded one of the oldest religious sites in the world. "My Prince Khalid want you good. You must have – if – pain my people you no food no water. Understand you what I speak you?"

The kafir had barely survived the five-day forced march through hostile terrain. It was no longer safe to travel any other way. Helicopters were shot down. The roads were crawling with bandits. The men escorting him were private security employed by Prince Khalid. They were loyal and efficient and deadly. He had been with them for about a month while the details of his exile were agreed. No one spoke to him. No one explained anything. If he kept quiet they did not hurt him. They reached north eastern Badakhshan by helicopter then set off on foot into the mountains. They had rendezvoused as arranged with a group of locals on a high pass that offered plenty of cover. The kafir had been handed over like a parcel. The locals appeared to be nothing more than nomadic tribesmen, rugged, turbaned, well-armed. They had livestock and guns. The kafir was too tired to care. He needed to sit down. He needed to rest. When he did not move fast enough, they just put a rope around his chest and dragged him. He had to follow them. He focused on following. His eyes filled with sweat and dust. His body accrued cuts and bruises. It might have been hours, it felt like days, he trailed behind them, not aware of his surroundings until they took him into a cave. The steep steps were beyond him. He fell and fell again. His feet and shins and knees were soon cut and bleeding. There were so many steps, and it was so very dark. They dragged him when he could not walk. Then there were miles of corridors, he was dead on his feet. He needed the gag to be removed. He could not breathe. He was so thirsty and so very tired. More uneven steps. More corridors. He stumbled along, dragged and pushed and cursed. Then there was a room. It was small and empty. He was allowed to fall down. They strapped his ankles together. They abandoned him without a word. He was alone. The only light was taken away. He had been left there for a very long time.

The isolated community did not want him. They understood only that he was infected with some unpleasant disease. They waited patiently for him to die.

"I want you must have speak understand you," the woman demanded.

The kafir filled his lungs. He had no idea what was going on. He had been left in the dark. He was no longer even sure whether strangers had come to him in the darkness and fucked him. So many men. Was it a dream? He had dreamed that his master had come to rescue him. They had made mad passionate love, but he always awoke alone, parched, starving, and in the dark. He took another moment to survey the dazzling room. It was so beautiful, so rich and fabulous. There was a turquoise pool of water. He would have sold his soul to be allowed to slip into that beautiful clean water. What little strength he had left finally deserted him. He slipped to his knees, and bowed to this powerful woman.

"I ask no you no two – twice."

He shivered, and looked up at her, feeling threatened, but then he bowed his head respectfully. "Yes." He looked around the amazingly beautiful room, and acknowledged that she was the most important person there: "Your Highness."

"You bad my brother. Him pain you must have. Break hearts of child." She was surprised by her hatred. Revenge had been an alien concept. She wanted him to understand that she knew all about his dreadful, unforgivable crimes. "My people speak you very bad. Devil."

No one wanted him there. That was obvious. But only God had the right to judge him. His arrival had caused a great stir. It was said that even his shadow would defile them. Even the priests were reluctant to have any contact. They lived in an exalted state, terrified of being touched by anything that was deemed offensive to their god. Even the air that they breathed was considered a threat because it might pollute the eternal fire that they had tended in their temple for thousands of years. So the priests stayed in the Fire Temples, praying and chanting for days and weeks, while the kafir had languished in the darkness. There was no one automatically in charge in this situation, who would know what to do with a prisoner, know how to arrange food and water while maintaining public safety. There was a great deal of talk about public safety. There were no prison facilities at all. In their culture, there was no need for a prison. In their religion, there was no such thing as guilt. Very few of the doors inside the mountain actually locked. It had taken nearly a whole day prowling around gloomy corridors to find a room where the kafir could be safely left. He could die there. No one would notice. People were openly talking about dumping his body to deny him even their sacred Towers of Silence. But he had not died.

"Betray. Yes? You betray my brother. My people speak you must have poison to them. My people want you must have dead near – soon. My priests want knife – cut you. You must have much need pain. You must have punish you."

"Please?" he gasped, knowing he was doomed. "Please?"

"You speak?" she demanded indignantly.

He grimaced, and struggled to find his nerve. There were a dozen priests, and many more men in splendid robes, all of them elderly. Almost everyone had greying hair and beards, many of which were coloured with henna. Every man was armed with a large dagger and pistol in his belt. Some had automatic rifles slung across their backs. The priests were not armed or bearded. They wore white and blue robes, and carried ceremonial staffs decorated with gold. They were not Muslim. That made them his sworn enemies. He could not begin to comprehend why he was there, but it was Prince Khalid's decision. This was his exile. All that he knew with any certainty was that he did not want to go back into the darkness and be alone. "Please?" he asked brokenly.

Though the Queen was a powerful woman, proud of her heritage, and her priests were very wise, none of them actually wanted to cast the first stone. They believed in charity and cherished peace. She knew that his crimes demanded that he be stoned to death or received the mercy of a sword. Yet the laws of her city's ancient and benign religion dictated that only God could be the final judge. It guaranteed that justice was always very slow and sure.

The creature's only saving grace was that it had been brought to her country as a slave. They understood what that meant. There were many slaves. They were common in the culture, in the country and in the religion. They belonged to their masters, and with permission, they married and raised children, and were all enslaved, yet they were cared for by their masters, who were as devoted and loyal as the slaves were in return. Loyalty was in their blood. That was the bond that held society together. This alien slave was different. It came disgraced. It had been disloyal. It had been banished for a crime so terrible that it must be kept a secret forever. Queen Leila wanted vengeance for her cousin, but she did not want publicity. It was for God to decide its fate. They had left the creature in the lonely subterranean room, and it had not died. That was a sign.

It was an increasingly foul smell that had filled the corridors inside the mountain, which now dictated the creature's fate.

"There is work. You must have work. My people. You no trouble no. No! No trouble. Understand?"

He dared to briefly look up into her unveiled face, and wondered what would happen if he confessed that he did not understand at all.

"My people will no pain no – hurt you, no hurt you. You work. No trouble. No pain. Yes?"

He lowered his gaze and bowed. "Yes, Your Highness."

The Queen nodded, uneasy at surrendering her need for revenge so cheaply. She explained to the audience around her that the creature would work as required, that they must make sure it was fit enough to work, and that from now on they had an obligation to take care of it.

"He is dirty, Your Highness. He must not live amongst us. He has sinned."

"What do you mean?" She gazed at the elderly man, who had spoken.

Dressed in colourful robes, with a scarlet sash around his belly, one man shyly stepped forward. He was in his late sixties with a smiling face, but he was red with embarrassment. He bowed graciously to the Queen. "Men and some boys have visited him scandalously, Your Highness."

The Queen turned quite pale. "Which men and boys? Tell me their names?"

The man bowed again. "I cannot, Your Highness. I saw and I heard only from a distance. It is a crime of darkness and stealth."

The kafir stared at the floor. He could not understand a word. He wanted to fall into the beautiful turquoise pool, and drown there.

Everyone in the room looked guiltily at everyone else.

She knew the wives and children of all the men there. It was inconceivable that a married man could do such a thing for pleasure. "Then we will find an incorruptible jailor, Josephus. A pious priest perhaps?" The collection of priests at her right hand shifted uncomfortably. "Yes. He will become your ward. He will work at night to keep our air fragrant, and during the day time, he will be in your care." She turned primly to gaze at the pale priests, and enjoyed their discomfort. "I want him to be blessed. If you have blessed him then his presence will not defile us. It will be safe to have him in the city."

"Your Highness, it is impossible. He would need to be blessed every day. He will be foul and wretched after such employment. He should be left food and water as we have done with the Dalits. It is a practical proven system that has worked for many years."

"No, he will be blessed every day. He will be kept safe with you, who are above reproach. It is not acceptable for him to be abandoned to faceless enemies."

"He will be castrated?"

"No." She looked at the creature. "He's harmless. Look at him."

They all stared at him, but he looked dreadful and smelt worse. He was nothing more than a grubby skeleton wrapped in rags.

*

It was Monday. The football kept intruding. It seemed to be on 24/7. But she had the garden, and now a hedgehog. There were the wheelie bins to drag down to the gate. That day the postman actually came up the potholed driveway to deliver a water rates bill. She caught the young man hiding in the curtains to watch the stranger poke the letter through the front door. He was frightened of something. She had never thought for a minute that he might be that afraid of anything. It just added to his aura of mystery. If possible, it made him even more attractive, and his silence even more intriguing.

She spent an hour with the hedgehog. It was dunked again into the olive oil bath. Several dead and half dead ticks had already fallen off. While the hedgehog remained determinedly curled up in a ball, she was able to pick up all the ticks, clean out the hutch, put in new bedding, and then return the significantly more fragrant little creature back into its private hospital ward. She put in fresh food and water. Within minutes of being alone, it was munching through the food enthusiastically.

Then she mowed the lawn with the blades set slightly lower. It still looked awful, but she persevered. At Wimbledon, they mowed the grass every day. She was not sure that she was that desperate to have a perfect lawn. She went to the shops. There was still money in the bank. She bought ice cream and more olive oil. One was frivolous, the other now a necessity. The divine young man liked the ice cream.

In the afternoon, she intercepted him on the way back from the bathroom. She slipped her arm through his, and steered him through the kitchen then out into the garden. It was the first time that he had actually been outside. They walked together slowly along the cobbled path. Neither of them had shoes. She took her time, gazing at the flowers and the swelling buds that would become fruit. He blinked at the sunlight, but placed his feet carefully, unsure of the ground, and wondering where she was taking him. She opened the old door, and invited him to step through into the wider garden. There was the long lawn, the deep herbaceous borders and the lofty trees. She tried to see it through his eyes. Her hours of toil meant that she knew every flaw and every weed. What he saw was a landscape drenched with colour and beauty. It all merged together into a perfect whole. She smiled happily as his face reflected wonder, then she took his arm again, and they walked on slowly. Holding his arm, she could feel his frailty. He was absolutely no threat to her. She drew him across the lawn to the ponds, apologising for the rough patches of grass, and not giving him the opportunity to say anything. But then he never said anything. She named the roses that were filling the air with fragrance. She pointed out the bumble bees that were busy around the foxglove spires. There were butterflies everywhere. She did not know the names, but named them anyway, confident that he was too polite to contradict her. They slowly circled the garden. Back near the wall, she pressed him to sit down on the bench. By then he was pale and tired.

They sat together in the sunshine, surrounded by colour and beauty and birdsong. She turned to look at him, and was completely blown away by his looks. He had shut down again. He seemed to know when he was being watched. She almost felt sorry for him, but it hardly seemed to be a disability that anyone could complain about. She smiled at his discomfort then gazed away across the garden.

"I found you over there in the woods." She pointed vaguely towards the treeline beyond the lawn.

He came to life. His head lifted. His eyes scanned the treeline. Of course, he was interested. His whole demeanour changed. They were both curious about his presence in her garden. He had to believe that she was not involved, but if she was an innocent then why had he been left there?

She searched his face as he searched the treeline. There was intelligence now. He had character and personality. He was no longer just a gorgeous vacuous mannequin. It was as if someone had switched on a light somewhere inside him. She reached out to touch his arm, wanting him to turn and look at her, sure that she would learn something. He flinched. The shutters came down. He stared at the ground.

"It's alright," she said. "We'll work it out. You'll get better and you'll grow stronger, and one day you will remember everything."

He looked at her sharply then lowered his gaze. He managed to nod.

"You could take off your jacket?" she suggested. "It's a lovely afternoon."

He breathed deeply then shuffled forward so that he had room to slip off his jacket. He moved carefully. It was obvious that he was still in pain. He was merely obeying an order. If she had asked him to do handstands and cartwheels, he would have done that too.

She took the jacket, and folded it over her arm. She could see the tension in his jaw muscles and furrowed brow. He was not enjoying being outside. She had hoped that he would relish feeling the sun on his face, and breathing the sweet fragrant air. She gazed away across the garden then surveyed her extensive range of derelict buildings. Perhaps, if she did not look at him? It had to be an absolute pain to be ogled at all the time.

Her favourite black cat emerged from a nearby flowerbed. It walked across the lawn like an emperor, its tail twitching, its yellow eyes on fire. She talked to it as it approached. It lifted its head. The yellow eyes gleamed brightly. It was indeed a handsome cat. Without hesitation, it forced its way on to the bench then took possession of her lap. She stroked it. She kept talking. It purred very loudly.

The young man watched the cat. He managed to relax a little after accepting that nothing unpleasant was about to happen. They were just sitting in the sunshine. It was not a trap. It was not a game. When the cat head-butted his chest, he actually managed to lift a hand and stroke it.

"Why don't you roll up your sleeves?" She held out her forearms to show off the scratches and modest tan. "It's lovely and warm today."

He hesitated. Everything was such an effort. Without thinking, he tried to turn back the cuff that was buttoned snugly around his wrist. When she started laughing, he stopped and turned away. She was still laughing as he fiddled the button loose then carefully folded back the cuff.

She realised that she had embarrassed him. "I'm sorry. You're tired.

I've made you walk too far today."

He carefully folded back the cuff on his other arm to reveal the fabulous Breitling wristwatch.

"It's alright," she said. He was rigid with tension. "Honestly, it's alright."

He glanced towards her then stared at the ground.

She patted his arm then rose to her feet. He needed space. She could see the weeds growing before her eyes. She slung the cat across her shoulder then walked away. The cat was comfortable. It was happy to drape across her shoulder for hours. The lily leaves were unfurling. Soon there would be flowers. There were hardly any frogs. The newts were even scarcer. She could see that the blanket weed was still spreading. It seemed to grow even faster than the brambles. She lifted the cat down onto the grass then stooped to pull out some weeds. She was watching the young man. She wanted to observe his reactions. She felt like a scientist studying a lab rat. Had she felt guilty about it then she would probably have felt like some seedy private eye, but she did not feel guilty. He was in trouble. She needed to know what was happening. It took much longer than she had hoped for him to relax even a little bit. For an hour, she pottered about dead heading and pulling out weeds. She needed a trowel and a refuse sack, but she was really just pretending.

When she felt he had settled on the bench, she turned and walked back towards him. He became visibly tense. His feet shuffled. He was ready to stand up. She went through the gate into the walled garden. She paused just inside the doorway. She could not hear anything. There were no sounds to suggest that he was following her. She waited. He did not appear. She went on into the house then filled two glasses with water. She went back out to find him still on the bench. Without actually looking at him, she forced a glass into his hands then walked away across the garden. He had been upset at being left alone. So he had not been lying. He really did not want to be on his own. She went to stand by the ponds. The handsome black cat was asleep in the bed of *Nepeta cataria*. It was feeling no pain. She sipped from her glass of water, and turned slightly to observe that the young man did the same.

She easily spent another hour quietly working. Eventually, she forgot to look at him. Whenever she remembered, he was sitting on the bench. At first, he seemed interested in the trees at the bottom of the garden. Later, he was just staring at the ground. He looked increasingly uncomfortable. It took her a long time to realise that something was wrong.

When she returned to the bench, it was obvious that he was in distress. She sat beside him. It was not until she took hold of one of his hands that he even noticed her. His face was grey and soaked with sweat. His eyes were glazed. She squeezed his hand tenderly. She could hear him breathing. He was dragging air into his lungs. She moved closer to take hold of his arm.

"Let's go inside."

He frowned and looked at her. He shook his head. He did not know how to stand up.

Her grip on his arm tightened. "Stand up. Come on, up you get!" She swept him on to his feet then wrapped her arms around him. He was so slight she could keep him upright and balanced. But as soon as he took a step, his knees buckled and he slumped down. She stooped over him. "Come on, baby. We need to go back inside. You can sleep on the sofa. You can watch the television. Come on, up you get."

He was on the ground. His head was swimming. He was aware of her. He could feel her pulling his arm, which hurt his back terribly. All the words were just noise.

She managed to lift him back on to the bench then pulled his arm across her shoulders. She was panicking. But his arm braced. He held on.

It seemed a million miles back to the house. She took him only a few steps at a time. She kept telling him that they were nearly there, that he would be able to sleep for as long as he liked, and that it really wasn't far. He had no idea what she was saying. The immense wound on his back was throbbing with pain. It was so overwhelming that he had to force air into his lungs. Every muscle was paralysed. Even his brain had stopped working.

She was exhausted by the time they reached the sofa, but she lowered him down carefully, and arranged the cushions. While he tried to open his eyes, she combed her fingers through his hair, pushed the wayward strands back off his forehead then pressed her palm to his cheek to feel if he was warm. He was ice cold and sweating. "You should eat more. You'll never grow stronger if you don't eat more."

His eyes closed. He was just breathing. Anything else was beyond him.

She loosened his tie and unbuttoned his collar. She had so many things to do, but she could not leave him. She felt that she had put his recovery back by weeks. For half an hour, she sat on the floor beside him, holding his hand, stroking his hair, listening to his breathing. Sometimes, he had his eyes open, but he never looked at her.

When his breathing steadied, she covered him in a blanket and crept away. She fetched his jacket and the glasses then fed the cats. She gave the hedgehog another olive oil bath while she sat in the lounge watching the young man. He did not die. Her confidence returned hesitantly. She had the hedgehog now. She knew what to do with a hedgehog. Over the years there must have been dozens. One winter, she had every hutch filled, and the whole house smelled of hedgehogs. That was a bit overpowering, but only one had died. That was technically a great success. The others had gone back into the garden full of energy and a good weight. She had always thought that ticks were an African thing, but they seemed to be everywhere now. She used the medicated drops from the Vet for the cats. She had never seen them on the cats, but Tick Bite Fever was a terrible thing. It had killed poor dear Elsa.

She missed her favourite programme. It was gone ten o'clock by the time she remembered to take her pills. Whenever the young man awoke, she spoon fed him jars of baby food or yoghurt. Once, she helped him to walk to the bathroom then lingered outside the door, terrified that he would fall down, and she would never be able to get the door open to rescue him. But he was recovering. She took his arm across her shoulder, and helped him to walk back. He was going to be alright. She could hardly believe it. When she was confident that he was just sleeping, and not at death's door, she went off and had a bath.

Later, she came down in a long dressing gown. She had her hair wrapped up in a towel. She made a cup of tea, loaded a DVD into the machine then pressed 'play'. She did not really need to watch it. From the first chord of the music over the credits, she knew every scene, every line of dialogue. It was majestic. It was reassuring. It was like going home.

Chapter 31

He was fine. He carefully stripped down to allow her to put more cream on his back. He was not bleeding. She was so relieved she wanted to shower him with kisses. He managed to feed himself with baby food. When she was happy that the cream had been absorbed, he folded his body back into the shirt, waistcoat and jacket. He managed the buttons. He insisted on wearing his tie. So he was fine.

She spent another hour soaking the hedgehog in olive oil. It was strong enough now for her to dribble some oil into the ball. It unwound a little. She poured more in, making sure to cover its eyelids, and a little in the ears. The eyes were firmly closed. There were still some ticks attached. It probably could not open its eyes fully. The hedgehog had already gained weight. It had shed nearly twenty ticks. They must have sucked it almost dry. No wonder the poor little thing could hardly walk. She worked quietly and patiently. One tick came away from an eyelid. She managed to dislodge another from an ear with the help of the point of a screwdriver. She poured more oil down across its tummy. When she released it back into the hutch, it hurried to eat the fresh food. It was not at all bothered that she was standing only a few feet away. That was definitely a victory. She was very happy, but there was no one to share the moment.

The young man was in the lounge. If he felt neglected, he did not say anything. She came and went. She gave him drinks. She had obviously moved on. He had the remote. When alone, he flicked through the channels absorbing information like a sponge. There was tennis on at Queen's. He assumed she knew. When she came to him just before lunch, and offered his shoes and socks, he was surprised. He did not have the reach to put them on, and was touched by her consideration when she knelt down at his feet to do it for him. But he could not say anything. When she drew him to his feet, he was overwhelmed with anxiety that he might be going somewhere new. He was almost relieved when she led him out through the back door and into the garden. He felt he knew what to expect. There would not be any surprises.

She had her arm through his. They walked slowly together. She was talking all the time, pointing to plants, explaining about this and that.

He did not understand. He was not really listening. He remembered about the peacock butterfly because he had seen real peacocks in the garden in Riyadh, but the butterfly flew away. She seemed very happy. They walked on. He was taken around the garden twice then they went to sit on the bench. By then his legs were shaking. He was sweating. He was ready to go back, and lay down on the sofa for a very long time.

"Are you okay?" she asked. She had taken hold of his hand, and was patting it gently.

He nodded. Yesterday had been unexpected. Today would be routine. He glanced towards her then stared away at the treeline.

"Did you live in a nice house in Paris?" she asked. She was smiling warmly. She had watched Big Shoulders through three times while he had been asleep. "Whenever I go, it always rains. Really, every time. It can be March or July or August, and it always rains." She knew every line, every scene, and still did not know why it healed her. It was brutal, harsh, poetic and beautiful. In real life, she probably would not have liked John Wayne. Apparently, he was a hard-line right-wing Republican, but Ethan and Nathan were the fathers that she had never known. "I thought that August would be great. It's so hot in August that the French all jump ship and head for the coast, but as soon as I arrive, it rains."

He glanced anxiously towards her. When she looked at him, he lowered his gaze to the ground, increasingly uncomfortable, waiting for her to stop talking and go away.

"Did you live with Omar? He was your friend. You told me." She was making small talk. Now and then, she paused to survey the garden or to count the clouds in the sky. His face was a mask. She could not read him at all. "He took care of you. That's nice. That's what friends do. They take care of each other."

He stared at the ground. He was ready to take off his jacket. He was comfortable about rolling up his sleeves. He was even prepared to be left alone there on the bench when she went off doing whatever she did in the garden. But he was not ready for a conversation.

"You can tell me anything," she said. She was smiling. She felt solid and substantial after months of being lost in a wilderness. "Really, you could lie. How would I know! I only want to help you. If you need to lie to me then that's okay."

He did not understand. How could dishonesty be okay?

"I'm going to call you Daniel."

He glanced towards her. Suddenly, he was in pain. He did not understand.

"Yes, Daniel. So you have a boyfriend? That's great, isn't it? How long have you two been together?"

He was staring at her now. He was absolutely speechless.

"Come on," she said, laughing. She jabbed him gently in the ribs. "Come on, lie to me. Tell me a story. Make it up. You can tell me anything. I can't keep talking to myself. People will think that I'm going crazy." She stopped to smile, waiting for him to find his nerve. "Come on, Daniel. Take a deep breath. It's alright."

He wiped his palms on his trousers. He just did not know what to say. He could not grasp the concept. Then he looked at her. "Please? Is my name Daniel?" The pain that went through his heart engulfed him.

Then she could not smile. "No, it's just a name, but it's a nice name. You said you didn't remember your name. That makes it harder to talk to you. I thought it would be nice. I'm sorry."

He nodded. He understood that. He took a moment to breathe then gazed at her shyly. "I have never had a name. Maybe, once upon a time, a long time ago, but not now." He took another long, deep breath. "When I was a child? Maybe, twenty years ago?"

It was obvious he was telling the truth. She just could not understand how it could be true. "What happened to you?" she asked gently.

He shook his head. There were so many stories in his head, and nothing made any sense. "It was a long time ago." He managed to look at her. "Please? I really don't know."

She stroked his hand comfortingly. "What do you remember?" She felt him travelling away from her. She watched as he shook his head then frowned. He was still sitting there, but in his head he was definitely somewhere else. "Were you happy?"

"You can ask me that?" he said quietly.

She patted his hand. She wanted to embrace him, and promise to make everything better, but he had become as insubstantial as a shadow. "Well, I don't know anything," she said in a soft whisper. "You haven't told me anything." He seemed to shiver. She squeezed his hand reassuringly. "May I call you Daniel? You don't mind?"

He shook his head. He was disintegrating emotionally.

She gave him a moment. All the time, she held his hand in her lap and stroked it gently. She waited and waited until she could not wait anymore.

340

"So you live in Paris?" she asked. "You said that you lived in Paris." She studied his lovely hand. They were the hands of an artist or a musician. His fingernails were immaculate. She felt that she was holding some very delicate thing in her ugly, clumsy, battered hands. "You've been ill?"

He nodded quickly. He was trembling.

"Was it a nice house?"

He nodded again. "Yes." He glanced down at his hand that she held on her lap. She was being so kind. "It belonged to my master. There were many rooms and many servants. There were high walls and tall trees."

She stroked his hand tenderly. "So it was a big house?"

"Yes."

"So your prince lived there?"

Reluctantly, he said: "Yes."

"And you lived there with Omar and the Pakistanis and your prince?"

"Yes," he said anxiously.

She felt the tension in his hand. She rubbed his palm gently. "So you were all his servants?"

He shook his head then nodded forlornly, only to shake it again with regret.

"And you had to go to a hospital because you were ill?"

He nodded. He did not dare pull his hand away.

"And the doctor did not tell you anything?"

He might have nodded. He did not know how to make her stop asking questions. He did not want to remember.

"But he spoke to your master? That was the prince?"

"Yes."

She wanted to know the name of the prince, but guessed that he would never tell her. "And you were his servant? You took care of him?"

"Yes." It was a confession.

She took a deep breath. She knew that she was standing on the edge of a revelation, and that she might not want to know the truth. "So what did that entail? As his servant, what did you do?"

His face was white. He managed to meet her gaze for the smallest fraction of a second then turned away. He started to speak, but his voice failed. He tried to breathe. He tried to swallow the anguish that was choking him. Without thinking, he lifted his hands to cover his face. She let him go. He needed to find his courage again.

She waited with trepidation. Now and then, she reached out to stroke his shoulder, but he did not know where he was anymore. "It's alright, my dear." She tried not to watch him. It seemed the right moment to go away, and make a cup of tea, but she did not dare leave him alone. He was in pieces. "It's alright. You're safe now. No one will hurt you anymore."

He filled his lungs with air then cleared his throat. "Please? They said that I was a valet. I helped him to dress. I took care of him."

There were tears in his eyes. She did not want to stare. "And that's what valets do. That's a respectable job. That would make you a gentleman's gentleman. There certainly aren't as many about these days as there used to be. Back before the war, gentlemen in great houses all had valets. It's become a bit of an anachronism, I suppose. Times have changed. But I expect royalty and rich men can afford to keep these old traditions alive."

"As old as Alexander," he murmured.

"Really?" She was surprised then reflected and nodded. "Well, yes, - possibly. I rather thought it was a French import with the Norman Conquest, but you could well be right."

He wanted her to stop now. He had had enough.

She tried to smile. "So you were right. You did take care of him. That is exactly what a valet does. He keeps his master clean and tidy." She knew he was not exactly being honest, but as she had invited him to tell lies, she did not feel able to challenge him yet. "And what did Omar and Mahmood and 'your Pakistanis' do for you? You said that they took care of you."

He nodded stiffly. She had to stop now.

"But what?" she asked quickly, but she was smiling. She was trying to be jovial. She did not want him to feel that she was interrogating him. "Were they all your valets?" She tried to laugh. "How many valets can one man possibly need?" She tried to gently poke him in the ribs, but he was rigid with stress. "Were they his servants?" She waited for a response, but there was nothing. "So they took care of you for him?"

His head bowed. He stared fixedly at the ground.

She had so many questions, but thousands of suspicions and assumptions. This was about sex. She almost felt vindicated, but was appalled to find any satisfaction in his condition.

"I am decorative," he said slowly. "I am expensive."

She studied his beautiful broken face. But for that expression, she would have thought he was being arrogant. "I'm so sorry." She watched him acknowledge the words. She wanted to smother him with reassurance, and make everything alright, but she could only sit there and feel useless. "I'm really so very sorry."

He covered his face again, and tried to erase the pain.

"You need to talk about it, Daniel. How can you possibly go home if you can't talk about it?"

"I don't remember," he said. "Please, I really don't remember."

She stared away at the garden. Looking at him was suddenly too hard. "It's probably Post Traumatic Stress. You need help, Daniel. You need real help. You don't eat. You don't talk. When you're asleep you have nightmares. Something terrible has happened to you. Something has just shut down your memories, but it'll come back." She tried to smile bravely. "It'll just take time. But you'll have to talk about it with someone. You really will have to talk about it or it will destroy you."

He managed to inhale. He stared down at her feet.

She leaned forward, convinced he was about to make a confession.

"I'm dying," he said slowly. "That's why I must go home."

It was her turn to be struck dumb. She did not want to believe him, but his sincerity was persuasive. "But you can't be dying! You're getting better. You must be feeling better. The infection's gone. The fever's broken." He stared resolutely down at her feet. "Well, you'll never be strong if you don't eat enough," she scolded. "You should be putting away about three thousand calories every day. I bought the baby food and milky drinks because they were easy for you to digest when you were so weak. You should be on real protein now, meat and fish, and huge amounts of carbohydrates."

He did not move at all. "Please? I can't eat."

"But you've been here weeks. You haven't eaten anything at all." She knew there was irritation in her tone, but she did not understand. It seemed logical that he was a faddy eater so he was obviously just being silly. "You must eat." She wanted to sound compassionate, but knew that it was just another whinge. "You won't ever grow stronger if you don't eat proper food."

"You've been very kind," he said mechanically.

"But you're dying?" she demanded. "You can't be dying."

There was his awkward shrug. As her gaze pieced him like a surgeon's scalpel, he stared steadfastly at the ground. When she drew away, he tried to smile. "I cannot eat," he explained carefully. "I am allowed water and milk, sometimes honey or soft fruit." He managed to look at her. His hesitant smile trembled. "And now strawberry milkshake."

"And banana," she said helpfully. She could not smile. This was the truth. She wanted to be brave and strong for him, but she was in pieces. "Well, no wonder you're so slim." She was utterly flummoxed. "Is it an allergy? I've never heard of it."

He was studying the treeline. When she stopped talking, his gaze dropped back to the ground. "I'm so grateful. You've been very kind."

"Stop saying that!"

He flinched. His hands clasped and unclasped. There was nothing else he could say.

"Is that why you were in Paris?" She stared at him for a long time, but he did not move. "You need to explain," she said angrily. "This is your prince? This is your lover? When you say that you can't eat, do you mean that you physically cannot eat because of an illness or that you are not allowed to eat? It's not that you don't want to? It's not an allergy?" She drew away appalled. "This is some weird homosexual thing. No food in. No food out. He's keeping you thin and empty. The bastard's killing you!"

He flinched again. He tried to shake his head, but he could not move.

She was cold to the bone. "He's bloody killing you. Can't you see that? Your damn lover is killing you. He's got you all wrapped up in this sadomasochism thing, and you can't see that he's killing you. He's bloody killing you. You can't all be like this. Why don't you leave him? He's killing you."

"Please, no. No, it's not like that. You don't understand."

"Well, when did you last eat anything?"

He shook his head. He could not actually tell a lie.

"But he's killing you!"

He looked into her eyes. "I just want to go home." He was a child again.

She backed off to give him the respect he deserved.

Feeling trapped, he struggled with his good manners and his nerves. He stared at the ground. She stared at the garden. "Please? I don't eat. I never eat."

She was chewing her nails. "But that can't be true." She peered at his face in anguish. "You'd be dead. You must be eating something. He might be starving you to keep you slim, but you must be consuming something."

He shook his head. "Please? I cannot. It's forbidden." He raised a hand to shield his face from her inquisitive gaze.

"I don't understand." She felt helpless. "I really don't understand." It had to be a cult. It had to be religious. He was just fasting. Fasting was different. Some religions banned some foods. His must have banned everything. Nothing else made sense. It was the weirdest diet ever, but it had to be religious. No lover would demand such a sacrifice. If it was common practice amongst homosexuals then she was sure that she would have heard about it before. No one was ever actually quite that Machiavellian. If it was a cult then it explained why he did not know about McDonalds.

"You don't believe me?"

"No. I'm sorry. It's not that I don't believe you. I just don't understand."

"Please, don't be angry with me."

"I'm not angry." But she was angry. She did not have the social skills. She did not know what to say. She had all the pat phrases from years of counselling, but they had never helped her. "You don't have to apologise for anything. Something terrible has happened to you. I want to help you. If we could talk about it together then it will help you to deal with it."

He shook his head slowly.

"What were you doing in Paris?" she asked. "I'm just trying to help you."

He shook his head.

"This is about your lover, isn't it? You can tell me. You're perfectly safe here." There was no response. She took a deep breath. "They say that everything today is about sex. We're surrounded by subliminal messages about sex. Little girls dress like prostitutes because they believe they'll be loved more. Little boys watch porn because that's what real men do. It gets hardwired into our brains from a very young age. Men think about it all the time, but that's by design. Now women take 'the pill' they can have sex three hundred and sixty-five days a year. It has certainly changed our lives, but it hasn't made us equals. Maybe, we're obsessed with sex because we don't have to go out and hunt for our food. All those primitive instincts that keep other animals alive are all focused in human beings on having sex.

Perhaps it is only during those moments that we truly feel alive." She glanced across to see if he was listening then stared back at the garden. "You obviously have a very intense relationship with your lover. You must love him very much. You've let him do all those procedures to your body. I know silly girls get breast implants to please their boyfriends, but what he's done to you is really extreme. He's controlling you, isn't he? That sheath? You wear that for him? He's obviously had a lot of fun with all that artwork. It must have taken weeks. And it must have hurt terribly. Is he like that? All decorated?"

He was too tired to respond.

"So it's just you."

He flinched.

"Is it a cult? Are there other people involved? I believe this sort of controlling behaviour is most often found in cults, you know, a group of like-minded people. It's usually introverted and isolationist. There's usually one powerful personality running it, and everyone else is just a disciple."

"Please? I don't understand. It wasn't like that. He wasn't like that."

She watched him imploding. He was actually shivering. She needed to push him just a little more. "The guy in charge just goes around fucking everyone. It's always about sex. The disciples are, in reality, nothing more than sex slaves. Most of the time, it doesn't seem to matter whether they're male or female, adult or child. There are some really sick people out there, and quite a lot of them are frighteningly charismatic."

He shook his head. He could not look at her. "Please, no. You're wrong. It wasn't like that."

She wanted to believe him. "So this is just between you and your lover?" It was difficult. In the sunshine, he glowed like one of the jewels that she had hidden away in a drawer. "You are so beautiful." She hesitated then shook her head. "Well, you are. You could have anyone. Why would you put up with such a controlling bastard?"

"You don't believe me?" He was heartbroken. He tried to lift his gaze. He needed to confront her, to make her stop, but his nerves were in pieces.

"You won't explain."

"Please? You're angry."

She reached out to capture one of his hands, and held it tightly to her breast. "I want to help you. You cannot possibly imagine how much I want to help you. Please, just let me help you?"

He inhaled deeply. "I'm dying." He tried to smile. "I've come here to find my family." Then he frowned and gazed away at the treeline. "Nothing else makes sense. They brought me here. There can be no other explanation."

"Who brought you here?" When he shook his head, she almost hit him. "You mean that there really were men here in my garden? I should damn well call the police!"

"Please, no. Please, don't do that."

She felt redundant. "I don't understand."

He looked at her. "I don't remember you. They've brought me here to you, but I don't remember you."

She was upset. "I'm sorry, but I don't understand. Who brought you here? This is madness. You're just tired."

He shrugged slowly. He did not even blink. His eyes were like shards of glass.

"How can you be dying?" she demanded. "From not eating? Well, that's your own fault, isn't it? You've got involved with some dangerous psychopath. Well, he is! You've fallen out with him. Well, good riddance. But you're safe here. We'll get you better. You're not going to die."

He shook his head.

"You say that you're his valet, but your clothes are very expensive. I've seen the labels. That watch probably cost more than my house. The crown jewels, really, they must be worth millions. You have great teeth. The manicure? The tan? You haven't done a hard day's work ever."

"He is a great prince."

"And he is your lover? Just admit it. Have the courtesy to tell the truth about that. You're a very attractive young man. It's only natural that you'll have a lover. And hey! He's a prince. That's kinda cool, you know. And he's totally obsessed with you. You must know that."

He was embarrassed, but politely shook his head.

She really needed a cup of tea. She studied his face as he quickly lowered his gaze. It was deference. It was not shame or a lack of masculinity. "The great prince is your lover. He is one of the richest men in the world? Well, the token he gave you makes the usual diamond engagement ring look insignificant and cheap." She smiled because he almost smiled. "But he flogged you? He knew that you had a heart condition, and he flogged you. That must have been some serious lovers' tiff. Is that the sort of thing that you guys do? Is that part of the thrill? This is real sadomasochism, isn't it? This isn't just playing games. It was real. He nearly killed you. My god, that's so sick!"

"Please, we're not lovers," he insisted firmly. "He is my master."

"But – then – why?" she asked, feeling increasingly stupid. "I don't understand. You could have anyone in the world. You are absolutely gorgeous. You have money. You said that you were expensive. You make it sound like you're just a whore, but look at you! Honestly, you could have the pick of all the gay guys in the world. Why would you put up with being treated like that? You can't possibly love him?" She leaned closer, daring him to deny it. "Just leave him! You're gorgeous. Go find some other guy, who won't hurt you like this. It can't be about money? If you're doing it for the money then you are no better than a whore."

"Please, you don't understand," he said earnestly.

"Well, obviously!" she retorted. "I'm not gay."

"Please, no. You don't understand. He is my master. I am his. I must obey."

"You are his what?" she demanded then wished she could take it back. "I'm sorry."

He nodded slowly. "I belong to him."

Her brain had seized up. The cogwheels had stopped going round. It was just too much information. It did not compute. "I'm sorry," she murmured. His face was a mask of misery. "I'm so sorry." She watched as he struggled to breathe. For a moment, he seemed inconsolable. "I'm really so very sorry." She had never loved or been loved on that scale. It was not some secret satanic sect or weird indoctrination ritual. It wasn't the Masons. She had always felt it was a bit extreme for the Masons. "And obviously you must love him very much."

He was surprised. "I belong to him. I must obey."

The shock had worn off a little. She stared away at the garden. In her head, she was repeating everything that he said, but it was still incomprehensible.

"Please, if you don't believe me then no one will." He took a deep breath. He was wilting in the sunshine. He needed a drink. He needed to go and lay down. He simply did not have the strength to endure sitting still. "No one will believe me."

"But you can't be dying," she insisted. "You can't. You are getting better. It will be slow and maddening, but that's because you don't eat properly. You'll always be weak if you don't eat properly."

He nodded. He wanted to look at her, but his nerve failed. "Please? I cannot. I cannot tell you anything. Please, don't ask me. I cannot explain."

"I don't understand. You're safe here. I'm trying to help you. Why can't you tell me what happened to you?" She wanted to sound compassionate, but her tone was cutting.

His heart was pounding. He was as white as a sheet. "I am starved to keep me weak so that I cannot run away. I belong to him. I am his property. He may do as he wishes." He shivered. He gazed across to check her reaction. Her mouth was open. Her eyes were wide. "If I tried to eat now it would kill me. Internal organs are failing." He nodded grimly. It took him a moment to find the words. "I belong to him. He is my master, my lord, and I must obey him."

"You mean you literally belong to him?" Her blood had turned to ice. "So this is the slave trade. You're kidding? The white slave trade? No, that's women." She stared at him while he tried to keep his nerve. "So you were abducted!" It was not a question. "You were abducted when you were a child." She was utterly appalled. "Twenty years ago! More? And you're still alive?" She wanted to disbelieve him, but it was painfully obvious that he was telling the truth. "Do your family even know that you're still alive?"

He died a thousand deaths just thinking about that.

Chapter 32

He was given water to drink, and more water and a coarse soap to clean his body. They left him a lantern, but he was alone again for a very long time. The room was crudely carved out of the stone heart of the mountain. The door opened on to a narrow stairwell. The steep steps were worn with age. There was no window. The stout door filled the frame, which was bolted into the walls. In all the days that he had been locked in that cave-like room no one had passed by the door. Not a sound had reached him. His sanity had crumbled. To be alone again destroyed him.

When they eventually returned, the lantern had burned itself out. He backed away from them like a cornered animal, too frightened to believe in hope or kindness.

Mansour was a jolly fellow. He was merely one of a group sent by the Queen to sort out the problems with the toilets. They had all piled into the small room to stare at the infamous foreigner, who shrank away from them to huddle in a corner, completely terrified. Many of the men were equally afraid. There was genuine concern that his sinfulness was a horrific virus that would infect them all. Mansour saw only a frightened young man completely at his wits' end. He pushed his way to the front, and stooped to offer his hand to help the kafir rise from the floor.

The kafir studied Mansour's face for a long time before reaching out to grasp his hand. The twinkling eyes and encouraging smile seemed genuine. Lost in a wilderness of self-pity and loneliness, the kafir was easily ensnared. He had to trust someone. It had been his Pakistanis, then his master, and now it had to be Mansour. He was drawn to his feet, and led from the room to go down the endless steps in almost complete darkness.

The ancient citadel's toilets were a scandal. The whole place reeked unpleasantly, and the ever-diminishing population were too precious about their dignity and status to contemplate doing anything for themselves. The Queen had talked to her elders and the priests about the toilets. The men were all convinced that the 'Untouchable' family, who lived in another cave further up the valley, would sort out the smell. They were, after all, descendants of toilet cleaners, and their children were destined to be toilet cleaners. They had served the people of the mountain for generations in exchange for being given food and water and refuge. It was a traditional arrangement. It had always worked very well.

As Hindus of the lowest caste, it fell to the Untouchables or Dalits to do all the unpleasant tasks. Not only the toilets were their domain, but dealing with the dead. They were scavengers. They were considered uncouth and uneducated, often having no knowledge of anything beyond their narrow blighted existence. They lived like brute animals in hovels with only the clothes that they stood up in, and no more furniture than they could cobble together with their bare hands. In legend, they were made of the earth beneath Brahmin's feet, unlike the other Hindu castes that were formed from his feet or his arms or his head, and took their position in society accordingly. Untouchables always lived apart, and in the shadow of the house or village that they served. They were not allowed to touch the community's water supply, and were paid a pittance, which kept them in servitude, if they were paid at all. They were considered the property of the community. Their children were often bonded from birth so there was no chance of schooling, not that any rural school would take them. Their women were not safe. They had no legal protection. They were tricked and deceived at every turn because they were beneath the consideration of other human beings, or so Hindus believed.

The religious community in the mountain believed that the arrangement that existed between themselves and the lowly scavengers of the 'night waste' was a fair one. They paid them with food and water. They allowed them to live and worship their own gods, which numbered thousands, inside the mountain. All that was required of them was the daily removal of the excrement from beneath the 'Turkish' toilets. The people were so comfortable with the arrangement it never occurred to them that the Untouchables would go on strike and withhold their labour. Within days there was a smell, but they assumed it was just a momentary event caught on the wind. Inside the mountain, a dust storm could pass unnoticed, but it was easy to blame an unfortunate draught for a sudden unpleasant aroma. The aroma, however, intensified. It had taken almost a week for the elders to nominate someone to go down and check the pits beneath the toilets. He quickly came back to confirm that the pits were choked with rotting excrement, and completely overrun with rats.

A deputation went out to speak to the men of the Untouchable family. It was explained quite stridently by the family that they had become Believers, which meant that with immediate effect they no longer had to submit to the indignity of cleaning other people's toilets. The deputation returned into the mountain, and reported this unexpected turn of events to the Queen. It was discussed at length. It was not just the problem with the toilets, but the loyalty of the Untouchables. They had converted to

Buddhism some years before, but no one took it seriously. They had now converted to Islam though not one member of the large family could read or write. As was often the case, poverty had made them cunning. It might have been just a wish, but if it was a threat, suggesting a loyalty to the Taliban, then it made them a very real danger to the non-Muslim community living within the mountain. They had offered to do other work. They offered to tend animals, to clean apartments, to prepare food, but the people from the mountain found all these suggestions completely and utterly abhorrent. The Untouchables were only suitable for cleaning toilets because they smelt foul and ate rats. No one could countenance them doing anything else. The city elders discussed sending agents to the Punjab to try and snatch a likely family of lowly Untouchable descent, who would do as they were told and be grateful. There were surely tens of millions of them in India. The fear was that any newcomers might be just as bad or might as easily be corrupted. The consensus was that everyone wanted the Untouchables to just stop being silly and go back to work.

The kafir was taken down the tightly coiling staircase that was carved in to the rock, and led down hundreds of metres through locked doors to the valley floor. He had arrived this way. The prospect of going home immediately lightened his heart. More than anything, he wanted to go home to Prince Abdul Aziz.

After the gloom of the stairs, they passed through the last fortified door, and emerged into the crystal blue light. The kafir squinted, lifting a hand to shade his eyes, overwhelmed by the towering opalescent mountains that filled all the horizons, and the brilliant sapphire blue sky. There were about twenty men there waiting for him. The group that had brought him down the stairs swelled the numbers to nearly thirty. At that moment, he was much more interested in the mountains that glittered in the crystal light. The air had a clarity. He felt as if he could reach out and touch the mountain tops even though he knew they were many miles away. It was like being at the madrassa. From those battlements, he could see further than anywhere else in the world. He looked desperately for familiar peaks, but had to accept that he was amongst strangers. Unhappily, he lowered his gaze to the mere mortals, who surrounded him. He was not going home.

They were men of the mountain with fair hair and pale eyes. Some of them had dyed their beards with henna. Others had no beards at all. Their clothes were vividly colourful and beautifully made. They all reminded him of the peacocks in the garden at the palace at Riyadh, except that every one of them had a gun and a knife in his belt, and carried a rifle slung across his shoulder. They talked to each other, and eyed him with varying degrees of contempt and suspicion. His reputation preceded him everywhere. He had brought the unmistakable whiff of scandal with him. None of the men spoke to him or touched him, and his hands were not tied so he was wary of their motives. Three priests in long white and pale blue robes, who were the only men not armed, moved to stand as sentinels around him. They carried golden staffs, but were otherwise quite plain in comparison to the others.

The kafir did not understand a word they were saying, but moved with them as they walked along the base of the cliff. He noticed the caves. There were several small ones in the cliff above him. As he peered further along, he saw that there were probably twenty in all, scattered across the vast expanse of cliff. He could see now that there were marks to show where there had once been scaffolding to hold up the external face of the original city, but all the evidence had been erased so long ago, it had become not even a legend but a myth. The scars on the cliff were all that remained of the vast city. What was inside the mountain were just the salvaged remnants of a whole civilisation carefully preserved. It was sad.

He had no idea where they were going. He was walking with them rather than being taken. Even at the palace, Mahmood and Waheed would have held his wrist, and led him about to underline their authority. Here, the priests were happy to stab and slap with their sticks when he slowed to look at something interesting, but as long as he kept pace he was left alone. He hardly noticed any of them. The quality of the light amazed him, and the clarity of the shining mountains filled his eyes with beauty. After being shut inside the windowless room for so long, it was quite intoxicating.

He did not even notice when a group of people emerged from a cave further down the valley.

They were all exceptionally dark-skinned with black eyes, and were thin. All of them were thin. There were two older men with white hair and beards, a woman, who looked frail and had silvery grey hair, two younger men and three woman of about the same age, and probably a dozen children that swarmed around the adults like flies. Most of the men and all of the children had unkempt wild hair. Their clothes were mostly drab and brown. The women's sarees were more colourful, but they were anything but fresh or vibrant.

The kafir was encouraged to step forward so that the decidedly unattractive group could have a good look at him. He understood that he was being exhibited, but the speech that accompanied his imitation of a shop-window mannequin was completely unintelligible. The tone was unmistakable, and the threats were very evident in the body language, but they were not directed at him.

"This man will do the work you shirk. You must decide now. Either you go back to work, and do your duty or you will all leave this land immediately. You cannot live here under our protection if you do not work."

The kafir gazed across the swarthy faces, and felt no inclination to bow or show them any respect. They were peasants. They were, in fact, less than peasants. He had never seen a collection of human beings so completely devoid of refinement or intelligence. Their eyes were black and dull. Their complexions were rough, and there was an unpleasant coarseness about their physical appearance. The children, almost all, had a slack-jawed glaring look of hostility that would not have endeared them to even the most tender-hearted philanthropist.

"We are Muslims. We do not have to do this work anymore."

They were Muslims. He understood that, but he was still loathed to bow down before them. The grandly dressed men and priests, who stood behind him, were in charge now. They were not Muslims, but he was their property. He understood what that meant. It hardly mattered as he could not leave even if he wanted to, at least, not until Prince Khalid gave him permission.

"He is a Muslim. He will do it."

The kafir glanced behind at the middle-aged man, who had spoken. He seemed a pleasant fellow with pale eyes and chestnut hair streaked with grey. His gestures informed the kafir that he was still the main topic of conversation so he turned back politely to regard the aggressive dark faces that were now all glowering at him. He wished he understood what was being said. It was a language he had never heard before, not even amongst the melting pot of dialects at the madrassa.

"You were Hindus. Then, you were Buddhists. Now, you are Muslims. God means nothing to you. You have no honour. This is your work. If you will not do it then you must leave. We gave you food and water and a place to live as payment for working. If you refuse to work then you forfeit this payment. Having a new religion today does not change what you are, what your fathers and their fathers or your children and grandchildren will be."

"No," one of the young men raged angrily. "My children will not do this."

"Then you will all leave."

An old dark-skinned man shuffled forward. "My son is searching..."

"He's been gone for months. If you return to work then you can stay.

We intend to board up the cave. There'll be no shelter, no food and water. If you don't leave we'll burn you out, starve you out."

The men from the mountain pressed on, walking through the group of Untouchables as if they did not exist. They walked along the base of the cliff until they reached the wide mouth of a cave. Not one of them wanted to go inside. The priests hung back too, covering their noses as if the air was poisonous to them.

There was conversation. The youngest of the men from the mountain was delegated to go into the cave. From the outside, it looked uninhabited yet at least twenty people lived there.

"We will set a fire to burn you out. We will come with guns. We will seal the entrance. You will work or leave or die. That is now your decision. This man will do your work."

The Untouchables hurried to fill the cave mouth, but the men from the mountain were armed.

The kafir felt the eyes on him again, but he was more interested in the snow-covered peaks and the crystal light. The air was sweet when he inhaled. After the dry, dusty, windowless room, he was happy to be outside.

"We do not need to tolerate your presence here any longer. Will you go back to work now?"

"No." The dark-skinned men all said, no, and shook their fists belligerently. The women shook their heads and mouthed words, but they were scared. They reached out to clasp their children to them.

The kafir was surprised when the youngest man from the mountain caught his sleeve, and pushed him forward towards the noisy, bristling protestors. With a gun in his hand, the young man followed the kafir. The crowd broke before the gun, and fell silent as the pair ventured across the threshold.

It was dark and cold, but the kafir crept forward, propelled by the hand nudging his back. He had no idea what was happening. He understood it was the dark-skinned Indians who were in trouble, but his part in it was still a mystery.

They found a few possessions: there were baskets and hand tools, which the kafir had to pick up; a platform that looked like a bed though it was as bare and hard as rock; a bucket of water that he was directed to empty on the ashes of a fire; a bundle of rags that might have been clothes; some dried dung; enough flour to make only a small loaf of bread, which he was instructed to scattered across the earthen floor; a broken comb; a broken shoe; some dead rats; some small idols hidden inside a niche in the cave wall; a very tatty silk flower with frayed petals; stumps of candles and a primitive lighter. It was pitiful. Even the kafir felt the sadness of such miserable poverty. It was his job, however, to carry off whatever the young man believed belonged to the people in the mountain, so that all that remained were the rats and idols and broken things.

As they emerged, the scene on the valley floor had changed. The men from the mountain had drawn their weapons and surrounded the Untouchables, and were ordering them to leave at the point of a gun. The sight of their tools being carried off must have settled the matter. In the clothes that they stood up in, they huddled closer together then set off walking south along the base of the cliff.

They were followed all the way to the moraine. Some of the men from the mountain followed them until evening to make sure that they left the area.

The kafir was directed back up the stairs. At the first landing, he was pointed to a door. He moved on to the landing, and put down the baskets and tools. One of the men took up a torch and gestured towards the door. The kafir opened it. A wall of poisonous air swept out and almost knocked him down. He closed the door again, and turned in alarm to gaze at the man. The gesture was repeated. It never occurred to him to refuse. Years of conditioning had erased his will and any sense of self-preservation. He took a deep breath, and opened the door. The man had done likewise, and moved to stand behind the kafir, holding the torch over their heads.

It seemed to be better, but the hot air seared their lungs and burned their eyes. They moved inside. The passageway was rough and unfinished, nothing like the corridors he had passed through higher up in the mountain. The only noise they could hear was the constant drone of a million flies.

Both of them opted to breathe through their mouths, but it still became unbearable as they moved deeper into the mountain.

The man made the kafir aware of the reason for the stench. The human excrement was beige and mushy where it was fresh. When it was older, it was darker and often covered in fungus and maggots. It lay as a thick carpet across the floor of the cave, and the distraught kafir stood in it barefoot. He started vomiting. The smell filled his nostrils again. His eyes burned and flooded with tears. Everywhere he looked, he could see the bloody-red eyes of rats. Then he could not breathe. His chest muscles had become so tight he simply could not inhale.

There was nowhere for the smell to escape except back up through the holes in the roof of the tunnels to the rooms and apartments above.

The man was retching too. He turned with the torch, and fled back to the staircase. The kafir raced after him, and collapsed onto the landing, vomiting bile and acid. After the tunnels, the air was almost sweet. They both lingered, sickened and revolted by the poisonous fumes, their heads thumping as their senses reeled in shock. The kafir had never imagined that such a place existed.

The man had to somehow persuade the creature to return into the tunnel to toil in darkness willingly and diligently without any supervision. The Untouchables were born to it. Their children worked alongside them, and it was understood that there was no choice. A thousand years of the caste system made their occupations predestined. There was simply no option. It might have been made illegal in India more than fifty years ago, but the Untouchables or Dalits, men, women and children, were still made to clean other people's excrement by hand. It was traditional. Ignorance and prejudice did not care about the law.

The man moved to stand over the kafir, and nudged him with his shoe.

Still overwhelmed and frail, the kafir struggled to remember where he was, and moved to his knees to bow.

The man frowned. This was to be an altogether new relationship. He commanded the kafir to pick up the baskets, and pointed at them when the kafir frowned in incomprehension.

The kafir moved on to his feet, and picked up the baskets and tools, desperate to believe that the tour was over, and that they were both going to continue up the stairs. The man, however, opened the door again. He pointed inside then gestured putting something in the basket. He manually counted the baskets that the kafir held. There were five of them. He gestured putting something into each of them. Then he took away all the tools but one scooper and one hand brush. He pointed into the dark corridor again then gave the kafir the flaming torch.

The kafir wanted to have misunderstood, but he could not be that dishonest. He breathed deeply, trying to suppress his revulsion and need to vomit. The man explained that he would wait there for him on the landing, but it was harder to explain with gestures. He tried anyway.

The kafir watched him, puzzled, and then nodded, then breathed deeply again, and still found himself a coward. But he went on leaden limbs, grimacing as his lungs burned, and the hot air made his eyes water. Behind him the door closed. That made his heart jump. For a moment, he panicked, dropped the baskets, almost dropped the torch, and then remembered to breathe. He was sick again. It did not matter how often he was sick. The smell did not go away. The door did not open. He became used to it simply because he did not die.

He filled the baskets. He had no idea how many minutes or hours it took him. His guts ached from continual retching but he was empty and totally dehydrated. It had made no difference that he had tools because he had fallen down and slipped, and dropped the baskets so often he was covered in human faeces. Knowing what it was only made it worse. Exhausted and almost asphyxiated, he staggered back to the door, and faced his true terror: that he would never be allowed to leave.

He banged and banged on the door, but it did not open. He called. He shouted. No one came. He was just about to try and set fire to it when it suddenly opened.

It was the same man. He looked as if he had had a bath.

The kafir burst out on to the landing looking demented. He was coated in excrement. The smell was appalling. He collapsed to his knees, coughing and retching again, desperate to fill his lungs with cleaner air, but there was none. He smelled as bad as it was possible to smell, and there was no escape.

The man stood as far away as he could, and covered his mouth and nose with a damp cloth. It was only curiosity that made him look into the passageway to check what had happened to the baskets. He was prepared. He was actually convinced that the white creature had failed because it was inconceivable that anyone but an Untouchable could do such disgusting work. Even with the light of the torch, he struggled to find the baskets in the gloom. He was surprised to find that all of them were filled, but it had been a sloppy piece of work. Every basket looked as if it had been dropped at least once. However, he had to admit that they were now brimming full. It was miraculous. He turned to look back at the kafir, who resembled a reptile more than a human being, his skin covered in slime and crust as if he had been wallowing in a swamp.

He told him to get up then threatened him with the torch. Understanding only that the white creature did not understand his language, the man relented a little, pausing to cover his face again with the damp cloth so that he could try and breathe without retching. He did not know if he had become used to the poisonous air or whether it had improved, but he survived for a few minutes, long enough to gesture picking up a basket and carrying it down the steep and uneven steps.

For the kafir, it was simple. He obeyed. He had no comprehension of refusing. He did whatever he was told with good grace and perfect manners. That was the way he had been brought up under the strict laws of the True Faith. Even though he was aware that these people were not Muslims, and were therefore rather suspect, he had no doubt at all that his master meant him to obey them, and not to cause him or his family any embarrassment.

There were fifty-four steps. He was to become very familiar with them.

He was relieved to emerge from the mountain into the clean sweet air and crystal light. The sunlight told him he had been inside the passageway for many hours. The man directed him to walk away across the valley floor, and idled along behind him. There was an obvious collection of dung on the ground about halfway across the valley, but it was all aged and odourless. The kafir stopped and half turned, waiting for the man to catch up, which he obviously had no intention of doing. He gestured for the basket to be emptied at one end of the existing carpet then pointed the kafir back to the mountain, and did an impromptu performance of carrying another heavy basket down the stairs. The kafir was reluctant but not stupid. He trailed wearily up and down the stairs until all the baskets of human faeces were emptied on the valley floor.

He had been tired before starting down the stairs hours earlier to be shown off to the Untouchables, and was a trembling wreck as he followed the man back to the landing in the late afternoon. His muscles were swollen and sore. Every step was an ordeal. Beneath the extra skin of crispy and flaking excrement, he was also covered in cuts and bruises. He had a headache. He was seriously dehydrated. All that kept him going was the single fact that no one told him to stop. He carried all the baskets, careful to keep them away from the man's beautiful clean clothes. And he stood on the landing, literally bracing himself for the order that would condemn him to re-entering the passageway, already hearing in his head the door being locked behind him.

The man closed the door and turned the key then gazed at the wretched white creature that had exceeded all his expectations.

He was told to put the baskets down.

He was told to sit.

The man nodded and smiled then turned away, and climbed the stairs, taking the torch away with him.

The darkness was like ink. The kafir crumbled under the realisation that he was to be left there covered in shit, unable to wash himself, unable to have a drink. He would have wept if he was not already too exhausted, so he lay on the ground on the edge of the landing, and stared into the darkness. It was the same whether he closed his eyes or not. He had never been so tired before or so dirty. He had never been so ill-used.

The man returned with a bucket of water with a tin mug floating around in it. He put it down beside the startled creature, and directed it to drink.

The kafir cautiously picked up the cup and filled it. He sipped it suspiciously then drained the cup. It was sweet and cool. He filled the cup a dozen times.

The man watched in silence. When the kafir paused to draw breath, he offered him a tablet of soap. The kafir took it and bowed uncomfortably. His despair returned to crush him as the man stuck the torch into a sconce on the wall above his head, and then disappeared back up the stairs. He sat for a while unsure of what was happening, but he had to accept that he was alone again. He drank more of the water, sensible enough to know he could not drink from the bucket after he had started washing in it. The water was delicious.

No one came to disturb him. He gazed around his new home: a barren landing on a narrow staircase carved out of the rock, and was resigned to being there for an indefinite period. He did not care to compare it with Prince Abdul Aziz's many sumptuous bedrooms. He pulled off his long shirt, and dumped it into the bucket then toiled with the soap to clean it, then used it to painstakingly wipe the foul scum off his body. His injuries stung, but he worked hard to restore his lovely white flesh. His beauty was precious to him. He had nothing else to treasure. The smell lingered, even after he had soaked his hair, even after he had washed out his nostrils so vigorously that his nose bled. He even put the baskets out on to the stairs and poured the remains of the water over and through them, but they remained gross and smelly.

He curled up and closed his eyes, resigned to waiting.

Chapter 33

He had been abducted. She could hardly believe it. There was no precedent for him being alive. But he was alive. It was almost easier to believe that he was lying. He should not have been able to survive. It made no sense. She had never heard of a kidnapper releasing their victim. There were cases of distraught women stealing babies after losing their own. The child might be found by the police and returned, but they were never sent home. The lost children were never seen again unless the police found them and found them quickly.

He was so damaged.

"How old were you?" she asked, but was dismayed when his furrowed brow and slight shake of the head declared that he did not know. "I'm so sorry." She wanted to embrace him and promise some miraculous salvation. He did not want to be touched. Now, she understood his aversion. "What sort of sick bastard could have lavished so much money on you - only to have flogged you almost to death? He knew that you were ill. Is that why he's let you go? Did he regret it? Why didn't he just take you back to the hospital? That would have been safer. Why on earth did he send you here to me?"

He shook his head. Her concern almost overwhelmed him. "I don't know."

"How on earth have you survived?"

"Please? I don't know."

She stroked his arm, marvelling at his demeanour. "He must have loved you very much. He's kept you all these years. He must have had some genuine affection for you." She nodded and smiled. "Of course, I know that doesn't mean anything when you're a captive." She wanted to console him, and be more upbeat. "And you seem to have had some friends. You liked Mahmood. I think you liked Omar."

He was staring at the ground again. He nodded stiffly. "They took care of me."

She bit her lip then sighed. "Did he hurt you?"

"My master may do as he pleases."

That sounded like a programmed response. She hardly knew what to say. Something terrible had happened to him. "We should call the police."

"Please?" He shook his head. He was remembering. At that moment, he was so very far away. "I cannot. I'm forbidden to speak. And no one will believe me. He is a great and powerful man."

"Forbidden?" She was in meltdown. She could not get passed calling the police.

"We must hold that forbidden which has been forbidden."

She was flummoxed again. "That's silly. We need to call the police. They'll have all the resources. They can protect you. They'll find your parents. Think about it: you could be talking to your parents within the next twenty-four hours. This nightmare could be over for you – and for them. Imagine what they have been through. All these years, they will have been grieving for you, not knowing whether you were alive or dead."

He could not believe it was so easy. It was too easy. There had to be a catch. "Please, I cannot." He shook his head. "I cannot do that. Please, don't do that." He could not think. "I'm – I'm." He shook his head again, and sighed. "I'm sorry. I cannot. Please? You don't understand."

"But you do want to go home?"

"Please, of course. Yes. But not the police. I cannot do that. Please, not the police. They'll find out. They will come after me."

"They?" She felt his fear. "But the police will be able to protect you."

He shook his head. He was trembling again.

She felt like a Nazi when he needed Mother Theresa. She hardly knew what to say to him. Some horrid little voice in her head was saying: "This is it! Ask him now!" She did not dare touch him. He looked suddenly old and withered. The grace and beauty had disappeared. "So what will you do now?" she asked gently. It felt totally inadequate.

He did not hear her. He was in hell. But it was the hell of loneliness. Whenever he thought about going home it was always about returning to the familiar. Home was his master. He could not conceive of a moment when that would not be true. He felt that he was a bad person for wanting to be allowed to return to the Prince and the life that they had shared. He knew that he should want to see his parents. He had asked to be allowed to see his parents. That he was dying had added weight to his request. It was his dream for so long, but he had never imagined that his master would acquiesce. Now, he felt that he had been banished like an unfaithful lover. The whipping felt like a justified punishment. He had been cast off like something foul and offensive. He was in exile, alone, adrift and rudderless. Everything had been taken away. The wistful dream of being reunited with his parents had suddenly become a real possibility, and he was terrified.

She touched his arm gently, startling him. "What will you do now?"

He stammered. He did not know what to say. "I want to go home," he said. "But please, not the police. Please, I cannot."

That silenced her. Of course, he wanted to go home, but if he would not speak to the police then she hardly knew how she could help him. Around them, the sun shone down on her beautiful garden, but they were both in hell. She felt literally sick. What could she do to help him when she was barely capable of looking after herself? Beside her, he was pale and motionless. He did not seem to be alive. She stroked his arm again, and watched as he grimaced then returned from his private thoughts. "I'm so sorry. I'll help you. Of course, I'll help you. You can stay here with me until you're ready to leave. I'll help you. We'll work it out. We'll find your parents." She tried to smile. "Apparently, you can find anyone via the internet. It must be an absolute godsend to stalkers." She patted his arm again. "We'll find them. Don't worry. It'll be alright."

"I'm very tired." He wanted to be left alone. All his deep existential wounds were hurting.

She shot to her feet. "Yes, of course. We'll go in. You must be thirsty. I know I could murder a cup of tea."

He hesitated, but she had taken hold of his arm so he had to stand up.

They walked back together. Neither of them said anything. They were both overwhelmed and preoccupied. She made a pot of tea. He was very quickly asleep. She wanted to believe that he would be safe there. She needed to believe that she could make it all alright. He would be alright. The hedgehog would be alright. She could do it.

The DVD was still in the machine. She had never needed Ethan more.

That evening she pressed him again. "You need to talk about what happened to you. Yes, I know, you don't want to talk to the police, but you need to talk to someone. You need a trained psychologist. A psychiatrist? I don't know, but not me. You won't tell me his name. I can't help you if you won't talk to me. I know you don't believe me, but it really does help to talk about it. I really want to help you, but I can't if you won't trust me." She tried her best smile. "It's supposed to be cathartic – talking about it. I know it sounds like nonsense, but it does help. It seems to sort it out in your head when you say it out loud. It's something about letting go of a bad secret. It takes away the pressure of keeping all that poison locked up inside your head. And it's like a poison. You have to let it go. Just saying it out loud makes it less important. I'm not trying to trivialise what happened to you, but if you share the burden then it's easier for you to bear. Keeping secrets is totally exhausting. I know that sounds daft, but it's actually true."

He shook his head. When she stopped looking at him, he resumed watching the television. It was another football match.

She ground her teeth quietly. She had to admit that her sympathy waned when he was watching the football, which was a terrible admission. "But," she said forcefully, then rose to her feet. She crossed the room to perch on the edge of the sofa, and lifted one of his hands. "You'll need to talk to a stranger. When you unburden all of your secrets, you'll find it easier if you talk to a stranger. That's why people go to psychiatrists. And we tend to choose someone that we'll never meet in our everyday lives. It's part of the process. You're giving away your secrets, and they're not coming back."

He lowered his gaze. The shutters came down. All his defence mechanisms suddenly made sense.

She watched him intently. Nothing but his extraordinary good looks could have kept him alive. She smiled, and stroked the habitual wayward strands of hair away from his eyes. It had to be surgery. No one had any right to be so beautiful. "You want to go home," she said. It was not a question. "You know that will be difficult. It's not just about finding them, but what will you say? How will you explain everything?" She stroked his hand. She would have liked to look into those lovely eyes, but he was staring at the floor. He did not seem to be listening, and he was very pale. "I want to help you. There must be something that you can tell me that will give me a place to start?"

He remained motionless.

"You lived in Paris?"

That seemed harmless. "Yes."

"You worked for a prince?" That seemed the least painful way of describing his existence.

There was a long pause. "Yes."

"You and some Pakistanis?" She waited in vain for an answer. "You and Mahmood and Omar?"

"Omar is not from Pakistan," he whispered, knowing that was important to Omar.

"So Omar and the Pakistanis? You lived with them for a long time?"

He closed his eyes for a moment. Emotion heated his face. With some difficulty, he said: "Forever."

She did not know how to process that. It was simply too immense in her tiny little world. She backtracked and regrouped then tried to find another thread. "You're safe here. No one is going to hurt you anymore. I promise." She stroked his cheek gently. "Tell me about Mahmood and his friends. What were their names? Did they all like football, or were they cricket fans like Mahmood?"

"They liked cricket," he said softly.

"Their home was Pakistan?"

"Yes. Pakistan."

She was trying to hold a smile, but it trembled on her lips. "So there was Mahmood and…"

He visibly paled. He tried to drag his hand away from her, but she held it with surprising determination. "Abdullah," he said in a low monotone. A storm of emotions battered him. His whole body shuddered. "Abdullah." He was so frightened.

She watched helplessly. He was remembering, but she needed him to speak. "You're safe here. I won't let anything bad happen to you. It's alright to remember."

He blinked then stared at her, not recognising her face. He gasped as a bolt of pain went through his chest again and again then it slowly ebbed away. He was breathless and sweating. His eyes were glassy. "Please? I don't know you."

"You're safe here," she reassured him. "My name is Jane Howard. This is my house. I won't let anyone hurt you."

He stared at her as if she was a total stranger. He was just a child. He had been abused and abandoned. He was helpless. "Please? I don't know what to do."

She squeezed his hand. She wanted desperately to embrace him. She wanted to be his mother, and protect him from all the evils in the world. "You're safe here. It's alright. Take as long as you want."

He shook his head. "Please, I cannot. I do not understand." He peered around the room as if it were a foreign country. "Why am I here?"

"It's alright. You're safe now. This is my house. No one is going to hurt you ever again. Just take a deep breath. You need to relax. You need to let go of all these secrets. You'll feel so much better afterwards."

"Please?" He shook his head again. "I cannot. You must not ask me. I cannot tell you. You must understand why I cannot tell you?"

"Because you were abducted?" she asked gently.

"Because they'll find me!" He did not understand why she did not know.

"No, it's alright. You're safe here. You can tell me anything. You have to trust me. Come on, Daniel, I want to help you, but you have to let me. You have to talk to me."

He shook his head.

"You have to trust me." She waited for him to look at her, but he was too tired. "Please, talk to me. Tell me about your friends. There must be so many things that you can tell me which won't offend anyone. Come on, Daniel. Please, talk to me."

"Mahmood took care of me," he said carefully. "He helped me with my English so that I might read poems for my master. Every evening, I read to him. He liked that." He paused to remember, and almost smiled. "Waheed, Famzi, Malik and Aziz. They all took care of me. I was never left alone." He took a moment to simply breathe. He tried to smile, but he could not look at her. "Omar insisted that they never left me alone. Then Aziz died. It wasn't my fault. They thought I had killed him, but I didn't. Please? It was an accident. He was very angry. He was shouting at me. Then he fell down and he was dead. But it wasn't my fault. You must believe me."

She patted his hand. "You're safe now. It's alright."

"Please? It wasn't my fault."

"No, I'm sure it wasn't. Was he old?"

He shrugged and shook his head, mystified.

"Was that in Paris?"

He hesitated to consider his answer. "Dubai. We were in Dubai." It sounded like a confession. He could not look at her. Another minute passed before he could continue. "They took me there when everyone had to leave the mountain."

She waited, hoping he would explain. "The mountain?"

There was an even longer pause. He started to speak then stopped. He had said too much. He wanted to take back every word. He was actually trembling.

"What mountain?" she asked.

He shook his head. He just kept shaking his head.

"It's only a mountain. You can tell me about the mountain, surely?" She tried to laugh. "Was it in France? I think Dubai is flat as a pancake and down at sea-level. Or was it in Pakistan? There are lots of mountains in Pakistan."

He looked at her as if she was completely insane then stared back at the floor.

"You had to leave the mountain?" she reminded him.

He nervously reclaimed his hand then covered his face. He was shaking quite badly. "After the Jews attacked New York – I was taken away. They came and took me away."

She doubted her hearing. Then she doubted his words. Even after she had repeated it all three times in her head, and very slowly, it still did not make sense. "And when did the Jews attack New York? I think I missed that."

He heard the change in tone. He knew he had made a mistake. He shook his head almost imperceptibly then stared at the floor.

"No, come on! You need to explain that one."

He shook his head again. His jaw was set. He was not going to say another word, but his nerves crumbled, and he whispered brokenly: "It was a long time ago." He felt her eyes piercing his brain. "The Zionists flew planes into the tallest towers of New York."

She was baffled then shocked. "That wasn't the Jews. Why did you say that? That's an awful thing to say. You can get into trouble making wild accusations like that."

He bowed his head as if ducking a blow. "Please? I'm sorry. I apologise, but everyone knows that it was the Jewish Americans who planned it. They are all murderers."

She could not quite believe that she was hearing him. "You're joking!"

He glanced searchingly into her face then lowered his gaze. "There is proof. It was all a Zionist plot. They killed some Americans to make sure that America started a war against Islam, which has allowed the Jews to stay in Palestine."

She was dumb with shock. So he was completely delusional. Was everything a lie? "You're joking," she repeated lamely. "No, I'm sorry, but you're completely wrong. They were Saudis. They were Arabs. They'd been in America learning how to fly a plane in a straight line. The man who planned it is locked up tight at Guantanamo Bay, and hopefully he'll stay there forever. Abu Dhabi Mohammed, something like that."

"Khalid Sheikh Mohammed," he corrected her quietly.

"You know his name," she said. A cold hand slowly crushed her heart. "Yes, Mohammed. He's a Saudi. They're all terrorists. It was a scandal that no one had realised what they were up to, but then no one had ever thought about flying passenger planes loaded with fuel into tall buildings. It was a miracle that the death toll was not twenty thousand. You cannot seriously believe that it was the Jews? That's just crazy."

He nodded, but he was not converted.

"Really, it's completely insane. Who on earth told you that? It's a complete and utter lie."

He did not want to elaborate. She was only a woman, so she was not clever enough to understand the ways of the world, and she was obviously unstable.

"It's not true," she repeated adamantly. "You've been conned. It's simply not true."

He had shut down again. He was holding his breath and praying she would just stop and go away.

She did not want to have an argument, but it was beyond her to let such a calumny exist. She studied his face in silence. He was still extraordinarily beautiful, but the attraction had died. "This is about Islam, isn't it? You've been told all this nonsense by a Muslim. Your Pakistanis, I presume?"

He was not prepared to acknowledge that.

She frowned. It was brainwashing. It was Stockholm Syndrome. It was Patty Hearst all over again. "Somebody's lied to you," she explained gently. "It's alright. I'm not angry, but you must understand that it was not the Jews. You can't go around saying things like that. It was Islamic terrorists. And they're not all Saudis, but most of them are. We had a terrible problem with disaffected Pakistanis over here last year. I guess your Pakistanis have probably taught you all sorts of nonsense."

He sat motionless, silently begging her to stop.

She actually wanted to shake him. "But it isn't true! You can't go around making anti-Semitic remarks. You've been lied to. It's not the Jews who want to take over the world. That's totally against their nature. They're exiles. It's in their DNA. They have a lovely saying that by saving one life you are saving the whole world." She recognised the cynical sneer. "It's the mad mullahs. It's Osama bin Laden. They really do want to take over the world. It's Islam. They want a caliphate. It's not the Jews."

He pulled a face and nodded, but it was obvious that he did not believe a word.

She hardly knew what to say. She moved closer to pat his hand reassuringly then leaned across to kiss his forehead. She wanted to tell him that he was completely insane, but as a woman living alone, it seemed rather inflammatory. "I'll make a cup of tea." She ruffled his hair. She did not want to leave him. She did not understand how anyone could believe such nonsense. Leaving it to fester in his head seemed a bad idea, but she had no idea what monsters lurked in there now. "I need a cup of tea." She took a deep breath then leaned down to gaze at his face. She stroked his hair. She smiled as the usual few ebony strands flopped back fetchingly across his forehead. "You're wrong," she said. "I can't imagine what you've been through, but you've been told a pack of lies. I think you'll find that you've been misinformed about a lot of things."

He did not look at her.

She drew away. There were so many questions that she wanted to ask. But she had other responsibilities too. She took her pills. She munched through a cheese sandwich while the hedgehog had his daily bath. The cats wanted attention. There were perimeters to check. She pulled on a pair of shoes, picked up a torch, and took a tour of the garden. There were still birds singing. She could hear activity in the bushes, which usually meant hedgehogs. She hoped they were alright. She must have spent almost an hour loitering about, trying to catch sight of them. There were frogs now in the ponds, and a surprising number of newts were still aggressively courting. She could not see any dead ones. On the way back to the house, she was annoyed to see how many of the bird feeders were nearly empty. It was too dark by then, and she was bone tired.

He was asleep. The television was still on. It was half time or full time. There were talking heads offering opinions. There were lots of new goals to study from every angle, but none of them were English.

She went up the stairs, and opened the door to the spare room. It was dominated by boxes, but in one corner was a comfortable bed with an almost new duvet and feather pillows. She could see him sleeping there. It was an attractive picture.

She woke him up gently. "Come with me."

He was barely awake, and she already had him on his feet.

"It's alright." She had him at the bottom of the stairs.

He looked around then peered anxiously up the stairs. He stiffened immediately.

She expected him to protest and plead, but he never said a word. Obviously, she had caught him off guard. She moved him to her right side so that he could hold the banister then she supported his left arm, and started him up the stairs. He was very quiet. She realised that he was probably half asleep and certainly very tired. They climbed the stairs together. She made sure that he never wavered. When he needed to stop, she stood beside him, keeping him upright. On the landing, she showed him the bathroom, explaining that the toilet seat must always be left down, that if the door was closed it meant that someone was inside, and that if he had a bath or a shower then he must not under any circumstances make his back wet. She lectured him about the danger of damaging the delicate new skin on his back. She wanted to lay down the law about masturbating in the bed, but did not know how to say it out loud. She did not let go of his arm until he was sitting on the bed.

"If you take off your clothes, and get into bed then I'll come by later, and put some more cream on your back. In the morning, you can go back downstairs, and watch the television."

"Please?" He gazed at the pillows then stroked the duvet. "This is my bed?"

"Yes." She sat down beside him and clasped his hand. "Yes, this is your bed. You'll be more comfortable here."

"My bed?"

She did not understand. "Yes." She stooped to try and read his face, but he was staring at the floor again. "It's alright. You're not alone. I'm just across the landing. If you have bad dreams then I'll be able to hear you, but honestly, you'll be alright."

"Thank you."

"Do you want to use the bathroom?"

He shook his head.

"I'll find you a light for here." She pointed vaguely at the small table.

"Thank you." He could not look at her. "You've been very kind."

She backed away. It was very confusing having him in a bedroom. "Well, you go back to sleep. You'll be more comfortable up here. You won't have cats walking all over you." She was at the door. "I'll leave the light on out here and the door open." She gave him a minute to answer, but there was only silence. "I'll come back with the cream."

He was still stroking the duvet. He had never had a bed of his own before.

Chapter 34

From the doorway, she could see he was asleep. He looked comfortable. His face was buried in the pillows. One arm was raised and folded - probably to shield his eyes from the light flooding in from the landing. Very quietly, she crept into the room, and carefully sat down on the chair. There was something immensely soothing about watching someone who was deeply asleep. He looked younger. He looked pristine. But he was so damaged. He needed so much help. She wanted to take the coward's way out, and hand him over to the police. It would take them hardly five minutes to put all the wheels in motion to find his parents and reunite them. His lack of memory would not handicap their efforts. They would run DNA tests, and their computers would spit out a dozen names of families who had lost a son in the relevant timeframe. That must have been in the late eighties. He must have been beautiful even then. She was almost relieved by her conviction that if all else failed then it would be so easy to find them.

For hours, she watched the blue moonlight move across him. He was not dreaming. He was at peace. In her head, she built and destroyed a thousand schemes. She had lost a child. She knew her own pain. She would not presume to trivialise what his parents must be feeling, but she knew loss and heartache. When her son had disappeared something inside her had broken. It was too trite to say that it was her heart, but she had to lock away everything that caused her pain, and it had blighted her life. She could not tolerate being around people because they might say something that made her remember. She could not chat. Socially, emotionally, she was dead. She filled up her existence with the cats, the garden, the woodland and the wildlife, but it was all just a placebo to stop her from slashing her wrists in the bath. She kept herself so busy to make sure that she did not lay awake scrutinising her life.

So she could not call the police. She could not ask for help. She could not open her own wounds for public viewing. While he was still and quiet, he would remain one of her waifs and strays. If he did not send ripples across her quiet life then he could stay. She could not interrogate him. What he had been through was probably worse than anything that she could imagine, but it was not some brutal slasher movie. He had a life. It was as complicated as any normal person's life. There must have been some awful moments, but he evidently had friends. There were people who took care of him, and he had a lover. Superficially, he had a charmed life. He had expensive clothes and accessories. Money appeared to be no object. He had a good dentist. He had access to a private clinic and good medical care. He had a beautiful well-trained body, and probably a good brain because he would have needed to be intelligent to survive. The psychological damage was more extensive. He lacked social skills. He had been isolated. It was more than living abroad in an alien culture. She did not want to dwell on what had happened to him. His body suggested the answers. It was about sex. His obvious physical beauty must have been a tremendous bonus to his abductors.

*

The Untouchables returned with a cunning plan. They kidnapped the white infidel. They crept up behind him and beat him until he was too battered to resist. He was quickly dragged away before anyone could raise the alarm. They made him run for the first time in his life. He could not breathe properly. He could hardly focus. Hours later, they dragged him into a cave, and he just collapsed. He was exhausted from running, and still bleeding from his wounds. The adrenalin coursing through his veins was not enough to carry him another step.

Then he saw the rest of the Untouchables, the Dalits, and knew he was in serious trouble. They emerged from the shadows at the back of the cave as dark-skinned and black-eyed as he remembered. Their clothes were thin rags. They looked wretched with hunger. As they all swarmed around him, they launched into a loud and bitter argument. He had no idea what they were saying, but feared that he was the cause. He remembered their rage at being driven off by the Parsi from the mountain. He could not possibly help them so their abduction of him was mystifying. He could not return them to their cave or restore their pitiful possessions. As the war of words raged above him, he lay very still, and hoped to be forgotten. They were so angry. It seemed certain that the slightest provocation would lead to more violence. On the ground, at their feet, surrounded, there was no escape. All the men carried sticks. They had already beaten him into submission. He no longer had the will or the energy to move. His scalp felt as if it had been torn from his skull. His feet were cut painfully, and every joint and sinew ached. He needed water and food and time to heal, but the shrill shouting and violent gestures continued. Their raw hatred shocked him. Not even the radicalised clerics at the madrassa had hated him like this.

One of the old, withered men stepped forward and lifted his hands, demanding silence. The others succumbed to his plea, however grudgingly.

Then he spoke softly to them as if explaining something complex and subtle to a child.

The kafir felt sure that he was still the topic of conversation. The men stood close around him. The women were back a little, but volatile and shrill. No one actually looked at him, but they were pointing and gesturing angrily. The children had wandered away. He was still breathing hard when the man in jeans suddenly grabbed him, and shoved his face into the ground. He closed his eyes. He groaned. He knew he could not walk another step.

The man pulled the belt from his own jeans, and stooped to lash it around the kafir's wrists. Then he pulled the kafir back to his feet, and shoved him out into the bright sunshine.

They set off in a procession: the young men kept the tall kafir close between them, they were followed by the two old men then the seething swarm of children, and the four women trailed along in the rear carrying their meagre possessions. They moved slower because of the children. Unfortunately, the children had the time and energy to pelt the kafir ceaselessly with stones that they were able to collect in great quantities. He ignored them as best he could. No one intervened so they ran wild, screaming with delight at every successful hit.

When he tripped, and fell tumbling down a slope, the young men went after him like wolves after a fawn, dragged him back, beat him viciously then cowed him into continuing. He obeyed. He knew nothing else. He moved as quickly as he could because they seemed to be in a desperate hurry yet his legs failed him. He went crashing down again, this time taking a child with him. Suddenly, the women were screaming. The children were all crying. The men were demented. The kafir just cowered beneath the renewed barrage of blows. It did not matter that it had been an accident. He could not lift a hand. He was not allowed to speak. The Dalits dragged him back on to the path, and held him still while the women accounted for all their children. No one was hurt. They were all present. That did not stop the kafir being beaten again until his face ran with blood. There was another loud argument. Everyone but the kafir had an opinion, and shouted it angrily. He just lay in the dirt grateful for a moment to rest, wondering why he was still alive. After a heated debate, the old men were sent on ahead, taking the women and children with them. The kafir was brought slowly behind. He could walk. Whenever they tried to make him hurry, he just fell down.

They walked all day and for more than an hour in complete darkness before they reached the tiny fire and their families. The kafir was almost unconscious with exhaustion, and needed no encouragement to fall down and lay still. He took no further interest in proceedings, and was generally ignored. The women cooked something that looked horribly like rats, but could have been marmots, and ground some seeds or nuts between rocks to eke out their starvation rations. The children huddled around the fire with dull eyes, beyond sleep but as hungry as worms.

Then something whistled.

The men started to their feet, peering into the darkness.

There was another whistle from the rocks above them.

One of the Dalits called a greeting into the night, and slowly from all sides, men swathed in dark clothes and black turbans appeared like ghostly apparitions. They encircled the huddled group, who clung to the fire like moths.

There were eight men, all bearded, all dressed alike. The youngest was a boy in his late teens. The eldest was a man in his late fifties with streaks of grey in his beard. All of them stared at the Dalets with suspicion. All of them had rifles or AK47s slung over their shoulders, cartridge belts draped across their chests, and Soviet army supplies packed around their waists.

"You have the American?" one of the Taliban asked. He had handsome chiselled features, and the soulful shining eyes of a poet. His fingers were long and slender, everything about him suggested a delicate artistic nature, but there was a golden dagger in his belt, and the heavy machine gun dwarfed him.

The Dalits parted submissively to reveal the white kafir, who lay on the ground as if dead.

The handsome young Taliban gestured his older comrade to take a look. No one spoke as the man limped through the anxious Dalits, who shrank from him and his bristling weapons, then he leaned down to stare at the kafir, squinting in the poor light to see his face.

The kafir was somewhere between sleep and death. He did not stir as the man stepped awkwardly over him so that he could take advantage of the firelight. The man stooped again to examine the kafir's ashen face then looked at his ragged shirt, his bound hands and his roughened feet.

"He is not American spy," the man announced, glancing towards the young Taliban, who was apparently in charge. With two calloused fingers, he probed in the kafir's neck for a pulse. "He isn't strong."

The kafir stirred. His blue eyes flashed. He saw the face of the man bent over him, and lapsed immediately into memories of his childhood. "Please? My lord, sir, please, by the Grace of God. Please, I am sorry. God is Great. God is Great. Please, my lord, forgive me. God is great. Praise be to the Prophet. Peace be with you, sir, my lord by the Grace of God."

His Arabic amazed them, but they all took up their weapons as he struggled grimly to his feet and bowed. He was confused and disorientated, but he bowed to each of them in turn until the man who had roused him, caught his arm, and shook him violently to waken him from what seemed like delirium. The kafir collapsed like a house of cards, and was unconscious before he hit the ground.

"He is not spy," the man said again. "Not American anymore. We should leave him here and forget him or kill him and burn the body."

"Why?" the young Taliban asked. He walked through the Dalits as if they were invisible to stare down at the pale white kafir in his tattered shirt.

"He is dancing boy. A beardless boy." The man spat in the kafir's ashen face. "A catamite."

There was a gasp. Even the Dalits turned to stare.

"A lady-boy?" The young Taliban gazed at him, ashamed of his curiosity yet curious all the same. "How can you tell?"

"I have seen them before," the older man explained. "Pretty boys. Beardless boys. Bacha Bazi, they dress the pretty boys like girls then fuck them. He is too old now. Perhaps, he fails to please."

The young Taliban turned on the Dalit men. "You tried to trick us."

The women drew back, clutching their children to their thighs.

The older men trembled.

It was the Dalit in jeans, who held his ground. "He is American. He is enemy. You ransom him. They will pay. They always pay. For his white skin they will pay."

The older man shook his head, and smiled ruefully. "No one will pay for that."

The young Taliban threatened the Dalit with a gun. "You tricked us."

The Dalit hardly knew what to say. He tore at his hair and thumped his chest. "We have nothing. We have nothing. There is no food for our children. We have no hope. He took our work. They drove us from our home because he would do what we had done before. What can we do? If you do not take him then what can we do? We have no food, and nowhere to live. How can we feed our children? How can we keep them safe?"

"Then you kill him. You wanted us to be his executioners?"

The Dalit shook his head in dismay. "We thought you would want to know about him. He might be American spy. He might be anything. You will be able to raise money with ransom. You need money. Jihad. Kill unbelievers. God is Great."

The Taliban agreed that God was great, but did not want to have anything to do with a filthy catamite especially a disgustingly filthy American catamite.

As a sign of goodwill, they agreed to stay the night, and opened their packs to share what food they had. They talked to the children like benign uncles, and let them gorge themselves without comment. The men ate politely. The women, who were now veiled, did not eat at all.

Some hours later the kafir stirred. He was lost and disorientated. He wanted to be with his master, but knew that he was meant to be picking up excrement, and scrubbing the pits beneath the toilets, so why was he surrounded by strangers and outside in the freezing cold? He struggled to lift his hands, but they were bound, and looking around, he saw that several people with big guns were watching him. He stiffened, and lowered his gaze, then tried to edge away.

The Taliban nearest him simply leaned over, and stabbed a rifle barrel into his abdomen. That stopped the kafir dead. He stared down at the weapon, its metal gleaming in the firelight, then cast a wary look at the man holding it. There would be no more looking anyone in the eye. He lowered his gaze and lay still. He was amongst Believers. The old rules applied.

"Why are you in the mountains?" the older Taliban asked.

The kafir breathed slowly, but found no courage. "Sir, please?"

"You understand. You speak Arabic. How many other languages do you speak?" The man was shrewd. "You don't speak Gujarati? These people speak Gujarati like the Parsi."

"Please?" the kafir asked anxiously.

"How long have you been here?"

"Please?"

"Water?" The man held up a Russian army canteen, and sloshed it about noisily.

The kafir focused.

"Free his hands. He'll need to eat and drink something. They won't have fed him." He turned to seek approval from the young leader, who nodded silently. "He's haram. He is filth. They will have fucked him. They've probably fucked his brains out already, and sent him here to die."

The kafir was released, but he still did not lift his head. Closing his eyes so that the Believers would not be insulted, he cupped his hands together to beg. Being considered spiritually unclean, he knew they would never allow him to touch their belongings, so he waited for water to be poured into his hands. He drank at first because he was obliged to, then he drank because he was thirsty, then he drank because he was afraid they would never allow him another opportunity. They all watched him. Perhaps, they understood. Every time he bowed his head and offered his cupped hands, he was rewarded with water. When the dented canteen was empty, he tried to withdraw then froze as someone unseen moved close behind.

"You feel better?" the older Taliban asked.

He nodded dumbly, head down, hands trembling.

"How long have you been here?"

The kafir shuffled awkwardly on to his knees then bowed down with his face in the dirt and his palms flat on the ground. "Please? God is Great. God is Compassionate. God is Merciful."

"Praise be to God and the Prophet. You haven't answered a single question. I can see you understand. You must be clever or you'd be dead by now."

"Please, sir, I know nothing."

"Here, have some bread."

The kafir's hunger shrivelled under the attention. "Please?"

"Eat," the young leader said encouragingly.

The kafir drew back to sit hunched over his heels, round shouldered and grovelling. He offered his hands again while bowing his head and closing his eyes. They had guns. He recognised their uniform. These were the legendary warriors of God, the Taliban, that he had heard about at the madrassa, and that were whispered about by the servants. Scraps of food were thrown at him. He ate it all though he had to scratch in the dirt for every crumb, which amused the Dalits. It tasted of nothing, and was hardly enough to provide nourishment. The Taliban watched his every move, but they talked amongst themselves in quiet amiable tones.

Slowly, one by one the Dalits and their Taliban guests lay down to sleep. The older Taliban bound the kafir hand and foot then lay down wrapped in a woollen shawl. There were two guards all night. It was quiet. Not even a wolf howled to disturb them. The cold was penetrating.

At dawn they awoke to find a few inches of snow. The Taliban laid out their prayer mats and knelt down to pray. Hearing the words again awoke a thousand memories in the kafir. Throwing caution to the wind, he desperately pleaded with the Taliban to take him with them. He begged to be allowed to travel with them. He would not eat or drink. He would not slow them down. He just needed them to take him through the mountains to Pakistan. He had no conception of how far or how difficult that would be. All that he knew was that he might be able to find a sanctuary if he could find Achmed Qadri. He bowed down and praised God and begged for mercy and compassion, but the Taliban did not want him. When he clutched at their feet, and tried to seize their clothes to make them listen, he was beaten off like diseased vermin. They prepared to leave, not remotely interested in the Dalits' dilemma. They were off to make war for God, and were determined to avoid becoming surrogate executioners. The kafir persisted. He knew the Dalits meant to kill him. He had to believe that the Taliban would respect the command to show mercy and compassion to slaves. But the Taliban had other priorities. They hammered a pistol against his head, and left him to his fate. They told the Dalits that all disbelievers were condemned to death, and it was their duty to carry out the punishment, and they had an obligation to teach their sons how to kill infidels before the infidels came to kill them.

The Dalits decided they would throw the kafir in the nearest river, the turbulent currents and freezing temperatures would quickly finish him off without leaving blood on their hands. After a few days, they would return to the mountain, and renegotiate their employment. It would take that long for the toilets to start smelling again, and the people in the mountain were far too precious about their sacred fires and cleansing rituals to ever get their hands dirty cleaning their own toilets.

The Taliban had hardly been gone an hour when a group of heavily armed Parsi from the mountain swarmed down to surround the Dalits. There was no need for any conversation. They knew why the Dalits had taken the kafir, and were determined to simply recover him. The kafir was freed and brought to his feet, then Mansour emerged from the crowd, and beckoned the kafir to join him. Though Mansour was visibly loath to touch him, he firmly took hold of the kafir's sleeve then walked him away to separate him from the besieged Dalits.

The kafir never saw the Dalits again, and could not be curious. He did not hear gunfire, and when the rest of the Parsi rejoined him and Mansour, none of them were injured or bloodstained. He had to assume that the Dalits had given up and moved on to find a new home somewhere else.

It was a long way back to the mountain. He walked placidly six feet behind Mansour, his adopted master. No one beat him. His hands were not tied. He was comfortable following Mansour. He was comfortable in the group. The men from the mountain moved like a unit. There was always someone half a mile down the trail, and another bringing up the rear. They were well armed. They were competent. There was no bickering or shouting or screaming. If they had been Muslims, he would have respected them, but they were heretics so he was not allowed to like them even though they had just saved his life. His true master had sent him to these strangers. Obviously, there was a reason. So he would obey them, and not run away.

The kafir was taken back to his small windowless room. No one said anything to him. It would have been pointless. He spoke many languages, but not theirs. They really did not want to have anything to do with him. He was dirty. They were obsessed with cleanliness. He was desperate to be a good Muslim. They considered all Muslims to be their mortal enemies. He was only permitted to leave his room because the Dalits had overplayed their hand, and a filthy Muslim was ideally suited for filthy work. Mansour brought him water, but he was otherwise left alone. His curious adventure left him confused. He would have gone with the Taliban. He did not understand that they would have cut off his head or burned him alive. The Islam that they preached was not the same as the one observed by Prince Abdul Aziz or even his Pakistanis. The Taliban forbade joy. There would be no more music or dancing boys. There was only the Word of God, which according to them was the truth, the whole truth and nothing but the truth.

He was asleep when they returned. It felt like hours had passed. He gave himself up without hesitation to Mansour, but the crowd that followed him into the small room felt like a vengeful mob. With a wagging finger, a loud voice and gestures demanding calm, Mansour compelled him to surrender. Mansour kept eye contact with him, and the kafir obediently deferred. In the absence of Prince Abdul Aziz and Prince Khalid, the kafir accepted without question that Mansour was his master. He had to obey him. Peace prevailed. It had nothing to do with the quality of the armed men who surrounded him. They had come prepared to violently take him down, but he stood quietly, round shouldered, and gazing at Mansour more in hope than expectation. He was taken from the room then down several steps to a nearby landing where he was compelled to sit on a lonely chair. Mansour stood in front of him demanding calm while he was hurriedly fastened to the chair with extravagant amounts of rope. Satisfied that they were all safe, the crowd around him thinned. Mansour patted his shoulder reassuringly then stepped back to let a stranger stoop over him. The stranger had a large pair of scissors. There was nothing the kafir could do as his long and filthy hair was cut off. He did not understand why they were doing it, but knew that his precious looks had already been completely destroyed. It should have been painless, and yet it hurt him terribly, reminding him again of his debasement. What had he done? Why had he been sent away? What was to become of him? They crudely shaved off all his hair, but left his fledgling beard which was already thick with sweat and grime. When it was over, he was too despondent to care what happened to him anymore. Back in his gloomy room, he was given a drab collection of garments to disguise him as a nomadic tribesman. His transformation was complete.

For a few days, men with guns followed him whenever he went out into the valley, but it bored them, and made the kafir nervous. The solution was a long chain, in fact several pieces of chain, fashioned together to make one long leash. One end was fastened to a stake driven into the cliff face just inside the cave. The other end was literally bolted around the kafir's ankle. It was long enough to allow the kafir to trail miserably up and down the stairs while he collected the baskets from the landing, and just long enough for him to take them out on to the valley floor where he was required to empty them. There were still men with guns, usually hidden somewhere high up in the mountain like snipers. The chain was only removed from the kafir's ankle when he was sent into the tunnels to clean the pits or returned to his small room to sleep.

He was given the same quantity of food and water that the Dalits had received. There was a little mutton every other day, bread and water every day, and soap and water provided for him to keep himself clean. They believed the chain kept him safe. It was not meant to make him a prisoner. To a society obsessed not just with wisdom, but cleanliness and purity, his reputation condemned him to total isolation.

Chapter 35

She was still in the chair when the sun filled the room with light. He was asleep. She crept away to her own bed. It was another four hours before he awoke. She felt vindicated. She was right about the bed. It was such a tiny victory, but she had needed one.

As soon as he was awake, she was in the doorway with the tub of Vitamin E cream. He was still sleepy. The bed was exceedingly comfortable. Nothing but the coolness of the cream on his delicate pink skin disturbed him. It made her heart leap with joy to find him so content.

"Did you sleep well?" she asked. Of course, she knew the answer as she had sat beside his bed all night.

He smiled into the pillow. He slowly stretched his arms out, then nodded

She could feel his muscles moving beneath her fingers. The skin was so very fragile. The slightest pressure would have swept it all away. "You need to be careful," she said again. "It'll be weeks before you can let this skin get wet, and you'll never be able to sit outside without a shirt on. You've been so lucky. It really was a horrible mess. Your skin was literally hanging off in strips. The infection was down to the bone. I still don't know how you survived. Well, you must remember how painful it was?"

His smile had disappeared. He did remember. "Yes, thank you."

She sighed. She could have sat there caressing his back for hours. The temptation to straddle him was almost unbearable. Her heart swelled. She yearned with every nerve and sinew. Her sanity was teetering on the edge of an abyss. But she resolutely screwed the lid back on the jar then stared away out of the window. She needed to be Meryl Streep again. She was calm and his mother. Her maternal instinct struggled back to life. She did not even know what day it was. That did not seem to matter. The sun was shining. He was alive, and she was still - more or less - okay. From the window, she could see to the horizon, and there was not a house or hamlet in sight. She put the jar down on the table then walked away to the door. "You should stay here for a while then get dressed and come downstairs. I'll be in the kitchen. Just give me a shout if you need anything."

He waited for her leave then swung his feet onto the floor. He did not need to stand up to know that he was still weak. He stepped into the shorts and trousers then slowly straightened up, and pulled them on. The view from the window amazed him. It was the first time he had been able to look out of a window. It was a Van Gogh painting. The yellow fields blazed beneath the clear blue sky. Without thinking, he slowly sat down again on the bed. There was no strength at all in his legs. He massaged his thighs, but even that was difficult because every muscle in his body seemed to originate on his back, and that was still incredibly painful.

She had been loitering in the hall. As soon as he appeared on the landing, she swept up the stairs. "Yes. Yes, I know, but I promised to make sure that you didn't fall down."

"Thank you." He leaned wearily onto the banister.

She had a couple of bottles of baby food and a milkshake ready on the coffee table. He wanted to sit down. She fussed around with the cushions. He leaned across the armrest. He completely ignored her. She eventually got the message and backed away.

She had to leave the room. She had so many questions, and he just was not ready. Even she knew that it was unacceptable to pump him for information when he was not really awake. So she went outside to fill the bird feeders. She thought about walking down through the woods to visit the shrine and then the pond where she had found him. Now, she was not afraid to go down there and find that it had been corrupted. Now, she was afraid to leave him alone in case he disappeared. It was irrational. She knew that it was totally irrational, but she could not believe that he would stay there of his own free will. He would leave. Obviously, he would leave. She would be alone. She did not want to be alone. He had ruined it for her.

He was still on the sofa when she returned. She had a cup of tea. He had a milkshake and some painkillers. He was watching another programme about antiques. She turned the sound down. "They took you to Dubai and Paris? You travelled a lot? All of you?"

His gaze fell again. He became anxious

She tried her best smile. "It's alright. We're just talking about you and your friends. They took care of you. That's nice."

He sort of nodded. He did not quite believe her.

"Mahmood and Omar and the others?"

"Yes."

"Were they all related? You know, brothers and cousins? It must have been quite a gang of you all travelling together." The smile was becoming a grimace, but she was determined.

He shook his head almost imperceptibly.

"So what did everyone do?"

He made his usual awkward dismissive gesture, but her silence compelled him to elaborate. He took a deep breath. "Omar and Malik were bodyguards. There were always bodyguards. It was always dangerous. Aziz, Waheed and Mahmood took care of me." He swallowed the anxiety that had tightened his throat. "He trusted them to take care of me. From the first day..." He hesitated then swallowed again with difficulty. "They taught me everything."

She gave him a moment. "So what did you do with Aziz, Waheed and Mahmood?"

His head went down. He shifted uncomfortably. "I had to work."

"But what did you do?"

He shivered. It took him a minute to find the right words. "In the beginning, I cleaned the floors. I cleaned their clothes. Then I cleaned them and dressed them. Much later, I had to bathe and dress my master. I was given nice clothes. I didn't have to clean the floors anymore. It was better."

She took a moment to consider what he was not saying. It would have been cruel to expose him. "And he never hurt you?" she asked gently.

His body language made every word a lie. "He never hurt me. He is a great prince. He never looked at me or spoke to me. He never hurt me. I am only a servant." He stared at her, challenging her to doubt him. "I am honoured to serve him. It is a great privilege."

"And how long were you his servant?"

He shifted again. "Please?" The tension aggravated the wounds across his back. "I don't know. Maybe, ten years. I don't know. It is a long time."

"And before that?" she asked quietly.

"For seven winters, I was at a school. Before that, I don't remember. I don't remember anything before the school. I don't remember my name. I don't remember anything."

She did the maths. "So you were very young?" She watched him slowly fall apart. He was shivering. She hardly knew how to console him. "I'm so sorry."

He buried his face in his hands. "I shouldn't have forgotten. It's my fault.

I was so frightened. Why did I forget my name? I don't know who I am."

"Because you were a child and you were frightened," she said soothingly. "It was a frightening situation. You did what you had to do to survive. You mustn't blame yourself for any of this. It wasn't your fault."

He stared at her brokenly. "I can't remember anything."

"You stayed alive," she said. "You stayed alive. You did what you had to do."

He sobbed once loudly then smothered his emotions. "I should be able to remember."

She wanted to fly across the room, and wrap him up in her arms, but knew that he would reject her. "Tell me about the school? Was it in Dubai? Was it a nice school?"

He inhaled raggedly. "It was in the mountains, in the north of Pakistan."

She hesitated. "Pakistan?" Her heart seemed to stop beating. Suddenly, there was a pain. "You were at a madrassa?"

He had heard the change in her voice. He was watching her now. He could read the obvious apprehension in her face. "Yes." He felt compelled to explain, but it was hard for him to put it into words. He sighed and fidgeted.

"You were at a madrassa?" she repeated in shock.

He nodded then filled his lungs to try and explain. "It is a school. I didn't understand the languages, and I wasn't like them so I was very unhappy for a long time." He nodded resolutely. "I was unhappy. I wasn't like them. They were Believers." He fidgeted then nodded again. "There were many boys. Some of them didn't have families because of the war. The school was their home. They thought I was their enemy. They..." He slowly shook his head.

"A madrassa?" she said bluntly.

"Please? It's just a school."

"Yes, I know what it is. So this is Islam? Hard-line mainstream Islam?" She paused to let him respond, but he was staring at the floor again. "So you learned to read the Koran in Arabic? All day, every day, seven days a week? Did you learn anything else?"

"There is nothing else."

"For seven years?"

His head bowed lower.

"You must know it by heart." She took a moment to absorb the information. There were alarm bells ringing in her head. Her blood pressure had soared. Suddenly, she did not like him anymore. "So you're probably pretty good with guns and explosives? Isn't that in the curriculum now? The wannabe terrorists are all running off to madrassas in Pakistan."

He wanted to deny it, but remembered how Jawad and his friends had been radicalised. "I was their enemy," he explained quietly. "I was the infidel. They are taught that all infidels want to destroy them. It is God's Will that all infidels must be killed." He shook his head slowly. "I was at a madrassa, but I was never... The other boys were encouraged to beat me. I was never allowed... I had to beg for food and water. When I tried to run away..." He shook his head. It was too painful.

She did not know what to say. This was about him. She did not want to hijack the conversation just to air her grievances while she had an audience. "How did you survive? Seven years? That must have been a nightmare?"

He nodded slowly. He felt her need for an explanation. "It is God's Will. It is a commandment from God. It was the last commandment from God, the All-Knowing and most Wise, to His Holiness, the Beloved Apostle, peace be upon him."

She was bristling, but reined in her temper. This was about him. "Was any one nice to you?"

He trembled and sighed then shook his head. "There was one teacher, Prof. Shah. He was very old. He hated the British, but he spoke English and German. He taught me to translate the Holy Book into English. He shouted at me, and was bad-tempered, but he was old and frail. When he became ill, I was permitted to take care of him. He called me Nazarene. He let me hide in his room when the other boys were..." His voice faded away.

She did not really want to comment.

He sighed. He wanted to tell the truth, but he knew she would not understand. "They are taught that they must fight everyone who does not believe in God and their Prophet or who does not acknowledge the Religion of Truth. They are taught that to be a martyr should be their one goal. Their family will be blessed with honours. They will go to paradise and be waited upon by beautiful virgins. They will dwell in paradise forever." He did not dare look at her. "They are righteous. What they are doing is righteous. It is a commandment from God. They must obey or they will go to hell and burn for eternity."

She was staring at him. She wanted him to break out into a smile as if it was all some big joke. It was shocking to realise that he was absolutely serious. But then he had obviously been thoroughly brainwashed if he had spent seven years at a madrassa in Pakistan. "So you are a Muslim now?"

He flinched. "I am a kafir," he explained gravely. "I must bow down before them. It would be unpardonable to allow me to be a Muslim now."

"That's what they call us, isn't it? We're all kafirs."

He nodded.

She sighed heavily, reaching out to pick up her cup of tea, but the cup was empty. She hardly knew what to say. "I don't understand how you could have possibly ended up at a madrassa in Pakistan?"

"Please?" He felt threatened. "Please? I don't know." He wanted her to leave him alone, but had never been allowed to have what he wanted. Under pressure, he sighed then shook his head again. At last, unhappily, he confessed: "They told me that I was a horrible child, and that my parents had sold me for money."

She wanted to believe that he was joking, but it was obvious that he believed every word. "I'm sure that's not true."

"I had to go to the madrassa to learn how to be a good Muslim. They punished me because I am horrible. They punished me because I am the son of imperialist swine. They punished me because I am a disbeliever. I have no honour. I am always the filthy kafir not good enough to wipe their feet. They must punish disbelievers because that is the Will of God. I had to learn to be a good Muslim, but I am always the Nazarene." He made a valiant attempt to smile. "My master's household is devout. It is important to him that I do not offend anyone."

"And did you offend anyone?" she asked mischievously.

He understood the question. "I am the evil blue-eyed jinn. Everyone is offended."

She tried to smile. She really had a problem with Islam.

"I think I was stolen away like the children in Kitgum. I think someone came in the night with a gun, and took all of the children away. It was so long ago. I don't remember what happened. Not my name. Not my family." He took a deep breath then looked at her. "I should remember, shouldn't I? If I was a good person...?"

"This isn't your fault. You mustn't blame yourself. Really, none of this is your fault." She wanted to suggest going to the police again, but did not want to scare him back into silence. "Well, that's a place to start: seventeen years plus probably five. We should be able to find a list of boys kidnapped during that timeframe." She really made an effort to sound confident. "It won't be easy, but it's a start." Then she frowned. "So what happened in Kitgum?"

He took a deep breath then drew his hand across his eyes. He was tired already. He felt obliged to answer her questions, but compelled by something stronger to stay silent. Being afraid was familiar territory, but now he was lost. "In Africa, a gang of drug-addicted fanatics were terrorising villages. They stole the children and killed the adults. They call themselves The Lord's Resistance Army. My master regularly visited the hospitals and camps. We all saw the children that had been rescued. I had never seen children hurt like that before." He wondered if he was a survivor. "It was horrible. They were - terribly mutilated. Many had lost limbs, but there were others that had lost their ears or noses or sometimes their lips." He shook his head again, still appalled by the savagery of the LRA.

There was a long silence before she nodded. "Ah, yes, I remember," she said. "That was northern Uganda. That was years ago. How did you hear about that? It barely made the news over here. Are those bastards still out there?"

He nodded. He had his face in his hands. "We went there. My master went there, and I accompanied him. I went everywhere with him. We visited some children that they had managed to rescue." He paused to try and control the sudden flood of memories. "It was horrible. They were just children." He rubbed his hands distractedly. "They were in a hospital. There were Peacekeepers and OAU soldiers. There were doctors. But there were no families. These children had no families or friends left alive. They were all dead." He tapped his forehead. "Traumatised by what had happened, they were just dead. And you knew that the children who were not disfigured were the ones that had become the killers. They tried to separate them. They were all victims, but some of them were also murderers." He tried to erase the memory by rubbing his eyes, almost gouging them from their sockets. But he gave up. "They are still hunting for Joseph Kony, but Africa is vast. They may never find him. Children are still being kidnapped and killed." He shook his head. "My master is a United Nations Ambassador. He was the Secretary General's Special Envoy." He glanced nervously towards her to see if she was impressed. "He is a very important man."

"Your prince?" She was actually shocked.

He nodded wearily. It was not the reaction he was hoping for.

"So you travelled together?"

He nodded again. His throat was dry. The painkillers were not killing anything.

She studied him intently. "So you must have had a passport? It might not have been your real name, but there had to be a name in that passport."

He smiled at her innocence, but continued his observation of the carpet. "No. I am a servant, who travels on his master's passport, which gives him diplomatic immunity. It is meant to protect me."

"He could do that?" She did not believe him. "No, there must have been a passport or a legal document. Even dogs have to have passports."

He flinched then admitted reluctantly: "I always travel as a female servant."

"A girl? Why?"

He could not answer. For a long time, he could not answer. He was ashamed and embarrassed, and squirmed like a guilty child. "I must wear the burqa."

She could not speak. He had a lovely face, but she knew the burqa had nothing to do with modesty. It was about control.

"As long as I am covered up no one interferes with me."

"A burqa? You mean that ghastly veil thing?"

"Please? I must wear the burqa to keep me safe."

She tried very hard to smile. "It's alright. I'm sure that's what they told you, but it also enables them to keep you out of sight."

"Please? No, you don't understand. No one may look at me without his permission. I belong to him. He would be offended if anyone tried to interfere with me." He breathed deeply. "He can be jealous. The burqa protects me." He sensed she was angry. "It is absolutely forbidden for a man to touch a veiled woman. It is supposed to protect her." He nodded affirmatively. "It is better for me."

"You wear a burqa?" She voice dripped with contempt.

"Please? You do not understand. No one may see my face." He was agitated and nervously ran his fingers through his hair. "It is about honour."

"So you travelled with him dressed like a girl?"

He nodded, staring at the floor in absolute misery. The tension made his head throb with pain. He was deeply humiliated.

"But in fact you were his valet?" She was struggling to be polite.

He nodded. "Please? You don't understand. It is to keep me safe. I would be taken away and killed if I was discovered. In the burqa, I am safe. No one has ever asked to see my face. That would have been disrespectful to my master. He is a great man."

"Yes, I'm sure, but as a woman, I have to say that no woman should need to hide behind a veil to guarantee her safety. A woman should be able to travel safely anywhere without the risk of being interfered with by anyone." She had upset him. She tried to smile, but he had withdrawn and was staring at the floor. Meryl Streep managed to smile, and asked pleasantly: "So you travel a lot?"

"Please? You don't understand. They must conceal themselves. They must cover their hair. They inflame desires in men which cannot be restrained. The women bring dishonour on their men. They must be veiled."

"That's surely more to do with men not being able to control themselves. They're at fault. Not the women!" He was staring at the carpet again. She wanted to shake him and shout at him, but it was pointless. "So why a burqa and not a niqab? Is that the right name? That's the Saudi version that hides everything but the eyes."

"I travel with the Pakistanis."

She watched him for a moment. He was trembling and pale. "I'm sorry," she said. "I didn't mean to upset you. It's just that as a woman I would find it totally offensive to have to wear a veil. It's so insulting. My modesty is my business. No one has the right to dictate that I have to put a bag over my head to be a modest respectable woman. And that any woman who doesn't wear a veil can expect to be interfered with is totally offensive." She took a moment to calm down then changed the subject. "So your master is an ambassador at the United Nations?"

He nodded, but could not look at her. "He is a great prince. He is an important man. I always take care of him. There are always meetings, hotels, airports. His work is vital. He visits the refugee camps operated by the United Nations. It is often very dangerous. So the bodyguards are essential. They keep him safe, but I look after him."

"You like him?" she asked gently.

He flinched. He shrugged. He stared doggedly at the floor. "He is my master."

She watched him for a while then went out to the kitchen. There were so many questions, but he was probably incapable of answering them truthfully, and she was not sure that she could hear the answers without completely losing her temper.

There was housework and gardening. She did not feel like doing either. Her blood pressure was much too high. She needed to calm down. She made a cup of tea then took another couple of pills then spent half an hour giving the hedgehog another bath while she waited for the pills to take effect. It was easier to focus on the hedgehog. Because she had not spent hours with it on her knee, it remained totally wild. It probably did not even consciously associate her with food so she was never disappointed when it remained curled up in a prickly ball while having its bath. It had gained weight which was tremendous, and she could not see any evidence of there being any more ticks. There were not even any dead ones in its bedding. Success! She grimly hung on to the positive with both hands.

*

It was late in the year, and at the high altitude, it was already very cold despite the crystal sunlight. He was swathed in the robes of a mountain tribesman with a scarf around his head in a crudely fashioned turban. On his feet, he wore a pair of sandals that were much too small with soles falling off and broken straps, all held together with knotted rags torn from the hem of his clothes. Other rags were wrapped around his palms and fingers, which he continually pulled and tweaked to provide cover and protection. He looked old and his beard was long. His once lovely hands were calloused and lacerated; the nails were torn and broken and permanently black with dirt. Where he lived now, alone in the darkness, there were no mirrors. His shining beauty had been utterly destroyed.

The work was not physically back-breaking anymore, but it never stopped being crushingly ignominious, and the smell permeated his whole body. He smelled as vile as the excrement that he had to scrape all night from the pits beneath the Turkish toilets then transport at dawn out to the valley floor where it was baked dry by the sun. Most of his day was spent inside the small windowless room that opened on to a staircase that no one ever used. He slept. He paced up and down. He was absolutely alone. There were infrequent trips to forage or to hunt, but he was merely the beast of burden. The men were always heavily armed. They wore the same clothes that he did, but he was the fetcher and carrier, and what he could not carry then he had to drag. At the end of each summer, he had to collect up the dried dung and carry it back up the endless steps to another room where the winter fuel was stored. When the snow was too deep, he piled the faeces at the cave mouth. As soon as the snow cleared, he had to move it across the valley floor.

He accomplished the tasks previously done by a whole family of Untouchables. The priests never blessed him. The Queen had forgotten that he existed. There were no more foul smells to offend her. He learned the language because he had to. Mansour was a humane man, and tried to make his life as comfortable as the circumstances allowed. There were no more lovers. Not even a blind man would have found him attractive now. He was lost again in a culture that was totally alien, and surrounded by a landscape that might have been on Mars. He had become an Untouchable.

*

After lunch, she took him outside to sit on a blanket on the lawn. He winced and grimaced as he went down on to his knees then settled a little more comfortably. She had forgotten about the delicate condition of the wounds on his back, but having committed him, she could not bring herself to make him climb back on to his feet, thus admitting she had made a mistake. She brought out a tray of tea. It was a lovely summer afternoon. The birds were singing. The bumble bees were bumping about from flower to flower. She looked like a jobbing gardener. He looked like royalty. He sat bolt upright. He had put on his jacket. The tie was in place. His shoes were still immaculate.

"So you were someone's lover," she said kindly.

He shook his head. He drew breath to speak then gazed away across the garden. "Please? It wasn't like that."

"That sheath that you were wearing, that was from a lover. It was a thing of beauty. It must have cost a fortune, and had probably been made bespoke for you." She watched him shift uncomfortably. "It was from your lover?"

He did not know how to answer that.

"It was strong and unbreakable," she said.

He breathed heavily. "Hitachi. The gemstones were added in Jaipur."

She leaned towards him, smiling. "Someone loved you very much."

He shook his head again, and stared down at his hands, which were clasped tightly in his lap.

"You're still alive because someone loved you. You must know that. If you were just some... if you were not loved then you'd be dead." She took a long moment to admire his beauty. Now, he was being enigmatic. It was an irresistible combination. "You were loved. It has to be the prince. Who else has the authority and resources to keep you like this?" She indicated his suit. "He has taken care of you, hasn't he? He's lavishly decorated your body. The tattoo, the tribal markings and the jewellery? All these years, he has kept you safe and well, and when you needed to go to the clinic, he paid all the bills. He must have loved you. These days, not many marriages last that long."

He flinched. "Please?" He tried to look at her, but his nerve failed. "You don't understand. It wasn't like that."

"So it was one of your Pakistanis?" she asked doubtfully. "They paid for those clothes? I couldn't afford the tie never mind the suit." She tried to smile. "Your prince? Your master? Your lover? They are one and the same." She waited for a reaction. "Come on, Daniel. May I call you Daniel?"

He nodded. His head went down even further.

"You didn't love him?" she asked. "That's okay. How could you after what happened? But he did love you. You must know that. I know it's difficult to understand, but it'll be so much easier for you if you accept that he did love you. He protected you and kept you safe. You said he never hurt you. Well, something happened recently, didn't it?"

He stared down at his hands. He had not moved at all. What could he say?

"So you were lovers. You were having an intense sexual relationship." She watched him for a while. "If he didn't hurt you, did he abuse you in other ways? Were you afraid of him?"

He carefully straightened his back which was suddenly painful. He really did not want to talk about it, but she would not let it go. "Please? I'm sorry. You don't understand."

"He loved you. That's the only reason that you are still alive. If he hadn't loved you, we wouldn't be having this conversation." He was trembling. She turned away to pour another cup of tea. It was hard to watch him when he was in such a state. He dashed a tear from his cheek. She sipped her tea. "You'll go insane if you deny the truth. I'm sure some terrible things happened. I'm sure there are things that you never want to tell anyone, but you must know that he loved you, because of or despite everything that happened to you. You have to acknowledge that he loved you, and hopefully that you did love him."

He shook his head. There was nothing he could say so he shook his head.

"You might not have been in love with him. It might not have been high romance. There probably weren't any flowers. But you were having a sexual relationship."

He just shook his head. He was struggling to remain calm. His heart rate had escalated. His head was pounding. He wanted to deny it all, but he could not be so dishonest.

"It's alright," she said. "Really, it'll be alright. Come on, Daniel. Just take a deep breath, and say it. You'll feel better, I promise. Just say it, Daniel." She tried to reach out and touch his elbow, but he lifted his arm away. "Just say it out loud."

"I'm not Daniel," he said. He could not look at her.

She felt the pain. "I'm sorry. I didn't mean to upset you. But you have to trust me." She wanted to say that she was older than him, and knew what she was talking about, but it seemed mildly patronising. "You have to trust me."

He stared down at his hands. The jaw muscles flexed. His brow furrowed. He was in turmoil, and he could not look at her.

"He loved you. You are alive so he must have loved you."

He shook his head. He was in distress. "Please? You're wrong. He could not love me. It's forbidden. It is forbidden. He does not." His eyes flashed as he looked at her then he stared at his hands, which clasped and unclasped anxiously. "He does not love me." He shook his head more emphatically. "He does not. Please, stop saying that. It is forbidden."

"I'm sorry," she said. She did not know what to say. It was impossible to avoid looking at him. He was in quite a state. "I'm so sorry." She felt compelled to touch his arm. "It'll be alright. You're safe here. Please, don't be upset."

He flinched then shook his head.

She wanted to give him a great big hug, but she couldn't. He would not like it. She would be humiliated and hurt and probably burst into tears. So she stroked his arm again. He seemed to be so far away, not just physically but mentally. "I'm sorry. Come on, baby. Come on. It'll be alright." She tried to tug on his sleeve, but he was so very far away. "We'll get you stronger." She tried to smile enthusiastically. "I have a great doctor. He'll find out what's wrong with you, and we'll fix it. You're not going to die. We'll find your family. They'll be so pleased to see you. It'll be lovely. You'll be able to put all of this behind you. Please, look at me."

He inhaled. He did not really believe her, but he managed to look at her, and he actually smiled.

She fairly blushed. Her heart fluttered a little. "I didn't mean to upset you."

He drew away sensing she was not being honest then withdrew into himself again like a snail in harm's way.

She gazed around the garden. Instinctively, she reached for the teapot to offer him another cup then saw him wince. "Would you like to go inside?" She waited for him to say something, but he had shut down. He was very pale, his face glistened, and he was shivering again. "I'll take you in." She quickly rose to her feet then reached down to offer him her hand.

He hesitated then reluctantly clasped her hand. She did not pull so he was allowed to take his time and gather his knees under him, then rise to stand. It took him more than a minute to regain his feet. He could stand taller now. The pain across his back had been aggravated. It slowed him down, it restricted some of his movements, but he could function reasonably well considering. "Thank you. You've been very kind."

She ignored the annoying words. It was not that he sounded insincere; she just felt he needed a bit of variety. Then she felt guilty.

They walked back to the house. She had her arm through his. They did not hurry. Various cats emerged as she neared the kitchen. From his gait, she could tell that he was growing stronger. He was not ready to try out for the track team, but he was able to walk almost unaided. She stayed with him all the way to the sofa, and smiled as he slowly lowered himself to sit close to the armrest. He was tired. She wanted to ruffle his hair. She wanted him to smile again, but he leaned away across the armrest.

While he drank a milkshake, she fetched in all the paraphernalia from the picnic then fed the cats. She carried the hedgehog back into the lounge in its olive oil bath. It was still a prickly ball, but it was healthy enough to be quite grumpy. There were still no visible ticks. She intended to keep it just a few more days then she would put the hutch out into the garden with the door open. For another few days, she would put food out, then the hedgehog was on its own. She knew the young man was watching her all the time. She was not embarrassed. She was in her element. It was certainly possible that the little hedgehog was a child or even a grandchild of one that she had saved in previous years. She could see its face now. The ticks had fallen off from its eyelids and cheeks and ears. It was altogether more fragrant, but its table manners were still appalling.

The young man was interested, but as soon as she moved to her feet, he lowered his gaze. She smiled at him then carried the bowl out to the scullery. When she came back, he was asleep. She pulled a blanket down over him, and silently admired his beauty for a while then went out to the shops. He had definitely earned an ice cream.

She was determined to watch her favourite programme. She had missed two episodes. She did not feel that she was being selfish. The World Cup had really only just started. She was sure it would be a marathon rather than a sprint. She had missed most of the tennis at Queens because she had wanted to spend time with the young man.

The news about Nadal was actually worrying. It seemed that he could also play on grass.

The young man visibly stiffened with tension whenever she glanced towards him for the rest of that day. She still had questions, but it was obvious that he was in no fit state to answer any more.

Devon was lovely. She really liked Bill's shirt. The Dabchick nest had been predated again, but Bill was sure that they would try for a third time. The Kingfishers were busy in the river. The male caught a fish for the female. They were behind a bush, but it was obvious what he wanted. She quickly swallowed the fish then did a bit of wing-shivering, and he was in or rather on. She accommodated him, but her tail was in the way. That did not slow down her suitor at all. The wings were flapping like mad. He was obviously hanging on to her flanks for grim death. It was definitely a wham bam. There was no foreplay at all. He was on her back and inside and gone in a moment. There was no fondness. He was not even tender. Having had his way, he was off. Bill observed that if only that happened in real life he would carry a tin of sardines around with him. Kate laughed. He always had a rejoinder. He liked to make people laugh.

The bird colony in Shetland was loud and crowded. The Fulmers at Sumburgh Head were busy feeding their chicks. They apparently mated for life, which could be thirty years, and were often seen preening each other's feathers. Their devotion to each other was not carried over into their relationships with their neighbours. There were fierce battles over nest sites. There was always at least one of them on the nest to protect it from marauders. Their beaks were very sharp, and they were extraordinarily gifted when it came to vomiting on their enemies, which apart from being unpleasant was seriously damaging to their feathers.

There was a golf course making sure that its 'rough' was wildlife friendly. They had even gone to the expense of building an artificial sand bank to attract Sand Martins. And now they had nesting Sand Martins. Everyone was very pleased. But there were no badgers anywhere. As usual the badgers had an aversion to being on live television, but they were everywhere when the programme was off the air. They took over the small mammal feeding station, which was certainly not designed to take their weight. Their table manners were actually worse than the hedgehog's. They seemed to spend most of their time just eating or scratching or sleeping, but never on live television. Bill was issuing ultimatums that if they did not put in an appearance then they would not be on Autumnwatch. Of course, no badgers. But they would be on Autumnwatch because everyone loved them. Farmers were adamant that they caused Bovine TB, but no one outside the industry really believed it, and if they did then they needed to be immunised. No one seemed to be prepared to pay for that. And if it was Bovine TB then, surely, the cows were the carriers?

The Pips were still not pupping. There were jokes about anyone knowing how to induce bats contacting the studio. The Red Kites in Rockingham were still doing well. The chicks were growing fast, and had not yet resorted to eating their siblings, which the Buzzards had done. A ranger had needed to go up a ladder and remove some plastic rubbish from the nest as it was likely to hurt the chicks. Casanova was a superstar. The Swallows were lovely. Runty was still alive.

The young man was asleep. He had had a tough day. She pulled the blanket up around his shoulders then went out to the kitchen to make a cup of tea. It was too early to go to bed, and she did not feel like prowling around the garden with a torch. Returning to the lounge, she put a can of milkshake down for him just in case he awoke. It did not even take a conscious thought for her to reach for the remote. She pressed 'play' and settled to share one hundred precious minutes with Big Shoulders. Later, she renewed her acquaintance with Nathan Brittles. Trooper John Smith was lovely, and Ben Johnson certainly knew how to ride a horse.

It was past midnight when Daniel awoke. She helped him back up the stairs, and hovered on the landing while he undressed. He was definitely getting better.

Chapter 36

She hardly knew where to start. She had no resources. She had promised to help him, and she really wanted to, but she was a lonely middle-aged woman, and she was ill. She would have to go out, and confront her worst fears, ask strangers for help, and then possibly find some obscure clue that might be the golden key to unlocking his past. There was no real hope of success.

She longed to be able to go back and change everything. When she found him, she should have driven into the village and asked for help. She should have faced her demons. The agony of having her space violated would have been easier than everything that had happened since. The invasion by the police would have been intense and harrowing. They would have asked questions she did not want to answer. For twenty-four hours, they might have made her life a living hell. Hindsight made it seem such a small price to pay, but confronting it then in the anxiety of the moment, she could not do it.

They would have taken him away so quickly that she would never have known him. That was the price that she was not sure that she could have paid. He had filled up her life completely. His mere physical presence had engulfed her. He had excited her sexuality when nothing more than an invalid. With only his eyes he had conversed with her heart and soul. He simply filled her up, but he was also the dynamite that had shattered her illusions. She was not in control. She was hiding from everything that signified a life. She would not see what upset her. She would not hear what contradicted her view of the world. She had built her defences so well that she did not see that they were the walls that she could not climb to escape the prison she had made so carefully.

For years, she had been shutting down all her femininity. She had focused all her emotions on the cats and the wildlife and her land. She had stopped thinking about herself as a woman. She barely remembered being a woman. Her life was completely contained within the rigid inflexible prison of her fears. No one could have breached her defences. She had been so safe. She had never considered for a moment that she was lonely or unhappy. There were not enough hours in the day for her to do all the work, care for all the animals, and live in her head where she could pretend

398

to be happy. Like a Trojan Horse, she had brought him into her home. She had surrendered to him because he was so fragile. She had become enslaved at the sight of his naked flesh. He had secured her devotion when he opened his eyes. He had only to look at her with those glittering eyes for a fire to ignite and burn throughout her body. He had made her a woman again. He had made her a flowering girl. The dead years had fallen away like old tree bark. She knew passion. In the solitude of his silence, she had recognised a hunger. She wanted him insanely, desperately, and lustfully when he was utterly defenceless. She had never experienced such an obsession before. Had he never regained consciousness, she might have loved him in that thwarted agonising way, and been happy and miserable, but never content. As soon as he began to speak, he was transformed again. He was vulnerable. He was sick and wounded and incredibly needy, but it was not until he actually said something that he became a human being. Her coarse and vulgar lust had died with shame. Her compassion focused. It did not matter who he was, he had become a human being, and had a right to be treated with respect. That he was a thing of beauty only intensified her desire to help him.

There were things that she could never tell him. She did not believe that anyone was capable of understanding why she had not been able to call for an ambulance or the police. Remembering how she had pushed and shoved him into her wheelbarrow still made her cringe with guilt. It seemed so appalling to keep making excuses, but who could guess that he had been hurt like that. She thought he had fainted. She did not know. How could she have known? There were so many secrets that she had to keep forever. He had secrets, but she had so many more. She felt like a hypocrite telling him that he must talk about what had happened. She never could. She reasoned that he was different. She was ill. She had always been ill. He had every hope of a full recovery.

His eyes were utterly mesmerising. When he looked at her, it felt like a kiss. The thrill of it never waned. It was like bathing in stardust. That he had made such an effort to avoid looking at her was irritating and puzzling. In the beginning, she had been offended. Her lack of self-esteem guaranteed that it felt like an insult. But with words came understanding. It was deference. His eyes were subdued. His quietness was respect. His docile manners were dictated by his circumstances.

"You were abducted," she said. She felt she needed to announce it so that he could prepare for whatever happened next.

They were in the garden again sitting on the blanket. He had taken off his jacket and rolled up his sleeves. He had even loosened his tie. But that was as far as he would go. He looked a picture. He was Narcissus, and she was captivated.

"I'll find out what we need to do." She smiled, and glowed when he looked at her. "No. I won't go to the police. We'll do it your way."

He nodded and smiled then his eyes strayed away to the treeline. It did not matter that he was hardly strong enough to walk across the lawn, he was simply not programmed to go off alone and explore.

She surveyed his face with admiration. It was actually a struggle to focus on anything but his extreme physical beauty. She found it difficult to finish her sentences. She was constantly just staring at him, and imagining that they were making love. Obviously, Meryl Streep would behave with decorum. So she tried to sit upright, and pull her shoulders back, and have all the sang-froid of the great actress. Being someone else had always been her best defence. When she was really under pressure, she could turn in a Katherine Hepburn that would have set the oceans ablaze.

"I think you're mid to late twenties. That means you were kidnapped probably in the mid-eighties. They told you that you are British? That certainly helps."

"Yes." He looked at her. It was still difficult for him to volunteer information. He frowned and stared down at his hands. "Achmed Qadri told me that. He said Prof. Shah hated me because I was British. He said it wasn't my fault."

She hesitated, acknowledging again that there were always more questions than answers. It was doubtful that she would ever be able to have a conversation with him that was not primarily an interrogation. "It's alright." She tried to smile nicely for him. "We'll sort it out, Daniel. You don't have to worry about anything. Honestly, it'll be all alright."

He gazed at her shrewdly, and nodded then stared back at his hands. He was still frightened. He did not know how to tell her that it really was dangerous. She was not equipped to fight his enemies. She seemed too naïve to understand what she was up against. "They're very powerful," he said quietly.

She frowned. She hardly dared to believe that he was about to reveal something significant.

He made his habitual awkward shrug. He found it difficult to quickly translate the maelstrom of words filling his head into coherent sentences. The only words he had ever been allowed to say were when he pledged submission. Sometimes, he was allowed to say 'yes', but never 'no'. He could not refuse or decline or resist. At the madrassa, Prof. Shah had him translating the Holy Book into English then German, and frequently shouted at him for being thick, but he had such a limited vocabulary that it was almost an impossible task. At the madrassa, he learned several languages, but only a limited number of words. Later, when Prof. Shah was ill, they spent a great deal of time together, and the professor told him stories about his home in Patna. They were magical stories of a golden childhood, which opened his mind to ideas and images that were totally alien at the madrassa. But he had never needed to be able to speak aloud until he was required to read poetry to the Prince. Mahmood had spent many hours every day coaching him. Learning to read English texts had opened his mind to the world, but sorting out his own thoughts and vocalising them still required a conscious effort. Half the time, he was thinking in three languages simultaneously. Having watched enough television to drive any sane man mad, he had expanded his vocabulary still more, and acquired a grasp of modern idioms. But under pressure, he was invariably mute.

"It's alright," she said. She reached out to squeeze his arm. He looked like a lost child. Her brain was sending out so many mixed messages.

He nodded slowly. He could not look at her. "My master's family are very powerful, very important. To prevent a scandal, they will kill us all without a second thought." He visibly shivered. "I don't know what to do."

"You're safe here," she insisted earnestly.

He shook his head. "You don't understand. How did I come here? They brought me here. They left me in your garden."

Her blood suddenly turned cold. "They know you're here?" But then she realised that they obviously knew. She had already worked that out for herself. She smiled again. "But it's alright. That doesn't matter."

He shook his head. "It has to be true," he said. "They know. It's the only explanation."

She wanted to reassure him. "Well, he knew you wanted to go home. Maybe, your family are living in this area? Perhaps, he was helping you?" She hardly believed it, but it was better than the other answer. "But if he was letting you go home why did he hurt you? It couldn't be more conspicuous. It was bound to raise red flags all over the place. It was guaranteed to bring in the police. And the police can't keep a secret to save their own lives so it would have been leaked to the Press, and been a sensational headline." She could not tell him why she had not called the police. It wasn't a morbid fear of publicity. "Was it someone else? Did someone else hurt you? I thought it was your prince. I assumed…"

He shook his head. He could not remember anything. How could he explain what he could not remember? "You don't understand. There'll be no scandal. It'll all be hushed up. They're so powerful that no one would dare write a story that might upset them." He paused to smile wistfully. He actually managed to smile. "My master is not like them." He nodded to underline his conviction. "He is a really good man, but many of his family are corrupt degenerates. They are all wealthy. They are so rich that there is nothing and no one that they cannot buy. They get drunk and make jokes about how they will steal more children or this actress or that supermodel. The young princes are the worst. There is absolutely nothing for them to do. If they get into trouble then they are granted retroactive diplomatic immunity. It doesn't matter whether they have a parking ticket or were caught raping a thirteen-year-old girl. Vast sums of money are handed over to shut up the victims or their families, but there is no justice."

She shook her head. She had to remember to close her mouth and breathe. "You're exaggerating, surely?"

"The French Secret Service and local police consistently turn a blind eye to the disappearance of underage girls onto yachts in the Mediterranean. The Cote d'Azur is one of their favourite destinations. They like Los Angeles. They like to go hunting were the girls are easy. They rape them then pass them around their friends. Then they just throw them away."

"That's terrible." She hardly knew what to say. "How do you know all this? It can't be true. It just wouldn't be allowed. Someone somewhere would be shouting about it. It would be on the news. The tabloid 'papers would be having a field day."

"In America, there are organised procurers. It's run like a business. They know exactly what sort of product is required. The US State Department condones it as an acceptable collateral cost of importing oil from the Gulf States. So many children go missing, and the local police are trained to deal with it as a local crime, but it's not local, it's a multinational business." He was staring at his hands. He was not really speaking to her. He was just talking aloud because she had said that it would make him feel better. "If they get caught then they go home to cool off for a while, but they always come back. They treat the girls like dolls. If they get attached to them or they're forced to leave the country in a hurry then they'll smuggle the girls back home. They might keep them for a while in their secluded houses then when the girls are finished, they're dumped out in the desert. They are never found because no one ever goes looking for them."

"No! No, honestly, that can't possibly be true." She shook her head. "No. It can't be true."

He frowned. "I read about it in an English newspaper," he said flatly. He took a moment to fill his lungs and anchor his courage. "People don't want to know that bad things happen unless it affects them directly. The price of oil affects everyone. These princes are above the law because they control oil production. They all have diplomatic immunity. They have so much money and power, and no reason to behave when the law allows them to do anything."

"I thought they were Muslims. Islam cannot possibly condone this?" She stared at him. "It simply would never be allowed. Most of the criticism of Islam is because it's so unforgiving." She tried to sound reasonable. "So you saw all of this happening?"

He leaned towards her. "You believe the myth. The public face of Islam are the clerics. Some Jews eat bacon. Some Muslims drink alcohol. Men are men. In your country is it not only the old women who keep Christianity alive?"

She had no answer for that.

"My master is not like them," he insisted. "He is a good man. He is a great man."

"But you say that you belong to him? You said he may do as he pleases?"

He flinched. "He is an honourable man." He felt compelled to explain. "I was given to him. I was a gift from an old friend. He could not refuse a gift. It was a matter of honour."

She drew a long deep breath to argue, but backed down. She did not want to burst the bubble of loyalty and perhaps affection that he obviously retained for his master. It might be the only thing that was keeping him sane.

"So all of this was going on around you?" she asked.

He frowned then shook his head. He took a longer moment to find his voice again. "I heard things. Servants like to gossip. Even amongst the servants there were those who went to pray five times a day only because they must. It is the law. It is Sharia. They must submit. There are many men who do not believe in God, but they go to the mosque. They pray. It is an unpardonable crime not to believe in God." He glanced across to read her expression. "He was offered a million dollars for me. He was given diamonds."

She was beginning to repeat everything in her head again.

"Yes." He tried to smile and failed. "It was not meant to be flattering.

My master had become increasingly isolated from his family. He was saying things that upset them. He was asking questions that no one was allowed to ask. There was one young prince, who would be denied nothing. He wanted me. He had had everything else that his heart desired, but it became a personal insult that he could not have me."

"He wanted to buy you?" she asked in shock.

For a while, he stared at his hands. He had stopped breathing. His face was a white mask. "Please? No. It wasn't like that." He grimaced then slowly shook his head. She was wrong. Saying it out loud did not make him feel any better. He filled his lungs again. He hardly knew how to put it into words. "He only wanted to fuck me. He could be... He had a reputation. I would almost certainly have died. Everyone understood the risk. My master did not want to send me to him, but it was a matter of honour. He had no choice."

She bit her tongue. It was obvious that he was telling the truth.

He was pale and trembling, and he was lost.

"That's terrible," she said, and felt useless and inept. She just did not know what else to say. "Why didn't they arrest him? He sounds like a serial killer. Surely, it didn't matter who he was if he was a murderer?"

He filled his lungs slowly then cleared his throat. "You don't understand. He was promising to pay blood money. That absolved him of any crime. The million dollars was not for using me, but compensation to my master for the loss of his property." He swallowed with difficulty. "I am a slave. I have no protection under the law except as the property of my master. This young prince could have paid one hundred million dollars. No one could refuse such a sum. It was about honour."

"Would your master have refused one hundred million dollars?"

He sighed and shook his head. "Everything has a price. They can offer so much money. But he could not refuse."

She was surprised. "But you said that he was one of the richest men in the world? He didn't need the money. Surely, he was incorruptible?"

He shook his head again. "You don't understand. The young Prince Bandar would have paid off the servants or the bodyguards or the chauffeur. If he had made up his mind, I'd have been pulled out of a car on the highway or carried off in the confusion at an airport. If he wanted me enough to offer such a ridiculous sum of money then my master would have given me to him just as a generous host must share his good fortune with his guests. If Prince Bandar wanted me so badly then it was good manners for my master to give me to him and not to take a penny."

"Even if he killed you?" She was aghast. "You can't be serious."

He grimaced and shrugged awkwardly. "It was a matter of honour. Prince Bandar would have been humiliated if he was forced to bribe servants to get what he wanted. My master would have seemed ungracious if he forced Prince Bandar to such lengths over such an insignificant thing." He glanced towards her. "You forget that in their eyes I am nothing. I'm a kafir. I'm nothing. The only value that I have is as a decorative object. When I lose my looks, I will have no value at all. No one will want me then. I will have no protection."

"He loves you. You must know that he loves you. I know you've been hurt, but he has loved you."

"They are righteous. They believe they are doing God's Will. I am an infidel. Everything they have done to me is God's Will. While I am beautiful, my master will keep me safe. I am not foolish enough to believe that he will want me when I am old and ugly. He will find someone younger. One of his wives sent an assassin to throw acid in my face. I was lucky. Omar saved me. If she had succeeded, I would have already been fed to the jackals." He frowned and nodded unhappily. "He might not have waited for me to die before throwing me away. I am decorative. That is all that I am."

She could not believe it. "I'm sure he's genuinely fond of you. He's kept you all this time. He found you a doctor when you were ill."

"I am his," he said simply. "He may do as he pleases. I am honoured to serve him, but I know he will abandon me."

"But he did protect you," she said with relief. "He didn't give you away. He did actually care for you."

He was engagingly embarrassed. "No. I am promised. Prince Bandar is still waiting. Had I not been ill, I am sure I would have been made available to him. My master is an honourable man. He would not do anything that might cause offense to a member of his family."

"A member of his family?"

"I believe you would consider them second cousins."

"No, I'm sure he valued you. You're free now."

He smiled, but shook his head. "This is about honour." He hesitated then looked at her. "Am I really free?"

Her brain was hurting. Her heart was in pieces. "Yes, of course. It'll be alright, I promise." She could not begin to understand how it must feel to be just a commodity. "I'm so sorry."

"I was a gift. He cannot give me my freedom. That is not possible. It is not possible so why am I here?"

"You talk about it as if you were just a piece of bric-a-brac."

He did not understand that.

"So he could give you to this Prince Bandar, but not sell you to him? But if you died then your master would be compensated? And you would have died because everyone knew that Bandar was a complete psycho?"

He shrugged. He wished he had not started the conversation. "You don't understand. This is about honour."

"So he'd give you to this psycho?" She was absolutely appalled.

"You don't understand. He threatened to sell me a thousand times. He could give me to whomever he chose. Sometimes, he was serious. He may leave me to slowly starve to death just because it amuses him. He does not need a reason. Every moment of my life is focused on making me necessary to him. He will never give me my freedom. The last Commandment from God to the Holy Apostle was to kill or enslave all disbelievers. There is nothing else."

"But that's barbaric. And it was so long ago. That's like saying we have to eat fish on Fridays or go to jail. It's ridiculous. No one can be expected to live their lives according to some unsubstantiated superstitious nonsense some guy came up with more than a thousand years ago. Could he even read and write?"

He shrugged again. He really did not know how to explain it to a woman. "We cannot criticise the Prophet. He is loved by God, the All Knowing. You just don't understand. I'm a kafir. They are taught from birth that disbelievers are their enemies. It is their duty to punish us because we do not believe in God or His Messenger." He knew she did not want to understand. "Who are you to say that they are wrong? If everyone believed in the one god and the true religion and obeyed Sharia then everyone would be happy and content. If you were a Muslim, you would not have to be alone."

"I don't care. It's barbaric. Religion should be about a freedom of intellect. No one should be enslaved. No one should be forced to submit to another's will. Don't you want to be free?"

"They throw away food all the time, but never give me any. They starve me. They say I must fast to do penance because I am an infidel. They believe that denying me food is righteous. I must submit. I am an infidel. I'm a kafir. God hates me. They all believe that." He took a moment to frown and shake his head. "So I must fast and bow down and I ask for mercy. And they insist that I am grateful because God hates me."

"How did you stay alive?"

He flinched then hesitated. It seemed such a ridiculous question. "They kept me alive."

"Yes." She lowered her gaze. He was in distress. "I'm sorry. Of course, you were a captive. You didn't have a choice. It must have been terrible." She reached out to rest a hand on his arm as a gesture of support. "You've been so brave. And you're safe now. No one will hurt you like that again."

He could not look at her.

"Do you remember anything about your past life? Are there any memories? Do you ever dream about it?"

He shook his head. He was tired. He felt he had said enough.

"Do you remember who whipped you?" She watched him shake his head again. "What was the last thing that you remember?"

"We were at the house in Paris. Omar was with me. We were waiting for my master to return."

"You'd been at the clinic?"

He was surprised, then remembered. They had already had this conversation. He nodded, suspecting a trap.

She tried to shrug. "It just seems odd to me that the Prince would have hurt you so badly. And you liked Omar so I'm sure he wouldn't have hurt you."

He fairly choked as he blurted out: "They beat me all the time!" He took a deep breath to steady his nerves. He took more than a moment to find his voice again. "My master insisted that I was beaten regularly so that I always carried the marks. It was done to protect the servants from temptation." He shook his head and trembled. It took him a minute to find the words. "In some tribes the men are very proud of their virility. They like to have sex. It is an important part of their culture." He hesitated to see if she understood then flinched. "They take great pride in their physical ability to perform. They talk about it all the time. They boast to their friends. They are obsessed with sex, but there are no women. They keep their women hidden away. There are never any women. But the men must have sex. It is about being respected. They are proud men, and to be considered men then they must prove their strength and their virility to have respect." He shook his head. "But there are no women so they must satisfy their appetites with boys. It is a great sport to rape young boys. Some believe it is more acceptable to fornicate with a kafir, but there are so many little boys..." He shifted uncomfortably. "There were many servants and soldiers. In the absence of little boys, I was available for the single men or those whose families were far away, but my master disapproved. He could not criticise them because it is traditional. It is part of their culture, but I was marked so that they would know they were offending God."

"That hardly seems fair. Why didn't he just lay down the law with them or keep you away from them?"

"In Pakistan and Afghanistan there are many old traditions. They like pretty boys. They are kept like pets. Bus drivers, lawyers, butchers and bakers, if they can afford it, they keep their boys with them, and pass them around their friends. There is much prestige and honour in possessing a pretty boy. To have the prettiest boy is a prize worth killing for. The families are paid off. The police are complicit. It is an accepted part of their culture."

She nodded. She did not want to believe it, but knew it was true. "Yes, I've read about it. And it was in a James Michener novel. And there have been problems in Afghanistan." She looked at him critically, and knew the answer before she had even asked the question: "Did you dance?" His face betrayed him. She took a deep breath, and tried to smile bravely. He was a victim. It was not his fault. He was not a filthy whore. She felt quite sick. He was a victim. He was absolutely and definitely a victim. He was helpless. It wasn't his fault. She tried another smile. "Well, the Greeks certainly did it. I believe it used to be called 'Greek Love'. Of course, young male prostitutes were all called 'Arab Boys'. I wonder why they were not 'Greek Boys'? I think men were more openly bi-sexual then, and family planning was non-existent. It was likely to be good practice, and probably saved many young women from an early death. The Romans were also bi-sexual. You have only to look at their art. The Turks don't exactly have a good reputation either. There is a classical history of men taking boys from their families and mentoring them. They teach them usually to be warriors, but there was always a sexual element. The boys were bound by a contract to the alpha male. They had to surrender their families and their childhood. From our perspective it's barbaric, but back then it was about survival. The best fighters became the best soldiers and stayed alive. The strongest alpha male was undoubtedly the best teacher and mentor. There was probably competition between the alpha males. Families paid a lot of money for their son to go to the toughest teacher.

When all the boys were being buggered it would not have been seen as a problem. It was normal practice. It was traditional. Those boys grew up, and if they survived as warriors then they became the alpha males that the next generation came to for an education. And who's to say that it wasn't a perfectly normal healthy relationship? Someone somewhere has decided that it's unhealthy. Someone else has passed a law. But if they were equals? If there was love? If both parties were in love? It is a completely different scenario if it's violent and abusive. But if there is love?"

He lowered his gaze when she looked at him. He managed to nod, but he did not want to comment.

"So he had flogged you like this before?" she asked quietly.

"He never hurt me."

"But…"

The pain in his chest was acute. He ground his teeth together, and waited for it to ebb away. His brain was on fire. He struggled to find the right words in English. There were tears swimming in his eyes. "He did not hurt me," he said with conviction. "But he enjoyed it."

She stared at him. "You mean…"

He shuddered violently. "He took pleasure in my wounds." He could hardly say the words: "He was always more interested when I was hurt and bleeding."

"So it was sadomasochism?"

He was too upset to even shake his head.

"And this was every day?"

He rallied slowly. "Yes, almost every day. I had to go to his study or to his hotel room. I stripped naked then one of my Pakistanis would thrash me across my backside until they were told to stop."

"He was there? He watched?"

His face crumpled up. "No. Sometimes. Occasionally. If he was not there then Omar had a camera. If he was not there, he wanted proof that I was being marked. He wanted them to stop committing a sin. It was to save them. It was not about hurting me. He told me."

"And it was Mahmood? Your Pakistanis? Your friends who took care of you?"

"It wasn't like that. They had to do it. I was never hurt like this." He trembled as all his wounds protested. "They did take care of me. It wasn't like this. I wasn't ever hurt like this. They did take care of me. You don't understand. I am a kafir. I am their enemy. You are their enemy. What they were doing to me was righteous. God has decreed that disbelievers must be killed or enslaved."

"And this has been going on for ten years?"

He stared at his hands. "You don't understand. He didn't hurt me. He would never hurt me."

It was obvious that he was lying. She turned away to stare at the garden. She did not want to see the tears in his eyes.

"I thought Islam was a religion of peace." She glanced towards him then gazed at the treeline. "We've had five years of people coming on the TV, and saying that Islam is peaceful. Is all that a lie? If they are all secretly planning to murder us then that isn't very peaceful."

He did not say anything for a long time, then breathed deeply. "Please? You only know the bad things. The Holy Prophet did say that they must kill Jews and disbelievers, but it was only a rallying cry in the midst of a battle. My master has pointed this out at conferences and in mosques. He has made enemies. The radicals have used these words to raise an army. My master says they are abusing children with lies. They are not taught about the community and compassion or that we are all the sons of Abraham. They are only taught about hatred and killing. My master says it is the teachers who are to blame. He says the teachers must be held responsible and put on trial. Only Muslims can do this. If the Americans invade even with the best motives, every Believer must oppose them."

"Which is totally infantile." She shook her head. "Saudi should have sorted this out years ago. How many people have died because they wouldn't sort out their mullahs?"

*

It was a warm day in New York and a cold day in Afghanistan. September 11th 2001.

He did not know what had happened. So much had changed recently. The arrival of dozens of uniformed Arabs with automatic weapons had upset the locals. They had been sent by Prince Abdul Aziz to protect the people of the mountain, but they were not welcome guests. They had set up a satellite dish, and brought the world into the mountain. At first, the locals had disdained to be impressed. Then on a Tuesday there were live pictures from New York. The world changed in a moment. The shock penetrated every heart. There were half finished sentences and disbelief. It was something about planes and buildings and possibly tens of thousands of

Americans having been killed. A war had begun. New York had been attacked by passenger planes. The tallest buildings had collapsed. And bin Laden? His name was mentioned a lot. There were arguments about him. Some of the newly arrived Arab guards refused to accept that a Muslim could kill so many. It had to be a Zionist conspiracy. A few suggested that bin Laden was insane. The Americans would drop nuclear bombs. The world would be destroyed in a fireball because bin Laden and Al Qaeda had attacked America. They said that the evil President Bush would retaliate big time. He would blow up the Middle East. He would hunt down and kill every Muslim on the planet. The kafir listened to the crumbs of information that reached his lonely existence, and he tried to work it out. He could not believe that any Muslim would kill so many innocent people. It was forbidden. It was absolutely forbidden. He was easily persuaded as the guards were persuaded that it was all a cunning Zionist American plot. It was typical of the Jews, who were all butchers and terrorists. They would kill anybody. They would tell such lies. They had made Israel from stolen Palestinian land. Everyone knew that killing a Jew brought one closer to God. It was written. It was halal. Half of America was probably Jewish or gay so perhaps killing all Americans was now halal.

There was more news the next day. The Arabs were so distracted by it they forgot to let the kafir out of his foul smelling hell until lunch time, and were too angry to be bothered with nurse-maiding him outside. They were talking about becoming holy warriors for Islam. They were loud about slaughtering Jews, infidels and crusaders. Jihad was a righteous duty. Any man who failed to fight was a coward and worse, he was not a Muslim. Bin Laden had declared war on America because of the oppression, tyranny and humiliation that America and the Jews had forced upon all Muslim brothers. America deserved what it got. Bin Laden had struck merely the first blow. He would make God the Lord of the World. There must be no law but the Koran and no God but Allah. His word is truth and Islam is perfect. America deserved ten thousand deaths.

Not for the first time, the kafir was ashamed of his white skin. When soldiers came that he knew from his days as the Pakistanis' dancing boy, he believed their rejection of him was because of his white skin. He accepted that he was a living insult to God. He had no mirrors to see the changes wrought on his appearance. He could not see that he was totally unrecognizable.

Chapter 37

He slept most of the afternoon on the sofa. She drifted in and out. The bird feeders needed filling up again. The Starlings were still monopolising the fat balls in the walled garden. The main garden was full of fragrance and flowers and weeds. In the space of a few hours, she had managed to fill up the wheelie bin. She was trying not to think about him, but after what he had said, she was bursting with more questions. Of course, she knew that she had upset him. What he had said was enlightening and horrifying. She wanted to know more, but it seemed cruel to keep on pressing him. Her rationale that he would feel better if he talked about it was probably accurate, but it was also selfish. Did she really need to know? She could certainly justify her need. While she was in the garden, it was easy to reel off a long list of imperative justifications. In the house, it was harder. His fragile features spoke to her heart. Making demands on him made her feel like a ghoul. In his presence, all her maternal instincts and her guilty conscience were in overdrive. Her poor old hormones were very confused.

During a tea break, she went to sit in the lounge. She had not made a sound, but he woke up, and twisted uncomfortably to sit upright with his feet on the floor. He looked pale and tired and old.

"It's alright," she said softly. "You mustn't worry. We'll get you better, and find your family. It'll be alright."

He nodded slowly, but did not lift his eyes from the carpet.

She wanted to give him a hug, and kiss him to make it all better as if he were some fretful child. But she could not touch him. He was not a kitten to be played with. He was still the most beautiful thing she had ever seen, but he was so damaged, and though guiltless, he had undoubtedly been tainted by his ordeal. It was all about sex. He was definitely compromised. She tried to imagine what it must have been like to be so completely enslaved.

"You've done really well today," she said and smiled. It was a great big Oscar winning smile.

He might have acknowledged her with a fleeting look, but stared at the floor with such rapt attention that she just deflated.

"You're tired," she told him. "Do you feel any better about what happened to you? You've managed to talk about it. You've been so brave."

He stiffened immediately. "I didn't tell you anything."

She blinked. She thought he might have been joking, but he was in deadly earnest. "But the degenerate princes? You said..."

"That was in The Times. That's in the public domain. I haven't told you anything."

She was surprised by his tone. "And Prince Bandar?"

"Please? I'm sorry. I didn't. I didn't say anything."

"But..." She shut up. He was very upset. She wanted to remind him about the million dollars, but changed her mind. He was lying stubbornly like a child so there was no reasoning with him. "It's alright," she said kindly. "It doesn't matter."

He knew she knew. "Please? You can't tell anyone. You've been very kind, but it's dangerous. If I say anything then they'll know. I swore an oath. They'll come here and kill us. I'm sorry, but you don't understand."

"It's dangerous?" she asked. She had not even thought about that. In her quiet, private world there was nothing to fear. Beyond her borders were the dragons. She was as short-sighted as the Flat-Earthers before 1492. She actually managed to laugh. "No one will come here. And who would I tell? The cats?"

He shook his head. His face was white. He really could not say anything else.

She read the vow of silence in his expression. "It's alright." She ruffled his hair, and smiled again. "You watch the television. There's an England game on. If we don't win this one, we should hang our heads in shame. It's one of those tiny principalities like Monaco or San Marino or Wales. Andorra, maybe? Anyway, you can watch it. I'm going back outside. Come and find me if you get lonely."

She went out to the garden. His fierce denial was a surprise, but she reasoned that he had every right to be anxious. When she came back in to feed the cats, and give him some painkillers, he did not even look at her. She gave him yogurt and a cup of tea then had a cheese sandwich on her own in the kitchen. The deaf old lady cat made a fuss until she had her fill of cheese crumbs. The black cat with the yellow eyes watched everything from the draining board. She talked to them about the state of the garden and the turnaround in the weather. Some plants were early and others were late. It was a situation she had never seen before. The terrible spring had turned into a hot summer almost overnight. She was still expecting the temperature to fall again and rain to come, and everything to be ruined, but so far the fine weather was holding. If it did not rain soon then she would have to start thinking about watering the garden with a hosepipe.

Later, she watched Springwatch. It was the last programme in the series for that year. She knew she would miss it terribly. She was even happy to see Bill had his England scarf, and had a string of flags draped across the studio. Apparently, England had won. They were through. She did not know exactly what that meant, but Bill was pleased.

In twelve weeks, there would be Autumnwatch.

She gazed at the young man, who was laid out on the sofa. As usual, he was protecting his back. He did not need her constantly reminding him to be careful. It was a huge wound that was still very painful.

*

Prince Abdul Aziz was in Manhattan that dreadful day. He could see the smoke from his hotel window. Like the rest of the world, he saw it all unfold on the television. He had never experienced such a cataclysmic event. He was shocked, alarmed, and ashamed. He was impotent. For the first time in his life there was absolutely nothing that he could do, and he was angry. The confusion and horror that everyone could hear in the voices on the television were not his. He knew from the moment that it was announced that a plane had flown into the Twin Towers: it was a terrorist attack. It was Al Qaeda. He had barely digested the news of Ahmed Shah Massoud's death in Afghanistan before the first plane hit. All that day he stood staring at the television. There were phone calls. His family called to make sure he was safe. Prince Khalid's mother phoned to shout and scream while informing him that his son was safe. They had both been living in New York, but never spoke. Since that other day more than two years ago, they had not exchanged a word. When the towers came crashing down, he understood that the world would never be the same again. Bin Laden had followed up on his declaration of war. At that moment, the death toll was estimated to be in the tens of thousands. Some of the biggest and most prestigious companies in the world had offices in the Twin Towers. Prince Abdul Aziz could count more than twenty close friends who worked there, and dozens of others that he had dealt with through his various businesses. His heart filled with pain. There were so many people. They were the fathers and mothers and sons and daughters of thousands of innocent people. It was horrific. He was ashamed. He was so ashamed. When the towers came down, he went to the window. A great billowing cloud filled the sky. Through the glass, he could feel the vibrations, and he could hear the rolling thunder that stopped the endless screaming of sirens. That was followed by the most awful silence, which seemed to last forever.

He called his people into his hotel suite. They were all nervous. They were afraid of reprisals. They wanted to go home. He asked them to stay in their rooms. If they needed anything then the hotel would provide it. They wanted to use the phones, but there were no phones by then. America was on lockdown. The Pentagon had been blown up. The President was probably in a bunker. Half of the firemen in New York were dead. The only good news was that thousands of pedestrians were swarming on to the highways walking home. That meant they weren't dead. But so many were.

The Prince and his people had to justify their presence in Manhattan, first to the Secret Service, who were polite and efficient. The local police were a bit more rabid. Someone at the hotel had reported a bunch of suspicious Arabs hiding in the penthouse suite. It took only a few calls to sort out the misunderstanding, but the bodyguards and servants were insulted. When the phones began to ring again, he received several calls from fellow Saudis who felt they were being harassed, and were now trapped in America because all flights were grounded. Nobody could get out, and nobody else could get in. Prince Abdul Aziz asked them to be patient. He asked them all to remember that they were just guests in a country that had been attacked without any warning. Everyone was tense. Over their heads, fighter jets were searching the skies. The power was still out on the west side of Lower Manhattan. The people in Battery Park had been evacuated. And all the time, the exhausted firemen and policemen and the National Guard and an army of volunteers were searching for survivors amongst the debris, hindered by fire and deep crevices in the ruins. But there was no one to find. It was total devastation.

Everyone watched the television. There just was no other story. There were hundreds of eyewitness accounts, and interviews with the bereaved. The President of the United States was almost speechless with rage. His quirky Texan charm had gone. He had the face of a man waking up from a nightmare to find out that it was all real. There were still rumours about other missing planes. Mayor Giuliani was everywhere. He was articulate and humane. When asked about the dead, he said there were too many to count. They were preparing for the figure to be in the thousands.

The next day and the day after that there was the merest semblance of normality. People woke up and ate breakfast, and if they did not look at another human being, it was possible to believe that everything was the same. Children went to school. People outside of Manhattan could go to work. In Manhattan, there was a shroud of dust. There were fears about asbestos. All the people were red-eyed and pale and so very tired. Every newspaper carried massive colour pictures. Every news channel vied for the most informed experts and most heart wrenching story of loss. Cynics would say that it was all about a ratings war, but it was about America at war. For many, it was the first attack on home soil since Pearl Harbour.

There was speculation about what Al Qaeda would do next. At some point, someone had made the decision to identify bin Laden. Suddenly, a lot of informed experts were being interviewed about Al Qaeda and bin Laden. Within twenty-four hours, everyone everywhere knew who he was.

Three days later when the airports opened there was a mass exodus of Arabs, and most particularly Saudis. Amongst them were bin Laden's relations. They had disowned him, but the name made them targets so they all had to go home. Local feeling had been heated up despite Giuliani's best efforts because of the reaction to the attacks in other Muslim countries. There was rejoicing. Every news show had stories about the celebrations in Palestine, East Africa and Afghanistan. It seemed that every Muslim fanatic wanted to ride on the coat-tails of the 9/11 bombers.

George W. Bush declared war, and demanded that Afghanistan hand over bin Laden. He also told Pakistan to choose sides. The trouble with Pakistan was that the mullahs believed the only law was Sharia, which put them on the side of the Taliban while the Military and the political elite were invested in a secular state built on Democracy, and law and order, so this schism meant that Pakistan was basically embroiled in a constant civil war.

Prince Abdul Aziz knew the clerics were gathering in Kabul to discuss Osama bin Laden's fate. He knew as well that the Afghans did not care about world opinion, they existed in a vacuum, and would not make a bargain with anyone they considered an infidel. They proudly boasted that anyone who invaded their country destroyed themselves, and history seemed to prove them right, not that the Americans would pay any attention to history. Musharraf was trying to pull the region back from the brink of war, and was being pilloried for his efforts. The Prince did not need to consult a map. He knew the wild borderlands like the back of his hand.

On the television, an American was saying: "We cannot tolerate any government providing a safe harbour, providing finances, providing training grounds, providing a safe headquarters for terrorism."

Prince Abdul Aziz sank his head into his hands, and prayed silently for wisdom. The nightmare that he had dreaded for ten years was now visited upon the world, not just America, but the whole world. The man he hated most had been transformed from some shadowy spectre into a very real person. His face was in every newspaper. He looked demure and spiritual, but the Prince knew that he was dangerous, cruel and quite literally insane, with a frightening ability to twist the hearts and souls of otherwise sensible people, turning them into bloodthirsty psychotic killers. Bin Laden had hijacked a religion based on peace, creating a bunch of ranting fanatics, who were such losers in real life that they were easily persuaded to die for the cause, even though Islam was against suicide and condemned the killing of innocents. They were desperate to kill themselves because they were failures. The promise of an eternal paradise populated by virgins would always be very attractive to miserable young men. It would certainly always be more attractive than a long life dedicated to hard work, self-sacrifice, and enduring all the whips and scorns of time without complaint. Bin Laden's own sect was merely one of more than seventy sects in the family of Islam, but it was an extremely narrow and puritanical interpretation of the Koran, which was alien to many, but he had the money and connections to humiliate and terrorise all Muslim brothers into his service. He believed that his interpretation of the Word of God was the true one, and Islam declared itself to be perfect so no one, on pain of death, was allowed to question it or criticise any part of it. So it was impossible to stand against bin Laden without appearing to criticise Islam as a whole. Anyone who disagreed with him was condemned as a traitor and a heretic. Now, he had the Taliban at his beck and call, and the mullahs in Pakistan were all stirred up. Musharraf had his hands full. The children of the fundamentalist, Zia, were now all grown up and intoxicated with his medieval view of Islam. Zia was to blame for the madrassas, and had rewritten history to portray Jinna as an Islamist, when in fact he spoke clearly for a secular tolerant state.

The trouble was Israel. It was always Israel. Islam had changed after Israel. The Prince still found that the word stuck in his throat. If only there had been no Holocaust. From the Muslim Brotherhood and Qutb in Egypt to Ayman Zawahiri and bin Laden, there was always the emotional blackmail of having failed the displaced Palestinians. Not that anyone liked the Palestinians enough to offer them a home. It was a rallying cry that excited every Muslim heart, and bin Laden and his acolytes played it ruthlessly. He attracted criminals like Zarqawi, and spoiled rich Saudis who could not hold down proper jobs, while inspiring disaffected refugees to attack the very countries that had given them sanctuary.

Yes, he hated bin Laden, but what could he say aloud? Bin Laden had the power to issue fatwas, and enough unstable followers to penetrate the most secure defences, and having no scruples at all would kill indiscriminately anyone in his way. If bin Laden was the chosen Warrior of God, then the Prince despaired of his God's love for his creations. Surely God wanted them comfortable, educated and generous of spirit, not miserable, maimed and suicidal. Martyrdom had become an obsession amongst the young. It was completely beyond the wit of an intelligent man to comprehend their insatiable hunger for death.

*

They did not talk at all that evening. She watched him attentively, understanding that he was distressed, and worried that he might do something reckless. He did not seem interested in anything on the television. When he went to the bathroom, she followed him quietly, and listened at the door. Nothing happened. She hurried into the kitchen as soon as she heard the door opening. When she offered him a can of milkshake, he hesitated, but she forced it into his hands then gave him some pills. His conditioning meant he could not refuse. Without further prompting, he swallowed the pills and drank the milkshake. Half an hour later, she suggested he go to bed.

He went quietly. She followed him up the stairs then watched as he stripped off his clothes, which he laid across the chair. He was not remotely shy, but not demonstrative either. He avoided looking at her while all the time aware that she was watching him. There had rarely been a moment in his life when he was not watched and scrutinised. His Pakistanis had monitored him closely. His health was their primary concern. When strangers watched him, it was different. He could almost feel their eyes pawing his flesh. The air crackled with excitement. Soon they would not be strangers. They would plunder his body like greedy children then shove him away when they had satisfied their appetites. She was confused. He felt it in the way that she touched him. There was a conflict that he did not understand. He lay face down on the bed then held his breath in anticipation.

She moved to sit on the edge of the mattress. She picked up the jar of cream. It was still quite shocking to see the extent of his wounds. When she leaned closer, and began to gently apply the cream, she was able to see the fragile new skin that was gossamer thin. He trembled under her fingers, but he never made a sound.

"In the morning, we'll wash your hair." She tried to smile.

"Please?" he whispered. "You have been very kind." He distinctly felt the irritation in her fingers. "Forgive me."

She hesitated, then continued spreading the cream across his back. She was struggling to be Meryl Streep. Knowing something was worse than knowing nothing at all. She would not acknowledge what he was because it was scandalous, and it was likely to influence her behaviour. She did not believe that she could be that open-minded. Even pretending to be Meryl Streep was not likely to give her the cover she needed to hide her delicate mental condition. He was the victim. He needed to be protected. That was her job now. Nothing else mattered. But he was so lovely. He was so beautiful. And he was... She shook her head. She drew away from him. In her belly the muscles were contracting. Her pulse was racing. Oh fuck! Fuck. Fuck. Fuck.

She went back downstairs then went for a walk in the garden. It was very dark. There was no sign of a moon. There was no birdsong. She did not even know where she wanted to go, but she kept walking until she reached the shrine. Her torch battery was failing. She kept having to tap the lamp to brighten the beam. When she stood still, she realised that she was trembling. She wanted to weep because she was ashamed. She did have the decency to recognise that she was a foul, heartless bitch from hell. She was the terrible spider that devoured her prey. She was the monster. She wanted him to make love to her. She wanted him to ravish her. It had to be him. It had to be initiated by him. She couldn't do it. She could not take advantage of him, but she desperately needed him to make love to her. He had to do it. He had to do it vigorously and wholeheartedly. She needed to be battered and bruised by the power of his love. Her heart convulsed. She needed somebody to love her. It could be him. Surely, it could be him. She sobbed wretchedly. She did not want to be alone. He had ruined it for her. Her stone cold dead heart needed to be set on fire again. She needed to be alive again. He could do that. He was a beautiful young man, and what was more, he was acknowledged a consummate whore. He was a million dollar whore. Did it matter that he was gay? She wanted to scream. It wasn't fair that he was so beautiful and so gay and a bloody whore. It just wasn't fair.

She sat on the ground and wept tearlessly. The medication had dried up her tears. All she could do was sob and grimace and wear herself out with stifled hysteria. She needed to cry, but that was impossible. Perhaps, if she had gotten drunk or had sex. She knew it was chemical. Eventually, she was just too tired to be upset. Her thoughts became dark and devious. In her world, she was never denied anything that she really wanted. The air cooled around her. Foxes barked in the woodland. She heard an owl. This was her land. She owned everything, but she knew that she would never own him. He was out of her league. He was a distant glittering trophy that she could not reach. Some Arab princeling was prepared to pay a million dollars just to fuck him. She could not work that out in pounds, shillings and pence, but she knew that he was worth more than her home and her land. That was sobering. Her nerves settled slowly. She had to help him. That was an imperative need, and an unfamiliar concept. No one had ever needed her help before. If she helped him, perhaps they could be friends. Perhaps, what they both needed most was a friend.

She walked back to the house. The torch failed before she reached the garden, but she carefully found her way. The kitchen lights were on. She made a cup of tea, then locked up the house, then went upstairs. He was asleep. She pulled the covers up across his shoulders then brushed the errant ebony strands of hair away from his eyes. He moved restlessly. She drew back, anxious not to waken him, but he settled again. He looked very comfortable. The painkillers were strong enough to knock him out for about six hours.

All night, she sat in the chair watching him. He was so beautiful. He still did not seem real.

Chapter 38

It was not Dunkirk, but it was complicated. Most of the men did not want to leave. The women would not leave without the men. Leila, the Prince's distant relation, would not leave without her people. They had lived in the mountain for thousands of years. The Temple was one of the oldest religious sites in the world. It was the focus of their culture, and the mountain had been a safe fortress throughout history. It had a core of lapis lazuli and gold. Nearby, there were rubies. They had been rich and ostentatious once, but modern prejudices required them now to be invisible. Their reluctance to leave was understandable, but American vengeance would bring down all the mountains, and while the world watched anxiously, millions of Afghanis were already fleeing into Pakistan and Iran. In the mountain, they had become so inward looking that they could not conceive the implications of what had happened in New York. Even with pictures, it was too much for them to comprehend. What should have been a simple extraction became a long, drawn out negotiation. More than anything, they wanted the Temple to be kept safe so that they could one day bring back the Sacred Fire, and no one could guarantee that if the city was abandoned.

President George W. Bush had made a statement on the 15th September announcing that the United States of America was at war against Terror. The world had held its breath at the thought of nuclear weapons in the hands of a president portrayed as unstable and idiotic by the media, so there was genuine relief that the unavoidable conflict would be with conventional weapons. Bin Laden had won already. He had forced America to recognise him, and by doing so had divided the world into Muslims and non-Muslims. Pakistan was told to get on side or be bombed. The mullahs were in uproar. Aggrieved Muslims began to take revenge on non-Muslims. A thirteen-year-old Pakistani boy, who sold food on the street, was killed by a mob simply because he was a Christian. In the small town of Isiolo in Kenya, two churches were burned down and the words, 'God is Great' and 'We condemn America' were carved into the charred remains. In Gaza, Palestinian women were dancing in the streets because Americans had died. There were isolated atrocities against Christians almost everywhere, but very few were actually reported.

Many believed that Mullah Omar had always been a stooge of the Pakistani intelligence services, but his home in Kandahar was bombed on the same day that the Americans began bombing Kabul. Negotiations were over. The Americans had drawn a line in the sand. Everyone had to leave.

The very next day, half a dozen of the Prince's personal bodyguards swarmed into the kafir's subterranean room. He was startled almost out of his wits. They were all aggressive as hell and armed to the teeth. He was sure they had come to murder him, but in his small bare room there were no hiding places. He hardly needed one. He was filthy. He looked and smelt disgusting. No one wanted to touch him. They sent for a bucket of water while he cowered like a cornered rat.

Some of the bodyguards knew him from before. As he removed his clothes, they made scathing comments about him to their friends. They were crude and offensive, and encouraged because they were amongst friends to be unbelievably gross. He did not expect privacy, but he had become used to a small degree of respect. Hot with embarrassment, he toiled to scrape the ingrained dirt off his body. There was no soap. The water was chillingly cold. When he did not move fast enough, they berated him with curses. His shorn head made him look like an escapee from a mental institution. His beard was thick and heavy with sweat and dust. He bore absolutely no resemblance to the beautiful creature that had once danced for them in a scarlet dress. No one wanted to fuck him now. Not one amongst them would admit to having paid money to take pleasure in his body. Long before he was clean, they hurled a bundle of clothes at his feet. He hurriedly pulled them on, grateful for the offer of some camouflage, and he was surprised to discover that he was to wear a military uniform just like theirs. He dressed quickly. There was obviously a deadline. He realised that he was leaving. He was leaving? After two years, he had given up hope. His heart was thumping. His hands trembled. He struggled with the buttons. He was leaving? They had even brought him army boots, but they were the wrong size. He did not care. Nobody cared. He was leaving.

With a man anchoring each arm, he was hurried up the narrow staircase then along a maze of corridors to the higher levels that he had only seen once before, and that had been years ago. There were the decorated tiles, the gleaming polished walls of lapis lazuli that were streaked with seams of gold. He remembered the stylised art and flickering torchlight that made the windowless corridors gleam and flash with light. It was all very beautiful, with a touch of faded grandeur. The carpets that had once been vibrant with colour were now faded with dust and worn. That was one of the first things that the kafir had noticed. Everyone wore shoes indoors. He had never seen anyone go barefoot. The bodyguards hurried him up more stairs, passing groups of agitated, chattering people, some of them priests, and exited on to the roof which was nothing more than an immense natural plateau surrounded by even higher peaks.

There were massive military helicopters. They sat like giant fat bugs on the snowy ground. They were being loaded with people and possessions. There were crates, sacks and even humble bundles. The kafir blinked in the dazzling light, and stalled at the sight of so much frenetic activity. He drew back, trying to lift a hand to shade his eyes while he tried to comprehend what was happening. There were so many people. They were loud and angry and frightened. There were more helicopters flying in. Two had already taken off, and were disappearing into the distance. The noise and the rotor blades made the air vibrate. He wanted to cover his ears, but the grip on his arms tightened again. He was taken away from the Parsi. He was separated from them. There would be no goodbyes. Suddenly, he wanted to find Mansour, he wanted to know that he was alright, but such consideration was not his to own anymore. Once again, he was just a piece of freight. There was a smaller helicopter parked away from the others. It was a Blackhawk. He had seen one before. He was immediately afraid. The rotors were already circling slowly. He was forced to bend down then hurried towards the steps. Two men leaned out of the dark interior to take hold of his shoulders then hauled him inside like a sack of grain. His wrists were quickly wrapped in sticky tape. The webbing that usually harnessed crates now harnessed him. His nerves were shredding. He had no idea what was happening. He allowed himself one last look around. There were familiar faces, but there were no friendly smiles. The old rules applied. In that moment, he was relegated again to the rank of an unbeliever, loathed by the Righteous because his existence was an insult to God.

They flew east to Pakistan. It was a perilous journey. The tension inside the helicopter was absolutely exhausting. All the bodyguards remained on high alert, ready to shoot anything that seemed threatening. The landscape was vast. The air was crystal clear. Every road had a trail of refugees. Villages had been abandoned. As they neared the border, the number of people on the roads increased from hundreds to tens of thousands. They flew over a refugee camp that was already teeming with people. There were tents packed shoulder to shoulder. More families were pouring in every minute. It seemed that all of humanity was on the move.

The kafir knew something momentous had happened in New York. He knew that the people from the mountain were fleeing their homes. He had seen the refugees. At the airport, he was in the midst of some cataclysmic event. He had never seen so much chaos and confusion and despair. There were hundreds of tents pitched in the fields surrounding the airport. Many had red crosses emblazoned on them. And there were more foreigners than he had ever seen before. In the confusion of refugees and mobilising armies, the Arabs transferred with quiet discretion from the helicopter to a private jet. They were not even asked for any documents. The airport's control tower was struggling to clear flight plans. There were a dozen planes waiting to take off, most were military, some were American. The Prince's jet took its turn, listed under his United Nations credentials even though he was not on board. That was to be the first of many flights that had been logged to airlift his cousin's people to safety.

They flew south to Karachi. The kafir sat on the floor becoming increasingly anxious. He had no idea what was happening. He was being taken somewhere, but it never occurred to him that he might be going home. It was inconceivable that either prince wanted him again after what had happened. He could still feel their hatred. The injuries had healed, but he had never been able to forget their hatred. Always in his dreams, Prince Abdul Aziz was his lover, but only in dreams. They had condemned him to a life of perpetual toil and sweat and filth and loneliness. Who would fuck him now? Who would beat their chest and swear undying love for him? He hated himself. He hated being alive. He had become an untouchable.

The only talk now was about the coming war. The Americans were obviously going to hunt down bin Laden, and rip his heart out. They would slaughter every Muslim. They would not rest until Islam had been wiped off the face of the earth. It almost did not matter whether individual Muslims believed in bin Laden; they had to defend their religion. They had no choice. They were all committed to laying down their lives to defend God and His Blessed Prophet. When the kafir tried to move because his leg muscles were cramping, he was smacked across the head. The coarse jokes flowed for a while then slowly ebbed away as everyone's thoughts returned to the impending calamity. No one wanted to guess at the death toll. The grieving Americans were still counting their dead. The scale of the attack had been shocking. The scale of America's vengeance was likely to be beyond belief.

The airport at Karachi was huge compared to the one upcountry, but there was the same tension and buzz of frenzied activity. The kafir walked quietly between the bodyguards. He kept his head down. He obeyed every command. If there was an altercation, he raised his hands passively and stood still. From the ordinary people around him, he heard snatches of conversations. There was talk of war, invasion and bombing. The people were afraid. Their families, their homes, their livelihoods were all at risk, and Musharraf was in league with the Americans. The mullahs were screaming for his death. Everywhere the kafir looked, there were soldiers bristling with weapons. The bodyguards had the right paperwork when they were challenged. The Prince's United Nations credentials carried a lot of weight. No one even looked at the kafir. In the pandemonium of the departure lounge, the Arabs were quiet and contained. They kept the kafir moving. They kept him isolated. Pakistan was a nuclear powder keg. At any moment, it might explode.

They crossed the tarmac to board another private jet. Omar stood at the top of the steps, watching as the creature was delivered back to him. It was limping, seriously dishevelled, and visibly overwhelmed by events. Had he not known that it was the blue-eyed kafir, he would never have recognised it. When it saw him, it stopped dead. It actually struggled, but the bodyguards just carried it forward like flotsam on a rising tide. It was swept up the steps. It was still fretfully wrestling against the unyielding grip on its arms when Omar stared into its eyes. They were as blue as he remembered, but hotter and wilder. That it might actually possess a temper was surprising. Omar smiled. He stepped back to let his men drive it on to the plane and out of sight.

The kafir's heart had stopped beating when he saw Omar. He could not think. He could not function. He just wanted to be sick. Mansour had taken the time to teach him Gujarati so that he could talk to the Parsi. He had admired them. They had treated him fairly. Mansour had been as kind as his circumstances allowed. Mansour had explained about their philosophy of "Good thoughts, good words and good deeds." The Parsi had treated him as a human being. As he was forced to climb the steps, he had to accept that he had lost everything. He had barely crossed the threshold before Omar struck him hard across the face. His head snapped back. For a moment, he lost consciousness. He tumbled back into the arms of the Prince's bodyguards. His temper flared then was smothered. He found his feet. He could taste blood. Every bone and tooth rattled. He managed to focus, and remembered unhappily that he was a kafir, and knew exactly what that entailed.

Omar leaned closer. "Don't ever look at me." He watched as the creature stiffened then bowed its head like a penitent before a priest. Omar stared at it disapprovingly while he slid the familiar Breitling watch around its wrist. The head came up. The eyes flashed hotly. It was quite overwhelmed, but did manage to keep silent, and did not look at Omar. Omar had never seen it angry, never imagined it requiring self-control. "Just calm down," he warned quietly. "We don't want to hurt you. We've just come to take you home."

The kafir shuddered violently. Only the bodyguards kept him upright.

Home? His whole body convulsed in shock. He was suddenly cold and shaking, and he wanted to be sick.

"Okay?" Omar asked. He reached out to seize the creature's throat, forcing its head up. The eyes remained firmly shut. "We're taking you home."

The kafir was under pressure, but he kept his eyes closed. He tried to breathe. He needed a moment to process what was happening. He did not believe it. He did not understand it. The fingers squeezed his throat. It hurt. He shot a look towards Omar, and saw his grim determination. He understood that Omar allowed him to breathe. At any moment, he might change his mind. The kafir managed to swallow. He tried to ease away, but the fingers sank deeper into his neck like iron pincers. He felt the bodyguards letting go of his arms. They were leaving him. The commanding grip on his throat remained. He just focused on breathing. "Please?" he whispered. It was so difficult to speak.

Omar took hold of its arm as it wilted under the strain. Its wild appearance was shocking, and when the doors closed, Omar was able to fully appreciate the dreadful smell, but the engines started up, and the plane rolled forward. Someone from the cockpit suggested that they take a seat. Omar steered the creature backwards down the aisle then ordered it to its knees. While Omar took a seat and fastened a seat belt, the pale creature was pinned between Omar's legs and the wall of the fuselage. The jet rolled smoothly out to the runways. Omar stared critically at the filthy bearded thing, wondering whether it could actually be returned to its former glory. "His Highness has sent us to fetch you."

The kafir was lost. "I can't," he said brokenly. "Please, I can't."

The engine noise magnified. Suddenly, the brakes came off, and the jet hurtled down the runway. The kafir was crushed against Omar's legs by the momentum. Then they were in the air. The jet shot upwards at an alarming rate. It started to bank away. The kafir huddled down, stretching his arms around Omar's ankles, and holding tightly. He was terrified.

Omar unfastened his seat belt. He reached down to take hold of the creature's lapels then rose to his feet, taking it with him. He marched it to the bathroom. There was a small, neat shower cubical. He efficiently stripped off its borrowed clothes then backed it into the shower. It stood cowed and trembling as it was squirted all over with liquid soap. Then Omar set to work scrubbing it until it was raw then he turned on the water jets. The creature stood mute, but it was still trembling. The flesh was blue and pink and scarred. The smell had lessened. He crudely shaved off the filthy dripping beard to reveal a pale youth, but it was hardly attractive.

This was barely a shadow of the creature he had smuggled though Paris to escape a princess's spies. It had certainly changed. He realised it had grown up, which might actually prove to be a serious problem.

Omar let it sink back onto its knees. He realised that they might not actually be able to restore it. Nearly three years in the wilderness might have changed it too much. It was certainly physically bigger and stronger. He filled a glass with water, and stooped to press it to the creature's lips. It seemed to come back to life. The hands lifted to clasp the glass then fell limply. Omar let it have a moment. He understood that it had been on a long journey. It had definitely picked up some bad habits. When it started to drink, he rested a hand on its head. He remembered how hard it had tried to please. He remembered how bravely it had endured their odyssey in Paris.

Omar resumed his seat. He stared at the naked figure that knelt beside his feet and leaned heavily against his legs. He could feel the tension and see the distress. "You've been away a long time," he said quietly. "You'll have to forget all that." He leaned forward to offer it another drink, but it grimaced irritably so he smacked it across the head. "Your master wants you back exactly as you were. We're going to make sure that he isn't disappointed." He felt the creature shudder. It lifted a hand to wipe its mouth. "You need to settle down. You can't stop this."

The kafir wanted to look up at Omar, but that was forbidden again now. He had to subdue his eyes. He had to bow down.

"It'll be easy. You know what he likes," Omar said gently. "You know what you have to do."

"Please?" the kafir whispered. "I can't do that."

Omar hesitated then smacked it again across the back of the head.

"Please?" the kafir begged miserably.

Omar struck it again, but much harder. "Can't is not a word you may use. You say 'yes' and 'please' and 'thank you'."

The kafir was knocked to the floor, his head ringing like a bell. He stayed there, feeling the power of the engines through the floor panels. He had the frail hope that Omar would not pursue him on the floor. He had no other hopes. The few, the very few that he had managed to cling to since leaving the mountain were all gone now. He felt sick to his stomach. He could taste the vomit in his throat. If he was doomed to being that thing again then he did not want to live. He was surprised by his conviction. But he knew with absolute certainty that he would do whatever they wanted. They would seduce him. And as long as his master plundered his flesh with that same imperious wrath then he was truly doomed because he craved that dark rapture like a drug.

They flew to Dubai. It was late when they landed. By then the kafir was stiff and sore. He had been huddled up on the floor for hours. It was difficult to stand. Omar folded him into a long shirt then covered him in a burqa. There was the usual intricately carved shell mask fastened over the eye-slot to emphasise the wearer's modesty. No one would ever be able to see his eyes. When Omar took his arm and guided him down the steps onto the runway, they looked like man and wife. There was a car waiting. They were still travelling on the Prince's diplomatic papers. No one questioned them. They had both been there a dozen times before. They travelled through the opulent neon-lit city. Every building was a marvel of architecture. There were expensive cars, beautiful people, and in the shadows of the false daylight were the misery and poverty of the migrant workers, who had built everything, but were not allowed to play with the expensive toys.

Prince Abdul Aziz had an apartment in the city, and a palatial house out on the coast. Once the kafir had recognised where they were going, he turned away from the window. The structure of the mask intensified the effect of the flashing lights. It was not because he was crying. He was not blinded by his tears.

The apartment was so high up that the kafir's ears popped in the elevator. He was totally subdued. He was too tired to cause any trouble. Omar kept hold of his arm merely to stop him falling down, which would have attracted unwanted attention. He was not hurting him, but the strength of his grip was a warning. When they reached the door, it opened with a flourish. Aziz stood there. The kafir's legs turned to water. He staggered against Omar. Before he could process the information, he was swept into the apartment. Aziz had his other arm. His heart had stopped beating. His legs swam beneath him. He could not co-ordinate his movements. He was dizzy and nauseous. He was so thirsty, but he was also terrified of throwing up on the marble tiles. They were walking him. Light bulbs were exploding in his head. He could not see anything but flashing lights. Then he was salivating. Sweat drenched him. Suddenly, he was trembling violently. He felt the heat of urine raining down his thighs. It was too late. He fainted and dropped like a stone. Aziz let go in disgust, but Omar gathered him up into his arms then carried him through to the servants' annex.

*

The red hoardings at the Queen's Club in London were advertising the sponsor, Stella Artois. The grass was beginning to look worn and dry. It had not rained, and the cloudless blue sky promised more of the same.

Every seat was taken. Many of the spectators were looking decidedly pink. The English were out in force. Well, it was Tim Henman. He was not even seeded. He was not really expected to win although everyone wanted him to. Even Tursunov seemed to be on Henman's side. He had let the first set slide away, and was approaching the second as if he really wanted to leave the court as quickly as possible. He was acknowledged as a difficult opponent. He was not elegant like Federer. He whacked the balls back into play rather than hitting them. He was a big strong guy. What he lacked in finesse, he made up for in grit and determination.

Henman had won the first set by playing carefully. In Paris, he had been accused of letting Tursunov off the hook. Under pressure, Henman served an Ace. The crowd were delighted, which must have annoyed Tursunov. It was a strange match. Henman kept almost winning, but did not seem to be able to close out. He seemed tired. It was early afternoon. There were almost no shadows. It must have been very hot. Neither of them was actually playing well, but while Henman was hesitant, Tursunov was erratic. He could string together a sequence of inspired shots then just blasted the ball off court. He actually managed to draw level in the second set, but it was hard to pinpoint how he was doing it. Some of his shots were so bizarre that Henman was left with a bemused smile and a point he had not actually won.

Then suddenly, Tursunov focused. He was alert. He started hitting winners. Henman hung on. When Tursunov completely mishit a ball in the tenth, Henman was able to break his serve. But Tursunov was playing now. He ran down balls, and his returns were like sledgehammers. But again another mishit into the net allowed Henman to hold. It is 6-5 in the second. Henman had to win the set. Tursunov was not winning because his game fluctuated between genius and just plain daft, but he was always fun to watch though it must have infuriated his coach. Henman had to stay focused. He might be still wreathed in smiles, and as entertained as the crowd, but he had to respect Tursunov. At any moment, the genius might appear. Henman played some good shots, but Tursunov was playing better. He held. They went into a Tie Break. It was a wobbly start for both of them then Henman forged ahead. The crowd became increasingly pensive. Henman was playing really well. He played every point calmly and patiently. And he won. He actually won. It was lovely. Everyone went potty.

She was smiling for hours after that.

Chapter 39

They went out to sit on the lawn. It was uncomfortably warm. It did not take much pressure to strip him down to his shirt sleeves. He looked lovely, but she knew from the body language and drooping gaze that he did not really want to have a conversation. She set him up with a pillow and a glass of water then left him to doze in the sunshine. The birds were singing their hearts out. The flower beds were alive with bees and butterflies. She had absolutely no problem getting stuck in with the gardening. Three hours passed in the blink of an eye. When she came back he was fast asleep. He could not have been more attractive. She sat down carefully beside him, and just smiled foolishly. It was a lovely, perfect day.

She knew enough to be concerned for his safety. Whether he found his parents or was found by his prince, he was in danger. Whatever happened, he would be hurt. His parents might be anything. They would surely be devastated by his disappearance, and delighted to know he was alive, but there was the possibility that they were just horrible obnoxious bastards. The fact that he had been delivered unconscious to her garden was quite alarming. There was no evidence of trespassers, but how else had he arrived there? Someone with dubious motives knew he was at her house. If it was some Saudi prince then it was truly bizarre. If it was someone else then she had no idea of their motives. As in all the other crises of her life, she knew who she could trust. She felt it was probably too soon to call in her Rottweiler. She would do a little detective work of her own. She felt she needed to check some of his facts. According to various movies and television programmes, she would be able to go on to the worldwide web, and speedily find the most obscure details about the weirdest things. She did not know how it worked. It was all binary code. She had never understood how a sequence of ones and zeros could be anything but ones and zeros, but she would give it a go. She might even be able to find out about Barbaro. Was he still alive? It would be a miracle.

She lay down on the blanket. She was close enough to gently sweep the few strands of hair back off his forehead. He was so pretty. He breathed heavily then slowly opened his eyes to look at her. She tried to smile. She had woken him, but he had been asleep for hours so it was hardly a criminal offense.

"Hi," she said.

He might have frowned. "Hi."

"It's teatime," she said.

He frowned like a dopey mere mortal. He had no idea what she was talking about. "Yes."

"How are you feeling?"

In his universe that was a loaded question. He tried to imagine what she might be telling him. It was obviously code.

She read his disquiet. "I thought we could go for a walk, but if you're tired we can go in. We could have a cup of tea."

He decoded that as meaning she wanted to ask him more questions. He started to move, intending to sit up, but the wound across his back had set solid in the heat. The pain was crippling. His whole body quaked. In a matter of seconds, he was drenched with sweat and gasping. He felt as if his brain had exploded.

She was quickly on her knees beside him, full of concern and anxiety. "Don't move. It's alright. Just take a deep breath."

He was at the madrassa again. A bucket of icy water had just been poured over his head. He could not function. His brain was totally paralysed.

She stroked his face then stooped to kiss his forehead. "It's alright. It's just shock."

He could just about blink, but his vision was blurred. He hardly knew where he was. The pain was overwhelming. He thought it would never stop. He thought he would die, but it did suddenly diminish. He managed to inhale. He managed to gently push her away. "I'm alright."

She was relieved. She quickly scrambled to her feet. "Shall I get you a chair or a walking stick? I'm sure I have one somewhere."

Using his arms, he very slowly moved to sit up then moved on to his knees then regained his feet.

She watched helplessly, grimacing for him, desperate to help but aware that it was easier for him to manage on his own. If he wanted her to help him then he could make that decision. He had only to reach out and take her hand. When he looked at her, she smiled. "A cup of tea then?"

He was not sure he was capable of walking anywhere.

"There will be setbacks," she said. "You've done so well."

He managed to stand upright, and slowly straighten his back. The pain was definitely diminishing. He filled his lungs then shook his head. "I'm alright."

She moved cautiously around him so that she could look at his shirt. There was no blood. It was obviously his damaged nerves that were protesting rather than the delicate skin. She took hold of his elbow, and drew him towards her. "Let's go in. You won't fall down. I won't let you. We'll make this alright. You're just very tired."

He did not believe her, but could not refuse. It took a few hesitant steps for him to find his confidence. The pain had almost completely disappeared. By the time they reached the back door, he was fine, just totally exhausted.

While he settled down on the sofa, and reached for the remote, she made two cups of tea. In his, she poured nearly half a cup of rum then lots and lots of sugar. She had Earl Grey. He was quite correct. She did want to ask him some questions. She hovered in front of him until he started to drink then went outside to fetch in the blanket and pillow. As soon as she came back she was poised to make him a second cup.

He had often been sedated. He understood that she was giving him something to make him quiet, but he had never had anything alcoholic. In his world, that was totally prohibited. He was not even allowed to have anything that contained a drop of vanilla essence. So when she pressed a second cup into his hands, he drank it down quickly without registering that it was very sweet and quite cool. He was not drunk, but he was suddenly relaxed and less cautious. His few defences were effectively overwhelmed.

She sat quietly waiting. The television was on. It was football. He was staring at it, but not really watching anything. She understood that it was not the game anymore, but a memory that he was clinging to like a life raft. After a few minutes, she walked across and turned the sound down. Then she settled on the sofa next to him. It was not too hard to pull him down into her lap. "How are you feeling now?"

He dared not struggle free.

"So we'll start looking for your parents. It isn't going to be easy, but you still need a few more weeks to recover so we have plenty of time." She could not see his face, and she could not fidget without disturbing his back. She could see his hands which rested on her knees. And she could fondly stroke his hair. "We have a lot of work to do. You need to think about what you can tell them. They'll have so many questions. They'll have been grieving for you all these years as if you were dead, but it will have been compounded by not knowing what happened. They will have been living in a void, trapped by the inescapable pain of loss, waiting for news, waiting for your dead body to be found or for you to come back. They will have searched for you. You can't begin to understand how desperately they will have searched for you. If you had just disappeared, the police might have been slow to believe it was actually a crime. People disappear every day. It's very easy. So your mother and father will have searched for you. It must have become an obsession. Every knock at the door. Every time the phone rang. They would have hoped it was you. They must have gone half mad not knowing what happened to you. There will have been days when they accepted that you were dead only to be followed by a thousand other days when they felt guilty for having lost hope. They will have gone over every minute of their last day with you, trying to understand if they said something or did something that might have made you run away. At the back of their minds, there has always been the conviction that it was their fault. It's a dreadful burden to bear, but until they find you murdered aged eight, they will always believe that it was their fault. You have to deal with that. You have to tell them something that will take away their pain. It should be the truth, but that's your decision. It's the most important decision you will ever make. They won't hate you, but you will have to justify what has been done to your body." She felt the tension in his limbs. Perhaps she had not given him enough rum. "I'm sorry, but you can't hide that body. All that stuff? What they have done to you? You have to be able to explain it all in a way that makes sense or there will always be more questions."

"Please?" He shivered and grimaced. "You're wrong," he insisted quietly. "They don't need to know."

"You can't hide that body, and the police will be involved. You might try to keep them at arm's length, but your parents will have to tell the police that you've come back. You'll be a case file somewhere. I think they have to tell them. And the police will want to interview you. They'll insist you are checked over by a doctor. There'll be blood tests. They'll want samples of your DNA. You won't be able to refuse to answer their questions. You can try the 'I don't remember anything' defence, but they won't believe you. It'll go on and on. You have to be ready for all that shit. It'll get ugly. You need to prepare."

He moved a hand to cover his ear in a childish attempt to not hear. "It won't be like that. I just need to talk to them. I just want them to know that it's alright now."

She clasped his hand. "We'll work it all out. You've been through a terrible ordeal. You can't deny what happened. It's not who you are, but it is part of your life. You have to own it. There will be lots of difficult questions, but we just need to work out what you can tell them. You really can't believe that you won't have to explain the marks on your body? That's irrefutable evidence. Even if you lie about everything else, you will have to explain why you are marked like that. You'll probably have to explain about the anal intercourse. I don't know, but I'm sure they can tell from the musculature that you have anal sex. But that shouldn't really be too difficult these days. Everyone is a lot more broadminded about homosexuality. It's not illegal anymore. There was a time when you'd have been put in prison and force-fed chemicals to cure you. They'll check you for HIV, but that's always a good idea, isn't it. You don't want to go home with undiagnosed AIDS."

He was hardly breathing. He could not see anything because his eyes were flooding with tears.

"Do you miss the sex?" She felt him shudder. "Well, you must know whether you miss it? You're not in any danger now. You can talk to me about it. You had a sexual relationship with one of the richest men in the world. He's indulged you with fine clothes and expensive accessories. You keep telling me that he never hurt you. Was that a lie?"

"Please? You don't understand."

"Because I'm a woman? That isn't fair." She fondly stroked his hand. She examined his fine-boned fingers and the perfectly manicured nails. "He has looked after you. He was your lover." She tried to smile. "If you didn't love him then that's okay. Relationships are never equal. But if you don't love him, if you don't like him then why aren't you running to the police to have him arrested?"

"Perhaps I'm a fraud."

That was not the answer she was expecting. His voice was so low. It was so frank and so honest. It felt like a confession. "So you did love him?"

"I hated him. He raped me then he made love to me then he just threw me away."

"Love and hate are just different sides of the same emotion." She smiled reassuringly. "If you hate him now, did you love him before?" He tried to move away, but she held him still. "It's alright. You just need to think about this. You need to acknowledge how you feel about him, and about your friends, Mahmood and Omar, and the Pakistanis. You have to be honest with yourself. If you are lying in your heart then no one will believe anything that you say. You need to have everything straight in your head. You have to have all your answers ready. If there are any inconsistencies in your story then the police will be all over you." She squeezed his hand gently. "You can tell lies, but you have to know the truth to be convincing."

He breathed deeply. "Perhaps it's all a lie."

"Do you like being fucked? Not that I'm offering. I don't think I'm equipped." She actually managed to laugh then patted his hand again compassionately. He did not seem to be listening. "I never liked sex. I was shy. I was never like you. I was never very attractive so I didn't have a lot of confidence. My husband was a complete shit. I don't know why I married him. I was frightened of him, terrified, I think. I think I was raped. It felt like rape. It was abusive and violent. I'm not even sure if you can have your husband charged with rape. The police are a bit slow when it comes to domestic violence. I had the black eyes and the broken ribs. If I had gone to the police then I would have had to run away. If I went home then he was there. The police would not have arrested him and kept him locked up forever. No. I really didn't like sex. I don't think I ever felt real passion. I don't think I was ever actually in love with anyone like that."

He squeezed her hand. "I'm sorry."

"Have you ever loved anyone?" she asked.

He did not answer. He did not know how to answer.

"So in a perfect world, when my brilliant doctor has cured you, when you have your whole life ahead of you, what will you do?"

He could not answer that either.

She felt really sorry for him. He was so unbelievably good-looking, but he had nothing else, not even hope. "So I believe you have a couple of weeks to think about what you want to do. You need to be brutally honest with yourself." She patted his hand again. "It'll be upsetting and confusing and painful. You're probably angry. At this moment, you probably hate me, but I'm trying to prepare you for what will happen when you go home. It's going to be really hard for you and your parents. All of you have been victims. All of you are damaged."

"What if it's true? What if I was horrible? What if they didn't want me? What if they did sell me to some collector?"

"No. No. Don't think about that. It isn't true. They just told you that to break your heart." She wanted to wrap her arms around him, but his injuries forbade such violence. "Never think that. No one would ever do that to you. Even your prince turned down a million dollars." Just saying the sum aloud took her breath away. This man in her arms was a valuable piece of merchandise. He had a specific monetary value. It was not existential. It was about his meat and bones. "You are loved. You must know that. You must realise how much you are loved?" His whole body was tense. "I'm sure that your prince loved you. He's kept you all of these years. That's not how these stories usually end. He's taken care of you. When you were sick, he took care of you. It would appear that he has allowed you to come here. He would not have done that unless he was genuinely fond of you, unless he really loved you. This must be a huge risk for him. He must trust you."

He moved restlessly. "Please?" He filled his lungs. He did not want to say anything but he just couldn't help himself. "You don't understand. It really doesn't matter what I say. No one will believe me, and if they did then they wouldn't do anything about it. I must be very careful. If I make a fuss then they'll kill me. I'll fall off a roof or get knocked down by a car. They are above the law. They cannot be prosecuted. No one will try."

"Do you miss him?" She gave him time to answer, but there was only silence. "What about your friends? Would you like to see Mahmood again? Or Omar?"

"That's impossible. I couldn't..." He sighed deeply.

"And what about Prince Bandar?" His silence was ominous. "Is he likely to come looking for you?" There was still no response. "That's surely the real danger?"

He did not answer.

She realised he had fallen asleep.

*

The kafir was trapped.

He was in hell.

After the nightmarish repercussions surrounding Aziz's death, they had moved out to the house on the coast. He had been there before with the Prince. He had never been there alone. He felt alone. He had the two people that he trusted with him. These were the people that he depended on for everything in his life, and they were being unkind. He was denied the companionship that he craved. He was denied the constant reassurance that he required to function. They knew he had not attacked Aziz. Something inside Aziz's head had burst. The doctor had said so. Omar knew the truth. The kafir had heard him explaining it all to Mahmood when he arrived to cover for Aziz. The kafir did not understand what was happening. He was ill. He felt so ill. And they were punishing him, but he did not know why. Every day was horrible. Every day ended in tears. His nights were miserable. Every morning when he was awoken to face a new day, he wanted to be sick. When he was coherent enough to process a thought, it was that he had never been so unhappy in his whole life. All too soon he was incapable of making any kind of decision. They were systematically pulverising his brain.

Omar rose at about 5am. He turned over on the bed to stare at the creature, which lay immobilised on the floor of his walk-in shower. He drifted across to the windows, and gazed out through the fine net curtains. It would be another beautiful day. He went into the bathroom to relieve himself. The creature did not move. It looked pale and haggard. He knew that it was awake. That it was pretending was proof of its deceit. It was thinking. It was not allowed to think anymore. Omar turned on the shower. A fierce torrent of cold water poured down. Omar watched as it twisted and turned in vain to catch the tiny drops of water in its mouth. Water was rationed. Omar turned off the water before it could drink. When the creature lay back on the tiles, it was desolate. It was trembling. Omar half-filled a glass at the tap then moved to kneel down beside it. He pulled it up close to his chest, and felt it sob. It was just about broken. In another few days, a week at the most, he knew it would be in pieces, and then they could start putting it back together. He pressed the glass to its lips. The eyes flashed. They were still blue. The face was beautiful again. The expensive surgeons had repaired the splendid flesh, a battery of drugs had cleaned its blood and various necessary organs, but its spirit was the problem. It was merely a device. It had a single function. Omar held it in his arms while it drank the precious water.

"Are you counting?" he asked.

The kafir nodded. He couldn't stop counting. He strained inside Omar's familiar embrace wanting to find the safe refuge that Omar had always provided. "Please?" He needed tenderness and affection. He needed to be loved. In absolute despair, he started crying.

Omar frowned. "Stop complaining!" He actually found it difficult to be so brutal. He had known the creature for a long time. It was more familiar to him than his children. Obviously, he understood the necessity of the tough regime because it had been in a totally different environment with radically different goals. It had to unlearn all of that. It had to forget or it could not survive. "We're not here to play with you. Now, start again at 'one'. I want to hear you."

The kafir trembled. "One," he said miserably. His throat was dry and sore. He had not even reached ten before he was coughing.

Omar cradled it in his arms. "Just stop coughing. You're only doing that to get attention. Now, start counting again. Start at 'one'. When you reach five thousand then I'll let you have some honey. You like honey, don't you. You have to try." He tenderly wiped its beautiful face. "If you don't make an effort then I'm not allowed to give you anything."

The kafir's throat was so sore he felt as if he had been strangled. "Please, my hands?"

Omar shook his head. He gently stroked the drops of water from its flawless skin. He ran his fingers through its alarmingly short hair. "You're shameless. You know, that's forbidden. That's only fair. What has been forbidden must remain forbidden."

The kafir's eyes were full of tears. He was staring at the ceiling. He could see Omar, and read the compassion in his face, but he dared not look at him. He was already counting. He had been counting for as long as he could remember. Even soundlessly, it damaged his throat.

"Start counting," Omar reminded him gently.

The kafir blinked. "I am," he whispered. A tear rolled down his cheek.

"We have to hear it."

The kafir shivered. He couldn't. He really couldn't, but the alternative was harrowing. "One," he said. "Two." His voice was full of pain and anguish. His face fractured into a mask of torment. "Please…"

Omar counted slowly but surely, instilling a rhythm and commitment. Even after Omar laid it back on the wet tiles, the creature continued counting. Omar washed at the sink. He put on his simplest white clothes then went in search of the other Believers, who would gather to bow down and pray.

The creature was still counting when Mahmood came to fetch it. It was no longer speaking aloud, but its lips moved as if it were talking in a dream. Mahmood freed it from the sticky tape, and unlocked the shackles. He had to help the creature to its feet then walked it to the sink. It leaned wearily while Mahmood shaved its face then brushed its teeth. It stopped counting then. It seemed to want to look at Mahmood, but the Pakistani focused on his work. He cleaned it, pulled on a new white shift then took hold of its arm.

"Please? A drink?" the kafir asked in despair. The toothpaste felt like acid on his sore throat. His fingers closed resolutely around the edge of the sink. "Please, I'm begging you. God is Merciful. Please, let me have a drink? I'm begging you. God is Great. Water? Please?"

Mahmood tried to wrench its fingers from the rim of the sink.

"Please?" The kafir suddenly grasped Mahmood's shirt. He stared into his eyes, desperate to persuade him. "Please... so thirsty. Water? Please, water?"

"You should be counting." Mahmood would not look at it.

"Please, I don't understand?"

"What is there to understand?" Mahmood demanded angrily. "You obey."

The kafir crumbled. He was unable to understand anything. His brain was full of numbers and a thousand memorised quotes from the Holy Book. Water was just an instinct. His body demanded it. There was no calculation involved.

Mahmood had taken care of the creature since it had arrived from the madrassa early in 1995. He knew it intimately. He had always been fond of it, but only because he was naturally kind-hearted, and there was no need for him to be anything else. Ordered to be stricter, Mahmood had struggled. It had always been so extraordinarily pretty and eager to please. But as the creature grew taller and stronger, Mahmood had to toughen up, and discipline it though never quite as harshly as the other Pakistanis. It had been Mahmood, who had to step into the role left vacant by Aziz's untimely death. He hated having to be so strict, but the creature had returned with some bad habits, which it simply had to unlearn. No one was being unkind. It had only to remember that it was a kafir, and that there were rules. He took hold of its wrists. "You ask for nothing. You are nothing."

The kafir was taken through the house to a corner of the terrace that overlooked the sea. Mahmood made him kneel down facing a blank wall. He pressed a worn copy of the Holy Book into his hands. The kafir had been reading it for days and weeks and possibly months. At that moment, his throat screamed with pain. He trembled violently. Mahmood smacked him across the head to get his attention, to make sure that he was holding the precious book securely.

"Now, read! I'll be sitting here, and I'm listening. I want to hear every word." Mahmood gazed at the creature. It was still trembling. "He will be back soon. He can tell when you haven't been trying. You really don't want him to hurt you."

The kafir shook his head. He could barely focus on the pages. His eyesight was definitely failing. "Please, I can't."

Mahmood hit him again, but not very hard. "You must read now." Mahmood lingered. "This is a blessing. These are the Words of God. Read them with love, and you will be blessed."

The kafir drew a long deep breath. He couldn't. He just couldn't do it, but he couldn't bear the thought of Mahmood turning against him. He sobbed and sighed, but he started reading. The pain immediately registered in his throat. He started coughing. He couldn't stop coughing, but he forced out the words.

Omar came back to sit on the terrace. He had breakfast then read through the local newspapers that had been collected at dawn. The international dailies would come later. All the while, the creature knelt a few feet away, reading the sacred texts. It was struggling. Its voice was breaking. The incessant coughing made many of the words unintelligible. But Omar had also learned the verses as a boy. His education had started at a school that was not really any different to the madrassa that the creature had attended for seven years.

When the kafir collapsed in a fit of coughing, he was ignored. He could beg and weep, and no one responded. If he persisted, he would be beaten. Not as Aziz had beaten him, which had been endless and pointless, and was simply abuse. Omar was subtler. Omar knew how to really hurt him.

"Why have you stopped?" Omar asked, still gazing at his newspaper.

The kafir was just coughing. He was genuinely in distress.

"Just pull yourself together. I can't hear what you're saying. Do you want me to hurt you?" Omar did not even look up from his newspaper. "Don't make me hurt you."

Feeling that he was being throttled, the kafir tried to swallow and lubricate his throat. The muscles were swollen and sore. It was so painful. He forced out another few words. He struggled to inhale. "Water. Please, water?"

"Don't beg. It's offensive when you beg." Omar shook out the newspaper, and turned to the next page. "Start at the beginning of the sentence. You disrespect the words when you don't read them properly. These are the Words of God. Say them with reverence."

"Please?" the kafir gasped. His whole body shook as he tried to quell his coughing.

"Read from the Book. Don't beg. Don't complain. I can't give you anything to drink if you don't attend to your lessons. Do you want me to hurt you?"

The kafir wilted. Just swallowing was acutely painful. He read. His voice was unrecognisable. The words were unintelligible. The coughing was incessant. Soon he was dripping with sweat. His throat felt as if it had been slashed by razor blades. Stooping over the Book, he traced the words with a finger. He felt ill. He was in serious distress. There were the words. There were so many words. Then there were the numbers. He was counting. His finger moved across the page but he was counting. He did not know where he was anymore. He was coughing and counting and weeping.

Omar patiently read his newspapers. Only when the creature passed out did he walk across the terrace to check if it was okay. He felt its forehead then checked its pulse, then satisfied that it was just being silly, he poured a glass of water over its face then gave it a slap. It came around quickly, perhaps tasting the water that it craved. Omar hauled it back on to its knees, and pressed the Book into its lifeless hands. "Read."

The kafir was barely alive. He could feel the water on his face. There were a few drops on his lips. He didn't understand. Completely overcome, he stared up at Omar. His eyes were shining. His face was white. He couldn't speak anymore. And he did not know how to think. All he had in his head were numbers. He knew this man. He trusted this man. But he couldn't remember his name. In absolute despair, he lifted his hands to touch Omar's chest, he wanted to speak to him, but there were only numbers, then he covered his face to weep, but the pain in his throat meant he could not even sob without choking.

Prince Abdul Aziz found them together on the terrace. He had just arrived after a stressful four day ministerial conference in Doha for the World Trade Organisation. He had a dozen lawyers and accountants and secretaries following in his wake. He had a headache. Somehow, he had completely forgotten that Omar and his creature were still at the beach. Seeing it again just stopped him dead. His heart swelled up painfully. He simply couldn't inhale. Omar pushed the creature away then turned to greet his master with respect, but he was ignored. He was totally ignored. The Prince only had eyes for the creature.

The Prince was struck dumb. His creature was safe. He could hardly believe it. He was shocked that it was still so astonishingly beautiful. He actually could not believe that it was really there, and it was looking at him, and it was so happy. He had never seen such a broad smile. The face was perfect. The eyes were shining with joy. His relief was so deep and so cool and so refreshing. He realised that he had actually been preparing for disappointment. He had not dared to hope that it might be the same. Yet here it was looking up at him with those glorious, shining blue eyes, and it was smiling at him. He could not believe it, but he slowly managed to recover his composure then the house was suddenly full of people, and they were all too busy to be interested in an emotional servant having a meltdown. The Prince frowned. He was momentarily distracted then quickly gestured Omar to take the thing away.

Chapter 40

He had dressed, and was loitering at the top of the stairs when she emerged bleary-eyed from her room. Still half asleep, she was brought to a standstill by his appearance. Clean shaven and groomed, he was a thing of beauty. She quickly raised a hand as if to shield her eyes, but actually hiding the fact she looked and felt a mess. She needed to go to the bathroom, and put on her war-paint before she was able to deal with anything.

He glanced at her then focused resolutely on the floor. He grimly held on to the banister as if his life depended on it.

"You should eat, you know," she observed crossly. "You'd be a lot stronger."

He nodded respectfully.

She shook her head. He would not eat. She was wasting her breath. "Go on down. Get yourself a drink. I don't mind. Take a can out of the fridge. Put the TV on. I'll be down in a minute."

He lingered.

"Off you go," she said. She shooed him away like a chicken. "You've been up and down a few times. You can manage on your own. I have absolute confidence in you."

This time he nodded grimly, his lips compressed, his brow furrowed.

She waited and watched as he approached the stairs.

He went down slowly. He was still very weak, and was obviously in pain.

She turned away, but waited until he was safely downstairs before breathing again. She definitely needed an alarm clock. Her fragile self-image could not endure being met every morning by Adonis when she felt like Medusa on a bad day. She went into the bathroom, closing the door and locking it. Her reflection in the mirror was not inspiring. He was more than just beautiful. There was something bewitching in his blue eyes. His voice was like a rich warm coffee after a cold late night. When he smiled, she felt blessed. She could blame her age or her hard life or the fact that she was still half asleep, but the truth was that she could never have competed with him. Few mortals could. He was extraordinarily beautiful, but that beauty had cost him dear. It had changed his life. She suspected that he would have been much happier to be merely ordinary.

Downstairs, he was standing in front of the television. He had waited for her to arrive before turning it on. She guessed that he had also declined to take a drink from the fridge. She opened the curtains, then admired the view, and then turned to survey the room. He lowered himself carefully on to the sofa. He was obviously in some distress so she went out to the kitchen to fetch some painkillers and a can of strawberry milkshake. He took it from her. He bowed his head, but he was still staring at the floor.

It was too early to start with the third degree again. She checked the hedgehog then quickly put down three dishes of food for the cats. She watched them eat. They were all there. They were all alright. She smiled. Perhaps, everything would be alright. Perhaps, there were happy endings. Like a good girl, she munched through a banana, swallowed her pills then returned to the lounge with a cup of tea. He was still leaning over the armrest, utterly quiet and becalmed. She put the remote in his hand then hurried away. It was too easy to just sit there staring at him as if he were some heathen idol, waiting for him to speak or for some flash of inspiration to provide all the answers, and there were so many other things to do. She went out to fill the bird feeders then spent an hour pulling out weeds. There were nettles growing again. The ponds were full of blanket weed. There was so much to do she hardly knew where to start.

At 10.30 the Trooping of the Colour began. She made another cup of tea. The scarlet uniforms were dazzling in the sunshine. The Bearskins were difficult to explain. The soldiers on parade were all hardened professionals. Some had recently returned from frontline duty. Others were about to be deployed. They were not just decorative foot stompers. All of them had drilled for months in preparation for the honour of marching before the Queen. Their uniforms were immaculate. Their buttons were buffed. Every collar was clean and crisp. The horses were turned out as immaculately as the men. It was an annual show full of pomp and circumstance, but for most of the soldiers, it was a once in a lifetime experience. She sat contentedly with the black cat on her knee. The visual spectacle was always worth watching, and the music was great. Wind or rain, the Massed Bands could carry a tune. There were all the standards, some classic movie themes like 'The Dambusters', then some newly commissioned pieces. The music was always superb, and seemed the perfect herald of the Proms concerts that ran through the summer at the Royal Albert Hall. The black Irish horses stood placidly amongst all the shouting and martial music. They probably had earplugs now. In the old days, it was just good training. At other moments, there was absolute silence and stillness with only the acres of flags disturbing the perfect peace.

She enjoyed the spectacle. He fell asleep about halfway through. She was not sure he had ever actually managed to watch anything right through to the end. He had no stamina at all. But then he was not eating, and he had been terribly ill. She almost did not want him to wake up until he was fit and well, and the nightmare was actually over. He was going to be hurt. There was not a hope in hell of him not being hurt. She made a cup of tea, and waited for him.

After lunch, they went outside. Two circuits of the garden were enough for him. He did not want to sit on the blanket. He was a coward. The pain was still a vivid memory.

She felt the tension in his body, and glanced into his face to see a fierce emotion that was somewhere between desperation and terror. That stopped her dead. "I'm sorry." She collected him into her arms. "Let's go back inside. You've done really well today. You should be proud." He leaned against her. She was not sure that he had gained any weight at all. "Please, let me call my doctor? He'll keep all your secrets. You don't have to worry about that. You'll have proper medicine. You'll grow stronger. I don't know if I'm doing the right thing."

He flinched. He really needed to sit down. "You've been very kind. You've saved my life."

She was flattered and embarrassed, but slowly lifted an arm around her shoulder then started back towards the house. By the time she was lowering him down on to the sofa, he was shaking. His face was unbelievably white.

For an hour, she sat beside him spoon-feeding him bottle after bottle of baby food then painkillers then milkshake. They did not even have the television on. Then he was horribly sick, and then he was embarrassed. He was hardly strong enough to sit up, but he could not stop apologising while she cleaned up the vomit then carefully scrubbed the carpet. The chemicals cleared the air. She opened the windows anyway. The sun was shining. It should have been such a nice day. Once she was satisfied that she had cleaned up everything, she went outside. He was terribly distressed, but she knew he would eventually calm down if he was alone.

After a great deal of soul searching, she knew she must face the shops. It was Saturday. It would be hell. The local village shop just did not have what she needed. The baby food, obviously, was not doing it for him anymore. He was not getting any stronger. If he had a relapse then his immune system might immediately collapse. Before she went out, she managed to make him drink a glass of water. He did not want to swallow the pills, but submitted again as usual. She ruffled his hair and smiled adoringly, but he just lay back across the armrest and closed his eyes.

Once she arrived in town, it took nearly an hour of queuing to reach the supermarket. It was bursting with inconsiderate and frustrated people. Like her, everyone resented the time it took to just do a bit of shopping at the weekend. On Saturdays, there were never enough parking spaces. The aisles were too narrow. There were screaming children, bored out of their minds. There were always long queues at the checkouts. Too many checkouts remained closed. At the weekend, it always took longer to pay at the checkout than to actually go around doing the shopping. She hated it.

She kept reminding herself that she was doing it for him. He needed nutritionally stronger drinks. He needed fortifying. She had picked up a dozen bottles of vitamin pills and super-food supplements. Of course, he needed omega 3. Apparently, everyone needed omega 3 and zinc and potassium and acai berries and green coffee beans. It cost a fortune. She just about remembered to buy some cat food. The ice cream was an afterthought. She was not sure whether that was for her or for him.

He was fast asleep when she returned. He was not hot. He was breathing evenly. She went outside, and sat on the blanket to eat an ice cream. Her beloved black cat came to join her. She could not comprehend how completely her life had changed. He had filled her up as no one had ever done before. She could not bear to think about what she would do when he went away.

*

Prince Abdul Aziz was busy all that first day, and too tired to eat, so there was no need for his creature to serve at dinner. He was involved in a dozen delicate negotiations. He was now the Americans' 'go-to guy' for introductions, and had been the facilitator when negotiations between Musharraf and the White House had imploded after a few misjudged comments were leaked to the Press. He was also regularly in touch with various ministers, who reported directly to the Crown Prince. He had become a conduit between the Crown Prince and the United Nations, and less frequently between the Crown Prince and the Americans. The King had not been well since 1995. The Crown Prince was slowly gathering the reins of power.

Prince Abdul Aziz had been so busy for so long that he had almost forgotten that his creature was patiently being restored for his pleasure at the house in Dubai. He trusted Omar implicitly. He knew that it was safe. He had put everything on the line to get it out of danger, and back into his life. For a while, that had been enough. Its image was indelibly seared into his brain. He did not need to have it in his hands to remember every detail. But then he had glimpsed it down on the terrace. Somewhere the lines of communication had been crossed. He had taken an earlier flight, but nobody in Dubai had been told. He and a dozen high-powered acolytes had swept into the house to come upon Omar and some pale servant having a scene. Only the Prince knew that the pale servant was not some poor Thai or Tibetan lured from their homeland with the promise of a well-paying job.

In the morning, he rose alone to dress, and went down to first prayers. He saw Omar across the room, and remembered. But then the day engulfed him again.

*

"You're looking at me," she said, smiling at the irony.

They were in the lounge. He had slept on and off all day. She had sat with the black cat on her knee watching him and Big Shoulders. Apart from the lingering smell of chemicals it was impossible to tell that he had been ill.

He understood, and correctly lowered his gaze to stare at something no one else could see on the floor somewhere between them.

She felt his anxiety. "What's the matter? Are you alright?"

He was embarrassed then surprisingly shifty. "Yes. Thank you." He took a deep breath then looked at her. "I was just wondering who you are?"

Suddenly, it did not seem so ironic. She found it difficult to smile. "What do you mean?" Her defences came up. She had already told him her name. She was not sure he was entitled to anything else.

He moved restlessly, telegraphing that he was about to say something difficult.

She was anxious.

"Well," he said carefully. He studied the carpet. "Why did they leave me in your garden? Why you and not someone else?"

She had toiled over that one herself, but it did not seem right to encourage his distress. "Well, why not me instead of someone else?" she asked blithely.

"Well," he said. "Yes, exactly. That's what I don't understand. It can't have been random. This house is so isolated. It would have made more sense; it would have been easier for them to leave me in London near the airport or in some other city where I'd just disappear. Why did they bring me here to you? How did they know about you?"

She was sure that she had anticipated that there would be just such a moment. It was only natural that he would question her existence. "But you're assuming that there was a plan. And you're assuming that we really are isolated here. In fact, we are only an hour and a half from London, and less than ten minutes from an airfield. You couldn't land a Jumbo Jet, but I've seen the old Dakotas landing there, and lots of small private jets. You can't actually see anything from my windows, but there are three large towns within walking distance. And tens of thousands of people live only ten minutes away by car."

"There's never any traffic," he said. "How did they find you? Why did they choose your garden?"

She shrugged, determined not to let his suspicions cause offense. "I can't explain it. There probably isn't any logic behind it. People come to this area from all over the world. You wouldn't understand why, but it's true. Anyone could have bought a map, and read the signs, and easily guessed that the lane goes nowhere. They'll have seen the woodland marked, and if they'd a mind to hide something or lose someone, they could have driven up here in the twilight, and walked unchallenged into the woods." She paused to watch him struggling to believe. "Aren't you glad that I found you?"

"Yes. Yes, of course." But his anxiety would not rest. "I just want to understand."

She felt empathy, but that did not help her. "Sometimes, there are no answers. Sometimes, things just happen. That can be the hardest lesson that we have to learn. Life is not organised or logical. Things just happen. Sometimes they're good and sometimes they're bad. Sometimes, everything makes perfect sense, but usually it's just bloody chaos, and you have to make the best of it because there's nothing else."

He nodded. That was not what he wanted to hear.

She took a deep breath then leaned towards him. "Of course, he might have brought you to this area because he knew that it was important to you." When he looked up, his eyes were swimming with tears. But he crumpled up; he wrapped his arms about his chest and began rocking to and fro. "Well, he might know where you came from," she explained. "He's obviously protected you; he's taken care of you, hasn't he? It's possible that he sent you here for a specific reason."

He suddenly focused on her. "Yes. He's sent me here to you."

She retreated under the pressure. "No, I don't think so. Not to me. But I think that it is possible that you come from this area. Maybe, one of the nearby towns? It makes sense, but it's not guaranteed. Please, don't get your hopes up. It just seems to me that your prince is an intelligent man, and if he was prepared to let you go then there is every possibility that he'd make it easier for you to find your home. Nothing that you've said suggests that he's a spiteful person. You said he hadn't hurt you so there is every possibility that he's trying to help you."

His face contorted. "He never hurt me."

She still did not believe him, but could not bring herself to call him a liar. "Would you go back to him?"

His whole body shuddered. His brain had exploded. He could not understand the words.

She tried to ignore him. "Well, if you stay here then you'll need to earn a living." It was so difficult to say the words: "A job. You'll need to get a job. You'll have to mix with ordinary people. You couldn't hide. Men's toilets are open plan. You'd have to line up at the urinals with all the other guys. I'm sure nobody looks, but… well, someone will. You can't go to a gym or a public swimming pool. You couldn't ever take your shirt off unless you knew that you were alone. That body's unique." She shook her head, blushing as she remembered it. "You know that you can stay here, but you can't live the way that I do. You're a young man. You're meant to be loved. I know you're gay, but whether you're involved with boys or girls, someone will betray you. It seems inevitable these days. The trashy magazines and tabloids are full of tittle tattle, and the confessions and revelations of jilted lovers. There seem to be quite a lot of girls out there who are basically professional girlfriends. They bed a celebrity then sell the story to the media. You're so vulnerable. I'm terrified that you're going to be hurt, and that you'll be exploited. The real world can be a truly horrible place."

He gazed at her unhappily. "Why are you saying this?"

"I'm trying to help you," she said earnestly. "I don't want you to believe that you'll live happily ever after. That only happens in children's stories. There will be good days, but as many more will be hard and painful. You have to be a realist. I don't know what happened to you, but you've been marked by it, and I don't just mean the patterns on your skin. You've lived through things that most people wouldn't be able to imagine.

You will never be like other people. You have to accept that, and learn to live with it."

He blinked then focused on her again. His heart was beating too fast. "I need to ask you something, and I want you to tell the truth. You have to tell the truth. Do you promise?"

She stared at him in dumbfounded silence. What could he possibly ask that could be so important? At last, almost fearfully, she nodded. "Alright."

"You must promise?" he demanded.

His tone was unnerving. She felt exposed and vulnerable. She just did not have the confidence to avoid feeling guilty. "Yes, of course," she said, but she was not ready.

His face contorted again. Suddenly, he was ugly and unattractive and not worthy of sympathy or respect. For a moment, he covered his face while breathing deeply, and trying to find some control. He could not look at her. Not then. "It would make sense if they brought me here because you are my mother." His voice died. The muscles in his throat were choking him. It was beyond him to look at her, but he needed to. It was imperative. "Are you my mother?"

It was surprisingly painful. She tried to smile bravely. She wanted to be composed and mature, most of all, she did not want to hurt him, but that was a forlorn hope. Her sympathy for him increased immeasurably. The poor boy. How long had he toiled under that misapprehension? "I'm sorry. No. You're not my son. I'm sorry if I did anything to make you believe that it was so. Somewhere out there, you have a mother. You have a family. We'll find them." She managed to smile, but it felt like a disaster. "I'm sorry. I had no idea."

He tried to conceal his despair, but understood that she saw through him completely. "Please? I had to ask. You don't mind? I had to ask. I didn't mean to upset you."

She shook her head, still hanging on to a smile, still revelling in the fantasy of having him as a son. But the cold grasp of reality slowly crushed her heart. "My son would be older than you are now if he was alive." She shook her head. "He's dead now. It was a long time ago. I'm sorry if I was sending out confusing messages. I didn't mean to."

He did not understand, and he was drowning in his own deep, dark, fathomless misery. He could not respond to her pain. In his consciousness, he was so small and so alone that nothing bridged the gap to allow him to forge a connection with another human being, and the relationship he had with his Pakistanis was very familiar but totally unequal. He did not know how to empathise. He found it difficult to believe that other people had problems as unsolvable as his own.

He went up the stairs in silence. She followed, hardly able to guess if he was disappointed or relieved. While he undressed, she went and sat on her own bed. She should not have been surprised by his question, but her reaction to it had been a shock. He was someone's child. All her hot sweaty fantasies had gone up in smoke. He had used the M-word. She was not his mother. She had nailed her colours to the mast on that point. It did not really matter that she knew that everyone who had ever had sex had a mother. It seemed silly that it had upset her. Was it because he was so vulnerable and a victim that she felt guilty? Was it because it underlined the difference in their ages? Did it just signpost what she represented from his perspective?

When she went into his room, she found him laying face down on the bed. He had tactfully pulled the sheet across his backside which denied her the tribal markings that she found so fascinating and intriguing. The shockingly pink new skin across his back grounded her. It was so delicate. It was the colour of watermelons. She perched on the side of the bed then opened the jar of cream. It was almost empty. The one thing that she needed urgently and she had forgotten to buy it. She wanted to reassure him. Gently rubbing the ointment into his terrible wounds went with tenderness and platitudes. She just did not have any words that she could say without feeling like a ghoul or a liar. She did not want to burst the bubble. He should not have survived. She was delighted that he had, but could not in all honesty explain it. It was a mystery. It felt like a miracle. She did not want to jinx it by over analysing what had happened.

He had turned his face to the wall. She did not need to study body language to understand that he wanted her to hurry up and go away. He flinched occasionally. She was too nervous to be playful, and she had to respect his injuries. "I'm sorry," she said as she screwed the lid back on the jar then placed it carefully on the bedside table.

After a moment, he turned to look up at her questioningly.

She grimaced with embarrassment. His eyes were wide. His eyebrows arched. She felt her cheeks burning. She did not know what to say. There was nothing that she could say that would not have exposed her to ridicule. He had already asked too many questions. That he was so far off the mark did not make any of them hurt any less. "You make me want to cry." She grimaced again. She tried to smile. "I can't cry. It just doesn't work. It's not that I don't feel anything. I feel everything. I just can't cry." She shrugged miserably. "No tears left. I'm sorry."

He blinked slowly like a cat. He stared into her eyes until the colour drained from her face, and she had to lower her gaze.

"I cry all the time."

Chapter 41

She woke first. She wanted to be ready. She was supposed to be taking care of him. He was her guest. It seemed terribly wrong that he could wake up earlier than she did, and then had to wait on the landing because he was still uncomfortable about going downstairs alone.

She pulled on some old clothes and tiptoed down the stairs like a thief. Going around with the vacuum cleaner was anything but quiet, but she did her best. She was in the middle of mopping the floor in the kitchen and scullery when he appeared. He had shaved and dressed. He looked elegant, and totally out of place.

"Come in," she said. She gestured him to sit at the kitchen table.

He was hesitant. He was hardly encouraged when she hurried out of the room to return minutes later with a cushion. She carefully placed it down between the hard chair and his tender wounds. He still sat bolt upright. His gaze was fixed on the table. She hurried away again then came back with a sheaf of paper and a pen. He became increasingly anxious. He had no idea what she wanted him to do.

She sat down opposite him, raking her fingers through her hair, and trying desperately to smile, and not be ashamed of her appearance. "I thought you could write down what you want to tell your parents. You could pretend that you won't be able to go so you're sending a letter. It'll help you to sort it all out in your head."

He just stared at the paper.

She tried another smile, which was frightful. "Really. It's a good idea."

His head moved. He was not convinced. "I don't think I can."

She was annoyed because it sounded like he was refusing, but that was totally out of character so she was confused. "I'm sorry, Daniel, but I don't understand. I'm just asking you to pretend to write a letter. It'll help you to prepare. You need to get this right. You need to be rock-solid. If you can't tell them the truth then you need to be word perfect. This will help you."

He lifted his hands an inch or two off the table top in a helpless gesture. "Please? I don't know how to do that."

She still did not understand, but she needed to leave. The chair scraped loudly as she rose to her feet. "I'm going to get changed. Help yourself to a drink."

He just shook his head. "Please? I'm sorry. I cannot write in English. I have never learned. I can read. I can write in Arabic. Prof. Shah taught me, but the script, the letters are not the same." He managed to look her in the eye, but only for the briefest fleeting moment. "It will help me to write it. You are right. But I can't. Please? I'm sorry, I don't know the letters. It's impossible. Please? I'm sorry."

She sat down heavily. "I didn't know."

He stooped, round-shouldered and defensive. He managed his awkward little shrug. "Please? I don't know anything."

"But…" She was at a loss to know what to say.

"Please? I never need to write. I have servants." He stopped then nodded gravely. His composure returned slowly. "They brush my hair, they clean my teeth, they do everything for me. I couldn't… I am not allowed to do anything. I am only decorative. I am to be admired. Their job is to make me beautiful so that I am always admired."

"And loved," she reminded him gently.

"I wasn't… It wasn't like that."

He could not lift his eyes. She felt so sorry for him. "But you can read? You said Mahmood taught you to read poems."

"Yes," he said.

"Do you remember any of them?"

He shook his head then shrugged evasively.

"But they were in English?"

He sort of shrugged again then admitted reluctantly: "Many were in English."

She wanted to swear, but not at him. It was not his fault. None of it was his fault. Feeling helpless, she rose to her feet again. She fetched him a new can of nutritional milkshake. It was fortified with every mineral and supplement she had ever heard about. It probably tasted horrible, but he was an adult, he did not need everything to be sugar-coated. "Here, drink this. It's much better for you. You're going to need to build up your strength."

He looked at the strange can. The words and logos were different. It was not pink, and it did not say 'strawberry' anywhere. "Thank you. You have saved my life."

She turned away irritably. "I'm going upstairs. You sit here and try to remember one of those poems."

He might have nodded. He was still staring at the can. "Thank you."

She lingered then turned away to leave him. For all her concern about his delicate mental condition, it would have destroyed her to stay there in her tatty work clothes with not even a smudge of makeup. She could not really focus on anything until she had the bathroom door closed. If he could remember a poem, she was sure that would help him to copy the text in his own hand. That would be mimicking rather than learning. She did not expect him to be literate by nightfall, but it was a major obstacle that he needed to overcome.

*

Prince Abdul Aziz stared gravely at his restored property, slowly unravelling his customary detachment, while all the time denying the depth of his curiosity, and the disconcerting and quite bewildering pangs that tore at his heart. It was a surreal moment. He had dreamt of it. He had imagined it, but it had always been something wistful and unachievable. He had never hoped. If he had allowed himself to hope then the temptation would have overwhelmed him. After 9/11, everything changed. He could not leave it unprotected in the middle of a warzone. That was unthinkable. In the days after the attack on New York, he had imagined personally leading a troop of commandos into Afghanistan on a daring rescue mission. That had been an exciting fantasy, but fortunately common sense prevailed. Instead, he organised the rescue of the Parsi community. He hired professional soldiers and a dozen Chinooks. The United Nations thanked him. Everyone thanked him. No one asked why. The Parsi were taken under the UN's wing. The kafir was quietly brought home. This exquisite creature was his again, and it was undoubtedly even more beautiful than he remembered. The certainty of possession warmed his flesh like a roaring fire. He wanted to be content and contemplative, but he realised that he was genuinely distressed, which was baffling. He had every right to be happy because he had achieved his goal, but he felt that he should be angry. His honour demanded it. Honour was everything. But it was his heart that hurt him, not his precious honour: here was the thing that had broken him and his son.

The kafir was bursting with joy. He had not been able to stop smiling since seeing the Prince on the terrace. He was dizzy with excitement. He could not sit still despite Mahmood's best efforts and Omar's empty threats. But hours dragged by. There was no summons. His fragile psyche had begun to implode. That first evening, he had been all dressed up with nowhere to go until news came down that the Prince had retired. By then he had become distressed. An army of doctors might have restored his physical appearance, but psychologically, all he had left on which to secure his sanity was the simple fact that his master had cared enough to bring him home.

The kafir bowed down, and softly kissed his master's feet then the ring and, finally, his hands. He was trembling. By then he was emotionally overwhelmed. He gazed up into the Prince's face, noticing the grey hairs and the tired eyes, and he knew that he loved him. "Please?" His voice was hoarse. He kissed the ring again. Omar had filled his head with numbers and words, but nothing made sense. "Please?" His throat was swollen and sore. He could barely speak above a whisper. There were so many words and numbers, but he could not remember the ones that he needed to salute his master. "All that I am." He turned the hand to kiss the palm then pressed it to his cheek. "Please?"

The Prince was drowning in the blue eyes. The dark rapture burned powerfully through him. He gasped, felt a pain like a knife then shook his head. It was tainted. It was not the same. He wanted to cherish it and kill it. He needed it like a drug, but wanted to erase it from his memory forever. "Be quiet!"

The kafir was too happy to be careful. All that mattered to him was that he had, at last, truly come home. He smothered the hand with kisses. His blood fizzed with excitement, and he knew absolute, perfect joy.

Somewhere in the house, a phone rang. They did not hear it. They only had eyes for each other, but they were poles apart.

The Prince took a moment to breathe then withdrew his hand. He was remembering not the thrill of plundering his creature's flesh, but the ignominy of humiliating his son. He had committed an unpardonable crime, and here was the cause. His shame flared up and burned through him like acid. Here was the cause. This beautiful thing had bewitched his soul and driven him insane. Here was the cause. It had corrupted him and his family. It had scarred them irreparably. His son and brother and brother-in-law had not spoken to him since that night. None of them could bear to be reminded of what they had done. Here was the cause. Here it was smiling triumphantly, which proved its guilt. It had corrupted them. It had orchestrated every despicable act. It had spun some web around them, and then played with them all like puppets. Here was the cause. In the glorious smile, he read jubilation. It was evidently delighted to have him in its power again. It had played him. From the beginning, it had played him. Here was the cause. Obviously, it had to die. He could not bear to give it away. To think of it with another man was agony. His soul was torn to shreds just imagining it being touched by someone else. He could not own his jealousy. He could not acknowledge that it was his pride that had been insulted by his son. Rage twisted his brain. Here was the vile thing that had broken his family apart, but he could not give it up. He would take his pleasure in other ways. It would be denied everything that it craved. It would suffer. He would find ways to make its every waking moment a torment, which would prove to his family that he hated it. He did. He was so sure. And he needed to prove to God that he hated it. Then there would be no stain on his honour. His horrible crime would be washed away and forgotten.

The kafir stooped to kiss his master's feet. There was something wrong. A dark veil had come down across his master's face. The light had gone out of his eyes. Unable to worship the ring, the kafir struggled to keep his nerve.

Prince Abdul Aziz knew he must kill it, but not yet. He wanted to see it suffering for a while, but knew that it would revel in every punishment that he could devise, which he found darkly challenging. His anger and pain became molten wrath. Unable to resist proving his resilience, the Prince moved almost imperceptibly to point at the floor before him. It was the slightest of movements. It was hardly even the flexing of one joint of one finger, but his creature stirred. Its eyes shone brilliantly, but now with tears of heartbreak. It literally started forward on its knees like a wretched beggar. It snatched at his hand, seizing it desperately before suddenly begging for mercy. The Prince was so incensed he tore his hand free then swung it back to knock the vile thing tumbling across the floor.

For some minutes, the only sound was the creature struggling to suppress its sobs. It lay on the floor, ugly, defaced and emotionally destroyed.

The Prince had struck out as a reflex, and was briefly horrified by his base behaviour. In that instant, he was transported back to that night nearly three years ago when he had been so arrogant and so insulted that he had betrayed his own son to provide a sticking plaster for his wounded honour. They had raged and shouted at each other like some seething mob, but it was the creature which was assaulted. The Prince could still remember the fire in his veins. It felt like a drug. They had all behaved like drunken barbarians. That they had not compounded their crime by triumphantly urinating on their fallen enemy absolved them of nothing. It was still difficult to believe that it had actually happened, but the floor of the entire room had to be ripped up. The long table had been burned. Even now, almost three years later, he could see the bloodstains though they existed now only in his head.

He was appalled at having struck it again, but quite overwhelmed by the excitement coursing through his veins like raw alcohol. He was aroused. He was shocked by how quickly he had become completely aroused. His mouth was dry. His heart was racing. Images of that night flooded his head. Echoes resonated throughout his body. It was so vivid, so intense, so immediate. He reached for his groin, and found his sex like a rod of iron. The certainty of rights over property in an ancient tribal culture enabled him to deftly sidestep his dilemma. There was no morality or equality or fairness. It was lust. It was simply lust. The creature was a just cipher. He had spent millions of dollars to possess it again. He owned it. There was not the slightest doubt that he owned it. He had the right. The Prince turned away, and walked to his desk then cleared a space. "Come here." His voice was husky and low. He watched as the overwrought creature gathered itself on the floor then crept to its feet and slunk closer, head bowed, tears still falling like diamonds from its lovely blue eyes. Without any prompting, it leaned down over the desk, and braced itself. It was shivering, but its quiet submission was shocking.

The Prince knew he had to fuck it. It was as essential to him as oxygen. He had to have it. He had to force his way inside. He had to go rampaging through it like a marauding army, battering it into submission, exploring every part of it so that he could be sure of rooting out and annihilating any resistance. Then he could walk away. Then he might be able to escape. It held his soul in its hands. He had to believe that he could kill it. It wasn't murder. He had the right. It had destroyed everything that he loved. Surely, that gave him the right. He wanted to see it broken and powerless. And more importantly, he had to restore his honour. He had to completely destroy it to save his honour. He had no choice. He searched for a weapon, and found only a ruler. His hands were shaking badly. He wanted to fuck the beautiful creature until it wept and begged for mercy, knowing instinctively that all its protests and tears were only to excite and tease. It really was insatiable. It hardly mattered that he knew that the creature would lie and deceive. Every gesture and every expression were calculated. There was nothing the creature could say that he would believe. But he needed proof. He needed it badly. The cold metal ruler hardly felt hard enough. He admired it for a moment then gripped it tightly in his right hand. His left pulled up the creature's shift then rested on its back. It flinched. He could feel it shivering, which made his heart quicken. Taking a deep breath, he gritted his teeth then laid two stripes across the creature's firm backside, counting them in a loud authoritarian voice. The creature writhed and gasped.

The pain was shocking. The kafir trembled. His legs almost gave way. Like a drowning man, he clung to the desk. He knew what he would have to endure. It did not make the pain any less. This was the price he had to pay. He had to be hurt and bleeding or his master would not love him. In barely a moment, he was shivering violently and drenched with sweat. He couldn't breathe. He couldn't think. He wanted to scream, but not because of the pain. He needed his master to fuck him. His whole body craved the brutal violence that he needed to feel loved.

Maddened by the soft cries that each blow drew from his creature, the Prince was soon struggling to focus. He was trembling. He hit it again. There was the same sweet heartrending gasp. His guts twisted into a thousand knots. He could hardly speak, but he thrashed it until his arm arched. By then he was shuddering. He was beyond rage, beyond sanity. He raped it there and then. He wore himself out fucking it. He wanted to destroy it, to tear it apart, and shatter it into a million pieces that would become nothing more than grains of sand in a vast desert. He had to defeat it. He had to dominate it. He had to carve his ownership into every fibre of its body. He had to be the master of his own soul, but he failed. It had bewitched him. He was compelled beyond madness. He fucked it until he was too weary to pull away. He filled it with seed. He beat it brutally. He battered every part of it, and still came away consumed by a need. He could not even name what he needed. Feelings of loss overwhelmed him. Something was missing. He was exhausted, drained of everything, but compelled to strive again, to drive back into the creature's flesh, and search again and again and again because he had to find what he needed to take away his pain. But he could not find what he could not name.

The creature remained elusive.

*

Most of Sunday was spent in the kitchen. They had several poetry books on the table between them. She loved her books. She handled them with respect, and expected him to do the same. Fortunately, he had been taught to treat all his master's books as if they were the Holy Book, which was sacred as it contained the Words of God. There was a volume of 'modern greats', another of love poems, and the collected work of Keats, Shelley, and Byron.

He was very happy to just sit there reading quietly, but the whole point of the exercise was to find a poem that he was familiar with. She had a ream of white paper and a couple of pens. After she had read the opening lines to a dozen of her favourites, and asked if he remembered them, she began to feel that he was not being entirely honest. "These are some of the greatest poems ever written. If you didn't read Keats then you weren't reading love poems."

He closed the book he was reading, and clasped his hands together then sighed. It took him a moment to deal with his emotions. At last, he managed to look at her, and he smiled a little wistfully. "How do I love thee? Let me count the ways. I love thee to the depth and breadth and height my soul can reach, when feeling out of sight for the ends of being and ideal grace. I love thee to the level of every day's most quiet need, by sun and candle-light. I love thee freely, as men strive for right; I love thee purely, as they turn from praise, I love thee with the passion put in use in my old griefs, and with my childhood's faith. I love thee with a love I seemed to lose with my lost saints – I love thee with the breath, smiles, tears, of all my life! And, if God choose, I shall but love thee better after death."

She was transfixed. His voice was rich and smooth. The words wrapped her in honey. And his eyes gleamed like white-hot embers. At last, she remembered to breathe. She managed to close her mouth. Some horrid little voice in her head reminded her cruelly that he was not speaking to her, but to some fondly remembered memory. She filled her lungs and almost said: "Wow!" But it seemed totally inappropriate and contemptuous. "That was lovely," she whispered. "Of course, Elizabeth Barrett Browning." She smiled easily. "Well, that was really lovely. And word perfect."

He had lowered his gaze. He might have tried to smile, but it was twisted with embarrassment and discomfort.

She stared at him for a moment, stunned by his performance, dazzled by his looks. "And you read to him every evening?" She was not sure how much she would have paid to have that kind of attention. "And you did love him." It was not a question. "You can deny it to everyone, but you have to be honest with yourself. You loved him, didn't you!"

His face flushed. For the briefest moment, he managed to look at her. "Yes. He was different. When he fucked me, it was different. Even when it was just sex, and when he hurt me, I felt that he knew who I was. With everyone else I was only a substitute for a girl. They slapped me around as if I was a girl." He nodded his head affirmatively. "He'd look me in the eye. He knew me. He was fucking me. And I loved him for making love to me." His head bowed. His chest tightened. "He made love to me. To me!"

She understood. There was nothing to say that would not have diminished him. Blushing hotly, she reached for one of the fatter books. She opened it at the index and searched for the opening line. Of course, it was there. It was one of the finest poems ever written. Every literate lover knew it by heart. She found the right page then gently pushed it across the table for him to see the words that he had just recited from memory so eloquently. He struggled to lift his gaze and focus on the printed page. She could not look at him. He was terribly upset. She pulled a few sheets of paper towards her then carefully wrote in longhand the same poem. It took only a few minutes. It felt longer. She felt he was watching critically. "This is what you need to copy. Once upon a time, we all learned to write in a very precise way. These days, kids seem to be illiterate when it comes to producing a legible letter. Anyway," she said, and smiled. "You know the words. You have the printed text. This is handwriting. You need to learn how to write like this. It's easy, but it takes a bit of practice. You need to be able to do this if you're going to stay here and get a job. Do you understand?" She nudged the sheet that she had written on across the table. "It's very easy. Just take your time."

With a trembling hand, he picked up the pen.

"You're left handed?" She was surprised.

He moved the pen into his right hand then moved it back into his left. "I don't know."

"When you wrote Arabic at the madrassa, which hand did you use?"

He shifted the pen between his hands. "I don't remember." He shook his head. "I don't remember!"

"When you brush your teeth or comb your hair or shave?"

He shook his head. "I never…" Then he remembered. His right hand rose to stroke his smooth face then swept through his mane of raven hair. He smiled then placed the pen confidently into his right hand. "I use my right hand. And with my master, I use my right hand."

"And it's comfortable?"

He nodded and smiled triumphantly. "Yes. I am right-handed."

Her heart tingled at his response. He was a child winning a prize. She watched as he studied the pen and then the printed text and then her handwriting. She realised it was going to be a long day. "I need a cup of tea." He was not even listening. She rose stiffly to her feet and went to fill the kettle. Then she stood at the window, staring out at the view. It was almost criminal to be inside. From the window, she could see that there were lots of birds in the fruit trees and shrubs. Many of them were obviously juveniles. Rising on to tiptoe, she could just about see that the distant feeders were all nearly half empty or worse. She went outside, sure that he did not even notice that she had gone. Of course, the birds disappeared rapidly, but she knew they would come back. It took more than an hour to go around topping up all the feeders. Many had birds back on them before she had returned to the house. Yes, she was making a difference. She checked up on the hedgehog in the scullery, and decided he could be released at sunset, then returned to boil the kettle again.

He had attempted a few words in a trembling hand. His assumption that it would be easy had been quickly undermined.

She heaped praise on him, offered him a nice hot cup of tea then ruffled his hair as he blushed. While he focused on his task, she sat opposite him, and browsed idly through her leather-bound volume of Keats. Were they all drug addicts? Were they the pop stars of their day? Byron was worshipped in his lifetime. She had a feeling that most poets starved to death in their garrets, and only then received the fame and glory that their talent deserved. They all seemed to be consumptives, but maybe it was not pulmonary tuberculosis at all, but opium or gin.

For her, it was a pleasant way to pass an afternoon. She did miss the tennis. Lleyton Hewitt beat Blake in two sets. She would have liked to watch it, but never mind. From her point of view, it was the right result. In only a few weeks, it would be Wimbledon. She could hardly wait. It would be Roger Federer all the way. She was almost rubbing her hands with glee.

Chapter 42

Monday morning, she walked him around the garden a few times then took him back inside. He was left stretched out on the sofa with the television on while she went into town.

There was an internet café. She only knew of its existence because it was on the way to the car park, and had once been a florist so she was used to looking in the window whenever she passed. It was decidedly less attractive as an internet café, but it was always busy. She braced herself and went inside, hands clasped together, eyes popping, and feeling like an old fuddy-duddy surrounded by juvenile delinquents.

A very pretty girl approached. She looked about twelve but was probably twenty. "Can I help you?"

"I don't have a computer." Most of the tables were occupied. Half of the rest had bundles of cables amongst the condiments. "But I wanted to come and have a go."

The pretty girl smiled warmly. "Of course, if you come over here." She indicated a few tables nearer the till and counter. Older people sat there. Most of them were staring at the screens as if extremely short-sighted.

A little offended at the assumption of her age, she followed the girl, and sat down. The chair skidded on the lino floor. It made a noise. She blushed. She did not feel that she was in the Darby and Joan demographic yet, but had to accept that as far as computers were concerned she was amongst the dinosaurs.

"Do you want to look up anything in particular?" the girl asked sweetly.

Jane watched as the computer screen lit up with advertisements for all sorts of things that she had never heard about. "It's very busy," she observed critically. "It's very confusing. How do you know what to look at?"

The delightful girl leaned down to tap on a few keys. The mouse darted about. Above the music and the noise from the street, there was the *click, click, click* of plastic on plastic that opened up an Aladdin's Cave of information. The screen was transformed. It was white and clean but for a toolbar across the top, and a box in the centre where the cursor blinked expectantly. The girl smiled again. She gazed at Jane, who was extremely nervous, then quickly typed in the name of the town. Instantly, there was a list of sites and some photographs covering a wide range of subjects connected to that town. The girl pointed at the toolbar, and explained about the images and the maps and the printer.

"Would you like something to drink?"

Jane pushed her handbag down on to the floor, and tucked it between her feet. "A coffee?" She managed to drag her eyes from the screen to gaze across the counter. "And chocolate cake?"

"Of course." The girl smiled then reeled off a list of the different types of coffee available.

Jane Howard did not know about latté. She knew espresso came in a tiny cup. "Just a normal cup of coffee."

The girl smiled sweetly. She still looked about twelve.

Jane stared back at the computer screen. She had already done some homework. She had a room full of books. It might have taken until the early hours of the morning, but she had established the parameters of her inquiry.

It was actually frighteningly easy to look up missing children on the internet. An American site listed more than seven hundred missing boys in the timeframe she was using. An equivalent British site had a much smaller number, but it was still utterly harrowing to click through all the photographs. Each one represented a whole family destroyed. So many of them were recent. She could not help suspecting that there were a great many more older cases that had not yet been loaded, or where perhaps the families had asked for their son to be withdrawn from the list. She could imagine that closure was impossible while the photograph remained on the internet. The photograph was their hope. How could they grieve when they still had hope? She found it all seriously disturbing. She went through all the files even though some of the children were black or Asian. Her heart ached for all of them. Her heart that had seemed so cold and dead for so many years was alive now and grievously wounded.

Every child had a photograph. Their names were listed, as well as date of birth, hair and eye colour, when and where they went missing. The recent cases had only recent photographs, but the older ones had two. One was a real photograph obviously from the family album, usually showing a happy child. The second photograph was a computer generated image of what they might look like now. They were all attractive and young and nice.

The various staff in the internet café hovered around anxiously when she lingered for an hour and then for another hour after that. The pretty girl refilled the coffee cup. The chocolate cake was not touched.

The American site was very upsetting. There were so many children missing. Some of them did not even have photographs, but raggedly drawn likenesses. It was so upsetting. She knew there was no point in looking through the files, but it was just so appalling; so many children. She had to look at them.

There were ghosts gathering around her. There were so many faces, and some of them seemed horribly familiar. They leaned over her shoulder searching for their own photographs, forcing her to look at every single file and acknowledge every name. It was cold and eerie on a warm summer's day. How could she explain to anyone why there were so many ghosts? She felt her husband's presence too. His shadow fell across everything. His sick predilection had cost countless lives and ultimately his own. She shivered. Her skin crawled. She felt her ribs cracking again. His filthy hands were around her throat. She was afraid again. She was absolutely terrified. But he was dead now. He could not hurt anyone else. She had thrown him to the fishes in the Wyre Estuary, and he was never coming back.

For a moment, she was at Knott Holme again. She was in that dark and terrifying house. Her husband was violent and abusive. He was sick. He was a psychopath. He had a thing for little boys, and no conscience when it came to money. Just remembering made her feel ill. He was a loathsome monster. His life was full of dark secrets. He had beaten her even when she was pregnant. Giving him a son just made it worse. She could not protect herself never mind her child. Her beautiful child withered then disappeared. She was sure he had murdered her son. And he had never denied it. That had been the catalyst. That had driven her insane. She had never been strong or brave. She could not fight him. Poison had always been a woman's weapon. She did not regret killing him, but she had run away and changed her name, and been hiding ever since. That was another life. She was somebody else. But she was still terrified.

She looked at all the little boys. Was she really only looking for her son? Had her son been swept up by the collectors, and whisked away to the Middle East? Had her vile husband sold his own son for a handful of coins? Had Daniel come back only to haunt her? She shook her head. She was cold and shivering. She was struggling to nail shut the door and deny it all. She was Jane Howard now. She was not the poor, demented wretch living in terror at Knott Holme with an abusive husband, and that host of strange men who always came in the night.

There were just too many ghosts. They were not real. She knew it was all a figment of her imagination, but the pain was real. Her fear was real. What she felt was authentic. But she felt like an intruder. All she was doing was looking through all the photographs and reading the brief, tragic, little stories. Whole lives were condensed into two or three lines. It was unbearably sad. The old photographs were heart breaking. They were all smiling, and they were all dead. She did not need to be a psychic to know that almost all of them were dead. She tried not to think about what had happened to them. Her husband would have known and taken delight in it. He was a paedophile, and while he lived she was culpable. She had known and did nothing until her own child was lost. She tried not to imagine the terrible suffering of the families. How many lives had been destroyed? It was not just the missing boys, but parents and grandparents and siblings. Her search criteria had been just a few years in the 1980s. There were hundreds of boys. After twenty years what hope was there left? Even the bravest parents must have been crippled by it. To carry such a burden for so long must have damaged them irreparably. Would they have ever been able to laugh again? Their ability to love must have been blighted by a cancer. It did not matter how many days or weeks or years passed, they were permanently scarred. They could not trust anyone. They could never stop wondering if this stranger that they were passing on the street was the murderer who took their son. There was no peace. There was no rest. They were given counselling and support and drugs, but nothing would ever fill the hole carved into their hearts.

It was absolutely agonising when she found a boy with startlingly blue eyes. He was attractive and grinning broadly. He looked happy. He looked so very happy. The photograph might have been taken on holiday. The background was hazy. It could have been the seaside. It upset her that he had been taken away from so much happiness. So many of the pictures were like that. She assumed that they had been chosen because they were smiling. It must have cost the families dear to have their boys on public display on the website. 'Anyone having information' – it was such a cold phrase. She wondered how many mothers still visited the site to gaze at their sons. Such devotion was admirable. The pain must have been extreme.

Her own pain was nailed down. She controlled her environment. No one was allowed into her life to ask difficult questions. That was her coping mechanism. She could not begin to understand how these other poor souls could survive knowing that the whole world could look at their son, and read the sad little piece of history. They were so exposed. She could not have survived that. So she had run away and changed her name and stopped being alive.

She wrote down the important details. It was good news really. Perhaps, the internet was a good thing after all, not that she wanted a computer in her house. That felt intrusive. She had a few bare facts. There was still a long way to go. And she hardly knew what she could safely tell him. The likeness was so good, she was almost certain, but it was not proof. And what would she do if he went completely off the rails, and ran away before she could explain that they must be so careful, and check every detail thoroughly? She could not help feeling that she had found just enough information for it to be seriously damaging.

The pretty girl came forward to ask if she wanted a printout. In barely a minute, she had all the information and two photographs. Looking at the pieces of paper, the girl was upset and curious but Jane could not explain.

She walked back to her car, and just sat there for a while. She had found him. She was sure, but she did not know how to tell him. The computer generated face was his face, but it was ordinary. The cheekbones were not so chiselled. The eyes did not gleam. The hairstyle was more laddish than stylish. She was actually frightened. She had found a huge piece of the jigsaw puzzle. It would change everything. It might destroy him. He was not ready. She felt guilty for wanting to keep it a secret. But he was not ready. She was not sure that he would ever be ready.

She drove home. She had meant to go to the shops. She had meant to find out about Barbaro. Her brain had turned to mush. She knew his name. She knew a little bit, but she could not tell him anything. He was not ready. She parked the car. She fussed about trying to decide whether to take the photographs and printouts into the house. If she hid them away he might still find them. He was unlikely to go near the car.

She sat for half an hour just staring at the photographs. The little boy was quite adorable. He was cute and pretty and so happy. He had been loved. He was still loved. That happy little boy had grown up, and been sculpted and polished into something extraordinary. She still believed that he was loved. It was not simply because he was so beautiful. He was another species, a divine being in a league of his own, and someone loved him very much. It might not have been a conventional relationship, but there was affection and passion and definitely love. She had to believe that he was loved.

*

The Prince was in his study. It was late. He had just broken his fast. All the doors and windows were open to let the cooler air flood into the room. The air conditioners were switched off. The guests had gone. His phone had finally stopped ringing. It was so quiet. He should have felt at peace, perhaps weary because of the hour, but he was distracted and confused which were unfamiliar to him. He paced the room. He stood at the open doors filling his lungs with the fragrant air carried in off the sea. He picked up a coffee cup then sighed because it was cold, then shoved it away because he was not actually thirsty. He could list the things that he did not want, but not acknowledge what he missed.

It was after midnight when he picked up a phone and dialled Omar. The call was answered promptly. Omar had not been asleep.

"What's happening?" the Prince demanded. "It's been three days."

"Your Highness?" Omar responded politely.

The Prince took a deep breath. "Where is my servant?"

Omar hesitated. That was enough.

"Bring it here now!" He angrily put down the phone. His stomach was dissolving in its own acid. His mouth was dry. He paced the room then sat down, then shot irritably to his feet. His heart rate had escalated. He was angry and upset and excited, but none of his thoughts or emotions made sense. He could hardly construct a rational thought for the storm raging in his head.

There was a knock at the door.

He turned impatiently. "Come in!"

Omar entered. He was respectably dressed as if he had just come from the mosque. Behind him, the creature remained obscured.

Prince Abdul Aziz reined in his temper at the sight of Omar. He moved to sit down on the sofa while Omar and the creature crossed the room.

Omar bowed. The creature sank wearily to its knees and leaned against him. Its wrists were handcuffed close together, which Omar held in his fist, preventing it from offering its customary pledge of submission.

The Prince stared at the creature. He could not breathe. He could not think. "What happened?" he asked. His voice was thick with emotion.

"Peace be upon you, my lord, Your Highness," Omar said respectfully. "May the Blessings of the Holy Prophet protect you and your family."

"Thank you," the Prince said distractedly, then remembered his manners: "Peace be upon you and to your family. Omar. And thank you." He actually managed to look at Omar then focused again on the creature. "Is it sick?"

Omar could not criticise his boss, but he did not approve of his behaviour. "Your Highness, I regret that we underestimated the damage done during its absence. Please my lord, Your Highness, forgive me."

The Prince rose to his feet, and advanced to stand over the creature, which shrank away from him to hide behind Omar. He did not understand. "What's wrong with it?" he asked irritably.

Omar had rarely stood so close to the Prince. He could not lie to him, but the truth was unrepeatable. "It fell down," he explained quietly.

The Prince's expression remained dark and forbidding. There was no guilt at all. The creature was his to command. He had spent millions of dollars to camouflage its return amidst the rescue of the Parsi. So far only one of his wives had complained, but she was hot-tempered enough to melt an ice cap. If she had her way, the creature would have been disembowelled and fed to her precious dogs. She had screamed abuse, and threatened to throw acid in its face. He threatened to divorce her. She swore that she would tell his father that he was screwing around with men. He had her locked up in her suite of rooms, took away her phone, forbade her visitors, and chose loyal men to guard her. That had been months ago. He could not keep her locked away forever just as he could not have left his creature in such terrible danger.

Omar cleared his throat politely. "We really don't know what happened in Afghanistan. It has taken months to recover. I don't believe it would hurt anyone, but I'm not a psychiatrist."

"So it's just nerves?"

Omar nodded reluctantly. "I think it fainted."

"It fainted?"

Omar nodded again. "There were cuts and bruises. But they're healing."

"Yes, good," the Prince murmured. He wanted his creature to look up at him, but he could not ask it for anything in front of Omar. "Can it stay here?"

Omar hesitated but knew he could not refuse.

The kafir was exhausted. He had not slept for three days. He had regained consciousness in Mahmood's arms, and then thrashed about like a demented lunatic. Omar had sent for some of the bodyguards. For the next seventy hours, he had been held still by various men. They were not comforting an invalid. He was held absolutely still so that he would know that he was powerless and yet safe. They allowed him to wear himself out, but there was no escape. There would never be an escape. It was like wrestling on the mats again. They simply outweighed him. They did not have to hurt him. It was not threatening. He was just held still. When he settled down they allowed him a drink of water. After twenty-four hours, he was resigned. After thirty-six, he was distressed. It was another thirty-six hours before Omar allowed him to stand up. By then he was totally subdued. Then the phone had rung. He implicitly understood that the Prince had the power and the right to dispose of him in whatever way he saw fit, whether it was by dropping him out of a helicopter over the Rub al Khali or allowing him to slowly starve to death. The manner of his inevitable execution was entirely at the whim of the Prince. No one would challenge his authority. He could have stood on a public street, and put a gun to the kafir's head then shot him dead; no one would have said a word. He was a prince. There was no restriction on his will. He was above the law in his own country, and shielded from it everywhere else by diplomatic immunity.

"I don't believe it is fit to serve you, Your Highness," Omar said bravely.

"And why is it skulking around?" the Prince demanded. "Get up!"

Omar brought the creature carefully to its feet. He knew exactly why it was frightened. Any fool could see that it was frightened. He kept hold of the handcuffs, and with his free hand, he straightened its shirt and tidied its appearance. It was trembling with fear, but the eyes flashed like moonbeams in the pale face.

They were close together. They were all about the same height, but the creature was stooped, and anxious not to be noticed. The Prince reached out imperiously to seek the collar that he knew his creature was obliged to wear. He recognised it immediately. It was the same collar that he had organised four years earlier. It was glittering brass and beautifully hand-stitched leather. It was heavy and unbreakable and tight. He forced up his creature's head. The face was a white mask of pain and distress. The only colour came from the cuts and bruises. The Prince paused. His temper subsided. He remembered unhappily that he had beaten his creature when it had faltered in its devotion.

Omar moved to support the creature, which was barely strong enough to stand. He held it under the arm. He did not look at the expression on the Prince's face. He did not need to see proof that the Prince was obsessed. Most men had a weakness of some sort, for the Prince it was this blue-eyed creature. The attraction was an open secret. Most of the other servants knew what was going on. Like Omar, they believed it was none of their business. The creature was acknowledged to be a great beauty, but its looks would definitely fade with time. There was no doubt at all that the Prince would eventually lose interest. Nature would take its course. That was inevitable.

"It's not going to hurt me," the Prince said firmly. He forced up its head again, but it would not look at him. "Leave us."

Omar stepped back, and bowed then turned away to quietly leave the room.

Prince Abdul Aziz jostled the collar playfully, and was rewarded when the creature slowly raised its eyes to look at him.

"You wouldn't hurt *me?*" the Prince asked gently. He was smiling. The moonbeams in its eyes had melted his heart to syrupy honey. He surveyed its face, returning constantly to stare into the gleaming blue eyes. There were superficial cuts and bruises, but much of the damage had been obscured by a tinted foundation. He eased the pressure on the collar then arranged it decoratively around the creature's neck. He straightened its shirt then smiled as he stroked a few stress lines from its forehead with a firm thumb.

"No, you wouldn't hurt me," he said quietly. A great smile spread across his face then he patted it affectionately on the shoulder as if it were a faithful hound. It blinked slowly. It did not look well. He turned away to sit on the sofa.

The kafir slid down heavily on to his knees. He had never thought to harm anyone. When the Prince held out a hand, he shuffled wearily closer. He was allowed the ring to kiss. All the time, he gazed steadily into his master's eyes. He was too tired to be afraid, too tired to played with. Somewhere in the recesses of his mind, he knew that his master could be kind as well as angry. He just did not know what to do. He moved in as close as possible to the sofa, and kept his master's hand pressed to his cheek. As he leaned against the cushions, he breathed deeply, then simply fell asleep.

The Prince was suddenly becalmed. His temper melted away as he gazed at it in thoughtful admiration. He was quite comfortable. He could gaze down at the pretty thing that asked for nothing more than to be allowed to hold his hand. It was still beautiful even with its shorn head and the cuts and bruises. He accepted unhappily that it had not fallen down or fainted. Omar had invented that to deflect attention from the truth. He did not like the truth. He always avoided acknowledging that his creature lived amongst them as a slave because it was more convenient than recognising that it was a human being. God the All Knowing and His Holy Apostle had sanctioned slavery, and demanded the humiliation of all the enemies of Believers. To question the legitimacy of the Word of God was blasphemy. To doubt was a punishable offence. To deny meant death and eternal shame for his family. The Prince's faith was private. He believed deeply and profoundly, but constantly found himself at odds with all the fundamentalists and even with some of the reformers. His country was isolated and isolationist. Sometimes, it seemed medieval. They could all claim that the creature's humiliation was approved by God. They had all the written words to prove it.

The creature was deeply asleep. The Prince smiled wistfully. It was the sleep of innocence. He had not been able to sleep that peacefully for years. The creature held on to his hand like a child. Its head grew heavier. It looked so peaceful. Watching it sleep was a soothing balm to his heart, and eased some of the guilt that the injuries had aroused. It would not hurt him. He had never been more sure of anything. He felt heavy with contentment. He felt its soft, warm hands like a glove around his own. Admiring it in silence gave him a rare pleasure. All his cares slowly drained away. It had come back to him. It would be a constant in his life again. It would never hurt him. He smiled foolishly at the thought. He had boasted once that it was as dangerous as a cobra when it was – in reality – gentle and kind and utterly devoted.

Prince Abdul Aziz leaned down carefully to study its strikingly handsome face. It was still fast asleep. He was torn between his responsibilities as a man of power and reputation and rank, and the soft voice of his heart seeing something vulnerable and hurt. It was difficult for him to acknowledge that he might have behaved badly or that his culture was flawed. That he had allowed it to be banished in a fit of pique remained a deep scar on his heart. It had done nothing wrong. It had never done anything wrong except not be a Believer. He could not quite remember when he had stopped treating it like a respectable servant. Something had happened. The invisible but unbreachable walls that separated servants from their masters, and were ostensibly for their mutual protection had been torn down, and not by his creature. It did not have the power to do that. It would never have been allowed to commit such a monstrous crime. He remembered believing that he had been tricked and seduced, but that was not true. In a foul temper, he had ravished it, and could not quite regret the experience. That had been a transcendental adventure beyond all his dreams. It would have been totally dishonest to say that he had not enjoyed every moment of it, and he could excuse it all because he believed that he had not loved the creature before or during or after. And afterwards he had hated it with the vengeance that his faith demanded, but that did not absolve him either. Gazing down at it now, as it slept like a child, he had to accept that it was his creature that had paid and was still paying, and that the price was too high for something so young and so fragile.

As his creature slept with its face resting in his hand, the Prince built his own little fantasy world. They would be happy together. He would buy it nice clothes. He would take it everywhere with him. The creature would be safe, and it would know that the Prince provided everything to ensure its happiness. It would be grateful. In its gratitude, he would find forgiveness. He was rich and powerful, and could buy a country for them to live in together. There were no obstacles and no limits. Everything was possible. And it was all so easy as long as he forgot about his God and his Prophet and his family. Then he was miserable. Then the beautiful creature was loathed again like a diseased pariah. His culture condemned them both.

Chapter 43

He had heard the car, and moved to the window when she did not come inside. She still did not come. He dared not open any door. The bay windows did not allow him a view of the garage so he learned nothing. His anxiety levels rose. He felt trapped and threatened, but he was alone in an empty house. There were cats asleep. They were not alarmed. But he knew that something was wrong. He tried to rationalise, but all he knew for sure was that he had awoken alone, and she was now sitting outside in her car. He moved through to the kitchen and gazed out of the window, but from there all he could see was the walled garden. He was still there when she opened the front door.

She was surprised to find him in the kitchen. It took her a minute to realise that he had been staring out of the window and waiting for her. He looked pale and shattered. She pointed to a chair, and he went meekly to sit down. "Are you alright?"

He was just breathing, but he nodded slowly then looked towards her. "I didn't know where you were."

She felt obliged to apologise, and managed to smile. "It's alright. You're safe here." She laid a hand on his shoulder. "It's going to be alright, you know."

He nodded, but was not convinced. He could not look at her, and felt sick and dizzy. The pains in his chest were bad again. He was reminded that he was dying, and that he was running out of time.

She hardly knew what to do. She could not tell him anything. Finding him in distress, any hope she had of going off alone for a long walk was scuppered. So they would watch television or rather, she would. Ascot had not started yet. She needed to fortify her nerves with something wonderful by Frank Capra or John Ford. It did not have to be Big Shoulders. Jimmy Stewart was adorable and Gary Cooper was just fine. She needed to cry. All the hormones that had been hysterically demanding that she physically devoured him were all now rewired to just make her cry like a baby. But she could not cry at all. "I'll put the kettle on," she said bravely. "You'd like a cup of tea." That was never a question.

He sat at the kitchen table chewing his knuckles, completely overwrought, while she pretended to be busy. Something had happened. He could not ask.

She made a pot of tea then loaded up the tray with cups and saucers, and she fetched some ice cream cones from the freezer.

He took the one she offered. He was never allowed to choose or refuse. But he did not pull off the wrapper. There was something wrong. She would not look at him. She was pale and red-eyed. She looked exhausted, but there were no shopping bags. He waited desperately for her to explain, but she was focused on tea cups and milk jugs and sugar bowls. "Please?" he said, at last. "I don't understand."

She felt it like a slap across the face, but she was being Meryl Streep so merely smiled then quickly carried the tray through into the lounge. In the kitchen, sitting at the table, she would have been too close to him. She would have told him everything, and been tactless and intolerant. In the front room there was space. If he sat on the sofa then she could be right across the other side of the room. In the no man's land between them, the coffee table marked the front line. She felt like Ripley confronting the Alien as she took her position in the armchair, and waited for him to advance.

He followed her on watery legs.

"I thought we'd watch a movie," she announced loudly.

He moved apprehensively to the sofa. There was already a cat there, but he carefully pushed it aside so he could reclaim his position next to the armrest. His back was throbbing painfully, matching his heart beat. Every nerve in his body was registering alarm. His flesh was cold. He was sweating. There were light bulbs exploding in his head.

She shot to her feet then stooped to carefully pour out two cups of tea. She passed one to him with another Oscar winning smile. He was shivering. His face was white. "Oh, you poor thing," she cooed. "Would you like some more painkillers?" She swept out to the kitchen with obsessive zeal to fetch him three pills. "Here, take these."

He flinched, and had to quickly put aside the ice cream as she advanced to force the pills into his hand. Every movement hurt. He waited until she was busy studying her DVD collection before struggling nearer the edge of the sofa so that he could lean down, and place the tea cup on the floor.

"Harvey," she said, turning to look at him. "Have you seen Harvey?"

He stiffened with his hand outstretched. He could not move.

She breathed deeply then shook her head. How could she explain a pooka to someone who was socially unaware of everything? "Baseball? The Railway Children?" She had already picked up 'The Searchers'. "We'll watch this. You look tired." She felt guilty and wanted to apologise, but there was nothing she could say. "You should really try to get some sleep."

He ate the ice cream then retrieved the cup of tea. He took a sip to gauge the temperature then tossed the pills into his mouth, and swallowed them down. She was not well. He understood that. He watched as she set up the television, and did her usual swift check of a dozen channels. Nothing caught her attention. The movie that she liked watching filled the screen. He had seen several parts of it, but never the whole. She always gave him the pills, which always put him to sleep. He watched the credits roll and listened to the music. By the time all the cows were dead, he was asleep again.

She sat on the comfortable chair hugging her knees. Big Shoulders went off on his quest to find Natalie Wood, but all she could do was stare at the lovely little boy, who had come back from a different quest as a very beautiful young man. Physically, he looked as if he should have the world at his feet. He was poised, polished, incomparable. But mentally and emotionally, he was actually handicapped. If he had been a girl, his future might have been more assured. Girls were taken in and rescued. They might be blatantly objectified in the media, and vulnerable to predators, but Society still believed that little girls were to be rescued and protected and kept safe from harm. That might not always happen, but the belief was cherished. The young man had been objectified and was vulnerable, but Society would expect him to pull up his socks and stand on his own two feet and get over it.

"Paul," she thought. "Your name is Paul." But she could not say it aloud. He was not ready. She was not ready. He would leave her. She could not bear to think about that.

*

While bombs rained down on Tora Bora, the Prince went to Paris. They stayed at the Ritz while he spent his days house-hunting. He took his creature everywhere with him. It wore Yves Saint Laurent, Hermes and Dolce & Gabbana. It carried his Ralph Lauren briefcase. It was the most elegant and beautiful accessory that any man could afford. It was always attentive and gracious. It was quiet and self-contained. The Prince had only to turn and gaze at its beautiful face to feel content. When it raised its blue eyes to look at him, he was aglow with pleasure.

Early in January, they flew to Kathmandu. They were in the room when

Pervez Musharraf actually shook hands with his Indian counterpart. Only a week earlier they had been on the brink of war. The Indian Parliament had been invaded by gunmen. There were twelve dead. India immediately blamed Pakistan. No one thought they would ever be friends, but here was Musharraf literally forcing Atal Bihari Vajpayee to shake his hand in public. Pakistan was having some trust issues. They were running a little low on friends. The American intelligence services did not believe Pakistan was a reliable ally, but the Bush Administration were trying to keep Musharraf onside. No one ever quite knew whose side Musharraf was on. After the Americans dropped the infamous Daisy Cutter, the Special Forces and Delta Force soldiers could hear bin Laden on the radio trying to rally his men, and then later he was apologising for leading them into such terrible danger. While the Americans and their allies were preparing to sweep through the mountains and round up all their enemies, the Pakistani Air Force was secretly airlifting the Taliban and bin Laden to safety. So the war went on. Bin Laden disappeared. It would be a decade before they were ever that close to him again.

The Prince went back to Paris. He and his creature were still exploring their boundaries. They were not lovers. It was a strictly orthodox relationship. The Prince was a Believer. His creature was not. In many ways, all the old rules still applied, they were just being gently finessed. The Prince wanted to reduce his entourage, but needed to stay safe so the group became predominantly made up of bodyguards. Leaving his creature behind was no longer an option, which meant Mahmood was constantly away from home and homesick. In January, there was a conference in Mecca where a group of respected Muslim scholars spent six days coming up with a definition for terrorism. The King had issued a statement calling for the eradication of terrorism in the Kingdom, and had declared that women must have identity cards, which meant photographs. Women were not permitted to be photographed because photographs of women allegedly aroused men into a sexual frenzy. It was assumed that the edict came from the Crown Prince. The King was unwell, and unlikely to be quite so radical.

They had still not found a house to live in. They flew to New York to attend a meeting of the Security Council, and had barely unpacked their bags when the news broke that Mount Nyiragongo, a two mile high volcano, had violently ruptured and caused catastrophic damaged to the city of Goma in eastern Congo. It was hellishly dangerous. Nyiragongo was classified as a super volcano. There were fears that the deep gas-saturated waters of a nearby lake would be heated up when the lava reached them, which would release clouds of lethal methane and carbon monoxide. And Goma had a huge population swollen to bursting point with refugees from constant warfare in the eastern part of the country, and from the genocide in neighbouring Rwanda a decade earlier. It was one of the most dangerous cities in the world.

In the old days, his creature would have been left behind with the Pakistanis. There was no question of leaving it anywhere anymore. The Prince kept it close even when they were in dangerous situations. It had the same boots, hard hats and bulletproof vests as everyone else. If the Prince wanted to roll up his sleeves and rough it then all of them had to do that too. The only times that it was actually put away were when there were visitors who might have been impolite and curious or when the Prince had to attend public meetings. But the creature was always nearby. It would be in a gallery watching or waiting in a nearby office with some of the bodyguards.

The Congo was a very dangerous part of the world. It had all the problems endemic in other African countries, and some that were all its own. The Hutu militia from Rwanda had fled across the border into the Congo after they lost power at home. They allegedly had launched a campaign of violence against the local population which were not Hutus. This included raping and mutilating women and children on an epic scale. The Tutsi militia had followed the Hutus. They were still fighting each other as well as the various Congolese factions. The genocide that had been headline news in Rwanda had quietly slipped over the border into the Congo, which was still the darkest heart of the Dark Continent so the violence went on more or less unchecked and unreported.

The Hutus' view of events, which was equally true, was that the Tutsis had not been massacred in quite such large numbers, and in revenge had driven a million and more Hutus into the Congo, and had been hunting them down like dogs ever since. The Tutsis were the victors, and they had written the history of the genocide. Anyone who contradicted their version of events was imprisoned for a very long time.

The damage from Mount Nyiragongo was considerable. The damage from the bloodiest conflict since the Second World War was inestimable. The United Nations and Red Cross were expecting a huge refugee crisis, which would place all their people in real life-threatening danger. They sent out rescue teams and scientists with monitoring equipment then rolled out all the emergency aid. The Prince's staff offered assistance. He dutifully flew down in the second wave of responders, his 747 loaded to the gunnels with barrels of water, tents, vaccines and latrines, but they were diverted to Kigali as lava had obliterated part of the runway in Goma, as well as many of the local roads. By then the first responders were finding their feet and knew what they needed. Amongst other things, it was UN Peacekeeper boots on the ground and roadworthy trucks. The official figures put the number of refugees at well over four hundred thousand, many of whom were actually armed combatants from the fighting. It was a tough situation. The danger of another rupture or of invisible clouds of poisonous gas never went away. The threat of simply being murdered was ever present.

The Prince's party ended up in northern Uganda almost by accident. A UN mission arrived to review the refugee situation and the security issues in Goma, but were actually destined for Kampala. The UN plane had managed to land at Goma. The Prince and his skeleton crew quickly begged a ride back to Kigali. He offered to fly the UN team on to Kampala, which freed up their plane for a return trip to Goma. The UN were going to be briefed about the Lord's Resistance Army, a violent fanatical cult that was terrorising and murdering villagers in northern Uganda. There were various UN and Red Cross projects in Uganda. The country had been crippled by the excesses of the Idi Amin era. It had started to make a recovery when it was blighted by the nightmarish drug-fuelled atrocities committed by the Lord's Resistance Army and even at times by the Ugandan army. It was a big UN team. For the UN personnel, Uganda was a significantly safer posting than the Congo.

They went to one village in open countryside with UNICEF and representatives from Save the Children's Fund. There were children there who had recently been rescued from the LRA after a carefully planned campaign by government troops. There were only a dozen children. Some were so badly injured they remained in their beds. It was supposed to be a hospital, but it was unlike any hospital that the Prince had seen before. Even by the standards of the hospital in Tindouf, it was primitive and lacked any useful equipment. Some of the children had lost limbs, and not because of accidents with landmines. They had been crudely mutilated. Some had their ears cut off. There were others who had their noses or lips removed. These were all the victims. They were all children. It was appalling.

While the Prince sat cross-legged on the ground with one of the horribly disfigured children, an interpreter related what had happened. Rebels had broken into her home in the middle of the night. She watched as her parents were both raped. Her father was castrated. She was given a gun and told to shoot him. There was a gun to her own head. She had cried and screamed, but one of the rebels squeezed her hand around the gun, and then her father was dead. She could still hear her mother screaming as she was taken away. She never saw her mother alive again. In the bush, she was raped repeatedly. One night she was ordered to hit another girl with a machete. When she could not do it they hacked off her arm with the same machete. She was left in the bush to bleed to death, but aid workers found her the next morning. Her family were dead. Most of her friends had been murdered or kidnapped. In one night, a whole village had been decimated. The little girl was not even ten years old. If she survived no one would marry her, and she could never have children. Her future was bleak.

Later, the Prince was shown other children. They seemed much older. They had the stone cold look of killers, but they were hardly ten or eleven. They had also been rescued, but these were child soldiers with barely a scratch on them because they had obeyed like machines and been rewarded with drugs and alcohol. They were not to be left with the other children. They were kept under guard. Eventually the police would come and take them away. The UN tried to talk about rehabilitation, and the fact that even these killers were just children and were also victims, but the wounds were too fresh. Even in a Christian community, the wounds were too fresh. If the rebels came back then the killer children were programmed to obey. It was just too dangerous to keep them in the area.

The Prince talked at length to the doctors and social workers. They needed so much, but what was imperative was stopping the Lord's Resistance Army and their leader, the former altar boy, Joseph Kony, who were all now wanted for war crimes. Kony believed he was God's Spokesman on Earth, and ruled according to the Ten Commandments. He declared that everything he did was sanctioned by God. With barely a few hundred men he had turned northern Uganda into killing fields. Because of disputes between the governments of Sudan and Uganda, each country had undertaken to support their neighbour's rebels with money and weapons.

Some of the pictures drawn by the children as part of their therapy proved conclusively that the LRA were actually indulging in cannibalism. The survivors whose faces had been mutilated were doomed. They would never be able to survive in isolated villages living basically in mud huts with no sanitation when their faces were covered in open wounds. The air was already thick with egg-laying flies.

In the plane, the Prince spoke to the leader of the UN mission. If they could find the children somewhere safe to live, he was prepared to write a cheque for the cosmetic surgery. At the very least, they needed skin grafts. The UN and the OAU and the WHO could surely sort that out between them. He assured them he could put together an operating theatre on a plane that surpassed anything that Medecins Sans Frontieres or the Red Cross could muster. He could bring the best doctors and surgeons. He could have it anywhere in the world in eighteen hours. He could not turn a village in the African bush into a sanctuary for damaged children. He could not command governments anywhere to accept such hideously disfigured children. The UN constantly reminded him of the moral imperative of children being reunited with their families, and staying in their communities despite the risks. Political Correctness always triumphed over common sense. The best anyone could offer was transferring the children to a two hundred bed government hospital in Kitgum.

The kafir had stood in his place all day. He had seen and heard all that his master had seen and heard. He was touched by the same emotions. On the plane, he sat at the back with Omar. They were all appalled by what they had seen. That was the first time that any of them had seen young children maliciously mutilated. They had seen the wounded and the dead in conflict zones and natural disasters, but never the wanton disfigurement of innocent children. As a father, Omar was particularly upset. His own children were only slightly older. When the kafir had turned to him, and asked how anyone could do such a thing, Omar had no answer. They would make many trips back to northern Uganda. The horrific and pointless injuries never lost their power to shock.

At last, in Paris, the Prince found a house. From the outside, it was just another modest chateau, but inside it had been completely modernised. There were five floors not including extensive cellars and a swimming pool. There was a three acre garden surrounded by impressively high walls. After endless meetings with interior decorators, the Prince left Omar to sort out the security, then took his creature away to Venice for a well-earned break.

Prince Abdul Aziz could not remember when he had last had a holiday. He was committed to going back to the Kingdom for the Hajj. His wives had combined together to make it a command. He could not deny that he wanted to see his children again. Some were away in boarding schools, but he was confident that there were enough to fill his weary heart with laughter and joy. There were expected to be about two million pilgrims in the Kingdom for the Hajj, but they would be in Mecca. Mecca was far away. And it would be hot. In Riyadh, it was always very hot. He had several houses there. He had yet to decide whether to stay with one of his wives. In the past, it had always been easier to stay in a hotel.

Venice was very beautiful and magical even in February. Grey skies were illuminated by a million lights, and by evenings of fireworks and music and gaiety. Visitors flooded in from all around the world. There were the most decadent parties, the most beautiful costumes, and everyone wore masks, which allowed a multitude of sins. The Prince had an exact copy of Othello's outfit in the Franco Zeffirelli opera production. He looked spectacular. He had open invitations to every dinner and ball and theatrical extravaganza. He knew several of his hosts. Everyone recognised the costume, and appreciated the effort and expense. His bodyguards were more discreetly attired, but they still wore masks. His beautiful creature had to give up a new Louis Vuitton suit for a rather severe pageboy's uniform that had been borrowed from the Grand Hotel des Bains. It was allowed no mask. The Prince had no intention of hiding his most expensive and exclusive possession. Everywhere the creature went, it attracted admiring looks. Men and women, all a little the worse for wine, fawned over the pretty thing that could neither raise its eyes nor speak. When in distraction, it sought its master, there was such an expression in its face and eyes that the Prince felt his heart quiver. It was sweeter than honey and more intoxicating than any wine.

In every dark alleyway and lonely gondola, there were scandalous sexual liaisons. Late at night, heading back to their yacht moored in the lagoon, the Prince and his party were often passed by naked youths fleeing from the police. The fabulous theatrical masks that they all wore encouraged everyone to be reckless. Venice was, after all, the home of Casanova and Lord Byron. In a mask, everything was possible, and during Carnival it was actually encouraged.

The very first night on the yacht, the Prince was still constrained by his pride and good manners. He could grin at his pale creature as it stripped away his costume then helped him to wash, but he did not think to touch it. It was so completely his now that there was no imperative need to take advantage of it when there would be a lifetime of such opportunities. But it was so beautiful. The eyes, the face and its whole body were perfectly sublime.

The following afternoon, the Prince had a guided tour of the Doge's Palace. His creature followed dutifully, never more than six feet away, usually only at arm's length. If the phone rang, the creature produced it from a pocket, and offered it graciously. It carried all its master's possessions, from a heavy briefcase to a wallet stuffed with one hundred dollar bills. All the Prince had to carry was a handkerchief. There were parades of dignitaries. There were theatrical pastiches. There were dancers and acrobats. There were regattas. Everywhere, there were crowds of tourists with cameras. From late afternoon, the costumed revellers began to appear. At sunset, the fireworks began again. The Prince was turned out in his red doublet and breeches. There was a concert in a palazzo on the Grand Canal. Several famous opera singers performed wonderful Italian arias. There was a late dinner at a local aristocrat's for a few select guests. The Prince knew many of them. They were the CEOs of banks and investment houses. He was introduced to their wives and families. It was a decidedly more respectable affair than some of the events scheduled in Venice that week. No one asked after his creature, which stood silently in the shadows. It looked exactly like a personal assistant. Why would anyone have suspected that it was anything else?

There were three naked, glistening men screwing on a row boat in the shadows of the jetty when the Prince started down the steps to find the launch that would ferry them back to the yacht. No faces were visible. They were consumed in their task. Their muscular bodies were hard and bronzed and shining in the twinkling harbour lights. It was startling to come upon them. The Prince barely hesitated, and strode on purposefully. The kafir was a little less worldly, but the bodyguards just swept him down the steps. They were giggling like children hearing a dirty joke.

That set the tempo. There was an awkward silence on the ride back to the yacht. The kafir had a sixth sense that ignited a need. When they boarded the yacht, the Prince went straight down to his cabin. The kafir only lingered to have the heavy briefcase removed from his wrist. He followed his master. He knew probably before the Prince had consciously thought about it. He stripped off his clothes, and folded them carefully across a press, then went through to the bathroom to make sure everything was ready. His blood was already on fire when he returned to the Prince. He found him in the dressing room idly pulling at the laces of his doublet. He looked as if he was in pain.

The Prince was in pain. He turned to seize the creature's face. He held it in awe, gazing at the beguiling eyes. Then he forced it down on to its knees. The breeches opened. The mammoth cock burst free to be plunged into the creature's sumptuous mouth. It struggled briefly which only encouraged the Prince to hold it tighter and plunge deeper. He experienced the most delicious agony then staggered as his legs gave way. They tumbled together into a heap. The creature made one last desperate attempt to escape, but the Prince quickly pinned its arms beneath his knees then sank into it again. The extravagant costume impeded him, but the pain was so terrible he could not stop. He battered the soft throat relentlessly then exploded like a canon. It was a brutal assault, but the relief he felt was so very sweet. His power simply vaporised. For a while, he continued thrusting into the lovely moist mouth. At last, elated and spent, he managed to edge backwards on his hands and knees until he was looking down into the creature's wild bright eyes. Without thinking, he stooped to tenderly kiss the lips which were the colour of pomegranates. Before he knew what was happening, the creature had reached up to lock its arms around his neck, and was kissing him back ardently, and it was laughing.

Perhaps because of the extraordinary atmosphere or his heightened physical contentment, the Prince carefully pulled the arms down, and pinned them back under his shins. He was intoxicated, but it was not with wine. His creature was radiant. It shone like the whitest diamond. And the smiles and laughter were entirely new. He stroked its face, and smiled as it smiled with unrestrained delight. Without thinking, he stooped to kiss it again. It responded happily. Suddenly, its hands were free. It was passionately embracing him again then began to hurriedly tear away his clothes. The ornate costume was unfamiliar and heavily laced. It was hard work but by then they were both laughing.

Hours later: it felt like days had passed, the Prince gazed down at the exquisite creature that lay in his arms. "You love me, don't you!" he said, reaching out to stroke the perfect face.

The kafir pressed the hand to his lips and kissed it tenderly. His eyes never left the hot coals that were his master's eyes. He had never felt so completely loved. He was happier than he had ever been before, happier than he ever thought possible. His heart was bursting, but he dared not speak.

The Prince kissed him again hungrily while the kafir was almost weeping with pleasure.

He stretched a leg across his creature to keep it still and quiet then gazed contentedly into the shining eyes. "I never thought that you'd be capable of such an emotion." He ran his fingers through the fine hair and caressed the soft throat. "I never dared to hope that you would love me this much. When did it happen?" He tenderly brushed a tear from its cheek. "How did we not foresee this? What did we do that changed everything? You love me." He blushed as he said the words. "How long have you known that you loved me like this? You are sweet and affectionate, and I've always let you take advantage of my weakness for you." They were both grinning like idiots. They were both sated, but the Prince needed reassurance. "I know that I have spoilt you terribly, but you've always worked so hard to make me happy." He stroked the beautiful face then traced the scarlet lips with his fingers. "You seem to understand me so well. How could I ever be angry with you?" He leaned down to whisper in its ear. "Yes, I know I can be jealous, but that's your fault. You must stop tormenting me. I know that you haven't betrayed me. I know that you haven't, but for my own sake, I have to be sure. It isn't meant to hurt you." He kissed it again powerfully. The creature struggled to capture him in an embrace. The Prince pulled away then pinned it down and held it still. It could not move, but its eyes shone like the moon, and there was a smile dancing on its lips. "Whenever I go away you must feel lonely and neglected, but you must accept that I can't always take you with me. You have to trust me. I only want what is best for you. No one else would understand. They would try to take you away from me. I couldn't allow that. You have to stay. You must wait for me. I will always come back." He moved away again to survey the perfect flesh then ran his fingers across it like a connoisseur admiring a sculpture. "If I lost you, I think I'd go mad. I know it's harder for you now, but you must believe that I'm suffering exactly the same anguish. At least, you are safe here with me. I will make sure that you are safe." He smiled as the creature smiled, and another tear rolled down its cheek. "I know that sometimes I do hurt you when I'm in a hurry or upset about something else. I want you to know that I'm never angry with you. It must feel that way sometimes, but it is never you. I do love you. I never say it. I don't know how to show it. You understand me so well. I don't have to pretend with you. You don't argue. You are never upset. I love your silence, and the way you graciously accept that I can be rough and demanding and inconsiderate." He stroked the beautiful flesh again with great tenderness. "I wouldn't change you. When I go away and have to leave you then my heart calls for you in the darkness. Does your heart call for me? I've never felt this way before." He sighed. "It is very strange for a man. I never expected to feel like this about you. I know you love me. I want you to be happy with me." He stroked his creature and petted it affectionately, then kissed it again with a hunger. Then he frowned. "Obviously, there's nothing that I can give you. I want you to promise me as you love me that you will never try to take advantage of my feelings." His hand strayed to the soft throat. There was no collar to thwart him. He could feel the creature's pulse. Its heart was beating powerfully. The flesh trembled with excitement. "That would be wrong. That would be intolerable. I am a prince of royal blood. I know that you will always obey me because you are mine and you must, but I want to hear you say it. You must say it. Swear it." He squeezed the throat gently. "You will love me and obey me, but you will never ask me to love you. You will not seek any such assurance. You will not make any demands that would be offensive to me. Say it!"

The kafir was breathing hard. He was so emotional, he hardly knew whether he would laugh or cry. It was a declaration of love better than anything he could have imagined.

"Say it!" the Prince insisted impatiently.

"I love you."

The Prince slapped it brutally across the face. Its persistent impudence infuriated him. "Never say that. Say that you'll never ask for anything. Say you'll never make any demands on me!"

With all his senses reeling, the kafir had lost the power of speech.

"Say it now! Swear it. You will never make any demands on me. You will never do anything to offend me!"

The kafir stared into the noble handsome face. He really did not understand, but he nodded. "I promise," he said quietly. "I won't ask for anything. I promise. All that I am. I am yours. I am yours always."

"And you'll never leave me!" the Prince leaned closer to glower into its eyes. He had his fingers around the soft, white throat. "Say it! Swear it."

The kafir could not breathe. He simply could not inhale. He could not make the words. When the Prince drew back to strike, he managed to quickly drag air down into his lungs and gasp: "Yes. I swear. I'll never leave you. I am yours." When the Prince relented, he reached up to tenderly touch his face. "Please, don't leave me. Please, don't ever send me away."

Chapter 44

Late in the afternoon, she went out to mow the lawn. She was upset and confused, and he was tense. There was nothing to talk about. She had commanded him to copy out poems so that he could improve his handwriting, and left him alone in the kitchen to do it. When she returned, hot and bothered from her exertions, he had barely written a paragraph.

"What..." she demanded. "This isn't enough. What are you doing?"

Her tone went through him like knife. He shrank before her eyes, and shivered. "Please? I'm sorry. I didn't...Please, don't be angry."

She started to deny it, but she was livid. All the emotions that had been fermenting in her heart turned to bile. She could not look at him. It was actually painful to look at him. She went to the sink to splash water on her face then took a long drink. All of the time, she could hear him apologising. In her head, she was screaming at him to shut up, but she could not speak. Still hot and breathless, she wrenched open the freezer to find some ice creams. He was still apologising when she sat down opposite him then threw an ice cream across the table.

Then he shut up. He realised he had made a mistake. He stared at the ice cream that was still neatly wrapped up then glanced anxiously into her eyes. They were red and sore in her white blotchy face. Moving slowly, he reached down to pick up the ice cream. It would be delicious. He removed the wrapper quietly. She had given him ice cream before, but never when she was angry.

They both ate in silence. Her mood slowly mellowed. Ice cream could do that. In her head, she had already had a long conversation with him about making an effort and being prepared, and most importantly, that she was only trying to help him. She wasn't angry, but she was. It wasn't his fault, but it was. He was going to leave her. She could not forgive that. His name was Paul Lawrence now, and he was going to leave her. She was so angry and so upset, and he was so vulnerable and so damaged. She couldn't hate him because he didn't know. She had to tell him, but couldn't do it because he would leave her without a second thought. He would be gone in a moment. She would be alone again. There would be no more ice creams. But he didn't know, and if she didn't tell him then he would never leave. The little voices in her head were whispering a dozen conspiracies.

"Please?" he said. "I'm sorry."

She blinked. He was looking at her with concern and regret. She tried to smile then slowly pulled herself back together. "Don't be silly. I should apologise. I was tired." Meryl Streep took over. "Your handwriting is improving. It just takes time, and lots of practice."

He regarded his wobbly script, and grimaced at his efforts, but smiled when he looked at her. "My hand shakes."

"You hold the pen too tightly," she said with assurance. "It should balance in your hand. Imagine you were holding a feather."

He picked up the pen. He had never in his life held a feather in his hand. That was beyond his imagination. Putting down the pen, he finished the ice cream then stared down at the table and waited.

She watched him for a while then rose to her feet. All she could say calmly was: "Just keep practicing." She could not ruffle his hair. She did not dare touch him. Her fingers were still stained green from the grass cuttings. She was hot and sweaty, and he was cool and perfect. It wasn't fair. But it wasn't his fault. She filled her lungs, and strained to produce a big smile. "It'll be alright, you know. It won't be easy, but it will be alright."

He nodded, but stared dismally at the table.

"I'm going to release the hedgehog, do you want to help me?" she asked with forced enthusiasm. "I meant to do it yesterday – but I forgot. I was so tired." He did not seem to have heard. "The little hedgehog that was sick," she explained encouragingly.

He struggled onto his feet then stared at the floor.

She was not feeling overwhelmed by his enthusiasm. "It doesn't matter. I'll do it on my own. You carry on here." She watched as he sank back on to the chair. He was obviously stiff and sore, which triggered her sympathy. "Do you want some more pills?"

He nodded. He still did not look at her.

She counted out two pills, and gave them to him with a glass of water. "You just need to keep trying. It'll be worth it in the end." She turned away to look out of the window. She needed to be outside. She needed to lose herself in the garden. He said nothing so she left him there.

It was not difficult to lift up the rabbit hutch, and carry it outside. Obviously, it would have been sensible to take out the dish of water before she started, but once it had split, she just carried on regardless. The hutch did not weigh much. The hedgehog was nearly 600 grams, which was its perfect weight. It was easy to carry the hutch along the cobbled path then put it down by the door in the wall. As soon as the sun set then she would carry it out into the main garden, open the hutch door, put in more food, then let the little creature decide whether it wanted to be free. She had set so many of them free, but it always tugged at her heart. She did not feel selfish. It was as much about a lack of confidence. Were they really ready? Was she doing the right thing?

She could have gone back into the house, but Paul Lawrence was there. He was different now. He had a name and a history and a family, who would still be devastated by their loss. Imagining their pain should have eased her own. He had filled up her life in such a way that she feared being alone again. It had taken her decades to build all the defences that she needed to survive. She had accepted being alone. She had not enjoyed it. She had not thought about it. That was the price she had to pay to feel safe. To hand him back to his family in the best condition possible, was a tremendous achievement that she could take pride in, but she did not. It was the right thing to do, but she wanted him to stay there with her. She had lost a son. Why couldn't she keep someone else's?

She sat out in the garden until the twilight faded. She sat on the bench. Beside her, the black cat with the yellow eyes kept her company. She was not really there. She was very far away and safe.

*

In Venice, they were lovers. The increasing possessiveness and jealousy were just the side effects of the Prince's dilemma. In some deep wordless, unconscious and primeval way, he was profoundly adjusting his perspective.

In Venice, it had kissed him. Up until that moment he could plunder its flesh callously with the authority and contempt of an owner. No power on Earth could deny him that. But with a kiss this thing that he could command so ruthlessly had declared its independence. Perhaps, it had been totally corrupted by its exile with the Parsi? Perhaps, it was just the heightened atmosphere of Venice during Carnival? Everyone wore masks. Everything seemed possible. The little harmless charades that he had played with his creature had changed. He had changed. The thing that he had owned, but not really valued, now had a specific price tag. And when it kissed him all of that was just blown away.

In Venice, on the yacht, they made love for the first time. They kissed. They explored their bodies like strangers. It was not just the pursuit of a moment's gratification. The Prince was gentle and anxious. For the first time, he hoisted the creature on top of him. He watched its face as he drew it down on him. It was transformed from happiness to pain then pleasure. When it looked at him, there were tears swimming in its lovely eyes.

"You're crying? I've hurt you?" He was embarrassed.

"No." It had smiled like an angel. "I'm crying because I'm happy."

The change in their relationship marked them both differently. The kafir became more devoted and more forgiving. He had found his nirvana. He was loved.

For the Prince, it was more complicated. Everything that he had ever believed in was under threat. In Venice, he could deny the danger. Everyone wore masks. Everyone could be someone else. He could avoid phone calls. He could avoid people. They were on a super yacht in the lagoon. The only human beings anywhere near them were the discreet bodyguards, a few sailors, a cook, and poor old Mahmood, who hated being 'at sea'. On the massive yacht, it was easily possible to avoid the crew. The lovers were naked. There were no clothes, no inhibitions, no guilt and no conversations. They kissed and cuddled and smiled, they even laughed, but there were never any words. To say anything might have broken the spell, and made it real. The Prince was invested in a hedonistic dream. While he feasted on the delicious flesh, he never thought about the consequences. None of it could be real. He was drunk with pleasure. He was blissfully happy. At any moment, he would wake up and know that it had all been just a foolish dream.

Initially, his creature had continued to behave with impeccable decorum in public, but the Prince was sure that he saw it being just a bit too friendly with a waiter, and another time he was sure that it smiled at a fellow guest. The first few times, he was irritated but let it pass. By the third morning of waking up with the creature asleep in his arms, he was feeling quite territorial. They might be sharing a bed, but he was the one fucking it. It was his property. He felt absolutely entitled to its loyalty and devotion. It was beautiful, and he took pride in possessing something that so many other people obviously admired. He was like a jealous child, and it was his favourite toy. He wanted everyone to admire it, but no one was allowed to touch, and the creature had to remain aloof from the adulation. When it stood next to him, he was at peace, but the moment it moved away he became irrationally suspicious. And it had to move away. When he was at dinner or at a concert, his hosts naturally expected the 'personal assistant' and bodyguards to withdraw. Not being able to see it always twisted his guts up like a kitten's ball of string. He was constantly looking for it, and heaven help the creature if it was not looking back at him. He demanded its constant attention. By the end of the fourth evening, he had counted seventeen occasions when he looked across the room to admire his creature only to discover that it was looking at someone else.

"They are permitted to look at you. They can admire you. They can even talk about you. You do not look at them. You do not speak to them. It doesn't matter what they do or say. You belong to me. You only look at me."

The kafir was pinned down on the mattress. The Prince held him by the throat. Another ounce of pressure would have snapped his neck like a twig. His master had been increasingly tense all evening, stalking around like a leopard after a buck. Now, they were alone, and all pretence of good manners had gone.

"They may tell you that you are the most beautiful creature in the world. They may tell you that they love you. They can promise to give you the most expensive presents. They can promise you anything and everything." The Prince's voice was thick with emotion. "You do not answer. You never answer. You belong to me."

The kafir held the powerful arm with both hands, trying to ease the pressure on his neck. He gazed up into his master's face with glittering eyes. He could not speak. He could not move his head. The grip on his throat was powerful and irresistible. It was increasingly difficult to remain calm, but he had to remain calm because the slightest show of anxiety would be construed as temper if not outright rebellion. He was using all his strength to hold back the hand whilst the Prince slowly became heavier, and his grip tightened.

"You will submit," the Prince warned. "You belong to me. I may kill you whenever I wish. There is no law to stop me. You will submit." He leaned closer to watch the creature turn white. Its pupils dilated. Beads of sweat adorned its beautiful face like autumnal dew. "Submit!"

The kafir's chest was crushed. He could not inhale. He was lost somewhere between blind panic and absolute terror. It was beyond him to understand what he had done wrong, but he knew his duty. He had to obey any order, even if that order was to lay still while his master murdered him. There was no shred of trust left in him. His pulse was hammering in his brain. His heart was rupturing. He dared not let go, but understood that was the command. He was not permitted to struggle for his life. He was not allowed to thwart his master's desire to choke him slowly to death.

The Prince glowered down into the luminous blue eyes. He knew that he held his creature's life in his hands. Through his fingers, he felt every heartbeat and every wretched fear. It did not really matter that it held on to his wrist so desperately. He could have crushed it as easily as a fly. It amused him to toy with his creature. That it might believe that it could hold him off was really just a joke. He would have laughed at it. Ha! Ha! Ha! But he was too angry to laugh at anything. "Submit," he whispered menacingly, and the creature's face melted. It blinked, and huge tears swam from the lovely blue eyes. He could have shaken off the grip on his wrist, but it fell away voluntarily. There was wild terror in the glittering eyes. He wiped the tears away brusquely. The face was whiter than white. The lips were grey. Dimly, he was aware of the sound of an animal choking. That was his creature. He slackened his grip then let go altogether. The creature cowered away, struggling to drag air down its crushed windpipe. He put out a hand to keep it from straying too far. It shivered, but took the minute allowed to catch its breath then lay back obediently across the mattress. The Prince leaned down to grip its throat again. He could see real fear in those blue eyes. "You don't look at them. It doesn't matter what they say. Do you understand?"

"Please?" the kafir managed to whisper. "I didn't."

"Don't insult me with lies. You humiliated me today. You know what you did. I saw you looking at that man."

The kafir did not remember looking at anyone. He knew that his master was possessive and jealous. That had grown worse since Afghanistan. "Please? I didn't. My lord, Your Highness, my master by the Grace of God, the Compassionate, the Merciful. Here I am. I am yours. I swear. I have never. I would never."

"You humiliated me in front of all those people." The Prince held his creature by the throat, but he did not squeeze. "All you have to do is stand there. It's not difficult. You should not be thinking about anything except what you need to do for me. It's your job." He reached down to lay a hand across the creature's genitals. "This can be cut off. Would that help you to concentrate?"

"Please?" The kafir was petrified. With the Prince there was no such thing as an idle threat. He had the power to do anything. The merest whim could be fulfilled by an army of retainers and limitless wealth.

The Prince removed his hand then wiped it across the front of the creature's shirt. "You're just a filthy little whore. You flirt shamelessly with everyone. I saved your life, and this is how you repay me."

"Please? No one, my lord, Your Highness, my master by the Grace of

God, the most Compassionate, the most Merciful, there is no one. I am yours. All that I am. I swear. Always. God is Great. Please? God is Great." The hand came back to caress his throat. The threat was obvious. "Please? I didn't." His nerve failed completely. "Please? I'm sorry. God is Great."

"You're a whore. You just want to be fucked all the time."

The kafir seized the Prince's wrist, and stroked it urgently. "Never by anyone but you, my lord. Only you, I swear it. I love you. You know that I love you. There's no one else. I swear. Please, think about it. Here I am at your service. You must remember. I'm with you. I'm always here with you. Please, just think about it. There's no one else."

"I've spoiled you, and you repay me with this deceit. It is unforgivable. You humiliated me. My dirty little whore humiliated me in front of my friends. What punishment can there be for that? Six hundred lashes? Castration? Beheading?"

The kafir was cold with sweat. All his escape routes were denied him. He was pinned down on the mattress. "Please? My lord, my beloved master, think about it. I wouldn't do anything to offend you. Please, just think about it. You're upset. You're tired. Please, just think about it."

"So it's my fault! How dare you?" The Prince surged closer. He had two hands around the creature's throat, and he was throttling it.

The kafir fought back, trying to pull the hands away. "Please? I didn't. No. Please, I didn't. Alright, yes, I'm a whore. But I didn't. It was an accident. It didn't mean anything. Please, you're hurting me. Forgive me. I'm begging you. Please, forgive me. I made a mistake. I'm a whore. I'm sorry. Please, I'm sorry. I promise. I won't do it again. I won't. I didn't understand. It was a mistake."

The Prince relieved the pressure, and allowed his creature to breathe. "And what about my honour? You humiliated me. There is no salve for that but your burned body left in a ditch for crows to feed on. Then my friends will understand that my honour cannot be trifled with."

The kafir could not speak. His life hung by a thread.

"For my honour?" the Prince murmured darkly. The beautiful creature was thrilling. "You have grossly insulted me."

The kafir reached up to tenderly touch his master's face. Pinned down on the mattress, he could not throw himself to his knees or smother the ring with kisses. "Please?" he begged. "I wouldn't." His hand was knocked aside. "Please, my lord, Your Highness, my master by the Grace of God, the most Compassionate, the most Merciful. God is All-Knowing, my lord.

God is Great. Please, be merciful. God is Great. Please, I'm begging you. I'm sorry if you were offended. It was a mistake. Please, I won't ever look at another man. It was a terrible mistake. I'm so sorry. I never meant to offend you. I love you. You know I love you. Here I am. Please?"

The Prince shook his head and sighed. "No man can forgive such an insult. It will live forever in the memories of my friends. You must be punished. It must be something that they will see and understand, and then my honour will be unblemished."

The kafir's heart was breaking. "But I love you."

"What do you know of love? You'd lay down with the devil if it would profit you." The Prince stroked its perfect face. "You are temptation. Perhaps, you are evil. Should I kill you? Yes, I think I should. It's inevitable. Will we all be safer from corruption if you are dead and gone?"

The kafir blinked. A tear rolled down his cheek. He had said too much. He did not dare risk more.

It was something about the eyes. They were extraordinary. While they looked at him, the Prince was at peace. He could not raise a hand against the creature. He might dream of hurting it, but that was merely a fantasy. They both played their little games. He knew that it could be blatantly insulting. No kafir was ever allowed to gaze into a Believer's eyes as if he were an equal. In women, that was forbidden because it was immodest, and immodesty was an insult to God. In a kafir, it was a surly insult that should be punished severely. Yet these eyes? He could swim in them like pools of moonlight. The light that shone in them had the radiance of an epiphany.

Another tear fell from the long dark lashes.

"I must punish you," the Prince said solemnly, but the moment had passed.

The kafir managed to grasp one of the hands. He pulled it to his lips and kissed it tenderly. "My lord, I'm yours. All that I am. Your Highness, my master by the Grace of God, the All-Knowing and most Wise. God is Great. God is Merciful. I am yours. Please, believe me."

The Prince pressed two fingers into the creature's mouth, and smiled as it immediately began to suck powerfully. He leaned closer and whispered: "I'm not going to fuck you because that's exactly what you want me to do. You get in trouble and you offer sex to absolve all your sins." But he was aroused. At that moment, he could have torn off the creature's clothes, flipped it over and plundered its body in every way that was humanly possible. "Abstinence is good for the soul. We've been remiss. We'll find you somewhere safe, a refuge where you can study and reflect on your shortcomings. You've obviously lost your way. Your old school is a ruin. We must find you another. You cannot be allowed to go to Mecca. That would be a sacrilege. We will devise a pilgrimage suitable for a whore, something educational, something that will challenge your stamina and courage."

The kafir shivered. "Please, don't send me away. You know that I love you." He stroked the Prince's face tenderly. "Please, I'm begging you. There's no one else. I've never loved anyone else."

"I'm not fucking you."

"Don't send me away." He knew he was in trouble. "Please, I'm begging you. You're upset. I made a mistake. It won't happen again. Please? God is Great. Forgive me. It was a mistake. It won't ever happen again. I promise, my lord. I swear before God. Please, don't do this. Just think about it. I'm at your service. I'm begging you. Don't send me away."

"You have no honour. You have no understanding of honour. When you swear before God you are blaspheming," the Prince explained patiently, and gently brushed a tear from its cheek. "You are insulting God."

The kafir trembled. "I'm so sorry. I didn't mean to upset you. Please? Please, I'm begging you. Please, don't send me away." An icy hand closed around his heart. "Please, don't abandon me. If you love me... if you love me, I'd rather you killed me here and now than sent me away."

The Prince stroked its lovely face. The eyes swam with tears. They were utterly beguiling. No power on Earth could have made him send the creature away.

*

Eventually, he went out to find her. He sat at the kitchen table quietly copying the words until it was too dark to see. It was not for him to switch the lights on. It was not for him to search the cupboards for cat food. They were all gathering. They recognised that he was not the woman, but they still cried and made a fuss. He had never seen them altogether before. To him they were all wild vermin, and they were hungry so he cautiously went through the scullery to open the back door. There was still some light in the sky, but it was dark and threatening everywhere. He could not see her. A few of the cats rubbed around his ankles. He carefully crossed the threshold, and started barefoot down the cobbled path. None of the cats followed him. He was relieved.

He found her on the bench. She was just sitting there. He hoped she would look up before he reached her, but he had to touch her shoulder.

"Please?" he whispered.

She turned to look up at him then smiled. "Your name is Paul," she said.

He literally staggered, but she quickly rose to her feet, and took hold of him. She had him sitting down in a moment. She had her arm around him.

"Your name is Paul," she said, staring at him, dreading his reaction.

He did not move at all, and then blinked as if he had been awoken from a dream by a strange noise.

"Paul," she said again. "Paul Lawrence."

There was no strength left in him. He exhaled loudly, and then turned grimly to stare at her. It was hard to breathe. The effort pained him. What she was saying hurt so much more.

"It's alright," she whispered. She could feel him shivering. "We should go inside. It's beginning to turn chilly." She turned towards him and caressed his face. He looked awful. He was white and broken and in pain. "Let's go inside. We'll have a cup of tea. I'll tell you what I know." She stroked his face, which was wet with tears. "I don't know much. Are you alright?"

He couldn't breathe. He could not begin to understand what she was saying.

She stood up then drew him back to his feet. He simply could not function. She had to pull him along, forcing him to move his feet. "That's it." She held his arm. "I'm sorry. I didn't mean to upset you. Just take a deep breath. It'll be alright."

She managed to get him back into the lounge then lowered him carefully on to the sofa. He fell back against the cushions then shuddered and cried out. She gently sat down beside him. She could not leave him in such a state. "It'll be alright. We have some time. Please, don't be upset."

He was in shock. He was shivering. He was unconscious with his eyes open. He did not know what was happening. The injury across his back had almost eclipsed everything else. The pain had gone through him like a lightning bolt. It had erased everything, everything but the name: Paul. Slowly, the pain began to ebb. As his senses recovered, he managed to lift his head then straightened his spine. He was soaked with sweat. He was trembling, but he managed to look at her.

"I didn't know how to tell you. I've been thinking about it all afternoon." She picked up one of his hands and crushed it against her chest. "It's alright. Don't get excited. Don't be upset. We know your name. Please, don't think for a minute that I know anything else. We know your name. It's a beginning. Please don't be upset, it's only a beginning. We have so far to go."

He nodded dumbly. He felt like a prisoner again. He could not speak. He did not know how to. His brain was burning up with a firestorm of explosions and blinding light. In his chest, his weakened heart accelerated alarmingly. "Paul?" he gasped in an agony of ignorance.

"Shush!" she pressed her fingers over his lips, staring into his eyes, trying to read his mind, seeing only the pain and confusion that were his element. "Paul," she whispered quietly. "Your name is Paul Lawrence. You went missing in October 1987. You lived in Chester. You were waiting for a bus. It was a dark rainy night. Does any of this mean anything to you?"

He managed to shake his head. He wanted to cry, but would not. He had a name now. It was important. It was essential. He had to find his nerve, and hang on to it with both hands. Life was going to get a whole lot harder. All the plans that he had made were suddenly ashes again. The name meant nothing to him. He had never heard of a place called Chester.

"There were so many boys listed," she said miserably. "I had no idea. It really upset me. I just wasn't prepared."

He turned his face away, and brushed the stubborn tears from his cheek.

"It's all right," she said. "You'll be fine. You're so brave. We'll find out everything you need to know. We'll find out where you lived, and where we can find your parents, and then we'll go up there together. It'll be fine. Just don't get upset. This must be so confusing for you. You must have even more questions. We'll work it out. Okay?"

He nodded, and managed to look at her, but his smile was weak and thin.

She was relieved that he was being so calm. She hardly knew what she expected, but at least something loud and aggressive. Then she remembered that exuberance and enthusiasm had probably been thrashed out of him years ago. "You poor thing," she whispered, stroking his face, longing for him to look at her again. "They stole your whole life. I'm so sorry."

He could not think. He felt as if he had been beaten to a pulp. He just did not know what to do. The name meant nothing to him. It meant absolutely nothing. He did not understand. If that was his name then why couldn't he remember it? The pains in his chest magnified. He felt dizzy and nauseous, and his head filled with noise. The muscles in his chest went into spasm. He couldn't breathe. He struggled away from her to fall from the sofa on to his knees. The pain just got worse. He was choking. He wanted to pull his ribs apart. His heart was exploding.

She dropped to the floor beside him. He was choking. She roughly seized his collar then slapped him brutally across the face. They both fell over. He hit the ground hard, and she tumbled heavily across him. The impact jarred every bone in his body. There was a strangled shriek of pain. His lungs filled. He cried out again. The agony engulfed him. He breathed again. He could breathe, but by then he had already lost consciousness.

She tried to arrange him comfortably on the floor. He was limp. His face had gone white. She pressed her fingers into his neck to monitor his pulse. He was breathing quickly. His heart was racing, but it was an even rhythm. After ten minutes, she was surrounded by her cats. They were really, really hungry. They were not remotely interested in the young man. He never fed them. She hardly ever sat on the floor so, of course, they were curious about this unprecedented event. She waited then waited a little more. When she was satisfied that he was alright, she climbed back to her feet, and went away to fulfill her duties. She had to feed the cats. She had to set the hedgehog free. Paul would be alright. He had just had a bit of a shock. It was her fault.

Chapter 45

The Queen wore blue. The horses were grey. The sun was shining. Royal Ascot was a perfect picture. She was determined to watch every damn minute of it. She was not being selfish. She was not ignoring her responsibilities as a decent human being.

He was still holding the photograph that she left him staring at in bed the previous evening. He had lost the power of speech. His face was a mask of anguish and sorrow as he gazed at the little boy in the photograph, and saw only a stranger. There were likenesses. She had pointed them out to him, but he wanted to disbelieve the proof. He had been staring at the photograph for hours, searching for evidence, seeking a clue, but there was nothing. It was just a picture of a little boy. It could have been anyone. He had believed that he would remember being that child. He would surely remember, but he did not.

She watched him quietly. She wanted to watch the horse racing, but she was experiencing empathy, and it hurt. His every frown and gesture were wounding. She did not know what to say to him anymore. She so wanted to watch Royal Ascot. She wanted to see the Royal procession. She wanted to see all the stylish hats and chic frocks, but the room was filling up with his pain. Her stone cold dead heart was breaking.

"Let's go for a walk," she said. She put aside her cup of tea then gently coaxed the cat off her knees. "You'll feel better in the garden."

He might have nodded, but he was lost in his scrutiny of the photograph. He had not heard a word.

She crossed the room quietly, not wanting to upset him, and he started in alarm when she gently touched his shoulder. "It's alright. We'll go for a walk." She knelt down to slide his shoes on over his bare feet. "Let's get some fresh air."

He could not drag his eyes away from the photograph.

She reached up to stroke his handsome face then combed his hair back. Her other hand firmly took hold of the photograph, and prised it from his grasp. He was reluctant to let it go, but surrendered it with another anguished frown. She carried the picture away to the mantelpiece, and propped it up against some books. He was still staring at it when she returned to help him to his feet. She had made up her mind so he really did not have a choice. He moved like an old man. He swayed on his feet, and held on to her arm. The photograph had knocked the stuffing out of him. She knew she had made a mistake showing it to him. That had been too much of a shock. Her many failings haunted her again. She did not know how to be around real people. She was inept, socially handicapped and always afraid. He needed a mother, and she had not been a mother for a very long time.

In the kitchen, she stood him beside the sink while she filled a glass with water then pressed him to take some more painkillers. He never looked at her. He did not even look out of the window at her beautiful garden. There were tears swimming in his eyes, and he did not want her to see them.

"It'll be alright," she said quietly. All she had were platitudes, and she had already said them all a thousand times.

Every fibre of his being resonated with pain. He could hardly breathe. He shambled along like a decrepit old man, holding on to her arm, terrified of falling down and increasing the pain. Beside him, she was firm and assured, much more assured than she really felt. She kept saying that it would be alright, but he could not begin to comprehend the words anymore. By the time they reached the door in the wall, he was wheezing.

They sat on their usual bench. She kept hold of his arm. They leaned against each other. She wanted to put her arms around him, but he was too fragile. For a long time, the only sounds were the birds singing and a gentle breeze rustling through the treetops and his ragged breathing. She stroked his hand. Now and then, she was sure she felt a teardrop splashing on her skin. He flinched and shivered as his thoughts ran away unchecked on the problems that he faced.

"It'll be alright," she said again. "We'll find your parents."

His head went down. He shuddered violently. "Please? I don't understand." It took all his courage to fill his lungs. The pains in his chest were almost crippling. "Why is this happening to me?" He gasped as another bolt of pain tore through his heart. "I don't understand why they did this to me."

She turned into him, lifting a hand to caress his face then ruffled his hair, subtly forcing his head down onto her shoulder. She could not look at him. Her whole body burned. Every nerve tingled. Her heart swelled painfully. She was sure this was maternal love. It was powerful and sure. It was totally appropriate, but she felt utterly helpless. "I'm so sorry. I wish I could explain everything so that it made perfect sense. You've been through a terrible ordeal. I wish I could make it all go away. I wish I could turn back time and make sure it didn't happen, but it did. You've been so brave and so strong. This must be so confusing for you." She held on tightly. "You will feel better. You will grow stronger. We'll find your parents, and they'll be so happy to see you again. You must believe me. It'll be alright."

A terrible sob tore through him. For a moment, he just wept like a child, and there was nothing she could do but hold him in her arms. Her shirt was soon soaked. She felt useless. He was in so much pain. He had so many wounds. She just held on, carefully patting him and stroking him where he had not been beaten to a pulp by some sadistic maniac.

"It'll be alright." She shushed him gently as she remembered her own mother doing when she had been a child with a grazed knee or a spiteful friend. "Come on, darling, everything will be alright."

His frailty and her pills smothered his tears. He was not physically strong enough for a full blown emotional meltdown. He pulled away slowly then stared at the treeline that he had studied so often before. His face was pale and blotchy. His eyes were red and raw.

She smiled. Only Gene Tierney could weep and still be gorgeous. He was human, after all. "Would you like to go for a walk?" she asked, and pointed towards the trees.

He lowered his gaze. For a while, he just focused on breathing.

She took his hand again, and stroked it affectionately. She wanted to look at him, but knew he was embarrassed though he had no need to be embarrassed. He was the bravest man she had ever met. "We have plenty of time."

"It was Abdullah," he said in a broken whisper. He seemed to shrink in size as he cowered. "Abdullah beat me. He hurt me. He said my master did not want me anymore." He shuddered again at the terrible blow. "Abdullah said I was to go to Karachi with him. It was arranged. I was to go with him. He said the men with ugly wives would come to fuck me. The men who fucked their donkeys and their goats would all come to fuck me. He said they'd all beat me. He said I would make him a rich man, a respectable man." He trembled again at the memory. He could still feel the whip slicing through his flesh like a filleting knife. "He said that I'd have to sleep in the cages with his dogs." He shook his head in dismay. "My master did not love me. We were not lovers. I made a mistake, and he threw me away."

"But you're here?" she said gently. "Abdullah did not take you to Karachi."

He flinched and grimaced. His eyes strayed back to the treeline.

She followed his gaze. "This is not Karachi. You know that."

He breathed deeply then sighed and shivered again. He was back there in the bathroom in Paris surrounded by sea nymphs and mirrors. "I made a mistake."

She leaned towards him, and tried to touch his arm with compassion. "What happened?"

He shook his head. "I made a mistake."

Knowing he was not interested in her beautiful garden, she stood up and offered him her hand. He rose obediently, and they walked together back into the house. He went silently to his place on the sofa while she made a fresh pot of tea. She would watch the television, and soon he would be asleep. She did not know what to do. He was so badly damaged, and she just kept making it worse. How could she keep him safe? Her heart ached for him, but there was nothing she could do that would not expose him to more distress. So she had a cup of tea and a shot of rum and lots of sugar. It was revolting, but she gulped it down. She wanted to throw up and run away and cry, but sat huddled in her chair staring at him. He was still shockingly beautiful, but he was doomed.

On the television, Alan Ball was talking about the World Cup. He was at Ascot. Apparently, England was playing Sweden that evening. She actually grimaced. According to the celebrated footballer, England needed to play better, but if they could beat Sweden then they would not have to face Germany or Argentina for a while yet.

She heaved a sigh, but focused on the television. It was Ascot. George Washington was supposed to be running in the St. James's Palace Stakes, but he was not there. Holy Roman Emperor floated across the ground like some magical being. He was beautiful and elegant, and he was the favourite. The draw bias had been a talking point on the completely reconstructed track. Hellvelyn had a low draw that put him on the stands side, which was obviously faster ground. Probably the fastest racehorse ever, Hawk Wing, had lost the 2,000 Guineas a few years ago despite being the most spectacular thing on four legs that season simply because he was drawn on the wrong side of the track. Araafa, another handsome beast, won the St. James's Palace Stakes. Apparently, he had beaten Gorgeous George in Ireland on soft ground. She had not seen that race. She was limited to the terrestrial channels, but suspected she had actually been in the garden on a rescue mission with her wheelbarrow when the Irish Guineas was being run. She had been distracted. It was not anyone's fault. According to the commentators, George was not well, and had not been well in Ireland. The winning trainer swept his wife up into an emotional embrace, brushed off her hat and kissed her. It was a lovely spontaneous human moment. Later, when the man said he was definitely looking forward to a rematch with George Washington, Jane had to agree. She was feeling rather cheated having missed a good race in Ireland, and a little jealous that she had never ever been kissed by anyone like that.

*

After the carnival, Venice emptied as if there had been another outbreak of Asiatic cholera. There was a clamour for the trains. The yachts weighed anchor. All the elaborate masks were cast aside. When Mahmood came with the heavy collar, the kafir knew it was over. There was nothing he could do. They were in his master's suite. Obviously, his master had summoned Mahmood. He just could not believe it. He retreated, shaking his head, his heart breaking with betrayal. When the Prince turned away, he felt it like a knife through his heart.

"Please? Why?" he asked. "Why now? You don't have to do this? No. Please, don't do this."

Mahmood started to reach for the camel whip that hung from his belt.

"You don't have to do this." The kafir went quickly to his knees. "Please? My lord, Your Highness, my master by the Grace of God, the most Compassionate, the most Merciful. Please, you don't have to do this." He was so sure that his master would spare him, but it did not happen. The Prince did not turn around. Mahmood moved to put the great collar around his neck. The kafir tried nervously to grasp it and push it away, but he could not refuse to wear it. He could not refuse. He could not resist. He could not believe the Prince would not turn around.

Mahmood did not want to hurt the creature. He tried to smother its feeble protests before the Prince noticed. Only a blind man could not see that it was terribly upset, but when it failed to submit, he struck it hard across the head.

It was a sharp blow. The kafir cowered in shock. He simply could not believe what was happening. He had been so happy. His heart broke as the heavy collar was cinched snugly around his neck. He did not understand. What had he done? Why was he being punished? His whole body shook as he tried to come to terms with submission. More distressing than the collar was that the Prince had turned away and abandoned him. Had none of it been real? He felt physically sick. He had believed that he was loved. He had believed it totally yet here he was being banished again. When Mahmood took hold of the collar, the kafir knew he was doomed. He struggled weakly on to his feet. To stifle the nausea that overwhelmed him, he bit his own hand and chewed until the pain erased his disappointment. He surrendered his wrist. Without further explanation, he was led away.

They went to Riyadh. Prince Abdul Aziz had several houses in a large compound on the outskirts of the city, but would have upset his wives if he had chosen to stay with any one of them. It was easier to stay at his hotel. The top two floors were always kept vacant for him. That was easier than dealing with the jealousy. He was just about up to date with his emails when he arrived, but there were still several hours of phone calls to clear before he could think of calling his relations. The news was still about Daniel Pearl, the American journalist who had been kidnapped in Karachi a few weeks previously then been brutally murdered, all of it filmed and broadcast on the internet. In the Kingdom, the news was all about the anticipated arrival of two million pilgrims for the annual Hajj, and flattering reports about the activities of the Crown Prince. It struck him again how cocooned life was in the Kingdom. He found it impossible to resist the daily five calls to prayer. The few women that were out of doors were heavily veiled. After the lively colourful extravaganza of Venice, the Kingdom was a complete culture shock.

His mother phoned first. She spent ten minutes telling him that he was not a good son, and then started telling him that she had been insulted by several of his wives. He put the call on speaker then settled to read various business updates and share forecasts. The copper mine in Chile was having labour problems. The gold price was rising as usual because of the war with the Taliban and Afghanistan, but production costs had risen alarmingly in the African subcontinent. Liberia and Sierra Leone were flooding the market with 'blood diamonds' to finance their civil wars. There were even more rumours about the UN and EU being involved in corruption, and the mismanagement of the Oil For Food programme set up to help the oppressed civilians of Iraq, who could not buy food or medicine because of the draconian sanctions. Even Kofi Annan's son was implicated. Despite winning the Nobel Peace Prize, Annan and the UN were being heavily criticised for their failures in the Balkans and Africa. Large companies in the US and Europe were still going to the wall. And his mother just droned on about how unhappy she was, and how all her daughters-in-law were selfish and lazy.

Venice seemed like another world. After final prayers, he lay down to sleep in an empty bed. He was alone. The sheets were cold. He was restless. He thought about his beautiful creature then erased it from his mind. His family came first. He had obligations. With an old photograph album, he sat for another hour putting names to the faces. It had nothing to do with not loving anyone. He was just rubbish with names, and as he saw them so seldom, it would have been terribly wounding if he made a mistake.

Taking them strictly in order, he called his wives in the morning, and invited them all to a lunch at the hotel. All but two came. Only one had not been invited. They all behaved impeccably. He did not invite his mother because she would not mind her manners. Twenty-seven children came, and he knew all their names. He should have been pleased, but he saw in their eyes that he was a stranger. Like his own father, he had taken their affection and respect for granted. They did not know him. They had obviously been told to behave in front of an important man. Not even the little girls would run to their father and give him a kiss. His loyal wives tried to appease him. They told him about his important work, and the many demands on his time, but he felt he had failed. He was never there on birthdays. When they needed the strength of a father, it had been a servant or bodyguard who stepped in to save the day.

It was Prince Khalid's mother who did not attend. No one mentioned her. No one suggested anything was wrong. She had been coldly polite on the phone, but the silence surrounding her absence suggested that something was seriously wrong.

The wife he had locked away, remained locked away, and was never mentioned by anyone.

By the end of the lunch, it was arranged that he would visit each of them. It would be in the same order. He would show no favouritism. As the women prepared to leave, he watched them put on the black cloaks and veils, which they were required to wear when they went outside. They all had chauffeurs and bodyguards. They lived quiet respectable lives, which should have been enough, but as a man of the world, he was very aware of the restrictions. Technically, it was not just the Hijab; they also required written permission from their husband to leave their home. Abroad, they could have been doctors or lawyers or teachers or taxi drivers. He remembered how he had fought to go to school in America. He wanted a different life. He understood that they might also have had dreams. He wished he could have granted them their dreams, but that was impossible. The Kingdom was not ready. The men might never be ready. He did not believe it would happen for his daughters or even for their daughters. Princess Noor was still in exile. She had more bodyguards than the Crown Prince. An awful lot of people wanted her dead, and not just because she had courted publicity to tell lies about the abuse of women in the Kingdom, and to expose what she believed was the suppression of women by men under the pretext of it being ordained by God. Princess Noor was only alive because the Crown Prince had issued an ultimatum, and she had sensibly taken heed. Now, she lived quietly in Vermont. Her father had offered her in marriage to various princes, but nobody wanted her anymore, and nobody expected her to come home because that would have been a death sentence. That did not stop her father from believing that he had the authority to sell her off to a husband. She was unmarried. She was still his to command. He refused to accept that she was beyond his reach.

Before dawn the next morning, Mahmood brought the creature to the Prince's suite. While the creature was sent off to run a bath, Mahmood lingered. The Prince was still half asleep. He sat on the side of the bed, dishevelled and bleary-eyed. He had only had a few hours' sleep after taking conference calls from Jakarta and Santiago and Denver. First prayers did not wait for anyone. It took him a moment to see that Mahmood was still standing over near the door. Stifling a yawn, the Prince pulled on a robe then rose to his full height. It was not that he was naked. It was just impolite to have a conversation with someone when only one of them had clothes on.

"Yes?" the Prince asked graciously.

Mahmood bowed low, twice, and then gazed at the Prince's bare feet. "I regret, Your Highness, my lord by the Grace of God, the most Compassionate, the most Merciful, I regret that my mother has passed away." He drew a deep breath. "I am so sorry, but I must take care of her. I am her only child. There is no one else. I must go. I am so sorry."

The Prince was stunned by his humanity. "Of course, yes, Mahmood. Yes, you must go." He straightened up and ran his fingers through his hair, trying to improve his appearance. "Where is she? Is she here in Riyadh?"

Mahmood was embarrassed. "We have a small house in Jeddah. My adopted son has taken care of her. I must make arrangements for him now. I am so sorry, Your Highness. I would not leave it alone here for anything less."

"Leave it?" the Prince asked, then nodded and frowned as the creature emerged from the bathroom. "Yes, of course, well…"

Mahmood bowed again. "And I would like to commemorate my mother's life by completing the Hajj." He dared not look at the Prince. "I can catch a bus from Jeddah to Mecca. If you would allow it, Your Highness, I would be most grateful."

The Prince knew he would go to hell if he refused permission. "Yes, of course." He tried to smile. "You must take as much time as you need, Mahmood. For the memory of your mother."

Mahmood turned to glance at the creature which stood docilely at the door to the bathroom. "And what of the blue-eyed jinn, Your Highness? There is no one to keep it safe. Waheed is now with your father. Aziz is dead. Omar is in Paris, not that he would know how to look after it properly. Perhaps, you could send for Waheed. If your father could spare him..."

Prince Abdul Aziz was not really keen to involve his father. There would be a lecture and disapproval and unacceptable advice. Then he remembered that they were in Riyadh, in the bosom of his family, which meant unwanted attention and criticism. He had just committed himself to visiting his wives and re-establishing a relationship with his children. His creature could not be included in any of that. "Damn," he said, then raised a hand to acknowledge that an apology was required. "What do you suggest, Mahmood? You know it better than anyone." He looked across to see that his audacious creature was watching him. He frowned disapprovingly. "What do you normally do when it's a pain in the arse?"

The kafir fumed, but lowered his gaze respectfully.

Mahmood, of course, knew everything. He had cleaned and groomed the creature during their long holiday in Venice. He provided comfort when the Prince cast it off after the holiday was over. He knew that it had been genuinely devastated. He had taken it into his own bed, and the creature had remained stubbornly inconsolable despite being beaten quite harshly.

"It's been difficult lately," Mahmood admitted. "I fear solitude will make it worse. Omar made it study the Holy Book when we were in Dubai. He was very strict. He believed it needed to go back to a madrassa to be cleansed after spending so long with all those heretics."

The Prince shook his head. "That's impossible now. It must stay here. You'll only be away a few weeks. What harm can it come to?" He shrugged. "It's not important. You must take care of your mother. If there is anything that I can do, please tell me? Was it your mother's wish to go back to Pakistan? I can arrange that. You have been a loyal servant, Mahmood, I would be very happy to do such a small thing to show my appreciation for all that you have done for me."

Mahmood blushed. He hardly knew what to say. "Your Highness, thank you. I am honoured." He bowed again. "You have always been very kind."

He drew a deep breath then sighed. "My mother had never mentioned going back to Pakistan. She left as a bride when she was thirteen. I would like to take her ashes with me to Mecca. She would like that. She was blind, you know. I think now she will be able to see."

The Prince was not sure he could have shown his own mother that much consideration. "You are a good man, Mahmood. She will like that."

Mahmood blushed even more. He indicated the creature that waited upon its master's whim. "It loves you, Your Highness. Forgive me, but it does love you." He tried not to see the Prince's indignation. "It doesn't need much. As long as it's fed and watered..."

The Prince surveyed his creature. The memories of Venice were still fresh. It was disturbing to imagine gloriously fucking it when he was supposed to be preparing to go and submit to God's Will. But his problems were all inconsequential compared to Mahmood's loss. He was momentarily ashamed. "You should go now. We'll be fine." He turned and walked away to his desk. Amongst the litter of phones and gadgets was a wallet. He took out all the cash that was inside, and pressed it into Mahmood's hands. It was a considerable sum. "If you need anything, phone Tariq. He always knows how to get in touch with me." He shook Mahmood by the hand. "If you need anything..." and he smiled. "Off you go."

The kafir had missed most of the conversation. Someone was leaving. When the Prince turned to look at him, he stiffened anxiously. He was across the room. Had he been summoned, he would have bowed down, and made his pledge of submission, but the Prince just stood there staring at him. His face was unreadable.

The Prince was lost. He had committed two weeks to his family, and had to fit his business commitments in amongst that as well as his role as a UN Special Envoy. At any moment, he might be called upon to fly to the other side of the world. He had already taken nearly two weeks to go to Venice, which had been completely self-indulgent. The two weeks was about to stretch into four.

"What am I going to do with you?" he asked.

The kafir just stood there

The Prince waved him away then went to pick up the phone.

The kafir waited by the bath tub. When the Prince joined him, nothing was said. The Prince stood in the tub while the kafir washed him. Everything had changed since Venice, but not necessarily for the better. They had been lovers, but only the Prince had moved on. The kafir had been relegated again to the rank of infidel and servant. He was invisible, and had to accept it in dignified silence because all the old rules applied.

When the Prince was dressed in his simple white robes, he went to his desk to find the handcuffs that had been delivered at his request. Then he went to find his creature. It was back in the bathroom, wiping around the bath and sink then collecting the dirty towels. When it saw the Prince advancing, it just stood still. It did not notice the handcuffs until the Prince demanded its wrists.

The kafir was suddenly nervous. He did not understand. He watched helplessly as his master clamped the cold metal cuffs tight around his wrists. The Prince steered him toward the shower cubicle. He backed him inside, made him kneel down then adjusted the handcuffs to incorporate a bracket that held the water pipe leading to the shower head.

The kafir tested the handcuffs then gazed anxiously up into the Prince's dark penetrating eyes.

"You love me, don't you?" the Prince demanded.

The kafir was too upset to answer.

"Then sit here quietly."

"Please, don't leave me."

The Prince raised a finger to his lips commanding silence,

"Please?" the kafir whispered brokenly. "Don't leave me here."

The Prince reached out to slap his creature's head against the tiles. It made an alarmingly loud noise, but had the desired effect. The creature deflated before his eyes.

For the kafir, his abandonment in a hotel bathroom in Riyadh was the death of all his hopes. He was broken from the moment that the Prince walked away and locked the door. He never made a sound. Everything that he had enjoyed in Venice became tarnished by the realisation that none of it was real. He had believed they were lovers. He had been so sure that he was loved, and therefore valued. It was all that he needed to anchor his sanity. And if it was false, then he became nothing.

The Prince had more important obligations. His creature was not even on his list of priorities, and if it had been then it would have been carelessly brushed aside as an inconvenience. He had indulged it in Venice. It could hardly expect that amount of attention when the holiday was over. He spent his days with the children. That was difficult at first. They had to learn that he was their father, and that he loved them all unconditionally. He brought small trifles. They already had all the toys that they wanted.

With the youngsters, he sat on the floor while they crawled over him and pulled at his beard. They were so uncomplicated. They were happy just to have his attention. At other moments, he sat in nurseries doing crayon drawings or telling stories of the great kings of old. He remembered the stories that his mother had told him. If she was bitter and lonely then wasn't that his fault? The older children were more reserved. They remembered that he had forgotten their birthdays. They knew that he would disappear again. Falling in love with his wives was easy. They were all as beautiful as he remembered, and they were devoted, uncritical and modest. He believed he was the luckiest man alive.

It was dark when the Prince returned. The kafir heard movement in the next room then heard his master's voice. It had to be a phone call. That would be someone in Asia. He could not make out the words. Then, at last, the bathroom door opened, and the room was flooded with dazzling light. The kafir's heart quickened. He could not hide his joy at seeing his master, but the Prince was tired and preoccupied. He irritably unlocked one of the handcuffs then turned away and left. It was all the kafir could do to struggle on to his feet, and dutifully follow him. He found his master impatiently waiting to be undressed. There was no kind word. He was ignored. He carefully stripped him of his clothes then followed him back into the shower. They stood close together under the torrent as the woes that filled all their days were washed away. The Prince remained aloof. The kafir tried to catch enough water in his hands to drink, but it was hardly enough. The kafir was confused. They were strangers again.

When his master took him into his bed, he dared to hope that there might be some physical contact, but the Prince wrapped his arms around him then placed a hand across his mouth. That was a warning. The kafir lay still. Even when the Prince had fallen asleep, he did not move. He barely breathed. To be in bed with his lover, and not be loved broke his heart. He had been abandoned, but not banished. That was agony.

In the morning, the kafir had to surrender his wrists again to the handcuffs. For ten days, he remained in the bathroom. If he could sleep the hours passed quicker, but did not ease his distress. Over the years, he had been left in much worse places, but he had never felt so alone. Every night he was taken into his lover's bed, and forced to lay there motionless like a corpse. Eventually, the Prince did remember to provide bottles of water, and had the hotel send up a late supper so that he could give his creature some food if he felt it deserved a reward. By then it had lost weight that it could ill afford, and it had become sullen and petulant and ugly.

Fortunately, Mahmood returned before any real physical damage was done. When he went to collect the creature from the bathroom, he was quite overwhelmed when it bowed down to him as if he were the Prince, and called him 'Hajji'. He patted it affectionately, while it kissed his feet and then his hands. It seemed so pleased to see him, but trembled when he pushed it back into the shower. It clung to his hand like a frightened child. Mahmood carefully extricated himself, and turned away to find a soap and razor. It needed a shave. It needed a haircut. As soon as Mahmood set to work, the creature began to relax.

Chapter 46

It was slightly cooler later in the afternoon. The garden was full of baby birds. The noise was deafening. She took some chairs down to the bottom of the garden then fetched Paul. He had a name now. He was walking easier. He had some strength in his limbs, but not much. He sat bolt upright. His back was still too tender to be pressed against anything harder than a pillow. So she watched him and sometimes, the birds. When a family of Goldfinches came down on to a nearby feeder, she explained what he was seeing. One family of Great Tits had eight chicks. They were all adorable. The garden was drenched with colour. The air was full of the heavy scent of old roses. There were bees everywhere. These were the moments that made all the hard work worthwhile.

"So how are you feeling?" she asked quietly. He had completely shut down. He did not even pretend to be interested in her garden or her birds.

He acknowledged the question by lowering his gaze. His head went down.

Her stone cold dead heart was put through the wringer. She felt sorry for another human being. It hurt. She felt helpless and a coward, but she needed to help him. It was an imperative need. "Have you thought about what you'll say?"

He breathed deeply. His face was white and haggard. His beauty had been diminished. He looked almost human. He started to speak then shook his head, and was engulfed again.

"I could help you." She leaned towards him. She wanted to touch him, but that still felt inappropriate. She wanted to assure him that she was not Blanche DuBois.

He managed to nod, but he could not look at her. He frowned and sighed, and did his awkward evasive little shrug. "I thought I would tell them that I was a servant," he said quickly, but his nerve failed. He took a deep breath, and shivered, then said: "I'll tell them that I was alright, that nobody hurt me. It was just a job. It wasn't anything bad." He flinched. Another minute passed while he stared at his hands, and fidgeted like a guilty thief. At last, he confessed: "I will tell them that I did have a lover. And I had friends." The wounds across his back protested as the tension ploughed through every nerve in his body. He grimaced then shuddered, which made the pain even worse. His hand was shaking as he raised it to wipe his brow. He managed to breathe, but he was terribly pale and visibly distressed. Then he looked at her. "In that culture what happened to me was not uncommon. It is a traditional pastime. I was lucky. To have been chosen was a great honour for me." His gaze sharpened. His eyes narrowed with desperate resolve. "I was lucky. I was asked, and I consented. I understood that it was privilege. I was flattered to be asked."

She was actually impressed. It had the ring of truth. She wanted to ask him about Abdullah, but knew that would upset him. "So you were a gentleman's gentleman?"

He nodded.

She had hoped he would smile and find his nerve. "You had a respectable job, and you travelled extensively."

He nodded again. His head went down.

"Did you ever come to England?"

He shook his head once. "He came here, but I was always left behind. Now, I understand why. It was never discussed. No one ever said anything. I did not understand that I might belong somewhere that was not at his side. I belonged at his side. That was my place. There was nowhere else that I wanted to be."

Whether it was brainwashing or affectionate loyalty, she did not know. "And the wounds on your back?"

He flinched then filled his lungs again. "I'll tell them that I was assaulted by a jealous ex."

She wondered if he had secretly been watching *East Enders*.

He took a moment to find the right words. "The world is a dangerous place." That was a pat phrase that he had heard on the television, but it still felt like a lie. He flinched again then shook his head. He swallowed the anguish that threatened to choke him. He was betraying everything he had ever known. And he was lying, which was unforgivable. "When my old lover found me, he made sure that I was given proper medical care, and then I was sent here to convalesce with you."

She frowned then offered her best smile. "So I have to tell lies as well?"

"Please? But I don't know how to explain you."

"I don't know either." She watched the baby birds for a while. They were emptying the feeders so fast she could almost see the seed level going down. "It might be better if you suggest that you think they were planning to take you home, but that something went wrong and you must have been left here by accident."

"Would anyone believe that?"

"Well, it meets your need to protect the prince, and you were very badly injured so you were unconscious. You would not have been aware of what was happening around you."

He glanced across to see if she was watching him, and being discovered, he stared back at the ground.

"Paul?"

He looked at her anxiously, and was rewarded with a smile.

"Did you ever believe that you would be able to go home?"

He shook his head. He managed to look at her, then lowered his gaze to search the lawn for the words that he needed. "I had forgotten everything... I had no past and no future. I was not unhappy." He took a long deep breath. "I believed that I was happy." He managed a fleeting wistful smile then sighed. "When I was young I was always hungry, but being hungry was my penance for being an infidel. They told me that, and I believed them... They are righteous." He sighed deeply. "I did not think about going home. That was my home. I worked and I danced, and if they were pleased then I was allowed to share their beds." He nodded uncomfortably. "That was my reward. I did not want to be shut away alone." He chewed his lips thoughtfully. "That was my life. I was lonely. I don't think I was consciously aware of being lonely, but I was happier to share their beds than to lie down alone on the cold floor without any covering. I had no bed, no blanket. I owned nothing. Most of them were kind. They gave me fruit, and sometimes – rarely – they'd bring chocolate. They were gentle." He paused to remember then nodded. "It was better than being alone on the floor."

She sat quietly. He had found his voice, at last.

"It was many years before my master noticed me. I did not... I was frightened of him." He hardly knew how to say it. "He had other servants. He did not need me. He was seldom at the house where I lived with my Pakistanis. They were afraid of him so I was afraid of him, but he was never unkind to me. One day there was a misunderstanding. I was confused. I made a mistake, and he forgave me. It was madness. It was unlike what the others did to me. It was not love. We were not lovers. He just fucked me, but it was different with him. I would have done anything to please him." He nodded affirmatively. "Once, he asked to be allowed to put a picture across my back. He had never asked me for anything before. He did not need to ask. I belonged to him like his slippers. I could not refuse, but he asked me if I would allow it." He smiled sadly. "He wanted my permission. He could have taken what he wanted, but he asked me to allow it." He stared down at his hands. "It took such a long time, and it hurt. I had no idea what would happen. It took hours and hours. I couldn't move. I was on my knees and bent forward. It was hard to breathe... He stayed with me, holding my hands so that I could not move, so I would not disturb the men with the needles." He was silent for a while, flinching as he remembered the needles being drilled repeatedly into his flesh. "He told me that it was agony for him to watch, but that he would endure it because the picture would be so beautiful. That would make me even more beautiful. Of course, he would love me more. He said so. He promised. But afterwards, I couldn't move. When he touched me, it was so painful. I couldn't bear it." He shivered. "But it healed. He was so pleased. When he came to me again, and asked again, of course I said yes. I am his. All that I am. But the pain was worse. They cut me and burned patterns into my skin. There was a lot of blood. He did not stay with me. He was angry. The pain was terrible. I fainted. That did not heal so quickly, and I wasn't grateful so he gave me to the Pakistani."

She was shocked: "To Mahmood and Waheed? Weren't they your friends? They wouldn't have hurt you."

He had turned white, and shivered helplessly. "Abdullah. I was given to Abdullah." He nodded again while he struggled to find his nerve. "He came from my master's father's house. My master had invited Abdullah to come and teach me. My education was important. He did not want me to embarrass him. Always, I was sent to a madrassa for Ramadan. It is the holiest month. I went to study and fast. We fast during Ramadan. It is very important. We are meant to measure ourselves against the example of the Holy Prophet, Peace be on Him. For my master, it was an obligation. He believed he had a duty to educate me so that I did not offend Believers. I was grateful. I understood that it was a great privilege. My master is a great man. He is very religious. He sponsors many schools in Pakistan because the children there are so poor." He lowered his head. "It was my fault. I had embarrassed him. I was not grateful. He had every right to give me back to Abdullah." He stared at his hands. He felt her disapproval. "It was my fault. You do not like Islam because you do not understand it."

She felt drunk with rage, but bit her tongue, and merely shook her head. Another family of Blue Tits had arrived. The parents were visibly worn. The juveniles were round and fluffy. The parents collected seed from the feeders, and distributed them around their young. She tried very hard to smile. "I understand. You're probably right. Only the bad things are reported."

He followed her gaze to the baby birds, and remembered again that she was only a woman. "You have a good heart."

"I have no heart," she said coldly. "You have no idea who I am."

He took the liberty of studying her face, which was a mask of resentment, then lowered his gaze. "Please? I'm sorry. I meant no disrespect."

She looked away at the baby birds. She focused on breathing and not being angry.

There was a long silence then he said: "Please? I'm sorry."

She shook her head, and tried to smile. It took her a moment to recover. "No. I'm sorry. What do I know? I just read newspapers and watch television. My opinion on everything is dictated by the people who run news channels and print newspapers. How do I know if any of it is true? I think I'm smart enough to know that journalists always go for the sound bite that will capture the attention of an audience. But that doesn't make it true. If the Second World War had been reported like the Gulf War then it would have been over before Dunkirk. It would have been over before Belgium."

He focused on the ground. He was never confused by such conundrums. His faith was so strong. The Believers were righteous. As the symbolic enemy, he was held to be responsible for everything, and accepted the blame. When the horrific conditions in Abu Ghraib were made public, he had to endure the same abuse, and as he was told at the time, it was 'his people' who were responsible. His people had sodomised defenceless Believers. His people had tortured them with electric shocks. His people had kept them in hoods and terrorised them with dogs. His people had treated innocent honourable men as if they were animals. His people had no honour. Whenever something bad happened to Believers, he had to deal with the reprisals. "He gave me to Abdullah. My master could be a little jealous, but it was my fault. It was always my fault. He had every right to do that. He had to send for Abdullah. What else could he do? I forced him to send for Abdullah."

She hardly dared to ask, but had to know. "What did you do?"

He shook his head. His guilt choked him. "I embarrassed him."

Her mind boggled.

There was nothing he could say that she would understand. "Please?

I'm sorry." He tried to meet her gaze, but that was beyond him. "You have been very kind. You have done so much. How can I repay your kindness?"

Could she count the ways? She managed to smile, and graciously shook her head. "I just want you to be safe and happy."

"Paul Lawrence from Chester?" he said quietly. It made his heart quicken to think about it. "Are you sure?"

"You've seen the photograph. There is an uncanny resemblance. But we can't be absolutely sure. I'm going to ask someone to find your parents. We'll know more soon. All you need to do is rest and get stronger. You must be feeling better. And your heart? Do you remember what they said about your heart?"

His head went down. "I heard Mahmood telling Omar that I would not survive. He said my heart had been broken. He said I was passing blood all the time because my liver and kidneys were wrecked."

She nodded her head thoughtfully while she dissected the information. He was definitely not passing blood anymore. Perhaps 'a broken heart' meant something else in Arabic. "My doctor will help you. You needn't worry about that anymore."

He looked at her anxiously then stared at the ground. "I'm frightened."

She felt that was probably an understatement. "Yes. You must be."

There was a long silence.

She stared away at the garden because he was literally shaking. She desperately wanted to offer comfort and support, but she was not sure she would be able to control herself. Her heart was palpitating. The muscles in her belly were tightening painfully.

"What if they don't want me?"

She turned to survey his beautiful face. It was impossible to believe that there was anyone anywhere with a heart capable of rejecting him. "They'll love you. You'll have to be patient with them. They'll be in shock. After all these years, they'll struggle to believe that you really exist. But as soon as they see you then they'll know. It's nearly twenty years. They must have just about given up hope. You'll have to be patient. You must be kind. They'll have so many questions, which you don't want to answer." She was distracted by a cloud of Goldfinches, and paused to collect her thoughts. "I shall miss you, but you must go home. Perhaps later, when you've settled into your new life, you could get in touch, and let me know that you're alright?"

He had not even thought about that. "Yes. Of course."

She fetched a drink for him and some more pills. He might not have known that there was a big football match on the television, but she was not prepared to take the chance. They sat together for another hour, but he was overwrought, and it was easy to persuade him to go and lay down on his bed.

*

They were all safely installed in the house in Paris when the ground invasion of Afghanistan began. The French were totally against it. They were even more enraged when the second largest airline in France went bankrupt. America was vilified in the French media. The French hated Americans more than bin Laden did.

For the Prince, the house in Paris was to be a refuge. He was completely jaded with the whole political situation. His role at the UN had worn him out. He had failed his friends in Western Sahara. He had bought so many latrines for the UN refugee appeals that he felt they were mocking him. He could not begin to count the millions of dollars that he had spent to eradicate famine, to combat drought, to provide shelter and sanctuary for the oppressed, but it always seemed to be his lot in life to provide the toilets. He had worked with three Secretary Generals, countless Special Envoys and High Commissioners, and by 2002, he was experiencing compassion fatigue. He knew he had been a failure as a father. Like so many fathers he had been so busy for so long, and just believed that his children would understand that their father had an important job. And like his brothers and cousins, he had made a phenomenal amount of money. Commercially, everything he touched turned to gold. He kept his wives in luxury to mollify them. He bought his children presents to make up for the days and weeks and months that he was never at home. When his first born, Prince Khalid, had married in New York, it had only been the speed of Concorde that got him there in time. The ten days in Venice, living quietly on the yacht with his creature, and only a few servants, had been some of the happiest days of his life. It reminded him of his time in San Francisco when he sat in the park with daisies in his hair, reciting poems to the tourists. In Paris, with all the phones off the hook, he was too tired to reflect on anything but his failures and broken dreams.

The kafir was permitted to wear his expensive suits in the house in Paris. He did not have to wear the burqa unless they were going abroad. The French hated the burqa. He could even look out of the windows, but he was not allowed to go outside. He was not allowed to swim in the pool. He had hoped they would be lovers again as they had been in Venice, but that had apparently been nothing more than a brief holiday romance. When he tried to engage the Prince's attention, he was irritably brushed aside, but he persisted gently and sympathetically. Even poor old Mahmood was feeling hurt and vulnerable. He had been brusquely instructed to find an assistant, which he misinterpreted as the Prince wanting to replace him.

It was not every night, but sometimes it felt like every night. Eventually, in Paris, the ritualised beatings began again. It was done quietly and tactfully away from the other servants, and for a while the Prince found some relief. Mahmood had brought in a young Algerian, who could be trusted to relish the duties that others resisted. The young Algerian was so eager to please that there were no limits to the tasks he was willing to perform. He took to brutally thrashing the creature's backside with embarrassing enthusiasm.

"I don't ask too much, do I?" the Prince whispered as he bent to kiss the creature's exquisitely tender wounds. "You know how much I love you. I can't help it. You are as beautiful as pearls. This flesh is so lovely. You wouldn't deny me this?"

The creature lay face down across the bed. Its long, lithe, burning body was liberally marked with dark welts, glazed by sweat and speckled with tiny drops of blood. The pain was unendurable, but it hardly moved as its master knelt astride, opened it and plunged inside the hot wet vault. It groaned and arched instinctively, opening itself to its master's desires. Great, strong hands pawed and pulled and gripped. They became one, bound to each other by a passion neither could renounce. Whether it was love or lust did not matter then. They both worked hard, sweating, groaning, and holding each other in a frenzy that denied life and logic and gentleness.

As the thrusts grew more powerful and intense, the kafir grimaced. It hurt. It hurt so much. Gasping, breathless and drenched by sweat, he forced the immense sex deeper into his body. Now, it was agony, but the kafir needed it. He wanted it. Yes. It was good. It was exquisite. It was always so painful. He twisted his hips and drove back again, trying to focus the hard sex that pounded like a steam hammer. It was so close. He felt it. Just a bit more. Just there. Just like that. Fuck. Yes. Again. For a brief moment, there was no pain at all. Oh fuck me. Please. Fuck. Yes. Come on. Fuck me. Please, fuck me. Don't stop. Please, don't stop. Don't ever stop. Fuck me. Fuck me. He moaned helplessly. It was over too soon. The pain of emptiness returned.

"You must never leave me," the Prince said, stooping again to kiss the creature's burning flesh. The wounds were sweet and salty.

The kafir groaned and gasped as his body was plundered. He knew exactly what to do to please his master. The pain was nothing. He needed to feel the immense, engorged sex boring into his body. It was splitting him open. There would be blood. His flesh was tearing. His teeth rattled in his jawbone as the Prince lunged into him. The great cock punched into his soft tissue. He gasped again. Something was broken. He was punctured. The pain was suddenly shattering. He was battered and pulverized. It was agony. He was being opened like a ripe fruit. Just a bit more. Just there. More. More like that. Harder. Harder! Push! He felt his master boring imperiously though his whole body. Nothing had ever belonged to him. Prince Abdul Aziz owned his flesh and his blood, and had carved his authority on every nerve and sinew. He wanted to be filled up. He wanted to be held powerless by the great strong arms, and be in agony because that was being loved.

Chapter 47

Wednesday was quite windy for June, which made the heat less oppressive. They walked around the garden. She was always trying to increase the number of circuits, and he no longer needed to hold on to her arm. As soon as she perceived that he was tired, she took him back into the house. They had a cup of tea, then she left him at the kitchen table, copying out poems, encouraging him to study new ones that were unfamiliar. His handwriting was improving. He found actual composition much more difficult.

She wandered in and out. She had not quite taken on window-cleaning, but she was keeping up with the vacuuming and the laundry, and had even taken the time to iron his shirts. Now, he had several shirts, and even more pants. Gardening was still her first choice.

He was struggling with his expectations. When she came in to share a pot of tea, he was disappointed and irritated by his failures. She offered advice. It was her house so she was entitled to offer advice, but he was obviously frustrated.

"I don't need your help. I'm fine. Honestly, I'm fine."

She leaned across his shoulder to look at the pages he had written, which he was suddenly trying to hide. He was still pressing too hard. The script was untidy, but there was evidence of a fluidity that had not been there before. "This is great," she said. "Really!"

He shook his head. "No. It's not good enough. I must keep trying."

She moved around to sit opposite him. "You've been doing this for hours. Wouldn't you like a cup of tea?"

"No, thank you. I'm fine."

She leaned on to her elbow, and gazed across the kitchen table. He certainly looked fine. "So what did they teach you at the madrassa?" she asked gently. She was smiling. "You were there for seven years?" She saw him flinch. "I went to eight different schools. We moved around a lot." She frowned distractedly. "That's probably why I don't have any friends." She focused on him again. "You said it was in the north? That's the Himalayas? No, that's further east." She looked at him. "You must have learned something."

He slowly put down the pen then pulled his hands beneath the table to clasp them in his lap. "I didn't..." He started and stopped. He drew breath to continue then hesitated. In a rush, he quickly explained: "I don't understand."

She watched him slowly disintegrate. Her confidence crumbled. She had put her foot in it again. She started to apologise, but he leaned across the table, round shouldered and avoiding her gaze.

"I don't know what you want me to say." It was barely a whisper.

She watched him for a moment. "People will ask you questions. They will be curious about where you have been and what happened. They'll be completely innocuous. There won't be a hidden agenda. They'll just be interested in you, and interested in a nice way. They'll be trying to help you." She tried smiling even though he was staring down at the table like a guilty schoolboy being told off in front of the whole class. "That's why we're doing all this. You have to be prepared."

He nodded dismally.

"You have to have a story ready. I'm not suggesting you have a completely rehearsed pack of lies, but there will always be questions. There'll be conversations. You'll learn how to deal with it. I've always found the best defence is to deflect and redirect. Someone asks how you are, and even if you're deathly ill, you should brush it aside dismissively as if your health is of no importance, and always ask them about themselves, about their health and their children, and keeping them talking so that they don't have a chance to come back at you."

"I don't know how to do that. I wouldn't dare." He slowly calmed down, and managed, eventually, to meet her gaze. "I don't know how to do that."

She smiled kindly. She was equally inept. "Go and wash your face. I think you've had enough for today. We'll have another walk. You'll feel better outside."

When he walked away, she went into the front room, and quietly picked up the telephone. She knew the number, and got through almost immediately.

*

They went to Dubai for the boat show, which encouraged the kafir to believe his master was also longing to rekindle their romance. He was interested in seeing all the facilities. He leaned over the Prince's shoulder to admire the beds, the bath tubs and the gold plated taps. The Prince, in a moment of insanity, bought the largest boat at the show. It made the super yacht he had hired for Venice look like an old tramp steamer. The Prince decided to change all the decor and the colour scheme, then insisted it was delivered to Cannes for September.

Only a few days later, at a late night camel racing meeting at Nad al Sheba, several princes were meeting informally. The kafir was there in his best robes and headgear, and still hot and distracted by his conviction that his master loved him again. There were other 'decorative' servants. They were all youthful males, usually blond and always stunningly attractive, but none compared to the blue-eyed jinn. He did not dare acknowledge any of them even though he had seen them at other private events. All of them loitered near their masters, but subdued their eyes, and kept their mouths shut. Not only the camels could change hands at the racetrack. Fortunately, Omar was always there and always paying attention. When a stranger suddenly lunged through the crowd, it was Omar who saw the danger, and threw the kafir to the ground before knocking the intruder away. The acid meant for the kafir's face was sent in a wide spraying arc. It burned through robes. It left a splatter burn across one side of Omar's face and neck. There was uproar. There was pandemonium. The intruder was dead long before the anxious and obsequious police arrived. Prince Abdul Aziz rushed Omar to hospital. A convoy of very expensive cars followed in their wake. There was outrage and fury. The Princes were grossly offended that someone had the bad manners to invade their private party. Their bodyguards were being interrogated. The caterers and most of the track staff had all been arrested. Omar was the acknowledged hero of the hour. It was possibly the most elegant of scars, if a scar could be elegant. In the hospital, Omar's wife was distraught. The kafir was devastated that he was the cause of so much unhappiness. He wanted to tell her just how grateful he was, but was not permitted a voice. To speak to a Believer was forbidden. To dare to speak to a woman was a death sentence. As soon as Aysha had arrived, the Prince and all the other male visitors had quickly withdrawn. She was devout. She was heavily veiled. Even with the doctor, she had to remain veiled. The kafir later realised that he was probably the only person there except Omar to have seen her beautiful face.

It was the following day when young Prince Bandar introduced himself. They were at the apartment in Dubai. The Prince was making arrangements for Omar to see the best cosmetic surgeons, and moving his family into the house at the beach. And he was realising just how much he relied on Omar to sort out the logistics of his life. Almost every question he asked his staff was answered with "Omar does that." So when Prince Bandar was brought into the Prince's study, no one was expecting him or had time to make an escape.

He was no more than mid-twenties, hardly any older than the creature, and it was not difficult to discern the motive for his visit. He offered his condolences for what had happened to Omar. He said security really needed to be tightened, but he kept returning to stand very close to the gorgeous creature, which dutifully stared at the floor. Prince Bandar was more than curious. He stroked its face, patted its shoulders then squeezed its biceps as if it already belonged to him. When he leaned in to smell the creature's neck, he managed to discreetly reach down and check that it was still entire. Startled and shocked, the creature stared wildly into his burning eyes then submissively lowered its gaze. Prince Bandar inhaled again, and smelt fear. "I'm not interested in geldings," he whispered quietly in the creature's ear. As soon as he started talking about money, Prince Abdul Aziz politely apologised, and explained that they were going away.

Omar recovered quickly. He kept the scar.

They flew to Beirut then New York, then went on to Japan to watch the national team play in the World Cup. In July, a close friend of the Prince died at the age of forty-three. The Prince and many of his generation were shocked, and promptly started reviewing their life choices. The Prince realised how finite everything was. He started to recognise that some things only happened once in a lifetime, and being wealthy was no guarantee of happiness and a long life.

They went to Addis Ababa, then Kampala, then Johannesburg. They spent a few days at the refugee camp in Algeria to talk to the Saharawi. Aba, his old friend, was recovering from a gunshot wound. The situation was tense. The Moroccans were still blocking the referendum. James Baker was being frustrated at every turn.

The few weeks down on the Riviera, drifting along the coast in September were definitely the highlight. The kafir enjoyed the lifestyle that the new yacht allowed him. There were seldom visitors. He was allowed to sunbathe naked on the deck, and was never left alone. The security around him had tightened significantly after the acid attack at Nad al Sheba. Omar's scar was a constant reminder to all of them to be vigilant. Many evenings were spent in the local casinos, and the kafir was always turned out in the expensive designer suits that he loved. The Prince's barber cut his hair. The same manicurist buffed his nails. But they were not lovers.

In Monte Carlo, Prince Bandar called again, and made his offer with a velvet bag of flawless white diamonds. The kafir was offended and humiliated, but he had to stand in silence while the young prince candidly announced his intentions, and proposed the value of the compensation he was willing to pay in advance. He did not just want to fuck the kafir. It was far more complicated than that. Apparently, he had a special place. He had various instruments and toys to test the kafir's range. When Prince Abdul Aziz did not immediately reject the offer, the kafir was suddenly quite alarmed. He was pawed again like a prize winning bull, and his master watched it all without complaining. The young prince said he had heard great things about the blue-eyed kafir. He said that he wanted to find out if it was all true. He did not want to brag about his conquests, but he considered himself something of an expert, and he had set his heart on exploding some of the myths surrounding the beautiful white infidel. The young prince was quite determined. He actually had the bag of diamonds in his hand. Prince Abdul Aziz knew he could not refuse. He let the young prince talk. He did not object when the kafir was turned about and touched and measured against – he did not know what. Prince Abdul Aziz smiled and agreed in principle, but again insisted that the young prince would have to wait a little longer. He gave vague assurances that he would make sure the young prince was satisfied.

With Ramadan approaching, the kafir was increasingly anxious about his fate. He did not believe that it was possible to return to the madrassa. Perhaps, it would be a different madrassa? He had only ever been excused when he was in Afghanistan with the Parsi community. He wanted to believe that the Prince needed him far too much to allow him to be sent off to waste four weeks at some school. Early in November, they had all gone to Sarajevo. He was almost certain that he was safe. He was absolutely devoted to the Prince. They flew to New York, and he was still hopeful. Around him, everyone was talking about their plans for Ramadan. That was the only time that grown men ever talked about food with real excitement. There were long conversations about chickpeas. In anticipation of fasting, everyone was very focused on their food. They were all ordering the traditional Palestinian dates by the tonne. Ramadan was a huge religious experience for all of them. Fasting naturally focused their attention. It was meant to be challenging. They were also obliged to be charitable and perform good deeds and be abstinent. The kafir just felt excluded and guilty. To him, Ramadan meant only four weeks of hell, which was a shameful confession. When they flew to Paris, he was convinced that the Prince would fly on to the Kingdom. The Prince was already speaking to his wives, and having extremely weird and unintelligible conversations with his younger children. He was happy. The kafir became paranoid, convinced he was to be left behind.

Mahmood, Famzi, the young Algerian, and the creature remained in Paris. There was no food or water or television from dawn until dusk. The creature spent its days reading aloud from the Holy Book. It was unhappy and ungrateful so it was constantly being disciplined. It was not even allowed to share Mahmood's bed. Famzi occasionally disappeared to visit his friends in Paris. He brought back sex toys, but Mahmood confiscated them as he found them. He explained to Famzi, for possibly the hundredth time that he was not allowed to play with the creature just because the Prince was away. His assertion that it was Ramadan, and therefore all that sort of thing was prohibited, fell on deaf ears. Famzi did not believe in God. Mahmood had never met anyone who openly denied the existence of God. He was absolutely horrified.

For the next two years, they lived on board a 747, flying almost constantly between New York, Darfur, Baghdad, and Paris. There were frequent dashes across Riyadh to catch a birthday party or an anniversary. The Prince was determined to not be a stranger to his family, but it was almost an impossible task. There were months when Mahmood and Famzi never stepped off the plane. The air was often stale. They all had headaches. The creature withered. Even when there were cleaners or engineers working on the plane, and everyone else had disembarked, the creature usually stayed aboard. It waited quietly in a sealed room expecting to suffocate as the air ran out, hoping somebody would eventually come.

Prince Abdul Aziz found less and less time to pray. He was failing to meet his obligations as a good Muslim. In the build up to the war in Iraq, they travelled to Ankara and the Azores. There were meetings in Riyadh and Jeddah and Mecca with various ministers, and once with the Crown Prince, which were followed by flights to New York or Washington then back to Baghdad and Teheran. The Prince tried to find moments to speak to his family, but time zones and endless meetings undid all his best efforts.

The situation in the Kingdom deteriorated rapidly. Blaming the expat community for all their woes worked for a while, but the increasing number of gun battles in Riyadh forced everyone to acknowledge that the terrorists at 9/11 were Saudis, and there was a real problem in their community that needed to be addressed. There was actually a war going on between Al Qaeda insurgents and the security forces. For a while, the news was carefully controlled. The gunshots that could be heard at night in Riyadh were not boisterous young men firing their guns into the air to celebrate a wedding or birthday. There were insurgents. There were dangerous young men. It took a while for them to actually be identified as terrorists. More alarming was the reporting of deaths. There were a considerable number of deaths, but no one ever seemed to be arrested. That suggested that the authorities did not want the embarrassment of any trials.

Baghdad, Basra, Teheran, Baghdad, Riyadh, New York, the Prince was clocking up the air miles. When he finally had a few days to rest it was too hot in Paris. The home he had bought as a retreat from the world stood as empty as the yacht. New York, Tifariti, Tindouf, Paris, Moscow, Grozny, Paris, Riyadh. It was exhausting. They went to Srebrenica for the unveiling of a memorial by ex-President Bill Clinton. The Prince spent time with old friends. The Balkans remained an open wound. Hardly anyone had a clear conscience. Some of the worst atrocities since the Second World War had happened there, and no one had intervened until it was too late. No one seemed to remember that it was one Serbian assassin, who had started the First World War, which had cost millions of lives, and changed the world forever. That the Serbians were now supplying arms to Iraq, ignoring all the embargos and sanctions, just reiterated how toothless the United Nations and NATO had been during the long and bitter conflict. And the Serbians took advantage of every weakness.

The Prince wanted to make the walk to Tuzla as part of his tribute to the tens of thousands of Muslims killed or raped by the Serbians, but he was warned that the whole area was now populated predominantly by the Serbians, and it was just too dangerous.

The creature spent another Ramadan in Paris with Mahmood and Famzi. Omar kept an eye on them. Mahmood had told him that Famzi was addicted to gay porn and sex toys. He had to rescue the creature from several unsavoury situations, but when challenged, Famzi always burst in to tears. The creature was never permitted to resist any of Famzi's advances. That would have been regarded as an assault on a Believer, which meant death. To complain would have been viewed as heresy, which meant at least one hundred lashes. The creature spent more and more time with Omar, who insisted that it read the sacred texts from sunrise to sunset.

The kafir knew that to read the Words of God was a blessing, which he should appreciate, but he found it arduous. He always had to read aloud, and the effort always tore his throat to shreds. When the Prince stayed a few nights to attend meetings, the kafir performed his duties with enthusiasm, desperate for a reprieve, but his master was too busy to notice him. By the time everyone else was celebrating Eid, the kafir was too sick to swallow anything, and still not allowed in to their beds. There were moments when being worked to distraction by Famzi's extraordinary toys was not altogether abhorrent.

They were in Addis Ababa when Saddam Hussein was captured near Tikrit. Even with the rather harrowing pictures on television, there were many who did not want to believe that he had been caught. Some hoped that Saddam had gotten away, and that it was just one of the lookalikes that had been dug out of the ground like a rat. The way that the President of Iraq was manhandled and examined on camera was disrespectful, but then some voiced the opinion that no one would have actually believed that it was really him if the pictures had not been shown on television. Had television become the arbiter of truth?

Only days later, there was a powerful earthquake in southern Iran. There were reports that it was the worst earthquake in history. A huge area around the city of Bam was flattened. An ancient citadel dating back centuries that had been recognised as a World Heritage Site was obliterated. The damage was catastrophic because most of the houses in the area were made of mud bricks, which had collapsed on the families still asleep in their beds. Iran initially declined the international offers of assistance that flooded in. However, once the scale of the disaster was known, the Iranians allowed aid and experts into the country. The Prince spearheaded the response from the Kingdom. He had the contacts, and the hands-on experience to qualify as a valuable asset on the ground in Iran. For weeks, he worked tirelessly to gather information, supply materials, and cut through the red tape that often handicapped committees. It quickly became apparent that the death toll exceeded twenty thousand, with even more suffering terrible injuries. In the depths of winter, it was essential to ferry the survivors away from the area as quickly as possible, though many had to endure freezing weather under canvas while the authorities struggled to find them homes.

The kafir remained on the plane with his servants. Every night, he lay in his lover's arms. He read poems and sonnets and soliloquies. He read from the Prince's cherished book until he knew all the pages by heart. Sometimes, he tried to find new poems, and when he came to an unfamiliar word then he lifted the book across his shoulder to show the Prince. Prince Abdul Aziz read through the few lines that had stalled the kafir. Sometimes, he would explain the definition of the new word. The kafir carried on reading until he or the Prince fell asleep. Prince Abdul Aziz held on to him like a child with a teddy bear. They were tender and quiet. They spoke in whispers. The Prince was unhappy again, and the kafir did not know why.

They remained in Iran for months with only infrequent trips to New York, Geneva or for children's birthday parties in Riyadh. The Prince was making a Herculean effort to be a good father. He was constantly flying from the twenty-first century to the Stone Age. The city of Bam looked as if it had been swept away by the Hand of God. The death toll had exceeded forty thousand. The injured were being cared for in hospitals that were not equipped for the number of patients coming through their doors. There was talk of moving Teheran away from the fault line. There was public unrest about the government's slow response to the terrible crisis. Months later, there were still thousands of people living under canvas. Even the Prince had rolled up his sleeves and moved into a tent. The news media had gone back to Iraq. Problems requiring slow hard graft were difficult to condense into ten second sound bites. Without the media attention, the aid money soon began to dry up, but the hard work continued through spring and summer.

Chapter 48

"Well, my dear lady, what may I do for you?"

She was flattered, and understood that she was meant to be.

"I have a problem, Mr. Watchman, and you've always been so helpful in the past."

He was a singular man. He was not tall or fat, but solid and impressive. His manner suggested that he had just come from the funeral of an old dear friend. He wore a black suit and a black tie. His shoes shone like polished ebony. He was a solicitor. He was her solicitor. If his clothes had been less expensive, he might have been mistaken for an undertaker. He often smiled, but it was always with an air of melancholy. When he did not smile, he had the most sinister and malevolent expression. When he did not smile, he was the most terrifying man she had ever met.

She had rehearsed the conversation. She knew exactly what she wanted to say, but being with him was challenging. He was so clever. Half the time, he seemed to know what she needed before she had even opened the conversation. It fuelled her paranoia, but as she was paying him rather handsomely, she could fool herself that she was in control.

They were meeting at a tearoom in a rather grand hotel down near the river. Mr. Watchman always took his ladies there. All the waiters and waitresses knew him. They fell over themselves to please him. He was known to be a good tipper, and everyone felt more comfortable when he was wearing a smile. He selected different tables for different ladies. Many were happy to sit near a window so that they could enjoy the view. He knew that Ms. Jane Howard would prefer to sit at the rear, and preferably in a corner with her back to the wall. Ms. Howard liked to know what was coming.

"And how are you, Jane?" he asked gently.

He was being polite so she assured him that she was fine. She did not feel that she knew him well enough to share such private details. In fact, she was a middle-aged woman, and sometimes life was just a pain in the arse. As a man of the world, he knew, of course, that her answer was somewhere short of the truth.

"So, my dear Jane, what may I do for you? We haven't spoken for some time. I'm always delighted to hear from you." His smile was warm, almost cherubic.

The rehearsed speech was succinct and articulate. Sitting across the table from Mr. Watchman, she felt like a schoolgirl before a headmaster. She could not remember one of her lines. Her brain had gone completely blank. Her trembling hands were moist with sweat. He had ordered cake, but she did not dare pick up the fork because he would see that her hands were shaking.

He waited patiently like a fond uncle as she twisted and turned in embarrassment. He ate his slice of carrot cake, and ordered a second while she tried to master her nerves and organise her thoughts. There was not the briefest fraction of a second when he was not smiling. It was a mask that he wore to good effect.

"It sounds so improbable," she said, almost in a whisper.

Mr. Watchman put aside the new slice of cake. He was watching her intently. The smile remained, but it was distinctly separate from the adamantine rigour in his eyes.

"A few weeks ago, I found a young man in my garden." She paused to study Mr. Watchman's face. She was almost relieved that he was paying attention, because she could not have endured incredulous curiosity. "He was unconscious. I took him into my home." She stopped again, expecting him to ridicule her foolish behaviour, but there was still the warm smile though he had not blinked once. "He wasn't well. He had been hurt. But he wasn't an addict or anything like that." She hesitated again then went on defensively: "Well, he had such lovely clothes and a Breitling watch. And he had proper hair. It wasn't all shorn off like a hoody or someone with an ASBO. He seemed so helpless, and he is helpless." She saw the glint in Mr. Watchman's eye. He knew too much already, but she did not know how to take it back. "I haven't done anything, Mr. Watchman. I couldn't. He's so damaged. You have to help him. I can't. I don't know where to start. You'll help him, won't you?" She heaved a sigh. She wanted to have a drink. Her throat was dry, but she did not dare pick up the tea cup. She was bound to spill it. She could not eat the cake because she did not feel that she should eat cake in front of a stranger. Mr. Watchman was her solicitor, but she was very intimidated by him. "And half of your clients are crooks so you'll know how to find people who might not want to be found."

"My dear Jane," he said. Fortunately, he was still smiling or she might have fainted. "I couldn't possibly agree with you. All of my clients are my dearest friends."

"So you'll help me?" she asked quickly.

"What is the young man's name?"

She sighed again. Even that was not an easy question to answer. "We don't really know. It's all very confusing. He says he was abducted when just a child. He doesn't really remember. He says he doesn't remember. He's been abroad. He has awful dreams. There are so many things that he won't tell me. It's easy to deny knowledge, isn't it? What he has said is very disturbing. He's frightened. He doesn't quite trust me because he doesn't know why he was left in my garden. What can I tell him? He says he was in Paris." She gazed into Mr. Watchman's killer eyes. "I didn't know what to do." She wiped her mouth. She needed to drink. It was Earl Grey. She recognised the aroma. But he was watching her now. The smile had almost disappeared. "I had a look at the Missing Persons website. I had no idea that so many people go missing every year. It must be less than one in a thousand who actually make it on to a news programme or are reported in the 'papers." She sighed again. She could not look at him now. She knew she was not feeding him information fast enough to satisfy his appetite. "I found this one child: Paul Lawrence. It's the right time period. And he has the most remarkable blue eyes. The picture of Paul Lawrence had the same blue eyes. I'm sure, but I don't know how to test my theory. I can't leave here. I couldn't... I wouldn't know how to find his family, and I'm not equipped to make contact. What would I say?"

Mr. Watchman studied her for a while then smiled as she looked up to meet his gaze. "Have you spoken to anyone else?"

"No. Of course not."

"Not the police?" It was just a question. He was not offering an opinion.

She shook her head. "He's really quite fragile. He's anxious to avoid publicity. I think he's frightened that they'll come and find him if there's any kind of fuss."

"Doesn't he want justice?" Mr. Watchman asked.

She shook her head. "He says he just wants to go home."

"And you believe him?"

"He's got it into his head that he's dying. I believe he just wants to go home."

Mr. Watchman smiled again. "We all want to go home, my dear Jane. It's a powerful motivation when we are near death."

"But he's going to be alright," she insisted. "I'm going to take him to my doctor. He'll be alright. He just needs someone to take care of him." She leaned down to pull a few sheets of paper from her handbag. "This is what I found out." She pushed the papers towards him. "If you could just establish that he is Paul Lawrence, and where we can find his family now. You'll know how to do that without causing a lot of fuss. I want to speak to them before they meet him. He's so fragile. I need to know that they're not going to ruin everything. He's been through enough."

Mr. Watchman was reading her notes. He looked sombre and serious. He was not smiling anymore. "Where has this young man been all this time?"

She frowned, and swallowed a lump of anguish. "The Middle East, I think. He's been through hell. I don't know how he has stayed sane."

"Is he sane?" He was utterly menacing, but suddenly smiled and the danger passed. "This is child slavery? Sex? Paedophiles?"

She nodded. "They've used him. He won't tell me anything, but he's a complete mess emotionally. I don't know any of the names. He won't go to the police."

"That's sensible. These people have a long reach."

"He just wants to go home." She studied the solicitor's face. "I'd like him to have that opportunity. It's important. He's never going to be able to have a normal life. They've done things to him. He..." She covered her mouth and almost sobbed. "They've marked him. I don't see how he'll ever be able to have a normal relationship with anyone." She tried to smile, but she was too upset. "He is the most beautiful thing you've ever seen, but he's marked in places that are, well, intimate. I can't think that any normal person would want to touch him. It's not something that can be surgically removed."

Mr. Watchman's eyes widened then narrowed. "And he wants to go home?"

She filled her lungs. "I don't think he's intending to take his clothes off. It's..." She just did not know how to describe his skin.

"So no police?"

She nodded then shook her head. "It would be all over the newspapers. He'd become a freak show."

Mr. Watchman folded her documents, and slipped them into a pocket of his coat. "I will do my very best for you, Jane."

She drew a deep breath. "There's just one other thing." Before he could answer, she pulled a bundle of tissues from her bag, and pushed it across the table.

Intrigued, Mr. Watchman carefully unwrapped the bundle, and was very surprised as a badly dented and scratched piece of metal fell onto the table, heavy with gemstones.

"They're all real," she said, matter-of-factly. She had recovered some of her composure. She had spent half the night cutting the metal and beating it out of shape to guarantee that no one would have been able to recognise what it was. Looking at her solicitor's expression, she was confident he did not know its scandalous origins. "I need to sell these. I'm sure you know someone who can do that. It's not hot. It's not stolen property. I'm told they are all very valuable. I just don't know who I could trust, except you." Mr. Watchman was still staring at them in shock. It was an expression she had never expected to see on his face. "Some of them must be at least fifteen carats. One of them looks to be about twenty. Do you know someone that you can trust that would give me a fair price?"

Mr. Watchman sighed, but he wrapped the tissues back around the bent and twisted metal. He had made several assumptions already. "I know of a man. This is a dangerous game. How do you know they are not stolen?"

She trembled at his tone, but her greed saved her. "I know where they came from. It's an unimpeachable source. I just need to sell them quietly to avoid giving offence." She picked up her handbag.

"Yes." Mr. Watchman smiled. "Of course."

"I want to go home now." She stood up.

Mr. Watchman rose to his feet, and offered his hand. "Ascot, I believe," he said, smiling warmly.

She blushed. "I have to be so careful. This has been so difficult for me, you understand?"

"Of course." He smiled with genuine empathy. "You know, I'm always here for you, Jane."

She nodded, and was completely flustered. "I'm not Blanche DuBois."

He leaned a little closer. "No one said that you were."

She nodded then drew away. The meeting was over. She had a date with Yeats.

*

The cracks first appeared at a hotel in Ankara.

They had arrived at the airport, and been waved through on diplomatic papers. In all the years that the kafir had travelled with his master, he had never known anyone question their documents or have the temerity to suggest searching them or their baggage. He understood though he had no proof that he was simply listed as a servant. He did not know if he even had a name. As usual, he was seen at airports only as a Muslim woman, heavily veiled, and too modest to be allowed to mix with strangers. Once they had checked into a hotel, he was turned out in one his expensive designer suits and gold watch, and introduced, if anyone ever queried his presence, as a valet or sometimes an interpreter.

That fateful day, he and his master had attended a conference across the other side of the sprawling city. They had travelled in a limousine, with an entourage of bodyguards in plain vehicles front and back. There was a lot of anti-Muslim feeling at that time, and their Turkish hosts had warned them that extra protection was required.

The Prince had been anxious because although he was a Muslim, his people had never been fundamentalists. He wanted to be seen as a moderate voice in a time of discord and misinformation. That day, he spoke at the conference of the diversity of the Muslim faith. He explained that Muslims could be Indonesian, Asian, African and European, not just someone who looked like an Arab. He was trying to underline the fact that the Middle East was not the problem. It was not about American Imperialism or oil. It was not about Arabs. He believed that Islam was in crisis. In a modern world, the unbending teachings of Islam needed to be opened out and explored and re-evaluated by the believers themselves. He insisted that they must want to do it. No one had the right to demand it. When he tried to justify his opinion by saying that the words of the Prophet had been written down over a thousand years ago for a very different world, in a land ravaged by tribal wars and roaming gangs of bandits, pursuing only profit and blood feuds, he was booed and heckled. He asked them why they were afraid of change. After that it did not matter what he said. The young delegates were enraged while older and wiser heads kept silent. As he had left the hall, someone had spat on him.

On the way back to the hotel, the Prince had made notes on his day, and recorded his thoughts into a laptop. He was annoyed with himself because he knew he had failed to clearly communicate his message when he had had the ear of the whole world. The PA sat in the front. Omar sat next to the creature, who stared out of the window, only now and then glancing at its master, knowing its duty, but fascinated by the brilliant and dazzling city that they travelled through like ghosts.

The hotel was an old fashioned, elegant affair, set back off the street, surrounded by palatial gardens, but the driveway was clogged with cars and coaches. Their driver honked and gesticulated, forcing his way through to the front door. There seemed to be hundreds of people milling around, neither coming nor going, and half of them were local tradesmen trying to sell souvenirs and postcards. Everyone seemed to be shouting. It was like the Tower of Babel.

The Prince sat calmly in the air-conditioned limousine waiting for his entourage to catch up, but the kafir was unnerved by the crowd. He had rarely been exposed to more than a few dozen people at any one time, and those occasions had been strictly controlled, and were so rare he could count them. As the bodyguards surrounded the vehicle, the Prince prepared to climb out, but as if remembering his manners, he turned to Omar. "Just keep it behind me."

Omar nodded. He knew what to do.

The door opened, and the Prince stepped out to stand for a moment surveying the bedlam that surrounded them. He was a prince of royal blood, and used to being treated with considerable respect, but here no one even noticed him. After the bad reception he had received at the conference, it seemed a natural progression. With a wry smile, he nodded to his senior bodyguard, who bowed respectfully. "Do we know what is happening?"

"I believe several coaches have arrived at the same time, Your Highness. It would seem they are all Americans."

The Prince nodded. "It can't be helped."

The bodyguard nodded and bowed then issued a few curt orders to his men. They formed a defensive wall on both sides of their prince, clearing a path for him through the seething drifts of people.

The kafir handed out his master's heavy laptop to the PA, then climbed awkwardly from the long black limousine. The noise was deafening. Grimacing, he paused to get his bearings, almost hoping that he could turn off the sound, and make all the people go away. The senior bodyguard took his elbow, and moved him away from the car so that Omar could climb out. A heavy security case was discreetly handcuffed to his left wrist. Omar took his other arm. The kafir hesitated. It was bedlam. He wanted to retreat back inside the safety of the limo where he had been comfortable and felt safe. There were too many people. Wherever he looked, there were tourists and locals shouting and complaining and laughing. He saw his master striding purposefully away, but he did not want to leave the car. He did not want to be swallowed up by the sea of humanity that swarmed around him. It was a hot sultry evening. He was already sweating heavily and agitated. His pulse was racing. He knew he was beginning to panic, and had no idea what to do.

"Come along!" Omar shouted in his ear.

Unable to resist, and still unnerved by the crowds, the kafir nodded dumbly. The bag attached to his left wrist was incredibly heavy. Gently but firmly, he was ushered in the footsteps of his imperious master. The bodyguards were extremely subtle. They appeared in every way to be protecting him. No one managed to come within arms' reach, yet the wall that kept the strangers out kept him neutralised within. He was in no way deceived, but he still found it overwhelming. The sound was bruising, and he could not help flinching and shying every time there was a shout or sudden noise.

The lobby was surprising small and cramped or, at least, seemed that way with so many people crammed into it. The Prince had not even crossed the threshold before he was hailed by two Turks that he had met earlier that day, and the three men stood together talking quietly while the bodyguards watched everything and everyone.

A little behind and to one side, the kafir waited with Omar within the wall of their bodyguards. He watched his master for a while then stared at the floor. He found all strangers intimidating. His life had conditioned him not to make eye contact. He studied the floor tiles and his uncomfortable shoes, only looking up to locate his master or to anxiously check that Omar was still beside him. When a group of Americans swept across the lobby, they careered into the human wall, but he did not look up or confront them. He quietly shifted his weight from one foot to the other, and looked dismally towards his master then bowed his head again.

It was incredibly hot and stuffy in the lobby despite the efforts of the droning air-conditioners, and the doors and windows that were thrown open to the night. He could smell exotic food and sweat, and the strong fumes of diesel from the coaches outside. He felt nauseous and dizzy. It had been a terribly long day. Looking at his master, he wished that the Prince would end his conversation so that they could go upstairs to their cool and spacious rooms. He was ashamed of his impatience and selfishness. He knew he was expected to wait obediently, but it was all so strange and distracting and hot.

Glancing around at the lobby, he looked at the architecture and décor, half remembering that he had been there before, but a really long time ago. It had been snowing then. He had wanted to go outside to see what snow was like, but his master had refused so he could only press his face to the window, and watch all the other people playing like children. Remembering the pain of his jealousy, he frowned bitterly and turned to check Omar, then gazed away at the tourists beyond the impenetrable wall of bodyguards. At first, they were just a loud and noisy, colourful blur. They seemed totally indistinguishable, but he had time. He had too much time. They were not just a seething, terrifying mob. These were people. He stared, focusing for the first time on their faces, and realised almost with shock that so many of them were European and about his own age, and they were laughing and smiling and shouting excitedly to each other.

It was a revelation. He had never seen people his own age before. They looked so happy. He did not understand. Why were they so happy? It was like a knife in his heart. He swayed on his feet, but leaned forward to peer through the bodyguards, desperate to have a closer look at these foreigners who seemed so much like him. Yes. They were like him. So many of them were like him. They were not like his master or his servants or the daunting bodyguards. They were just like him with fair skin and pale eyes. Their excitement was infectious. He longed to know what made them so happy. Then he realised. Then he trembled, and closed his eyes, and turned his face away.

A hand reached out to steady his elbow. It turned his blood to ice. He came back to attention, and bowed his head, half nodding, keenly aware of Omar, who had moved threateningly closer.

"Just stand still."

The kafir nodded uncomfortably, and stared at the floor.

"Don't do anything foolish." Omar squeezed his elbow again.

He nodded quickly, feeling his limbs thickening as his despair increased. It was too irresistible to imagine disappearing into the night with the tourists. He could be like them. He could be happy. He could be free. His heartbeat quickened, but in vain. He was too afraid to take any risks. Glancing once more at his master, he was defeated by his own conviction that no matter what he did or how fast he ran they would always find him, and that he would want to be found.

Time passed achingly slowly.

"Hey, are you famous or something?"

He was standing on the terrace at Haqi, high above the baking hot beach, and it was so still and so silent. If he closed his eyes, he could be there, and when he turned around he saw only his master, who smiled affectionately, and beckoned him to come closer.

"You're so cute."

The bedlam was forgotten. He was at home, the only home he knew. Rising on to his toes, he imagined flying out over a desert like a mighty eagle.

"Hey, you! Are you famous?"

He opened his eyes, and lifted his head, perplexed by the intrusion.

There was a bright and dazzling girl. He blinked, believing he was dreaming. She was standing just to the right of the Prince, who had turned to stare at her with something less than admiration. She was beautiful with cropped brown hair, a perfect figure, and the uniform of youth; hipster jeans and a very tight T-shirt that emphasised the swell of her amazing breasts. She stood with her arms akimbo, and she was staring shamelessly at the kafir, and laughing at him. "Yes, you silly! Are you famous?"

The kafir froze. Even as he stared at her in shock, he was aware of his master turning to regard him with a withering look. Without prompting, the kafir turned away and stepped backwards, and was relieved when Omar and the bodyguards swarmed to shield him.

She laughed brightly, encouraged by the positive proofs that he was indeed important, and therefore worthy of her interest. "I'm in room 348. Lose the goon-squad and come up."

The kafir could not help himself. He turned again and lifted his head, not quite able to believe that she had spoken so frankly to him.

She was still there and still smiling.

Though completely confused by her behaviour, he was so thrilled to discover that she really was addressing him and no one else, that he could not suppress his own sudden smile. Never in his life had he been so close to a woman, and she was so sexy. That was a shock, but the most pleasant of shocks. For one brief glorious moment, he imagined them alone together, flying through the air like birds, and he was free to take her in his arms and kiss her. He kissed her! He had never dreamed of doing that. His fingers sank into her breasts. That was another new sensation for him. His heart raced. He kissed her again. It was intoxicating. Heedless of the consequences, he tore off her clothes, and sank into her body, and she embraced him with a desire he had never imagined a woman could possess. They spun around through the hot air, plummeting down to the earth, too happy to notice that they were doomed.

She grinned and laughed, calling: "Room 348."

He nodded, calling: "Yes."

His bodyguards suddenly propelled him forward, brushing aside the girl, and hurrying him into the nearest elevator. He tried to turn around and find her again. It was hopeless. He saw her wave, and tried to reciprocate, but his arms were pinned at his sides, and then the doors closed, and he was whisked away. The carefully constructed illusion that the bodyguards were there to protect him ended abruptly. He was just a treacherous infidel and their prisoner, and they wrestled him from the elevator into his master's suite of rooms.

He did not really resist, though he liked to struggle just to stop them taking him for granted. He knew all of them, and they certainly knew him. Many of them had fucked him more than once. They understood his tantrums, and let him sweat and struggle to his heart's content. He was known to be a better fuck when his adrenalin was flowing. It was all part of the foreplay. But when the game began to bore them, he was just swatted like an annoying fly. They certainly never hurt him intentionally. He was much too precious to be damaged like that.

Inside the suite, he was forced to his knees, and held still while the heavy case was unlocked from his wrist then his own servants pulled up his jacket and shirt to reveal a broad studded belt. His wrists were locked to it, then on short tethers his ankles were shackled as well. Completely immobilised, he struggled irritably. The bodyguards merely laughed at him, and patted him on the head as if he was a mischievous child.

Famzi tried to bathe his face and brush his hair, but he was completely overwrought, and did not want to be still. Exasperated, Famzi was forced to set about him with the camel whip that all the servants carried like ceremonial swords. His head and face were not touched, but Famzi beat the crap out of him then put the heavy collar around his neck, and carefully fixed his appearance.

His frustration destroyed him. He did not understand the trick life had played on him. Why was he not free and happy? How had he come to be there? What crime had he committed that merited his total enslavement? He had always believed that there were many young people like himself. It had never seemed unnatural to him that he belonged to another person. He remembered no other life, and had never been made to feel ashamed of his condition. The culture that he lived in accepted him as a piece of property. It seemed entirely natural. He had always assumed that there were many other people living a life exactly like his own, and that because they were so inferior and unimportant compared to their masters, no one ever mentioned them. But it dawned on him painfully that he might be almost unique. He could count on two hands the number of white slaves he had seen. Were they really such a rarity? Only their white skins and their price tags separated them from the countless labourers that toiled until death in every shadow. Perhaps, the other world that he had glimpsed downstairs was the real one. Perhaps, he might have been free and happy, once upon a time. The laughter and excitement that he had found deafening now sounded bittersweet.

Chapter 49

Prince Abdul Aziz returned to his suite. He walked past the creature and the servants without acknowledging them, and went to sit at the desk. All his possessions had been arranged as he liked them. The computers and printer were already set up. His keepsakes and mementos were on the mantelpiece and sideboards. There were flowers and fruit on every table. His creature waited for him on its knees, a collar and leash about its neck as if it were a family pet. An elderly retainer brought in a tray of tea and a selection of pretty cakes. While he was in the room, no one moved or spoke. When he left, unbidden, Famzi dragged the creature across the floor, and dumped it back on its knees immediately before the Prince.

The Prince waited for the overwrought creature to look at him. That was forbidden, but it was one of the many rules that the creature always chose to ignore. Its treatment had been harsh even by the usual standards employed when they were far from home. At a signal, Famzi wrenched the creature's head back, almost pulling hair from its scalp. It gasped and shuddered, but refused to make a sound. The Prince waited, confident his precocious creature could not resist looking at him, but the creature delayed and evaded. It would be a guilty conscience, the Prince thought, and nodded to Famzi. The whip slid down between the collar and the creature's neck. Famzi turned the whip, and the collar became a tourniquet.

The kafir struggled violently. His blue eyes opened. He was furious, yet as the collar tightened by degrees, and his hair was wrenched again, his heart began to break. He could not resist them. How could he dream of escape? With a terrible wounded cry, he tried one last time to tear his hands free, but it was hopeless. Thoroughly defeated, he looked miserably to his master for mercy, but there was to be none. Famzi forced him to bow down, beating him with the camel whip until he was soft and pliant.

The kafir waited despondently until he heard the other servants leave the room, and firmly close the door, then he moved stiffly to sit back on his heels. He knew he was in trouble. He almost did not care.

The Prince regarded it scornfully. "Do you want to live in darkness, and suffer pain and torment?" he asked.

The kafir stared at the carpet. He did not know how to answer. His whole body ached from the abuse he had just received, and he did not want to incite more.

"You embarrassed me today," the Prince explained. "You betrayed my trust. A stupid, shameless girl smiles, and you humiliate me." He jerked the leash, causing the creature to hurtle forward and crash against the chair frame.

The shock and pain startled him. If he had been thinking about the girl at all, he stopped then. He tried to pull away, to lift his hands, to do something to protect himself, but he was helpless. "Please? I beg you, please my lord, Your Highness, by the Grace of God, the most Compassionate, the most Merciful. Please don't hurt me," he whispered miserably. "God is Great. Please, God is Compassionate." The leash slackened a little. With difficulty, he eased back on to his heels, but could not raise his eyes. He did not dare look up at his master. He knew the Prince would be angry, but was too unhappy to want proof. "Please, forgive me, Your Highness," he murmured, almost in a whisper. "Please, my lord, forgive me. I'm sorry. I'm so sorry. I meant no harm. All that I am. I am yours. I am here only to serve you. Please, forgive me."

The Prince leaned forward, sliding his hand down the leash until he held the collar in his fist, crushing the creature's neck. He stared at it, willing it to look up. He knew that it was afraid. That was clearly evident in the white face and shivering limbs, but he wanted to look into those ravishing blue eyes. Forcing up the creature's head, he traced a thumb across its lips then breached them.

The kafir looked at him, startled, sweating and distressed, tearing himself against the straps that held him still, yet revelling in his subjugation. This man was his only lover. His whole body throbbed as echoes of their intense passion pulverised him again. Every nerve and sinew burned with pleasure. His first and only thought was that he loved him wholly and completely and forever.

"You dishonoured me."

The kafir tried to evade the thumb. He tried to shake his head. He wanted to declare his love and protest his innocence, but the thumb rendered him speechless while the fist crushed his throat. He was terrified of being hurt, and of having his hopes destroyed again. He wanted to be loved. All he had ever wanted was for his master to love him.

"I was ashamed of you today. I thought I could trust you." The Prince smiled coldly, reaching further into the creature's mouth, supremely confident that the white teeth would never bite him even by accident. "I thought you loved me."

Trapped by the leash, the unhappy kafir whined as he tried vainly to pull away. He wanted to shout and scream at his master to tell him how much he loved him. He wanted to promise the moon. He would have sworn his life away, but could not say one word.

"I can't send you home, and I can't leave so we will have to be creative. How shall we keep you occupied?"

The collar drew him closer. There was no escape though he tried to wriggle free like a feral cat in a cage.

"What are you doing?" the Prince asked, actually laughing at its torment. "You're mine," he said while toying with the collar, and contemplating breaking the damn thing's neck. "You can't refuse me anything. These clothes! This body! This flesh! It belongs to me. You belong to me. Your heart belongs to me. I own it." And he smiled because it was true.

Struggling to breathe, the kafir slumped against his master's knees. His head was swimming. He could not inhale or loosen the grip on his jaw. It occurred to him that this might be the day that he died.

"Did you think that girl would come to you?"

The kafir had stopped breathing, and a sixth sense warned him that his master was not just dangerously aroused. This was something else. He was so unnerved, he peered up at his master with genuine concern. The expression he saw filled him with foreboding. There was something terribly wrong.

"Room 348, wasn't it? Shall we bring her here so that you can fuck her? Isn't that what you want? Do you want to fuck a woman? We could all watch. I'm sure it would be very entertaining."

The kafir trembled. He struggled to drag air down into his lungs. It was so hard to breathe. He could not even shake his head. The threat was obvious. It was in the words and in the strength of the Prince's unyielding grip.

"Do you?" He suddenly seized the creature's head, crushing it between his hands. "Would you like to fuck her?" He forced it to nod. "You must never lie to me. You want her, don't you!"

It was true, and the kafir was transparent. He wanted to fuck a woman.

"Shall I show you what we do to shameless whores?" The Prince suddenly released the creature's head. It collapsed on the floor, gasping. The Prince was embarrassed by his temper, and ashamed of his jealousy, and he knew in his heart that his creature would never betray him, yet the knowledge gave him no peace. He was angry. He could not shout at the young hotheads who had heckled and booed his speech. He could not stand up and declare that Osama bin Laden would be the death of Islam. It seemed he was unable to explain to a rational world that Islam needed to grow up and evolve from its roots in the desert. Who could he blame for his irrational rage and ugly jealousy if not the despicable creature that he was forbidden by God to touch, but could not kill? He had a sudden almost subliminal image of himself plunging into the creature, and it gave him intense nerve-jangling pleasure. His breath caught in his throat. Staring down at those blue eyes, he almost succumbed, but managed to catch himself, and in his relief nearly struck down the thing that he loathed to touch, but could not bear to be parted from. He sighed, almost forgot what he was saying then was embarrassed again. "Would you like that?"

The kafir trembled. He was hurt and confused. The wild emotions that had passed across the Prince's face were there for all to read. "Please, my lord, Your Highness, beloved master. God is Merciful. Forgive me, my lord. I meant no harm. I never meant to upset you. Please, my lord. Please, forgive me? I beg you, please?"

"You have embarrassed me," the Prince explained gravely, nodding to emphasise his disappointment. "I was humiliated today!" The blue eyes glittered. He wondered if the creature could just turn on the tears at will. He wondered what the tears would taste like. Were they sweet? Were they as sweet as ambrosia?

"Please, my lord, I'm so sorry," the kafir persisted quietly, knowing it was not his fault, knowing he was only caught in the crossfire.

The soft voice was very persuasive. The Prince's temper cooled a little. Without malice, he reached down to grip the collar then hauled the pretty thing back on to its knees. He stroked the beautiful face, and tried to brush the tangles from its hair. "What can you know of honour? You're just an outcast thing. Wicked. Perverted. Deceitful. You have no honour. Why do you bother me so much? I don't even need you, not really. You mean nothing to me."

"Please my lord," the kafir begged anxiously. He strained against the shackles that held him powerless. He could not take hold of the ring or stoop to kiss the Prince's feet or perform any of the other ritualistic salutes that always earned him forgiveness. Unable to move, he felt impotent and threatened. "Please my lord, I beg you. I meant no harm, Your Highness, my master by the Grace of God. God is Compassionate. God is Merciful. Please forgive me, my lord, Your Highness. I love you. You know I love you. I meant no harm. Please be merciful, my lord. God is Great. I beg you. Please, don't hurt me. Please?"

The Prince smiled slowly. "I have decided," he assured him, still stroking his face, and trying to tidy his hair.

The kafir was truly frightened. He could not breathe. His heart began to implode. His imagination reduced him to cowardice. He had never had any real dignity, and he could not pretend now. "Please, forgive me, master. God is Merciful. Please, don't hurt me. I am yours. I understand. I belong to you. All that I am. Please! Please, don't hurt me."

The Prince pressed a finger to the creature's lips, demanding silence. "You will never travel with me again without a pacifier. I have made up my mind. You will willingly submit to these conditions or you will be locked away in the dark for the rest of your life."

As his nerve collapsed, the kafir whimpered in shock and disbelief. Part of him wanted to believe that his master was joking, but looking into his black, pitiless eyes, he knew with certainty that he was in deadly earnest. "Please," he whispered. "Please, don't do this. I'm begging you. I am yours. All that I am. Please, my lord. God is Merciful, please be merciful. Please, my lord. I'm begging you. I'm begging you. God is Great. I'll do anything. Please…"

"That is the problem, isn't it! The very moment you feel threatened, you offer us your vile flesh as if we were all whoremongers." The Prince smiled grimly then stroked its beautiful face again. "You are nothing better than the worst of whores. Everything about you is an insult to God. That you enjoy your depravity is appalling. So you will wear the pacifier. You will ask for it or you will be locked away in the dark until you die."

"If you love me," the kafir implored desperately.

"Love you?" The Prince laughed at him. "I abhor you. If you had not been gifted to me I would have cast you off years ago."

The kafir stared at him, unable to believe that he could be so cruel, yet all that he saw in those black eyes was bitterness, rage and hatred. He shivered. His few frail beliefs in love and justice died. This man that he served loyally and adored beyond measure meant to extract a terrible revenge. He hesitated. He tried to find some reasonable argument that might spare him, but there was nothing he could say. He was not allowed to speak, only to answer, and he had been told what that answer was to be. Yet still he hesitated. The pacifier filled him with terror.

The Prince forced up the creature's head, and gazed into its raw eyes. "You will choose," he said coldly. "Do you know what it is to live in the dark without hope of light or companionship?"

"Please my lord. I have not betrayed you," the kafir insisted desperately. "Please..." He was slapped brutally across the face. It almost knocked him down.

"Choose!" The Prince smiled again, enjoying his power. He felt righteous in punishing a filthy sodomite. His fingers closed around the creature's soft throat. "Choose now."

In a small, eerily strange voice, the kafir submitted as bravely as he could: "Please master, if you wish it. I am yours. All that I am. To please you... Please, master, don't hurt me. I will wear it. Please..." He could hardly speak the words, but they tumbled out then he wept, emotionally destroyed.

The Prince wiped his tears, appreciating the irony. But the creature was inconsolable. When it became unsightly and excessive, he pushed it down to the floor.

It took several minutes for the pacifier to be sent for and found. During that time, the Prince sipped his sweet tea, and checked his endless emails. The vanquished creature remained trapped on the floor. With all its limbs harnessed up to the belt, it could not move at all. It wept silently, unable to find the courage that it needed to face its fate. Time moved much too quickly. Famzi returned long before the creature was ready to deal with him.

"Set it free," the Prince said, hardly lifting his gaze from his paperwork to regard Famzi. "It must submit willingly."

Famzi put the frightful contraption down on the desk. Then he loosened the shackles and straps that immobilised the creature, ordered it to its feet then commanded it to remove all its European clothes so that it could wear a simple white thobe. The creature was visibly overcome with emotion, but stood there dumbly as it removed the shoes, the clothes, everything.

Everything that gave the kafir an identity was taken from him. He shook involuntarily as every muscle in his body responded to his fear. He constantly glanced towards his master, hoping there might be a reprieve, but his master did not look him.

Famzi was a slight figure. His authority over the creature came solely from the presence of the Prince, and the creature's overwhelming fear. He wanted the creature kneeling down, but the creature's nerves made it unpredictable and consequently dangerous. When Famzi tried to restrain its wrists, the creature shied away then capitulated then shivered violently and drew away again. It was in a terrible state.

The Prince lifted his head, but declined to look at it. "Be still. You want this."

The tone brought the kafir up short. Beyond shaking like a leaf, he stood motionless staring at his master. He flinched whenever he was touched, but he did not impede Famzi, who attached his wrists back to the belt then guided him down on to his knees. His face was contorted by his fear and shining with tears. He had never looked less attractive.

They called it a pacifier. In truth, it was a bridle. Its origins were purely equestrian, but it had been enhanced in ways that were too cruel to be used on a horse. At the sight of it, the creature's nerve failed again, and it shrank away, struggling violently to escape. Famzi set about it with the camel whip then wrestled it back, pulling on the collar and yanking on its hair. Adrenalin flooded its body. It was simply maddened by fear.

The Prince rose wrathfully from behind his desk. With a forbidding expression, he walked around to stand over the terrified thing, then stooped to gaze into its reddened eyes. "Open your mouth." The creature cowered. A huge hand grasped its throat and squeezed. "Assist. You want this."

The anguished kafir stared up into his master's face, unable to believe that this man that he loved, and that he knew loved him, could hurt him so easily. "Please? Please, my lord. Please, don't do this. God is Merciful. Please, I beg you. Please, Your Highness. Please, be merciful, I beg you. God is Great. God is Great." But his hopes were dashed. His throat was squeezed until he was unable to speak.

Prince Abdul Aziz was furious. He was determined to have his way. His will was cast in stone. "Open your mouth!" As the bridle came nearer, the creature quailed and baulked. The Prince drew back then explained darkly: "You will ask for this. You will say that you want to wear it to please me."

The kafir could not do it. His face was ugly with misery. His heart was breaking, and he felt betrayed.

"Open your mouth," the Prince insisted.

The kafir broke down and wept.

The Prince struck it sharply across the face. "Open your mouth. Don't make me tell you again."

The kafir gasped and blinked, stunned by the unexpected ferocity of the blow. His whole body fought to escape. Every muscle twitched and shuddered in a paroxysm of terror. Only his sense of duty wanted him to obey. Weakly, helplessly, he gathered himself back onto his knees. "I can't do this," he thought, then peered up at his master. He saw the next blow coming, but could not avoid it. His senses reeled again. There was the sweet taste of blood after the bitter taste of fear. The pain would come later.

"You chose this," the Prince explained, then directed Famzi to bring the bridle closer. He waited barely a moment. "Open your mouth! You asked for this. We are giving you what you wanted."

The kafir trembled. He was devastated, and squirmed pathetically as the bridle was brought closer to his face. He had no options. He had never had a choice. He obeyed placidly. That was what he did. But he could not look at it. He turned miserably to stare at his master, and knew that he was lost, completely lost. Closing his eyes, he breathed deeply to steady his nerves. He opened his mouth, then grimaced and almost threw up. He was grateful to be allowed a moment to recover, but it was not long enough. A lifetime would not have been long enough. He shivered again and breathed deeply again then he grimly tried to open his mouth. It was his duty. He obeyed. That was what he did. He shook his head, but there was no escape. The rubber bit was violently forced into his mouth. The heavy leather bridle was dragged over his head. As the straps were fastened tightly around his skull, he knew absolute heart-stopping terror. He was trapped in a box within a cage within a prison.

Chapter 50

He was restless for a while. He could not settle to watching television, and did not have the energy to do anything else. His injuries frustrated him while his nerves kept him awake and miserable.

At first, she did not understand, but as the days passed, she realised he was incapable of curiosity, elation or just plain selfishness. She had thought he would be pleased to know his name, but he seemed almost disappointed. She had given him a gift, and he did not know what to do with it. She realised slowly that he had probably been hoping that it was a key to a door that would open to reveal everything. His name might have been a key. He still had not found a door. "It's alright," she said with compassion. "This isn't going to be easy. You must have known that it would be difficult. You've been away twenty years. It's a long time."

He was pale and his eyes were raw with stress. He could not process anything anymore.

She took his hand then led him through to the kitchen. He sat uncomfortably at the table. She put the pile of books down in front of him again then found the much depleted packet of paper. She pressed a pen into his hand. "Practice your writing." When he grimaced, she became insistent. "This is important. It doesn't matter how handsome you are if you're illiterate. You'll need to get a job. You need to be able to read and write."

He stared at the pen.

"You have to do this. I know you're confused and unhappy. That's only natural, but you need to focus. Right now, this is the most important thing that you have to do." She picked up a book at random then opened it and passed it to him. "Copy this out. Learn it."

He took the book reluctantly then stared at the page. "I don't know it."

"Yes, but you should be able to read it, and if you can do that then you can copy it in longhand." She felt like a school teacher. She could not resist pointing to the open page with a sharp pointy finger. "If there are any words that you don't understand then use the thesaurus." She pointed at that as well. "It's very useful. In fact, you could spend a few hours reading it every day. It would expand your vocabulary enormously."

His face was a mask. Only his reluctance to look at her registered his lack of interest.

"I understand that you're upset. You must have known that this wouldn't be easy."

He stared at the open book then sighed heavily. "I never imagined having to think about a life without him." He took a moment to control his emotions. "All of my life." His voice broke. He tried to smile bravely, but he could not look at her. "I can't remember ever being happy unless I was with him. Even when he did not touch me, I loved him. He was all that I wanted. He was everything to me. I loved him. He was jealous and possessive. If I looked at another man, he would be so angry. To me that was proof that he loved me. I wanted him to be jealous. I wanted him to want me. When I was beaten by the Pakistanis, I knew that afterwards he would be gentle and kind." He hesitated, then shook his head, then frowned. "Sometimes, I made them beat me harder to make sure he would come to me. I needed him to make love to me."

She sat down opposite him, moving some of the books so she could lean her elbows onto the table. "So you loved him?"

He nodded slowly. He could not look at her, but he nodded. "Yes. I needed him. I wanted him. I loved him. He was everything to me."

"And you still love him?" she asked quietly.

For a moment, he shivered, then filled his lungs with air and what felt like courage. But he sighed then acknowledged: "Yes, I belong to him. I want him to love me as I love him. If he needs to hurt me – I don't care."

She watched in silence. He was trembling. He was hot and glowing. His eyes glittered. He had never looked more attractive or more distressed.

"I never thought that he'd leave me. But he has. I must be too old now. He doesn't want me anymore. They've found someone younger." He stretched his fingers across his face. He was in shock, and heartbroken. It took him a minute to find his voice again. When he looked at her, he was almost in tears. "He's left me here. The doctor must have said something. I must be very sick. He was bored with me? I don't know what happened. Why was he shouting at the doctor? He'd never done that before. I must have done something. I don't remember. They took the briefcase. That wasn't my fault." He trembled. "I don't know what to do now. I don't know where to go."

She leaned across the table. "Someone is looking for your family. You'll go home, and be loved by your mother and your father. They'll be so happy to know that you're alright. You'll get better and grow stronger.

Everything will be alright. You will be happy, I promise."

"I miss him so much. I should hate him. Why don't I hate him? He gave me to Abdullah. I should hate him. Abdullah hurt me as no one had ever hurt me before, and I believe I did nothing wrong. I made a mistake. It was an innocent mistake, and there was no harm. My master sent for Abdullah. He meant me to be hurt like that, but he forgave me. We were lovers again." He smiled briefly, tearfully. "But he did not send Abdullah away. Why didn't he send him away? I was so frightened. I only felt safe with my master – or with Omar. Omar always took care of me. But why wasn't Abdullah sent away? Why did he keep him there? We didn't need him. We were lovers again. We were happy, weren't we?"

She hardly knew what to say except to keep assuring him that he was safe, and that everything would be alright.

"He asked to be allowed to decorate my skin." He shook his head in anguish. "I was allowed to say 'no', but how could I refuse? He had never asked me for anything before. My body was his property, but more than that, he owned me. I knew that. I understood. He could do what he wanted. He did not require my permission, but he did ask for it. I was so desperate, and so afraid of being abandoned again. He had sent me to the Parsi. He had given me to Abdullah. At any moment, he might send me to my death. I couldn't trust him. He was proud and jealous, but I loved him even though I couldn't trust him. I loved him even though I knew he would never love me enough." He breathed deeply again, trying to keep his nerve. "He'd go to the mosque, and come back, and hate me again. And he was always right to hate me. His god told him to hate me. It didn't matter how much I loved him because he had to hate me and punish me. His god demanded it. It was righteous to hate me. I'm an infidel. I'm a disbeliever. They are taught to hate us."

"Let's go outside," she said. "You'll feel better in the garden."

"Please?" He stared at her. "Please, I'd like to be alone. I need to think. I don't know what I want anymore."

"You'd like to go back to him?" she asked gently.

He nodded, but said: "I don't know. I don't know Paul Lawrence. Why can't I remember him?"

"You are Paul Lawrence. He will be whatever you want him to be. He is you." She reached across the table, needing to reassure him, but he lifted his arm away. She felt the chill of loneliness. He would leave her. That was the only certainty that she knew. Rising unsteadily to her feet, she moved away to lean against the sink and stare out of the window at her garden.

She would be alone again. She could not bear it. To her surprise, he came to stand beside her.

"You have been very kind," he said. "You have saved my life."

She managed to smile, but could not look at his beautiful face. Those luminous blue eyes would have broken her aching heart. "You must be so confused," she said quietly. "Everything that you know has changed so much. You're in a different country, a different culture and a new language. You've done so well, but you must be confused and exhausted and sometimes, you must feel completely lost. But it'll be alright. We've plenty of time. You don't need to make any decisions yet. The most important thing now is that you are sure that you know what you want."

It took him a long time to answer, but he said: "I want to go home."

He was staring at her so she turned from the window to face him. She also needed a minute. "But you need to decide where that is."

He flinched then stared down at the floor.

The phone started ringing. They both started in alarm. It was the first time it had rung since he had arrived there.

"It's alright." She reached out to squeeze his arm reassuringly. "You sit down before you fall down." She managed to smile. "It'll be someone trying to sell me double-glazing."

He did not understand, but returned to sit at the table, and picked up his pen.

She left him with a heavy heart. It could only be Mr. Watchman. No one else had her number.

*

Prince Abdul Aziz rose from his chair and walked across to stare down at his beautiful golden creature with its silky hair and glittering jewellery, which knelt tamed and humbled. He wanted to see its eyes, but it was unseemly to ask, and wholly inappropriate for the creature to look up at its lord and master so disrespectfully. The lovely flesh bore the savage marks of camel whips. It had been properly punished. Was it too much to expect the creature to be bold and brazen with so many fresh wounds? "I am not under any obligation to explain my decisions to you, but I know you, and I know that you will fret and worry, and make everyone around you unhappy. I have decided to make some changes. You're no longer a child. I think you need a stronger hand. Your behaviour lately has been embarrassing to me. You've disrupted the household. The servants think you've become possessed. You've humiliated me. This – all of this is unforgivable, and it is not Famzi's fault, or anyone else's. I must take some responsibility. I have indulged you. I have spoiled you. We all made allowances for you because you were a kafir. You were obedient once. We all loved you then. But you have taken advantage of my weakness, and it must stop now. You know what is expected of you. You know what you are. If you do not understand why this is necessary then you are being wilful and childish." He paused to gaze at the glowing creature, who stared at the floor, mute and motionless and bleeding from its wounds. "I don't know what has upset you. We've taken great care of you. Young Famzi and the others have looked after you very well, and you have rewarded their kindnesses with this betrayal."

The kafir ached all over. He wanted to go away and hide in a dark place, but his master's words turned him cold with fear because he knew he was vulnerable. He was not allowed to speak. He was not allowed to rise from his knees. He knew that if he looked up at his master, even to appeal for mercy, he would be struck down again.

"For more than a thousand years, kafirs like you have served their betters. It is written. The Holy Apostle received these instructions from God, the All Knowing and most Wise. You do not seem able to comprehend the gratitude that you should feel to have been chosen to live amongst us. Why have you strayed from the path set for you by God? It is written. You cannot change what you are. You must submit. Your foolishness has forced me to take this drastic action. I want you to be happy and content, but you must be easy to my hand. I cannot tolerate disobedience. There was a time when you gave me a great deal of pleasure. You were very useful to me. I hoped – I believed that you loved me. I simply cannot keep punishing you. I do not have the time to indulge your moods." He walked across to sit on the sofa, which afforded an excellent view of the creature's profile. "I'm trying to help you. I want you to be happy again. It is important to me that you understand that I am only doing this to help you."

The kafir inhaled deeply and shuddered. He had no idea what to expect. He had a vague conviction that he would be able to survive anything because he was hardened by the recent constant and gratuitous beatings. He hated the whip, but never resisted being whipped because his master always derived so much pleasure from his wounds, and he bathed greedily in the attention. But his body trembled again. His flesh remembered and doubted and feared.

Prince Abdul Aziz frowned. He wondered why he was bothering to explain. No one else spoke to the creature, but he needed it to acknowledge that it was to blame. It had betrayed him. It had offended him. "I want you easy to my hand again. I want you gentled. You loved me once. Why are you forcing me to do this? You will submit. You must. You will not merely condescend to obey me. There will be no more of these grimaces. You are here to serve – willingly – gratefully – happily. There is no other reason for you to exist. You are my property. This is what you are. I know you loved me. What happened to us? Do you want to leave me?" The Prince suddenly leaned forward. "Is that it? Do you want to leave? Do you actually believe that you can?" He was terribly upset then incredibly angry. "You cannot leave. You will not leave. I forbid it. I forbid you to even think about it. Perhaps this is my fault for spoiling you. I have indulged you far too much. But you forget yourself!" He filled his lungs to try and regain his composure. "I hope it is not too late. You break my heart with this sullen temper and ingratitude. I have given you so much. How can you repay my kindness with this treachery! You are a kafir. You are just a kafir. I should sell you off the block in Djibouti! You'd end up in a filthy brothel and be raped until you died."

The kafir glanced anxiously at his master, dreading to see the rage that he could hear so clearly in the words. What he saw made him pause. Trembling, he bowed down and salaamed and struggled to find a voice. "Please? Please, my lord, Your Highness, my beloved master by the Grace of God, the most Compassionate, the most Merciful. Please? God is Merciful. Please, my lord."

"This is what you are," the Prince said, waving a hand towards his abject posture. "Consider how much you need my good opinion. This is what you are. Your only protection is my goodwill."

"Please, my lord," the kafir persisted. He knew his master required constant reassurance. "I love -"

"This is Abdullah," the Prince said, rising to his feet, completely unmoved by the creature's plaintive tone.

Suddenly realising he was in grave danger, the kafir sat back on his heels then turned awkwardly to look for a stranger.

Abdullah was behind him. He had come quietly into the room to stand right behind him.

The kafir shuddered and flinched. His heart was pounding painfully in his chest. Every fear he had ever known came back to destroy him again. He had endured so much. He was overwhelmed by his injuries, and knew there would soon be more.

Abdullah stared down at the creature with unblinking eyes. He was no taller than the other Pakistanis, but built like a street fighter, and much darker skinned. His clothes were black, and of a slightly different style as if he was from another region. He was dangerous. Everything about him proclaimed that he was dangerous.

Prince Abdul Aziz walked across to stand in front of his ungrateful creature, intending it to feel crowded and threatened on its knees on the floor. "This is Abdullah," he said again firmly. "He has come here to help you recover your good sense." The creature cowered not knowing where to look. "From now on, he will be your constant companion. You will see no one else. You will talk to no one else. And you will learn from him. He is an expert. He knows what to do with ungrateful kafirs. He believes all kafirs turn into monsters. It is your age and your hormones, apparently. I have asked him to help you. He will not tolerate these tantrums. I have let you be wilful and selfish because I'm sentimental, but he will not permit it. You will submit willingly. You will not resist or complain. I don't want you to be hurt needlessly, but I am willing to endure it if that will bring you back to my hand. This body, this flesh belongs to me. It's perfectly legal. I own you. You know that. You are mine and no one else's. You must submit. It is the law. You must understand that this is your fault. Abdullah will help you, and he will make sure that you never forget again."

The magnitude of his peril made the kafir genuinely tremble. Whatever stubborn courage or misplaced hope he had possessed just abandoned him. "Please, my lord," he whispered. "Please, my lord. I haven't done anything. I am yours." He could not remember the words. "All that I am – I love you. Please, you know – always - I love you. I always – I haven't - please my lord. Forgive me -I beg you. Please, think about it. I am grateful. I have always been grateful. And I love you. You give me life. Please…" He stooped awkwardly to try and kiss his master's feet, but there was not enough room. He was trapped between his master and the menacing Pakistani. They loomed over him like giants. "I am yours. God is Merciful. God is Compassionate. Please, my lord, Your Highness, my master, I beg you. I am yours. I would never betray you. You know that."

"He is going to hurt you," the Prince warned severely. "You must expect that. You know the rules. It is unseemly for me to punish you directly so Abdullah is now my instrument. He has my permission to discipline you as often as he feels it is required. He will beat you until you demonstrate to us that you are capable of controlling yourself. You loved me once, and I spoiled you because I was so sure that you were devoted to me, but you have betrayed my trust. You must submit now completely."

Chapter 51

"There's a car," he said, rising to his feet, and walking to the bay windows.

She thought she had misheard, and came through from the kitchen to join him. "Are you sure? Who could it be?"

He pointed out of the window, not extending his arm, not moving his hand, merely straightening a forefinger as if he were afraid of being seen.

She rested a reassuring hand on his arm. "It's all right. I'll sort it out. You stay here." She was so busy reassuring him that she forgot to hate all trespassers and to treat them all with chilled aggression.

It was a Honda Civic, pale blue, five doors and a few years old. Easing its way around the potholes, it came slowly down the drive.

She opened the front door, but did not move from the shadows, preferring to remain hidden until she knew who it was.

He was a tall, slim man in his late fifties with a good head of longish grey hair. He wore pale denims, a white open-necked shirt with sleeves rolled up almost to his elbows. His face was lightly tanned; his forearms much more so. There was a big heavy wedding ring on his left hand and a solid practical watch. He moved with surprising grace and vigour, suggesting to her that he was possibly an ex-soldier or something equally physical. His grey hair and worn face proved his age, but everything else belonged to a strong, healthy younger man. He was ruggedly handsome. She had never felt such an instant attraction. Then she realised that this was his father.

She turned back to gaze into the hall, and saw him standing just beyond the door leading into the lounge. There was an obvious likeness. "It's your father."

He started forward then lost his nerve, and retired back behind the doorframe.

With an understanding smile, she turned back to meet her guest.

The stranger hesitated too. He stared up at the house. He was unsure. He started to lock the car then changed his mind then locked it anyway.

She walked out from the shadows and descended the steps. "Mr.

Lawrence?" she asked politely even though she was sure of him already.

He hesitated again then came forward to take the hand she offered him. He was taller and enigmatically handsome with pale blue eyes. There was a smile, but he was distracted and uneasy.

"You spoke to Mr. Watchman," she explained, quite willing to hold on to his hand forever. "Jane Howard." She smiled again trying to reassure him. "You must have set off straight away."

He nodded, searching her face, and discounting her completely before turning to look back at the house.

Though she was familiar with rejection, it still hurt. She let go of his hand, which had become cold and dead. "Of course, you'll want to see Paul. I can't get over how much you look like him."

He focused on her sharply. "Really?"

She nodded and smiled again, recognising that he was scared and confused. It would have been too easy to gush.

"Is he here?"

"Yes," she said, trying to imagine the turmoil he must be experiencing. "He's hiding." She paused to let him look at her, but he stared distractedly at the house. "He's petrified. This is really a big moment for him. You'll need to be patient and understanding." She wanted to seize his shoulders and shake him to make him listen. It was inappropriate. The poor man had probably suffered as badly as her guest, but in so many different ways. "He has been through a terrible ordeal."

"Yes." The man nodded. His face set in a mask of resolve. Only his eyes betrayed him. "I understand. Can I see him now? I'd given up..."

"Yes," she said. "You and your wife must have been heartbroken." She turned, wondering why he had come alone.

"I'd like to see him now," he said flatly, ignoring the unspoken question.

She smiled again then stepped aside, and waved towards the house. "Please come inside. I'll make some tea. You can have a nice chat and get to know each other again." Then she put a hand lightly on his arm. "Please don't expect too much today. He's very fragile. He's lucky to be alive. I don't think he realises just how lucky he has been."

The man stared at her as if she was speaking a foreign language. "Do you live here?"

"Yes," she said, smiling again and withdrawing her hand.

"And he just turned up here after all this time?"

She nodded again, frowning. "Yes. He'd been badly hurt. Heaven knows how he got here. I think he just wandered in quite by chance. I'm so pleased to have been able to help him."

"You were too kind."

That seemed such an odd thing to say. She frowned again. "Yes, well, it was just by accident really. I couldn't have turned him away. He was in a terrible state."

The man nodded, staring at the house, unable to approach.

They both waited. She almost called to Paul to draw him out, but he finally appeared in the doorway. The two men stared at each other in a strained silence. She had several pertinent things to say, but they seemed suddenly inappropriate. The men were not aware of her at all. She looked from one to the other then backed away like a passer-by escaping from the line of fire in some Wild West gunfight. "I'll put the kettle on." No one was listening. She watched them. It was like looking at a photograph. They did not move. They did not acknowledge anyone else in the world except each other. The likeness was amazing. But for the difference in their ages they were mirror images of each other. She looked from one to the other, then back again. There was no doubt in her mind. They were father and son. It made her smile. Perhaps there would be a happy ending?

She did not want to leave them, but knew she was not wanted there. The still figures had not moved at all since setting eyes on each other. She felt compelled to leave them alone. They had drawn a wall around themselves and shut her out. They did not want her there. They did not need her. At that moment no one needed her. It was oddly hurtful. After having made a connection with another human being, she felt the rebuff sharply. She went into the house, and disappeared into the kitchen. She filled the kettle then stared out of the window. The bird feeders were almost empty again. The Starlings had disappeared. It was not too hard to waste five minutes, but after that she was beside herself with curiosity. If the young man had not been so vulnerable, she was confident that she could have walked away and let them talk together for hours. But he was so vulnerable. He did need her even if he had totally forgotten that she was alive. He was not equipped to deal with any kind of interrogation, especially if the inquisitor was his father.

They were in the lounge, standing far apart, staring at each other.

She put the tray down on the table, and knelt down to sort out the cups and saucers and teaspoons. "Do you take sugar, Mr. Lawrence?"

He looked suddenly angry. "No, thank you."

She glanced at Paul. "Offer your father a chair. He's come a long way to see you."

The young man blinked and nodded then just stared at his father with a look of complete bewilderment.

"He was abducted, Mr. Lawrence," she explained, hoping to open a conversation. "They took him abroad. The shock and trauma of what happened has blanked out most of his memory. He's very fragile, Mr. Lawrence. It may take quite a long time for him to fully recover."

Paul blinked and swayed then sank on to the nearest chair. His usually pale face was ashen. He looked as if he had been mortally wounded.

His father just stood there staring at him.

"I thought Mrs. Lawrence might come with you?" she asked, hoping there would be a good excuse for her absence. The young man's disappointment would explain his dreadful pallor.

"She died," the man said, rather coldly. Then he seemed to realise what he was saying. His face melted. His eyes glazed. It took him a minute to recover then he half turned to stare out of the window. "It was difficult after Paul disappeared. We drifted apart. It was impossible. We tried to get on with our lives, but just reminded each other of what had happened. She couldn't bear to look at me. I couldn't cope with her pain. We got divorced. She moved south. I heard from her occasionally. About ten years ago she was killed in a car. Some drunken scumbag jumped a light and hit her. She didn't have a chance." He breathed deeply then turned back to stare at his son. "I wanted to forget. I thought I had forgotten. I erased everything that reminded me of him. Now, it's started again. I can't believe I'm standing here looking at him."

Paul lowered his gaze. He was shivering.

"He was barely eight years old. Look at him. Look at him!" He pointed feebly at the young man, relieved that he did not have to look at his face or see his eyes. "Where did all that time go? I was in hell. What did they do to him? Look at him! They've had him longer than I ever did. I don't know who he is now."

She gazed at Paul, hoping he would say something, but he was hunched over, hugging himself, traumatised. "He's been badly hurt, Mr. Lawrence. He'll need a lot of help to readjust to a normal life, but he's a good boy. He wants to know you again. There's so much he doesn't remember. He just wants to come home."

The man shook his head. "I don't live there anymore. I don't know how you found me. Why doesn't he say anything?"

She smiled pleasantly. "He's still listed on the National Missing Person's Bureau website."

"Yes," he said, as if he was remembering something from another life. "They told me. I was surprised. I'd given up. After his mother died, I couldn't carry on alone." He stared at his son. "Is he dumb or something?"

"No," she corrected gently. "He's just a little overwhelmed. He didn't expect to see you today. You've just told him that his mother died. All these years, he has been hoping to come back to you both. This must be a terrible shock. He's been kept a prisoner. He must have spent a great deal of time imagining this. You need to be patient, Mr. Lawrence. You must be patient and understanding."

"Why is he so afraid of me? He looks scared to death."

"No, I'm sure you're wrong. He doesn't remember you, Mr. Lawrence. When he first arrived, he did not know his own name. He's terribly damaged," she said.

"So he might not be my son?" he asked coldly. "The likeness might be coincidental."

She hardly knew what to say. "I'm sure DNA tests will prove it, Mr. Lawrence, if you feel that it's necessary."

The man nodded. "What did they do to him? He doesn't look right in the head."

"He's just scared, Mr. Lawrence."

"Of what?" he asked, still staring at his son with no empathy at all. "If there's nothing wrong with him then why doesn't he say something?"

"You need to be a little more understanding, Mr. Lawrence."

"I don't know who you are, lady, but if he is my son then I want to talk to him and not to you."

That felt like a sharp slap in the face. She had to tell herself that she was not afraid of him, but she had lost control and that was terrifying. "He was abducted and held captive for almost twenty years, Mr. Lawrence. Put yourself in his shoes. This is so very hard for him."

The man turned away to stare out of the window. He was so angry and so upset and so afraid of daring to be happy that he felt physically sick. "I've remarried. I have a new family. Does he want money?"

Her heart began to break. She was not brave enough to look at Paul. "No, Mr. Lawrence. I'm sorry. It's nothing like that. He just wanted you and his mother to know that he was alright. He was worried about you both. He took a great risk coming here to find you again."

"Why is that?" the man asked coldly. He glowered at her, then stared in naked distress at his son.

She could hardly begin to imagine his pain and anguish. "The people who took him will still be looking for him." She lied fluently. It was easier. The truth was so unpalatable and too complicated. Perhaps later, the young man would be able to explain, but she knew it was beyond her capabilities to do it justice.

"Why?"

She breathed deeply. "Well, he wasn't meant to get away. He can identify them. They'll want to shut him up before he's strong enough to face the police."

"What did they do to him?" he asked again.

She shuddered, and turned unhappily to gaze at Paul.

"What did they do?" the man demanded furiously. "Look at him! What the fuck did they do to him?"

Paul shrank lower, turned his face away, and tried desperately to disappear.

"Please, Mr. Lawrence," she said quickly. "He needs you to be calm. He's so damaged. Please don't shout at him. He can't help it. It wasn't his fault."

The man loomed menacingly, but could not cross the room. He did not want to look at his own son yet could not drag his eyes away. "Look at him! What did they do to him? It's been twenty years! Two decades! I don't know who he is. If he doesn't know who I am then how can I know who he is? What happened? What did they do? Why is he so afraid of me?"

She rose to her feet, determined to protect the young man. "You need to leave now, Mr. Lawrence. We all need more time. We all need to go away, and think about what we want to say, and how we really feel."

Paul rose too and stood swaying like a drunk, staring miserably at his father. He was afraid of him, but did not know why because he did not remember the face except that it was his own face. "They raped me," he blurted out like a hurt child. "They raped me every day. I couldn't stop them. Why didn't you come? They beat me and starved me and raped me.

Every day. I was fucked. Totally fucked. Why didn't you come? Why didn't someone come?" His knees folded. He collapsed back into the chair, trembling violently. "Okay? You know now. Are you happy?"

His father turned away to hide the absolute abhorrence that registered on his face. The nightmare had returned. His worst fears were realised. Closing his eyes, he covered his face with his hands, and tried desperately to disbelieve him.

"It's a miracle that he has survived, Mr. Lawrence. They hurt him badly, but he will recover. You have to give him time. He needs you to be patient and kind. He came back because he did not want you to worry about him. He came to tell you that it will be okay. You just have to give him time, Mr. Lawrence. He's been so brave."

The man turned from the window, pale with shock and grief. "Who did this to you?"

Paul looked up, shattered, broken, barely able to focus. "I can't tell you." He grimly sucked air into his lungs. It hurt. It was so unfair. "They'll come after me. They'll find me again."

"Paedophiles?" Lawrence demanded, struggling to say the word aloud.

"Yes," she said, moving to stand beside Paul, placing a hand on his shoulder, feeling him shiver, sensing every nuance of his distress. "It was an organised gang. He didn't stand a chance. They probably had him out of the country before the police started looking for him."

The man groaned and turned away to stare out of the window. "He just vanished. We looked everywhere. No one had seen anything. There was no evidence. We were treated like suspects. They wouldn't believe us. There was blood on one of my shirts. They were convinced I had hurt him. It took weeks to make them understand that it must have been someone else. But they never found anything. He was just gone."

"It was a professional gang." She watched the man turn back from the window to stare at his son. "You have to forgive him, Mr. Lawrence. It wasn't his fault. He's been through enough. Don't make this worse. It isn't fair."

The man inhaled deeply, and rubbed his forehead as if to erase something horrible. "Where has he been all this time?"

She shrugged and turned to gaze sympathetically at the pale and distraught young man. "I don't think he knows. They seem to have kept him completely isolated. He's never mixed with other people his own age. When he came here he had no idea what a strawberry milkshake tasted like. He's never heard of the Simpsons. He doesn't know anything. He needs time, Mr. Lawrence. He's not sick. He just needs time and a little patience, and he needs someone to love him. I think he's earned that, Mr. Lawrence."

The man shook his head. There were so many dreadful images in his head. He was going mad. He could not make it stop. "But they've had him – they've used him like that for nearly twenty years? They're paedophiles. He should be dead. Why didn't they kill him? Why didn't they just kill him?"

She sighed, and squeezed Paul's shoulder. She realised that Mr. Lawrence was not going to be the answer to her prayers. "It's not his fault. He's been so brave and so strong. We should respect that. Surely, the important thing is that he has survived?"

The man shook his head dismissively. "I know enough about psychology. Twenty years in the hands of those bastards? No one would survive that unscathed. He's more their thing now than he was ever my son."

She was appalled. "I'm sure he fought to survive, Mr. Lawrence. He wanted to come home. It must have taken great courage. You can't condemn him for still being alive. You should be proud that he endured all that abuse, and never gave up. You should be so proud, Mr. Lawrence."

The man shook his head. "I have another family. I have young children. I can't risk it. He's not my son anymore. He's their thing."

She stooped to whisper into Paul's ear: "Why don't you go outside, and wait in the garden. Your father is upset. I'll talk to him. He's just upset. It'll be alright." She pulled him to his feet. "Off you go. We'll come and find you."

Paul leaned against her, hanging on every word, not able to acknowledge his father at all.

"Off you go," she whispered.

He slunk away reluctantly like a condemned man.

She watched him go then moved to pick up the forgotten tea cup, which she passed to Mr. Lawrence. "I'm sorry. It's probably cold. Would you like to sit down? You can't go now. You're too upset to drive. Here, sit down. It's alright. I guess we both knew that this would be hard and unpleasant."

He stared at the tea cup, but did not move away from the window.

"He's a brave boy, you know. I guess he gets that from you. This must be so hard for you. After all these years – to have him turn up like this? It must have been a terrible shock. Did you come expecting to find someone else?"

He nodded. "I was so sure that he was dead. I've rebuilt my life. I have filled it up with so many new things so that I'd never need to think about him again."

"It's not his fault," she explained quietly.

He turned to put aside the tea cup then stared at her with his lips compressed and his jaw set like granite. "Does he want money?"

She was shocked. "No. It's not like that. He doesn't want anything from you. He just wants to come home."

The man groaned and shook his head. "I have children. He's – I don't know what! After twenty years, he'll have become totally assimilated. They will have conditioned him. That's how it works, isn't it? He'll be like them. He'll be a paedophile. He doesn't know anything else. He's certainly not normal. I don't want him. I can't take the risk. I'm sorry."

Her heart sank. "I almost wish we'd never found you."

"I'm sorry."

She believed him. "And I'm sorry. I think this will destroy him."

The man winced and groaned again. "Do you think this is easy for me? I'm just glad his mother is dead." He shook his head. "She never recovered. I think she died that day. Maybe, we both died. I'm sorry, but he isn't my son anymore."

She nodded. She understood even if she did not want to. "Will you speak to him? Will you explain?"

His face paled. Then he drew his shoulders back and stood up straight. "Yes. He needs to understand."

She smiled compassionately. "He'll be in the garden. It's through there," she pointed towards the kitchen, "he likes being in the garden."

He started to walk away then turned to look at her. It was a strangely critical look, full of suspicion and malice, then he turned again and walked away.

Chapter 52

It was no surprise that Waheed received the pictures. He was on everyone's mailing list when it came to lurid pornography. Mahmood was shocked to receive it..

He was still working for the Prince, but had moved back to the old fortress after a great deal of trouble with Abdullah. He was happier. Abdullah had forced his hand, but Mahmood needed a change. He was too old to cope with all the emotional turmoil, the threats and the politics. Abdullah was a cunning opportunist, and he did not want to share. As far as he was concerned the creature was his own personal property. He set a trap for Mahmood, who he saw as a rival, and Mahmood stepped into it because he was a thoroughly decent human being, but Abdullah informed the Prince that Mahmood was undermining his authority and had ruined the creature with kindness and treats. It was not true, but Mahmood had to leave. The length of his service allowed him a reprieve, but he had to keep away from the blue-eyed kafir.

He kept busy. He could spend time with his son. He had a family, at last. Waheed had been promoted to the Prince's father's household in Jeddah. He was still running a few boys, and had fingers in several lucrative pies. The set of photographs were well thumbed and grainy, but Waheed had felt the need to reach out to his old friend. No one else saw beyond the Abu Ghraib genre. The media everywhere were full of those revolting pictures. Mahmood had quickly tossed the packet in a drawer without looking at them. He could not understand why Waheed had sent them to him, literally, out of the blue. They had drifted apart when Prince Khalid took the blue-eyed jinn away. When it had reappeared in Dubai some years later, Mahmood had been called up briefly to take care of it, but by then Waheed was long gone. When the photographs arrived, Mahmood was actually insulted that Waheed had sent him such horrible things. It seemed like a really bad, tasteless joke.

It was only later, when he sat alone in his room ready to burn them that he recognised the victim's blue eyes. He was shocked and upset, and finally understood why Waheed had sent them to him. Had Aziz been alive, Mahmood would have gone to him at once, and protested, but Aziz was long dead. His family had returned to Pakistan. His name was seldom mentioned anymore. Those that had known him were scattered across continents. In Dubai, there had been Omar. Omar had protected the white kafir from a lunatic with acid at Nad al Sheba. Mahmood was not sure if Omar would still be interested as the white kafir was, obviously, no longer with the Prince, but he was upset, and could not let the matter rest. As the man in charge of the laundry, Mahmood knew everyone, and they were all happy to help him with a phone number, and then with access to a phone.

Omar did not remember him until Mahmood explained about Dubai and the kafir and when Aziz had died.

"Yes," Omar said quietly. He was New York. He had been awoken from a heavy sleep. "Yes, of course. What time is it? Oh, is everything alright?"

"I am sorry to trouble you," Mahmood said. "It might be nothing at all." He was embarrassed. He was not sure how to explain his concern without sounding like some soft-hearted kafir lover. He was not a racist. Kafirs were actually condemned by God and the Prophet. They were destined for Hell. It was almost a criminal offence to feel sorry for them.

Omar was just about to go back to sleep. He was yawning. He was so tired.

Mahmood lost his nerve. "Perhaps, you've already seen them?" He shook his head helplessly. His self-confidence had never been particularly resilient. "I'm always the last to know." He shrugged. "I didn't know what to do. It's really none of my business, but I felt that I must tell someone."

"Tell someone what?" Omar asked without conviction.

"About the photographs," Mahmood said, sure that he had already explained about that.

"What photographs?" Omar had opened his eyes. In his world, photographs were always connected to scandal and blackmail. "What photographs?"

Mahmood distinctly heard the change in tone. His nerves shredded a little more. "I didn't know who else to call. I'm so sorry," he said weakly. "Maybe, it isn't important."

Omar had sat up. He had the lights switched on. His feet were firmly planted on the floor. "What photographs?"

"It's that kafir. The one from Dubai. The one with the blue eyes," Mahmood explained quickly. After all, during his career, there had been so many pretty kafirs, but they did not all have such extraordinary blue eyes.

"Where are you?" Omar asked.

"Hejaz."

"I need to see these photographs. Find Suleiman al Bashir. He can scan the photographs and send them to me."

Mahmood was relieved. "Thank you."

"Is he alone?" Omar asked. "Is the kafir alone?"

"On the back of the pictures there is a number and a price. I think someone is selling these pictures," Mahmood said anxiously. "Who would do such a thing?"

"Is the kafir alone, Mahmood? Is there anyone else in the photographs?"

"No. But there are dogs. I believe they are fighting dogs, but the kafir is alone. They're attacking it." Mahmood took a deep breath. "In some of these pictures... It might be dead."

Omar could not reassure him. That would have been dishonest. "Go and find Suleiman al Bashir. Go now, Mahmood. I must see these pictures."

Two weeks after acquiring the lurid set of photographs, Omar threw open the door. He had tried to take an early flight back to Riyadh to confront Abdullah, but the Prince had refused to let him go, and he could not explain the necessity. Deep in the basement, beneath the car parks and utility areas, it was always as dark as Hades. He heard the tuneless whistling from the stairwell. There was only one light bulb, but he could see Abdullah standing over what looked like a heap of laundry. His malevolence filled the room. As Omar approached, the strangely sinister whistling stopped, and Abdullah turned angrily to confront him.

"What the fuck do you want?" he demanded.

"I came to see you," Omar answered. As he watched, the heap of laundry became the creature. It could barely lift its head, but very slowly twisted around to look at him. The expression on its face was beyond despair.

"I'm busy," Abdullah said dismissively, and lapsed back into his tuneless whistling as he stared down at the broken thing at his feet.

Omar watched as the creature flinched and cowered.

Abdullah turned slowly to study Omar again. He saw the acid scar, and touched his own face to acknowledge it. "I'm busy. This is fucking private. You shouldn't be here."

"What exactly are you doing?" Omar asked. He was polite but firm.

"My fucking job," Abdullah announced with a leering smile.

On the floor at their feet, the creature tried to move.

Abdullah put his foot down heavily on one of its hands. "What the fuck are you doing? Where are you going? Did I say you could fucking move?"

Omar watched as the creature cowered again, unable to retrieve its crushed hand. "So what exactly is your job?" Omar asked. "Are you trying to kill it?"

Abdullah slowly stepped back, which allowed the creature to snatch its hand free. "I teach these fucking kafirs to be grateful. As they get older, they start to get funny ideas." He poked the creature with his foot then turned to regard Omar with open hostility. He knew about Omar. He had recognised the scar, and understood what it signified. "Your boss is just like his father. He gets attached to the bloody things. He wants to fucking keep them. And anyone with half a brain knows you must let them fucking die. I've spent thirty fucking years doing this shit." He kicked the creature again. "This little fucking bitch should have been euthanized five fucking years ago. What is it with you bloody Arabs? Don't you see how dangerous these fucking things are?" He moved his foot again, and grinned when the creature flinched and shrank away. "Just because it's got a pretty fucking face, you think it doesn't have long fucking teeth and sharp fucking claws. It's a fucking kafir! As soon as its balls drop, you put a fucking bullet in its fucking head!"

Omar hesitated, expecting him to laugh at his little joke, but it was obvious that the Pakistani was being absolutely serious. "Prince Abdul Aziz will not approve of this. He might have been angry months ago, but not enough to justify this. No one has ever questioned the kafir's loyalty. It never did anything to deserve this. This is a mistake. You need to stop right now."

Abdullah merely shook his head. "And you need to fuck off. You need to mind your own fucking business. Your prince sent for me. He asked me to come here to sort out this fucking bitch. He was furious. He'd been insulted. You weren't fucking there. You don't fucking know what happened so you should just fuck off, and mind your own fucking business. This is what I fucking do – all day – every day. He personally asked me to come down here and sort out this fucking piece of shit. He invited me. I have my reputation to protect. And I'm not stopping until I'm damn well satisfied that this fucking kafir has learned that it can't insult us."

"It looks half dead. I think it's had enough." Omar remained polite and calm. He would have liked to punish Abdullah for his foul language, his arrogance and his disrespect, but he did not have the authority to do that.

Abdullah nodded slowly. He was really pumped up and angry. He was staring down with raw malice at the broken thing laying at his feet. "I'm killing its fucking will. When I take it up to the fucking roof, and order it to jump, it must fucking jump. It must go right to the fucking edge, and want to fucking jump though it knows it will die a fucking horrible, painful death. It must obey any fucking order. It must jump to its death. It must submit. If I decide to move it back from the fucking edge, it must be fucking grateful. It must acknowledge that it only fucking lives at that particular fucking moment because I've decided that it will."

Omar hardly knew what to say. His own attempts at conditioning the creature seemed pathetic and amateurish. Looking down at the thing on the floor, his compassion stirred. "No, you're wrong. I can't speak for the others that you've destroyed, but you're wrong here. This is not what the Prince intended. You need to stop now."

Abdullah gazed down at the creature. "I haven't fucking finished with it yet. You should leave."

"You're finished," Omar said.

Abdullah smirked. He glanced towards Omar then focused on the creature at his feet. "Fuck off."

"You're finished," Omar repeated resolutely.

Abdullah glowered. "And who the fuck are you to say that?"

On the ground, the kafir was almost blind. He could hear voices but not words. Every inch of his body hurt. He hardly knew how to breathe. He could not believe that his prayers were answered: here was Omar. Here was his saviour. But it was too late.

"I'm the man with the Abu Ghraib photographs. You should have been more careful. You didn't hide its face very well."

Abdullah studied Omar speculatively then shook his head. "So fucking what? No one gives a shit. It's just a fucking kafir. It's the fucking kafirs who are doing this to us. Those poor fucking bastards in Abu Ghraib were totally fucking innocent. They hadn't done anything wrong, and look what the fucking kafirs did to them. I'm making a stand. It's about time somebody makes a fucking stand. We need to see that the fucking kafirs are getting fucked. They're doing it to us. They're fucking killing us. So I took a few fucking pictures. So fucking what! You've no fucking idea how much people will pay to see some bloody white kafir getting fucked. D' you want a cut? I'll let you have 20%."

"This is not about revenge," Omar said angrily. "You're not here to take revenge."

Abdullah was furious "You don't fucking know anything. I'm doing my fucking job. For all you fucking know, I'm saving your boss's life. How do you know this fucking kafir won't revert to bloody type, and kill your master and his family and anyone that gets in the fucking way? That's what these fucking kafirs do. They're all treacherous bloody bastards. Given half a fucking chance they'd cut all our throats and rape all our women. If you were a Muslim, you'd fucking know that's the fucking truth."

"I am a Muslim."

"No, not a practising Muslim, not if you're a fucking kafir lover."

Omar shook his head. "It's not true," he said carefully. "It's a fallacy. There is no great conspiracy. There are no crusaders." He really did not want to start hurling obscenities about. "They're not killing us. We're killing each other."

Abdullah was livid. No one was allowed to contradict him. "Just fuck off. I'm doing my fucking job. Your boss asked me to fucking come here, and sort out this fucking piece of shit, so that's what I'm fucking doing. You don't fucking like it? Who gives a fuck? This is what I do. I'm fucking good at it. When I'm finished with it, this fucking kafir won't even fucking piss unless I tell it to."

"Prince Abdul Aziz will not approve." Omar gazed down at the creature. It jerked and twitched as if it was dying. "The Prince regularly sent it to a madrassa for Ramadan. He spent a great deal of money on its education. He can't do that anymore. You were not supposed to torture it like this, and then sell the photographs on the internet. It's scandalous. If the Prince finds out what you've been doing, he will be furious."

Abdullah was hardly convinced. "You don't fucking know that. You weren't fucking there. I was asked to come here, and sort out this ungrateful piece of shit. I've worked for the prince's father for thirty bloody years. I know how to deal with these fucking things. I break them. I beat the fucking heart out of them." He grinned malevolently at the creature. "And I'm fucking good at it. They should be so fucking grateful. Because of me, they might actually live longer." He laughed. "Yeah, they should be so fucking grateful."

"Nevertheless, you have miscalculated. Prince Abdul Aziz will not approve." Omar paused to gaze down at the creature. "I'm taking it away. You will not lay a hand on it. You can stay here and get paid, but you will not have any further contact with it." Omar gazed witheringly at Abdullah. "If you do anything to cause trouble, I will show the Prince the photographs, and then there will be repercussions. I can assure you that he will not approve. He is an honourable man. He will find this offensive. He will find your language offensive. There will be repercussions. No one will employ you." He held Abdullah's steely gaze. "You will also remove the photographs from the internet. There must be no evidence for anyone to find, and nothing that leads back to the Prince."

Abdullah shrugged then grinned like a gargoyle. "It's just a fucking kafir. Who really gives a shit about these fucking disbelievers?"

"Prince Abdul Aziz gives a shit," Omar insisted. "He will be outraged. And he will believe me. And I have the photographs. Now, go away!" Omar glowered at Abdullah until the short, surly man shrugged and turned and walked away. He did not seem remotely fazed by what had happened. He started whistling again. It still sounded like nails on glass. He could be heard whistling all the way down the long empty corridors.

"Please?" the kafir gasped. He hardly had the strength to speak.

Omar stooped to examine it. Up close, it looked even worse. He turned away to find something to wrap around it, but there were only old crates and dust and spiders' webs. Its clothes were so ragged, it was really naked. Omar removed his bisht to cover it then lifted it into his arms.

He could not carry it through the house in its present condition without causing offence. After passing several men, who all glowered and hissed, he found his way to the laundry, and commandeered a trolley. The unconscious creature was lowered into the basket then quickly covered with soiled linen. Using service lifts and back corridors, he moved like an anxious thief up to his own room then laid the creature out on his bed. It was still lifeless. Its body was covered in bruises, and varnished with sweat, and more than twenty pounds lighter than when he had last seen it.

Omar used the excuse of 'security issues' to allow him to go to the house in Paris, taking Famzi and the creature with him. He was ostensibly taking advantage of a gap in the schedule to have the creature's blood checked for STDs at the clinic. They settled in quietly on their own while the Prince went on to Geneva to listen to Annan's speech about the changing role of the UN. Omar had a lot of demands on his time, but he kept a close eye on the activity around the creature. Abdullah was never very far away.

Weeks later, the Prince was pleasantly surprised to find his creature waiting in a smart valet's uniform to serve him dinner. He had not seen it for months. It was lean and lovely. It worked hard. It never missed a cue. The Prince was completely satisfied. He made a mental note to thank Abdullah for all his efforts. The creature had obviously remembered its manners. After an hour or so, he noticed that its hands were shaking, its face had turned grey, and it was registering distress. When he kindly offered his hand, it went down on to its knees and kissed the ring, but it would not look up at him. He ruffled its hair affectionately, but it would not look at him. His pleasure turned to annoyance, and he pushed it away.

*

Mr. Lawrence and his son walked in silence, neither able to speak, both consumed with anxiety and despair and pain. Paul stayed a few paces ahead. He did not dare to turn and face his father, but he listened intently, desperate to hear his name called or a kindly word. The man stalked him, staring at his back, feeling his adrenalin levels rising as his mouth dried and his heart raced.

After several minutes of walking beneath the towering trees, they reached the shrine. Paul stopped and stared at it, sensing this was the place. He felt sick and frightened, but turned slowly to face his father.

Mr. Lawrence just stared at him. He was in agony. He tried to speak, but choked on the words. Now and then, he managed to shake his head. His son had died twenty years ago. This stranger was not his son. Nothing in God's Creation could induce him to own this thing as his son.

"Please?" Paul asked quietly. He was disintegrating.

Lawrence just shook his head. He did not want to hurt him, but his son had died. This was not his son. That was impossible. Yet his eyes and his heart told him otherwise. He needed to pound his fists on something - anything. Incoherent with distress, and grieving again, he stared at the little boy who had died so many years ago. Understanding was impossible. The man who faced him now was so very different and yet the same. It could not be him, but it was. It was a trick. It was some deception.

Paul reached out to lean against the shrine. He had never felt so weak. In his heart he knew he was never going home. The little dream that he had clung to just melted away like acid through his soul. His mother was dead. Her suffering was over. Where there should have been sadness there remained the void. He did not remember her, and now she had gone. He gazed at his father's overwrought face. He had come back, believing that he was dying, to tell them that everything was alright. He did not want them to suffer anymore. The pain that was so clearly etched into his father's face told him that he had been naive. Jane Howard was right: they were all victims. The vague half truths that he had rehearsed were just lies.

"I'm sorry, I don't remember you," he said slowly. He wanted to explain everything, but could not. This was his burden. They were his scars.

Lawrence filled his lungs then shook his head again. He was screaming and shouting like a madman but no one could hear him. He turned slowly away then turned again to look at his son. His son.... Just acknowledging it tore his heart in two. "I have other children now," he said as if that explained everything.

Paul absorbed the information with regret. He knew he should have been pleased for him. His father had gotten on with his life. He had not been destroyed by the loss of his first born. That was a good thing, but it hurt Paul. He made his awkward evasive shrug. "That's alright. I don't remember you."

They stared at each other is silence.

Paul shivered. He almost collapsed. He clung on to the slabs of Cotswold stone that formed Jane's private shrine. The scattered ornaments and trinkets meant nothing to him. These were her scars. He turned back to stare at his father. "I just wanted you to stop worrying. I wanted you to know that I was alright."

Lawrence nodded. He was completely overwrought. He was in pain – almost in tears. All he could see was his late wife and his late son. They had both died so long ago. His eyes were deceiving him. Shaking his head, he gulped down a sob then turned away.

Desperately, Paul took a step closer. "Please? They told me I was sold. They told me you didn't want me."

Lawrence was staring at the ground searching for answers and explanations and excuses. The words seeped into his consciousness like mercury. At first, he did not believe them. There was so much noise in his head. He lifted his hands to rub his eyes then raked his fingers through his hair in agitation. Then he turned to look at his son. "Didn't want you?"

Paul shrank back, seeking the shrine for support. His legs wobbled. His heart quaked.

"Didn't want you?" his father demanded furiously. "We looked everywhere for you. We never stopped looking for you. Do you have any idea what it was like? The bloody police were convinced it was me. It destroyed your mother. How dare you say that!"

Paul could only stammer and cower.

"How can you say that?" his father demanded again. He started towards his son then suddenly stepped back. "I have another family. I have children. They won't understand."

Paul clung to the shrine. He was to be abandoned again. He was doomed to exile. At that moment, he grieved for the loss of everything, but it distilled alarmingly into his need to be overwhelmed and compelled and burned to the bone by his master's imperious wrath. His whole body flushed. Every nerve quivered like a taut guitar string. The rapture that he craved almost brought him to his knees.

Lawrence was still struggling with his guilt. He was shaking his head again, distracted and bereaved. "We looked everywhere. We couldn't even bury him." He stared at this stranger, who claimed to be his son. "What happened? Where did you go?"

Hot and breathless, Paul gazed at his father. He wanted to throw up and run away or just weep for everything that had been taken away from him. There were so many things he wanted to say, but all of them were accusations and protests, which were always forbidden. He was not allowed to refuse or resist. Complaints were blasphemy. He shook his head slowly then nodded then sighed. "I don't remember you. I don't remember what happened." He took a deep breath to steady his nerves. "Please? It wasn't meant to be like this. I just wanted you to know that I was still alive. I didn't want you to worry anymore."

Lawrence could not hear the words. He was absolutely lost. This stranger was definitely a threat. He had to be a paedophile. This was not his son. He could not overcome his conviction that he would have been assimilated into that brutal and perverted underworld that every parent feared. "I have children," he said. "They're very young."

"Please?" Paul asked. "It wasn't meant to be like this." His father drew away. "I'm ....."

"You're not mine," Lawrence said. He took a deep breath. He raised his hands to announce that he had finally made a decision. "Don't come looking for me. You should have died fighting them. Every bloody day you should have fought them. Now, I don't want you. You aren't mine. Don't ever come looking for me again. You are dead to me. Never come back." And he walked away.

Paul was shattered. He could not believe the words. He could not believe that his father was leaving him. It was over. It was really over. All his hopes and dreams were shattered. He was totally alone. His mother was dead. His father did not want him. The pain in his heart became crippling.

His muscles seized up. He could not breathe. He struggled desperately in inhale. He was choking. He felt as if someone was throttling him, and stumbled helplessly to his knees.

Chapter 53

She was so busy with the cats and the washing up that she did not notice the car driving off. The cats were doing the usual routine of pretending that they were starving to death, but they did it so sweetly and affectionately, that she had temporarily forgotten that there was a strange man in the garden. Then she had looked at her watch, and happily imagined that father and son were being reconciled. She would not think about what her life would be like after the beautiful young man left her. From the beginning, she knew he would leave. No one appeared. She leaned across the sink to stare out of the window into the walled garden. It was empty. She was surprised then nodded, knowing that they would be sitting on the bench having a good chat. They would not want her there. Even if she went out with a cup of tea, she would be intruding. She was quite pleased with how she was dealing with the situation. Of course, she was performing. She was being Meryl Streep. She was ticking boxes. It did not make her any less curious. She looked out of the window again then turned away to wander through the house. Opening the front door seemed a little too brazen so she slipped into the lounge, and moved furtively to look out through the bay windows. The driveway was empty. Realising that she had made a mistake, she retraced her steps, and went to open the front door. Obviously, she had miscalculated where he had parked the car. But opening the front door, she realised that the car had gone. She stepped down on to the gravel, and ventured across the driveway. The car was definitely not there.

For a moment, she was completely powerless. She could not move her feet. She knew that she was incapable of another rescue. Paul was out there somewhere alone. He had not gone with his father. She was sure that he was incapable of such an abrupt departure. He might have been coerced, but it seemed highly unlikely. His father seemed reluctant. It took her a while to find her courage, and it was not even conventional courage, but sheer bloody-minded determination. Full of dread and regret, she turned away from the driveway, and started on shaky legs towards the garden. The path led her down behind the garage, past the wheelie bins and yellow broom to the lawn and deep herbaceous borders.

He was not on the bench. Her nerve wobbled a bit as she turned to gaze at the treeline. He had never ventured that far on his own. He had never set foot on the grass without her beside him.

She was almost convinced that he would not have left of his own free will. His father had not been friendly. The reconciliation that she had orchestrated had floundered at the first obstacle. She kept telling herself that he would be fine, but she did not believe it. He would have come back to the house. He would have come back to find her. She kept taking deep breaths to find her resolution, then sighed it all away in despair. Could a father murder a son? Yes, of course, always. She started walking again. The garden seemed incredibly big. There were no birds singing in the tree tops. There was not a breath of wind. She began to hurry. A dozen shrill voices screamed in her head. Something terrible had happened. She started to run.

He was in a heap on the ground. He had his eyes open, but he looked dead. She fell to her knees beside him, seizing his clothes, shaking him. He was limp as a doll. She frantically searched for his pulse. He was alive. Inconsolable, she cradled him in her arms, rocking him like a child, her child. This was all her fault. From the beginning it had been her fault. She grimaced and sobbed, but could not produce a tear. She could not leave him there. There would be no rescue this time. She had to wait for him to come back to her. She had to wait for him to want to live again.

*

They had a few busy weeks in Paris then settled into the usual routine of life aboard the Prince's 747-400, which had been completely refurbished. The Prince had a private suite, there was a boardroom then the rest of the space was divided between offices and sleeping quarters. Omar was housed near the Prince. Abdullah and Famzi were stuck away at the rear, sharing a very small room. The creature customarily slept on the floor. Omar could not interfere. The Prince had shaken Abdullah by the hand, and thanked him for his efforts with the insubordinate creature. As Mahmood had warned, Famzi knew every sex shop in Paris, and was pleased to be able to demonstrate his knowledge and resourcefulness to Abdullah, whom he greatly admired.

They travelled constantly between New York, Moscow, Chechnya and Paris. When two British journalists were gunned down on the streets of Riyadh, they were far away. One died and the other was left paralysed. Expats started packing up and leaving in droves. When James Baker resigned as the Special Envoy in charge of sorting out the Saharawi problem, the Prince dropped everything, and flew down to Tindouf, then Tifariti, then went back to New York with some of the Saharawi leaders to demand an explanation. The United Nations had apparently spent $600 million dollars on the Western Sahara problem, and were no further forward than they had been in 1981. The King of Morocco and the Saharawi government-in-exile were intractable. The situation was complicated now by oil prospectors drilling offshore, which promised wealth to whoever was in power. Prince Abdul Aziz was taken aside, and advised that there was nothing to be done until one side or the other agreed to renegotiate their position. He argued again that it was the UN's duty to protect the rights of the indigenous peoples of Western Sahara, but the King of Morocco had powerful friends.

The situation in the Kingdom was deteriorating rapidly. Almost every day there were gun battles. The security services were still trying to defuse the problem by suggesting the Americans were being killed fighting amongst themselves, then they identified the troublemakers as insurgents, but eventually they had to recognise that there were actually terrorists operating in the Kingdom. It was a real wakeup call. No one had ever thought that there would be real trouble in the Kingdom.

Prince Abdul Aziz was busy on UN business in Bosnia when he started receiving distress calls from his wives. He tried to reassure them. He sent his best man back to hire the contractors to make sure that all his houses were totally secure. The compound had its wall reinforced and built another two metres higher. The best high tech surveillance was installed. Huge concrete blocks were placed strategically all around the perimeter to deter car bombers. The standalone houses were also strengthened. Omar organised alarms and safe rooms, and selected the best men from the ranks of the bodyguards to provide additional personal security for all the women and children. And still they worried and fretted that they were all to be murdered in their beds.

"They're anxious," the Prince explained.

They were in the boardroom on the 747.

Prince Khalid was technically there under duress. He had driven upstate to the quiet airfield where the 747 parked during their stays in New York. He could not bring himself to look at his father. It was not so much hatred as betrayal. He wanted to loudly criticise his father for having brought that disgusting degenerate creature back from Afghanistan after giving his word that he would never see it again. At any moment, he expected the damn thing to appear at the door, which would have completely sent him over the edge.

"Would you be willing to give them your protection?"

Prince Khalid had not been listening. "Who?" he grunted inaudibly.

"Your mother and sisters? I will rent a house for them here in New York. Will you give them your protection?"

Prince Khalid nodded stiffly then finally managed to speak. "Yes, of course."

"I have opened the house in Haqi. Jeddah is still reasonably quiet. Your brother has an apartment in Hyde Park which he only uses for a few weeks in the summer. I feel I am being encouraged to buy property all over the world, which I am reluctant to do. The Kingdom is my home. I like to believe that it is still your home." He looked at his son, who continued to stare at the highly polished table between them. He wondered what he was remembering. "I am sorry that I have been a disappointment to you. As a father, it is distressing to know that your children no longer like you."

Prince Khalid looked up at his father expecting him to jeer, but he was being completely genuine.

"I have failed in so many ways," Prince Abdul Aziz said quietly. "I had such hopes. I had so many goals, and have achieved none of them." He met his son's gaze. "I have been arrogant and foolish. I am but a man with all the weaknesses and faults that such a condition entails."

"We are all arrogant," Prince Khalid responded. "It comes with the territory."

Prince Abdul Aziz nodded. "I am moving out of the Paris house. I'll move my office back to the Ritz. My family are more important to me than anything else."

Prince Khalid threw a challenging look, his eyebrows raised quizzically, but his father shook his head. The white creature was not on the agenda.

"I'm very proud of you," Prince Abdul Aziz said. "I was never there for you when you were growing up. I have tried to learn from my mistakes. Your younger brothers and sisters see more of me. I understand this might cause offence, but you will forgive me for learning late in life my responsibilities as a parent. There are so many things I would do differently if I had a second chance." He stopped speaking when his son looked him in the eye, then he gathered his courage in both hands. "There was a time that I feared I had lost my faith. I could not understand how God could allow so much death and destruction in His Name. How could He permit bin Laden and his followers to kill so many innocents? They did not want to die. They wanted to stay with their families, and grow old surrounded by love. God cannot require so much death. It is illogical. Murder is a crime. It is a sin. No death can be sanctioned by God. He tested Abraham, but spared his son. I have not sought money or power or fame. All the time that I have spent away from you and your brothers and sisters has been invested in trying to do good works. I do not wear my religion on my sleeve, but I have never denied who I am. I have worked hand-in-glove with the United Nations to provide for refugees, irrespective of their faith, and peacefully tried to end oppression no matter who the perpetrator. They have given me honours that have humbled me, but it means nothing compared to the loss of my children's affection."

Prince Khalid shifted uncomfortably in his chair. He could not speak. His heart was wounded, but his brain was being bombarded by images he had striven to erase. He could barely shake his head.

"I have never forgiven myself for what happened. You believed you knew the truth. I simply could not surrender something that was entirely innocent. I am responsible for my people. They made the myth – but none of it was real."

Prince Khalid rose to his feet. He shook his head again. He could not look at his father. "We are all guilty men. I can remember every moment. You were not my father. The things you said. Your voice. You hated me. I can still hear you shouting: 'Fuck it! Fuck it! Make it bleed!'"

Prince Abdul Aziz stared down at the table. He could see his son's reflection in the highly polished surface. "I behaved appallingly. I was insulted. You understand about honour. You believed you knew the truth." He sighed deeply. "And afterwards, we made it the truth. We all fucked a kafir. And it was still innocent."

"Innocent?" his son demanded angrily.

The Prince nodded. "Yes. Innocent."

Prince Khalid shook his head again. He managed to look at his father then turned away and left the room. He stormed off the plane, determined to avoid another confrontation. He knew, of course, that somewhere on the jumbo jet, the white creature lurked like a spectre of doom.

Omar had driven up from New York to rejoin the Prince's entourage. He had a long flight. Commercial jets were never as comfortable as the Prince's personal 747. His car had swerved to miss Prince Khalid's chauffeured limo on the narrow road leading to the airfield. He rolled down the window, and showed his face to the bodyguards stationed around the plane. One of them offered to carry his bags up the steps.

Prince Abdul Aziz was still sitting in the boardroom. When he heard the knock at the door, he assumed it was his son returning, and looked up hopefully, but it was Omar.

With great respect, Omar bowed and offered the correct salutations to the Prince, who looked very tired and worn. "I have written a report detailing all the changes made, and the costs."

The Prince nodded. He watched as a fairly fat file was placed on the table. "My son has been here. I have not spoken to him since that night. I believe I have lost him forever."

Omar could not comment. He bowed again. "My lord, Your Highness by the Grace of God, the most Compassionate, the most Merciful. May the Blessings of God and the Holy Apostle be with you always."

The Prince nodded, completely lost in his own thoughts.

Omar lingered, but realised that the Prince did not actually know that he was there. He withdrew quietly then went to his own room.

Abdullah was sitting comfortably in an armchair. A glossy magazine was open across his knees. "You're back?" he asked carelessly.

Omar was incensed that his sanctuary had been appropriated, but knew it must have been at the Prince's command. "Yes, I'm back."

Abdullah smiled. "We fucking missed you." He understood that Omar was irritated. He enjoyed it. "While you were away we had a few problems with your precious fucking kafir. You should go and take a look at it. It was a complete fucking mess." He laughed as Omar turned away and left the room. "I'll pack up my gear. You won't even know I was fucking here."

Omar hurried down through the long corridors, which became narrower as he reached the rear of the plane where the less senior servants were housed. He knew where Abdullah and Famzi and the creature lived. There were two beds, whereas other rooms of the same size had bunk beds. He threw open the door, fearful of finding something scandalous afoot.

Famzi was rummaging in a cupboard.

Omar saw only the creature, which lay on one of the beds, covered by a sheet. It did not stir as Omar moved closer then swept away the covering. "What have you done?" Omar demanded.

Famzi burst into tears.

The creature still did not move. It was barely breathing. Across its back was an intricate painting of a lush, leafy tree. Its backside and thighs were covered in blood. The skin looked as if it had literally been peeled away. Omar had not seen that much blood since he had accompanied the Prince to a field hospital in Baghdad, when they were visiting the survivors of a car bomb attack. "Famzi, what happened?" Omar demanded. "What have they done?"

Abdullah squeezed into the room behind him, and tactfully closed the door. "Your boss wanted a big tattoo. Three men came up from New York. It's fucking huge. It took ages…"

"You did this?" Omar insisted. "The Prince would never have thought about this unless you put the suggestion in his head. And all this blood?"

Abdullah shrugged and grinned. "That was last week."

"What have you done?" Omar demanded.

Abdullah was enjoying the moment. He had orchestrated everything, but could blithely deny any responsibility. Even the Prince believed that he had made the decision himself. "The skin has been pierced and cut and burned. When it heals – if it ever heals – it will be fucking amazing."

"You did this," Omar insisted. "I know you did this." He turned to seek confirmation from Famzi, but the young Algerian had almost climbed inside the cupboard to avoid a confrontation. Omar reached down to feel the creature's ashen face. It was cold and clammy. "Is it sedated?"

Abdullah shrugged. "It was upsetting everyone. It just wouldn't shut up."

"How long?" Omar demanded. He turned to tower over Abdullah. "How long has it been like this? A week? Has it seen a doctor?"

Abdullah smiled, and shook his head. "It gets morphine."

Omar was horrified. "What about infection? How much blood has it lost?"

Abdullah shrugged carelessly.

"And if it had died?"

"It didn't fucking die. It won't die." Abdullah laughed. "It knew the risks. The Prince asked the fucking thing to give him this. He asked its permission. It was so fucking sweet. He said: 'I ask this of you because I love you. You wouldn't deny me this one small thing.' And the fucking kafir kissed his hands. I could have fucking cried. Well, I could have fucked it until it fucking cried."

Omar turned back to survey the mutilated flesh. He felt completely useless. He had no idea what to do, but could not bear to leave the creature in Abdullah's hands. "I'll take it to my room," he announced irritably, and started to pull the sheet back.

"You can't fucking move it," Abdullah said with authority. "It has to lay still. It mustn't move at all or the fucking pattern will be fucked up."

"I don't give a damn," Omar said, and turned to Famzi. "Bring the medicine to my room." He rolled the creature into his arms, and lifted it from the bed. Abdullah blocked the door. "Get out of my way. I know you've done this. You think this is some little victory for you, but I'll win in the end. You're a sadist. The Prince will see you for what you are. You won't win in the end."

Abdullah was grinning, but he stepped aside, and opened the door with a flourish. "I've carved my fucking name into that fucking kafir's soul. In the end, it will be mine, you'll see."

No one stood in the way as Omar hurried back to his room. His main concern was that the Prince would appear and confuse the situation, so he was relieved when he was able to lay the creature down on his own bed. Rescuing it was becoming a dangerous habit. He was again appalled that no one else had stepped in to protect it from Abdullah. But then Abdullah was a Believer, and no one would dare criticize his treatment of a kafir, whose continuing existence was acknowledged to be an insult to God.

Chapter 54

"The police believe that you actually ran away from home." She had consumed a few glasses of wine and was feeling authoritative. "They say more than seventy thousand kids run away every year. It's about drugs and abuse and just bad parents. Sometimes they are not even running away by choice, they have been evicted, and locked out by their own parents. There are a lot of young children living on the streets because it's better than living with mum and dad. They're not wanted anymore. It can be broken homes. Sometimes there's no dad: the mother gets a new boyfriend, and he might not like having another man's children living in the same house. Boys are particularly vulnerable to being evicted. It's probably some instinctive territorial aggression. If she's weak or a drunk or an addict, then the children have no protection at all. They're probably dysfunctional anyway, why should a stranger put up with them when he's already got the woman under his thumb? Sometimes it doesn't even take that much abuse to drive the children away. Of course, he might hang on to the girls if they are malleable." She sipped her wine for a moment then continued: "It's bad parenting. They're inadequate. Often poorly educated, living on benefits, with no aspirations for themselves and no hope for the children, they seem incapable of keeping any kind of discipline. You can see them sometimes in the shops, and they all seem to hate each other. It must be a miserable existence." She waved the wine glass to emphasise her opinion. "Sometimes, it's not even mistreatment; it is just a careless form of neglect. They often don't teach the children to keep clean or to eat properly. They turn them out in clothes that haven't been washed in months. They have fleas and things living in their hair. And they smell. It's like no one ever explained about toilet paper and soap. And the children copy their parents. There's violence and abuse at home so they take it to school. They get into trouble. The teachers write to the parents. The parents don't care." Talking was making her thirsty. "And they're damaged. Before they were even born most of them were damaged. If their mothers drank or took drugs or even smoked cigarettes during pregnancy then they were poisoning them. It's brain damage. They have all these weird things like 'attention deficit disorder'. It's brain damage. I'm sure most of it is because their mothers were stupid and irresponsible. It's a total catastrophe. Really, they should not be allowed to have children. It's too precious a gift to waste on drunks and addicts. And the children always turn out worse than their parents. It's been proved. It's never ending. We'll end up with a mob of violent, uncontrollable people, who'll never hold down a job so the rest of us end up paying for them. We pay! Most of them end up being serial offenders. They are in and out of prison. And still we're paying for them. And they can't help it. We are supposed to feel sorry for them. We are supposed to feel guilty because we worked hard at school, and earned a living and were responsible human beings. We should feel guilty for doing that. They can't help what they are yet everyone knows that stealing and violence are wrong. We don't need to be lawyers. We know that it is wrong yet we are expected to make allowances for them. Well, I think that there are now more of them than of us. Does that sound arrogant?"

"I don't know." He had not been listening. "I'm sorry."

She smiled bravely for him, not wanting to overwhelm him with sympathy. "Yes, of course. How could you know? You don't even live here. It's just such a mess. I wish it didn't upset me so much, but it does. We're going down a toilet. These poor damaged children must be so unhappy. No wonder they run away. Living in a ditch in the bleak mid-winter, must seem infinitely more attractive than being beaten and starved in a loveless home."

The young man lifted his head then lowered it again, and turned away to conceal his wounds. "Yes. I suppose so."

"It must be very strange for you." She sighed, hardly knowing how to apologise. "You didn't even recognise him, did you? He must have been drunk. You should give him another chance. It must have been a terrible shock. After all these years, it must have been a huge shock. You must try to forgive him. Tomorrow, he'll hate himself. If he doesn't come back then I'll write to him. He just needs some time. You have to give him another chance."

He nodded. He wanted to throw up.

They were in the lounge. Eventually, he had come around, and she had bullied him to his feet and made him walk back to the house. That had been yesterday. She had made him some soup and put him to bed with enough pills to sedate an elephant. She sat beside him, holding his hand, desperately unhappy.

He would not say what had happened. The shutters had come down again and he was somewhere else.

Later, she phoned Mr. Watchman and explained that things had not gone well. He gave her Lawrence's address. While the young man lay on the sofa and stared at the floor, she made several attempts to write a letter, but it was in vain. She was so angry; she could barely compose one civil sentence. Then she just started to have a rant about life, the universe and everything, but as usual, no one was listening.

*

The Riviera in September was as beautiful as ever. The light was golden. The colours were rich and luscious. The Royal party were following the yachts down the coast. It was late September. Monaco was even more splendid and crowded than usual with the unbelievably rich and famous, and the glamorous Yacht Show in town. The Prince had a yacht big enough to fill an Olympic sized pool. It was moored offshore amongst a flotilla of super-yachts. Guests were ferried to the jetties in small motor launches. There were boats bobbing about everywhere. The annual show brought in buyers and agents, pimps and hookers and tens of thousands of ordinary tourists. All the beautiful people were there. It was almost impossible to walk down the promenade without seeing a film star or footballer or an oligarch. On the beach there were topless girls surrounded by photographers, all of them on the make. It was chaotic and crowded and expensive, but the sky was blue and the light was extraordinary.

The Prince liked living on his yacht. It was convenient and comfortable. He could pull up the anchor, and move on whenever the mood took him. And wherever he went, so the servants and bodyguards went too. He spent most of his day working in his study, dealing with his businesses and his obligations to the United Nations. The Prince complained that he was really too busy to be bothered with the wild parties and the jet set scene, but he had simply outgrown them. He knew that many of his countrymen, who frequented such places, led less than savoury lives. There were too many stories about sex with underage girls. The young princes boasted openly when they were away from home, but were very discreet in the Kingdom. Worse were the rumours about paedophile rings, and allegations of endemic corruption. It was common knowledge that the local girls were willing to come aboard the big yachts to party. Single Arab men were considered a desirable catch. They were free with their money. The girls that prowled the beach-front bars might not have all been prostitutes, but they were all looking for a good time and presents. They were certainly more sexually active than any girls that the Prince had met before, and many had the pinched needy faces of addicts. So he chose his guests with care, and was very selective about the places he chose to visit ashore. This gave him a reputation for being a recluse, which just guaranteed that he received more invitations. At such moments, he usually weighed anchor, but Monte Carlo in September was a difficult place to leave.

In Monte Carlo, Prince Abdul Aziz often enjoyed a few evenings at the casino where he was received as an honoured guest. The kafir accompanied his master in the role of a personal assistant, and stood behind him holding a briefcase and his phone. He stood silent and still, watching his master, waiting for his cue. He knew which games his master liked to play, and understood that he was a mere pawn in one of them.

One hot evening they were at the casino. The Prince and his party had spent the day on the yacht. They were relaxed and enjoying themselves. Even the bodyguards were turned out in their best suits. Around them were glamorous women and powerful men. Even in the more public rooms, the guests were handsomely dressed and perfectly behaved. After all, this was not Las Vegas.

The kafir always stood behind his master's left shoulder. He carried the usual weighted briefcase attached to his left wrist. He wore a dark blue suit that had been made for him in Rome. His tie-pin and cuff links were art deco and solid gold. His face was lean and handsome. Occasionally, he lifted his head to survey the room, and was always rewarded with the smiles of both women and men, who had been watching him with frank admiration. Over the years, he had become accustomed to being looked at. A great deal of time and money were spent on his appearance because he was on public display whenever he went out with the Prince. No one questioned his presence because no one noticed anything but his beauty. It often left them dumbfounded. He remained aloof. It was not in his remit to acknowledge the attention he received. Under pressure, he sometimes smiled but always deferred to his master, always lowered his gaze, and always stepped back into his master's shadow. If he did not defer, he knew his master would be upset and jealous, and threaten to leave him at home. He was on display, but strictly on his master's terms. The public were allowed to look, but modern technology increasingly allowed surreptitious photographs. The Prince was always irritated when there was a camera flash. It usually only happened once or twice before someone intervened and asked them to desist. But the cameras were always improving, and eventually the kafir had to stare down at his shoes, and not lift his head at all. He was always kept away from the paparazzi. They were as despised as mosquitoes, and as difficult to avoid. The bodyguards had been known to smash cameras whether or not any pictures were taken. This all added to the Prince's reputation as a recluse.

It was after nine when the kafir shivered. He felt a sharp pain in his belly, but tried to ignore it. He moved to dab the sweat off his face. Even that slight movement made him dizzy, and it immediately focused Omar's attention. The kafir never moved. He never looked hot or bothered. For another hour, the kafir stood there, turning grey, his breathing becoming ragged, his stomach dissolving in its own acid. When the pain was unbearable, he shivered again. He could taste the vomit in his mouth. Suddenly afraid, he took a step backwards then turned slightly to locate Omar. Had the briefcase not been locked to his wrist, he would have reached out to seize Omar's arm.

"I'm ill," the kafir whispered. "There's something wrong." He staggered against Omar, who quickly caught him around the waist. The pain magnified again. He shuddered violently, his face creasing as the pain overwhelmed him.

Omar knew it was genuine. He needed only one look into the creature's grey face to know that something was terribly wrong. It had never really recovered from the physical trauma of the immense tattoo and the artwork that had literally been carved on to its body. It had lost so much blood. Abdullah had destroyed its spirit. He had ripped out its heart. It was still beautiful, but it was as fragile as a fawn. Omar stretched his arm around it, and turned it away from the crowded room. It began to fade, growing heavier, but Omar was strong enough to remove it from view without causing a fuss or attracting attention. As they left the throng around the roulette table, the creature's legs gave way. Another of the bodyguards took the creature's other arm. They held it upright, but the weighty briefcase now hung like an anchor from its wrist. Walking it away, Omar sent another bodyguard to whisper to the Prince that they were taking the creature outside.

The kafir's head was swimming. He was aware of nothing but the pain that tore through his stomach like a knife, and his sudden need to vomit. He tried to walk, tried not to pass out, but with every second, he grew weaker and sicker. Staff at the casino rushed to assist, ushering the little group to a private lounge. He was laid out on a chaise. Omar carefully loosened his collar then wiped his face with a damp cloth. The kafir was barely conscious. He was mumbling incoherently.

Omar sat beside the creature, attentive and listening while the Prince's car was fetched to a side door. The casino management had a doctor on call, but Omar did not have the authority to allow a stranger to examine it. Always courteous, Omar thanked everyone for their good wishes and assistance, but explained that the young man had sunburn, and probably needed nothing more than a few days rest.

From the corner of his eye, Prince Abdul Aziz had seen his creature stagger. His immediate alarm was quelled by his iron will, and the demands of his ego. Good manners allowed him to turn his head slightly and establish that Omar had everything under control, then he returned his attention to the spinning wheel, and his fellow guests. It was unseemly for him to appear to be overly indulgent with his staff. If it had been a life or death situation, he would, of course, have risen to his feet, and given it his full attention, but not some silly fainting fit. His fellow guests were of the same opinion. No one mentioned it. One or two smiled sympathetically. A grand-dame with a chest full of diamonds leaned a little closer, and apologised for the very hot weather.

The Prince was not by nature a gambler, but he enjoyed the convivial company. There were some loud crass Americans in the room, but none at his table. He had an Argentinean, who was quite a famous polo player, two German bankers, a princess of a country that no longer existed, and the Finance Minister of an African nation that was now a complete basket case. The Prince made polite conversation, but never initiated one. He preferred to listen. He liked to observe human nature. But that evening, he was disturbed by a strange and unyielding emotion that was almost unknown to him. It was disconcerting. He felt loss. He was missing something. In quieter moments, his thoughts focused not on the game or the pleasant company, but on the absence of the creature that was always beside him, never further than the reach of his arm. He felt the lack of it as surely as he would have missed a limb. At the very moment when he had been thinking about his creature, and idly pushed a pile of chips across the table, and resigned himself to losing it all, the ball had dropped for him. The muted cheers and congratulations of his fellow gamblers brought him back to the table. He was almost embarrassed by his good fortune because it was born out of a moment of complete self-indulgence. In his head, he had been plunging into his creature, devouring it, rampaging through it, destroying it and loving it, and all his senses were reeling with joy and the darkest rapture. It was still his drug of choice. He was still an addict. Then he resented the creature for having cast its spell over him, and he vowed to punish it because it had no right to his affection. And he felt no obligation whatsoever to take care of it because it was the vilest whore, and beneath the consideration of any decent man. But he smiled, and tipped the croupier, and received the admiration of his companions. There was a hush as everyone placed their bets again. The wheel spun. The ball whizzed around then jumped and bounced. Everyone but the Prince leaned forward. The ball dropped into another slot. He had lost. He was relieved. The attention shifted away from him. Turning slightly, he sought solace from his exquisite creature, standing in its place. It was always there, silent, motionless and utterly beautiful. But it had gone. Of course, he knew it had gone, but it had become a constant that he relied on. The longing wounded him again. He wanted it back. He struggled to justify his need. Every thought and emotion was wholly inappropriate, but he was fixated now. He worried that it was sick. It might even be dead. In his hatred, he reasoned coldly that a dead body could be easily disposed of at sea whereas an invalid required care and attention. Then his longing pierced his heart again. Was it ill? Was it dead? Forgetting himself, he earnestly offered a silent prayer that it might be saved, then remembered, and cursed the damn thing for bewitching him.

He tried to focus on the game. He distracted himself counting the chips. The wheel spun. The ball rattled around its track then collided with the channels and bounced. He was very familiar with the soundtrack of a casino. Across the room, there was a crowd gathering around the craps table. Whoever held the dice was playing to the audience and raising the tension. His croupier asked if he wanted to make a bet. The Prince picked up half a dozen chips, and put them down on a number. He had not counted the chips or looked at the number. He lost. He did not notice. Every fibre of his being, every neuron in his brain, every drop of blood in his veins hungered for the creature. He had never wanted it as badly as he did at that moment when there was the chance of losing it forever. He could not wait. He had an imperative need to hurry back to it. His lust was base and ignoble, but he could satisfy it easily by fucking the creature until it was vanquished. He had to crush it into submission. He could not bear to be parted from it yet he resented its power over him. Simply acknowledging it made him angry. He hated it. Even their love making was a poisonous marriage of jealousy, guilt, and doubt. There had been too many nights when he fucked it and fucked it until he found proof of its depravity, and then cast it out of his bed like a leper only to spend long hours alone wondering if he had become the slave. Was he gratifying the creature? Was he serving it? Had he become so obsessed with it that their roles had reversed? And this vile thing pulled at his heart like a child, which infuriated him. He hated it yet wanted nothing more than to know that it was safe and well, knowing with certainty that only he could make sure that it was absolutely safe and well.

The Prince did not return to the yacht until long after midnight. He asked for Omar, who came to explain that they had safely returned the creature without incident, but that it was still unwell. There was absolutely no question of calling for a local doctor so the decision was made to hire a private ambulance, and send the creature back to Paris. As the arrangements were made in the Prince's name, the two paramedics assumed that the creature was a prince which everyone else found very amusing. By dawn, the sedated creature was already halfway to Lyon.

Famzi and two bodyguards accompanied the creature while it fell to Omar to take a commercial flight to Paris to organise its reception at the other end.

Chapter 55

"Sometimes, the only choices we have are bad ones." She did not know if he was listening to her anymore. He was pale and worn out. He had nothing left to give. "So what do you want to do now?"

He shook his head. It had been a week. His body was healing, but he was broken inside.

"You could stay here," she said quietly, trying not to sound desperate. "There's plenty of room."

He lifted his head and smiled. The sunlight from the windows lit up his eyes like beacon fires. "You have been very kind."

"You'll be safe here," she said. "I promise. No one will hurt you if you stay here."

He looked at her again, smiled again, then combed his fingers through his hair. "But I am their thing." The smile turned into a frown. "That's what I am."

She did not want to understand. "That doesn't matter. That was the past. You have your whole life ahead of you." She tried desperately to find the right words, but they were all the wrong ones. "Your father didn't mean that. He was upset and in shock. He didn't mean it. Let me write to him again. The first letter might have gone astray. We don't know that he received it. Let me try again. He's your father. He does love you. He'll come around." She needed to be Meryl Streep now. Her voice was high and hysterical when she needed to be calm and collected. She was almost beside herself, and when he turned away to lay down with his back to her, she was choking back tears. "Please, don't give up. You have plenty of time to work this out." There was no response. She felt as if she had been dismissed. It hurt, but her concern for him overwhelmed all her own problems. She could not help him anymore. He had to work it out. "I just want you to be happy," she said, but there was no answer.

She made a cup of tea and took her pills. She was a good girl. She absolutely had to stay sane. All her hopes and dreams were in ashes. There was Wimbledon on the television. She should have been happy. The sun was shining. Federer was playing like a god. All she could think about was the beautiful young man who had come crashing into her life, and changed everything forever. There was only reality left for him.

He watched television. He even watched the tennis with her although he did not understand the game. Most of the time he was just looking at people – other people – people who were not like him. They were happy and animated. They leapt to their feet and raised their arms above their heads to cheer in jubilation. There were no veils or masks. No one subdued their eyes or bowed their heads. The sun was shining. Everyone looked alive and alert and happy. They were absolutely terrifying. They were a mob, and he remained an outcast. He did not know how to feel exuberance. The only excitement he had ever tasted had been when he was with Prince Abdul Aziz. When they were together he knew happiness. Other people found happiness watching a ball being knocked to and fro over a net in a game where the scoring was incomprehensible. What was Love? Love apparently was nothing. It was zero. Losers had Love. Winners had fifteen – thirty – forty then game.

He thought about his life, which amounted to nothing. Everything he had experienced had been as a shadow of someone else. While his master travelled the world and was feted everywhere, he was always behind him carrying his bags or hidden behind an intricate shell mask and a burqa. It was not for him to admire the view or marvel at a work of art. He looked at his master or he looked at the floor, and he always kept his mouth shut. All that was his alone was the pain. Abdullah suddenly loomed large. No one had ever hurt him like that before. Worse than the pain was knowing that his master had brought in Abdullah to punish him for simply looking at a girl. It had all started with the girl in the hotel lobby in Ankara. It was more than the usual jealousy. It was brutal, spiteful, vengeful. His master wanted a terrible revenge and brought in a sadist to guarantee it. That he knew he was only caught in the crossfire did not make the pain any less. Abdullah had destroyed him. He knew it. He could not go back. His master obviously approved of everything that Abdullah had done. Of course, his master was under no obligation to explain. The kafir did not need explanations. He understood. His Pakistanis had never been shy about discussing his performances or his prospects. He was too tall. He was too old. He might be pretty now, but one day he would be old and ugly. They hoped the next one would be blonde. They liked blondes. They were only waiting for the Prince to lose interest, which would happen as soon as the kafir was no longer attractive enough to be admired. Perhaps he had been lucky. His Pakistanis had always assumed that he would end up being dumped out of a helicopter over the Empty Quarter. They discussed his fate while brushing his hair or fucking him as if he was deaf, dumb and blind. Mahmood had been more sensitive, but only much later when they were alone. He had never liked helicopters. He had other fears too. There were the constant threats of being sold. His master had given the young Prince Bandar certain assurances that he was honour-bound to keep. So why had he been left in someone's garden? He did not understand, and the more he worried about it the worse it seemed. He felt he should be doing something. He just did not know what to do. It was an unfamiliar concept. He had never had to think about anything. His life was arranged. It was regimented. They brushed his teeth. They combed his hair. He was led around by his wrist or marshalled by a vice-like grip on his arm. He kept in step. He stopped when they stopped. He was not even permitted to think that he might be thirsty. As far as they were concerned, he only needed what they provided, and was allowed nothing else. Wanting something was still an alien concept. And he had become so used to it that he did not rebel. He did not even get angry. The madrassa had ingrained into his brain that he was a worthless infidel, and hated by God. It was not the Pakistanis who were mean to him. God, the most Compassionate, the most Merciful, the All-Knowing and most Wise, hated him as He hated all disbelievers. Everything the Pakistanis did was righteous. Everything Abdullah had done was righteous. It was not unfair. It was not cruel. If anything, they were generous to allow him so much. To know that God hated him was a dreadful burden to bear. He valued every kindness. He was grateful for everything they allowed, but God hated him. He never doubted that for a moment.

Somewhere along the way, Paul Lawrence disappeared again. He had died. He should have died ten times over. That the kafir was still alive was easily explained. Prince Abdul Aziz wanted him to be alive. It had been arranged. It was not accidental. It was not a miracle. His master still wanted him to live.

*

It was the most ordinary of days. The Prince had several meetings, which was not unusual. His diary was always booked up solid often months in advance. They had travelled slowly across Paris in a convoy from one conference to another. There were all the usual bodyguards as well as several security guards on motorbikes supplied by the French Secret Service. There was no indication that anyone was in any kind of danger, but as they came out of a restaurant, suddenly, there were very loud bangs. Someone was firing a gun near enough to be threatening. Everyone turned. The bodyguards swarmed around the Prince, making a solid human wall between him and the direction of the noise. The Secret Service turned on the sirens and the flashing lights. In the few seconds it took to react and acknowledge the incident, the kafir was gone.

Only Omar said that the creature had not run away. Everyone else believed it had fled. Some said it ran away because it was a coward. Others suggested it was just hiding. It was even declared to be a common little thief.

The kafir had literally been lifted off the pavement, and swept into a van that suddenly appeared through the traffic at the very moment the gunshots were heard. It happened so quickly that no one could be really sure what happened. Almost everyone was staring off into the distance in search of the shooters when the van sped away in the opposite direction. The kafir was unconscious moments later, smothered with chloroform. He never saw his abductors. When he regained consciousness, he was lying in a skip covered in rotting food and garbage. The heavy briefcase that went with him everywhere had been cut from his wrist. Fortunately, no one had noticed the Breitling watch. He was still coming around when Omar and a few of the bodyguards arrived. The GPS tracker was working perfectly. He was dragged from the skip and brushed down then bundled into an SUV.

"They took the briefcase?" Omar asked.

The kafir nodded. He was feeling very muzzy and wanted to throw up. He did not feel well enough to worry about his master's briefcase, but knew there would be a reckoning.

"Did you see them?" Omar demanded. "Would you recognise them?"

The kafir shook his head unhappily, and stared down at his hands.

"Did you see anything? Did you hear anything?"

He shivered. He hardly dared to shake his head again. "Please? There were many, but it was dark. They wore – ski-masks, I think."

"Did they say anything?" Omar watched as the creature almost disintegrated under pressure. He reached out to tip up its head so he could look in its eyes. The smell dissuaded him from moving any closer. "They held something over your face?"

The kafir focused. He gazed desperately at Omar. "Please? I fainted. And now I feel sick."

Omar relented then reached out to pat him kindly. "It's alright. It wasn't your fault. The case was heavy. It was a great temptation for thieves."

The kafir nodded then groaned as he started to throw up. They went to the clinic, entering through the basement. He was cleaned up and examined. When the Prince arrived, the kafir was sent away.

They went back to the villa. It had been empty for months because the Prince's family had moved down to Antibes. Famzi was waiting. Omar handed the kafir over with the explanation that "something happened. The Prince will be back soon."

Famzi had barely finished stripping off the kafir's smelly clothes to put it in a thobe before Abdullah appeared at the door. He was very drunk. He swept in, seized the unhappy creature, and dragged it away. There was no one to interfere. The great house was almost empty. The safest place for a bit of undiluted vengeance was in the rooms used only by the Prince, and the bathroom was the safest place of all.

Abdullah started with the whip that had always been his favourite. He laid several sweeping cuts across the creature's back, slicing through its shirt and skin. The poor trembling thing collapsed across the marble counter, panting heavily and dripping with sweat. It was too afraid to meet Abdullah's searching gaze, but Abdullah combed his fingers through its hair then wrenched its head up so that he could leer into its ashen face, and enjoy its torment.

"Soon you'll be mine. He won't ever fucking touch you now. Not after this." He slobbered over the face like a drooling hound, his tongue as quick as a snake's, his breath heavy with the foul odour of cigarettes and alcohol and bad teeth. That it was visibly revolted only encouraged Abdullah to spit into its eyes. "You will come back with me to Karachi. I have a house." He pulled on the hair again to bring the creature's face back close to his own. "It's down near the harbour. It's the most dangerous fucking street in Karachi. We run the drugs. We run all the bloody whores. I'll run you. You'll make me a rich man." Leering, he leaned closer, one hand caressing its throat while he slavered over it again. He thrust his sex hard against its backside. "I'll put a thick iron ring through your pretty white nose to advertise that you're just a fucking whore. You'll work the streets. You'll suck cocks in cars. Your white arse and your mouth will be available to every fucking man in Karachi." He laughed as it shrank away in terror, letting it slide down on to its knees. Gloating with triumph, he gazed down at it for a moment, imagining the life it would lead in the crowded slums of Karachi. Then he reached down to seize its hair, and dragged it across the floor to send it sprawling under the torrents of icy water in the shower.

They were in the master bathroom at the villa in Paris. It was a large shining room with harsh white lights. Every surface was marble flecked with gold or glass. It was lavishly decorated with carved shells, ornate tiles and references to Neptune and naked sea nymphs. There was a large free-standing tub on ball and claw feet, an even larger sunken tub with seating for six, surrounded by Grecian benches upholstered with golden damask, three sinks, two toilets, two long dressing tables heavy with glassware and flowers, and everywhere immense mirrors. The fittings were gold. One corner of the room was a spacious walk-in shower with a drain recessed into the floor. Water came down in a steady stream from a large flat shower head that extended across the whole area. Powerful water jets were set randomly into the walls. The pressure was unrelenting. Abdullah had every tap turned on, and the temperature set at zero. There was no shelter anywhere from the icy deluge.

Abdullah stood grinning as the creature crumpled into a heap, instantly drenched and battered by the water. He had no intention of getting wet, but he was conscious of the need to keep the blood splatter down to a minimum.

From corrupt politicians to the most ignorant beggars, Abdullah did not know of anyone who would be too proud or prejudiced to screw such a nice piece of arse. He turned the water off. The silence that followed was only interrupted by the odd intermittent drip. Abdullah leaned down to seize its hair then whispered into its ear: "I'll be a bloody rich man. Addicts. Perverts. Murderers. They'll all fuck you. You'll do whatever I fucking say. Twelve, twenty, even thirty fucking men will pay to fuck you every bloody day. Blow jobs. Arse jobs. An' you'll still fucking dance. You'll seduce them. You'll be the most vulgar fucking prostitute in Karachi. They'll be queuing up to fuck you. I fucking guarantee it." He smiled jubilantly. "I've heard about the giant fucking cock of a bull. Yes, you'll become the most famous fucking whore in all of fucking Pakistan. I'll have a great big bloody house. I'll be rich and respected." He pulled away from the creature then cuffed it across back of the head. "Get up!"

Abdullah turned away for a moment, and picked up something from one of the dressing tables. It was the bridle. He hurled it at the creature, who caught it before realising what it was, then recognising it, let it fall to the floor in horror.

"Please, no. Please, don't hurt me." The kafir trembled. He was already in agony, but it was the bridle that terrified him.

"Put it on!"

Traumatised, the kafir shook his head. He could not do it. He dared not look at Abdullah, and could not bear to look at the bridle. "Please, I beg you. I won't make a sound. I swear before God. You don't need to do this. Please, God is Merciful."

Abdullah snatched up the bridle then forced the large rubber bit deep into the creature's mouth, then roughly pulled the thick straps over its head, and buckled it tightly in place. He slipped a zip tie around its wrists then bullied it to its feet, and fastened the wrists to an ornate golden hook embedded in the marble wall.

"You'll live amongst the fucking paedophiles and queers. They'll open your bloody mouth and your arse quicker than fucking rats. Sometimes, it will be many men at once. They'll fucking tear you apart. You'll grow sick and diseased because all of your precious fucking customers will be sick and diseased." He laid several lashes across the creature's exposed back. The thobe now hung in rags from the seams across its shoulders. "You'll be raped every fucking day by those same men who fuck their bloody donkeys and goats because their wives are so fucking ugly. Some men will pay just to fucking beat you like this." The whip sliced through the bloodied wounds. The creature writhed like a demented animal. "Some will demand that you fuck their dogs while they are fucking you. In Karachi, your fucking life will be worthless. You'll beg and steal and do any fucking thing to buy my protection."

In the bridle, it was very difficult to breathe.

"And when you're so fucking ugly that not even the bloody freaks and perverts will pay for your mouth or your arse then there will be animals. They're not so bloody fussy. My cousin has a fucking bear. I've never seen a man fucked by a full grown badass bear. It must be possible. You were fucked by a bull. Everyone talks about it. How the fuck did they arrange that?" Abdullah paused from his labours to laugh as he pictured the scene. "By then all of Karachi will fucking know what you are. They'll know I own your fucking arse. I'll make sure you're famous. I'll be able to sell bloody tickets. There'll be fucking crowds cheering. We'll run sex shows between the dog fights down in the warehouses by the docks. I'll be rich. Really?" Abdullah laughed again, enjoying his own jokes, moving closer to admire his handiwork. The bridle concealed most of the creature's face. It was breathing hard. It was still trembling. "You're just a bloody whore." He leered at the monstrous bridle that encased the creature's head. "And when I'm old and fat and respectable, and you are too fucking ugly to be a whore anymore, then you'll be a bloody beggar in the streets. I'll give you a tin fucking cup to fill and a broken fucking leg to slow you down. Every fucking day, you'll fill the cup, and bring it back to me. If it's full, I might let you fucking sleep alone in my cellar with a blanket. If you don't fill the cup then you'll spend the whole fucking night in the cages with my dogs. Every fucking day, you'll go out. If you ever dare to fucking run away the fucking police will bring you back to me. In Pakistan, the police belong to the bosses. They'll fuck you over. It won't fucking matter what you say.

They'll always find you and bring you back to me."

Abdullah stepped back and stretched his arm, sweeping the whip through the air. The creature twisted and turned desperately to seek some protection, but there was to be none. He thrashed it until his arm ached. With spittle and blood dribbling through his beard, he turned away from the mutilated creature to find Prince Abdul Aziz watching him. Without hesitation, the Pakistani went to his knees and bowed reverently. He bowed as the kafir had to bow, but he was allowed to rise to his feet and look at his prince. "My lord, Your Highness, by the Grace of God, the Compassionate, the Merciful. May the Blessings of the Holy Prophet be upon you," he said rather breathlessly. "Peace be upon you."

Prince Abdul Aziz was speechless. He regarded Abdullah then stared at the bag of bloodied flesh hanging from its wrists behind him. "Did it offend you?" he asked quietly.

Abdullah bowed again. "Yes, Your Highness. It insulted God, and it tried to attack me."

Prince Abdul Aziz could not doubt his word. It was a sin to lie. He looked again at the creature, recognising the bridle that it wore, and the flesh hanging from its back. "Have you satisfied your honour?" he asked.

Abdullah ran the whip through his fingers, and took a moment to admire the thick bloodstains left on his hands. "Yes, Your Highness. I have punished it harshly for offending God. I am sure it will never be so insulting again."

"Is it still conscious?"

Abdullah barely turned to look before answering confidently: "No, Your Highness. God has been satisfied."

The Prince nodded distractedly while he searched his robes. He did not wait for Abdullah to turn away before pulling out a pistol, and shooting him in the head. The sharp bark of the gunshot filled the room. Distantly, there were cries of alarm. The Prince walked calmly passed the dead man then carefully lifted the bloodied creature into his arms.

When he turned, he saw Omar standing breathlessly in the doorway.

Omar took in the scene. The sound of the gunshot had brought him. He was shocked, but nodded to Prince Abdul Aziz then stepped forward to assist. He held out his arms to take the creature, but the Prince lifted it away, crushing it to his chest. He could not surrender it. Omar gazed into the Prince's anguished face, and nodded again then bowed. "Let me remove this thing?" Omar indicated the bridle. The Prince was almost incoherent with grief, but he managed to master his emotions and allowed Omar to touch his beloved creature that had been tortured almost to death. He watched protectively as Omar found the buckles then gently removed the cruel device. To see the ashen face was beyond painful. The Prince gasped as the head fell limply against his chest. He had killed it. He had murdered what gave him joy.

Chapter 56

The young man stood alone in the anteroom. There were no windows. There was not even a chair. He wore blue jeans and a fresh white shirt. His hair was neatly cut. The delicate tan that made his skin glow with health was perfectly natural. He looked superb. But his hands shook and his heart raced. He was nervous. He had been pacing up and down for half an hour, but now stood facing the ornately carved doors. Everything in his life had brought him to this moment. Now, his limbs were leaden. He could not advance another step. He could not grasp the handle and open the door. He could not confront his destiny. Beyond the door lay not only his future but his past. All the pain that he had ever suffered came back to engulf him again. Could he really endure it twice? His nerves said no. He gazed at his trembling hands. His flesh remembered. His heart and soul and brain were in conflict, but his body shivered with fear at the price it would have to pay. His testosterone levels were escalating. Adrenalin already flooded his body. Deep in his belly, his guts twisted into a thousand knots. Had he anything but bile in his stomach he would have turned away and thrown up. A cold sweat drenched him. He knew that he was a coward. What he did not know was whether he could face what would happen after he had opened that door. And if he never crossed that threshold then where could he go? What could he do when so completely alone? He was in hell already. He knew all about hell. There was no escape at all from his own personal hell, but beyond the door?

To summon them, all he needed to do was try to remove the wristwatch. It had brought Omar to him to Paris. Now, it would take him home. He waited in the lounge, gazing out of the window. Jane Howard was busy in her garden. He had told her he was going to lay down. He said he was tired, which was true: he was tired of waiting. When the SUV came up the driveway, it drew her in from the garden. He could hear her shouting a warning as he went out to meet them. He raised his hands and turned around so they could search him while she stood on her doorstep and wept. Sticky tape pinned down his arms. The last thing he saw before the burqa came down to cover him was her collapsing on the ground. His legs turned to water. His nerve failed, but they bundled him into the SUV, forcing him down on to the floor. His shoes were pulled off and thrown away. All the old rules applied. So he was taken to London, to one of the oldest and finest hotels, and he was left alone in an empty room, and told to wait. And he had waited while his courage was worn away and his resolve turned to ashes.

In despair, he reached out to take hold of the door handle. It was surprisingly cold. It was stiff. He feared it was locked. He leaned against the door almost too frightened to try and open it. All his hopes were being destroyed one after another. Had he come back, and put himself through this ordeal only for them to have locked the door against him? He had no understanding of indignation. He was never allowed to be so self-indulgent. Somehow, he found the strength to turn the handle. There was the heavy click of the mechanism. Under his weight, the immense door shifted a few inches. His nerves shredded a little more.

"Come."

Had he imagined it? The voice was known to him. It had spoken so often to him in his dreams.

The room was very large and well lit by immense windows. The colours were all muted creams. The furniture was classical, yet looked new. It was a reception room. There were three suites of sofas arranged around coffee tables. Most of the walls were covered in bookshelves or artwork. One man sat on the far side of the room. He looked up briefly from a newspaper to acknowledge his visitor then turned away.

It was Prince Abdul Aziz.

Devastated by the cool response, the young man clung on to the door, daring to hope he had not been recognised, and that he might still be able to run away. But he could not move a step. The door had become a crutch. What little strength he possessed melted down through his flesh. It pooled in his feet. He was stuck there like a butterfly skewered by a pin.

The Prince continued reading his newspaper. After a few moments, he lifted the paper and shook out the creases, then folded it over, turning to the next page. He seemed totally unaware of his visitor, but after a while, negligently, offered the ring.

It was so far across that lofty spacious room that the young man might have completely missed the small and almost insignificant gesture, but that he had been looking for it. All his training spared him the need for conscious effort or thought, but a thousand memories vanquished him. Every belief in his independence was erased. He turned to close the door behind him then slowly walked across the void to meet his fate. His heart grew heavier. Before he had reached the Prince, his legs were completely useless, and he found it difficult to sink gracefully on to his knees then to bow. When he raised his eyes and reached out to clasp the hand, it and the ring had been withdrawn. He felt it like a dagger through his heart. Unhappily, he sank down again to press his forehead into the carpet in an appeal for mercy. They had set a trap for him. He had walked into it with his eyes wide open.

The Prince put aside the newspaper, and gazed down at his creature. He was not unmoved by its beauty or its distress, but he hardly knew what to say to it. There had been days when he had not remembered its existence, but too many nights when it had haunted his dreams in ways that no other living thing had ever done. For more than a decade, it had been a constant in his life. It had infuriated him, and provided moments that were so perfect and sublime that he could not share them with another living soul. To see it again made him feel a joy that few grown men were allowed. He was covetous and consumed by jealousy. A dizzying melting pot of seething fluctuating emotions slowly robbed him of reason. His breathing was heavy and laboured. His fists were clenched. That it had come back willingly was both thrilling and mystifying. It still carried the wristwatch with the GPS tracker that had broadcast its location faithfully during its long absence. He had never lost it. There had not been one brief moment when he did not know its exact location. Staring at the tracking data, he had often smiled, imagining the creature's happy delusion that it was free and safe when it was always and forever on a hook. Now, it had come back. Now, it had to commit to him again. The Prince kindly offered the ring.

The kafir heard rather than saw the gesture. He rose slowly to sit back on his heels then leaned forward to kiss the ring. The fear that had paralysed him dissipated somewhat, but he was not brave enough to test his master's capacity for forgiveness.

The Prince was breathless. The face was even lovelier than he remembered. The eyes shone luminously. The kiss was electric. In the clean white shirt and jeans, the creature was transformed. Yet it must be the same. It had to be. The Pakistanis would quickly strip away all the new artifice. It would be reduced again. Reduced and reduced back to the merest bones of existence because it required nothing else to serve. The Prince drew a long deep breath. He wanted it so badly. His whole frame convulsed. His weakness was humiliating. Deep in his soul, he understood that the creature was nothing less than the personification of sin. He could not have it. He knew it would destroy him. His spiritual salvation lay in resisting the constant temptation. That meant never surrendering it, never letting it go. The blue eyes flashed as the creature watched everything but looked at nothing. The Prince lifted a towel off the sofa, and tossed it down on to the carpet between them.

The kafir flinched. He understood. When the ring was offered, he kissed it again then bowed gravely. He still felt sick and his muscles were shot, but he picked up the towel, and edged away from the Prince. When he regained his feet, he stooped respectfully to reduce his height then backed away. He returned to the anteroom, which was still deserted. There, he stood for a moment. He wanted to throw up. His legs shook so violently he almost collapsed. It was imperative that he surrender his will. Once he accepted that he possessed no opinion, that it was not in his power to want anything or to refuse anything, then the agony of his helplessness became nothing at all. The towel smelt of the Prince. He pressed it to his face and inhaled. He remembered vividly the last time that his master had given him a towel. It had been so many years ago. It had been a remarkable gesture of consideration. It had been immediately followed by the hottest and most awesome sex that he had ever experienced. His total lack of self-esteem did not allow him to dream that he might be so blessed again. But his mouth was dry. His heart pounded in his chest, and endorphins were firing off like rockets in his brain.

When the Prince looked up as the door opened, he saw his luminous creature standing there. It was a thing of beauty. It had the muscle tone and proportions of a heathen god. The towel was wrapped tastefully around its waist. Despite the amount of flesh on show, it was demure, almost chaste. It stared at the floor. It was submissive. He offered the ring again, and smiled as the creature diligently crossed the room then sank down to worship the gem. As it bent over its knees to perform all the rites of submission, the Prince saw for the first time the damaged skin across its back. The dreadful wounds inflicted by Abdullah had all healed, but the scars were unmistakable and permanent. Unable to resist, the Prince leaned down to trail his fingers across the delicate, soft, new skin. The creature flinched but submitted to its master's curiosity as it was probed and explored. It was not allowed to deny its master anything.

The Prince leaned back on the sofa. He wanted it, but he had sworn that he would never use it that way again. His hand touched the collar, which had been hidden beneath the towel. The brass twinkled and glinted like jewels. He picked it up from the sofa then tossed it down between its feet. This was the test. His guts twisted as he heard the creature pick up the collar. He watched as it sat back on its heels to fumble with the stiff leather and the kilos of brass chains and decorations that had been added to it. He found it difficult to breathe as the creature struggled to arrange the various strands of chain and the dozens of snagging charms. The noise excited him. The extraordinary face reflected dismay and confusion. It frowned and pouted. The flash of white teeth was almost as startling as the brief glimpses of the dazzlingly blue eyes. He could see that its hands were shaking. Its nerves were obviously strained. He hoped it was from anticipation. Could it be suffering as he was suffering? He sank his teeth into his lower lip as it lifted the heavy collar against its neck. He stopped breathing. He actually stopped breathing as the creature tried to buckle the garish collar about its own neck. It was his again. It belonged to him. The collar was so heavy. Every movement produced a delightful ringing chime of bells. As the creature failed in its task and wearied of trying, it gazed miserably up at its master. They stared into each other's eyes. The Prince felt his guts tighten. He filled his lungs. He wanted to fuck it so badly.

And the kafir wanted to be fucked. He needed it. He put aside the collar, but knelt at his master's feet, silently begging him to want him. He needed to be touched by another human being, and his heart longed for it to be the Prince. He needed his master to plunder his body so utterly and completely that not an inch would be left un-violated or available for others to touch. If his body was to be invaded and conquered by someone then for his sanity it had to be the Prince. If his master abrogated his responsibility, and abandoned him again to Abdullah and his other faceless enemies, then he was condemned to dwell among the living dead.

With his eyes locked on to the creature's, the Prince moved forward to open his knees around it. He picked up the collar. He brushed imagined dust off the fine shoulders. He finger-combed the hair, stroked the neck, then lifted the chin. The lips parted. The perfect teeth gleamed white. The creature was breathing hard. Every inch of its body registered anxiety. The Prince carefully pressed the collar across its chest. That he had been proved right thrilled him even now. The shining brass set off the creature's looks perfectly. He raised the collar around its neck then threaded the buckle. The creature was drawn closer.

The kafir shuddered as he was bent into his master's groin. The smell intoxicated him. Had they been lovers, he could have slipped his arms around his master's waist, and hugged him while nestling closer, but they were not so he must wait like a lamb. He did not need to wonder whether his master had the same thought. He felt the tension. At that moment, they were both remembering exactly the same encounter on a yacht off the Italian coast.

The metal tongue was forced through the hole. The Prince manhandled it callously, confused by his memories, but it never complained or showed any temper. With the collar securely fastened, the Prince forced the creature back away from him to survey the heavily decorated leatherwork. He ran his fingers around it, forcing up the creature's head, smiling as it lifted its head higher and higher, then submitted reluctantly to being admired. He was not satisfied. He pulled the creature closer, forcing it down on to its hands and knees, burrowing its head deep between his thighs, then roughly unbuckled the collar. The leather was thick and reinforced with hinged metal plates. As an equestrian noseband it was simply not designed to be repeatedly unbuckled. The holes on the band suggested that only two of the half a dozen holes had ever been breached. One was probably for the horse that had originally worn the noseband as part of its bridle. The other was deeper along the collar, and fitted the proportions of the creature's neck. There were other holes. He reached down to feed the collar back around its neck, and threaded the leather end through the gate of the buckle. He let the creature take the weight while he gazed across the ugly mutilated skin that covered its back. Beneath the damaged skin he could see every bone in its spine, the ribs and musculature. He could watch the creature breathing. There were tremors. Now and then, it actually shuddered. Whenever it moved the brass decorations tinkled beguilingly, and its skull brushed against his groin. He tightened the collar. He watched as the breathing quickened. He pulled the collar even tighter. The creature's body registered distress. The head lifted, but it was shoved back into the vice that was its master's thighs. It started to choke. The collar had never been so tight before. The hole the Prince had chosen was virgin. It was not so much a hole as a dimple. The metal tongue was thick and blunt. The Prince would not be denied. He would have it. He drove the leather down over the tongue leaning down onto the exposed neck. It surrendered slowly, but it sank into place. He quickly threaded the strap through the buckle then pushed the wretched creature back onto its knees. Now, he could not slide one finger between the stiff collar and the soft white throat. There was now real anxiety in those glorious eyes. The Prince smiled greedily. He arranged the brass links and chains and charms. The whole collar probably weighed three or four kilos, but it was very attractive. He did not care that it was heavy or uncomfortable or even that it was too tight. It was about ownership. It was more than mere domination. The creature might be tame, but he knew that it had changed. That was only natural. It had been on a journey. Physically, it had certainly matured. If possible, it was even more attractive. The Prince stroked it affectionately, but he understood that he must continually imprint his ownership on it again. That would be unpleasant, but it was essential. He drew back to lean against the sofa, and wrestled with his emotions while he surveyed his restored property. He could not count the occasions or the diverse and astonishing ways in which he had explored its exquisite body. Obviously, it was not allowed to withhold anything. Perhaps, that was what had made it seem without limits. No other events had ever touched him so profoundly. Thinking about it had always distracted him. Having it in his hands was overwhelming like a mind-expanding drug. To have it back again, and not be allowed to resume his conquest was burning a hole through his heart. But he had sworn an oath. He had made a deal with God, and God had come through.

Despite the tight collar that crushed his throat, the kafir's heart warmed. He stared up into his master's eyes. He saw what he hoped was pleasure. He dared to hope that it was because he had returned. He dared to imagine that they might make love, there on the sofa, on the floor, in a bed, in every bed of every room in the luxurious hotel. He needed to feel his master inside his body. He needed to be ripped open and consumed like a great feast. The muscles in his gut were cramping. He was already aroused. He was hot and feverish and going insane.

The Prince read the body language. He leaned forward to smile. "You know better." Without warning, he brutally slapped the creature across the face. It slumped on the floor, broken and betrayed. He watched it slowly recover. It clutched at its face then at the collar then remembered its duty, and returned unhappily to kneel in exactly the same place. He hit it again. It took a little longer the second time. It was visibly stunned. There was blood on its lips. What colour it had, drained from its face, but it obediently returned to sit on its knees though it was shivering from fear. There was no evidence anymore of arousal. The eyes remained fixed on the floor. It was submissive and enslaved. All hope had gone. When the Prince reached out to caress its face, it cowered miserably. The marks of the blows reddened and burned. "It is forbidden." The Prince smiled, his fingers tenderly brushed the flushed cheek, but as soon as the creature settled, he struck it again. "What has been forbidden by God and His Messenger must remain forbidden."

His head was ringing. The kafir could taste blood in his mouth. He did not dare look at his master. He did not want to move if he was to be hurt again, but his master was waiting for him. He felt sick with dread. He could not refuse his master's command. It was encoded into his DNA. Gathering the towel around him, he crept back to kneel before his master. He was shivering as much from fear as from the shock that almost paralysed him. His flesh was weak. He bent to press his forehead into the carpet then slid forward to kiss his master's feet. Bolts of pain were tearing through his heart. It was so hard to breathe. The collar was so tight. A varnish of sweat gleamed across his skin. Raggedly, he rose to kneel before his master. He was still shivering, still frightened, but he settled so that his master would be able to hit him again and again and as often as he desired.

The Prince caressed the creature's face tenderly, but did not strike it. He took a moment to arrange the chains and trinkets that hung from the collar. It was so very tight, gouging into the soft neck.

They were so close. The kafir could feel his breath. He could smell the conditioner he used on his hair. At that moment, he would have consented to anything. But nothing happened. The Prince was content to study his face, and to admire his features as if he were simply a work of art. Quite overcome, the kafir slowly lifted his hands to embrace his master's hands. "Please?" he said. "Please, my lord, Your Highness, my master by the Grace of God, the most Compassionate, the most Merciful." He risked one brief look into his master's deep dark eyes. "I am here." His voice was breaking. It was difficult to breathe properly in the tight collar. "Please, my lord. All that I am." He gazed into his eyes again. "I am yours, my lord. Please? All that I ask is that you don't hurt me anymore. Please, don't hurt me. Do not give me to Abdullah. I will do whatever you wish, but please don't hurt me."

The Prince was more than surprised by the nerve of the creature. It had no right to ask for anything, but its reverence touched him. The scars on its back bore testament to the terrible wounds that Abdullah had inflicted. It must have been in agony. Basic human decency perhaps allowed it to vocalise a complaint, but only once. "You do not speak. You do not ask for anything." He explored the beautiful face, the fine lips, the perfect teeth. The luminous eyes shone. Was it the tears that made them glitter like diamonds? "This is all mine. I own it. You may deny me nothing." He squeezed the soft throat. There was a sudden flash of panic in the eyes. The hands started to close. He stared into the blue eyes. They were extraordinary. There were so many different shades of blue and green. He did not blink. He did not say anything until the creature slowly lowered its hands. Then he smiled. "You are no more precious to me than my old slippers, and as easily replaced."

The kafir wanted to swallow a lump of anguish that threatened to choke him, but the hand on his throat and the collar made that impossible. He tried nervously to lift his chin, but there was no escaping the grip. "Please?" he begged, utterly broken.

The Prince leaned down closer. He held the face in his hands. "But my slippers do not vex me. So I must hurt you. I must punish you. There can be no peace for you." The Prince's voice was husky. He was trembling. His heart thundered like artillery. His guts were twisted up into a lump of raw agony. Every part of his body had become enslaved to his need to fuck this vile thing. He could not think about anything else. "For every man that comes to spill his seed in you, you will be beaten tenfold. And every man that comes to beat you will be righteous before God."

"Please, Your Highness," the kafir said anxiously. "Please, my lord by the Grace of God. Have mercy, my lord, Your Highness. Please." He felt his master's desire. It radiated from him. It was in the tension in the hands that held his head in a vice. It was undeniable. He had never been so sure of anything. "I came back to you. Please."

"Don't speak to me," the Prince warned thickly. His sanity was under threat. "You do not speak to me. How dare you speak to me! I will break you. You do not make demands. You never ask for anything."

The kafir trembled, but he did not lower his gaze. "Please, God is Merciful. Be merciful."

The Prince was insulted. He could have crushed the skull with his bare hands. He could have lifted the lithe body into his arms, and carried it off to gorge on it like a ravenous beast. And then he saw compassion in those shining blue eyes. "I can't love you. Don't you understand? I can't. It's a crime against God. It would be abhorrent to all men. I can never love you."

The kafir's heart was breaking. "I know."

The Prince pulled the creature closer. He trembled violently. The lips were parted. They were both breathing heavily. He placed a finger against the perfect lips as a barrier. "Don't talk to me." He sucked air into his lungs, and held it there. He hardly dared to breathe. He knew he would fall. The mouth was so inviting. Every fibre of his being, even his soul, wanted to swim in the sublime, delicious creature. "I can never love you."

"I know." The kafir reached up slowly to clasp the hand, and drew it away from his lips. "I will stay with you. I will never leave you. I won't run away. Please, don't make me a whore. I will do anything, but please, I'm not that thing anymore."

The Prince was appalled by his own weakness. He needed to step back and review, but he could not bear to let go of the beautiful creature. If he was not allowed to taste it then he needed to hate it. He needed the compensation of punishing it for corrupting him. He needed to vent all his rage and frustration on it, but knew that he held joy in his hands. His voice was torn from his throat. "You are that thing. No one can change what you are." He held the face up close to his own, and peered into the eyes, searching for evidence to prove his assertion. He found nothing that he could believe or trust. The absolute truth and sincerity had to be the most cunning of deceits. He drew back dismayed. It was beyond him. It would have to be destroyed.

"I will stay with you," the kafir promised faithfully. "I will do whatever you wish, but please don't hurt me. Don't share me with other men. Please, Your Highness, my master, my beloved master by the Grace of God, the All-Knowing." The collar was hurting now. It was so tight and so heavy.

He held it in both hands to ease the pressure on his neck. His eyes never left his master's face. A perfect storm of rage, wounded pride and bitter frustration darkened the usually noble features. "Please?" he asked again. "I'm begging you. I'm begging you, my lord." He was desperate. He needed to agree terms before he capitulated. There was not a hope in hell of him surviving the old regime. "Please?"

The Prince drew away to regard him wrathfully. "You insult me. You forget yourself. You may ask for nothing. You may refuse nothing." He took a moment to find his resolve. "This is outrageous. You have no right to make any demands. You will submit. You do not ask me for anything. You do not try to take advantage of me or my feelings for you. That I may lay down with you and caress you does not give you the right to make any demands on me. This is rebellion. The Pakistanis will teach you to be grateful again." He grimaced. "If you fail to satisfy them then you must be destroyed."

The kafir leaned closer. He caught the Prince's hands and crushed them against his chest. "You cannot love me, I understand. It's forbidden. But you can use me. You can treat me like a whore if that is your wish. The Holy Apostle has sanctioned it. It is written. It is the Will of God. I am a possession. I am your property. All that I am. No one can deny your right. Please," he whispered. "If you give me to Abdullah, I will die. If I am sold amongst the Pakistanis, I will die. Please, be merciful. God is Merciful." He kissed the hands passionately. "Please, be merciful. I'm begging you. I came back to you. Please, don't send me away."

Prince Abdul Aziz pulled back his hands. "I cannot love you."

The kafir shivered. He sank back on to his heels, bereft. Instinctively, he reached up to support the collar that was a crushing weight around his neck. It was hard to breathe, made harder by his distress and agitation. "Please? My lord, please, will you not keep me?" He stared at his master, tears filling his eyes. "I came back to you." He found no solace, no hope at all.

The Prince rose to his feet.

His voice breaking, the kafir said: "Don't leave me. Please, don't leave me. I came back." He shivered. "Please, don't leave me here alone."

The Prince regarded him sorrowfully. He wanted to explain, but what could he possibly say that would not condemn them both. "God is All Knowing," he said then turned and walked away.

The kafir waited, staring at the floor, not knowing if his master would ever come back to him.

Chapter 57

The phone rang.

"You did very well." The voice was familiar and commanding.

Jane Howard turned cold. "Your Highness?" She trembled. "How did you find me?"

"You'll be well paid."

"I don't know how you found me." She had to sit down as her knees gave way.

Prince Abdul Aziz smiled. "I needed to send him to someone I could trust, Catherine – sorry 'Jane'. There was no one else."

"No, look, I'm really sorry." She took a deep breath, and said resolutely: "I don't do that anymore."

"You have no choice, Catherine. You'll be well paid."

"No, please, I can't. You don't understand. I've been ill."

"He looks splendid."

"Please, don't do this to me. It was my husband. It was never me. He collected your children. You know it wasn't me."

"Has he been with anyone? I couldn't bear it. Even if it was a woman – I'd rip his heart out, and make him eat it." There was a long pause. "I'm sure he wouldn't do that to me. I love him so much. Did you like him?"

"Yes, he was lovely, but please don't do this to me."

"Don't you want to see your boy again?"

She felt a knife go through her heart. "My son is dead."

"Really? Do you really believe that?"

She trembled. "You're lying. He's dead."

"Can you take that chance?"

*

Slavery exists today. At this very moment, there are 27 million slaves in the world. Half of these are in India. Human trafficking is the second largest illegal trade after Drugs. A slave can be purchased today for $15. They are cheap and plentiful and disposable. Because they are poor, nobody cares. During the 350 years of the European Slave Trade 13 million slaves were taken from Africa to the New World. They were a Capital Purchase. They were listed as assets. In today's terms those slaves were valued at $40,000 each. In the New World, the slaves were emancipated and went on to form large, vibrant communities. Three times as many slaves were taken to Muslim lands.

In Great Britain, more than four hundred children disappear every year. They are never found.

Lightning Source UK Ltd.
Milton Keynes UK
UKOW06f1041210116

266832UK00002B/115/P

9 780993 471308